The Oracles
And The Jewels
The Academy, Vol. I

C.S. Stanford

Stanford Publishing

@Copyright 2005

All rights reserved

SAN 256-9175

ISBN 0-9771814-0-5

9-780977-181407

Dedicated to Lizzy, who believed in Entos even before I did.

Thanks, Stanford kids, for the use of your names, as if you had a say. Also thanks for your help making sure the story was told correctly.

Thanks, Airman R.W. Stanford, for the great cover design, the drawings, and maps. Well done.

The Oracles And The Jewels

Table of Contents

Prologue - Entos and Ektos I

Chapter One - Examination Day.. 1

Chapter Two - School's In.. 19

Chapter Three - "Honorably Retired"... 41

Chapter Four - Cooperate and Graduate... 81

Chapter Five - The Great Declaration.. 91

Chapter Six - He's Been Chosen.. 105

Chapter Seven - The Work Begins... 123

Chapter Eight - "Hasan Horan"... 157

Chapter Nine - The War Begins... 181

Chapter Ten - The Three Rings... 205

Chapter Eleven - A House Divided.. 213

Chapter Twelve - The Invisible Army... 225

Chapter Thirteen - Expelled... 259

Chapter Fourteen - Skattos Forest... 317

Chapter Fifteen - Make Ready.. 343

Chapter Sixteen - King Ashkelon Attacks....................................... 371

Chapter Seventeen - The Aftermath... 461

Appendix.. 473

Prologue

Dawn in Entos was always beautiful. It made no difference under what conditions the sun set, each morning Entos was born anew. Sometimes, as the day wore on it became dark, cool, windy, and wet, but at dawn Entos always began in the bright and majestic light of its glorious sun. Entosians had long ago lost interest in why the days always began in such glory, but that did not change the promise of dawn. They knew that no matter how dark, cold, and wet the afternoon, the night brought peace and the next morning brought a new and bright beginning.

The Land of Entos was itself radiant. At night, Entos glowed with a soft enchanting light, which fell upon the city from its three small moons and millions of stars. Even though the Land of Entos was surrounded on all eight sides by the darkness of the Land of Bohow and the despair that was the Kingdom of Ektos, the Entosians could yet sleep safe and secure behind Entos's eight great walls and eight great towers, which stood as a strong fortress against the evil that was always seeking to destroy the marvelous light called Entos.

Entos was an oasis of beauty, light, life, and love in the midst of a dark, ugly, and brutal world. Within the walls of Entos, the land was rich and full of the colors of life. And in the middle of the Land of Entos there was the great and glorious city of the same name - - Entos.

The eight walls surrounding and protecting the Land of Entos were joined together eight towers, which each held ten thousand Entosian warriors. These towers served as home for the eight mighty armies of Entos which, at the blast of the battle horn, stood ready to repel any attack from King Ashkelon, the Lord of Bohow and the King of Ektos. The land on the eight sides of Entos belonged to King Ashkelon, but

The Oracles And The Jewels

all the land inside the eight walls belonged to the King and to the Entosians whom the Creator had made.

The walls and towers of Entos were protected by ninety thousand warriors of noble birth and the best training. Another ten thousand warriors collected from the eight tribes of Entos, were scattered throughout the Land of Entos, ready to destroy any creature of Bohow or soldier of Ashkelon who might breach the walls. Another ten thousand were found in the city and working at the Academy of Ancient Warring Arts. The Entosian army was an impressive one hundred thousand strong. Yet it was still only one tenth of one tenth of all the creatures and soldiers in Bohow and Ektos, all of whom sought her destruction.

As for the city of Entos, she was a noble and royal city. She was a bright and resplendent light set in the center of Entosian land. Her beauty and wonder were a stark contrast to the dark and dispirited land of Bohow. The buildings of Entos were wonders to behold. They were modern and ancient styles, yet the differences between them were subtle. The buildings on the edge of the city were only one and two stories high, but as one worked his way to the heart of the city, the buildings grew higher and grander. The buildings near the center of the city rose into the clear, blue sky and spoke of the Entosian love for beauty, harmony, and perfection.

As the sun rose each morning the gold, silver, and colorful metallic facades shone with a brightness almost as glorious as the sun itself. Their outer brilliance was only exceeded by their inner magnificence. Decorated with great works of art of every description, each room was a tribute to the Giver of all good gifts and to the creativity of the Entosian people.

The city sat on the Great Plateau as if to watch over the fields and valleys that rose to meet the city's edge. Some of the fields rose slowly and gently toward the city. Other valleys, like the Fortian and Pithosian Valleys, rose sharply, yet gracefully to the city's edge. In each valley well-kept paths ran from the plateau's edge through the fields of grass, gardens, flowers, crops, and woodlands into the hamlets and humble abodes that dotted the fertile lands of all eight valleys. Rivers and creeks, whose sources were the

Prologue

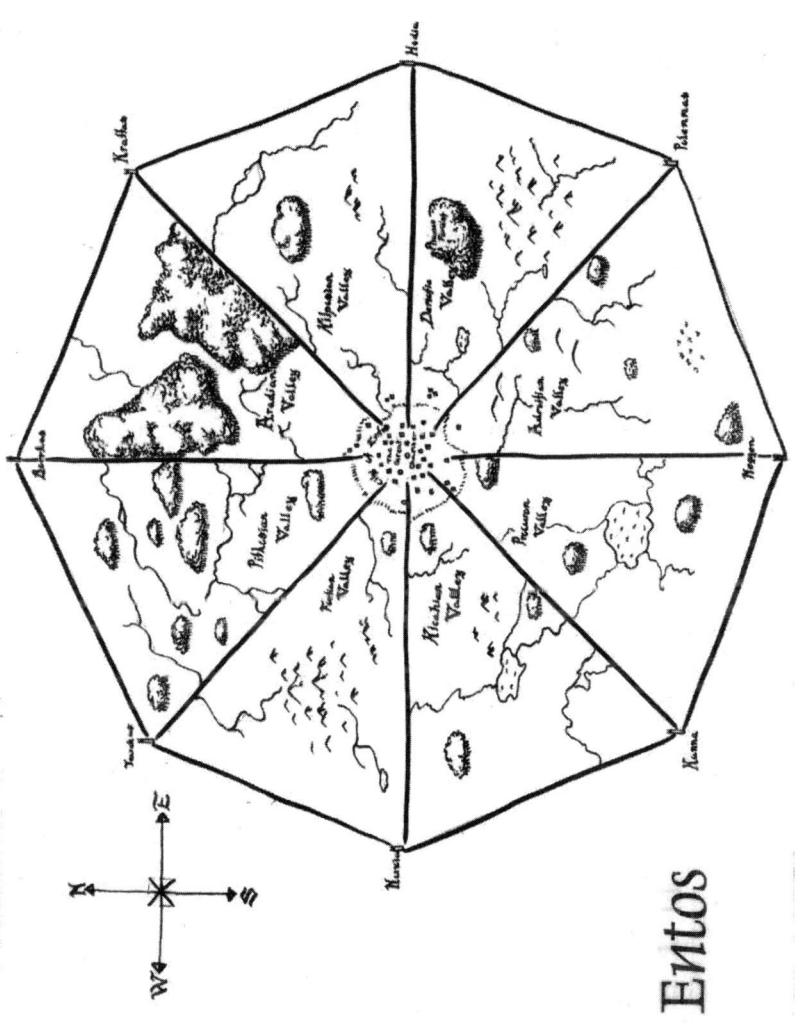

The Oracles And The Jewels

springs and great geysers that sat upon the plateau and fields, wove their way through the valleys and provided a cool drink to refresh any thirsty Entosian.

In the middle of the city stood The Great Chamber. It was the tallest of all the buildings and reached twenty-five stories into the sky. Three hundred feet high, it towered over all the other buildings in Entos, standing more than one hundred higher than the Performing Arts Theater, and one hundred twenty-five feet taller than both The Academy of the Building Arts and The Academy of the Ancient Warring Arts.

The foundation of The Great Chamber sat on a solid mass of granite that rose one thousand one hundred twelve feet from the floor of Bohow's desert. The Great Chamber could be seen from almost any place in Entos.

To the northwest, the mountains of Entos rose five thousand five hundred seventy-two feet from the desert floor. These were the mountains of Tarchus. It was from them that the people of Entos mined the minerals and rocks from which they forged the metals needed to build the city of Entos. The mountains of Entos were a wonder to behold. They were not only grand and stately, but like the forests that grew on them, they were always regenerating with the coming of each year. With the passing of each season, the scars inflicted upon them healed and offered anew her bounty of minerals and stone.

Before the city of Entos was created, the Maker of Entos had caused the ground to take its shape. By His speaking, the eight great plateaus were created. Each plateau went forth from the Great Plateau. As they stretched outward from the Great Plateau some sixty leagues, each plateau became narrower until it ended in a point, upon which a great tower was built. The towers were connected by eight imposing walls, fortifications which had protected the Land of Entos from the Early Ages.

Each plateau had been given a name. The plateau that pointed toward the east was called the **Hodia Plateau,** for it pointed to the rising of the sun. The color of its flag was white for the purity of the sunlight that rose over her each morning. The plateau to the west pointed to the setting of the sun, so it was called the **Nuxia Plateau.** It pointed to the end of the day and the beginning of yesterday. The color of Nuxia was

Prologue

gold for the setting of the sun and the gold that could be seen on the cliffs of the plateau from the Fortian and Pithosian Valleys.

The **Borrhas Plateau** moved out straight north of the city and the **Neggen Plateau** reached toward the south. Purple was the color of Borrhas' flag, for Borrhas pointed to the north and the Oracles made reference to a land of great kings who had once lived in the North. The color of Neggen was green, for the greatest forest and the finest timber came from the forest of Neggen. Of all the woods and forests in Entos, none were as filled with life and wonder as the forest of Neggen. The Neggen Forest covered forty of the sixty leagues between the southern wall of the Adroitian Valley and the city of Entos. These four plateaus were fair and friendly to the traveler and were marked by small rolling hills, gentle springs, trees, and peaceful lakes.

The other four plateaus were much more rugged. The **Tarchus Plateau** was the most rugged and difficult landscape in all of Entos and ran to the northwest between Borrhas and Nuxia. The plateau's name was taken from its ruggedness. Yet, its ruggedness was beautiful to behold with its mountains and forests, but difficult and dangerous to traverse. The metals for the Entosian swords were mined in the mountains of Tarchus thus its color was silver.

Opposite Tarchus and pointing to the southeast was the **Plateau of Polemmas,** so named because it was the place where one of the earliest and greatest battles was fought. The flag of Polemmas was red so as to serve as a reminder of the blood that was once spilled upon its ground to purchase the freedom for Entos.

Pointing to the northeast between Borrhas and Hodia was the **Krattos Plateau,** so named because it had often provided help and strength to Hodia. Its flag was yellow, for it too greeted the morning sun each day. The last of the eight great plateaus was the **Plateau of Kanna**, which means "to be humble," for those assigned to this Plateau were often called upon to assist their fellow warriors and were often overlooked for their great service to the people of Entos. The color of Kanna was blue, for it was the color of loyalty.

Each plateau and army bore its own color, but upon each flag only one symbol appeared. It was the symbol of

The Oracles And The Jewels

Entos, an eight–pointed star with an $\mathcal{E}$ in the center, for although they came from eight tribes they were all one; Entosians were born of the same Oracles and touched by the same Jewels.

Three thousand years earlier the priests of Entos had commanded that a great tower be built upon the point of each of the eight plateaus to serve as watchtowers against Ashkelon and the creatures of Bohow. Over time the inhabitants of Entos connected the eight towers with eight great walls one hundred feet tall in their middle and nearly three hundred feet high at each end where the walls met the towers and the cliffs of each plateau.

One hundred and fifty feet below the surface ran a mighty aquifer, a large river whose source was a great mystery to the Entosians. The aquifer was thought to be a powerful underground spring that welled up beneath the granite rock in the center of the Great Plateau. The water from that great spring spilled into eight underground rivers that ran beneath each plateau, spilling out along the cliffs and facades of the plateaus, and creating waterfalls that poured out into the valleys and springs of living water along the length of the plateau. After the Oracles and the Jewels, it was the water of Entos that kept her people and the land alive.

Between the plateaus the ground gave way to slopes, valleys, and hills. On the slopes and in the valleys were streams, springs, lakes, farms, small forests, and rolling hills. As Entos grew, hamlets spread out over the country side and the eight tribes took up living together, each in their own valley. The names of the tribes of Entos were as follows: Adroit, Aradian, Demotic, Fortian, Kicah, Kilpos, Pithosian, and Procuron.

The **Adroitians** were the smallest of all the Entosians. In appearance they looked very much like the Demotic people, but rarely did a male Adroitian reach five feet tall, and women averaged about four feet four inches. Their diminutive size made the Adroitians very nimble and quick. An Adroitian could shoot and place another arrow on the bowstring with such speed that the eye could barely comprehend it. They were also excellent disk throwers and could throw cutting disks even faster than they could rearm a

Prologue

bow. As a people, they were clever and quick in rendering judgments. They were very good at distinguishing between civilians, fellow warriors, and enemy soldiers.

The Aradians were of darker skin than all the others. Their ears were pointed and bowed out. They could hear a whisper before it was even spoken and most males stood seven feet tall. Their height made them great runners, especially for long distances. The Aradians could be found in every vocation, but they were particularly well suited as messengers. They could average one league every five minutes and could keep up that pace for hours.

The Demotic tribe was the most numerous off all the tribes. They were of lighter skin, generally had a strong build, and were the most evenly proportioned. Men were commonly six feet tall and women averaged around five feet five inches. Of all the citizens of Entos, Demotics were well suited for any station. While other tribes had specific qualities that enabled them to excel in certain fields, a Demotic was considered a general practitioner and suitable in all vocations.

The Fortians were short and stalwart, no more than five feet tall, had broad shoulders and mighty arms, and made good swordsmen and spearsmen. Of all the Entosians their eyesight was the best. They were fearless, passionate, and loved humor. They threw the best parties, drank the most spirits, and spent their spare time playing practical jokes on one another. They were born warriors and loved to fight for that which was good and right.

The men of the tribe of **Kilpos** were of medium build, swift of foot, and gentle of heart. Kilposians were men of good temperament and deliberate in their judgments. They looked for consensus and made good diplomats. From their line many City Fathers and priests had arisen. They too made good warriors and officers, for they followed orders well, but their tendency toward diplomacy and hesitancy for battle prevented many a Kilposian from rising to the highest ranks in the military.

The Pithos tribe was few in number, but they were physically the largest of the Entosians. The men stood an average of six feet eight inches tall. They were shorter than the Aradians, but their frame was broad and very muscular.

The Oracles And The Jewels

Pithosians who entered The Academy of the Ancient Warring Arts made the best foot soldiers. In strength, they could match even the strongest creature that Bohow could field. The swords they carried were longer than the average Fortian and certainly heavier than the average Adroitian.

Of all Entosians, the **Procurons** were the most unique in appearance. They were easily recognizable by their round, big blue eyes and their small round ears. They were logical creatures, driven most of all by balance, completeness, and symmetry. They made excellent builders and the best administrators. Even though they constituted less that ten percent of the population, they composed nearly forty percent of the student body at The Academy for Governance. They also featured prominently in the planning detachments of the armies, since they had a remarkable ability to analyze, predict, and anticipate. Few other Entosians played table games with a Procuron because in such things Procurons rarely lost.

The eighth tribe of Entos bore the name **Kicah**. These Entosians possessed a gift of great value. The Kicah had the ability to mask themselves by blending into the environment around them. When unmasked they resembled a Demotic, but were albino in appearance. In all of Entos there could not be found more than five hundred Kicahians.

Kilposians and Aradians reached their physical peak later, around their nineteenth year. Fortians, Adroitians, and Procurons attained adulthood by their fourteenth year. Pithosians and Kicahians reached adulthood by their seventh birthday. Each Entosian in his own time and according to his own tribe's custom celebrated his entrance into adulthood. Fortians and Pithosians welcomed the milestone with great festivals, which included food, drink, loud music, and dancing. Kicahians and Procurons celebrated the milestone in solitary contemplation of what had come before and what would follow. Kilposians, Demotics, and Adroitians celebrated the event with family and friends in smaller parties, which included cake, frozen cream, small gifts, and well wishes. Aradians didn't mark the event in any way, since they believed that they had made no contribution to the original event.

Prologue

Even though each tribe lived in their own hamlets and each celebrated life's milestones in their own way, they were still one community. They held to different customs and practiced different ceremonies, yet they were all Entosians, made thus by the Oracles and the Jewels and kept that way by their participation in the Great Rituals.

In the time before the Days of Old and the Ancient of Days, the tribes of Entos were grotesque creatures, inhabitants of Bohow, and in bondage to Ashkelon. But now they were one people, who had been translated into fair and glorious creatures. From time-to-time the tribes differed in opinions pertaining to the governance of Entos, but in matters touching the essence of Entos, they had been united since the Days of Old when the Oracles where first written and the Jewels were taken from the earth. The women of Entos, regardless of their tribe, were always lovely and the men, regardless of their tribe, were always handsome.

In the sun's morning light, the city of Entos always looked new and bright. Yet it was a city as old as the sun itself. Established of old, carved out of Bohow, Entos was always new and full of life. Between the grand buildings of the city of Entos there were streets of fine brick, pools of clear water, beautiful parks, gardens, small orchards, statues of great heroes, and the homes of the leaders of Entos.

The Land of Entos was filled with animals of every kind. Fauna abounded and lived in harmony with Entosians. Although many creatures hunted prey for their own sustenance, none could ever recall an Entosian animal taking the life of a citizen. In Entos, nature worked the same way as in other places. Birds of prey patrolled the air and larger beasts of the fields fed on the smaller. The penalty for injuring an Entosian citizen was immediate expulsion from the land. So terrible a curse was this, that no creature of the forests, mountains, and valleys dared bring an injury upon even one of the King's kinsmen.

The glory of Entos was not in its sun at dawn, or the three moons of night. It was not in its citizens, even though Entosians were different from the creatures found everywhere else in King Ashkelon's earth. The glory of

The Oracles And The Jewels

Entos was not its buildings, or art, or its traditions. The glory of Entos was found in the middle of Bohow, in the heart of Entos, and equidistant among the eight points and the eight towers of Entos' plateaus, in a stately hall surrounded by stained-glass windows that told the story of her beginning. There in the middle of The Great Chamber was found a marble rail of eight sides and in the center of the eight-sided rail, resting in a cradle of marble draped with a white bloodstained robe lay the true glory and power of Entos – The Oracles and the Jewels.

The Oracles and the Jewels were the life, light, wisdom, and power that was Entos. Without them Entos and all Entosians would vanish into the gloom of Bohow and the utter despair that is Ektos. Without the Oracles and the Jewels no Entosian could endure and all would return to the darkness from whence they came.

In the Ancient of Days before Entos, the Giver of the Oracles and the Maker of the Jewels came into this dark and gloomy land that is Bohow. In the midst of this great and terrible land the King and the king of Ektos made war in Ashkelon's dark earth. When they had finished their first great battle, the King and Creator of Entos and Giver of the Oracles and Jewels prevailed. In that place where there was nothing but chaos and darkness, in that place where King Ashkelon reigned his terrible reign, a great and glorious, although small land had been born. Into that place that was not, the Maker of Entos created the great and radiant land that is the Land of Entos. And it was into this new and glorious land that the King of Entos placed His new creatures, the Entosians.

The King of Entos took creatures of Ektos, spoke His Oracles to them, and touched their heads, mouths, and breasts with the Jewels. At that moment those hideous creatures of Ektos were transformed into the good and

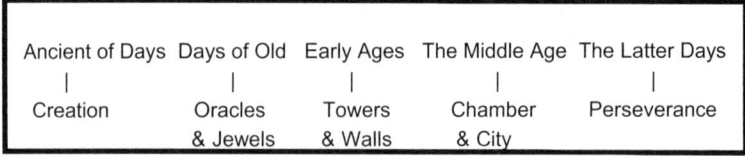

Prologue

humble creatures of Entos. The King placed His new creatures in the Land of Entos by the speaking of His words. So thereafter, the creatures of Bohow, the warriors of Ektos, and King Ashkelon himself waged their first war to drive the King of Entos and His newly-made Entosians from the face of Ashkelon's earth.

This is the story that the stained-glass windows in The Great Chamber told. This is what Entosians gathered to hear on the Eighth Day of every week. In The Great Chamber, the citizens of Entos gathered to see the windows and to hear the priests tell the story of the great battle and speak the Oracles. It was also at the Eighth Day Festival that the mothers and fathers from all the tribes brought their newborn creatures to hear the Oracles and to be touched by the Jewels. On that day, when all the citizens of Entos gathered together, the old became new, and the grotesque became fair. That is how Entosians were created and how they were made in every generation.

As the people sang, the priest took in his hand the Jewels and spoke the Oracles to the creature. As the words were spoken he touched the first Jewel to the forehead, the second to the lips, and the third to the breast. It was at that moment that a great and glorious Entosian was born. And in those places where the three Jewels touched the creature there was left an almost indistinguishable little mark in the shape of a drop.

Entos grew quickly in the Days of Old. When the King of Entos departed, He left eight small tribes whose total number did not exceed one thousand. In the three millennia that followed the King's departure, Ashkelon continually attacked the land and city of Entos, but after each attack was successfully repelled, the land and city of Entos grew. By the end of the third millennium Entos had grown from one thousand to a half million Entosians.

It had been five centuries since King Ashkelon had waged such an attack. The last time King Ashkelon tried to destroy Entos it had ended in a horrible defeat. In those days Entos was clear and unconfused. In those days the warriors, and even the children, knew how to make use of the Oracles and the Jewels and how to defeat the king of Ektos.

The Oracles And The Jewels

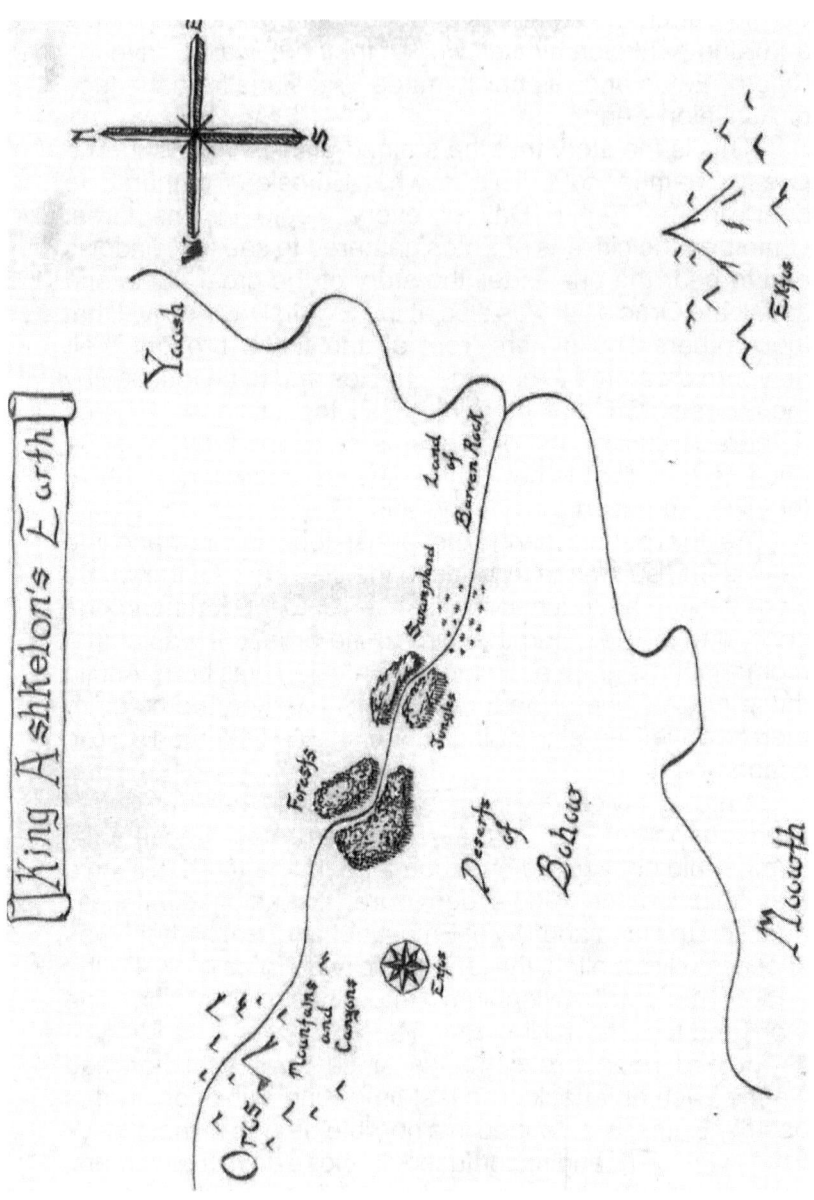

Prologue

In that day five hundred years ago when King Ashkelon attacked, one-third of his army fell, one hundred five thousand creatures in all. In the same day, Entos lost nearly two thousand Entosian warriors to the steel of Ashkelon and it was said that sixty Entosians were reclaimed by Ashkelon and walk with him to this day. For such fallen Entosians, it is said there can be no redemption and now they live in a fate worse than death.

The creatures of Bohow were of three kinds. Some creatures were evil, wild, and lived off the flesh of other creatures. These creatures were mere beasts of low reason. Their days and nights were filled with but one thought, to satisfy their hunger and passions. Other creatures in Bohow were creatures of reason and cunning. They were masters of the beasts and by virtue of their reason they were more dangerous. Reason served their hate. But reasoning or not, all who lived in Ashkelon's earth were under the domain of Ashkelon and all hated Entos, but loved Entosian flesh.

The third kind of creature was one that had been made by Ashkelon's priests and was forged from the fire and colly of Ektos. These were the soldiers and priests of Ektos. Of all the creatures in Bohow, they reigned and were lords. They were the most dangerous of all the creatures of Bohow. They existed so that Entosians might die. They were slaves for the purpose of enslaving others. They were soldiers of the most barbarous kind. They did as they were ordered to do by their masters and King Ashkelon and did so with no thought of their own well-being and possessed no fear.

In the beginning all the creatures of Entos had come from the creatures of Bohow. It was as if the words of the King of Entos and the power contained therein had taken Ashkelon by surprise. As a result, King Ashkelon lost many of his creatures and soldiers to the King. In the speaking of the King's words, at great and mighty army had arisen, where first there was none.

But as the glory and Land of Entos increased, so also did the evil and hatred of Bohow, Ektos, and Ashkelon. Over the centuries, Ashkelon had instituted safeguards and had taught his creatures well to guard against the hearing of the King's words. Through an ever-increasing enmity, it had become more difficult for Entos to make Entosians from

The Oracles And The Jewels

among the creatures in Ashkelon's dark earth. For the creatures themselves had long ago learned to flee from conjurors of Entos. Ashkelon too had learned that he would have to take from the Land of Entos the Oracles and the Jewels so that they could no longer be spoken and used in his earth.

Examination Day

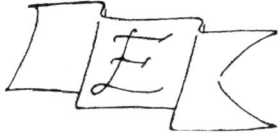

Chapter One
Examination Day

The morning sun rose and, like every morning since the first day of Entos, the light exploded across the whole land. The sun's rays struck the faces of the towering buildings high atop the Great Plateau, and the buildings replied with a reflected light more colorful than the sun itself. In that moment many Entosians, and all the creatures of Entos awoke to greet the beginning of a new and glorious day.

So it was with Rieve Waynwright, a young first-year student of The Academy of Theological Sciences and Ancient Conjuring Arts. On this morning, like so many before it, Rieve Waynwright awoke in the bedroom that had kept him safe and warm during his youth. It had been a year since he had slept in his bed and it felt good. By Entosian standards, Rieve had become an adult, albeit a young adult, but an adult with all the rights and responsibilities of an Entosian citizen. The time for childish things had come and gone, but the boy in him still took a quiet pleasure in being home.

The cottage in which Rieve had been raised belonged to his father, who had inherited it from his father, who in turn had inherited from his father, and so on. For five hundred fifty years that cottage had been handed down from one generation to another. For more than five centuries earlier, four generations of the Timaho Clan had occupied the furthermost cottage where the field of the Demotic Valley met the Mellii Woods.

The front door of the cottage faced the Great Plateau and The Great Chamber. Rieve's room consisted of the northern half of the upstairs attic. His younger brother's room occupied the southern half of the attic. Each room had three windows.

The Oracles And The Jewels

Rieve awakened every morning to the sight or the sunrise breaking over the Hodia Plateau, which could be seen from the eastern window of his bedroom. His younger brother, Thayer Taggert, had begged him for years to swap bedrooms. It had been Thayer's heartfelt desire from his earliest days to join the Hodia Army. After Rieve moved to the dorms at the academy, Thayer would often sit at Rieve's bedroom window on the north side of the room and stare at the Hodia Plateau and dream of great battles he would one day win.

Rieve had always declined the request to swap bedrooms because his room gave him an unobstructed view of The Great Chamber and the beam of light that shone from it each night. The window at the southern end of Thayer's room faced the Polemmas Plateau and, while his western window faced The Great Chamber too, his view of the city was obstructed by a weeping willow tree that stood in the front yard. Rieve had once promised that if Thayer obtained permission from their father to cut down the willow, he would grant Thayer's request and swap bedrooms. Thayer had often asked his father for permission, but his wish had never been granted.

It had been almost a year since Rieve had slept in his old room. Time had answered Thayer Taggert's request. Rieve had spent his fifteenth year away at school living in the dorms at The Academy of Theological Sciences and Ancient Conjuring Arts. While he was away Thayer Taggert had granted himself his heart's desire and made Rieve's room his own.

It was Rieve's sixteenth birthday and of all the birthdays in the life of a Demotic, the sixteenth birthday was the most significant. By the time a Demotic reached his sixteenth birthday he had reached physical adulthood. A sixteen-year-old Demotic was pound-for-pound every bit the physical match of those ten or twenty years his senior. What separated a sixteen-year-old Demotic from his older peers was the knowledge and skill that time and experience instilled in a fertile mind. His mother had planned a small party for family and friends that evening, but Rieve's birthday wasn't the reason he had returned home. He had come back

Examination Day

to be with his younger brother, who on this very day would take his placement exam and receive his vocational calling.

Rieve rose from his bed and began to ready himself for another day at The Academy of Theological Sciences and Ancient Conjuring Arts. It had been a year since he had walked from his father's cottage to the academy. He was confident that the journey would only take thirty-five minutes and he did not want to be late.

Rieve had been one of the chosen few who, by virtue of both natural gifts and hard work, had been selected by the Academy and the City Fathers to become a priest and conjuror. In time he, like the ancients before him, would teach, protect, and lead Entosians in the way they ought to go. He would one day preside over the Great Eighth Day Festival and sing of the stories of the creation of Entos and of the King's gracious protection. In times of peace, Rieve would serve in The Great Chamber. But in times of war, he might be called upon to serve as a warrior conjuror. The priesthood was an ancient order, the first of all the orders, and when stirred by great evil it could unleash the true and awesome power of the King's mysteries.

Rieve washed and readied himself for the day ahead in a little room that was connected to his bedroom. As he washed he heard his mother call for his younger brother.

"Thayer. . . Thayer. . . Thayer Taggert! Are you getting ready?" There was a pause. "Thayer!"

"Yes, Mother, I'm up," Thayer replied in a muffled voice, then buried his face into the pillow.

"All right then. See you at breakfast in a few minutes," his mother replied.

Rieve knew better. They were brothers, but in almost every way they were different. The window under which Rieve slept faced the sunrise. The window under which Thayer Taggert slept faced the sunset. The light of Entos held the brothers together, but at opposite ends of the day. Rieve was a constant and predictable personality, never too anxious, yet never too placid. Thayer Taggert was a study of extremes; sometimes too impulsive and at other times too meticulous; sometimes too engaged and at other times too detached. He was prone to moments of brilliance only to be followed by moments of stupidity. He possessed leadership

The Oracles And The Jewels

qualities, but could sometimes be easily swayed. Rieve had spent his whole life either pulling his younger brother along or holding him back.

"Rieve Waynwright," his mother said in a much softer voice, "You're up, I suppose."

"Yes, Mother, thank you for checking," Rieve replied as he dried his face.

Rieve walked to the western end of his bedroom and, poking his head through the door that joined his room to Thayer's, Rieve barked, "Tag, Tag, get up! Exam day . . . remember? Today is the day. Do well and one day I will be calling you 'captain,' or 'colonel,' or Entos forbid, 'general.' Sleep in and foul up and you might turn out to be a priest, or something much less exciting."

"No! Never! Entos forbid!" Thayer shouted as he threw his pillow in Rieve's direction, striking him on the side of his face. "I want my life to mean something!"

"Then get up and get ready for your exam. The priesthood is my station, not yours. I'm not sure even the King of Entos could protect Entos against a priest like you."

"My hands were meant for swords and daggers. Give me an Entosian sword and dagger and the city will be just fine. You can take the sacred scrolls in your hands and keep all that conjuration to yourself. Besides, if you were any good at that conjuring stuff you would have stopped the pillow before it hit you in the face."

"I haven't had the class on flying pillows yet. Besides, a conjuror uses his power to save others, not himself. For example, lethargic warriors who are caught unawares in their sleep."

Thayer jumped from the bed, looked to his brother nearly three years his elder and said, "No, thank you, your holiness. Preaching, teaching, incantations, conjuring, and creating little Entosians isn't for me. I was born a warrior and a warrior I will be! And when it comes to saving one's brother, it will be me who saves thee!"

"Me who saves thee?" Rieve laughed. "You're even talking like an old conjuror."

"A good warrior should know something of the old ways," Tag replied with an air of superiority. He ran his fingers through his blonde hair and shook his head.

Examination Day

"That depends on the exam today doesn't it?" Rieve replied.

"Brother, you've trained all your life in the classics, languages, and the incomprehensibles. When exam day came for you, you slipped right through like the little prodigy they said you were. What you are to the theological sciences and to wizardry, I am to warring arts and physical combat. I am as ready for my exam as you were for yours. Don't worry about me, big brother. If there is any saving to do around here, I'll do it." He walked over to the washbasin and mirror, leaned into the mirror and continued. "One day I will be a lieutenant . . . captain . . . a colonel, and finally the general of the Hodia Army, the master of the Hodia Tower. Big brother, you are looking at the future replacement for General Witticor himself." Thayer dipped his hands into his washbasin and splashed some water onto his face.

"It has been a very long time since a Demotic has been the commander of the entire army. Fortians seem more suited for that work," Rieve said as Thayer thrust the top of his head into the washbasin and scrubbed his hair with his fingertips, then shook his head like a dog.

"What a beast!" Rieve said as he moved for cover. "Hodia. You're more suited for the mountains of Tarchus or the forests of the Pithosian Valley."

"As long as I am at the Hodia Tower, you and all the rest of Entos will be safe and sound in The Great Chamber," Thayer replied.

"You talk too much for a warrior," Rieve said, then disappeared into his room to finish dressing. Ten minutes later the two were sitting at the breakfast table with their mother, Arete, and father, Tedmund.

"Good morning, boys," their father said.

"Good morning, Father," the two replied in unison. Their greeting bore the sound of respect and formality, but had the air of familiarity.

"Exam today, Thayer?" his father asked rhetorically.

"Yes, father. You know it is."

"It was a rhetorical question," Rieve explained, then continued, "and is intended to introduce the topic for further conversation."

The Oracles And The Jewels

"You're starting to sound like River Kiernan," Thayer snapped.

"I like that young lady," Arete said. Her voice was sweet and gentle.

"Mother, you like everyone," Rieve replied. "It's what everyone loves about you."

"Still," their father said. "One of you would do well to take her or a woman like her for a wife one day."

Tedmund was a temperate man. The boys could not remember a shout or a moment of true anger. Nor could they remember an outburst of joy or laughter. Tedmund was steady, patient, and stoic in all things. His comment was meant as sober advice, but "settling down" was the furthest thing from his sons' minds.

"He's talking to you," Rieve and Thayer said in unison as they looked at each other and smiled.

"How do you boys do that?" Arete asked shaking her head and adding, "It is the only evidence I have that you're brothers."

"Thayer Taggert," his father said again in a tone of sobriety, "are you ready?"

"No problem, Father."

"Now to a more important question," his father said. "Are you sure soldiering is what you want to do? You know your mother and I don't like the idea. We're Demotics from the Timaho Clan and our clan has produced very few warriors over the centuries. Those we have produced did not work their way up the ranks. It is said that only once a Timaho rose to the rank of major. History tells us that Timahos seem better suited for governing, teaching, and the priesthood."

"I'm a warrior," Thayer said as he beat his fist against his chest, "and a warrior I will be!"

"Son, do you have to act like such a beast?" Arete asked with a tone of disgust.

"Rest your mind, Mother. It's just an act," Rieve assured her.

"I know, but it seems so . . . so," his mother began.

"Undignified," Rieve said.

"Yes, undignified," Arete repeated, "like a Fortian who has been out in the wilderness too long."

Examination Day

"One of these days, Mother, your second-born son will be an officer and gentleman," Rieve said as he cut his eggs into small pieces. "I know it is hard to see that now, but it is true."

"By the way, Father, with all due respect," Thayer said, "Entosians are warriors. Our enemies are called soldiers."

"Father didn't say soldier. He said soldiering." Rieve commented.

"What's the difference?" Thayer snapped.

"One is a noun and the other a verb," Rieve replied. "Since 'warrioring' isn't a word, soldiering is an acceptable way of speaking about what an Entosian warrior does on the battlefield."

"There you go again, sounding like her," Thayer said as he looked in Rieve's direction. "If 'warrioring' isn't a word, it should be," Thayer said, then took a bite of his eggs, swallowed, and continued. "Father, today the Timaho Clan starts a new tradition. I am the birth of a new legacy. Today is the beginning of the Thayer Taggert warrior line of the Timaho Clan. Tell me, prophet brother, isn't there a prophecy about a warrior who arises from a humble clan, the first-born in a great line, who shall come and deliver a great defeat to Ashkelon?"

"Yes there is, but the likelihood that it speaks of you is very, very, very small," Rieve replied.

"Isn't that the way the King likes to work . . . taking small and unlikely things and making them great?" Thayer replied.

"Indeed, but I don't recall any prophet or warrior boasting beforehand that he was the chosen one," Rieve responded, then added, "besides, you're the second-born son."

"That just confirms my suspicion that you're adopted. But mother and father aren't talking about that," Thayer replied.

"Oh, he is not. I've told you before," Arete said with tone half serious.

"Boasting," his father injected, "usually disqualifies the candidate. The King smiles upon the humble and looks unfavorably on the proud and, even if you speak in such ways out of jest, it simply is not proper."

"Yes, Father," Thayer said.

The Oracles And The Jewels

"Can we return to the conversation at hand?" Tedmund asked.

"Yes, sir," Thayer said feeling the sting of his father's rebuke.

"Son, there is no doubt that you have the heart and intellect for The Academy of the Ancient Warring Arts, but you have always lacked the discipline. The Academy of the Ancient Warring Acts is not like grammar school. It is the most demanding of all the schools, for it requires what all others do not. A discipline of body, soul, and mind. If you try any of your boyhood pranks there, they will remove you immediately. They train for life and for death."

"Don't worry, Father. I will not fail. I'm sure I will make you all proud of me," Thayer said with a tone of proper respect, but then added, "Besides, it's not like anyone has a choice in this city. The prep schools train you for everything, then test you in all things, and finally they place you into the vocation you seem most suited for and more importantly, the one most helpful to the city. It seems pretty well decided even before the test is taken. It's just in my case, the City Fathers have it right. I'm a warrior. That's the station to which I will be called." Thayer scooped up the egg on his plate and swallowed the egg whole, then took a drink of juice.

"Let's see if you make it past the first lesson, the lesson in humility. That is the place where your mother and I have failed you," his father said with a tone of disappointment.

"It's just an act," Rieve replied. Rieve looked to his mother and said. "Don't worry Mother, you didn't fail. It is just an act and a bad one at that."

"Be it an act or not, I just want to make sure. We don't like the idea of having a Timaho in the military, especially these days, but we will yield to Entos as usual. Remember, I can write an appeal on your behalf," his father added.

"It doesn't hurt that you are Professor Tedmund of The Academy of Theological Sciences and Ancient Conjuring Arts, does it Father?" Rieve replied with a bit of lighthearted sarcasm.

"Membership has its privileges. It certainly helped when I made your appeal," his father said, returning the sarcasm.

"Appeal? Big brother needed an appeal?" Thayer said with a tone of surprise and glee.

Examination Day

"There was no appeal," his mother said. "Your father is just kidding. Now off with you both, and Thayer Taggert, don't be late getting home. The celebration tonight is twofold; Rieve's birthday and your placement."

"Me late! Oh, Mother! When have I ever been late?" Thayer said as he put a few items in his lunch pouch.

"If you really want an answer to that question, I can retrieve your school records from my office," his father said. "Then there is the question of obedience."

"Never in all of Entos has there been a more obedient son than me Father," Thayer replied with a slight roll of the eyes.

"My willow tree still bears the scar of your disobedience," Tedmund replied.

"The tree is still standing," Thayer answered.

"Thanks to your brother," Arete said.

"If I hadn't stopped you, you would have felled that tree right through your window," Rieve said.

"That was yesterday. Today is a new day. That's what you tell us every morning at breakfast, Mother."

"I'm thankful that I've taught you something, Thayer," Arete replied with a grin.

"From this day on, I am going to be the model of discipline and punctuality," Tag said.

"That would be different," his mother said as she brushed his damp hair from his forehead. The touch annoyed Thayer. His mother had fussed over his hair from the day he was born. That was okay when he was a little boy, but it wouldn't do from this time on. Tag leaned slightly back in a small effort to escape the touch.

"Mother, as soon as I am in the Warring Academy, you need not fear any creature from Bohow or soldier of Ashkelon. You have my word," Tag said then placed his fist over his heart to seal the pledge.

"Your first duty is to Entos and then to your mother and me," Tedmund added. "Don't forget that."

"Yes, sir," Thayer snapped and beat his fist over his heart a second time before he kissed his mother on the cheek and headed out the front door. Rieve shook his father's hand and gave his mother a hug and kiss good-bye.

The Oracles And The Jewels

"Mother, don't worry. I will make sure he gets to the test on time," Rieve said.

"Thank you, Son. See you tonight."

Rieve and Thayer walked side-by-side down the path from their front door to the small road that ran from the valley behind their cottage to the entrance of the Great Plateau. It was a twenty minute walk from their cottage to the edge of the plateau and it was another fifteen minutes to walk to The Academy of Theological Sciences and Ancient Conjuring Arts.

Rieve and Thayer had traveled that path almost every morning since they first learned to walk. They had walked the path every day to school and on the eighth day they would walk with their parents to the Great Festival. On school days Rieve and Thayer talked about the ordinary things that normally occupied the minds of young boys. Some mornings the pace would be slow, but on other mornings they would race from the cottage to the Great Plateau. In recent years, Thayer had made their races a real competition. But there would be no race this morning. This morning was different.

Rieve knew that Thayer would have his mind on the upcoming test. Thayer, like all other Entosians, had looked forward to exam day, but that did not mean he was in a hurry to arrive. Examination day was a day filled with anxiety and high tension. Even though all the students had been well trained in the classical disciplines of Entos, they were still in competition with one another. The City Fathers controlled access to the various academies so they could make sure that the Land of Entos would not want for priests or warriors. Nor did the land lack engineers and artists, rulers and servants, farmers, and artisans. The educational system trained for citizenship first and vocation second, but both were tied together on exam day. When it came to an Entosian's career, however, all depended on the test score. Second only to the day of their Entosian birth, exam day was by far the most important day in the life of an Entosian boy or girl.

Ideally, Thayer wanted to arrive right on time. He didn't want to be late and unsettled, but he did not want to be too early either. That would afford him too much time to over

Examination Day

think the exam. He wanted to arrive right on time, which in itself was a signal that this day was different from all the mornings that had come before.

As they walked down the path toward the city, everything appeared the same. The landscape was still beautiful. The sun shone brightly and the breeze blew gently. Their cottage was on the ridge of the eastern slope of the Demotic Valley and from it they could see the entire valley leading up to the Great Plateau. Before them was a handsome mixture of farmland and wild prairie through which a crystal-clear stream ran. Behind their cottage was a thickly wooded area and a second creek that ran toward the Phanos Forest and the Demotic Wall on the eastern edge of Entos.

The path to the city emerged from the woods behind the Timaho cottage, made a gentle bend to the right, then back to the left, and around a handsome stone formation, which in ancient times had been named, "The Three Faces of the King." One face bore the expression of deep sorrow for all the creatures who would never know the light of Entos. The second face was filled with joy for all who had been brought into the light. The third face was filled with great resolve, as a king whose face was set toward his enemy. The formation was not large, but had come to be a local symbol to the Entosians in the Demotic Valley.

The path made its way around "The Three Faces of the King," turned toward the city, wound its way down the gentle slope to the stream, then straightened itself out to take the traveler up to the Great Plateau.

Once Rieve and Thayer rounded the stone formation, the city was in plain view. The valley was filled with small fields replete with crops, almost ready to be harvested, and hedges that lined each side of the road. Wildflowers and bushes formed the borders between the fields and homes and framed one neighbor's property from another.

Rieve and Thayer laughed as they watched two snopes playing a game of tag in an open field. Snopes were cute and comical looking little creatures. They were small, no bigger than a Demotic's foot, but they had a thick coat of soft fur. They had long, large, floppy ears that dwarfed their bodies and big brown eyes, which seemed strikingly like that

The Oracles And The Jewels

of a Procuron. There was even an old fable that said that the Maker had taken from the Procuron race a measure of lightheartedness and gave this quality to the snopes. This was offered as the reason why Procurons were, of all Entosians, the most sober.

Because snopes were equipped with four large and powerful paws, they did not run as other four-legged creatures. Their powerful paws, short legs, and natural quickness fooled the eye. As they bolted around the field, they appeared to float and their movements were like that of a hummingbird rather than a normal mammal. Snopes were free creatures. They lived wild and came and went as it pleased them. It was not uncommon for a snope or an entire family of snopes to adopt an Entosian family and make their home in their yards and gardens. They were partial to the young and to the old and lonely.

To the right of the path the Hodia Plateau was clearly visible. Its rock face was white and at some points reached three hundred feet from its base to its top. To the left of the valley stood the Polemmas Plateau, which was somewhat shorter, but no less beautiful. Cliffs of the Hodia Plateau consisted of white granite, while the cliffs of Polemmas shone with red granite.

"Look!" Rieve said, then pointed skyward, "Another one." Thayer looked up and saw a large, monstrous winged creature soaring high above the valley and heading toward the city.

"That makes three this past week," Thayer said as he shielded his eyes from the bright blue sky.

"Three? I wonder what that means."

"It can't be good. When I saw the first one I thought the creature was lost or confused. I've never seen one of Bohow's creatures so close to the city before. When the second one appeared a couple of days ago, I thought it might be the same creature. But this one is reddish in color. The one I saw last time was as black as Ashkelon's soul."

"They say that Ashkelon can see through the eyes of such creatures if he so desires."

"That's what they say. If that's true, I suspect those creatures are scouts."

"Doing what?" Rieve asked.

Examination Day

"Scouting. That's what scouts do. That's why they're called scouts. And you're suppose to be the smart one in the family?"

"You will make a fine military officer, little brother," Rieve replied with a tone of sarcasm. "You see things with military eyes, even when those things might have nothing to do with military operations."

"When I see creatures of Bohow, I see enemies. What do you see when you look upon such creatures?"

"I see a lost and hopeless race, slaves to the evil one," Rieve answered.

"What do you feel?"

"Pity. Just pity," Rieve replied. "What do you feel?"

"I feel . . . I feel nothing. It just is."

"I suppose that is how a warrior ought to think. But I can't bring myself to it," Rieve replied.

"You have been chosen for the right vocation brother. You see things with the eyes of a priest and conjuror."

As they approached the city, Rieve started counting the cottages that dotted the landscape. The closer to the city they drew, the more crowded the valley. Rieve and Thayer liked the location of their cottage. It was far enough out in the valley that they enjoyed a large yard and a variety of terrain. As the ground rose to meet the Great Plateau, the yards grew smaller and the cottages were built closer together.

As they began their way up the slope to the Great Plateau, they saw two girls coming up a path that merged with the main road.

"Oh great. Look who's coming," Thayer remarked.

"What do you have against River Kiernan?"

"She is too . . . well, she's too smart for one thing. She thinks she's always right. And she's too . . . too . . . proper, formal, prissy," Thayer said.

River was accompanied by her sister, younger by eighteen months, Blisse Maia. The two sisters were Demotics from the Arria Clan and lived in the western part of the Demotic Valley.

"She's always been nice to you. Without her as your tutor a couple of years back what kind of score do you think you'd be looking at today?" Rieve asked as he raised his hand and waved to the two girls.

The Oracles And The Jewels

"That's exactly what I mean. Most girls would use that fact. But she has never once reminded me that she taught me how to avoid logical fallacies and how to construct valid arguments and how to diagram grammatical constructs. That's just not natural for an Entosian girl."

"Quiet now, they'll hear you," Rieve said as the two girls approached.

"Good morning, gentlemen," River said greeting the two.

"Good morning, River Kiernan. It's good to see you too, Blisse Maia," Rieve said with a smile. "Thayer was just telling me how grateful he is that you were his tutor."

"I hear it's a big day for the two of you," River remarked. "Happy birthday Rieve Waynwright, and I hope you do well on your exam today, Thayer Taggert."

"Tag, please. Everyone calls me Tag. Everyone except my parents and you and even my parents have started calling me Tag lately."

"I like Thayer Taggert. It has the ring of a warrior and gentleman," River said. "Besides, Thayer Taggert, an officer in the military is addressed by his rank first, then his first name and followed by his last, at least until he reaches the rank of colonel or higher. At that point it is customary to use only his last name. For example, General Witticor."

"I know the protocol," Thayer said and rolled his eyes just enough for Rieve to see. "But how would you like it if I went around calling you River Kiernan all the time?"

"I would prefer it. It is my name after all. That's the problem with young Entosians these days. We don't pay as much attention to formality as is right and good for Entosians to do."

"Excuse me. My name is Blisse Maia, just in case anyone noticed that I was here," said Blisse in a tone much like that of Tag's.

"Sorry Blisse," Tag said, "I know what it's like being upstaged by a slightly older sibling."

"Blisse, when do you turn thirteen?" Rieve asked.

"In a couple of months," she answered.

"So you have to wait another six months before you take your vocational exam and receive your calling," Rieve said.

Examination Day

"No. I am taking the test this morning. Thanks to a little help from my sister, I was able to move my test date up. I took the pre-qualifying exam. By 2:00 this afternoon, I will be finished."

"You're taking your exam today?" Rieve replied with a bit of excitement.

"What are you testing for?" Tag asked.

"The healing field," Blisse answered.

"Well between the four of us, I think we have the Land of Entos covered. Rieve Waynwright will soon be a priest and a full conjuror. Thayer Taggert will be a warrior for all that is good and true and right. And Blisse Maia, a healer . . ."

"Who can dress Tag's wounds," Rieve interrupted.

"And me," River Kiernan said, "a teacher of the liberal and the performing arts so that the beauty of the arts will continue among us. That's just about everything an Entosian could ask for."

"Well, I would appreciate a roof over my head," Blisse snipped.

"I suppose a builder would be helpful," River replied, "but I think we can all agree, we could do without a graduate from The Academy of Governance."

"Every vocation has its place," Rieve said.

"Of course, but I don't know anyone at The Academy of Governance, do you?"

"No, I don't, River Kiernan," Rieve replied. "They tend to be the children of the government workers and I don't think too many of them live in the valleys."

"Quite true," River replied. "Blisse Maia and Thayer Taggert, all you need to do is pass the exam today and Entos will pass once again into the hands of capable servants."

"Well, the master builder you suggested a moment ago might come in handy," Rieve commented as they walked over a bridge that was showing some decay. He rubbed his finger over a bit of rust and then he rubbed the rust from his finger.

"What is that?" Blisse asked.

"Rust," Rieve answered.

"Rust?" She said with a surprise. "I never noticed that before."

The Oracles And The Jewels

"I haven't either and it is unusual to see decay on such a young bridge," Rieve answered.

"Young indeed. I believe this bridge is only 700 years old," River added.

"Too young to be showing signs like this," Rieve answered.

"Perhaps we should report it to The Academy of Governance so they can fix it," Blisse suggested.

"The last person we want to call about a rusty bridge is a graduate from The Academy of Governance. They would call for a study," River said.

"A study of rust," Rieve added.

"Then a study of metal," River said quickly.

"A study of the water that runs beneath," Rieve replied matching the speed with which River spoke.

"Of the ground and air that surrounds it," River said.

"And the birds that fly above it," Rieve added.

"And the animals and Entosians that walk over it," River quipped.

"Okay, okay, we get it," Blisse said putting an end to the game.

"We'll just call an engineer to fix the bridge," Tag said.

The four walked down the path a bit further. The conversation quieted as Tag and Blisse began reciting in unison their declensions, dates, quotations, and the Articles of Faith upon which the Land of Entos was founded. The only break in the pattern was the occasional correction by River when an errant recitation occurred. As the two approached the testing center, they didn't seem to mind being corrected. Tag even caught himself thanking River for one corrected answer.

The four approached the part of the path that always excited people. The valley sloped downward toward the city and dipped to its lowest point, then it rose gently but quickly to meet the Great Plateau. In the last twelve steps to the crest of the plateau, The Great Chamber came into view. With each step, more of Entos' buildings manifested themselves from the top to the bottom. In just a few small steps a Demotic would be transported from the peaceful rural existence of cottage life in the Demotic Valley to the busy excitement of the urban center that was the city of

Examination Day

Entos, a city comprised of impressive buildings, facades, and busy streets.

As they reached the place where the Demotic Valley met the Great Plateau, Rieve said with the tone of an elder statesman, "Well, there it is, Thayer and Blisse," as he nodded his head to the right of the street. "You have five minutes before the test begins. You better get in and get a good seat. I will be here at two when you get done."

"Me, too," River said. "I am sure you will both do fine. After all . . . ," River paused.

"After all, what?" Blisse asked.

"After all, you both had the best liberal arts tutor in all of Entos," River replied with a slight look of embarrassment.

"Natural enough for you now Tag?" Rieve asked with one corner of his mouth turned up.

"That doesn't change a thing," Tag answered.

"Come on Tag. It's time," Blisse said.

"Yes, it is," Tag answered. Tag and Blisse melted into the crowd of students rushing into the testing center and then disappeared through the threshold.

"I have to go too," River reported. "My class on the great literature of the middle period starts in about ten minutes."

"That sounds exciting," Rieve quipped.

"It is much more exciting than debates over useless speculation on utterances of ancient teachers whose manuscripts have long been lost," River replied.

"You better run. I think you're going to be late," Rieve said.

"I'll make it. You're the one who is going to be late." River said. "Good-bye, Rieve Waynwright."

"Good-bye, River Kiernan. Have a good day," Rieve said.

It was uncharacteristic of Rieve to be late for anything, especially a class on the unfulfilled prophecies of the Oracles. He knew that beneath the seemingly arrogant attitude of his younger brother, there was a boy who was as nervous as any Entosian on test day. He let Thayer set the pace of their walk and in so doing had fixed the time of his arrival. There was no avoiding it. For the first time in his life, Rieve would be late for class. As River ran down the path to

The Oracles And The Jewels

the left, Rieve headed off to the right at a full run shouting, "Excuse me! Pardon me!" for several city blocks.

Thayer entered the testing center and took a seat at the table nearest the door. Blisse found a spot near the front at the opposite end of the room. Packets of papers had been neatly placed atop all the mahogany tables. Pitchers of cool water and glasses sat along side of each test packet, which contained the exam, several booklets filled with blank pages, and the writing tools needed to complete the test dotted the table tops. Soft sounds of music played in the background. It was just loud enough to be heard, but not loud enough to disturb the test takers.

"Good morning, scholars," the administrator, a Procuron said. "Welcome. The first thing I would like to say as way of advice is to relax. This is a very important day for all of you. We all know that. But you have spent the past ten years preparing for this day. All that you have studied, learned, and done in pursuit of academic excellence will serve you well this day. The teachers of Entos have spared nothing. They have done all that was needed to prepare you for this milestone in your life. By the end of this day, you will know where you are needed and what you will become. You will know your place in Entos and will find therein your true calling. For Entos is a living being and we are her servants. It is better to serve in the lowliest station in Entos than in the grandest halls of Bohow."

Several of the students started to open their test packets. Tag reached for his as well. The administrator held up a hand. "I know you are anxious, but please don't open your test packet until I have finished giving you the instructions. There are several sections to the test. Each section is timed. You will turn in each section as you finish it so that they can be scored. You will be given a break every ninety minutes. You will be finished at 2:00. The results will be posted on the bulletin board at 3:00 this afternoon. Any questions?" The administrator looked around the large room. "Seeing none, let us begin. Please start Part–One: The Articles of Faith. At this time open your packets." The room filled with the sound of shuffling of paper. "You may begin now."

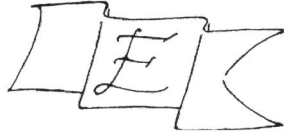

Chapter Two
School's In

The Academy of Theological Sciences and Ancient Conjuring Arts

Winded and sweating, Rieve tried to make his way into the nearest unoccupied seat in the lecture hall, but the effort was in vain. He had to push his way around three other students and took a seat in the second row from the back between Brenna and Yorrath.

Brenna Jossef was a Fortian from the Clan of Irisan. In the short time Brenna and Rieve had known each other they had become good friends. They hit it off from the very start. Rieve and Brenna shared an intense interest in the theological sciences, traveled in the same social circles, attended the same lectures and parties, and often found themselves arguing on the same side of an issue. Brenna's chief weakness was his willingness to entertain too many new ideas before rightly sifting through them. Brenna's excitement for new ideas sometimes put Rieve and Brenna on opposite sides of a question. Yet the two shared a common humor and humor often bridged the gap of their differences.

Yorrath was a Pithosian of the clan of Tommos, a noble and pious tribe who lived in one of the open fields of the Pithosian Valley. Yorrath was a gentle giant among the students at the Academy and humble of heart, and had the rare talent of befriending nearly everyone he met. He had taken particular notice of Rieve and Brenna in their first year at the Academy. He was loyal to the ancient ways, but did all within his power to avoid direct confrontations over the issues that were now dividing the students.

The Oracles And The Jewels

"Good morning Candidate Rieve Waynwright," Headmaster Sandor said, interrupting his lecture. "We thank thee for joining thyself to us this morning."

"My deepest apologies, Sir," Rieve said in a low and embarrassed tone.

"I believe this is a first for Candidate Rieve Waynwright," Sandor said. "Perhaps, Candidate Brenna, thou can help Candidate Waynwright grow a bit more comfortable with a casual style of life."

"I will do my best, Headmaster Sandor," Brenna answered with a boast. The class chuckled.

"I make no excuse for my tardiness," Rieve replied, "nor do I regard it as a matter for boasting."

"Very good indeed," Sandor said. "Perhaps, Candidate Waynwright, thou canst teach Candidate Brenna to be more comfortable with a life of formality."

"I do not believe such magic exists in all of Entos," Rieve quipped.

"Thus thou shows that it is not the power of the Oracles that is lacking, but rather our faith in them that is deficient. Yet, thy point is well taken in regard to Candidate Brenna."

"I think I am being insulted," Brenna said again with a tone of boastfulness.

"Ah, Candidate Waynwright thou hast already made progress. Candidate Brenna has begun to think."

"Sorry Headmaster," Brenna said, "but I get confused easily."

"Thou speakest rightfully," Sandor said with a faint smile. With each exchange the class laughed a little harder and Brenna's complexion grew more red.

"Still, Candidate Rieve Waynwright come and see me after thy morning classes have concluded," Sandor ordered.

"Yes, Headmaster. Again my apologies for the delay and the interruption."

Being late was a way of life for Tag and for Candidate Brenna. They would not have given the exchange another thought. But Rieve thought of tardiness as a sign of disrespect and that bothered him greatly.

Headmaster Sandor was considered the greatest teacher of his generation. Even though Sandor had never had an opportunity to use his power in a direct conflict with

School's In

Ashkelon, Entosians believed that Sandor was one of the most powerful conjurors in the history of Entos.

Sandor was so well read and learned in the Oracles that even his speech patterns and vocabulary mirrored the ancient tongues. Those critical of the ancient ways and language sometimes used the Headmaster's peculiar way of speaking as a basis for their mocking, but there was power in the old words and in Sandor's way of speaking. The words he used had shaped who he had become and he had become what the words he spoke had made him to be.

Sandor was also known for his tenacious defense of students, especially those who struggled in their academics. Sandor was kindly, unpretentious, and very ordinary. Though he had earned the right to command the greatest respect and the deepest address, Sandor had an air of familiarity about him. He was a statesman and grandfather to all who came into contact with him.

He was of humble origins, a Demotic. His hair, as with most Demotics, was blonde in his youth, but had grayed in his old age. He spoke in a rhythmic, musical style, which was a common trait among those who had spent their entire lives serving in The Great Chamber.

Sandor wore the customary priestly robes, but his robes were of the older style. They were plain, contained the eight colors of Entos, and were embroidered with an 'E', the symbol of Entos. He had been fitted for his robes fifty years earlier, when he was taller and walked erect. Time had shortened his stature and bent him a bit, but he had never taken the time to have his robes altered to fit his declining stature. Since a priest's robes never wore out, a priest did not need to buy new ones. But as the shape and size of the priest changed over the years, their robes needed to be tailored from time-to-time if they were going to fit properly.

"Gentlemen," Sandor began as he restarted his lecture, "there are among us a number of Entosians who make the claim that the prophesies of the Oracles are a map of and to the future. About this statement there is no doubt. The Oracles do speaketh of the future. What ought to be questioned is whether any Entosian can, based on what is written of the future, reproduce the details in the form of a map. I tell ye the prophesies are given us that we might have

The Oracles And The Jewels

hope and that this hope might carry us through days yet to come. I tell ye the words of the Oracles are not a map, not in the sense that there exists a map of this fine city, or of the land, or of Ashkelon's earth. The words concerning what is to come are words of promise," Sandor paused for a moment, "and words of warning. Take heed of both, but be particularly attentive to the words of promise for they illumine the words of warning."

Sandor paused and surveyed the room. "Yet this is not the greatest trespass in the new way. There is a greater trouble. In the new way of speaking, the words of the Oracles are understood as words of praise for all that is good and right in Entos . . . and in thyself. In the new way of speaking, the speakers give great attention to how Entosians ought to behave, the origin of the tribes, and the potential power of the words in thy speaking and living accordingly."

As Sandor spoke some of the students among whom the new ways had found favor dropped their eyes and bowed their heads toward their desktops. Too many of Entos's students had given ear to the new ways and to rumors that had arisen in the Academy. Many had begun to make alliances with other faculty members for the sake of their careers. Sandor was old and his influence in matters concerning the future was waning. Weaker hearts and minds had infected the Academy and were producing offspring in their likeness.

"Excuse me, Headmaster," one student interrupted. "Do you deny that there are things worthy of praise or that Entosians ought to speak and act as Entosians, or that the Oracles speak of things to come?"

"Lest ye think that I preach heresy, or deny the historical character of the words, let me say that the words do speaketh of the future, as prophecies always do. The words of the Oracles speaketh of the things to come, great battles, great saints, and great sinners," he paused again and took a drink, "the rise and the fall of creatures and nations, and of course, they speaketh of the King. I suggest in thy hearing no mythological interpretation, but rather of a higher history and a deeper understanding."

School's In

"Thou must think this way about the Oracles' words. The words about the future are to be comprehended in the same way as the words about the past." Sandor said then paused to stress his point, "We wilt know that a prophesy has come to pass only after the prophesy has come to pass and not a moment earlier. When it does come to pass, it still remains, in part, always unfulfilled. . . As for things worthy of praise or speaking and acting as Entosians, I find nothing praiseworthy in me or in my conduct. Art thou able to live in a manner worthy of praise? If so, do so."

"This is the good stuff," Yorrath whispered in Rieve's ear.

"Yes, it is," Rieve whispered back.

"Do you understand it?" Yorrath asked, "because I don't."

"We'll talk about it later," Rieve whispered. Rieve was annoyed with the interruption, but he hid his frustration.

"The greatest of all wars is coming," Sandor continued. "The prophesies tell us this. King Ashkelon will have his way with us for a while and the city will fall for we are not as praiseworthy as most now think, yet Ashkelon will not prevail. But think ye not this to be something new or greater than the threats that have come before." Sandor paused. "The threat is the same. It is always the same. There is nothing new under the Entosian moons. It is as it has always been. Ashkelon and his beasts have always been on the prowl for Entosian flesh." The room was silent. The students struggled to understand, and those that did not want to understand simply pretended as if they did.

"The soldiers of Ektos and the creatures of Bohow," Sandor continued, "have not breeched the gates and walls of our glorious land in many centuries, but the enemies of Entos are already within the city. It has been this way almost from the very beginning and so it will be this way today and all thy morrows."

This revelation further stunned the class and the students looked at each other and waited for someone to ask the obvious question. Brenna looked and pointed at Rieve. Rieve, having already drawn attention to himself by his entrance shook his head no and motioned with his lips, "You ask." With a shrug of his shoulders Brenna interrupted.

The Oracles And The Jewels

"Excuse me, Headmaster Sandor."

"Speaketh, Candidate Brenna," Sandor replied, "after all Candidate Waynwright and some others want to know too."

Brenna paused for a moment as he debated within his own thoughts as to how he ought to ask the question. "Are there agents of Ashkelon on the faculty of the Academy?" "Do they know themselves to be spies?" "Who among the faculty were the spies?" "How could these spies be identified?" These were the questions that students had debated in quiet and safe places. But to ask such questions out loud would draw undue attention to the one who asked the questions and no one, not even Brenna wanted that.

"If the prophesies speak of things that have always been, in what sense do they speak of things to come? And how is it that those that have been fulfilled remain unfulfilled? And . . . can they been seen in this place at this time?"

These were not the questions that all had hoped for. They were safe, given the atmosphere of the campus and came as close to the questions as one dared to get. Brenna was not known for caution and moderation, but when it came to one's career, timidness was the order of the day.

"Indeed," Sandor said with a tone of disappointment. "I thought thou might ask different questions, yet thy questions are pregnant with meaning. . . Candidate Rieve Waynwright, wilt thou dare to answer such pregnant questions?" Sandor asked.

Rieve paused for a moment to think. "It is a matter of degree, Sir," Rieve answered.

"Indeed," Sandor said. "Art thou able to speaketh more?"

"Things are as you say, Headmaster," Rieve continued. "The battle has always raged. Sometimes it is seen clearly, as is the case when Ashkelon or the creatures of Bohow attack our land and kill us. At other times the battle is unseen, hidden, even disguised as good deeds, so that most Entosians don't even notice that we are being undone."

"Thou hast spoken well. So well," Sandor said, "I will reward thee with another question. Concerning the future: how shall it be different in those great days?" Sandor asked.

School's In

"The prophesies predict that both good deeds and wars go together and that the wars will grow worse and good deeds shall become greater. But I do not know if these days are worse than those that came before. It was not until my arrival here at the Academy that I became aware of divisions and intrigue among us. It has been a disappointing and troubling revelation."

"Indeed," Sandor said as he moved away from the podium. As he moved he took his staff in hand and began to pace before the class. "The enemies of Entos walk among the friends of Entos in the light of day. They live in the valleys, in the hamlets, in our forests, upon mountains, on the plateaus, and even here in the city." As he spoke he lifted his staff in the direction of the most famous landmarks of Entos. "The enemies of the King walk in the streets and do business with fellow Entosians. They teach and study at every academy and always have."

"Including this one," Brenna blurted out.

Sandor smiled a small smile then continued. "They occupy important places in the halls of governance and always have. In your own homes they do reside and within The Great Chamber they do dwell. They, too, offer their praise to the King and think highly of themselves for having done so. They are filled with good intentions and seek to make Entos and all Entosians better than they found them."

"Headmaster," Brenna interrupted again, "I'm confused. Are we left only with mistrust? Do we trust one another or do we hold one another in suspicion?"

"Trust, of course, until we have ample reason to trust not," Sandor answered. "Is this not the ethic of Entos? Thus, it is to be. But either way, the battle that will be seen with the eyes will join the battle that has always been hidden."

"Are there teachers here at the Academy who cannot be trusted?" Brenna asked forsaking the caution that he had shown moments earlier.

"Trusted?" Sandor replied. "Dost thou trust what I teach because I teach it? Or dost thou trust what I teach because it is true?" It was obvious to all that Brenna did not know how to answer the question.

"Candidate Rieve Waynwright, dost thou have an answer?" Sandor asked.

The Oracles And The Jewels

"Both, Headmaster. I trust it because you teach it and I trust what you teach because it is true," Rieve answered. "As for trusting all on this faculty, I would rather not answer those questions for I know not how to answer them."

"Indeed," Sandor said, then continued. "Candidate Brenna, the Oracles foretell of the days when one Entosian will turn against another in a great and terrible battle. The words prophesy the day when the forces within will join with the forces from without to divide Entos. Once she is divided, she will be driven from the land from which she was created. When this will happen, we do not know. We do not have the time or the date. We only know that it will happen. When we are in the midst of these days, only then will it be known and thou wilt know it when we are in the midst of those days. They will be terrible. They will be wonderful."

As Sandor spoke, Rieve thought he detected a tone of joy in Sandor's speaking. Brenna thought he heard sorrow in the Headmaster's presentation.

"The scholars have always divided the words of the Oracles into three classes. Some of the Oracles told of the things of the Ancient of Days. These words speaketh of the first great battle between King Ashkelon and the King of Entos. They tell of the first great victory and of how the King and Creator made the good out of the bad. So it was with each of thee.

"The second kind of words teacheth Entosians what they are to believe and how Entosians live. These do not teacheth how it is that we became Entosians, but they teacheth how we remaineth what we are."

Candidate Devon, a Pithosian, spoke. "Headmaster, some say that the difference between the ancient ways and the new school is that the new school simply emphasizes certain words more than other words. What harm is there in that? You just acknowledged here that this is the proper function of the Oracles."

"So tell me, Candidate Devon, how are they doing, those who say such things? Are they living up to their own words or do they, like the servant before you now, fall short of the Oracles' commands?" Sandor did not allow the student to answer. He continued on.

School's In

"The third kind of words are the prophecies concerning the things to come. As we have just discussed, these words are hidden in the language of the mystery. They tell of unseen power and a war that has raged since that time when the Light first pierced the darkness. They tell of victories and defeats, past, present, and future; of loyalty and of betrayal; and of the rise, fall, and rise of Entos."

"Headmaster, which of the words do you say are most important?" Devon asked. Devon was a sincere student. He, like many students, found the new ways exciting and loved the optimism of a greater and more glorious Entos. He did not ask the questions in an effort to trap Sandor in a controversy, although that is how his questions sounded and how Sandor's answers might be used.

"Strange question. Why dost thou ask such a thing?" Sandor replied.

"Some of the scholars seem to stress the second, others have devoted their attention primarily to the third, but you are known for devoting your life to the first class of words," Devon said.

"Indeed, it is so. Yet I teach classes in all three," Sandor replied. "To speaketh of which is most important and which is the least important is the wrong way to think. The first words tell how it is that we have come to be. The second tell how it is we remain. The third tell what we shall become If we remain and if we fail to remain." He paused for a moment, walked to the desk, took a pitcher of water, and poured a portion into a glass. "Is the water that thou didst drink yesterday less important than the water thou didst drink today, or the water thou wilt drink tomorrow?" Sandor walked over to the student and offered him the glass of water. The student drank from the glass. "Is the question answered to thy satisfaction?"

"Indeed, Headmaster," Candidate Devon replied.

Throughout the history of Entos, many had tried to master the third kind of words in the hope of seeing the future. Some of those were scholars, others ordinary priests, and many laity, but no one had succeeded. No one, no matter how powerful, had pierced the veil of that which had not been revealed. But many longed for the power to do so.

The Oracles And The Jewels

Yet even Ashkelon left undisputed one fact in regard to the Oracles and Jewels. They possessed and conveyed a strange and mighty power that changed all things. As long as the Oracles and Jewels remained in Entos, Ashkelon could not prevail for the speaking of the words themselves had the potential to change and direct the future. All had been ordained from the Ancient of Days. Still the speaking and directing of the Oracles by those trained in the sacred arts changed all things from the moment of speaking, even if the change was undetected by the eye. It was the task of The Academy of Theological Sciences and Ancient Conjuring Arts to instruct the priests in the art of speaking the words. In those rare cases when priests showed exceptional skill and knowledge of these arts, the Academy was to make sure the priests used the skills to the glory of Entos.

Of all the vocations in Entos, the vocation of priest was the most demanding and required the most vigorous training. Priests not only needed to learn the ancient languages, history, music, the metaphysical arts, the warring arts, and the Oracles, but they also had to have a workable knowledge of mathematics, engineering, and the liberal arts.

The Academy of Theological Sciences and Ancient Conjuring Arts consisted of instructors of three ranks. The first rank was that of professor. These were men who were qualified to teach one or more subjects such as history, art, music, and interpretation.

The middle rank consisted of priests. They were ordained to serve in The Great Chamber and temples in the villages and hamlets throughout the land. The priests taught, spoke, and sang the liturgy. They handled the Oracles and the Jewels in The Great Chamber and practiced the mysteries in Entosian villages scattered throughout the land.

The highest rank in the Academy was that of conjuror. When a candidate, professor, or priest showed extraordinary skill, he would be selected from among his peers, adopted by a conjuror, and tutored in the skills of conjuring. Only the most skilled were accepted into the classes of conjuring arts.

School's In

Headmaster Sandor was one of the few Entosians who, by virtue of his wisdom and skill, had been trained and placed into the office of conjuror, priest, professor, and city father. This is the path for which Rieve had been chosen, although he did not yet understand the significance of that appointment.

Rieve spent the morning following his normal schedule. He attended classes, each at its appointed time. He took notes and passed the time, but his thoughts were directed toward his brother. The first part of the test should have been easy for Tag, Rieve thought. He had worked with Tag to make sure he had a thorough understanding of the religious and moral teachings of Entos.

The Articles of Faith should have been instilled in the minds of every citizen from his youth. In earlier times the words of the Oracles were commonly heard in the home of every Entosian. In addition to the training in the homes, families were expected to tell the stories of the Ancient of Days and the Days of Old. These were stories of folklore, told again and again in the language and rituals of each tribe. Many of the rituals were still practiced among the tribes, but even these celebrations were beginning to wane and lose their meaning.

The Articles of Faith were also taught in many Entosian songs and became themes in many Entosian plays. The priests spoke the teachings in the most eloquent of terms in The Great Chamber during the Eighth Day Rituals and visited schools to retell the great stories of old.

But in recent times, families had not been as diligent in the telling of the stories in their homes. The home had been the nursery for such instruction. Now the burden of teaching Entosian history and beliefs had shifted to the schools and the academies, but the academies were in decline. They expected less of their students and the students did not disappoint.

The decline had made it easy to confuse the people. New opinions had evolved and the teachers of Entos, once united in their understanding and purpose, often differed in what ought to be believed and done. At first the differences found expression in private conversations, studies, meeting rooms, and hallways. In time, the differences made their way

The Oracles And The Jewels

into the classrooms. From the classrooms the disagreements made their presence known in every school and in the streets of Entos. In public the professors pretended as if these differences were little more than pious variations of the same perspective, but the cracks that had appeared a generation earlier were growing into a great chasm in the present one.

The formal examinations were still based on the ancient ways and the old teaching. But pressure was building to make changes in the testing. If the examination was changed to accommodate the new ways of speaking and thinking, then all the schools would have to change accordingly.

For the moment the test remained as it had always been and very few students had mastered the teaching of the ancient ways as had Rieve. Tag had become the beneficiary of Rieve's knowledge and the test results would reflect the Timaho tradition.

The Liberal and Performing Arts Academy

River had arrived in the lecture hall with a few minutes to spare. The building for The Liberal and Performing Arts Academy was one of the newer buildings in the city. In the Days of Old the original theater had been the third building constructed, preceded only by The Great Chamber and The Academy of the Ancient Warring Arts. The theater had been one of the most valuable tools for learning and it had housed The Academy of the Liberal and Performing Arts. The poems, songs, paintings, and plays told the stories of the great heroes of old and taught lessons of love and virtue. The original theater had been abandoned and a new theater and academy had been built. The new theater was young, only one hundred fifty years old, housed the liberal arts academy, and was one of the most elegant and ornate buildings.

The building stood one hundred twenty feet high and was crowned by a large octagonal dome roof, under which was the main theater. The theater could hold up to twelve thousand and was decorated in gold and burgundy. Dozens of smaller theaters, art galleries, museums, and classrooms

School's In

filled the rest of the building. The main entrance was a prodigious porch, the roof of which was supported by four columns that each stood eighty feet high. In both beauty and size the Liberal and Performing Arts building was second only to The Great Chamber.

River settled into her seat and took out her notepad. She sat still and erect and waited for the start of the lecture.

"Hello, River Kiernan," Breille said in her usual cheerful tone. Breille was an unusual Procuron. She possessed all the qualities of the common Procuron. She was attractive, had a reddish tint to her blonde hair, a large mouth and large lips, which frequently turned to an almost overwhelming smile, big round eyes, and the Procuron's round ears. She was tall and shapely, polite and well reasoned, and devoutly loyal. Absent from her was the distance and formality of most Procurons. She had the intellect of the Procuron and the wit of the Demotic.

Breille had been the product of a mixed marriage. Mixed marriages in Entos were not unusual, but they were still uncommon. Most Entosians married within their own tribe. Shared tribal traditions and loyalty to one's family history made such marriages more likely, but occasionally

The Oracles And The Jewels

marriages between tribes were arranged and sometimes couples simply fell in love. When this happened, the couple always sought approval from their parents and clan leaders and permission was always granted.

While marriages between tribes were the exception, mixed marriages carried no stigma and the offspring of such marriages were treated without any predisposition or discrimination; after all, all within the Land of Entos were Entosians and this was where true unity was to be found.

Breille's mother was a Demotic and her father a Procuron. This mixture created an intellectually superior personality who was also warm, witty, and passionate. Breille liked equally the silence of thought and the company of friends.

"Hello Breille Clarrice," River replied in true form, "And congratulations on taking first place in the fencing competition."

"Thank you, although the competition this season was not very strong" Breille said.

"Still, it is quite an achievement."

"It is not as if I were fencing a professional warrior. It was only the amateur division."

"Humility has always been one of the Procuron's strongest virtues," River said. "But athletic achievements have not. Has a Procuron ever won the fencing competition before?"

"Yes. In the year 3467, Tate of the Morley Clan then Polemmas of the Sefton Clan prevailed in 4062," Breille answered without hesitation. "Both were full-blooded Procurons."

"Still your tribe must be proud."

"Yes, but since I am half Demotic the Procurons were well pleased to share the honor with the Demotic tribes."

"And I congratulate you on your achievement," River repeated.

"Isn't your sister taking her exam today?" Breille said, changing the subject.

"As we speak," River said. "How did you know? After all she is taking the test a few months early."

"Thirteen and a half months ago you told me that you were tutoring Blisse and that she would likely finish a bit

School's In

early. If I recall, she was on Chapter Eleven in Traditional Logic. Given the pace you set for her, I concluded she would be taking her exam today."

"Impressive, Breille Clarrice," River said and sighed. "I wish I could retain and remember information like that. Procurons are truly amazing creatures . . ." River paused a moment then completed her thought, "even when you're only half Procuron."

"The best of two worlds. Although sometimes my father would prefer that I only live in one." There was sadness in her voice and she knew it and overcompensated for the emotion with an overly cheerful tone. "I really hope that Blisse does very well."

"She'll do fine. I have been drilling her for days. We've covered the Articles of Faith, reason and logic, grammar and composition, history, governance, and her field of speciality,

The Oracles And The Jewels

anatomy and the healing arts. She's probably as ready as any Procuron at this point," River said with a smile.

"I wanted to be in the healing arts too," Breille said. "But I needed to pick. Last year they started pushing the schools and administrators to produce more builders and designers, so I spend most of my time in the building academy and take liberal arts courses as the schedule permits."

"I am surprised they let you do that," River said.

"That's one of the advantages to being a Procuron-Demotic mix. It doesn't hurt that my father is a man of influence either. It also helps that the two academies are across the street from one another."

"Still you must have earned privileges through an impressive academic record," River said.

"That's true, but those days are coming to an end. I hear there are big changes coming. New technologies, machines, and entertainment seem to be the trend," Breille said.

"Well, let's hope those changes don't take effect before you get your double major. That's a rare thing these days."

"All work and no play," Breille whispered. "Liberal arts is my play."

"Ladies and gentlemen, please take your seats," the professor said as she walked slowly to the podium. The lecture hall grew quiet.

The tone of Professor Marika's voice was uncharacteristically sober and the students could tell that something was wrong. Professor Marika was a beautiful and elderly Kilposian. In her youth she was one of Entos' leading ladies of the theater. But age had weakened her voice, so she gave up the theater and had taken up her second love, literature and theater from the early and middle periods. Professor Marika lifted her head and took a breath.

"Students," she said and paused, "I have an announcement to make before we begin our lecture on great literature of the middle period. I have been directed to make an announcement this morning. This announcement is being made in all the academies today. The City Fathers want to make sure that all of Entos is kept well informed on changes that will soon take effect." Marika was doing her duty and although she was trying to hide her dissatisfaction

School's In

with it, her dissent could be heard in her voice and seen in her tense features.

"As you know, this is examination day and a few thousand of your fellow Entosian students are taking their placement exams at the examination centers throughout the land. What you may not know is that over the past few years the City Fathers have been examining ways to build Entos into an even greater and larger kingdom.

"The City Fathers believe that Entos will be stronger if she is larger. They hope that by making a some changes we will soon be able to expand her exterior walls and will be able to take more territory from Bohow and claim more for her own, as was done in the Days of Old. In their wisdom and for the sake of growing Entos, the City Fathers have decided to make some changes, and these changes will have their greatest effect on the academies and on all future graduates, beginning with you."

"Here comes the bad news," Breille said in a whisper. River nodded.

"It has been decided," Marika continued, "that enrollment in the following academies will be decreased. The Academy of Theological Sciences and Ancient Conjuring Arts, The Academy of the Ancient Warring Arts, and The Academy of Healing Arts will all be reduced by one-third their present size at the end of this term. The Academy of Building Arts, The Academy of the Liberal and Performing Arts, and The Academy of Governance and Administration will all be increased twofold."

"But Professor it's unfair . . . just unfair to change the rules!" one student objected.

"It is about time that this academy be given its due," another student blurted out. The classroom erupted into open disagreement.

"Excuse me!" Marika said in as strong a voice as she could manage. "Excuse me!" she said a second time as she struck her cane on the floor. "You are Entosians. You all have been taught better than this. I disagree with the ruling as well, yet, it is my duty as an Entosian to yield to our leaders. As to 'unfair' this is not the language of a mature Entosian. Nor is one academy to be valued above another. The Academy of Theological Sciences and Ancient

The Oracles And The Jewels

Conjuring Arts is the queen of all the academies. All else in Entos is to serve this institution and the priests, teachers, and conjurors it produces." Marika paused and looked around the lecture hall. Several of the students who had behaved poorly bowed their heads in shame.

"I am very sorry," Marika continued "that this decision has been made. But it is the will of the City Fathers and in the absence of formal dissent from The Academy of Theological Sciences and Ancient Conjuring Arts, it is our duty to obey. As to the reason for these changes, they are part of the program of modernization. Under this new program, the practical arts will be the trend of the future. I'm the messenger, playing the role assigned to me, as is true with every academy this morning. The City Fathers have spoken. It falls to you to obey as best you can. It is your duty to obey as is right and good for all Entosians to do." Marika moved to the side of the podium and placed her hand on it as if to steady herself.

"This means that many of you will be reassigned to a new academy at the end of this term. The decision as to who stays and who is reassigned will be made on the basis of your academic performance and the scores from your entrance exam. You will be notified at the end of the term as to which academy you will attend the next term. Until then, we will continue and make the best of the present situation. If you find yourself in dissent, I encourage you to stay within the system and work for change down the road."

"Normal." River uttered under her breath, "Things don't sound normal to me. We belong to Entos. She does not belong to us."

"This is true," Breille whispered back. "My father would say this is exactly why we ought to yield to the will of the City Fathers. We serve where we are needed."

"But have the needs of Entos changed so drastically and suddenly that we must change that which has served the needs so well for so long? I think not. For eons this land has been governed and ordered in a particular fashion. Our own generation has now decided to alter the balance?"

"River, don't you think you're exaggerating just a bit?" Breille replied in slightly more than a whisper. "It's one thing to ruin my life a second time by changing my station again.

School's In

It's quite another to suggest that there is a cosmic shift taking place that could threaten the very existence of Entos. It's bad enough that I will likely be restricted to the building academy."

"Maybe I am exaggerating, but think about it," River replied. "This is at least a very bad idea." Professor Marika glanced in their direction. River and Breille fell silent and sat erect. The Professor turned and took her place behind the podium.

River whispered, "And Breille. . . . don't worry about your life being ruined. A Procuron as perky as you will always land on her feet. I think that is written in the stars someplace."

The two ladies settled into their seats, took their writing tools in hand and began listening to the lecture in earnest. Professor Marika tried to proceed with her lecture as usual, but the announcement had changed the atmosphere.

The Testing Center

"Ladies and gentlemen," the Procuron administrator declared. "Your time for Part One has expired. Please put your writing tools down, and pass the first part of your exam to the middle aisle where the recorder can collect them. Take a five minute break, then return to your tables to begin Part Two: Reasoning and Logic." The room was filled with the shuffling of paper and the sliding of chairs, which gave way to the sounds of anxious students querying one another over the exam.

"Well," Tag muttered to himself, "Part Two should be manageable enough. I just hope River Kiernan knew what she was doing." He passed Part One to his right, filled his water glass from the pitcher, and took a drink.

"Hey Tag! Tag!" a voice shouted in half a whisper.

"Hello, Brenz. I didn't see you over there." Brenz Clinton was a Kilposian of the Clan of Lalage. Few Kilposians sought a career in the military, but Brenz, like Thayer, had grown up with only one desire – he wanted to be a warrior. Brenz was two years Tag's senior and had had the foresight

The Oracles And The Jewels

to create his own physical training program to compensate for a Kilposian's physical weaknesses.

"Any problems so far, Tag?" Brenz asked.

"No problem. How about you?"

"So far so good. I saw you walk in with Headmaster Sandor's granddaughter, Blisse Maia. What's that about?" Brenz asked.

"Not what you think," Tag replied with a frown. "Her older sister tutored me for a while, and occasionally when Rieve and I are running a little late, we bump into them on the road. It's been that way all our lives. That's all there is to it."

"Sure," Brenz replied. "You might not be interested in her, but she looked interested in you."

"She's over there. I'm sitting here," Tag said, then picked up a writing tool and threw it at Brenz.

"Throwing things! Are you trying to get yourself kicked out of the Warring Arts Academy before you get there?" Brenz asked with a big smile as he returned the tool in the same manner in which he had received it.

"How confident are you?" Tag asked.

"I feel pretty good. I think I am going to do okay. And you?"

"I intend to set the academic record today," Tag said and smiled.

"An academic record? Pretty confident. That's held by General Witticor and is more than fifty years old," Brenz said.

"Hodia only takes the best of the best," Tag replied.

"I'll be happy if I make it into Krattos or Polemmas. To do that I am going to have to do well on the rest of the exam, but logic and languages aren't my strongest disciplines."

"Krattos or Polemmas! Come on, you can do better than that," Tag countered.

"What's wrong with Krattos or Polemmas? They're among the best armies in all of Entos."

"Yes, but they are not Hodia. Why settle for second or third best when you can be the best? The Hodia army will bear the brunt of Ashkelon's full attack when that day comes. Entos will stand or fall with the performance of the Hodia Army."

School's In

"Krattos and Polemmas might be a disappointment to you, but one of the marks of a good warrior is to serve when and where he is placed. Kilposians are not well suited for combat."

"Brenz, you're a good student and I'm looking forward to serving with you. But one of these days I will be standing guard over the Hodia Tower and your message will come. 'Captain Thayer Taggert, the army of Polemmas needs reinforcements immediately! Save us! Desperately Yours, Captain Brenz Clinton.'"

"In your dreams, Tag," Brenz said as students began filing back into the testing room. "I am not your average Kilposian. I've trained my whole life to be a warrior."

"Good, you'll need it to keep up with me."

"Do you have any plans for lunch?" Brenz asked.

"I was going to eat. What do you have planned?"

"I was thinking about watching you eat, if that is all right with you," Brenz said.

"That's something we both can look forward to. Talk to you at lunch. Do well," Tag said.

"Good luck to you too, Tag."

"Brenz, I don't need luck. I've got me," Tag replied with a grin. "You keep the luck. Kilposians need it in this vocation."

Brenz made his way through the crowded hall. As he walked toward his place at a table, the hundreds of conversations that had previously filled the hall began to soften and within a few moments had settled into a quiet hush. Even the noise of chairs being slid across the floor came to a quiet rest.

"Ladies and gentlemen, please take your seats," the administrator said. "You will have sixty minutes to complete the second part of your examination – Reasoning and Logic. You may open your test packets and begin."

The hall erupted with the sound of envelopes being opened and paper being shuffled into place. Blisse approached the test with little concern, but with a very specific strategy. She started with the first question and worked her way through in sequence. Tag, on the other hand, surveyed the exam, skimming each page just long enough to get an overview of its difficulties, then returned to the beginning and started with the easiest questions first.

The Oracles And The Jewels

Brenz took a third approach. He reviewed each page carefully. When the answer made its presence known in his own mind, he stopped to write the answer the corresponding question.

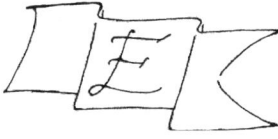

Chapter Three
"Honorably Retired"

The Academy of Theological Sciences and Ancient Conjuring Arts

    Rieve pulled open the large wooden doors to the faculty building and entered. He turned to his left and started down the narrow but brightly lit hallway to the Headmaster's office. It was a short walk. The Headmaster's office was three doors down from the main entrance on the first floor of the building. Headmaster Sandor liked the location of his office. As he had grown older, he had become more sociable and enjoyed frequent visits from faculty members, and Academy graduates.
    Rieve walked slowly down the hardwood floors. Each step echoed in the hallway and Rieve was self-conscious about the noise of his own footsteps. He walked slowly, gently, and nervously toward the office door. "What could Headmaster Sandor want with me?" Rieve thought to himself. "Surely students have been late to his class before?" although he couldn't recall anyone other than Brenna who had done so during his time on campus. "Am I in trouble? No, that can't be it," he thought. "Headmaster Sandor is not the kind to take offense at a rare incident of tardiness." Before Rieve could go on to his next thought, Professor MulLord stepped out of his office and bumped into Rieve with such force that the professor's books and papers spilled onto the floor.
    "Candidate Rieve Waynwright! What are you doing sneaking around here!" Professor MulLord shouted in a flash of temper. "Students don't belong in this part of the building without an appointment."

The Oracles And The Jewels

"Excuse me, Professor MulLord, it appears you didn't see me in your way," Rieve said with a touch of humor. Rieve was surprised at the tone of his own statement. He meant the comment in jest, but his words did not carry the sound of humor. As soon as Rieve had finished the sentence, he felt MulLord's arrogance bite him.

"You find fault with me? Is this not my office and does not this hallway belong to those with degrees? Degrees you have not yet earned!" MulLord said. Rieve looked at his eyes and saw what all others before him had seen. At that moment Rieve learned that what others had said of MulLord was not without foundation. He was a mean Entosian. Mean Entosians were rare creatures, but, sadly they did exist. In these latter days, it seemed that there were more of them than in the days gone by and MulLord was said to be one of the meanest. He had earned his reputation as he climbed the political ladder. As he climbed the ladder, he shamed as many on the way as was needed – and a few just for the pleasure of it.

"Out of the way," Professor MulLord said as he pushed Rieve aside. Rieve stepped back and debated as to whether he ought to help MulLord pick up the mess or move on. Staying and helping would certainly invite more abuse, yet staying and helping the professor was what would be expected under normal conditions and he did not want to give Professor MulLord any excuse for an accusation against him.

"I am terribly sorry, Professor MulLord, for both my inappropriate humor and for my share in this mess," Rieve offered.

"Again I say, you don't belong here. Move on!" MulLord snapped.

"But sir, I do have an appointment with the Headmaster," Rieve replied. Rieve knelt down to help pick up the papers.

"Oh you do – do you? An appointment? What does Headmaster Sandor want with you?" MulLord snapped again.

"I was wondering that myself," Rieve replied. He reached over to collect some of the papers into a pile. "May I help you pick . . . "

"Honorably Retired"

"No! No! Definitely not!" MulLord grabbed Rieve's wrist, twisted it a bit, and pushed his hand away from the papers. "These are none of your business! They are faculty business!" MulLord said as he stepped over the papers and tried to shield their titles from Rieve's view.

It was too late. Rieve's eye had caught the title of two of the documents. The title on the first paper was partially obscured by another that lay on top of it. "A Report on the Administration and Conjuring of. . ." The second document bore the heading, "A List of Unsuitable Cand. . ." A third document was plainly visible. It bore the title, "The Recommendations for the Reorganization and Growth of Entos."

"Now move along, Candidate Rieve Waynwright, and learn to watch where you're walking in the future," Professor MulLord said as he gathered the papers to himself and clutched them to his breast.

"Yes, Professor MulLord," Rieve said with less than an apologetic tone. He rose and stepped carefully around MulLord and the mess on the floor. "Have a good day, Professor MulLord." The comment was offered more as a formality than a genuine wish. MulLord didn't utter a word in reply.

Professor MulLord was not one of the Academy's brightest lights. He was, unfortunately, one of the Headmaster's biggest mistakes. MulLord had graduated from the Academy four decades earlier and he had spent the first ten years of his career as a priest traveling through the hamlets and villages in the countryside of the Pithosian and Fortian Valleys. Once he had worn out his welcome among the Fortian and Pithosian tribes, he spent a few years traveling the Nuxia and Tarchus Plateaus. MulLord had managed to convince Sandor that he was much better suited for the academic work of the Academy and that he would be of a greater value to Entos if he could work along side of Sandor.

The Headmaster had always been bad at administrative work. He loved the classroom and found administrative work to be harmful to theological reflection. He was a terrible bureaucrat, so when MulLord suggested that he could relieve Sandor of some of the administrative responsibilities

The Oracles And The Jewels

to give Sandor more time to visit with his students, Sandor created a position for MulLord at the Academy. Soon after taking up his administrative post, MulLord set his sights on teaching and much more. The appointment turned out to be a great mistake. Sandor had underestimated just how influential and dangerous an efficient bureaucrat could be.

As a thinker and teacher, MulLord's understanding was flat and dull. Even the most eloquent and comforting passages of the Oracles fell from MulLord's lips with the weight of lead. By the time MulLord had finished a lecture, that which was given in the Oracles to encourage and comfort had become burdensome, at least to those who were astute enough to understand what MulLord had said.

Headmaster Sandor and MulLord seemed to be at opposite ends of the Entosian spectrum. While firm in his teaching and convictions, Sandor was relaxed with the circumstances around him and was sometimes too passive, at least in the judgment of many. Professor MulLord, on the other hand, never seemed relaxed or content.

Sandor had increased in power and had grown in wisdom and in the conjuring arts over his tenure as a professor and in the office of Headmaster. Professor MulLord had changed barely a word in his lectures in more than twenty years. For all his years of service he hadn't grown a bit. Time had hardened him and he thought that the passing of the years had earned him the right to act in an unkindly manner toward those he considered his inferiors. By the mere passage of time, he thought he had earned the right to subordinate all with whom he came into contact. He was the kind of man who took control even when it was not his job to do so. MulLord always had a better plan. He was full of ideas about how to improve Entos or his fellow Entosians. Worst of all, MulLord had come to believe that it was his duty to rid the Academy of any student he thought a potential threat to his vision for Entos. Sometimes he tried to remove students simply because he didn't find their personalities suitable for the work of a priest.

Sandor was content to let all things run their course and although he had the power, by the force of his personality and by virtue of his conjuring skills, to change circumstances around him, he had never done so. By the time Sandor realized what kind of person MulLord was, he could not rid the Academy of the man, so Sandor settled into a pattern of disallowing any harmful decision made by MulLord. On occasion he disallowed MulLord's rulings just because he could.

MulLord had become one of the chief supporters for modernization. He was a pragmatist and an opportunist who sided with the group he believed would emerge victorious. If there was going to be a fight between the ancient ways and the new, MulLord would fight on the side he believed would ultimately prevail.

The new school, while not completely dismissive of the old, encouraged Entosians to rely more on their own inclinations and instincts. The new school wanted Entosians to take a more active role in shaping the future of Entos and to do so on the basis of good will and feelings, with unthinking obedience to those in authority. The new approach emphasized the service of the individual and urged Entosians to take pride in their personal sacrifices. The new way judged things according to results and what the eye could see. And what the eye could see was a more visible enthusiasm for a grander vision of what Entos could become under the new measures. These measures included a new kind of spiritual song, messages that urged the people to look to their own works and intentions so they would feel good about themselves, and a promise of an improved quality of life for all of Entos if everyone would dedicate themselves to Entosian moral improvement.

The new approach had been gaining greater acceptance among the City Fathers, several of the Academy's professors, and an increasing number of priests in the city. In those places where the new measures were instituted, revenues and activity increased. This kind of success fueled greater and greater interest in change.

MulLord had become closely affiliated with the City Fathers who favored the new approach. They wanted modernization and believed that in time and under their guidance Entos could move beyond its primitive customs and emerge a larger and more sophisticated land. The boundaries of Entos had not moved since the Ancient of Days. The population had not increased in two thousand

The Oracles And The Jewels

years and the land remained dependent on the ancient arts of the conjurors and warriors for protection.

In the early days of Entos after the King had left, Ashkelon, his underlords, and a great multitude of dark creatures waged a second war against Entos. In those early days, the priests of Entos led the armies against the forces of Ektos. The priests and the warriors of Entos were greatly outnumbered. Yet they, like the King of Entos before them, prevailed against an enemy of greater size and might.

In those Ancient of Days, many battles had been fought and many Entosians had fallen. But with each battle, the conjurors grew stronger and wiser in the ways of the Oracles. It was only in the battles of war that the conjurors perfected their craft. They became proficient in fighting the evil forces with supernatural powers. In those days in the midst of the battle, the Oracles had also created many converts from out of Bohow. The words of the Oracles had been spoken and new Entosians had been created where none had existed before.

In those early battles it appeared that Ashkelon would prevail against his new enemy and wipe Entos from the face of his black earth. Then the conjurors led a counterattack and drove Ashkelon and his army from the plateaus and valleys of Entos, across the desert, through the Skattos Forest and the jungles and swamps beyond, over the Land of Barren Rock, and into his city, Ektos.

Still the Oracles foretold of a day when Ashkelon would leave Ektos and again emerge from the Skattos Forest to march against Entos and leave the city in ruin. From his youth, Sandor had foreseen these things in the words of the Oracles in the translation of a long disputed passage. Tηε χιτψ σηαλλ φαλλ βψ τηειρ ηανδ αλονε, βυτ βψ ηισ ηανδσ ωιλλ ασχενδ ον ηιγη. (The city shall fall by their hand alone, but by his hands will ascend on high.) Sandor's translation confused and unsettled many in Entos and had even become the subject of many students' research papers. They studied everything about the original text and the grammar of his translation – "by their hand alone" and "by his hands" – were of particular interest.

"Honorably Retired"

While Sandor did not know the time of the great battle, he knew that the passing of each year brought the great war nearer. As it drew closer, Sandor's powers and foresight grew greater. But his power was more felt than seen. Though his appearance was that of an ordinary priest, when Entosians came into his presence they knew they were standing in the presence of a powerful conjuror. Ashkelon's creatures had fled in his presence. He animated the inanimate. With one sentence he settled disputes, brought about reconciliations, and changed hearts and minds.

With the increase of Sandor's power, there had also been an increase in the raids upon the land. As the raids increased, divisions arose within city. In some strange way, Sandor's power and Ashkelon's evil were linked together. While it was left unsaid, some believed that Sandor was responsible for the discontent and Ashkelon's increasing anger, and that Entos would be a better and safer place once Sandor had moved on to the Hidden Lands.

Professor MulLord was one of the leaders who believed Sandor was responsible for the strain that was being felt in Entos. MulLord was also envious of Sandor's conjuring skills, and was even more frustrated by the fact that Sandor had captured the hearts and loyalty of many of the Academy's finest faculty members, apprentice priests, candidates, and graduates. The Headmaster himself had placed many of the graduates into their orders. With one word Sandor could raise an army and take control of Entos. But this was not his way or the way of Entos.

Compared to Sandor, MulLord's weaknesses were obvious to everyone. But as weak as MulLord was in the presence of Sandor, he was not without means or without friends. He was a powerful man in the Academy and had become so in the affairs of the city. His power was of a different nature than Sandor's and, unlike the Headmaster, MulLord did not hesitate to use it. He had the ears of certain City Fathers, and those City Fathers had a willing servant in Professor MulLord.

It had been rumored among the students at the Academy that some of the City Fathers and some of the Academy's faculty wanted to be done with Sandor. Rieve had dismissed the rumors as idle talk, but when he saw

The Oracles And The Jewels

MulLord's documents lying on the hallway floor, his spirit stirred.

The politics of Entos had traditionally been kept from the students in all the academies and the commoners of Entos were quite naive about the unseemly side of Entos. The internal politics and intrigue were a reality, but a reality that most did not want to think about and so they didn't.

Rieve took a couple of steps down the hall and readied himself to knock on the door of the Headmaster's study.

"Come in, Candidate Rieve Waynwright of the Clan of Timaho," the Headmaster said. The voice startled Rieve. He nervously entered the study and moved slowly toward the Headmaster who was seated at his desk peering out his study's window.

Sandor chuckled quietly under his breath as he thought about the encounter in the hallway. "Do not give that matter in the hallway any more thought," Sandor said. "It was Professor MulLord's fault and not thine."

"Yes, I know," Rieve said.

"Thy offer to help him was very kind."

"Thank you. It didn't seem to help," Rieve said quietly.

Sandor turned away from the window and rose from his old wooden chair. The chair creaked when he stood. Sandor stepped toward Rieve. This time the wooden floor creaked. Rieve now stood two feet away from Sandor. Rieve had never been so close to Sandor before. For the first time he could see Sandor's face in great detail. He looked upon Sandor with great interest and began to study his features.

Rieve had only known Sandor as a professor, a priest in The Great Chamber, and as the Headmaster of the Academy. All his life Rieve had seen him presiding over the Eighth Day Festival. He had listened to him lecture in the classroom and watched him march in parades with the military. Now it was as if Rieve was seeing Sandor for the very first time.

Rieve was surprised by what he saw. Everything about Sandor was intriguing. Sandor's face was more wrinkled than he had noticed before. His hair and beard were more silver than grey. His stance and posture were that of an old man, but his eyes had of the look of youthful energy. They were blue, a bright blue, warm, and they seemed to possess

"Honorably Retired"

the ability to look into the soul of the person upon whom their gaze fell. Yet, in so many ways Sandor had an ordinary appearance. His frame was bent, his hands wrinkled, and his head often cocked to one side.

As Rieve looked at Sandor, he seemed to be a bundle of contradictions. Sandor looked old and frail, yet there was a presence and energy about him. He was gentle, gracious, and patient, but he was steady and there now seemed an urgency about him. He was common, but he carried himself with an uncommon dignity. Sandor's appearance put Rieve at ease. The young Candidate felt so relaxed in Sandor's presence, he had to remind himself formality was expected even in this circumstance.

While Rieve studied Sandor, Sandor studied Rieve and had rendered his judgments in a much shorter time than had Rieve. Rieve was unimpressive to the eye, lanky, and he had a shyness about him. Nothing about him looked ready for battle. He was young and looked the same. Silence hung in the air as the two studied each other and as the silence lingered Rieve began to feel awkward in Sandor's presence and Sandor noticed.

Rieve, too, seemed to be a bundle of contradictions. There was a maturity in Rieve's disposition, a politeness in his manner, and it was easy to see that Rieve had never been tested. There was nothing about Rieve that would cause others to follow him. He carried himself with a quiet confidence, but it was so subtle that only the wisest teachers could see it. "Young, too young, too naive, too innocent, and too inexperienced for this matter. Still the King has ordained thee to be," Sandor thought but dared not speak it. "It is so. The King uses the lowliest and in thee my young friend, He has found the lowliest."

As they stood looking at each other, they could hear MulLord huffing and puffing under his breath and heard him as he stomped down the hallway. Sandor smiled at the sounds coming from the hallway.

"Thou may smile too," Sandor said to Rieve and Rieve complied.

"Please sitteth here," Sandor began. "I have something to talk about." Sandor spoke in a tone different from the one

The Oracles And The Jewels

Rieve had heard so often in the lecture hall. They sat. Sandor's chair creaked again.

"Yes, Sir," came a soft reply. "Again I apologize for being late to class this morning."

"Thou hast already apologized . . . twice if I remember. Dost thou think that offering a third time earns more forgiveness?" Sandor asked with a smile.

"No Sir, but I supposed this was the reason for our visit."

"Thou art here to talk about things far greater than tardiness – although tardiness is no light matter. But thou has been brought here by the King to talk about Entos and the Academy."

"Two of my favorite subjects, Sir," Rieve said nervously.

"They are changing," Sandor said with a firm and serious voice. "Change is an interesting thing. Dost thou agree?" Sandor asked. Rieve did not respond. "Some change will happen. Some change should happen. Entos was meant to be a place of ever-changing constants, not a place of constant changes."

"Sir?" Rieve asked.

"For some time now I have seen changes coming. All of my life really. These things do not just fall from the sky. These things of which we now speakethhad their seeds planted long ago, by naive, young, and foolish teachers. We are today what yesterday produced." Sandor paused and sighed.

"Yes, Sir," Rieve said to fill the air with sound.

"The times in which we find ourselves fit well with some of the words of the sacred texts and the prophecies. Dost thou agree with this too?" Sandor asked as he picked up his pipe and put it to his mouth.

"I don't know. I am too young to measure such things."

"I took notice of that fact," Sandor said. "But dost thou agree that some of what is taking place in Entos is spoken of in the prophecies?"

"I do not understand what you mean."

"The time is coming. I thought once that I would be called home before the hour came upon us. But now, I see. It seems, I alone see and I have often wondered if, since I am the only one seeing, if I am indeed seeing. But now there is no doubt in my mind, just the doubt that comes from my own unwillingness to face it. But some of the prophecies will come true soon."

"The prophecies?" Rieve said in a tone of curiosity.

"The prophecies are always coming true. Thou, thyself said the same this morning. The prophesies are always on their way. They are ever moving backward in time toward us and we are ever moving forward toward them. The prophecies are inescapable. That is why the time has come for a meeting such as this. The Academy is in trouble. Entos is in trouble. Soon it will be up to thee and to thy friends to do thy duties."

"What kind of trouble?" Rieve's tone stiffened.

"The worst kind of trouble. The kind of trouble that can drive Entosians to fear and despair. It is the kind of trouble that will pit father against son and brother against brother. Good friends will find themselves at odds. Confusion will reign and error will be accepted as truth. The truth will be called opinion and betrayal of one's friends will be called a virtue."

Rieve felt as though he had entered the room in the middle of a conversation. He knew of what Sandor spoke, but did not know his role in the matter. He looked uncomfortable and Sandor saw it.

"Sir," Rieve said in a soft tone, "the students are aware that there are differences of opinion among the faculty. The students themselves mirror these differences. But we are encouraged by teachers on both sides to treat these matters as open questions and minor things. We are encouraged to comply with the expectations of our teachers and to reserve judgment, at least until we are ordained."

"Indeed. There are too many on both sides of these questions who worry themselves over protocol and work too hard to observe brotherly collegiality. Sadly, this has been my own sin and I indulged too much foolishness myself. Now those who teach the truth are so busy trying to be nice to those who err that they forget that there is a place for righteous outrage," Sandor explained.

"Every student knows that the faculty is divided over these matters and the faculty treats the student accordingly. Professors Etam, Langward, Worett, Atteowe, Nestor, and Scarre represent the old school. We also know that

The Oracles And The Jewels

Professors MulLord, Ellery, Millaran, Suedos, Bozzez, Proditor, and Paddan advocate the new doctrine. We know that the others, like Professors Labban, Octavius, and Tedmund, my own father, don't seem to fit into either group." As Rieve spoke his father's name he made an intentional effort to sound as objective as he could, so as not to distinguish his father from any other. But he also looked to Sandor to see if he would offer a word or a gesture in defense of his father. But Sandor gave no indication as to the validity of Rieve's assessment and offered no assurance of his own father's position.

"What of this new way of speaking? What say thou of this?" Sandor asked.

"I am no scholar, Sir, just a student and only an adequate one at that," Rieve replied.

"It is not a scholar's debate," Sandor said. "Is it?"

Rieve paused then agreed, "No, sir. It is not."

"It is a matter for all Entosians. Is it not?" Sandor asked as he gently corrected Rieve's attempt to brush the debate off as member scholasticism.

"Yes, Sir, but the people do not seem up to the task, let alone interested in the debate," Rieve answered.

"Now what say thee of this new approach?" Sandor asked again. "What say thee, young scholar?"

"At best, it is a great risk and a departure from all that has been spoken before. I believe the new speaking will prove harmful to Entos. It is different from the words that have kept us safe these five thousand years," Rieve answered. He paused for a moment hoping that his reply would meet with Sandor's approval and satisfy his interest so that he could relax a bit.

"But?" Sandor said. Sandor's utterance added to Rieve's anxiety.

"But, Sir," Rieve continued, "Professor MulLord and others deny they are teaching anything new. They maintain that they are simply restoring a proper balance to the Academy and Entos. They believe that you have moved the Academy and Entos into a rigidity and formality that is strangling Entos' ability to grow and improve. They believe that their way is a restoration of the original way. They have even made up a little rhyme, which they speak mockingly in the classroom. I suppose you have heard it," Rieve said.

"No, I have not," Sandor said with a gleam in his eye. Rieve was instantly sorry he had spoken of the rhyme and he was surprised that something that was so commonly known among the students was unknown by the Headmaster.

"But I would like to hear the rhyme." Sandor said as he leaned forward. His chair creaked.

"I don't feel comfortable, Sir, reciting it," Rieve said. "It strikes me as disrespectful to you."

"Then speaketh it with good humor as if thou were a Fortian who has partaken at a victory celebration," Sandor said.

"Very well," Rieve cleared his throat. The lyrics of the song were well known to him, but in the presence of the Headmaster he had trouble remembering both the words and the melody. Rieve's eyes rolled upward as he struggled to recall the words. Then his eyes fell to the floor as the lyrics came to mind.

"Sandor's doctrine tried and true, shall bring to Entos nothing new. Old and gray he's here to stay, a relic of a bygone day. No growth, no love, no joy, no play, just status quo we know and pray."

There was a moment of silence.

"That's it, Headmaster," Rieve said softly. "That's all there is."

"Only one stanza?" Sandor said as he smiled a gentle smile. "I have only merited one stanza?"

"Sir, for all their claims of creativity, those of the new school seem limited in talent," Rieve said. "The new school is not known for good hymns."

"Indeed, thank you, Master Rieve, I enjoyed that very much."

"Sir, some of us have made up a rhyme in reply," Rieve said quickly.

"Indeed," Sandor said.

"Yes, Sir."

"Well then, speaketh it so I may hear."

The Oracles And The Jewels

"Very well, Sir," Rieve cleared his throat.

"Sandor's doctrine tried and true, shall bring to Entos nothing new. Tho old and gray his doctrine stay and leads no Entosian astray. No relic of a bygone day, but meant for love and meant to pray, yes meant for love and meant to pray."

Again silence followed.

"We only have one stanza too, sir. But I am sure we can write another," Rieve said.

"Thou and thy friends do me great honor, an honor greater than I deserve," Sandor said as he looked to the floor. "I wish it were true. But in some ways all that which is coming upon us is coming because I failed to stop it."

"Sir, how can you think you have any part in this matter?," Rieve asked.

"I am a conjuror and some say the most powerful in all the land, but I am still only an Entosian and I have not been exempt from foolishness. I have from time-to-time been foolish. I did not see what so many others saw . . . the yeast. And when I was told, I chose not to believe what my ears had heard. I listened to bureaucrats instead of theologians. I closed my eyes so that I did not see.

"But let us return to thy judgment and see if thou hast discerned rightly the menace that now threatens our beloved Entos. What else do these new theologians of Entos say?"

Rieve was glad to return to the topic at hand. He was uncomfortable playing father confessor to Sandor and did not understand Sandor's part in the present crisis. It was not the place of a candidate and apprentice priest to hear the confessions, formal or informal, of his teacher and Sandor's self-evaluation was starting to sound like a confession. Rieve also knew that anything that he said in reply to Sandor's comments would be spoken in foolish ignorance of the historical facts.

Rieve continued, "They say that once the balance is restored, Entos will grow as it did in the Days of Old. They take offense when others accuse them of departing from the words of the Oracles. They assert that as language and the times change, the words of the Oracles need to be explained in different ways to create a more uniform and better understanding on the part of the people."

"A 'uniform and better understanding' concerning the mysteries of Entos?" Sandor chuckled. "Understanding is overvalued. What dost thou say of these arguments?" Sandor asked, expecting a particular answer.

"At first I had hoped that Professor MulLord and the others were right. But the more I heard of their words and the more I saw of their effect, the more convinced I became of the danger inherent in the new way of speaking."

"So thou agrees . . . Professor MulLord and the others are guilty of error?" The statement surprised and panicked Rieve. There were things that a candidate simply did not do. Priests, conjurors, City Fathers, and professors were held in such high regard that students and ordinary citizens did not dare approach them on an informal basis. A candidate did not simply drop in to say "hello" to a faculty member. Accusing a sitting professor of an outright error was unthinkable, unless of course it was true. Even if it was true, a candidate placed his career at risk in making the statement. Saying such a thing out loud was dangerous. Rieve hesitated.

"Candidate Rieve . . . agree or not," Sandor said in a softened tone, "that Professor MulLord and the others are guilty of error?"

"With all due respect Headmaster, I would rather not answer that question at this time," Rieve replied.

"Huh . . . I understand," Sandor said with a slight tone of disappointment. But no sooner had the Headmaster pronounced the 'nd' on the word 'understand' when Rieve said in a surprisingly firm voice, "Yes Sir, he is. . . they are. . . guilty of a great error."

The Headmaster grinned proudly. "Thou dost understand the significance of these matters. It would also appear that thou understands that a price will have to be paid if these new speakings are going to be opposed."

"Sir, do you expect me to lead some kind of attack upon the offending faculty?" Rieve said in protest.

"Of course not. They will attack thee," Sandor said. "They won't be able to resist the temptation. They seek control of the Academy and they will have it."

The Oracles And The Jewels

"But Sir, you are in control of the Academy and whoever controls the Academy controls the destiny of Entos."

"That is an interesting statement. What does it mean?" Sandor asked. His voice raised to a higher pitch.

"Each season more and more advocates of the new way graduate and each year they take their place in the leadership of Entos. Each year there are always more of them and fewer and fewer of us. Some believe if we can take back full control of the academies, we can undo what they have done."

"That which is done can never be undone." Sandor said.

"Headmaster, you are the most knowledgeable teacher in all of Entos. You are not only the Headmaster of the Academy, you are also one of the City Fathers. You are the most powerful conjuror Entos has seen in one hundred years. You must have the power and political influence to set things right. If anyone in Entos can fend off the darkness, it is you," Rieve said. "Why don't you use your power and influence to unseat the enemies of the old ways?"

"Power and the language of politics is the language of fools. A fine student thou art, but here thou hast made the same mistake so many of our friends make. They are always trying to preserve Entos through the political structures. Tend to the heart and mind," Sandor said as he stood and looked out his window at the courtyard, then repeated the same words in a softer tone, "Tend instead to the heart and mind. This is our jurisdiction."

"Sir, many from the old way supported the election of President Botha. They say that most of the City Fathers favor the old way. Surely these men all owe their positions to you and they will listen to you if you command them to remove those who speak in these new ways," Rieve said.

"No one can stop what soon is to happen here. We have not reached this moment in isolation of all other moments. Botha and the others were supported by the practitioners of the old ways. But that was long ago and this present moment was begotten of all the moments before it. No creature born in this earth can alter the past. It is the past that is always begetting the present and the present never lasts."

"But surely," Rieve said, "Ashkelon cannot prevail."

"Honorably Retired"

"Not even Ashkelon can change the past. He cannot change what he is. He cannot change the place from whence he came. It is hubris that causes Ashkelon and some of our Entosians to think that they can undo what has been done. Our tomorrow will only change by changing the present and all the moments from this one to the one tomorrow. History will run its course," Sandor said as his eyes fell toward the floor. He paused for a moment. Rieve thought he heard a tone of despair in Sandor's voice and the pause did not help. A chill passed through Rieve and his heart sank.

"But what of the Academy? Surely we can win the day through the Academy," Rieve said, trying to sound hopeful.

"It is as thou says. If they control the academies, they control the future of Entos. The opposite however, is never true."

"Sir, but if the first is true, the second should also be true," Rieve said.

"Again thou speaks in the new way," Sandor said. "Thou has fallen prey to the error again." Sandor sighed and looked Rieve in the eyes. "That is easy enough to do. I myself have fallen prey to such ways of thinking in the past." Sandor swung his chair in the direction of the window and sat down. He watched MulLord hurrying across the courtyard and toward the tribunal hall. MulLord's walk was filled with self-importance, yet at the same time looked like a school boy late for class. It was a walk filled with arrogance and anxiety. Sandor chuckled at the sight, but said nothing. He turned his chair back toward Rieve and with a deep breath continued, "It will fall to thee, my son, to Candidate Rieve Waynwright son of Tedmund of the Demotic Tribe of the Timaho Clan. It will fall to thee and to a few others like thee. Ye shall find yourselves put to the test soon."

"What test? And why me?" Rieve said with a tone of alarm.

"Aaah. . . that's always the question isn't it? 'Why me?' Tell me why not thee? Everybody always says, 'Why me?' That's not the question. Why not thee? That is the question," Sandor said.

The Oracles And The Jewels

"Sir, I am so young. I'm no one important. I haven't been placed in my station yet. I haven't even had my first class in real conjuring. And who would follow or believe me?"

"It is not about thee. It's not about thy qualifications. It is not about thy own strength or weaknesses. It is not about whether thou is liked or disliked. It isn't even about whether Entosians will follow thee. It's not about thy timing. It's not about what thou wilt do or not do. That's the mistake and that is the mistake that is made by teachers of both the new and old ways."

Sandor turned to his desk, blew into the palm of his right hand, reached into a dish filled with silver and gold glitter, and took a fistful of the glitter. He repeated the process with his left hand. He turned toward Rieve and tossed the glitter into the air, where it remained suspended like two clouds. Sandor placed his index fingers in the middle of each cloud. He spun his right finger counterclockwise and his left clockwise in the midst of the glitter. The clouds flickered and rotated and each began to take its own unique shape. The cloud on the right appeared as the image of the scrolls, upon which the Oracles were written. The cloud on the left took the shape of the city's skyline.

"It is always about these and the King's plan for our history," Sandor said. "It is never about thee. It is always about these. Those who scheme for good and those who scheme for evil think that it is about them and what they do. That is not the way of the One who gave us the Oracles and Who put the light into the Jewels."

"But Sir, it is a truth that we are made by the Oracles and Jewels, without any part in us, but if we are to remain what we have become we are to do something. 'We are made,' the teachers teach, 'without our cooperation, but we do not remain without doing our part.' The same can be said of Entos. Surely you can and are to do something," Rieve said softly.

"I am doing something. I am talking to thee. This very act will soon place me in bondage and thee and thy friends, in the midst of danger." Sandor placed his index finger on the birthmark on Rieve's forehead and in a softer voice continued, "For this I am sorry, but I do only what must be done."

"Honorably Retired"

Sandor held his hands, palms up, under each of the glittering clouds, then blew gently across the floating images. Immediately the glitter lost its form and its weightlessness and fell into his hands. As Sandor returned the gold and silver glitter to the dish, Rieve continued.

"Danger? With all due respect, Sir, I think you overstate the case."

Placing a cloth over the dish of glitter, Sandor continued. "I'm afraid I do not. Entos is in danger and in times of danger, He Who gave us the Oracles and the Jewels and made us out of the darkness of Bohow has used the youngest and most foolish of all Entosians to save His peoples. This is our Maker's way."

"Still, Headmaster," Rieve said objecting to his impending call to arms, "I am an unlikely candidate for this mission." But Rieve's words were ignored and Sandor continued on as if Rieve hadn't spoken at all.

Sandor reached for a jar filled with ashes black as the night. He unscrewed the lid and poured a fistful into his left hand. He tossed these into the air with a more violent motion than he had used previously. The ashes hung in the air as a small, thick, black cloud. He stirred the cloud with his finger and spoke.

"On the other hand, King Ashkelon uses the mighty, the cunning, and the powerful to achieve his ends." As Sandor spoke the cloud of ash began to take the shape of a great battlefield divided by the eastern wall of Entos. "He has already set these things in motion. Ashkelon will amass his forces opposite the eastern wall between the Polemmas and Hodia Towers. When the time is right, when Entos is at her weakest, he will send his army against the wall and General Witticor will do what must be done. He will send the armies of Entos against Ashkelon. They will fight valiantly and all the eyes of Entos will look to that place."

Rieve looked into the cloud and saw the great battle that was to come. He gasped for air and looked to Sandor for comfort. In that moment he saw the horrible things that would take place at the eastern wall. Sandor provided no comfort, but only continued. "But don't be fooled; fight here the warriors must – if Entos is to be spared. But this is not where the battle will be won or lost." Sandor looked at Rieve

The Oracles And The Jewels

and then nodded his head toward a place a few feet behind and off Rieve's left shoulder. "It will be won or lost in The Great Chamber in the middle of the marble rail, where the cradle holds the Oracles and the Jewels." Rieve turned and looked to the spot where Sandor had pointed and there suspended in the air was a glittering cloud in the form of The Great Chamber.

"My son, thou wilt be tempted to look in the wrong place for victory. If thou and thy friends do, Entos will be lost." When Sandor said this the cloud of glitter fell to the floor. Just then someone knocked on Sandor's office door.

"Headmaster . . . Headmaster are you in there?" a voice called out from the hallway. The cloud of ash fell to the floor.

"It's time my son. It begins," Sandor said without emotion. Rieve looked to see if there was a smile, a sigh, a chuckle, or some sign from which he could take a cue, but there was only the statement.

"Headmaster, please open the door now!" the voice demanded with an unusual firmness.

"Enter captain," Sandor said. Four guards entered the study and stood before Sandor who had sat down to receive his guests. As the four entered the room, Rieve retreated toward the table.

"Headmaster, we've come to escort you to the council," the captain said.

"I am in no need of an escort," Sandor said. "I was not aware that a council meeting was scheduled for today . . . and so early."

"We've been ordered to retrieve you, Sir," the captain replied.

"Retrieve me? That's an all together different matter now, isn't it?" Sandor added.

The guards were from the newly established Praetorium Order. Six months earlier the City Fathers voted to create a new class of guards. This new order was created primarily for ceremonial purposes, but a provision had been included in the resolution that made the Praetorium guards responsible for the personal safety of the City Fathers. Unlike the regular army, the Praetorium guards were under the authority of the City Fathers rather than the army's generals. Up until this moment, they had been used only for

"Honorably Retired"

parades and civil ceremonies. Yet they were warriors in every way. They trained and drilled like every other warrior. In skill, they could match any seasoned veteran.

Retrieving Sandor marked a first for the guards. The sight was a strange one to behold and Rieve could hardly believe his eyes. An arrest in Entos was almost unheard of. One hadn't happened in Rieve's lifetime and he could not think of any Headmaster who had been treated in such a fashion. As he watched the sight unfold, it struck him as a historic moment and he felt a great shadow fall over the future of the Academy, although he did not yet fully comprehend the significance of the event.

"Yes, Sir. We've been sent to retrieve you," the guard said.

"Retrieve me?" Sandor said. "Have I been lost?" Professor MulLord entered the study and stood just inside the threshold and behind the guards.

"Headmaster Sandor," MulLord said in a voice that the Headmaster had never heard before, "the City Fathers desire your presence in the hall of the tribunal – immediately."

"Headmaster," the captain said, "Please come with us immediately."

"What's so pressing that this old man of eighty-five years must rush? It is not as if Entos is coming to an end .. now is it?" As he spoke he looked at Rieve, gave a slight smile, then a wink. Just as quickly, the smile disappeared and his countenance took on the look of a prophet. He set his face firmly toward MulLord and spoke.

"So the time has come, Professor MulLord, to do your deed. This is the day for which you have long waited. So have I. Let us go to this tribunal of yours to see their great resolve."

"Bring this Candidate too!" Professor MulLord said. The four guards hesitated and looked toward one another, then to Sandor.

"I said bring this Candidate so we can question him!" MulLord shouted.

"Question him about what?" growled Sandor. His voice rattled the window and stunned the guards. "Question him as to why he comes late to my class? Leave this Candidate

The Oracles And The Jewels

alone captain. Thou has what the fathers sent thee to retrieve. Does Professor MulLord have the authority to order thee about or dost thou belong to another?" Sandor looked sternly into the eyes of the captain.

"Professor MulLord," the captain said, "Headmaster Sandor is right. I have orders from the council to bring Headmaster Sandor to the hall. Those orders do not include this Candidate."

"I am a member of the City Fathers and I order you to bring this boy with us. It will save us trouble down the road."

Sandor stared into MulLord's eyes, lifted his eyebrows, and in the growling base voice that had shaken the room a moment earlier, Sandor said, "Professor, leave this Candidate alone and today it wilt be well for thee. Take this Candidate and it will not. Thou came for me and not for this lad." Sandor took his staff in his hand and set its base down on the floor with such firmness all in the room felt the power in his staff.

MulLord paused for a moment. The anger welled up in his face and his mouth opened, but not a sound came out. Sandor took his staff and held it between Rieve and MulLord.

"Very well!" MulLord said, retreating from his prior resolve. "Leave the boy. He is of no concern to us. He isn't even one of my better students."

"That's welcome news," Sandor said. Rieve grinned at the insult. "Now go about thy business Candidate Rieve Waynwright. Remember all that I have taught thee this day. Be in the right place at the right time from now on and all will be well with thee," Sandor said as he placed his index finger on the birthmark on Rieve's lip.

"Yes, Sir," Rieve said as his voice cracked.

"Now gentlemen," Sandor said, "the City Fathers are waiting. Move along and try to keep up please." Sandor pushed his way through the guards and MulLord. He entered the hallway first. The five others fell in behind him. "What a strange sight," Rieve thought to himself. "They came to take him, yet it is he who leads them."

Sandor led the way down the hall to the entryway. One of the honor guards reached around from behind Sandor to take his arm to help him through the main doors and over the step outside. "I thank thee," Sandor said, "but I am just fine. I know I look older than eighty-five but still, this step is quite manageable for an Entosian my age. Very kind of thee though."

"Yes, Sir," came the reply. Two of the honor guards quickened their pace and reached the doors first. They pushed on them. The doors opened, and as they opened, they gave out a squeak that echoed down the hall and out into the courtyard.

"I thank thee, gentlemen," Sandor said as he nodded his head. "Professor MulLord, when thou takest over the Academy, do something about those squeaky doors."

"Thanking servants for just doing their job!" Professor MulLord said with a tone of disapproval. "It is their duty to open doors for members of the city council."

"I did not thank them for doing their job," Sandor said. "I thanked them for doing their job well. I gather that this would seem a strange custom to one such as thee."

Professor MulLord quickened his pace and took the lead in the courtyard. He wanted to put a little distance between the Headmaster, the four guards, and himself. It wouldn't do for his purposes to have Sandor reach the doors of the Tribunal Hall before him. This was to be an exercise in humiliation.

As they crossed the courtyard MulLord made sure that he was a good four steps in front of the others. The configuration pleased him. He looked back to make sure the formation would give the right impression. Several students were sitting in the courtyard. Most were reading. Some were talking. But as MulLord, Sandor, and the guards made their way through the courtyard, everyone stopped what they were doing and watched the parade walk by. MulLord wanted to leave an impression and so he did. The Headmaster appeared to be a prisoner being led to his trial.

As they approached the door to the Tribunal Hall, Professor MulLord turned to make sure that the formation had held its shape. His foot caught the bottom of his robe and he fell into a newly planted flowerbed. Sandor and the guards tried to hide their pleasure at the sight, but were only slightly successful in the attempt.

The Oracles And The Jewels

"Professor MulLord," Sandor said as he moved to help MulLord up. "Didst thou hurt thyself?"

"Of course not! Don't touch me!" MulLord barked. "I'm fine!"

"Indeed. But thy robe is torn . . . there on the bottom," Sandor brushed the dirt from MulLord's robe and pointed to the place where the robe had been torn.

"I said don't touch me!"

Sandor took a step forward to mirror MulLord's movements. MulLord took a step away from Sandor and finished brushing himself off.

"Excuse me," Sandor said. He stepped aside so MulLord could resume his position at the head of the line. "I believe thou wanted to lead the way," Sandor added. MulLord pushed Sandor to the side and stepped in front of him.

"Captain. Do I look presentable?" MulLord asked.

"Yes, sir," the guard replied choosing to ignore the last remaining dirty spot on the backside of MulLord's robe. MulLord turned, took the last remaining steps to the door, pushed the doors open, and burst into the hall with the energy of a child. The guards smiled as they watched the arrogant, but soiled, MulLord enter the hall.

MulLord's youthful burst of energy left Sandor and the guards far behind, but MulLord assumed the others would follow closely on his heels. The guards paused for a moment and allowed the gap to widen.

Sandor turned to the guards and said, "I suppose we should follow or the whole scene will be ruined."

"I suppose so, Headmaster," the captain replied. "After you."

Sandor and the guards entered the hall well behind MulLord, who was just coming to the realization that he had become the object of amusement. As Sandor walked toward the large table at the opposite end of the hall, he walked between the eight large pillars that lined the right and left sides of the hall. The hall fell silent. Sandor looked around as he walked. The hall was filled with all the normal dignitaries. The participants were appropriate to the historic nature of the event.

"Honorably Retired"

Sitting at the judging table were the eleven City Fathers, various members of the Academy's theological faculty, some of whom were favorable to the Headmaster, but most of whom were not. Representatives from various government and religious agencies stood along the walls of the hall.

The tribunal hall table was large and made of solid oak carved from ancient trees from the Pithosian Valley. The table was in the shape of a large "C" and in the middle of the "C" there were two podiums. One was used by the accuser and the other by the accused. It was obvious to all that the defendant's podium belonged to Sandor this day. It was obvious to Sandor as well and he took his position at the defendant's podium without a word being spoken. He stood in the podium and looked at President Botha, a Kicahian, who sat in the presiding judge's seat. Seated to the president's right, was the secretary of the city council, Scoderan, an Aradian. To the left of the president was seated Vice President Mohhan, an Adroitian. The chair next to the secretary was occupied by General Witticor, the Commander of Entos' armies. He was a Fortian through and through and second in command in all of Entos. Only the City Fathers have the authority to counter an order given by Witticor.

The Oracles And The Jewels

The chair next to Witticor was empty. That was where the Headmaster of The Academy of Theological Sciences and Ancient Conjuring Arts was normally seated.

To the right of the Headmaster's empty chair were the presidents of the other three academies. President Fradden from The Academy of the Liberal and Preforming Arts, President Larrence of The Academy of Governance, and President Kuchen of The Academy of the Building Arts filled out the left side of the large table.

To the left of Vice President Mohhan were seated the rest of the City Fathers by order of their tribe: City Father Derson, the Procuron and Breille Clarrice's father; City Father Simmjer, the Pithosian; City Father Bennser, the Fortian; City Father Rolif, the Demotic; and the last seat was occupied by City Father Klemmond the Procuron.

The entire complement of the honor guard, fifty in all, stood at attention around the hall. A few faculty members of The Academy of the Theological Sciences were also present along with some other dignitaries, all of whom the Headmaster knew.

Sandor looked to his left to see who would play the role of his accuser. MulLord did not take up the position. This did not surprise Sandor. MulLord did not have that kind of courage or talent. He had the kind of courage that worked behind closed doors, where he could issue orders and avoid facing those whom he sought to harm, unless his prey were of a lower rank and generally defenseless. On such occasions MulLord could muster up courage to harm his victim. For such things he had courage, but courage was lacking when he had to confront those who were more than his equal.

Professor Ellery, one of the newer faculty members, stepped into the podium. He did so without looking at the Headmaster. He had only been at the Academy for two years. The Headmaster approved his transfer to the Academy because he thought Ellery had shown promise as a speaker of the words. In truth, Ellery was as much a practitioner of the new school as anyone on the faculty, but had managed to mislead most until this moment of betrayal.

Sandor looked around the room and saw many professors and statesmen whom he had known. Many of

"Honorably Retired"

those in the room owed their positions to Sandor. Throughout his long career Sandor had helped and appointed many of them to positions of influence. He had given them opportunities that they might have never had but for Sandor. Some he had rescued from unfortunate circumstances. Others he believed would be helped by regular contact with some of Entos' most brilliant thinkers. Tragically, many had not used the opportunities to their full potential.

Standing opposite Sandor and behind the judging table Professors Millaran, Suedos, Paddan, Bozzez, Proditor, and Timaho stood against the wall. Few were able to look Sandor in the eyes. Those who did could not maintain it for long. MulLord walked over to them, looked at each one, nodded his head, and then walked over to the empty chair next to Witticor and sat down to represent the Academy in this matter.

"Seeing all present, we are thus convened," President Botha said and dropped the gavel on the table. "Welcome Headmaster Sandor and thank you for being with us this afternoon."

"I thank thee and all who have come here on my account. I want to thank the City Fathers for the manner in which I was 'retrieved.' It was most interesting and most exciting. Quite a sight to see, I imagine."

"Sorry, Headmaster, if the manner in which Professor MulLord carried out his duty left you or anyone else with the wrong impression. Please know that we appreciate your cooperation," Botha commented.

"Anything I can do to help resolve this matter, anything within reason of course," Sandor said respectfully, "I shall do."

"We appreciate that as well. The first thing that I want to make clear to you, Headmaster Sandor, is that all of us in this room are deeply grateful for the decades of your service as a teacher, priest, and conjuror of Entos. I think I can say that there isn't an Entosian in this room or in all of Entos that does not recognize your many years of service to Entos, The Great Chamber, and the Academy, not to mention your great contributions to the study of the Oracles and to the Ancient Conjuring Arts. I also," the President continued,

The Oracles And The Jewels

"want you to know that this is not a trial. It is not even a hearing. You have been charged with no offense. No one here is accusing you of erring doctrine or of any offense that would justify your removal as the rightful Headmaster of The Academy of Theological Sciences and Ancient Conjuring Arts. Nor does anyone here seek your removal as a priest in The Great Chamber."

"This puts my mind at ease," Sandor said, "Yet it raises many questions. For example, why are we here?"

"We are here to bring resolution to an impasse, an impasse that many believe is harmful to efforts to unify Entos and to Entos herself. The City Fathers and the faculties of the various academies, especially of the Academy entrusted to you, are aware of the division among the conjurors, priests, and professors. This division has worked its way into all levels of service in Entos. Even villagers in the outer most parts of Entos at odds over these differences of opinion." Botha paused for a moment.

"In order to bring resolution to the problem, we thought it best to have a quiet meeting and to hear the concerns of some of the faculty members of your Academy, then to move in a way to bring resolution to the problem at hand. With your consent may we hear from Professor Ellery, who speaks on behalf of several faculty members, apprentices, and candidates of the Theological Academy?"

"Permission granted," the Headmaster said. "Who am I that I should keep men from making fools of themselves?" Professor Ellery's face turned red with anger. That was one of Ellery's weaknesses as a Kicahian. He could not control his passions and this weakness often manifested itself in full public view.

"Please, Headmaster. We could do without the harsh rhetoric," Botha said in a calm voice.

"Indeed, rhetoric. Yes, the most important thing these days. I apologize for my offense against modern sensitivities," Sandor replied.

"Apology accepted. Professor Ellery are you ready to begin your oration?" Botha asked.

"Yes, Mr. President. I am ready," Ellery said.

"Begin," Botha said nodding his head.

"Honorably Retired"

"Mr. President, City Fathers, fellow Professors of The Academy of Theological Sciences and Ancient Conjuring Arts, and Entosian Dignitaries, on behalf of the faculty and students of The Academy of Theological Sciences and Ancient Conjuring Arts I want to thank you for this opportunity to offer words of praise for our beloved Headmaster, who is without a doubt one of the greatest teachers in the history of Entos and a powerful conjuror, a faithful priest, and a fine leader. He once led our city and the Academy through difficult days. Many of us in this room owe our standing in Entos to his aid. He has given many of us opportunities to serve Entos in ways that we might not have had without his support. Headmaster Sandor, speaking for myself, I thank you for bringing me to the Academy and I hope that the words I am about to speak will not diminish the confidence you put in me by bringing me to this place.

"We have not gathered here to defame or to harm our beloved Headmaster. Rather, we have come to help him preserve that which he has earned over these many years – respect, love, and loyalty. We have come to speak to the greater glory of Entos. We have come to this hall to restore true perceptible unity to our grand city and noble land."

As Professor Ellery spoke, Sandor stood erect with his head slightly raised toward the ceiling and his eyes skyward. He stood stoic and seemingly without breath as he listened to the oration. Everyone's eyes moved back and forth between the two men.

"This meeting is not about the past. It is not our intent to harm or to diminish what the honorable Headmaster has done. We stand before you asking that the Academy and Entos be allowed to move forward into a new and more glorious day." Ellery paused and took a drink from the glass of water that had been placed on a shelf in the podium, then continued.

"When we speak in such ways other members of the Academy, even the Headmaster himself, are quick to claim that we are bringing a new way of speaking to Entos. They believe it is a teaching that will harm Entos and bring her to ruin, as if that were possible. It is not. The Oracles themselves teach that Entos can never be felled, not even by the King of Ektos himself.

The Oracles And The Jewels

"It is true. The Academy is hopelessly divided and, as a result, Headmaster Sandor's leadership as one of the City Fathers of this glorious city has also been hindered. The Academy's representative to this esteemed council has acted in such a way as to slow your deliberations and has impeded our progress as a city. I admit that the Academy has not been alone in this matter. The military and its representatives have also been obstructionists in this regard.

"But the matter of the military is a matter for the council and not the Academy. We are to be about the business of the theological Academy. For our part, many faculty members believe it would be best for the council to establish its own theological and military commission to offer advice in light of these impasses. Such a committee could offer its opinion on the practical matters facing the people, while the theological Academy can concern itself with the spiritual needs of ordinary Entosians. But I digress. Do as it pleases you.

"Mr. President, City Fathers, Priests, fellow Professors, and Entosian dignitaries we bring no new innovation to Entos. There is no new doctrine in our speaking. We value and uphold the place of the Oracles as the source and fountain of life for all of Entos. We maintain that the Jewels are to be used in accordance with the instructions set before us in the Oracles.

"The arguments against our position are many, but have the weight of a feather and ought to be silenced for the sake of unity. As I have said, we have invented nothing. We bring that which is ancient and old into a new and brighter day."

Botha interrupted, "If it is as you say, Professor Ellery, then why are we here? Why are the students of your Academy so deeply divided? And why is more and more of the City Fathers' time spent in debate over these matters?"

"We understand that it is difficult for the Headmaster and those who follow in his way to see these truths. We know that he and others see our way of speaking as a threat. But if we would only be given an opportunity to implement our programs of reform, all would see that we represent no threat to the ways of Entos. The differences are, in reality,

"Honorably Retired"

differences in style and emphasis, not in substance or formulation, Mr. President. It is one of emphasis, but not of content. It is one of style and not of substance," Ellery answered.

"It is my judgment," President Botha began, "that there are significant differences between the way in which City Father Scoderan and Professor MulLord speak and the way in which City Father Simmjer and Bennser Fortian speak. To deny these differences is disingenuous."

At that, the council erupted into shouts of "yea, yea," which was the custom of the council when a statement was made upon which all could agree.

"Order! order!" Botha shouted as he slammed the gavel on the tabletop. "Given the gravity of the matter before the council, I would ask that we suspend the customary partisan responses."

"Mr. President, City Fathers, distinguished guests," Ellery said, "I do not mean to suggest that we are not divided. It is our contention that we are divided over secondary matters that are not constitutive of what makes and keeps Entos great. We find ourselves in a new set of circumstances. The Land of Entos needs to expand. It needs to grow. It also needs to call its inhabitants to a higher form of existence. It is true, Entosians do not participate in the Great Festival as they once did. Those who do, do not speak and sing the words with the same passion they did a generation ago. It is our duty to awaken in the hearts of Entosians a zeal for the work of Entos.

"If one does not see the new circumstances in which we now find ourselves, then such a person can never understand the danger in which we now find ourselves. Headmaster Sandor's eyes are old and accustomed to seeing things in very specific ways. We understand why it is hard for the Headmaster and those instructed by him," Professor Ellery nodded his head in the direction of the Headmaster, "to see our approach for what it really is."

"It's death to Entos," Sandor said staring into Ellery's eyes.

"Headmaster," President Botha said, "you will be given an opportunity to reply."

The Oracles And The Jewels

"The Headmaster," Ellery continued, "has been unwilling to listen and accept our teaching at the Academy, as you can hear for yourself. He allows only those who share his views to sit as heads of the departments. We only ask that our way of speaking be treated as equal to their way of speaking, since we speak of the same thing."

"But in a different way," Botha replied.

"But of the same thing, Mr. President," Ellery answered, then continued. "Many among us are very loyal to the Headmaster. We are asking for this action as a way of saving him and the Academy from public embarrassment. He is in part causing the divisions at the Academy. Such actions are unbecoming an Entosian. They are not only unbecoming, they are also planting seeds of distrust among the students and faculty."

"In Entos," Sandor said, "distrust must be earned. It is not something that I can create in others."

"As a result of his critiques," Ellery continued, "as misguided as they are, we are distrusted by many students. As long as Headmaster Sandor remains the functioning Headmaster at The Academy of Theological Sciences and Ancient Conjuring Arts, we will be at an impasse and we will be divided."

"Mr. President," Bennser interrupted. "I invoke the question."

"Granted, Father Bennser," Botha replied.

"What are these new circumstances, Professor Ellery, that require new ways of speaking?" Bennser asked.

"In our history Entos has known great periods of expansion. It has been a very long time since any expansion has taken place. We should also note that before each of these periods of expansion, new things and ways were generally instituted. It is our view that change must come as a precursor to expansion."

Simmjer spoke. "Mr. President, a corrective point if I may Sir?"

"Is it essential to the argument at hand?" Botha politely asked.

"Yes, Mr. President, it is," Simmjer replied. "I would not interrupt otherwise."

"Very well."

"Honorably Retired"

"The connection between any supposed changes, if there were any changes at all, and the expansion of Entos' territory is superficial. One cannot say, as you have indicated before this esteemed council, that the former . . . change leads to the latter . . . expansion. Expansion of this kingdom is due only to the choice and movement of the King."

"Father Simmjer," Botha interrupted, "a corrective point is a corrective point, it is not a theological debate and lecture."

"Indeed, Mr. President," Rolif the Demotic interrupted, "but it is a point that must be corrected nonetheless."

"Objection, Mr. President!" Vice President Mohhan shouted. "If the supporters of Headmaster Sandor will not allow Professor Ellery to speak, this matter will never be resolved. It would appear to me that those opposed to this tribunal are about to engage in a filibuster and I, therefore, ask the President to limit the questions and corrective challenges to those that have already taken place!"

"We should have seen that coming," Klemmond the Procuron, said in a soft but firm voice.

"Mr. President," Kuchen interrupted, "There are rules, laws, and procedures. We have all agreed in love to keep these procedures – they are our love agreement and, while I am sympathetic to the Headmaster's perspective, Vice President Mohhan asks only for what the rules allow. It is now in the hands of the President."

"Limitation has been asked and given," Botha ruled. "Continue, Professor Ellery."

Ellery started again. "Mr. President, City Fathers, and distinguished guests. We merely desire to start a new era in the history of Entos. If we are permitted an equal standing with others, centuries from now our descendants will look upon what we have been allowed to do as one of the great movements in Entosian history. We will be remembered as the generation who ushered in the greatest of all epochs in history. We will usher in a period of growth and wealth unseen before our generation.

"But this cannot be done if the Headmaster and other faculty continue to question our motives and our approach. His opposition to our pious desires is creating divisions

The Oracles And The Jewels

within our great city. And what are our pious desires? We desire to make Entos even greater than she is and to welcome in a period of acceptance, prosperity, and peace unparalleled since the Days of Old. What is so evil about these desires?

"We are loyal subjects of Entos and we wish to remain loyal to our Headmaster, but as long as he remains an active part of the Academy, lecturing and training students in the classroom, his influence will continue to shape the thinking of many priests and conjurors, thus multiplying the divisions among us.

"A few minutes ago the Headmaster called me a fool. I have come here to keep the Headmaster from exposing himself as such through his continual critique and opposition to our approach. I do this out of love and devotion to him, to the Academy, and to Entos.

"We are not asking for the Headmaster's removal as Headmaster. We are asking him to retire from certain functions of the Office of Headmaster. We would like him to accept, happily and willingly, the Office of Headmaster Emeritus. In this office he can devote more time to studying and writing the many books he has begun, but has been unable to finish due to his many duties. As Headmaster Emeritus, I can assure you his advice will be sought and given due consideration when needed.

"It is therefore our request that the City Fathers act upon our recommendation." Ellery looked at Sandor who stood still and silent, but who also had a slight tear in his eye. Ellery continued, "We request that Headmaster Sandor step down and retire to the Office of Headmaster Emeritus."

"Beloved Headmaster," Botha began, "will you now accept this office voluntarily and in the spirit in which we make the offer? Will you honor us and yourself by accepting the Office of Headmaster Emeritus of the Academy?"

The hall was silent, except for the heavy breathing of Professor Ellery. Sandor did not move a muscle or say a word. He stood with his hand holding his staff and his eyes slightly upward.

"Headmaster Sandor," President Botha said. "Headmaster," he said a second time with a voice more firm and certain than the first.

"Honorably Retired"

"Yes, Mr. President," the Sandor replied.

"Did you hear the gracious offer of your faculty?" the President asked.

"I heard no gracious offer."

"I heard such an offer, Sir," Botha said. "I am of the opinion that you should accept this gracious offer for your own well-being and that of the Academy. You could accomplish many great things for the Academy and Entos if you were to devote yourself to finishing your books," President Botha explained. "This, Headmaster, is an honorable retirement. There is no shame associated with it. Again think of the great things you could accomplish."

"Great things? Great things? Why would I want to do great things when I have so many ordinary things to do?" Sandor asked. The hall fell silent again.

"Sir, I must insist that you answer the question put to you. Will you accept this offer or will you draw us into a battle over the governance of The Academy of Theological Sciences and Ancient Conjuring Arts? Will you allow us to move forward?" President Botha's voice took on the tone of a parent.

The silence in the room was deafening. City Fathers Derson, the Procuron; Simmjer the Pithosian; Bennser the Fortian; Rolif the Demotic; and General Witticor, the Fortian listened with as much interest as those who sought the retirement of the Headmaster. These City Fathers were on record opposing the proceeding and opposing the forced removal of the Headmaster from his office. They were critics of the new approach, but could not stop the inevitable. The fate of the Headmaster was sealed long before the meeting was held.

The Headmaster's silence seemed to last hours. "Headmaster," President Botha said again, "Will you accept this offer or not?" Sandor lowered his eyes and his head. He peered into the eyes of President Botha and said in a firm and low voice that shook the air.

"I cannot accept this offer for never in the history of Entos has such an offer been made or accepted. In these matters, that which is new cannot be of Entos. Under circumstances such as these, such an offer is likely to have been crafted by Ashkelon himself," Sandor said. The hall

The Oracles And The Jewels

exploded with the shouts of those who favored Sandor's removal. "Outrage!" one shouted. "See . . . see what is in his heart," another cried. "Silence him!" still others shouted.

"Order! Order!" Botha yelled as he struck his gravel on the tabletop. "Silence, all of you!" The hall fell silent. "Headmaster Sandor, I will not allow you to defame the good names of those who only seek to do you good!" Botha said, as he peered into Sandor's eyes.

"Nor will I yield to this new teaching," Sandor asserted. "For if I take part in this offense, soon every priest, prophet, and conjuror who speaks the King's truth to the dissatisfaction of those who have lost their way will be retired as if he were little more than an attendant. Do, therefore, what thou must . . . for thou has bound thyself with an oath. Let the deed be done, but be ye all prepared." His voice rolled around about the hall like thunder. The force of Botha's shout was paled by the words of Sandor. A cold chill raced up the spines of friend and foe alike. The hall was silent as the echo of Sandor's voice faded. Many of the members of the council looked to Secretary Scoderan. Sandor's eyes shifted from Botha to Scoderan.

"They are waiting, Mr. Secretary," Sandor said. "Do what it is thou hast been assigned to do. Thou has not the courage to change it now?"

Scoderan spoke the motion: "Let it be that Headmaster Sandor be honorably retired and placed into the Office of Headmaster Emeritus in appreciation for his decades of fine service to The Academy of Theological Sciences and Ancient Conjuring Arts; and in recognition for his decades of service to the Land of Entos, be it also that Headmaster Emeritus Sandor be removed from the classroom, from his study, and from his duties as Headmaster."

As Scoderan spoke the hall fell so silent each person heard his own heartbeat. For all knew they witnessing something unprecedented in the history of Entos.

"Let it be also," Scoderan continued, "that the city council direct Headmaster Sandor to spend his time toward greater endeavors such as writing and research so that future generations may have his wisdom preserved for study to the greater glory of Entos."

"Honorably Retired"

President Fradden supported the resolution. Vice President Mohnan called for the vote. Seven voted "yea" and six "nay."

President Larrence of The Academy of Governance wasted no time in placing a second resolution before the council: "Let it be that Professor MulLord serve as the new Headmaster of The Academy of Theological Sciences and Ancient Conjuring Arts, granting him the full authority to deal with the Academy, the apprentice priests, and candidates as he believes best for the greater glory of Entos." President Kuchen supported the resolution. The vote was eight to five.

President Botha followed with another resolution: "Let it be that the City Fathers formally endorse and implement The Great Declaration as has been outlined, presented, and discussed in prior meetings, and let The Great Declaration be posted throughout the whole Land of Entos with great rejoicing." Vice President Mohnan supported the action. The third vote passed by the same margin – eight "yeas" and five "nays."

"Let it also be resolved," President Kuchen began, "that the council of the City Fathers establish a Theological Advisory Committee, appointed by the City Fathers to consult with the City Fathers on practical matters, so that The Academy of Theological Sciences and Ancient Conjuring Arts may dedicate itself to training future priests and conjurors in spiritual matters, while allowing politics to be practiced in a more pure form." The fourth vote passed by a larger margin – nine "yeas" and four "nays."

President Botha rose from his chair and walked slowly toward Sandor. The hall was so silent that his steps echoed throughout the hall. Botha stopped just a couple of feet short of Sandor.

"We regret," Botha said with a sigh, "that all this has become necessary. As for my part, I am in favor of modernization, but firmly believe that modernization and the ancient ways can go hand-in-hand. I will make sure that the whole Land of Entos is aware of your fine service these many decades and I bear no ill will toward you. The climate in which we now find ourselves calls for some new innovations and, as long as you remain the active Headmaster of the Academy, there will be an atmosphere of

The Oracles And The Jewels

intimidation, although no one has been able to show that you have contributed to this atmosphere. The fact that some feel it is now enough to require action. I have done what I have done so that we can at least hope for a greater unity and a greater hope for peace in the Land of Entos."

"Peace, peace, when there is no peace. Hope, hope, where there is no hope. Unity, unity, at the price of peace and hope," Sandor said as he looked into Botha's eyes.

"You quote the Oracles rightly Headmaster . . . Emeritus," Botha said stiffening his voice, "but at least half of the scholars in this room think you have applied those words wrongly in this case."

"Huh," Sandor groaned.

"As for your formal duties, you will cease your public opposition to the new approach. The 'new ways' as you and others call them have the blessing of the fathers and they are to be brought to the Academy and to all of Entos. They will, we believe, lead to a new and brighter day."

Sandor now stood silent before Botha once again.

"What has been done has been done!" Botha said in a loud and firm voice. He turned and faced MulLord. "Now I expect that all of you will show Headmaster Sandor proper respect for his many years of service. You shall conduct yourselves as inferior to the Headmaster. You shall extend to him all the courtesies and customs befitting the position of Headmaster, priest, and master conjuror. If he calls upon you to aid him in his writing and any other duties that may fall to him, you are to give him your utmost attention. If anyone, including you Professor MulLord, fails in this duty, we will be back in this chamber seeking your removal," Botha declared. "Honor Guard, please escort the Headmaster Emeritus Sandor to his new office. Meeting adjourned.

The guards immediately took their positions on each side of Sandor, who stood still and straight. Inwardly he worried for the fate of Entos, yet, his face wore the look of contentment.

Once all the guardsmen had taken their place, one of the guards spoke, "Headmaster Sandor. It is time to go."

Botha heard the address and moved to correct the guard. "Headmaster Emeritus," he thought to himself, but thought better and elected not to make a issue of it.

"Honorably Retired"

"Yes, it is done as was needed to be done," Sandor said then titled his head slightly upwards. "Lead me as Thou wilt."

"Yes, sir," the guard snapped. "I am honored to do so."

"I was not addressing thee," Sandor replied. The guard blushed with embarrassment.

"But the saying is no less appropriate in thy ear," Sandor said as if to relieve the guard of his embarrassment. "Let us be about our duties and be on our way."

Chapter Four
Cooperate and Graduate

The Academy of Theological Sciences and Ancient Conjuring Arts

The events of the morning had left Rieve confused, nervous, and concerned for the Headmaster. Yet he had told no one what had happened for he didn't know what had happened. The Headmaster had commissioned him to act, but in what way and when? "Be in the right places at the right times." It sounded so simple, but now that it had been said, it was no longer simple. In the absence of any clear order, Rieve resumed his normal day which, in his understanding, consisted of being in the right places at the right times.

It was midday and time for lunch. Each day Rieve and four of his classmates met in the commons for lunch, casual conversation, and theological debate. From time-to-time other students like Yorrath would join them, but in these trying days fewer and fewer felt comfortable in doing so. The disciples of the new school had given the table a nickname – the sinners' table because those who gathered around it were known as critics of the new school and had been branded by MulLord and others as violators of the Oracles' command to be obedient to those in authority. The candidates who gathered around the sinners' table were quietly referred to as the sinners' club. The sinners' club returned the compliment by referring to those who avoided the table as the righteous, for it is the righteous who give others such names.

While the students who gathered around other tables talked of love, getting along, and pious hopes, the candidates who sat at the sinners' table debated theology, history, philosophy, incantations, and Entosian politics. They laughed and roared. They played jokes and poked fun

The Oracles And The Jewels

at their teachers. While being accused of narrow-mindedness, those who sat at the sinners' table were not yet of one mind. What held them together was their increasing suspicion of the new school, their criticisms of the changes, and their love of humor, which was not often welcomed by those whose positions they criticized.

Rieve had arrived for lunch first. He sat down and unpacked his lunch pouch and arranged the items in front of him. Two sandwiches, a large piece of cake, a tomato, an apple, and his canteen filled with juice were all neatly arranged on the table. As he unpacked his lunch and waited for his friends, he replayed the conversation with Sandor in his head again and again. Rieve tried to parse Sandor's words, but the more he replayed the conversation in his head and the more he parsed the words, the more confused he became.

"Are you going to eat that?" Brenna asked. Rieve did not hear him.

"It must be a profound theological thought," Brenna said.

"Oh, sorry," Rieve replied. "I was just lost in thought."

"Like I said, it must have been a profound thought. I don't think we are supposed to have any of those anymore."

"Have you ever had even one profound thought?" Rieve asked jokingly.

"I don't think so. But then I get confused. Besides, it's lunchtime and I never have profound thoughts during lunch," Brenna answered. "Let me ask again. Are you going to eat that? You know there are creatures starving to death in the deserts of Bohow."

"Let them starve."

"What kind of reply is that? It is true what they say about you old school disciples. You are a bunch of heartless Entosians."

"Help yourself," Rieve replied as he pushed a sandwich in Brenna's direction.

"Brenna and the creatures of Bohow aren't the only ones who are hungry," Akimm, a Demotic of the Clan of Haystack, complained. Walking along side of Akimm was the fourth member of their party, Pandar, a Kilposian from the Clan of Vittis.

Cooperate and Graduate

"Hello, Akimm and Pandar," Rieve said as the two approached the table.

"It's bad news, Rieve, but it's no reason to stop eating. He's only been retired," Akimm said.

"Honorably retired," Brenna said as he prepared to swallow his first bite.

"He hasn't died or been convicted of anything," Pandar said. "He's just being retired." All three had assumed that Rieve would have heard the news by now.

"What are you talking about?" Rieve asked. By now all three had their mouths filled with Rieve's lunch.

"Headmaster Sandor. From the look on your face, I thought you knew," Brenna replied. There was a pause while they attempted to swallow Rieve's meal.

"Knew what?" Rieve asked. He waited for the first one to empty his mouth.

"The Headmaster. Don't you know? The City Fathers and MulLord finally got their way. They forced Headmaster Sandor into retirement," Brenna reported.

"Honorable retirement: don't forget the word 'honorable'," Akimm said.

"Yes, the word 'honorable' makes everything all right. The Headmaster was so honored, they removed him from the Academy," Pandar commented.

"Is there such a thing for a Headmaster and conjuror? Retirement I mean," Rieve asked. "I have never heard of a Headmaster and conjuror retiring or even quitting for that matter. I just thought they died in office."

"You haven't heard of it because it has never happened before," Akimm said.

"For better or for worse, we are witnessing history in the making . . . ," Pandar added, "the breaking of a pattern that was established long ago."

"I guess a forced honorable retirement is part of the new teaching. You'd better be careful or they will honorably retire you from your career, even before your career is started," Brenna commented.

"Let this be a lesson to us all. If you do your job too well, they might very well honor you as they have honored the most learned, wise, and powerful conjuror in all of Entos," Pandar said with an unmistakable bite of sarcasm.

The Oracles And The Jewels

"When did this happen?" Rieve asked.

"I was in the courtyard when they took the Headmaster into the Tribunal Hall. When he entered he was the Headmaster. When he left he was the Headmaster Emeritus. I wasn't there when he came out. I had to get to class, but a couple of the professors were talking about it between classes and I listened in a bit," Brenna said.

"Don't forget the 'honorable' title. He entered as Headmaster Sandor. He left with two additional titles, the Honorable Headmaster Emeritus Sandor." Akimm said.

"Agreed, don't forget the 'honorable' thing," Pandar said.

"Yes, the 'honorable' part makes it okay," Akimm added, then continued. "Pandar and I saw the honor guard taking Headmaster Sandor back to the faculty offices after the trial."

"During the trial I wandered into the faculty building for a few minutes and saw some of the students and maintenance people removing Sandor's books and furniture. They were taking the stuff from his office on the first floor and moving it upstairs," Akimm reported.

"Didn't you have an appointment with the Headmaster this morning?" Brenna asked.

"Yes. I was late for class and he wanted to talk with me about what I missed," Rieve replied. Instantly Rieve felt conflicted over the lie he had just told and carried on a quick debate in his mind over the lie. For now, he resolved it would have to stand.

"Did he give you any hint that something was wrong?" Pandar asked.

"I figured that out myself when MulLord showed up to the Headmaster's door with the Praetorium Guard to retrieve him," Rieve told them.

"You were there!" Brenna said.

"MulLord saw you in the office?" Akimm asked.

"Yes," Rieve answered.

"Well, it was good having you as a classmate and study partner," Pandar replied.

"That was a bad career move," Brenna said. "Some new school faculty don't like you already. This is only going to make you even more unpopular."

Cooperate and Graduate

"It's common knowledge that MulLord, some faculty, and the City Fathers wanted the Headmaster to step aside," Akimm said. "They just couldn't wait another twenty-five years for his death," he added.

"That's the problem with the new way. They are always in a hurry to get rid of the old," Pandar added.

"You don't think they are going to stop at the Headmaster do you?" Brenna asked. "The Headmaster is only the beginning. They want everyone who supports the old way gone. They want everyone who is loyal to Headmaster Sandor out of here."

"Yep. We are now an endangered species," Akimm said. "And you, Candidate Rieve Waynwright, will be the first."

"The Honorable Rieve Waynwright . . . Candidate Emeritus," Pandar said.

"It doesn't have the same ring to it as the Headmaster's new title, 'Headmaster Emeritus'," Akimm replied.

"An Emeritus Candidate. Is that a paid position?" Brenna asked. "If so, sign me up!"

"You guys are pretty funny," Rieve said. "You're worse than a bunch of old bored Entosian women. One thing happens and the rumor mill goes wild."

"You have spent the last year telling us to wake up and see things for what they really are. Now that history is proving you right, you think it's just gossip?" Brenna asked.

"Hello my brother Entosians," a voice cheerfully sounded. The four turned toward the voice.

"Hello, Yorrath," Rieve replied.

"Have you heard the news?" Akimm asked quickly and with a tone of excitement.

"What news?" Yorrath replied.

"About the Headmaster," Akimm answered.

"Is he ill? Has something happened?" Yorrath asked. A look of concern fell over his big Pithosian face.

"He's fine. His health is fine," Pandar said.

"But his career is dead," Brenna said.

"What's happened?" Yorrath asked.

"They removed the Headmaster from his office," Pandar answered.

The Oracles And The Jewels

"They did what?" Yorrath's look of concern turned to one of disbelief.

"They forced him into retirement," Akimm answered.

"They can't do that, can they? I mean I don't think such a thing has ever been done," Yorrath said.

"There's a first time for everything, I guess," Brenna said.

"I am sure this must all be a big mistake," Yorrath replied, then added. "Who replaced him?"

"MulLord," Rieve said with as much objectivity as he could.

"Oh, gee. That's not good," Yorrath responded as he sat down at the table.

"You might want to be a bit more careful about where you sit and with whom you sit these days," Brenna said. "Sitting at the sinners' table marks you as an undesirable."

"I'm sure that's just an unfounded rumor," Yorrath replied.

"Just mind yourselves gentlemen. Study hard and don't give them any reason to seek your removal. That's my advice," Rieve answered. "We can't do much about what happened this morning now, can we? We can't change what we know to be true. While we all enjoy good humor, it is obvious that those of the new school don't seem to have much of a sense for it."

"What do you think is going to happen around here with MulLord in charge and the Headmaster locked away in his office?" Pandar asked as he helped himself to Rieve's juice.

"The Academy is going to become an unpleasant place. Academic disagreements will turn to fights and the fights that should be fought will be suppressed." Rieve replied.

"Don't you think we ought to do something about this?" Brenna asked.

"Do something? Like what?" Pandar asked. "We are nothing but students. Cooperate and graduate. That's what they say."

"I've heard that too," Brenna said. "It doesn't sit well with me."

"It's not only them who say it," Pandar nodded his head toward a group of candidates sitting across the room. "It's

Cooperate and Graduate

not just supporters of the new way that say it. Many of our own priests and friends say it too."

"How different it is from what the Headmaster always said," Rieve replied, "seek the truth, especially when it opposes the powerful."

"All I am saying is that we let the faculty who support the old way fight this fight. They know more about what's going on. Let's face it, we don't have all the facts." Pandar paused for a moment, then said in a softer tone, "Maybe the Headmaster did something wrong. I mean, really, all we know of the Headmaster is what we are permitted to see." The other three were stunned by Pandar's comments. Pandar saw the shock in his friends' eyes.

"Look," Pandar said trying to prove his loyalty to the old way, "I am as strong a supporter of the old way as anyone. But let's not confuse support for the old way with a blind loyalty to Headmaster Sandor."

"So we support the old way, but not those who champion the old way," Rieve said with a tone of rebuke.

"Loyalty to one's master is part of the old way," Brenna added.

"The old way, the Oracles and the Jewels, are always right and good, but we are not infallible in these things," Pandar replied. "Don't tell me that you haven't had your doubts."

"Doubts, yes, but silent ones that should remain so unless otherwise proven," Brenna added.

"Unless there is clear and public evidence that Headmaster Sandor has indeed committed some great wrong or taught some error, we are bound to him as our teacher," Akimm said.

"So what do we do? Destroy our standing in an effort to restore Sandor's?" Pandar asked. "His fate has already been decided. Isn't it better if we simply do what needs to be done to graduate and to receive our orders? Then once we are safe within our office we can challenge the rising tide."

"We are to do our duty always and in every circumstance. We are to become the best theologians, priests, and conjurors we can be. We are to do that by learning and speaking the truth concerning the old way and concerning the new ways. We are to speak and defend

The Oracles And The Jewels

those who are wronged and befriend those who are punished for doing the same." As Rieve spoke his voice increased with power and clarity. "We cannot sell our doctrine or our integrity in this moment so that we can pretend as if we have them in the next."

Several other students in the commons ceased their studies and conversations to listen to Rieve's brief oratory. Several pairs of eyes turned in his direction.

"Rieve," Akimm said quietly and nodded his head. "They are listening to you."

"Good," Rieve replied unhindered. "For if we fail at the very point of the attack, the whole battle is lost, even if the point of attack is a small point. In this moment, the point of attack is against Headmaster Sandor and the battlefield is this Academy. This is not about Sandor. This is about what it means to be an Entosian and a student of the theological sciences and ancient conjuring arts. So I will stand and speak well of Headmaster Sandor, especially in the face of injustice."

"Careful, my friend," Akimm said, "Speak the truth yes, but you don't need to shout it."

"A few moments ago he was completely ignorant about the Headmaster's fate. Now he is a prophet and gives away free advice," Pandar added.

"It's good advice," Brenna said. "Give ear to it and it will be well with your soul. I pray that I could make such a bold statement amidst spying ears."

"Agreed," Pandar replied. "Here is some advice for you, Rieve. Eat some lunch. Maybe that will put you in a better mood."

"Time for class, boys," Brenna said as he looked at the clock at the end of the hall. Brenna looked around the hall and noticed several students still listening in on their conversation. "The lecture is over, gentlemen. I hope you all learned something." At that several of the candidates turned their heads and pretended as if they had heard nothing. A few others smiled and nodded their heads in humble agreement.

"Rieve, Brenna, Akimm, and Yorrath, enjoy the rest of your day. I have to go to MulLord's class," Pandar said as he started to walked away. "Guys, don't get me wrong, I'm with

Cooperate and Graduate

you all the way. We just need to think before we speak. See you later."

"Enjoy MulLord. I bet he is in a good mood today!" shouted Brenna as rose from the table. Brenna wove his way between the tables and chairs scattered about the dining hall.

"No doubt! But that won't make him a better theologian." Akimm said as he headed off in yet another direction.

Rieve was left behind to clean up the mess his friends had left for him. Once he finished, he headed off to his last class of the day with Professor Etam. Rieve entered the lecture hall. Professor Etam was a good and humble professor. He was an advocate of the old way, but had the kind of personality that prevented him from acting in an impolite manner, even when confronted by the arrogance of Professor MulLord. Rieve sat down, took out his notepad and writing tool, then began to doodle as Etam began to lecture.

"Candidate Rieve. . . Rieve Waynwright!" Professor Etam said in a firm voice.

"Yes, Professor Etam," Rieve shouted as if awakened from a dream.

"Candidate Rieve, are you all right?" Etam asked.

"Yes, Professor. Why do you ask?" Rieve answered.

"This is the first time you have sat through an entire lecture and never once raised your hand to interrupt me, or make a point, or ask a question. Besides, class ended a few minutes ago and you are still taking notes."

Rieve looked down at the tablet on the table. To his surprise he had written this phrase, "Be in the right place and at the right time," dozens of times. He closed the pad before the professor was close enough to see what he had written.

"Oh, sorry, Professor Etam. My mind is not as focused as it ought to be," Rieve said.

"On the contrary," Etam replied. "It is exactly where it needs to be."

"I heard about what they have done to Headmaster Sandor and I guess that bothered me more than I expected."

"Yes indeed, a bad thing has been done this day, but we must continue. We must keep an eternal perspective on such things." Etam began to erase the notes he had put on

The Oracles And The Jewels

the board during his lecture. As he did he repeated, "Keep an eternal perspective. Always take the long view in such matters. The long view always wins out in Entos."

"Is that your way of telling me not to get too excited?" Rieve asked. "Is our trouble just beginning?"

"Yes it is, but things will work out somehow. Candidate Rieve, didn't your brother Thayer take his placement exam today?" the Professor queried. "Your father was bragging about that in the faculty room earlier."

"Yes, he is."

"No, Candidate Rieve Waynwright. He was. He took the exam today. Past tense . . . perfect, completed action. It is 2:05 and unless the City Fathers have changed the rules, your brother finished his test five minutes ago. It's done. It can't be undone. If Thayer Taggert is like every other Entosian who has taken his exam, he is now standing outside the center with hundreds of others waiting for his final score and his placement assignment."

"Oh no! I promised him I'd be there when he finished. Thanks, Professor. Sorry, I've got to go!" Rieve grabbed his tablet and his books and ran into the street. He dodged his way through an almost equally hurried crowd before disappearing into the masses. Etam walked to the door and watched Rieve disappear into the crowded street.

"No need to apologize my young friend. Many will owe you an apology before this battle is done," Etam said, then whispered, "If Sandor is right."

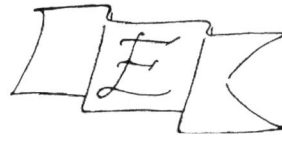

Chapter Five
The Great Declaration

The Testing Center

A large crowd of students had gathered just a few feet from the posting boards. Most exchanged answers as they each tried to guess how well they did. Tag separated himself from the crowd and paced nervously. Blisse wandered through the crowd looking for Tag. When she saw him, she paused for a moment to watch him. The over confident youth she had always known looked anxious and worried. He paced back and forth uttering phrases to himself and occasionally striking his right hand against the side of his head. A moment later she called out.

"Oh, there you are, Tag!" Tag didn't respond.

"Thayer Taggert!" Blisse called out.

"Oh, hello Blisse Maia," Tag answered.

"So, Tag," Blisse said, "how did you do?"

"Well . . . I think," Tag said in an uncharacteristically humble tone.

"Well enough to make the Hodia army?" Blisse interrupted.

"I don't know," Tag said. "I had a little trouble in a couple of spots."

"I'm sure you did fine." Blisse's statement was followed by an awkward silence. "In case you're wondering," she said, "I think I did pretty well too." Silence followed Blisse's announcement.

"I said, I think I did pretty well too," Blisse said in a slightly more forceful voice. But still silence. Blisse frowned and rolled her eyes in frustration. "Oh good, I'm happy for you Blisse Maia," Blisse said. "I am sure you are going to make it into The Academy of Healing Arts."

The Oracles And The Jewels

"Oh, sorry, Blisse, I didn't hear you," Tag said as he looked around.

"Obviously."

"I thought Rieve would be here when I finished," Tag said as he turned back toward Blisse.

"River was suppose to be here too," Blisse said as she looked around. At the moment the only person who caught her eye was Brenz Clinton, who was weaving his way through the crowd and heading straight toward Blisse.

"Hello Blisse Maia," Brenz said with a smile. Brenz looked relaxed and confident.

"Hello. You look pleased with yourself. I assume you did quite well," Blisse replied.

"I think so. But there isn't anything that I can do about it now. I'm just glad the whole thing is over." Brenz gently pushed his way around Blisse. "Hi Tag," he said.

As Brenz pushed around Blisse, she huffed and rolled her eyes, then asked, "Did you do well enough to make it into Hodia?"

"I doubt that. But I think I did well enough for an assignment to Krattos or Polemmas. I'm hoping for Polemmas. It has a grand history and is one of the finest armies in Entosian history. Tag," Brenz said, "how did you do?"

Before Tag could answer, Blisse piped up, "In case you're wondering, Brenz. I think I did pretty well too."

"Oh , sorry, Blisse, how rude of me," Brenz said.

"Yes, it was, but you're just being a boy," Blisse remarked.

"You're right. Ladies first. So, how did you do?" Brenz asked.

"Like I said, I think I did pretty well. As for Thayer Taggert . . . Well, you know that air of confidence that normally emanates from Tag?"

"It's hard to miss," Brenz replied.

"It's strangely absent at the moment," Blisse said with a smile. "It appears he's a Demotic after all." Tag had been so intent on spotting his brother in a crowd he heard the conversation, but did not listen to it.

"Here comes River," Tag announced. The three stood silent for a moment as River approached.

The Great Declaration

"What took so long?" Blisse inquired.

"There was an announcement made at the Liberal Arts Academy that created quite a stir," River reported. "I apologize for being late, but the announcement warranted some additional information."

"What kind of announcement?" Brenz asked.

"The City Fathers are making some big changes," River replied.

"Big changes?" Tag repeated with a mild tone of alarm.

"They are changing the configuration of the academy system," River said.

"They can't do that!" Blisse responded loudly.

"They can and they are," River replied.

"What kind of changes? They aren't changing The Academy of the Ancient Warring Arts are they?" asked Tag.

"Yes, Tag, I'm afraid they are," River responded.

"How so?" Brenz asked.

"If you would just relax for a moment I will explain the whole thing," River said with some frustration. Before she was able to continue, a city official approached the public bulletin board and posted an official declaration from the City Fathers. As he was posting the notice the four students looked around and observed that notices were being posted on all the public buildings. The testing center, the grammar school for general learning, the vocational academies, the museums and theaters, government offices, the gymnasium, and even the public park were all receiving the same notice at precisely the same time.

"I have never seen anything like this before," Brenz said.

"What's this all about?" Blisse asked.

"That's probably the news of the new reforms," River answered.

"It pains me to say so," Tag began, "but it looks like River Kiernan is right."

"It must be something really big if they are going to the trouble of posting the notice like this," Brenz said.

Brenz and Tag looked at each other and bolted toward the notice in the park, which was across the street from the testing center. River and Blisse followed. In each place the

The Oracles And The Jewels

announcement was posted, a small crowd instantly gathered to read the notice:

By Order of the City Fathers

On this, the fourth day of the eighth month of the year 5782 after the Creation of Entos, The Academy System is hereby Reorganized to reflect our new initiative, which bears the name; "Toward the Growth and Expansion of the Great Empire of Entos."

All Entosians are hereby called upon to embrace this effort by yielding in all humility and devotion to the wisdom of the City Fathers. To this end and to the greater glory of Entos we ask all Entosians to aspire to greatness and to undertake his tasks as he has been assigned (or will be reassigned), embracing this sovereign and mighty mission with all joy and enthusiasm.

For every foot of ground claimed by Entos is a foot lost to Bohow. For henceforth the fourth day of the eighth month of the year 5782 shall be known as the day of

The Great Declaration.

The Great Declaration

As the four read The Great Declaration, Rieve approached from behind. Out of breath, he asked "What's going on?" No one responded.

"It must be important," Rieve said.

"Read for yourself," River said and stepped aside to give Rieve her place. Rieve stepped into the open spot and leaned forward to read the announcement.

"The world is coming to an end as we know it," Blisse said with a pout.

"The Hodia army! They can't change the Hodia army . . . . . can they?" Tag said.

"It looks to me like a lot more is changing here than the academy system," Brenz mused.

"Indeed," said River.

Rieve read The Great Declaration and as he did the color rushed from his face. "Indeed. Something is going on. Headmaster Sandor knew what he was talking about."

"What do you mean?" Tag asked.

"I had a very strange day," Rieve replied.

"How frustrating," Blisse blurted out. "When the three of us walked into the Testing Center this morning the world was just fine. Everything was just as it ought to be, just as it had been for thousands of years. We studied. We were assigned our primary area of interests. I declared my major for the healing arts. Tag has his heart set on the Warring Academy and the Hodia army. And Brenz, well . . . What did you want to do Brenz?" she said as her tone of frustration grew more passionate.

"Warring Arts with some Theological Sciences," he said in a voice much softer than Blisse's.

"Ooops," River said.

"Oooops!," Brenz shouted. "What does 'Ooooops' mean?"

"They are cutting the enrollment of those academies along with The Academy of Healing Arts, so that they can double the size of the Academies of the Building Arts, the Liberal Arts, and Governance," River reported.

"Guys, we might have to change our plans," Blisse said in an overly dramatic fashion. "Thayer Taggert and Brenz Clinton, our chances of getting into the academy of our

The Oracles And The Jewels

choice is about to be cut by one-third from what they were when we entered the Testing Center this morning."

"So I am thirty percent less likely to get into the Warring Academy and thirty percent less likely to get into the Academy of Theological Sciences. I guess that means I'm sixty percent less likely to have a future," Brenz said with a heavy dose of sarcasm.

"That's fallacious reasoning. I hope you did better than that on your exam," River commented.

"How can they reduce the Warring and Conjuring Academies?" Tag asked, "without compromising the security of Entos?"

"They can't," Rieve answered, "but that is the essence of the new teaching. In the new world we put the emphasis on modernization, techniques, innovation, and on what we do, rather than on the ancient powers of Entos as practiced by the priests and warriors. Our leaders would rather place their trust on machines and gimmicks than the words and the practitioners of the ancient arts."

"That's exactly what I mean," Blisse continued. "Everything is changing. We are tied up for five hours and the next thing you know the whole world has gone crazy."

"Rieve, what happened today at the Academy?" River asked.

"Headmaster Sandor called me to his office."

"Grandfather called you to his office?" Blisse said as her voice moderated. "What in the world did you do?"

"I was a little late for class. That's all. But that didn't have anything to do with my meeting with the Headmaster," Rieve added.

"So tell us, what did you talk to Grandfather about?" River asked.

"Entos, the Academy, the new teaching, and the coming war," Rieve reported.

"The coming war! There's a war coming and the City Fathers are cutting The Academy of the Ancient Warring Arts?" Tag exclaimed.

Rieve debated within himself whether he should tell his friends what the Headmaster had prophesied concerning them and the coming danger. But since he was still confused

The Great Declaration

over what Sandor was asking of them, he decided to keep quiet.

"This can't be good," Blisse said.

"No it isn't," Rieve replied. "But this change has been coming for some time. It is just being made official."

The posted announcement was attracting a lot of attention. The students who had just taken their exams were outraged at the changes. They complained that the rules were being changed just as they were about to receive their assignments. But among the general population The Great Declaration was receiving mixed reviews. Many Entosians, mostly those who had been engaged in their stations for some time, were excited about the prospect of a greater, larger, and more powerful Entos. The people had grown bored with ordinary things, perhaps because so many of the priests and leaders had persuaded them to be bored, or perhaps because so many priests and those who played music for the ceremonies had themselves grown weary of the rituals. The ceremonies and music associated with the faith was supposed to be filled with expression and vitality, but had at times and in some places become flat and lifeless.

" 'New' is the catchword," Rieve said. "Growth is the goal. Innovation is the tool. That is what The Great Declaration is calling for."

"I don't like it one bit," River said placing her hands on her hips. "Who are we to change what has been for thousands of years?"

"I don't think change is always a bad thing," Brenz said. "I don't like the idea of having to change my plans, but it is not supposed to be about what we want. It is supposed to be about what's best for Entos."

"I see your point," Blisse said.

"River is right," Rieve countered. "There is no place like Entos in all of Ashkelon's earth. The city has survived for thousands of years because the Oracles and Jewels have guided our forefathers in the ministrations of Entos. Now our generation has decided that it's time for change?"

"I'm with you Rieve! I have changed my mind, Brenz! I'm on Rieve's side. Sorry," Blisse said defiantly.

"I'm on Rieve's side too," Tag said. "We can't afford to experiment with Entos. We are surrounded on every side by

The Oracles And The Jewels

Bohow. King Ashkelon has plotted for centuries against our land. Entosians are born and they die. At best an Entosian can live one hundred twenty five years. But Ashkelon has been around for eons just waiting for his opportunity to drive Entos from the face of his earth and make us slaves again. Change means instability. Instability means opportunity for those who seek to harm Entos."

"You make too much of this. Entos isn't exactly the same as it was. Every time we build a new building, or add a new piece of art, or write a new hymn for the Eighth Day Festival we change Entos a little bit. I am a Kilposian and you are Demotics. Our tribes have different traditions and customs. Differences and changes can be good things," Brenz argued. "Perhaps it is time for some new ideas. Who could be opposed to growing Entos?"

"I think I am starting to agree with Brenz again. Rieve, help me out here," Blisse said.

"There is a difference in things of this nature. In matters set forth in the Oracles there can be no change. In those things in which we place our trust, there cannot be change. In traditions and customs there can sometimes be change, but even here we ought to be careful in what we change and how we change it. We live in a dangerous world: Ashkelon's world. In these things it is important to adhere to the principle of the 'ever changing constants.' Principles and their practice are closely tied together."

"That is the problem they think they are solving," River stated.

"What problem?" Blisse asked.

"Practical versus theoretical. They are doubling the size of the so-called 'practical academies,' while cutting the academies that devote their time to theory and ideas. They are attacking the institutions that speak to the soul and mind of Entos, not to mention those things that keep her secure. To change a skyline or to refine metal is one thing, but they are meddling with the very things that make us Entosians and protect us against the evil one. After all, even King Ashkelon builds great cities and machines," River argued, "but Ashkelon cannot become something that he is not."

"Well that theory has one problem," Blisse responded.

"What problem is that?" Brenz said.

The Great Declaration

"The Academy of Healing Arts has always been understood as a practical academy. Why reduce that academy?" Blisse asked.

"I haven't figured that one out yet. I don't think I am going to today. It's late. We need to be getting home," River answered as she looked toward the afternoon sun.

The four had become so involved in their discussion of The Great Declaration, they hadn't noticed that the test results and the placement assignments had been posted on the information board just next to The Great Declaration.

"We have to get home too," Rieve said, "but don't you think we ought to at least wait for the test results?"

"Oh look, there they are!" Blisse said. "River Kiernan, go and look for me."

"Go yourself. They are your results," River replied.

"I'm afraid to find out. Go and tell me how I did. But if it is bad news, break it to me gently," Blisse whined.

"I'm sure you did well Blisse Maia. Go and look yourself," River said with a tone of complete confidence, "and break the news to us boldly."

Brenz and Tag were already at the board frantically searching through the thousands of code numbers. There were three numbers all together on the result sheets. The first number was a student identification number. Tag looked for his number – 506. Once he found it he looked across at the number indicating his score. That number read 47, which was a very, very good number. Rieve had scored the same two years earlier. River had scored a perfect 50. A perfect score had not been recorded in ten testing cycles (five years). Surely Tag thought with a 47 he would make it into the Hodia army. Tag closed his eyes for a moment, then opened them and stared straight at the third and final code – WAH01.

"I've done it!" Tag shouted as he turned and ran in the direction of his older brother. "I've done it! The Academy of the Ancient Warring Arts, the Hodia army, Officer First Class! I've done it!"

The process was universal. The grammar and general learning academies were so good that very few students ever did poorly. Under the system that had been in place for centuries, more than ninety percent of the students were

The Oracles And The Jewels

placed in their preferred vocational settings. The system was so arranged that virtually everyone passed the general knowledge requirements. The only question was whether the student was going to do well enough on the specialized sections of the test to earn his place in his preferred academy.

Second to that consideration was their rank within the academy. WAH01 meant that Tag would enter the Warring Arts Academy and be in the Hodia army with the opportunity to become a ranking officer immediately upon graduation. All the academies had the same system. It had worked well.

Entos was very clear about its educational goals. First, Entos produced a well-rounded and learned student.

Second, she trained the students for areas of specialization and placed the students in their vocations as Entos needed.

It was Brenz's turn. He looked for his code 398. Then his score – 43. Finally his placement. WAP02. Tag would have been disappointed with such a score and a placement (The Academy of the Ancient Warring Arts, Polemmas army, with a rank of officer second class). But Brenz greeted the news with the same enthusiasm as his friend. Such a placement and ranking was very good for a Kilposian with military aspirations.

"Me too!" Brenz shouted. "I've done it!"

"Hey, Brenz, why don't you come to our party tonight? It would be great to have a fellow cadet there," Tag shouted as he began to run down the path toward home.

"I'll try! Good-bye!" Brenz called out as he ran down the path toward his hamlet.

"Good-bye who?" Tag shouted.

"Good-bye, SIR!" Brenz shouted with a smile.

"It's your turn, sister," River said.

"All right! All right! Don't rush me." By the time Blisse got to the board, the crowd had decreased significantly. She held her breath, closed her eyes, then opened them. Student 641. Score 45. HAW01. Blisse let out a scream of such excitement that it drew the attention of everyone within earshot. The scream also had the effect of embarrassing her older sister.

The Great Declaration

"Sssshhh!" River whispered loudly. "It's not like it was unexpected."

"Leave her alone," Rieve said. "It's not every day that she gets to be . . . gets to be what Blisse?"

"Healing Arts Academy! White Section with the highest rank," she shouted.

"Good for you, Blisse. Good for you," Rieve said with the sound of maturity. "Well, I have to go. I'm not going to catch up with Tag, but I should arrive in plenty of time for his party," Rieve said, then added, "Good-bye ladies."

As they all headed home, the breeze shifted and dark clouds were gathering just east of the Hodia Tower. A storm was coming and they knew it, but they could not comprehend the severity of it.

As she walked home, Breille Clarrice replayed the conversations she had had with River in her head. Since she was a student in both The Academy of Liberal and Performing Arts and The Academy of Building Arts, she couldn't lose. Certainly there would be a great need for builders under the new plan and the changes would increase the stature of builders in the eyes of Entosians. Conjurors, priests, and City Fathers had sat at the top of the social ladder for centuries, while builders had been largely overlooked. There were advantages to the new plan, but the more Breille thought about what River had said, the more troubled she became.

As a Procuron she was a student of every discipline and thoroughly enjoyed the great theologians, historians, and philosophers of Entos. But she had regarded those studies as more of a hobby. She had dreamed of the day when her buildings would give shape to the skyline of Entos. Her father, she thought, would help settle the matter. After all, he was one of the City Fathers. Certainly he would explain the wisdom of their action.

Breille's father usually arrived about two hours after she arrived home from the academy. She spent the afternoon studying geometry and the shapes she would one day incorporate into her architectural masterpiece. The time passed quickly, at least more quickly than she had expected.

The Oracles And The Jewels

"Breille, I'm home," her father announced, to which Breille would always reply, "Is that you Father?" Since the death of her mother the announcement and its reply had become a part of their daily liturgy.

An early death was rare in Entos. Most people died between the ages of one hundred and one hundred twenty five years old and Entosians were still known to have offspring well into their seventies. If a person did die before turning one hundred, it was usually the result of an accident or an act of war.

It was an accident that had claimed Breille's mother and the reason for Breille's status as an only child. Breille's mother had died while on a family picnic when Breille was seven. They had climbed to the top of the Kanna Plateau and on their descent part of the rock face gave way and Breille's mother and the child she carried in her womb fell to her death.

Death was not regarded as an evil thing. It just was. Death was an occasion for sadness, but it was a sadness without bitterness or anger. The Oracles taught that those who died were immediately reunited with the Creator and Giver of Entos. Breille and her father mourned the death of her mother, but did not question why such a thing happened. It just did. Breille and her father missed her mother and the sister she never had, but this kind of missing did not produce bitterness and this kind of sadness was short-lived.

"Father," Breille said, "Did you know about the reorganization of the academies?"

"Yes, Daughter, I did," he replied.

"Did you see The Great Declaration?"

"Yes, I knew about that too," he confessed.

"Why are the City Fathers changing everything?" Breille asked in a tone not normally heard in a Procuron's voice.

"They're not changing everything, sweetheart. They are making a couple of changes, changes they hope will produce a greater and stronger Entos," her father reported.

"I think the changes are a bad thing," she said as she looked into her father's eyes. The statement was meant to test her father's commitment to the idea. Much to her surprise, her father's eyes dropped to the floor.

The Great Declaration

"I have spent the past months arguing against these changes. But as time went on, one City Father after another came to accept the arguments. Soon the majority became the minority. A stronger and larger Entos means we have increased food production. It means that we will have more territory to mine. And it will show Ashkelon and his minions that the King of Entos is greater than the king of Ektos. We hope this will lead to fewer attacks. At least that is the theory some have advanced," her father explained. "The advocates of the new approach worked very hard to get a unanimous vote. I must admit, Daughter, I grew weary of fighting over it. Besides, it was becoming clear that the average Entosian wanted to see some kind of change too. I know that The Great Declaration isn't popular among cadets, candidates, and other students, but it does have the support of most established Entosians."

"That's because it doesn't really affect them. They already have their stations. It is really unfair to us," Breille objected, "who have not yet graduated."

"Yes it is, but that, young lady, is one of the poorest arguments I've heard against the changes." Breille's eyes fell to the floor with the same feeling of shame that had marked her father's movements earlier. Selfishness was not the way of the Entosian. From the moment of their creation, Entosians took pleasure in serving their neighbors and filling their assigned stations. They did so with a sense of duty and selflessness.

"How many City Fathers supported the changes?" Breille asked in a more humble tone.

"Eight. Five of us opposed The Great Declaration. So you see, there is not a lot we can do," he explained with a tone of resignation.

"So what does all this mean for Entos?" Breille asked.

"I don't know. I had hoped that the priests, conjurors, and professors of The Academy of the Theological Sciences would see their way clear to correct this, if indeed we were doing something wrong," Breille's father said, "but they are even more divided than we are over the old and new things. It appears Entos herself is being torn asunder." As he spoke these words a gust of wind slammed the door shut and a

The Oracles And The Jewels

loud crack of thunder and a bolt of lighting came from the dark and enormous cloud that had settled over the land.

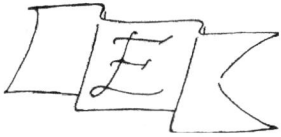

Chapter Six
He's Chosen

Nine months had passed since examination day. Despite the changes to the academy system, Rieve and his friends were still on schedule and in the right places as far as they were concerned. Tag, Brenz, and Blisse had all scored high enough on their placement exams to guarantee their places within the academy system. Breille and River had secured their positions within their respective academies. With the exception of Rieve, the authorities had not yet taken notice of the others. That itself was an accomplishment. A new spirit had entered the academy system. Many faculty members had come to believe that they were the gatekeepers of Entosian virtue. Obedience, rather than trustworthiness, was becoming the chief virtue and any students who did not comport themselves in complete obedience to the academies' administration could find themselves on disciplinary probation.

While the changes had brought about an oppressive atmosphere within the educational and governmental systems, the changes were sitting well with most Entosians. As for the students, they were cooperating to the best of their ability in order to graduate. Among the practitioners of the old ways, objections to the changes were still common, but those objections were now the minority opinion and were more symbolic than effective.

All but one of the academies were now in full cooperation with The Great Declaration. The Academy of the Ancient Warring Arts and the military establishment did not welcome the new direction and emphasis of the City Fathers. The Great Declaration meant that the army would begin planning and training for offensive campaigns and rely less on the ancient ways and more on machines. To a man,

The Oracles And The Jewels

the leaders of the warring academy opposed the changes, but they were still obligated to obey the City Fathers.

Rieve, Tag, Brenz, River, and Blisse had agreed that they would meet once a month. In this way they would be able to check on one another and to share information they might have from their respective academies. They met religiously for nine months, but reliable information was hard to come by. In former times rumors and gossip were rare in Entos, but in light of all that was starting to happen, there was no shortage of rumors and gossip now.

As students, they did not have access to halls of government or industry. So the information they were able to get concerned only the changes within the academies. This little they did know, the way to change Entos was through the academies. If one could control the academies, then one could control the future of Entos. Still it would have been helpful to have someone from the inside, someone whose father was a city father.

In prior meetings River has suggested that Breille be brought into their fellowship, but the rest of the group believed that it was too risky, at least at this stage, to involve others. Her father was a City Father and they had no way of knowing whether her father supported the changes or opposed them. In the months since the removal of Sandor, a quiet intimidation had fallen over the city and academies. The unity upon which Entos was governed was beginning to give way to a tribalism, a rivalry between the tribes, that highlighted the differences between the Entosian clans.

At the same time a new and seemingly contradictory atmosphere was taking over. A form of triumphalism was taking hold and the people were openly encouraged in a new type of pride. Many began to think more highly of themselves, of their clans, and of Entosian abilities. The gracious humility and unity that had once marked public life in Entos was being replaced, almost imperceptibly, with a subtle selfishness and self-righteousness.

Under the influence of the new teaching and the reorganization of the academy system it was only a matter of time, or so most thought, before Entos would have to expand the walls and take ground from Bohow, as The Great

He's Chosen

Declaration said, "For every foot of ground claimed by Entosians is a foot lost to Bohow."

As for the faculty of The Academy of Theological Sciences and Ancient Conjuring Arts, it remained deeply divided over the changes. Some, like Breille's father, had hoped that the Academy would issue a corrective to what the City Fathers had done. He was convinced that if they spoke with one voice, surely Entosians would listen and they would reconsider their actions. But the division in the faculty had paralyzed the Academy's ability to speak with one voice and each City Father invoked the name of whichever faculty member supported his own position. Any correction that might have been forthcoming had been blocked by Professor MulLord and other faculty members.

The division that existed among the faculty of the Academy and the City Fathers was mirrored in the student population. The division was seen everywhere. Candidates openly debated one another over the virtues of the new approach. In the nine months since the Headmaster had been removed from the classroom, the first-year candidates had been completely indoctrinated into the new teaching.

The new way was quickly becoming the majority position and, under the leadership of MulLord, the Academy's atmosphere had been poisoned by distrust and division. The seed of change had been growing for some time, but the fruit that now appeared had come into full bloom and it had done so in a very short period of time.

Rieve and some of his other classmates had become well-known for their commitment to the old ways and teaching, criticism of the new teaching, and their loyalty to the real Headmaster of the Academy. By now Rieve had entered his first class in the conjuring arts and was proceeding toward the day when he would be placed under orders. That day was not far away. Rieve was considered an upper classman. He was also becoming a target. Professor MulLord and others were keeping an eye on him.

River was continuing her studies at The Liberal and Preforming Arts Academy. Throughout her academic career she had distinguished herself as a thinker of the first order – equal to any Procuron. Now she was showing that she was also a particularly gifted talent. She excelled in music and

The Oracles And The Jewels

performance, something for which Procurons were not well known. Not only could she perform, but she had also begun composing music for the Eighth Day Festival.

Breille, the Procuron, was already distinguishing herself as an engineer and designer. As a Procuron she lived in a different hamlet than the others. Yet she enjoyed the arts more than most Procurons and often watched River perform.

Blisse was attending The Academy of Healing Arts and was doing very well. Most of her time was spent studying basic anatomy and the natural elements and incantations necessary to heal. Such a study was not as easy as one might think. She had to learn eight anatomies. Some elements and incantations would work for one tribe, but not for another. While all Entosians were basically humanoid, there were many significant differences between the tribes. Not only did healers have to concern themselves with healing illnesses and repairing injuries, but each tribe also had unique physical abilities that needed to be cared for and strengthened in the healing process. Second to the gift of conjuring, the gift of healing was most highly treasured in Entos. Conjuring and healing had some common elements.

Healers joined an incantation to a physical or material element to bring about healing. The same principle applied to priestly conjuring. In that case the conjuror would join a versicle from the Oracles, sometimes in a shout and sometimes in a whisper, to a physical element.

That is why the healing arts and healers were held in such high regard. In addition to the skills of healing, the men and women who entered the healing arts were well known for both their skill and their tenderhearted temperaments. It was said that the best healers often would feel the pain of their patients.

As for Tag and Brenz, they took to the life of a military cadet like birds to the air. As a result of their different ranks their academic classes were different. But three times a week they found themselves competing against one another in the physical arts of combat.

He's Chosen

The Academy of the Ancient Warring Arts

"Attention cadets," shouted Colonel Fornoff, a Pithosian with an unusually large nose. Immediately each cadet of every shape and size, Aradians, Fortians, Demoticans, and Adroitians, all stood erect and firm. "It has been nearly five hundred years since the last attack of Ashkelon. Some think that Ashkelon will never again attack the city of Entos. I don't believe that, nor should you. If that wretch doesn't attack during your lifetime, it will be because you don't believe that either. There is only one reason why that scum does not attack. Do you know why he won't attack us, cadet?"

The cadet was a Fortian and slow of tongue. As the Fortian opened his mouth Colonel Fornoff continued, "I'll tell you why they won't attack. It has nothing to do with the prophecies. Ashkelon doesn't care about those prophecies. He doesn't study them and decide what he will or will not do because the prophecies have ordained this or that. No cadet! That's not how that dirtball works!

"He studies us. He studies Entosians. He studies Entos. But most of all, he studies you cadet," the colonel shouted as he looked at an Aradian. He paused for a moment then stepped to the right and looked down at the Adroitian standing next to the Aradian. The colonel continued, "He is waiting. He is waiting for you to fail, to falter, to leave your post and forsake your duty. Should you fail, Ashkelon and his legions will be right there and he will kill you, or worse yet, he will convert you, turn you back into the miserable creature you could have been and once were."

Moderating his voice the colonel said, "Cadets, in the last great battle Entos prevailed. Entos prevailed because the Oracles were rightly used by the priests and conjurors, but so was the sword, the spear, and the bow. Entos prevailed because for every Entosian that fell, one hundred and ten creatures from Bohow fell as well.

"That is the strength of Ashkelon. It is in his numbers. If needed, Entos can field an army of 100,000, but Ashkelon can raise an army of millions. We come from eight tribes, but they come from eighty. Their strength is in their numbers, brutality, and evil. Our strength is in the Oracles as used by the conjurors and priests. It is also in your wits and your

The Oracles And The Jewels

training. It is in your weapons and in your courage, discipline, and devotion to duty. Entosian warriors are the finest and most noble warriors on Ashkelon's earth.

"In your reason, speed, courage, weapons, and cause we find our military strength. Ashkelon commands armies of brutes and morons. Those brutes and morons can crush you if they get close enough. Don't be fooled by some of Ashkelon's soldiers. Despite their appearance, they are terrible fighting machines. Fear not, you can defeat them as long as you remember your training and keep your wits about you. As long as you draw strength from our hope. As along as you remain steadfast we will be victorious.

"In this Academy, under my direction, you are learning to think faster and more clearly than you have ever thought before. Here we train your arms and legs, your head and feet, and even your heart and lungs, your whole being, to move without thought while you think and do what must be done when all else tells you it can't be done. Here we train you to be warriors through and through.

"There is no new teaching here. Here there will be no new order or grand experiment. There is nothing here but study, training, drilling, and very hard work. Here there is only duty. Each of you has been fitted with your own weapons. Each has been custom-made by the finest Entosian craftsmen. So, cadets, are you ready to do your duty?" the colonel shouted.

"Yes, sir!" the shout came in one loud voice.

"Cadets, are you ready to die well?" the colonel shouted.

"Sir, yes, sir!" the cadets shouted even more loudly than they had the first time.

"So be it, and so it will be. I commend you into the hands of the sergeants. Take over, sergeants," the colonel barked as he marched from the hall.

The Academy of Theological Sciences and Ancient Conjuring Arts

As he walked with two others into The Great Chamber, Rieve felt a tingle run up his back. He had been to The Great Chamber for every Eighth Day Festival since his own

He's Chosen

transformation into an Entosian. But as a layman he had never been permitted, nor had he ever thought himself worthy of standing on the inside of the eight-sided marble rail. Only the priests entered therein. Priests and priests alone read the words of the Oracles and handled the three Jewels. These were sacred things. To misuse them or to treat them with anything other than dignity was believed to cause death.

Legend had it that centuries ago a small rebellion took place wherein some laymen and laywomen charged the rail, claiming to posses a priesthood of their own. This priesthood, they believed, gave them the right to stand in the place of the priest and to transform their own offspring.

The legend said that as soon as they leaped over the rail and reached for the Jewels they were transformed into creatures from Bohow, a fate worse than death, and struck blind by the light of the Jewels. As is true of all creatures from Bohow, they could not stand the sound of the Oracles or the light of the Jewels. They took their offspring, whom they sought to save, fled from The Great Chamber and the city, and now served as slaves of Ashkelon. Since that day no Entosian had made such a claim and every Entosian was very careful in how they used the word rights.

Rieve recalled the legend as he approached the door to The Great Chamber. The three candidates were accompanied by Professor Langward. Professor Langward was a Procuron, one of the few Procurons who was well suited to and pursued the vocation of priest and professor. It was a good fit, for in the lyrics and the responses of the Great Rituals of The Great Chamber there was a symmetry and balance of great beauty. The Oracles were spoken and sung by the priests, and the Entosians replied in equal beauty. Professor Langward's task was to train the candidates, three-by-three, to lead the Great Ritual and to use the Oracles and the Jewels in the Rite of Transformation.

Rieve's training had begun in an ordinary classroom. Rieve, Akimm, and Brenna had grown comfortable in speaking the sayings and singing the lyrics in that setting. Every step and every movement of their arms and hands and every turn of their head was choreographed in the

The Oracles And The Jewels

classroom as the candidates learned to speak and sing the words of the Oracles and to speak the incantations of the Rite of Transformation.

In the classroom the students practiced the rituals with a book of about the same size and weight of the real Oracles. They also practiced with three stones cut in the shape of three large diamonds, and glued together in one brass mount. The brass mount formed a handle. The stones and the brass mount were a replica of the real Jewels. They were very pretty stones and the brass mount was also well kept, but they were just props.

"Now," Rieve thought to himself, "the props are gone. This is the real thing." He felt uncomfortable and disappointed in himself that he had just thought of the Oracles and the Jewels as 'things.' That mistake only made him feel more unworthy of the tasks that soon would be assigned to him.

Professor Langward opened the door to The Great Chamber and the four of them entered. The Professor led the way, Rieve was second, Akimm was third, and Brenna fell in behind Akimm. The Great Chamber was enormous and this was the first time Rieve had ever seen it empty. The chamber, like the city of Entos herself, had eight walls and each wall contained three beautifully detailed stained-glass windows. The Great Chamber was made of marble, granite, and glass. The main floor was surrounded by three levels of balconies. The walls and the balconies each possessed a tinge of the colors of Entos. The wall and balconies whose backside faced the Borrhas Plateau held a hint of purple. The wall and balconies whose backside faced the Krattos Plateau were yellow. Hodia was white. Polemmas was red. Neggen was green. Kanna was blue and Nuxia shined with the brightest gold. Tarchus was a soft brown.

Light streamed in from the stained-glass windows and from the light that came through the skyline window with its eight sides in the ceiling of The Great Chamber. But the greatest light, the light that lit the chamber, the light that never permitted The Great Chamber to grow dark at night, came from the cradle in the very center of the chamber, where the Oracles and the Jewels lay. But this was not the kind of light that caused a person to squint. The light from the

He's Chosen

Oracles and the Jewels fell evenly throughout the entire chamber. The light did not discriminate between one section or another. The balconies did not even cast a shadow upon that which was below. At night the light showed through the skyline windows so brightly that its beam could be seen from all points in Entos, even from that place where the desert and forest of Bohow meet. Empty, the Great Chamber looked even larger . . . and yet, they . . . much, much smaller.

The Great Chamber was so large that a breeze could be felt from time to time when the conditions were right. Today was one of those days. As Rieve entered the chamber, the breeze caught his hair and ruined his part.

The professor-priest led them down one of the aisles, his robe and academic vestments moving to the rhythm of his walk. The pace was brisker than Rieve expected. Soon there was a wide gap between Rieve and the professor. Rieve tried to pick up the pace, but soon discovered that only an unacceptable increase of speed would close the gap completely. His situation was made more desperate by the fact that the three candidates had been adorned in the proper ritual vestments which limited the length of their gate. On rare occasions a candidate would trip and fall in the aisle so Professor Langward was careful not to get too far ahead of them.

By the time the professor-priest had reached the marble rail, a gap of some thirty feet had opened up between him and his students. This was intended. Professor Langward had been the teacher of the rituals for decades. It was common for students to pause and marvel at the size and beauty of The Great Chamber. If the size of The Great Chamber did not serve as cause for a pause, the windows of The Great Chamber did. But that did not stop Professor Langward from beginning his brisk walk toward the rail. He enjoyed the chase and grinned all the way. The students, of course, couldn't see the grin. That was another unique feature to this particular Procuron. He had a sense of humor, subtle as it was.

Two scribes sat copying the scripts of the Oracles. Each year the Academy selected the very best translators and writers of the sacred language to work on copies of the Oracles. The copies were to be an exact duplicate of the

The Oracles And The Jewels

original texts. Some of the copies were so good, only the most trained eye could tell them apart from the original scrolls. It took years to complete just one perfect copy. Once completed, the copies were sent into the hamlets and villages throughout the countryside so that the priests could conduct Eighth Day Celebrations for those who were too far away to travel to The Great Chamber.

"Thank you, scribes, for your work. May we now have the chamber?" the Professor said. The two scribes gathered their scrolls and writing tools, stood up, bowed toward the Oracles, then toward Professor Langward and departed.

Having arrived at the rail, the professor turned and began to speak as if he expected the candidates to be just behind him. He would speak just one word, "Candidates . . ." then pause as if surprised. It was part of the fun. Rieve, Akimm, and Brenna accelerated their steps as their title was spoken. Slightly winded, the three arrived and the professor started again.

"Candidates, as you know the duties of a priest are primarily two. First and most importantly a priest is the leader of the Great Ritual. Without the proper use of the Jewels, an Entosian cannot be created. Without the proper and regular application of the Oracles, every Entosian will eventually cease to be an Entosian. Some will cease to be an Entosian sooner and others will cease to be an Entosian later. But without the regular and right use of the Oracles every one of us will become the creatures we were born. "Always, always remember, Entosians and Entos are not indigenous creatures to Bohow. The Maker and Giver of Entos has created this place where it does not belong. Where there was once no goodness at all, now there is goodness, and the evil hates this goodness with all its might. This is why," the professor continued, "Entosians are faithful in their participation in the Great Ritual. On the Eighth Day, every ninety minutes, from sunrise to sunset this hall is filled with Entosians who have come here so that they will remain the good creatures they have been created to be. Those who cannot attend, like warriors and other officials, have been assigned their own priest and conjuror to keep them safely within the arms of Entos.

He's Chosen

"It is therefore incumbent upon you who will be priests to take on this responsibility with the utmost sobriety, humility, and devotion. What rests before you in this cradle is the life and light of Entos. Indeed, your life and light. The Great Chamber and the Great Ritual are the chief and most important of all priestly tasks. To tend to The Great Chamber is to tend to the Great Ritual. For this place was given to us so that we gather to participate in the ritual. These are your priestly chores and it is here we will sharpen your priestly skills.

"The second great task of the priest is to master the conjuring skills. While these skills are secondary to the skills I will teach you here, they are essential. It is through the conjuring skills that the warriors of Entos are supported and it is through the conjuring skills that the invisible forces sent forth by Ashkelon are held at bay.

"Outwardly these look like two different activities, presiding over the rituals of The Great Chamber and working with the army in our battle against Ashkelon. But this is a distinction without a difference. They look very different and each has its own protocol, but the conjuring arts are closely tied to and are dependent upon the ritual arts. Many priests make the mistake of honoring one while devaluing the other.

"Some will devote almost all of their attention to performing, not perfecting, the ritual arts and sometimes speak disparagingly about the conjuring arts because they are tied to the warring arts. Others take great pleasure in practicing the conjuring arts, but they do not attend to their ritual skills. But these two must go together. No priest can truly master the conjuring arts unless he has mastered the ritual arts. Without regular practice and participation in the ritual arts, the conjuring priest will be slow and sloppy, and his wizardry will be of an inferior quality. If a priest has not perfected his ritual arts, he places not only himself in great danger on the battlefield, but he also places the legion he is responsible for in great danger as well.

"Professors in this Academy are charged with teaching doctrine and the history of Entos. The priests are charged with the responsibility of teaching you the arts of the rituals so that you can lead the people through the rituals. The

The Oracles And The Jewels

conjurors teach the skills of conjuring. I teach the former. Other faculty members teach the latter. So let us begin.

"The Oracles and Jewels are not for private use. They are not to be used for personal convenience. The power in them is too great. The few in our past who have forgotten this important lesson and who sought to harness the power for their own advantage have fallen prey to a fate worse than death. They became priests of Ashkelon. This is why even Ashkelon's priests know the words of the Oracles and sometimes invoke their incantations to harm and deceive.

"The Giver intended that they be spoken and applied to creatures, be they Entosians, creatures of Bohow, or even Ashkelon himself. But the Giver never intended all creatures to speak and to use them. Never enter this hall for the purpose of speaking the Oracles to anyone. Never ever go behind the marble rail for the purpose of invoking the Oracles without other Entosians present to hear the invocation. There must always be someone else. The ritual requires a speaker and a hearer, a giver and a receiver. There is always to be at least one inside the rail and at least one outside the rail. Even in this setting, as you learn to practice the rituals, the Academy takes the extra precaution of bringing citizens and fellow candidates into The Great Chamber to hear you practice the rituals.

"On to lesson number two. Strictly speaking you do not speak the words of the Oracles. Rather the Oracles speak through you. At first it will seem as though you are reading them and that you are speaking them, but as you perfect your skills you will soon realize that you become less and the Oracles become more. Soon it will seem that the words of the Oracles and the words of your mouth are one and the same. As you grow old you will simply find the Oracles speaking through you when the time comes for them to be spoken. When this happens you will know that the Oracles speak, not you." Langward paused a long pause. The candidates knew what that meant.

For two years they had studied. They had borne the title candidate. But candidates did not hold the office. They were still very much laymen and thus not authorized to touch the scrolls upon which the Oracles were written or to take into their hands the Jewels. Only those under orders and placed

He's Chosen

into their station could stand inside the rail, touch the scrolls, and handle the Jewels. This was the moment for which they had spent their lives preparing. Upon completion of their vows, all three would be priests. They would bear the title, apprentice priests, but they were still priests. The adjective 'apprentice' designated them as priests who were still under the formal instruction of other priests or conjurors until one of those priests or conjurors released them to operate as a free agent, as a priest and conjuror equal to all others.

"Kneel here," Langward said. The three did as instructed. Placing his hand upon the top of Rieve's head, Langward simply asked, "Do you vow to speak the Oracles in truth and purity?"

Rieve replied, "I will."

"Do you pledge to lead the Great Rituals in accordance with the Oracles?"

"I will."

"Do you vow to use the Jewels in the way prescribed by the Oracles?"

"I will," Rieve said in a soft voice.

"By the authority granted to me by Entos and the Academy, I now place you under your order and in your station," Professor Langward said.

Professor Langward repeated the ritual two more times. Rieve, Akimm, and Brenna were no longer the candidates, they were priests; apprentice priests, but priests still the same.

Professor Langward called for the hearers to be brought into The Great Chamber so that the three apprentice priests could begin to practice the Great Rituals in The Great Chamber. Each apprentice priest took his turn. Two took hold of the large and heavy scrolls, while the third spoke the words, incantations, and performed the rituals. The hearers offered the appropriate replies. Once they had finished practicing, the hearers were escorted from The Great Chamber and the apprentices soon followed in the same manner as they had entered. This time there was no gap between Professor Langward and Rieve as they exited The Great Chamber and headed to the stairwell.

The professor slowed his step for a moment enabling Rieve to walk along his side. The other two apprentices

The Oracles And The Jewels

excused themselves and headed down the corridor to the left and then outside into the street. The professor and Rieve entered the stairwell and started their descent to the tunnel that connected The Great Chamber with the Academy.

"You have a question, apprentice priest?"

"Yes, sir, but it has nothing to do with ritual arts."

"The Headmaster then?" Professor Langward stated.

"Yes. How did you know?" Rieve whispered.

"I have spent every day for the past three decades instructing students in the Great Rituals. The three of you are my first three students today. I have two more sets of three. That is six more hours of hearing the Oracles and the rituals. I do that seven days a week, in addition to my own participation in the Eighth Day Festival. I have probably heard the Oracles spoken in the rituals more than anyone else alive in Entos. Imagine what that does for an Entosian.

"I see your point," Rieve replied.

"Besides, I had breakfast with the Headmaster this morning and he told me that you might want to talk today."

"How did he . . . never mind." They both smiled. "How is the Headmaster? It has been months since he has been allowed to teach."

"He is doing well. He misses the lecture hall and the students. But he says that all things are as they are supposed to be."

"There have been many rumors about the Headmaster. Some of those rumors say unkind things about him."

"Rumor says nothing. Entosians who are losing their way say such things. The Headmaster, myself, and a few others are from the old school and the ancient ways are viewed with suspicion by many these days. Some believe that Headmaster Sandor is the single greatest threat to the new order of things and the reason for Ashkelon's increased hostility to Entos."

"He is the most powerful of all the conjurors," Rieve replied.

"There's the mistake," the professor answered.

"Mistake?" Rieve said with a slightly raised voice.

"That word power. They have not accused the Headmaster and banned him from the lecture hall because he is the most powerful conjuror in Entos. They haven't even

He's Chosen

banned him because he holds opinions from the old school. They accused and banned him because of you."

"Me!" Rieve exclaimed.

"Because he produces candidates, priests, and conjurors like you. Under his direction this place provides a continual flow of Entosians who practice the old ways, ways that many believe stand in the way of brighter and better days. We produce Entosians who stand in the way of their progress. Their views have taken hold in the various academies and in the halls of governance and priests and conjurors like you are a potential threat to their grand plans. You are growing too great in number."

"But we are so few. The new speaking is the majority opinion within the walls of Entos these days," Rieve said.

"New things are not always new." Professor Langward lifted his hand, then his index finger ever so slightly, and pointed straight ahead at Professors MulLord, Millaran, Suedos, Bozzez, Paddan, and Timaho who were walking toward them. "My father, my own father," Rieve thought, but dared not speak.

As the six faculty members drew within earshot, Professor Langward said in a raised tone, "Apprentice Rieve Waynwright, please try to be on time for ritual practice." Obviously Sandor had told Langward of Rieve's office visit months earlier, but the humor was lost on Rieve as he glanced at his father. Timaho heard the comment and gave Rieve a disapproving glance in return. As each group passed in the corridor they exchanged pleasantries.

"Good morning, Professor Timaho," Rieve said.

"Is it, Apprentice Priest Rieve Waynwright? . . . Late?" Professor Timaho replied.

While Rieve was still a son to his father and Timaho a father to his son, Rieve now belonged more to Entos and the Academy than he did to his father and mother. In the second year of the Academy the candidates moved away from home and took up residence at the Academy. Once placed into the station of priest, fathers and mothers no longer had the kind of relationship or authority they once did. Rieve only saw his mother on holidays and his father with the same frequency as he did any other professor at the Academy. Yet

The Oracles And The Jewels

beneath the formality there was always the undeniable reality of blood relation.

Rieve went to speak, but Professor Langward lifted his finger to his mouth signaling Rieve to remain silent for a moment longer. When sufficient distance had been put between the two groups, Rieve spoke.

"My father? Is my father one of them?"

"Them?" the Professor repeated.

"A practitioner of the new school. Is my father with Professor MulLord? Did he help ban the Headmaster?"

"Help ban the Headmaster? No, he had no part in that and he could have done nothing to prevent it. From such things he tends to hide. They use him to give the impression that they have more support than they do. Is he 'with' Professor MulLord? He was walking with him. Professor MulLord avoids walking with me and I with him. We do not stroll together and I certainly do not follow him around like a household pet. As for a practitioner of the new speaking, that's hard to tell with some, at least at first. It is hard to tell with your father. Perhaps when the occasion arises you can ask him yourself. The answer would be most interesting. Now to more important matters."

The conversation produced a firestorm of conflicting thoughts and emotions within Rieve, but Professor Langward was not going to let the revelation of Timaho's association with MulLord distract them from the task at hand.

"Apprentice Priest Rieve Waynwright," Professor Langward continued, "it is true Professor MulLord and others are in charge of the Academy and things do not look good for Entos, although most are unaware of the change that is now underway. There has been a coup d'etat, a silent coup, but still a coup d'etat. As you are well aware Headmaster Sandor has been banned from teaching in the classroom. He has been removed as head of the faculty and the Academy. He is no longer on the council of City Fathers. Professor MulLord now holds those positions, wrongly but he holds them nonetheless. But Headmaster Sandor is not dead and still lives here at the Academy. He is not without friends. So I have made arrangements for both you and for him.

He's Chosen

"Professor Etam, as good a man as he is, will no longer tutor you in the conjuring arts. He is not powerful enough, and he cannot bring you along as quickly as is needed. Only Sandor can do that and he is going to take over your training immediately."

"Can that be done?" Rieve asked.

"Yes. Will MulLord and the others like it? Hardly. But you need to take your place and you are years away from being ready. We do not have years. Besides, the Headmaster is old and without so much as a candidate or an apprentice to keep him young, he will grow older and, I fear, will die before his work is done, if such a thing is possible," the Professor answered.

"But will they permit him access to the conjuring lab?"

"He has everything you need in his study and since they have seen fit to banish him to the sixth floor at the end of the hall, they have provided the two of you with the seclusion necessary. There's just one more thing."

"I sense a catch coming," Rieve smiled.

"You will be tutored at the eleventh hour when the three moons shine bright. Find a place during regular lab hours to nap. After all, you are now on the accelerated conjuring program," the professor said with a chuckle. "You will need your sleep and you will need those skills soon."

"What of the Academy, Professor? Can she be saved from those who seek to change her? Are there enough good professors left to reclaim the Academy for the old ways?" Rieve asked in quick succession.

"Her future is unsure. Can she be saved? Not really. The weeds that have been planted here cannot be uprooted. Words that have been spoken here cannot be withdrawn, only opposed. The deeds done can't be undone, but only reversed. As for the faculty members of the old ways, you know yourself that Professors Worett, Atteowe, and Scarre all speak openly for the true way and critically about the innovations. I must also tell you," Langward said as he came to a stop. Rieve stopped too. Everything about the moment seemed hushed and weighty. "There is risk in what we ask of you. Sandor is sure that you are the one upon whom we must rely, at least at this moment. We cannot guarantee your safety. You may be discovered and removed from this

The Oracles And The Jewels

place. Under the system established by Headmaster Sandor, it takes a majority of faculty to remove a candidate from the Academy. All too many were graduated and placed in an office into which they should not have been placed. They have saved many of theirs from expulsion and we have saved many of ours. We will defend and protect you as we can. But with MulLord in charge we cannot prevail. With MulLord in charge you could be thrown out simply because you're not likeable. The faculty could not save Sandor from exile."

"Did they try?" Rieve asked.

"Fair question. No, they did not, at least not as valiantly as their offices called upon them to do. But remember, it has been a long time since any real threat or battle has been waged in this place. The warriors on the walls are tested far more often than we are and their enemies are easy to recognize. But here our enemies are sometimes our own friends. Many in this place have never had to do battle before."

The two parted company for the day, but their thoughts were not far apart. Rieve felt a loneliness and a burden unlike any he had ever felt before. Although he tried to avoid thoughts of self, concern over his professional standing, and worry over how his name might be spoken and used among fellow priests and Entosians, he could not help himself. For the first time he felt truly conflicted. He longed for the clarity that he had long admired in his younger brother Thayer Taggert. "Professor Langward is right," Rieve thought to himself, as he entered the Academy's courtyard. "Tag's enemies are easy to identify and to slay. Mine are not. Why couldn't another have been chosen? Why me? Why not me?"

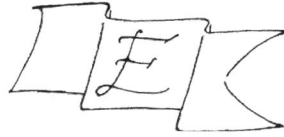

Chapter Seven
The Work Begins

"Hello, River Kiernan," Breille said as River exited the Performing Arts Building.

"Hello Breille Clarrice."

"I hope you don't mind. I have been attending your recitals, performances, and even a couple of your academic presentations."

"I am flattered that you find them worth your time" River said again with a tone of humility.

"Very much so. Since the reorganization of the academy system, I have had to choose between The Academy of the Liberal and Performing Arts and The Academy of the Building Arts. Architectural design is still my first love, but the performing arts are a close second."

"Am I to conclude that since you can't attend classes here, your more creative nature is living vicariously through me?" River asked.

"You got it. I hope you don't mind," Breille said with a rising voice.

"Not at all Breille. This reorganization hasn't worked out so well for you," River said. It was part a question and part an observation.

"It hasn't worked out badly, but I still don't like it," came the reply. River thought for a moment. Should she take the risk or not? Rieve was probing to find out where Breille stood in regard to the changes. The conversation was showing promise. River continued, "Why? Because you can't do both?"

"No, that's more of an annoyance than anything else. Once I am done with my studies and I start working I will have plenty of time to spend at the theater," Breille said.

"So what's the problem?" River asked.

The Oracles And The Jewels

"Haven't you noticed?" Breille said in a hushed voice.

"I have been pretty busy," River said.

"Entos. It's different. People are happier, but Entos doesn't seem to be. She is decaying. Things aren't working like they did even just a few years ago. I took a walk in the woods of the Neggen Valley yesterday and I was shocked at the decay I saw there. I often walked in those woods when I was little."

"When was your last visit to the woods, besides the one yesterday?" River asked.

"It has been a couple of years," Breille replied.

"Well maybe it's because you are older and just notice more now. I notice a lot of things these days that I didn't just a couple of years ago. Rooms are not as big as they once were. Entosians aren't as big as I once thought either."

"It's not that. I doubled-checked," Breille replied.

"Double-checked?" River asked.

"Yes, when I was young I used to go into those woods with my father and we would do calculations on the rate of decay."

"And that was fun?" River asked.

"Yes, try it," Breille said.

"Procurons have a strange sense of fun," River quipped. "So what did you discover yesterday?"

"That the rate of decay is nearly five times greater than when I took my last calculations just five years ago. Now, I admit a five year comparative study for a woods that is hundreds of years old can only give a snapshot of a moment in time, but that discovery in the woods started me thinking. So I have done some other comparative calculations. Even the metals of bridges and buildings seem to be showing some wear ahead of their time. I tell you something is wrong with Entos. If I were a healer I would say that Entos is sick with a strange sickness. The Entosians seem happy, but Entos does not."

"That is a profound insight," River complimented. "But I would have thought you to be rather supportive of the whole endeavor. Builders will soon be the most respected of all the vocations. You will replace old decaying buildings with new. Bohow will shrink. Entos will get larger and since your father

The Work Begins

is one of the City Fathers everything should work out pretty well for you. I mean no offense," River said.

"I take no offense. It's not supposed to be about me or you . . . is it? No offense intended."

"No offense taken," River replied. River wasn't the only one testing the waters. Breille wasn't going to blindly trust River unless River proved to be just as concerned about Entos as she was. By now they both sensed what the other was up to.

"You're right about that. It isn't about us. But what of your father?" River asked.

"My father is a critic of the new changes. He is no theologian, but he knows the difference between right and wrong. He argued against the changes until it was obvious that he couldn't stop them. Without a clear word from the Academy, he and the other three who opposed the changes were powerless to stop them. Now my father believes that these changes are here to stay and it is our duty to make the best of them for the sake of Entos. Is that what you wanted to know?" Breille said in a firm and clear voice.

"Yes, it is and it pleases me so," River said with a smile. "But, your father is wrong. Those changes are not here to stay and if you're interested in getting into a little trouble, I would like to take you to meet some people tomorrow."

"What kind of trouble?" Breille said with glee.

"The kind of trouble a good Entosian ought to be getting into these days," River said without a smile. River looked into Breille's big round eyes. The girlish smile disappeared from Breille's face.

"I'm a good Entosian. I'm in," Breille said.

"There is just one thing, Breille Clarrice. Your father must not know anything about this."

"You have my pledge," Breille said with sobriety. Giving a pledge was a sacred act in Entos. An honorable Entosian was willing to die rather than break a pledge or betray another. In the Days of Old, Ashkelon had enticed some priests to betray their fellow priests and warriors into his hands. They did and the death Ashkelon inflicted upon his prey could be heard throughout the whole land of Bohow.

Betrayal was the first great sin committed in Entos. Since that time Entosians had made an extra effort to be

The Oracles And The Jewels

honorable and loyal to one another and sealed that loyalty with their solemn pledge.

"Tomorrow meet me outside The Academy of Healing Arts. We will meet Blisse Maia at 4:00 and go to the meeting of our little fellowship."

"See you tomorrow, River Kiernan," Breille said as she started to depart.

"Tomorrow, then," River said as a moment of doubt welled up within her, but only for a moment. The pledge dispelled the doubt. "The pledge is given," River uttered to herself as she walked away. "Now I hope the rest of the group doesn't mind. Besides, a builder type with a father on the inside can only be a benefit to the cause."

The Academy of the Ancient Warring Arts

Brenz and Tag stood opposite one another in the war academy training hall. Their newly custom-made swords were safely tucked away in their scabbards. They no longer looked like the boys they had been just a few short months ago. They now stood as young warriors, cadets, arrayed in their fine armor and armed for battle. They looked the part - warriors - and they stood at attention, fitting the role perfectly. Twenty-four sergeants walked along the dozens of rows of cadets reviewing their respective charges as the cadets stood at perfect attention.

The hall was long, very long, and narrow by design. Entosians were rarely ever afforded the luxury of a wide battlefield. In the five thousand years of her existence, almost all of her battles were defensive in nature. For her part, Entos was content to live in peace amidst the dark world of Ashkelon. With the exception of the first war when the light pierced the darkness, Entos was the object of attack. Her borders and time in this world had long been fixed, although only known to the King. While possessing the power of the King, it had long lost its passion for expansion. In these latter days, the kingdom was content to survive her enemies.

From the Days of Old, Entosian warriors had always been about the business of defending the land and the citizens of the great city. Throughout her history, Entosian

The Work Begins

warriors were almost always surrounded by superior numbers and forced to do battle in tight quarters. So it was that Entosian warriors had learned to fight in confined spaces and against great odds. From the very beginning it had been designed this way and the design had served Entos well.

    The floor upon which the cadets stood was marked out with circles, some large and some small, and many in-between. From the Days of Old, Entosian warriors were taught to fight within those circles as if surrounded on all sides. This circle was called the "striking field." The size of the circle varied according to the size of the warrior, but the formula was always the same. The "striking field" of an Entosian warrior was no greater than twice the length of the distance from his nose to the tip of the sword when the arm was fully extended. An Adroitian fought within a much smaller "striking field" than did a Kilposian. A Pithosian by the same rule would have the largest "striking field" of all by virtue of his size.

    At this level of training the sergeants made sure to match Entosians of equal size and relative skill. Once each cadet had mastered basic fighting skills, that cadet would learn how to fight those smaller and quicker or larger and more powerful than themselves. The speed of an Adroitian warrior was superior to any other. Likewise a Pithosian warrior was so strong that even a Fortian had to learn specialized techniques to offset the natural physical advantage of his opponent. But in time, every Entosian warrior would learn the skills necessary to do battle and emerge victorious. What the Entosian warrior lacked in physical ability to meet the challenge of superior numbers and superior strength would be provided by the conjurors assigned to each legion. It was through his power that the natural inequities of the warrior would be neutralized.

    At each end of the training hall stood a healer. The time for games was over and cadets were trained to handle hard cold steel. Children played with wooden swords. By the time the cadets had entered the training hall, they had mastered many of the most basic skills. At this level two cadets could engage in swordplay with such skill that it looked as if they were engaged in a real fight. But each cadet was so skilled

The Oracles And The Jewels

that he could stop his blade before it cut into the skin of his opponent. However, as skilled as they were, on occasion a cadet would get sloppy and miss, so healers stood ready at all training sessions.

Short of an amputation, decapitation, or the piercing of a major organ like a Demotican's heart, the healers could easily repair the damage. It was very rare for a cadet to die in training, but it was not unheard of in the heat of battle. Every student of the healing academy had to spend time at The Academy of the Ancient Warring Arts. For they too had to learn the art of war so that they knew what to expect and what was expected of them in the heat of battle.

"Pair up!" one of the sergeants shouted. "Take your place within your assigned circle, cadets!" Immediately three hundred cadets broke down into one hundred and fifty groups. The cadets took up their positions opposite one another and within the circles drawn on the floor.

"You are now standing in the only universe under your control. It is of no concern to you what takes place outside this circle. Your job is to control and dominate the circle in which you stand. Your commanders will control the battlefield. They will direct your movements." As the sergeant shouted he walked between the circles and looked into the eyes of each cadet as he passed them.

"Your commanders," he continued, "will tend to matters of strategies and troop movements. Your job is to strike down any enemy that finds its way into your universe. Nothing exists outside your circle. We are few. They are many and the only way for us to prevail is for each of you to master your own universe. If you can defeat your equal in this place, in your universe, you can defeat any creature of Bohow." The sergeant paused. "Cadets, stand at the ready!" Three hundred cadets drew their swords from their scabbards and pulled their daggers from their belts. The sound of the steel echoed in the large hall.

"Cadets!" another sergeant shouted, "that is the sound of steel. The steel you will one day thrust into the breast of a beast. Your wooden swords have been destroyed in the fires of a smelter's furnace. You have fought your first fifteen matches with children's toys. Today is your first match with steel . . . It is the finest steel in this world. It has been forged

The Work Begins

from the mines of the Fortian Valley. It is unequaled by any steel in Bohow or in Ektos. Today you can take life or preserve it. The healers at each end of this hall are here for a reason. If you are sloppy, if you err, if you forget the teaching, you will be hurt or you will hurt another."

Tag and Brenz stood still, perfectly still, opposite one another. They stared into each other's eyes. A small smile leaked out onto Tag's face. The same happened to Brenz. They had been keeping score. In the fifteen official matches that they had fought, Tag had won seven. Brenz had taken five. Three had been declared a tie. A tie in Entosian military training meant neither cadet would have survived the fight.

Brenz and Tag, as well as every other cadet, stood motionless waiting for the sound of the battle horn. It was still and perfectly silent. Not a breath could be heard from any of the three hundred cadets. The only sound was the shuffle of the sergeants as they paced the floor weaving in and out between and through the cadets, checking their stance and their concentration. One cadet moved his head to see where his sergeant was.

"Cadet!" the sergeant shouted. "What are you looking for!" The sergeant charged toward the cadet. "What's your name, cadet?"

"Cadet Kelila! I was looking for you, sir," she replied.

"You aren't suppose to be looking for me!" As the sergeant charged toward Cadet Kelila, every other cadet stood absolutely still. No one dared look in her direction. The battle horn could blow at any moment, even in the middle of a sergeant's tirade. "You're supposed to know where I am at all times! If you have to look around to find me, you're dead! Dead, I said! Hear me, cadet! If you want to see me, then see me from the corner of your eye! Look for me through the back of your head! Feel my presence. Hear my presence! But never, I say never, turn away from your opponent. Not for a moment! Are you clear on that point Cadet Kelila?"

"Yes, Sergeant!" the cadet shouted. Just then the battle horn blew and immediately the smiles disappeared from both Tag and Brenz's faces. Tag was the first to swing, but Brenz met the blow before it really started. The two swung their swords flawlessly and fearlessly as they ran, jumped, turned, twisted, and even flew, or so it seemed, within their

The Oracles And The Jewels

striking field. They thrust, jabbed, and blocked. They advanced and retreated, but they always stayed within their circle. As the match went on their speed increased. Second only to a match between two Adroitians, Tag and Brenz were among the quickest and most skilled cadets in the academy. The sergeants watched their progress and were amazed at their skill. They fought with great speed. But more than that, they fought with great artistry. Neither cadet wasted a movement or a moment. They fought like veterans, not like students. They were smooth in their execution and the sound of their swords clashing fused into a melody.

It was as if they both had been born for this work and the sergeants watched Tag and Brenz with great pleasure. From the very first match, the sergeants had seen the potential in them. Their kind of skill was rarely seen in Demoticans or in Kilposians. In order to improve their skill, the sergeants had paired up the two from the earliest matches and had often wagered on the outcome.

In the narrow hall there were one hundred fifty matches, three hundred cadets. The clash of the swords, shouting, and grunting roared on for almost ten minutes. But one-by-one matches ended and the roar and clashing of metal began to fade away. In each match one was declared a victor and the other the victim. Their scores were recorded and their techniques critiqued.

Usually the Pithosians were the last to finish, but as their skill improved Tag and Brenz's match was almost always among the last to finish. This day was one of the usual days.

"Brenz," Tag shouted as they twisted and turned, striking their swords against the other's. "I'm hungry . . . and ready for lunch. Make a mistake and let's finish this."

"I'm not hungry," Brenz retorted. "It's your hunger. You do something about it."

"Okay!" At that Tag moved forward with a quickness that startled all who looked on. Brenz stumbled back a half step. But before the spectators could act upon their surprise, Brenz had successfully regained his footing and defended against the move with almost equal quickness. "Good recovery, Cadet Brenz," one of the sergeants shouted. No one was more surprised at their match than Tag and Brenz,

The Work Begins

although in the heat of battle this was no time to consider the matter.

The battle was now approaching thirteen minutes, which was a length almost unheard of in such a match. Entosians were taught to strike and defeat their opponent within the first forty-five seconds. In this way, they could move to the next creature and achieve the needed casualty ratio to win the day for Entos.

Smart, quick, and flawless execution was the key to survival and victory. If an Entosian warrior was going to fall in battle, he would have to strike down at least fifty of Ashkelon's soldiers or beasts in the process.

The entire regiment and the two dozen sergeants now stood in a large circle watching the match. No one had noticed that an old conjuror had entered the hall. His name was Conjuror Stratia, the dean of military conjurors. He was to military conjurors what Sandor was to the conjurors of The Great Chamber.

He had heard the reports of the unusually gifted Kilposian and Demotican and wanted to see if they were as talented as some of the officers had boasted. He had also

The Oracles And The Jewels

heard that Cadet Thayer Taggert was in need of a little spiritual disciplining – humbling. It was obvious to everyone connected to The Academy of the Ancient Warring Arts, including Thayer, that Cadet Thayer Taggert would one day be a great warrior and leader. But great warriors and leaders also must be humbled if they are going to be great.

Cadet Brenz Clinton had been a good counterbalance to Tag, but Brenz was reaching the fullness of his potential. Tag, on the other hand, still looked like he could go much further. Brenz had humbled Tag on several occasions, but those occasions were starting to become rarer. Conjuror Stratia believed the time had come to show Cadet Thayer Taggert that his skills were nothing compared to the power of a well-cast incantation.

Stratia walked slowly across the hall toward the match, which was now approaching fifteen minutes. The two were now breathing very heavily, yet still they seemed to pick up a little speed with each blow and move.

"Are you hungry yet, cadet?" Tag shouted. Brenz was indeed very hungry and starting to get a little tired, but he had a more serious problem at the moment. He began to notice that either he was slowing down or Tag's rate of acceleration was moving at a faster pace than his own. Either way, in another thirty seconds or so Brenz knew that the match would be Tag's, unless Tag made some mistake that could be exploited.

"You didn't answer Brenz! What's the matter, cat got your tongue?" Brenz wasn't the only one who noticed that a gap was beginning to open. Tag knew what was happening too and was enjoying the moment. "I'm getting faster Brenz," Tag said with a smile as he pushed Brenz toward the back of the circle. "You're not getting faster," Brenz said, "I'm slowing down. I'm hungry." Brenz was still blocking the strikes and jabs of Tag's blade. By now Brenz was fighting an almost purely defensive battle.

"Just a few more seconds, my friend . . . and you're all mine," Tag said with supreme confidence.

Suddenly a ball of light and glitter flew across the room and hit Brenz square in the back. Two seconds later, Tag was lying flat on his back and Brenz had his right foot on Tag's chest and his blade at Tag's neck.

The Work Begins

It was hard to tell which of the two was more surprised. Brenz had countered a thrust from Tag's blade, turned three hundred sixty degrees, hit Tag's blade with a reverse swing, knocked him to the ground, and placed his blade at Tag's throat. The sergeants yelled with excitement. The two hundred ninety eight other cadets stood in stunned silence.

"Yea, I'm hungry," Brenz said in disbelief and with his sword at Tag's throat. "Are you hungry too?" Tag didn't know what to say.

"Match to Cadet Brenz Clinton," yelled the sergeant.

"Very impressive for a Demotican and Kilposian," the conjuror said as he made his way through the crowd. "Very impressive indeed." Tag's eye floated to the left and looked up at an old and gray conjuror who bore a youthful smile.

It was customary to remain still at the end of a match until the sergeant had an opportunity to verbally critique the cadets. Something told Tag that the sergeant wasn't going to be the one offering the critique this time.

"Cadets, this is Conjuror Stratia. He is the chaplain here. As you can see, Conjuror Stratia moves a little too slowly these days to take the battlefield, but he still has conjuring powers second only to Headmaster Sandor. It is his job to teach the warrior conjurors to look to your souls and use the power of Entos to help improve the skills we teach you here so that you may defeat the evil foe. Welcome Conjuror Stratia," Tag's sergeant said.

"Thank you, Sergeant. I enjoyed the match very much. These two are very fine cadets indeed. They are developing their battle skills well. But to be fine leaders more is needed than a fast sword. I assume, sergeant, the one on the bottom is Cadet Thayer Taggert, of whom many speak so highly." Stratia looked down at Tag with a big smile. "In that position he doesn't look so impressive, do you my son?"

"I imagine not, sir," Tag said with a touch of embarrassment.

"When you fight with Ashkelon's warriors will you invite them to lunch?"

"No, sir, I will likely not," Tag replied.

"You are indeed impressive. Both of you are. Cadet Thayer Taggert you have just been the victim of a small dose

The Oracles And The Jewels

of conjuring. Cadet Brenz Clinton, you were just turned into a conduit for the power of Entos."

Stratia turned to address the whole assembly. "In that moment when the wizardry hits your opponent, even if he is the poorest of all warriors, he can kill you in an instant. Your power and skills are impressive. But they are nothing compared to the power that comes through the conjuror. You natural ability and your training can't save you if your opponent is so empowered by the mysteries of Entos," explained Stratia. "This is a lesson for you all. A conjuror is a warrior, but he can never use his power to take a life. As warriors of Entos that is your calling, not the conjuror's. You take life when you must in order to defend Entos or her citizens. A conjuror can only employ his wizardry through you. Of course, the more skilled you are, the better for the wizardry and for you. You have skills to defeat many of the creatures of Bohow. But you cannot prevail against the armies of Ashkelon unless you are so empowered. You are the means. I am your servant. But you are also my tool." Stratia paused and took a step.

"By the way, Ashkelon has the same power and more. The difference is twofold. His power is evil and, unlike the conjurors of Entos, he takes life directly when presented with the opportunity and when it serves his purposes. Sergeants carry on." Conjuror Stratia made his way out of the hall.

"At ease, men," the sergeant said with a smile. "Sharpen your swords, lick your wounds, and go to lunch. Tag and Brenz are hungry. Dismissed!" Brenz helped Tag up from the floor. "Relax, Cadet Thayer Taggert, the conjurors are on our side," his sergeant said.

"All of them?" Tag uttered under his breath.

"We'll see," Brenz said in an equally hushed voice.

The Meeting of the Little Fellowship

At dusk the following day, the time came for the monthly meeting of the little fellowship. The group had met under the decaying bridge in Rieve and Tag's hamlet every month for more than a year. On this night Rieve arrived first, as he almost always did. Tag and Brenz showed up a few minutes later.

The Work Begins

"Rieve, I have a newfound respect for what you conjurors and priests do," Brenz said.

"Really? To what do I owe this newfound respect?"

"Have you ever met Conjuror Stratia?" Tag asked.

"No, but he is well known at the Academy," Rieve answered.

"Yesterday we met him under the most exciting circumstance," Brenz said. Tag grunted.

"What does that grunt mean?" Rieve asked.

"It means that Tag lost in a great match yesterday," Brenz proudly announced.

"Without the conjuror I had him, Rieve!" Tag said.

"Sure, you did," Rieve said with a smile.

"I did. Tell him Brenz," Tag insisted.

"I am telling him. I will tell it my way, then you can tell him your way," Brenz replied. Tag drew his sword from its scabbard. Brenz responded by reflex and did the same. Their blades met in the air and made a loud clash.

"Come you two. Quit playing around. This is suppose to be a secret meeting," Rieve said laughing. His words did not hinder the game. The two went back and forth for a few seconds while Rieve reached into his pocket and pulled out a very small amount of gold and silver glitter. He whispered three words under his breath and threw the substance, hitting Brenz in the back. Once again Tag found himself on the ground with Brenz's sword waving over him. "Is that how it happened, Tag?" Rieve laughed.

Tag didn't find it funny. To be humbled by Stratia was one thing, to find himself on the ground at the hand of his brother was another.

"I could get used to this, Tag," Brenz said. "I bet you could get used to this, too."

Rieve reached into his pocket a second time and again a little ball of light flew through the air. This time its target was Tag. In a matter of just two seconds Brenz found himself in Tag's place and Tag in his.

"Learn anything yet?" Rieve asked.

"Now, now boys," River's voice called out. "Play nice."

"Is everyone all right! Are you hurt Brenz!" Blisse called out.

"Only their pride is hurt." Rieve responded.

The Oracles And The Jewels

"Oh shoot," Blisse said. "Today we worked on the incantations and natural elements to close an open wound. I had hoped at least one of them would have had an open wound."

Brenz got up from the ground and dusted himself off. "Sorry to disappoint you."

"Who did you bring with you?" Tag asked as he continued to dust himself off and looked at Breille.

"This is Breille Clarrice. I have talked about her before," River answered.

"You're this season's amateur fencing champion for the female division," Tag said.

Breille smiled and nodded her head affirmatively. Tag smiled.

"It's a shame you're a female," Tag said.

"Why?" Breille asked.

"Well, if you were a male I would issue a gentleman's challenge," Tag said.

"Are you sure it is a good idea to bring her along?" Brenz interrupted.

"Yes. She has given a pledge and she shares our concerns," replied River. "Is there anything else needed?"

"Sorry, Breille," Rieve said apologetically, "but we don't want to place anyone unnecessarily at risk."

"I understand. That is very reasonable." Breille stated. A typical response from a Procuron. There was a moment of uncomfortable silence. River had brought Breille into their little fellowship, but River did not want to divulge any secrets or confidences without the approval of the group. Blisse had known of Breille for the better part of a year now, but did not know exactly what her role would be in the little fellowship. They had been five, but now there were six. It would take a little time to figure out just where Breille Clarrice, the Procuron, would fit in.

"Breille," Rieve began, "we aren't sure exactly what we are doing here. We meet once a month and have been for several months now. At first it was just to keep in touch with each other's progress in our studies and vocational development. But as time has marched on, we began piecing together the events that are changing Entos. Of course our picture is pretty limited. We don't even know why

The Work Begins

we are putting the picture together. We are certainly in no position to reverse the decisions of the City Fathers. It is not our place," said Rieve. "We have no interest in inciting unrest or anything like that. We are simply educating ourselves about the nature of things."

"I am pleased to hear that we aren't about to launch a military take over. Such a thing would be both irrational and contrary to the very nature of Entos," Breille said.

"The only thing we can say about our situation is that we gather here to prepare for that day when, by virtue of our stations and our desire, we will be in the position to protect Entos and her citizens," Rieve explained. "That day might never come. At least we hope so. It simply seemed wise to us to educate ourselves."

"Here is what we can say with some confidence," River added. "We know that The Academy of Theological Sciences and Ancient Conjuring Arts is deeply divided and there is a great deal of infighting. Headmaster Sandor has been pushed aside and others are in control," River reported.

"Do they control the Academy completely?" Breille asked.

"No. They control the official offices, but there are still many fine faculty members and some fine students. Unfortunately, some of them are afraid to take a public stand against the current regime," Rieve reported with a tone of disappointment.

"Breille," River continued, "also know that the military is critical of the changes and is being very slow at instituting even minor reforms. They consider the changes to be a threat to the security of Entos."

"We also believe," Blisse offered, "that the City Fathers are banking on an increase in the frequency of small raids, but don't seem to believe that Ashkelon will ever launch a full frontal attack on Entos. We believe this to be the case because they are reducing the enrollment to the military academy and in The Academy of Healing Arts. If we do suffer a large attack, we will be hard pressed to tend to both noncombatants and combatants. A major engagement in the next few years will only accelerate the problem."

The Oracles And The Jewels

"Add this to what you know and believe the following," Breille volunteered. "The Academies for the Building Arts and Governance are very pleased about what is happening. Both institutions are making internal curriculum changes to bring their program more in line with the City Fathers' new emphasis.

"Some of my instructors now teach that the doctrines of the Oracles and the views of the priests and conjurors need not be reflected in our architectural forms or in the governance of the city. The distinction between theory and practice is being made with greater enthusiasm than ever before."

"That's more information than I need," Blisse quipped.

"I'm no theologian either. That's big brother's department. What does that mean in plain Entosian?" Tag asked.

"It means that some are pushing for a division between the Articles of Faith and the everyday ordinary operation of Entos," Rieve answered.

"That can't be good," Brenz said.

"No it is not," Rieve said. "It means that in practical everyday matters of life, the Oracles will become less and less important in the operation of Entos and in the lives of Entosians. Eventually, if such a thing continues, Entos will no longer be governed by the Oracles and our leaders might stop listening to the wise counsel of the priests and conjurors."

"What could possibly take the place of the Oracles?" Blisse asked.

"Any number of things," River answered.

"Technology, for example," Breille said.

"Entosians' likes and dislikes," Rieve added.

"Political and military power," Tag said.

"As I said, any number of things will fill the vacuum," River repeated. "But all of them will eventually lead to the fall of Entos."

"In our lifetime?" Blisse asked.

"Maybe," River replied.

"You can also add this into the mix as well," Breille said. "The vote for the changes fell in this way. Seven City Fathers voted for the changes. Six City Fathers voted against. My

The Work Begins

father also believes that the majority will eventually move for the removal of the minority."

"How can they do that?" Brenz asked.

"Under a call for unity and brotherhood those in power can justify any kind of political move," Rieve answered.

"Breille's father voted against it," River offered without hesitation, as if she knew what the others were thinking.

"Well then, we have one father on the right side of this fight in the halls of governance and one on the right side in the Academy," Tag said. Tag assumed his father would be on the right side. Rieve thought about correcting his younger brother at that moment, but he decided it was best to keep the day's events from the others, especially Tag. Secrets were rare in the little fellowship, but sometimes keeping secrets was necessary to protect the fellowship and Entosians like Headmaster Sandor.

The balance of the evening was filled with stories from their lives and with their hopes for the future. It was also filled with play. Tag and Brenz felt compelled to show off a little and the girls enjoyed watching the competition. But the girls did not remain passive participants. Tag and Brenz taught the three girls some basic elements of swordplay. The time flew and before they knew it, it was 10:30 in the dark. Rieve looked at his timepiece and remembered that he had to be at the Headmaster's office in thirty minutes.

"Sorry to be the one to bring this party to an end, but it's getting late," Rieve said.

"I have to get going too," Blisse said. "I have an exam in the morning. It just so happens that the exam is on the anatomy of a Procuron."

"Can I be of any service?" Breille asked with a grin.

"Where were you yesterday when I really needed you?" Blisse said. "Thanks for the offer, but I think all I need at this point is a short review. See you guys later. Oh Breille, thanks for joining us." River and Blisse headed down away from the city and toward home; Breille headed back to the city where her father kept a small apartment near the building academy. Tag and Brenz waited a little while, then returned to the barracks at the Warring Academy.

Rieve ran up the path toward the Academy, passed his dorm, and approached the courtyard. He slowed his pace as

The Oracles And The Jewels

he approached the faculty offices, in part because he was winded, but he also wanted to be careful as he went by the faculty housing. The closer he got to faculty housing and to the courtyard, the slower he walked. He was careful to stay in the dark shadows, or what passed as dark shadows. The three moons and stars made it hard to find such shadows, even at the darkest point of night.

The most difficult part of the entire affair was the one hundred fifty foot courtyard through which Rieve would have to pass to reach the main doors of the faculty building. The courtyard was surrounded by apartments in which several priests and professors lived. If Rieve were seen entering the building by the wrong faculty member, his private lessons would be over before they started.

Rieve looked up and saw the light on in the Headmaster's office. Sandor did not keep normal hours. As a matter of fact, other than his appearance, there was nothing normal about Sandor. The fact that his light was still on at this late hour was not strange.

"At least once I'm in the office," Rieve thought to himself, "I can relax. It's just getting there without being noticed that's the problem." Rieve walked quietly through the courtyard. He tried to appear casual, but not sloppy. He wanted to sneak his way through without looking like he was sneaking. As he made his way, he was conscious of every step, every movement of his arms and head, and of every breath he took. He used every object in the courtyard to conceal his presence. Bushes, trees, benches, and statues provided Rieve with protection as he moved through the yard.

"So far so good," Rieve thought as he reached the main entrance to the faculty office. The doors were very large and heavy. Rieve remembered that on his last visit the doors gave out a loud squeak when he opened them. As he took the handles in his hands, he remembered the squeak.

"Here's a problem," he thought. "How do I get in without waking the other faculty members? Surely, the sound of the hinges would draw some attention." Rieve had no incantation for squeaky doors. He had nothing, not even water to pour on the hinges.

The Work Begins

"Do I do this fast or slow?" he debated in his own head. "Is there another way in? No." He answered his own question and continued, "Not at this time of night. Which of the two doors is louder than the other? Which one do I pick? Well, here goes," he whispered under his breath. Rieve took hold of the door on the right and pulled it. At first he pulled slowly, then yanked it quickly. It made not a sound. "That was easier than I thought it was going to be," he whispered. Rieve wasted no time. He stepped into the lobby area, made his way quickly across the floor to the stairwell, and ran up the stairs, taking two steps at a time. By the time he reached the sixth floor, Rieve was breathing very heavily. He held his breath for a moment and poked his head out of the stairwell and into the hall. There was only one light on. It was the light in Sandor's study.

The hallway looked very long and it was dark, except for the light that spilled into the hall through the glass in Sandor's door. "Why couldn't they have put him at this end?" Rieve asked in a rhetorical tone. "Why? Because that would make it too easy for students like me to get to this office and we can't have that can we, Professor MulLord?"

Rieve stepped into the hallway and walked slowly toward Sandor's study. As he got closer, the light from Sandor's office made it easier to see, so his pace quickened. Before Rieve had a chance to stop and knock on the door, Sandor spoke.

"Come in, my son." His door was cracked a bit.

"Good evening, Headmaster Sandor," Rieve said in a whisper.

"There is no need to whisper, young man. There's no one in the building. Just thee and me. If there are, they won't come up here."

Rieve entered the study. As he entered, his eyes surveyed the room. Sandor's study was a large room. It was also dusty, disorganized, and cluttered. Books were piled everywhere. Many were on the bookshelves, standing as intended. But many more were piled up on two small tables. Still more were piled on the chairs that were scattered about the room. There were books on the floor and mixed in with all the books there were jars and cans filled with colorful dust and liquids of different shades and colors.

The Oracles And The Jewels

"Headmaster, I believe you have the entire history of Entos lying about your study," Rieve said. "Not to mention every conjuring book that has ever been written." Rieve lifted one of Sandor's largest and oldest books from the table. It was so large he needed both hands.

"Books don't make you wise, my son. They make one knowledgeable. Knowledge is only one-third of what is needed to produce a wise conjuror," Sandor said. "There are three components to wisdom." Rieve put the book down on the table from which he had taken it.

"I would greatly benefit from the recipe. What are the other two ingredients of wisdom, or is that a great secret?" Rieve asked.

"It is no secret, but ye have not yet been filled with the first ingredient, so there is no reason to introduce the other two," Sandor said gently.

"I thought I was going to have trouble getting in the place unnoticed," Rieve said changing the subject. "The last time I was here the main doors were very loud. At this time of night, I thought I would wake the entire campus pulling on those doors."

"Hasn't thou heard, I am the greatest conjuror in all of Entos," Sandor said.

"There's an incantation for squeaky door hinges?" Rieve asked.

"No, but there is a great magical substance that takes care of such things," Sandor said in a low and serious tone. The Headmaster held up his right hand and showed Rieve his fingers. They were blackened with a shiny substance.

"What's that?" Rieve asked with excitement. "I've never seen a substance like that in any conjuring book."

"It's called grease. I went down to the doors earlier today and greased the hinges. Professor MulLord thanked me himself as he passed me in the doorway." Sandor chuckled. "Entosians are funny these days," Sandor said. "They are always looking for the most mysterious and exciting solution to any given problem." Rieve felt foolish for being taken in, but Sandor's humor was not lost on him.

"Are we safe up here? Or do you have some good, old-fashioned earplugs to put into the ears of anyone who

The Work Begins

might enter the building at night?" Rieve asked injecting a little humor of his own.

"Most of the faculty leave me alone these days. They're ashamed."

"Ashamed of themselves I hope, not of you," said Rieve.

"Either way, they stay away."

"They won't bother us, even if they hear a couple of voices?" Rieve asked.

"I have taken care of that problem too," the Headmaster said with a chuckle, "and I have done so without using good old-fashioned earplugs."

"How so, sir?" Rieve asked.

"I have spent the past six months talking to myself out loud. Professor MulLord and his friends have become convinced that the solitude has driven me mad. They believe that the students and faculty have largely forgotten me. Rumors and gossip harm, but they can also be used to one's advantage. I chose the latter. There's more to conjuring than conjuring," Sandor said.

"Headmaster, may I ask you a few questions before we get started with my formal training?" Rieve asked.

"Yes, after all, this is thy battle too. Please sit down," Sandor said. Rieve looked around for an empty seat, but none was found. Rieve took books from one of the chairs and relocated them to the nearest table. The chair was dusty. As he wiped the chair with the sleeve of his robe, he continued.

"Sir, why have they removed you from the classroom and from your duties as Headmaster?" Rieve asked in a soft and humble voice and sat down.

"What do they say?" the Headmaster inquired.

"They say you've done a lot of things. None of them are very complimentary," Rieve reported.

"What dost thou think?" Sandor asked as he lifted his left eyebrow.

"I think you're in the way of the new teaching and that they needed you to retire so they could move on."

"What makes thee think that?"

"On the face of things, it appears that the faculty believe and teach basically the same thing. But it is equally clear that different faculty members have different ways of talking

The Oracles And The Jewels

about those things. It's not that some faculty deny the reality and purpose of the Oracles or the Jewels. It's just that they speak in different ways about them," Rieve explained.

"Are the differences great or small in thy judgment, Apprentice Rieve?" Sandor asked.

"Some faculty members believe that thinkers like you have lost their balance." Rieve continued, "They believe that all they are doing is putting a freedom back into the thinking and rituals of Entos. They think that they can produce an Entos that will always grow larger and become greater. Their teaching also seems to find favor with many Entosians and the way they speak certainly makes Entosians feel better about being Entosians."

"Is that how we are supposed to feel?"

"I don't know how we are supposed to feel. Perhaps there is something wrong with me. I don't walk around thinking about how I feel. I just do what I am supposed to do and feel badly when I don't."

"What doth thou thinkest of the new teaching?"

"I think that the new teaching is new and that it draws our attention away from the things that give us our freedom and balance. Faith in faith is foolish. Faith and love have to have an object outside of themselves." Rieve stood up, walked over to the light and turned it down. Then he walked to the window. Sandor stood as well and joined Rieve at the window. The two looked out on the buildings that shone so softly in the night sky.

"These great buildings of ours do not rest on their own foundation. They are sunk and built upon one solid granite floor that was here long before the buildings were made. Faith and love are the buildings. Faith and love are not the granite foundation. They rise up from Entos." Rieve paused for a moment to glance at Sandor for some look of approval, but he glanced so quickly he could not see what he was looking for.

"Professor MulLord and the others want to fix our attention on the buildings, not the ground upon which those two great buildings of faith and love sit. It is the ground that is Entos, forged out by the Oracles. The buildings are not Entos. Entosians don't even constitute the true nature of

The Work Begins

Entos. Although, Entos cannot be Entos without them and they can't be Entosians without her. Am I wrong?"

"Thou has spoken well," Sandor replied. "But thou still have not described the true nature of Entos. Keep speaking. Perhaps in thy speaking the answer will be revealed and thou wilt convince thyself of the rightness of our conclusions."

"Entos, I believe, is a living creature. In some mysterious way she is alive, but not because we give her life. She is alive. The water that wells up from within her is her life blood. Every day we take her beautiful stones to build our city and bridges. We use the trees for our homes, to keep us warm, and to cook our food. We eat the fruit and animals that grow in her valleys and forests. All of these things she renews so that we make take again the next day. Even the ground upon which we walk is alive. As we sleep she renews herself. Every morning is a new birth. It is as if she heals herself so that we might sustain our life for another day. Entos is alive. She is not just a place. Amidst Ashkelon's earth of darkness and death, Entos is a living part of the earth . . . and if she is alive . . ." Rieve paused for a moment, "then can she die?"

"If asked that question, how would thou answer?" Sandor asked.

"I do not know. The books say she is eternal, yet temporal. But I see the signs that mark old age and death in her." Rieve said and in saying so he felt sadness come over him.

"I am certain of few things," Rieve continued, "but I know that the Maker, Giver, and King made Entos and has kept her alive through the Oracles and the Jewels. I know together they created me. I also know that I am nothing unless I'm tied to something greater, to my mother Entos. Entos doesn't belong to me. It does not even belong to us. We belong to her and it is our sacred trust to pass her onto those who follow. I am sorry, Headmaster. I ramble too much, but to speak like this at the Academy brings contention and division. It does feel good to speak in such a way and to do so without fear of contradiction or penalty."

"Ye ramble well, ramble more," Sandor said.

The Oracles And The Jewels

"The new teaching is tearing the Academy and Entos apart. They keep saying that all we have to do is learn to trust and that our differences have arisen because we do not trust the teacher. But it seems to me that we do not trust the teacher because he is saying and doing things that breed distrust. It's a circle that cannot be broken. We distrust because they speak and we distrust because it is them that speak it. Unless we all return to the clear instruction of the Oracles, but the clarity of the Oracles is what is in question."

"Thou has stated the problem well," Sandor said. "Now we have a lot of work to do and very little time to do it. You cannot solve MulLord's problem. You can only speak and fight against him. So let's begin learning how to fight shall we?"

"Yes, sir." Rieve walked across the study and turned up the lights. Then he returned to his chair.

"Under the tutelage of Professor Etam how far didst thou manage to make it in your conjuring textbook?"

"I'm through chapter six," Rieve answered.

"Good, very good. Six. . . hummm. . . now that's an interesting number," Sandor said.

"Sir?"

"Six, an interesting number," Sandor said with a smile.

"Eight and three are interesting numbers, sir. Six is six. What's so interesting about the number six?" Rieve asked.

"There are six now, aren't there, in the fellowship?" Sandor asked. Rieve did not know what to say. "Take care of the other five. Thou wilt have need of them, each one in his own way and each one in his or her own time. Do not separate and do not leave any behind."

"Yes, sir. I won't," Rieve responded as if he understood, but the statement both frightened and comforted him. He was frightened because it was becoming obvious that the little fellowship would be key in the coming battle for the future of Entos. It was comforting because Rieve was coming to see that he would not have to bear the burdens of his office alone.

"How do you know such things?" Rieve asked. "Are you so powerful that you can see the future at will?"

The Work Begins

"Oh no," Sandor replied. "I am limited to bits and pieces. I see pictures of what may be. I only know that which I am permitted to know."

"How does this knowledge come to you?" Rieve asked.

"It comes in different ways, according to the type. Not all knowledge is of the same type. There are four types. There is the type that comes from the study of the Oracles and the great teachers of the same. They have much to teach us about ourselves and the nature of things. The Academy is suppose to be about imparting this first kind of knowledge, for it is the foundation for all other kinds of knowledge."

"What of the second type?" Rieve asked. The chair creaked as Rieve leaned forward to listen more intently to the answer. Sandor took his time in answering the question. He reached for a small glass of water that had been sitting on his desk and took a small sip, then continued.

"The second is a knowledge of the future that comes from the study of the past. I know, for example, that thou wilt face great temptations and that thou wilt fall to some of those temptations. I know that soon enough thou wilt be betrayed by those whom thou trustest. They will wound thee deeply and thou may well harm them in reply," Sandor paused. "I pray not, but such temptations are hard to resist, even for the strongest among us."

Sandor continued his discourse, "I know that because it has always been true that when Ashkelon discovers his equal, he will do all he can to turn you before you discover that you are his equal. I know that should he fail to turn thee, he will try to destroy thee.

"I also know that Ashkelon is not the greatest threat to thy success and well-being. For Ashkelon is a threat that comes from without. It is the threat within that is far more powerful. If thou prevails against thyself, thou wilt prevail against Ashkelon.

"These things I know because this is the way it has been with all the great conjurors. It is the great battles that make such men great."

"Have these things happened to you?" Rieve asked.

"Most certainly," Sandor answered. "I know these things because this is the history of Entos and the history of every conjuror who has had to do battle."

The Oracles And The Jewels

"What can be said of the third type?" asked Rieve.

"Sometimes a conjuror knows because he sees the world around him with the eyes of the conjuror. Where others simply see stars, or colors, or natural elements, the conjuror/priest sees signs and pictures. In time thou wilt see things that others simply do not notice. Such things are not magical. There is no mystery in such things. These things have been in the landscape and sky scape from the Ancient of Days. Most Entosians pass them by each day and never see them. They live their entire lives and never see them, because they have been taught not to see them."

"Like, the Three Faces of the King?" Rieve asked. Sandor smiled and nodded. "You said there are four ways by which you know something of the future. What is the fourth?"

"I know other things because I have been given the opportunity to see them as if I were standing on a great stage. This way of knowing is very rare and the least certain of the four types. I see only what I am meant to see and I know only what I am permitted to know."

"Do they always come true? . . . Your visions, are they always right?" Rieve asked.

"I do not know. Perhaps, one day thou wilt answer that question for me," Sandor replied. "Now my son, there is much work, study, and thinking we must do. Thou hast much to learn in the conjuring arts. Sooner or later all four types of knowing will be required, so let's get more thoroughly acquainted with the first two types of knowing. Retrieve that book from the table, the one thou didst pick up when thou entered the room. That is where we shall make our beginning." Sandor pointed to the large book that Rieve had picked up from the table. Rieve did as instructed and returned to his chair. He opened the book to the cover page.

"Read it. . . translate it," Sandor ordered.

"*Adan Yaddann Palanan Adon Entos an*," Rieve read. "The Knowledge of the Wonders of Entos."

"Indeed," Sandor commented in a reverent and hushed voice. "Continue, my son."

The night passed quickly. Rieve read and translated each section of the sacred book. After each passage was completed, Sandor would speak of its meaning, use, and value. Rieve sat in the chair all night reading, translating,

The Work Begins

and listening to Sandor. Where appropriate he asked questions. He took in every word that Sandor spoke. He wanted to take notes for fear that he might forget the teachings that poured out from the Headmaster's lips and from the sacred book, but Sandor forbade him. "It will come when it needs to come," Sandor said, then added, "I promise."

At 4:00 in the dark Sandor ended the session. "Time to go my son. Light will soon break over the city."

"Already?" Rieve said as he stood up from his chair and checked his timepiece. Suddenly his body felt the time and he yawned. As he yawned he said, "I will be back tomorrow . . . I mean tonight, Sir." Sandor smiled.

"Thou art young. Thou wilt endure thy training well."

"If I don't, do you have a potion or incantation that does away with the need for sleep?"

"Yes, but the side effects are very unhealthy. I suggest thou use the old-fashioned method."

"Naps?"

"Thou doth learn quickly," Sandor smiled again.

"Thank you, Sir, for your time."

"No, I thank thee for thy life," Sandor said.

"Sir, I wish you wouldn't say things like that. It makes me a little paranoid."

"It makes me sound profound," Sandor laughed. Rieve headed down the hall repeating the process that had brought him to the office some six hours earlier. As he left the faculty building he realized that it was the Eighth Day. The little fellowship had agreed that they would attend the 8:00 Festival. That left Rieve three hours of rest before he had to rise for the service. He returned to his bed for the balance of the morning.

At 7:00 Rieve awoke, but was still very tired. He cleaned up and dressed in his priestly robe and headed across the street to attend the Eighth Day Festival. He stood at the east entrance as thousands walked up the stairs and into The Great Chamber. He didn't have to look for the others. The little fellowship had made a game of attendance. The first to wake and make it to The Great Chamber would lean against the middle pillar on the right side of the main entrance. Each

The Oracles And The Jewels

entrance on each of The Great Chamber's eight sides was framed by three white pillars.

Rieve was almost always the first to arrive. He had a great advantage. The Academy of Theological Sciences and Ancient Conjuring Arts and his dorm were across the street from the northeast entrance.

Rieve stood at the pillar and watched River and Blisse approach. The two sisters had changed a great deal in the past year. As Rieve watched the two weave their way through the crowd and up the steps, it dawned on him that they were growing into beautiful young ladies. Rieve looked upon them as his sisters. He noticed, as the two made their way through the crowd, that several young men took a second look at the sisters. Dressed in their best and adorned in a fashion appropriate for the festival, they were a pleasure to any young suitor's eye.

"Good morning, Rieve Waynwright," Blisse said.

"Good morning, Blisse Maia," Rieve replied.

"Good morning, Rieve Waynwright," River said with her customary tone of formality.

"Good morning to you, River Kiernan," Rieve responded, echoing the same tone.

"You two look very lovely this morning," Rieve added.

"You look very priestly," Blisse replied.

"Good. That is how I am supposed to look," Rieve said with a smile. "Are those dresses new?" Rieve asked.

"No, just fixed up a bit," River replied. "Have you seen Cadets Thayer Taggert and Brenz Clinton yet?"

"Not yet, but they will be here soon. They are going to be relocated to the training field in the next week or two. This might be the last time all six of us are together for the festival for some time."

"I bet Thayer Taggert is looking forward to that. He will get to live like a real warrior," River added.

"Living in a tent, hunting, bathing, and cooking all outdoors, sounds like a lot of fun to me," Blisse said. "I prefer to see them like that." She pointed toward Tag and Brenz who were now weaving their way through the crowd. "Now those boys look like warrior gentlemen and officers."

Tag and Brenz were dressed in their parade uniforms, which was the customary dress for cadets and warriors who

The Work Begins

attended the Great Festival. In fact, every Entosian adorned themselves in their best robes and uniforms for the Eighth Day Festival. While many other traditions and customs had fallen away, there was still some respect for the dignity, formality, and beauty of the service.

It was still common for Entosian mothers to dress their little girls up in their prettiest dresses and tribal gowns. Many spent the evening of the seventh night fixing their hair and shining their tribal jewelry and family crests.

"Good morning, my priestly brother," Tag said with a smile as he ran up the steps, taking two to three steps at a time. "You look beat. Late night doing homework or something like that?"

"Something like that. Good morning, Cadet Brenz Clinton," Rieve said.

"Good morning, Priest Rieve Waynwright. And you don't look that bad," Brenz replied.

"Thanks," Rieve said.

"Good morning, cadets," River said.

"Same for me," Blisse added quickly.

"Good morning, ladies," Brenz said. "You look lovely."

"We know. Rieve already told us," Blisse said with great confidence and a smile. "You boys look pretty handsome too."

"Has anyone seen Breille yet?" Brenz asked.

"Yes. She's over there. Standing with her father," Rieve reported as he nodded his head in Breille's direction. Breille was looking at her five friends and signaled that she would be over in just a minute. Her father, City Father Derson, was talking with City Father Simmjer the Pithosian. Breille interrupted her father's conversation to give him a kiss on the cheek. She said something to him. He nodded in reply and gave her a kiss in return. Breille made her way to the little fellowship as Derson and Simmjer entered The Great Chamber still involved in a conversation.

"Sorry, I was delayed," Breille said. "My father and City Father Simmjer were discussing some of the issues before the council. I never miss an opportunity to get a good education on the politics of Entos."

"We have plenty of time," River answered.

The Oracles And The Jewels

"Breille, I have always found Procuron women stunningly beautiful. That is particularly true of you on this fine morning," Rieve said.

"You're just a robe full of compliments this morning," Blisse said.

"I don't want anyone to feel left out," Rieve replied. "Besides, a priest is a truth teller."

"Thank you, Rieve, for the compliment. May I say you look rather priestly this morning," Breille said returning the compliment.

"Yes, I have heard that too this morning. I guess that's a compliment," Rieve said.

"Now that we have all agreed that we are stunningly handsome and beautiful Entosians, don't you all think we ought to get inside?" River said as she took a step toward the entrance. The six of them walked through the east entrance of The Great Chamber. It was not as full as it once was, but it was full none-the-less. As the little fellowship entered, the noise and conversation of the street outside faded away with each step and the sounds of music and the choirs filled the air and their ears.

Entosians from every tribe were present and, while tribes tended to sit together in the sections designated by their traditional color and pointing toward their respective hamlets, it was not uncommon for Kilposians to sit in the section dominated by the Fortians, or a Fortian or two to sit with Pithosians and so on.

Rieve led the group around the outer hallway to the left. They passed through the red, green, and blue sections. They walked quietly and in single file until they came to the section colored with a tint of gold. It was known as the Procuron section.

Breille was the newest addition to their little fellowship. Breille had been their guest under the bridge just a few hours ago. Now they would sit among her tribe as a symbolic gesture. The symbolism of the moment was not lost on Breille.

The main floor was full, so they headed up the stairs. They reached the second balcony, but were unable to find a block of six seats. Rieve proceeded to lead them to the third and top balcony, which was about half full. The six took their

The Work Begins

seats and sat down. They remained seated and silent, taking in the grand sight. Entos was a beautiful land, but its beauty was pale in comparison to the inside of The Great Chamber. And The Great Chamber was most beautiful on the Eighth Day – it was, as Entosians liked to say, "holy other, almost other worldly."

The light that lit The Great Chamber made all within its pale radiate with its glow. When the seven priests entered The Great Chamber and took their positions inside the rail, the entire assembly stood in complete silence.

The little fellowship was so high up it was difficult to tell who was presiding at the festival on this particular morning, with one exception. Headmaster Sandor was easily recognizable. While Sandor adorned himself with the traditional white priestly robes of The Great Chamber, he also wore his academic hood which displayed the colors of every tribe.

Sandor had been removed from his duties at the Academy. That could be done easily enough. It was an internal matter. But to remove him from The Great Chamber would require an expulsion from the office of priest, professor, and conjuror. That would take a full public trial and would place their plans at risk. They had made a calculated decision that it was not worth the risk, at least not yet.

As the entire assembly stood in silence, two priests took in their hands the large scrolls upon which were written the words of the Oracles. The priests began to chant the words written on the scroll in the sacred language, *"Koboon, Paaran, Pission Etum Sammar Emen Eppon Ad Borran, Borranon, Ad Mellom Eoppon Entos an."* The entire assembly replied in unison the vernacular and in song, *"Glory, honor, fidelity, and praise belong to the Maker, Giver, and King of Entos."* These were the words that signaled the start of each Festival and those words triggered a series of proclamations and responses, which had been performed on the Eighth Day, every Eighth Day since the Days of Old. Entosians learned the words of the priests by listening to the choirs and to the sung replies of the Entosians week after week.

The Oracles And The Jewels

On this morning the Great Festival was the ordinary festival, yet its power, mystery, beauty, and order was always a sight to behold. In that hour, all Entosians were renewed and in so being renewed, they came to understand that they belonged to something far greater than themselves.

The little fellowship joined in the replies, songs, and chants as the ritual required. The entire assembly knew their respective parts. The choirs entered as the ritual required. Different sections of The Great Chamber replied in proper order. At an appointed time parents of the newborn creatures would bring them to the rail, where the priests would speak the words of the Oracles to them and touch their foreheads, mouths, and breasts. After each creature was transformed, the priests would hold the newborn Entosian up for all to see and all would reply, *"Glory, honor, fidelity, and praise belong to the Maker, Giver, and King of Entos."*

The incantations of the conjurors were only understood by the priests and they worked very specific works. But the sacred language of the Great Festivals was understood by all. Incantations had a power. Incantations helped those who fought to fight better. The incantations helped those who ran to run faster. They helped the weak to become strong, the fearful to be brave, and the sick to be well. But the words of the Oracles and the responses of the Entosians in the Great Festival were understood by all and had the greatest of all power. The Great Festival had the power to show Entosians the truth about their own natures and to bury the dark creatures within; the creatures from whence they came.

As the little fellowship stood side by side, singing and speaking their part, they all, each in his own way, understood that if they failed to remain true to the task ahead, whatever it might be, the Great Festival, like so much else around them, might be changed or even lost. Rieve understood this far better than the rest. But he knew that soon enough they would all have to pass their tests, for Sandor had prophesied it to be so. If all else changed, one thing would have to remain the same. The Great Festival must remain. As the festival goes, so goes the rest of Entos.

The Work Begins

As the ritual came to an end the people fell silent and only the voice of the Presiding Priest would be heard. *"Laccam sussim orad gabbom koboon or Entos an."* The entire assembly replied with one voice. *"Fight well for the glory of Entos."* That final reply dismissed the assembly to go about their ordinary eighth day business.

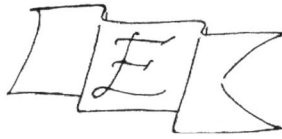

Chapter Eight
"Hasan Horan"

Twelve months had elapsed since exam day and a little more than three months had gone by since Breille had joined the little fellowship. Every day of the past three months Rieve had kept his nocturnal schedule. It was a demanding schedule, but being tutored by Sandor himself was a great honor. In those three months under Sandor, Rieve had learned more than he could have ever learned in his regular conjuring class. Professor Etam made it a habit to meet with Rieve to check on his progress and to help maintain the illusion that Rieve was still in the regular conjuring lab program. Rieve looked forward to their meetings. Etam and Rieve had grown quite fond of one another. Their meetings usually consisted of Professor Etam asking a few easy questions, which Rieve answered easily. Then Rieve would ask some questions of his own, usually of a political nature and Professor Etam would answer. That daily ritual would last about thirty minutes, then Professor Etam would conclude the session with one simple statement, "Nap time," and Rieve followed the order obediently for ninety minutes each afternoon before resuming his normal daily schedule.

Tag and Brenz were spending less time together at the Warring Academy. Tag was an officer of the first order and Brenz of the second class. They had both excelled in the physical arts of combat and had done very well in field training and tests. As they moved through the academic process their rank dictated differences in their education. Most of their time was now spent training in the shadow of their respective towers.

The battle between the old and new schools intensified with the passing of each month. The city council had passed several innovations that were designed to reform the five academies. The Academy of Governance and The Academy of the Building Arts were quick to accept the changes. The Academy of the Ancient Warring Arts had all but ignored the resolutions. Under the stewardship of Professor MulLord, The Academy of Theological Sciences and Ancient Conjuring Arts formally accepted its commission to update the theological curriculum, but since half the faculty remained loyal to the ancient ways the changes were not only ignored by the same, but were often critiqued and the target of theological humor.

"Modernization" was becoming a regular theme in the debates of the city council. The leaders wanted all things "modernized" and "contemporized." Even the language of Entos was undergoing a change. The words, doctrines, and images of the Eighth Day Festival were being restricted to the Eighth Day Festival and new ways of speaking were being introduced in some of the classrooms of the academies and in the city council meetings.

City Council

"General Witticor," Vice President Mohhan shouted, "we are growing tired of the delays. This esteemed council has directed you and your military planners to modernize the military with due diligence. We have passed several resolutions directing you to work with The Academy of the Building Arts and we still have yet to see one significant change in the training of our warriors. Not one new weapon has been incorporated into your training regimen."

"With all due respect, Vice President Mohhan, President Kuchen and I have had several meetings to discuss modernization," the general said in a calm but firm tone.

"Yet we have seen very few results," Mohhan replied.

"To the contrary, President Kuchen and I have developed a very extensive list of projects. A list of those projects was forwarded to each of you last week."

President Botha interrupted the exchange. "General, I admit the list is quite extensive. But it appears that you don't quite understand what is meant by modernization."

"Hasan Horan"

"Mr. President," General Witticor stood up and leaned forward placing his hands on the table, "what do you find unacceptable about the list President Kuchen and I have developed? We have agreed to work together to produce a metal that will be twenty percent lighter and will require less sharpening. A metal stronger, more durable, yet lighter, has greater application than just military use." Witticor's voice took on a tone of excitement and energy. "We also have several new weapons under design. The prototypes are being forged as we speak. We have agreed to develop a better communication and transportation system so that we can more effectively move our troops between the towers and within the interior of Entos. I really don't understand the council's frustration. I think we are making great progress," Witticor said with a big smile. "President Kuchen," Witticor began as he turned toward Kuchen, "perhaps you could shed light on the work being done toward modernization."

"General Witticor," said President Larrence, the president of the Governance Academy, "you are not an uneducated man. You know very well that this council means something more when it speaks of modernizing. What we are calling for is a shift in thinking about how Entos ought to move forward. The ancient ways have served us well, but if we are going to meet the challenges of our own day, as our forefathers met the challenges of their day, we need to utilize more contemporary means."

Simmjer, the Pithosian, could not restrain himself a moment longer. He had sat through meeting after meeting, offering resolution after resolution in an effort to save the old ways. But every motion had failed and every political plan had been undone by either those who disagreed or those who had lacked clarity of mind to comprehend the brilliance of his strategy. Simmjer was an old war horse, older than most in the room. The years had taught him patience, but they had robbed him of his passion. He had heard enough of talking around the issue. Now he rose and slammed his fist on the top of the table. "Our protection is not found in metal and engineering. Entos has survived and thrived these five thousand years because the priests, conjurors, and warriors have remained true to the ancient arts. Your way threatens Entos and I will stand opposed to it until the day I die." His

The Oracles And The Jewels

deep base voice shook the chamber. "If you had any sense at all, you would do the same, Mr. President!" When the echo ended, silence fell hard, if not long, in the hall. Whether it was Simmjer's words or the silence that followed, passions were stirred.

"Ashkelon is the father of machines, innovations, and cold metal," Bennser the Fortian added in a softer voice but no less firm. The softness of his voice could not tame the harshness of the indictment. The statement was more than the others could take. Moorre, Scoderan, Fradden, Larrence, and MulLord jumped from their seats and the room erupted in shouting and chaos.

"How dare you compare us to Asheklon!" Scoderan shouted.

"Cease then thinking like him!" Simmjer thundered. Shouts and insults from every direction bounced off the stone walls.

"Fathers, fathers," Botha shouted as he waved his left hand up and down calling upon all to take their seats, while banging the gavel on the tabletop with his right hand. He repeated the appeal several more times before order was restored. "We have had this debate several times before. The matter of modernization has been settled! We are going to bring Entos into a new and better day. We are going to expand her territory and bring her into a stronger position in her ongoing war with Ashkelon. More for us means less for him! We are not going to continue to fight among ourselves on the question of modernization!" Botha took a breath and calmed himself. "Gentlemen, I have tried to remain fair and neutral in this debate . . ."

"Ah," Simmjer groaned, but Botha ignored the sound and continued.

"But now that the council has decided the issue by a majority vote, I must support the council and the effort to modernize. Now everyone is expected to do their part to make sure our present course is undertaken in the wisest, most effective, and most efficient manner."

"Mr. President, the problem, it seems to me, is that during our debates on modernization, the advocates for it did not take sufficient care in offering us a precise definition," Klemmond, the Procuron, offered in a reasoned and calm

"Hasan Horan"

voice. "In the absence of such a definition, each of us comes here with our own. To accuse a man of General Witticor's status and intellect of having a philosophically contorted definition of modernization is unacceptable. If any of the advocates of modernization would like to offer a definition, then please do so. If one of you could answer our concern that the ancient ways will continue to hold their preeminent place among us, we would come to a quicker agreement on what modernization will look like."

"It is not our fault," Professor MulLord answered, "that some of you have failed to listen and have spread such distrust throughout our land."

"Professor MulLord and City Father Klemmond, may we return to the subject at hand?" Botha said with a sigh of frustration. "General, I apologize if any statement made questioned your intellect."

"Thank you, Mr. President," Witticor replied.

"The panels, the moveable walls," Botha began, "what is the status of the moveable walls. If we are going to engage in a program of expansion and establish outposts, as this council has so voted to do, then we are going to need a moveable fortress. So, President Kuchen, what of the walls?"

"This council gave us direct orders to design and build a moveable fortress and we have poured ourselves into the task. If we had had more cooperation from The Academy of the Ancient Warring Arts we would be a little farther along, but that has not been the case, Mr. President," Kuchen said. All eyes turned to Witticor, who sat stoic and still. "Be that as it may, we have assigned two of our best design engineers and several of our very best students, among them I might add, is City Father Derson's daughter, Breille Clarrice. She has been a great asset to the project. You should be very proud of her."

"Thank you. I am," Derson said.

"Be assured, I take the project seriously and I personally check the design and modifications every couple of days. I am very pleased with the progress."

"Thank you, President Kuchen," Botha said. "Given the current impasse over modernization of the military, I would suggest that we adjourn for the evening. General Witticor and I will meet with you before our next meeting to discuss what modernization might mean for the military. If that is agreeable to all concerned, then let us adjourn."

The Academy of Theological Sciences and Ancient Conjuring Arts

Professor MulLord had taken notice of Rieve's growing confidence and his increasing popularity among students of the old school. MulLord started to consider him a threat to his own future. Though he only suspected it, Rieve was making powerful enemies at the Academy. Yet, Rieve was not without friends and protectors. He enjoyed too much support among the faculty and this support had made it difficult for Professor MulLord to remove him without convincing evidence. MulLord and his supporters had made two attempts to have Rieve removed from the student body under an obscure rule which read, "Any candidate or apprentice priest who is found guilty of disrupting the learning environment of the Academy, or conducts himself in a disrespectful manner toward faculty members, and who persists in this offensive conduct is subject to removal by a two-thirds majority of the faculty." MulLord had twice failed to achieve the two-thirds needed, but since these efforts were generally held behind closed doors, the efforts to remove Rieve went unnoticed by even Rieve.

It had been another normal day and again night had fallen upon Entos. It was approaching 11:00 in the dark and Rieve went about his nocturnal ritual. He left his dorm a little early that night and took an extra long walk around the city, then he headed for the courtyard. Once there he looked around and saw nothing unusual. The trees, the white marble benches and statues, and the bushes were exactly as he had found them dozens of times before. The courtyard was empty. Lights were on in some apartments, but off in most. It was quiet and on this night the air was still.

Rieve followed his usual route. As he entered the courtyard, he thought for a moment about deviating from his regular routine. The trip was becoming old and the excitement of the journey had long since passed. But upon reflection, he decided to repeat the same exact route he had taken dozens of times before. "This is no game," he thought to himself, "getting caught could prove harmful not only to me, but to the Headmaster as well." He made his way across the yard and into the faculty building setting his feet in all the familiar places. But not everything was exactly as it had been the dozens of times before. This time he was seen.

Professor Bozzez, an Adroitian, was an associate professor. He had no conjuring skills of which to speak. He taught the practical arts and spent most of his time teaching oratory and priestly protocol to those who would find their life's work outside the city in the hamlets and villages that dotted the countryside and foothills.

Professor Bozzez did not enjoy his work. He thought his talents were being wasted on simple priests who were being trained for simple tribes. Bozzez had grander aspirations than these. The last thing he wanted to do was to spend the balance of his life among common villagers and priests of the same. He wanted to be among those who were shaping the future of Entos and, with MulLord as the new Headmaster, he was certain to ride the reforms to the top.

Professor Bozzez saw the rivalry between Professor MulLord and Headmaster Sandor as an opportunity to strengthen his own position and to secure a place of importance and influence. Bozzez was a supporter of the new ways and had been pretty effective recruiting students to the new way of thinking.

When Rieve had first arrived on campus, Professor Bozzez had made an effort to persuade Rieve to reconsider his position on the new teaching, but his effort did little more than to strengthen Rieve's commitment to an understanding of his own position. Professor Bozzez took the rejection personally and it angered him greatly.

Professor Bozzez had just recently moved into his new apartment on the top floor of the faculty apartment building overlooking the courtyard. The apartment was much larger than his prior abode. The fact that it was on the top floor said something about his status within the school. Professor Bozzez was enjoying the good graces of MulLord and was expected to be even more helpful in the future.

Since it was Bozzez's first night in his new abode, Rieve was unaware of the change. As he entered the courtyard he

The Oracles And The Jewels

had glanced over to Bozzez's old window and had noticed that the curtains were drawn. He assumed that Bozzez was fast asleep.

Bozzez was too proud of himself to sleep that night. He wanted to enjoy the view and take in his newly acquired station, not to mention the view high atop the courtyard. He was standing at his bedroom window with the lights off when he noticed a student enter the courtyard. At first he could not identify the shadowy figure and did not consider it odd to see a student out for a stroll. But as soon as Rieve stepped into the fullness of the moons and before he could reach the safety of the first tree, Bozzez recognized him and his heart stirred with excitement. When he realized that it was Rieve in the courtyard, he took a half step back to conceal himself in the window, but not far enough back so that he could not watch every step Rieve took.

As soon as Rieve disappeared into the doorway, Professor Bozzez immediately put on his robe and headed down the stairs to follow. Once he entered the courtyard, Professor Bozzez looked up at the Headmaster's window. The light was on. That was not unusual, but by now he could make out two silhouettes in the window.

Professor Bozzez made his way through the courtyard with the same stealth as Rieve had and entered into the faculty building through the same set of doors. He passed through the lobby and made his way up the stairs. He was excited at the prospect, but paced himself as he climbed the stairs. He wanted to reach the top, but he did not want to reach the top floor so winded that he could not breathe quietly. Since Rieve would have to exit the same stairwell at this time of night, there was no hurry. Bozzez's own excitement was the only force dictating his hurried pace.

As he entered the hallway, he heard voices coming from Sandor's study. He moved slowly down the hallway and tried to get a better listen. The process frustrated him. The closer he got to the door of the study, the louder the voices grew, but that didn't make the words any clearer. The solid wood door muffled the words.

Inside, Sandor was quizzing Rieve on advanced conjuring, especially on avoiding conflicting incantations. Many things could go wrong in conjuring, but one of the

"Hasan Horan"

worst things is the colliding of forces. If two different conjurors send out two contradicting incantations, all other things being equal, these incantations do not cancel each other out, rather their power is squared and the effects could be disastrous.

"Tell me Apprentice Priest Rieve," the Headmaster asked, "what kind of room would be the most dangerous kind of room in which a conjuror must never send out more than one spell at a time?"

"A room of glass and mirrors," Rieve answered.

"What ought to be done when confronted by a wizard of Ashkelon who sends forth his force?" Sandor asked accelerating his speech.

"Do likewise at the same moment," Rieve's answer came as quickly as the question.

"When confronted by such a situation, what is the best thing to do?" Sandor asked even more quickly.

"Let all things take their course. Launch a counter movement, followed by an offensive move, and repair the damage from the initial strike as the circumstance dictates."

"If the damage can't be repaired?" Sandor asked, raising his voice.

"Receive what has happened with quiet resignation and move on," Rieve replied.

"Very good. Now Master Rieve, are thou prepared to do that?" Sandor asked.

"Do what, sir?" asked Rieve.

"Receive what has happened with quiet resignation and move on, even if the one who has fallen is dearest to thy heart?" Sandor asked.

"I would hope so, Sir, but I don't know. I suppose it depends on the injury or on who has been struck down. I don't know if I can be that . . . . that clinical. I don't even know if I can help a warrior kill another creature."

"Indeed," Sandor said. "That is an honest answer. As for killing another creature, be not confused if thou hesitates even for the slightest moment, it is thy warrior, thy comrade, perhaps even thine own blood relations who shall perish from our King's good earth. Thou do not kill that which is alive. As a conjuror, thou is dedicated to keeping alive. But

The Oracles And The Jewels

thou must aid the warrior in killing thine enemy, for thine enemy is already dead."

At that moment Sandor heard the breath of an interloper outside his door. Sandor held his finger to his mouth to signal Rieve to silence. Rieve and Sandor looked to the door, then to the doorknob. It was turning slowly.

"It is the pant of an Adroitian," Sandor whispered. "Be thou still."

Sandor had been banned from the classroom for more than a year and even though the City Fathers had not banned him from giving private tutoring lessons, Sandor's critics would see such an activity as a distinction without a difference.

Sandor leaned toward Rieve and whispered again, "Be thou very still. No matter what happens. Be thou still." Sandor quickly reached his hand into a seemingly empty jar tainted by dust. As soon as his hand exited the jar, Sandor threw the haze above Rieve's head and whispered, *"Hasan Horan."* Rieve stood silent, still, and stunned. Nothing happened. Rieve heard the utterance and saw a small puff of dust float through the air above his head, but nothing happened. "Has the incantation failed?" he thought to himself. Sandor turned away from Rieve and toward his bookshelves.

Just then Professor Bozzez peered through the now open door. He stood silent as he watched Sandor take an old book from one of the tables and settle into his hard wooden chair. He set the book on his lap and began reading out loud in the sacred language, *"Boothos em Entos on, Borranon em ad kalloson*, paaran *yaddann . . . "*

Sandor looked up from the text and called out with an enthusiasm that took Bozzez by surprise. "Ah a visitor! How wonderful! Welcome to my humble abode. Do come in." Sandor stood to greet his uninvited visitor.

"Come in Professor Bozzez. Do come in." Bozzez was stunned at the greeting and shocked to find only Sandor in the room. Bozzez zipped about the room, frantically looking for the source of the other voice he had just heard moments ago. His head flew to the right, then to the left, then back to the right again.

"Hasan Horan"

"Where is he?" Professor Bozzez asked in a loud voice that carried with it more of a demand than a question. "Where is he?"

"Who?" Sandor replied.

"Apprentice Priest Rieve Waynwright! That's who! I know he's here. I saw him in the courtyard. I saw him in your window. I just heard him when I was in the hallway." Bozzez walked quickly around the Headmaster's large office for a second time.

"Are you hiding him on the ledge?" he asked as he grabbed the window and tried to open it.

"That doesn't work. I have asked that it be fixed several times, but my requests have all been in vain," Sandor said with a smile. "It gets terribly warm in here. Dost Thou agree?"

"Not as warm as it will be when I find him!" Bozzez snapped in an anxious and high pitched voice. "I only care about finding him . . . I know he is here." Bozzez waved his finger in Sandor's face. "I saw him in the courtyard."

"This is not the courtyard. Dost thou see him in this place?" Sandor asked with a soft but mocking tone.

"I saw him in the courtyard I said," Bozzez repeated.

"Indeed, thy hast said," Sandor replied.

"I saw him enter the building. I heard you talking to him," Professor Bozzez's voice was becoming more insistent and his face more red. "Now tell me where he is! He is not supposed to be here! You're in a lot of trouble I tell you. A lot of trouble."

Rieve stood still and in disbelief. He could see and hear everything, but Bozzez could not see him. Rieve stood straight and upright, clearly visible, or so he thought, to Sandor. Rieve looked cross-eyed to see if he could spot his own nose. He could. Yet, Bozzez could see nothing of him.

"Again I ask? Dost thou see the lad here?" Sandor said. "I don't know what thou thinks thou saw in the courtyard. As for my talking to the young man, I can only assume that thou have heard the rumors. I'm crazy, so the people say. Do not the people say I spend my days and evenings talking to students who are not here?"

"I don't believe those rumors. You're up to no good. I know it!" Bozzez scolded.

The Oracles And The Jewels

"I am but a teacher and have been for many decades. Thou can take the teacher from the classroom, but taking the classroom from the teacher is quite another matter. How nice though to be visited by a real person, even under such suspicious circumstances. Thou is a real person, aren't thee?" Sandor poked Professor Bozzez in the side with his staff.

"Stop that," Bozzez yelled.

"Ah, thou is real," Sandor said with a giggle and a shout. "Goodie. Please sit down and let's visit. I have all night to visit. Let us talk about how the Academy is getting along these days."

"The Academy is none of your business!" Professor Bozzez circled the study yet a third time. He checked the closet . . . twice. He looked under the desk . . . twice, he leaned over and looked under the two little tables, first on the one side, then for good measure on the other. Finally, he came to a stop just in front of the place where Rieve stood. Bozzez peered right through him as if he were thin air.

Rieve began reasoning to himself. Had he become truly invisible or had Bozzez been blinded to Rieve's presence? Was it the case that Sandor had simply used Bozzez's own desire against him, or had the incantation done something to Rieve's body? The answer, he thought could be found in the incantation, *"Hasan Horan,"* which literally means, "Be made unseen." But then Rieve wondered, had Sandor said, *"Hasan Horren,"* which means, "Be made unseeing." "If only," Rieve thought, "I had heard the incantation clearly, then I would know how this wonderful spell is done."

One step closer and the debate being carried on in Rieve's mind would be mute. "If he takes one step further, one question will be answered," Rieve reasoned to himself. "Can two Entosians occupy the same place at the same time when one of them is unseen or unseeing?" Bozzez turned toward Sandor and put his hands on his hips.

An Adroitian, Professor Bozzez was considerably smaller than Rieve, but Rieve was sure that Professor Bozzez was too large to walk between his legs. Rieve was tempted to move and his eyes looked desperately for an escape route, but Sandor looked over Bozzez's head and straight into Rieve's eyes. Sandor shook his head ever so

"Hasan Horan"

slightly, but enough to reassure Rieve. Two things were now evident to Rieve. Professor Bozzez could not see him, but Sandor could. "He must have said, *'Hasan Horren'* – *'be made unseeing*,'" Rieve reasoned and continued, "Perhaps the Headmaster is simply guessing where my eyes might be."

"I am sure I saw him!" Professor Bozzez said with a huff as he turned toward the Headmaster. Rieve breathed a very, very quiet sigh of relief. The Professor's back was now to him. This was an arrangement much more to Rieve's liking.

"Did I call the statement into question?" Sandor replied. "I believeth thee. Thou did see him in the courtyard. I have no reason to doubt this. Has MulLord banned evening walks in the courtyard?" the Headmaster asked.

"Headmaster MulLord!" Bozzez said rebukingly.

"Indeed. I stand corrected. Has Acting Headmaster MulLord banned evening walks in the courtyard?"

"No, he has not!" Bozzez replied.

"Then please sit thee down and let us talk about the Academy." Sandor's eyes opened wider and a large grin over came Sandor's face. The grin only appeared for a moment and was followed by a slight look of panic.

The material element that Sandor had bound together with his incantation was evaporating and Rieve's head was beginning to materialize. Professor Bozzez stood just in front of Rieve and only four feet tall. Professor Bozzez was a balding Adroit. As Rieve stood behind Bozzez, the top of Rieve's head was becoming visible again and it gave the appearance that Professor Bozzez had been separated from his hair. The sight tickled Sandor and, if the occasion had not been so serious, he would have had a great laugh at the spectacle. But in the present context, the unveiling of Rieve's hair could lead to Rieve's premature removal from the Academy.

"So tell me," the Headmaster continued as he moved toward his jar of air, "how are the candidates handling all the changes?"

"Fine," Bozzez snapped. "They are doing just fine. They are in good hands."

The Oracles And The Jewels

The sound of a thump came from the hallway. It was faint, but loud enough to catch Sandor's and Bozzez's attention.

"Didst thou hear that?" Sandor said as he looked toward the hallway. Sandor took a step toward the door.

"Yes!" Bozzez replied quickly. "Out of the way!" Bozzez pushed Sandor aside and rushed the door. "Apprentice Rieve!" he shouted as he bolted into the hallway. The quickness of his movement reaffirmed the fact that he was an Adroitian, albeit an older one, but still an Adroitian nonetheless. The opportunity was not wasted. Sandor reached into the jar of haze and mumbled, *"Hasan Horan."* The unveiled portion of Rieve vanished again.

"There's no one out here," Bozzez said as he reentered the study. He found Sandor standing in the spot he had just vacated. "Headmaster Sandor it is my duty to inform you that I intend to report this incident to the tribunal."

"What incident would that be?" The Headmaster asked.

"This one!" Bozzez said as he stood looking up at the Headmaster.

"Dost thou really mean to file a report that says, thou didn't see Apprentice Rieve in my study and that I was not talking to him," Sandor said with more than a little sarcasm.

"That is exactly what I mean!" the professor replied.

"That makes as much sense as anything else around here. That is why I will never understand the new ways of thinking." Before Sandor had finished his sentence Professor Bozzez dashed out the door and down the hallway.

Sandor turned to Rieve and smiled. "Don't just stand there my young disciple, move thou quickly. We will have to forego the lesson this evening. Thou hast work to do, while it can be done."

Rieve hesitated. He was trying to formulate a series of questions in the hope that he could learn what Sandor had just done. "Thou can move. Moving breaks the spell."

"Headmaster, what just happened?" Rieve asked.

"He didn't see thee," the Headmaster said. "The question really ought to be formulated in this fashion," Sandor said calmly, "What didn't happen? Agreed the answer is still the same. Professor Bozzez didn't see thee,

"Hasan Horan"

but still sometimes the way the question is formulated makes all the difference in the world."

"Why? Why didn't he see me? Did you do something to him or to me? Did you say *Hasan Horan* or *Hasan Horren?*"

"I didn't do anything to Professor Bozzez. He inflicted himself with blindness. He can't see things as they are. The new way of thinking blinds those who adhere to its tenants. Very few these days can see things as they truly are. I simply used his condition against him and for thee."

"So, you did it to him and not to me?" Rieve asked.

"It was done to both."

"But the jar was empty?"

"It wasn't empty. It had the most transparent thing in all of Entos – air. Cloudy air, but air is a substance – thus it can be a means. That is one of the problems with the new generation of conjurors. They don't think to use the ordinary things. They despise the ordinary. They think that they have to use fancy, shiny, and glittery things, unusual things, and extraordinary things. There's a place for such substances, but the key to becoming a master of the ancient conjuring arts is to see the potential in all elements – even the most common and plentiful. The Creator of Entos can attach His power to anything He so chooses.

"In the Days of Old, the masters did not have glitter and shiny things. They did not use metals and colorful liquids. They did not have high walls and fortresses to protect themselves against the attacks of Ashkelon. They only had the words of the Oracles, warriors, and ordinary elements. Enough of the lesson. Professor Bozzez will be knocking at thy dorm room soon. I think it would be best if he finds thee there." Sandor said.

"It makes no difference. I can't possibly beat him back to my room. He's an Adroitian," Rieve said.

"Indeed, but he is not a very patient or a very bright one. He will waste the time allotted to him. That is what he does. First he will have to tell someone else. He won't let this opportunity go by without an audience. I suspect he will go to Professor MulLord, who lives off campus and is not going to take kindly to being awakened at this late hour. They will march over to thy room at MulLord's pace, not Bozzez's. MulLord would never allow anyone else to set the pace. He

The Oracles And The Jewels

is contrary in those ways. Still, this is no reason for slothfulness." Sandor took Rieve's arm and walked him to the door. "Hurry now!"

As Rieve stepped into the hallway he said, "Thanks, Sir, for everything."

"Thou is very welcome Apprentice Rieve. And oh . . . Apprentice Rieve," Sandor said raising his voice.

"Yes, Sir," Rieve said softly.

"Dost thou knowest an Aradian thee can trust?"

"Yes, Sir. I think I do," Rieve answered.

"Very good then. Once thou is finished making Professor Bozzez look foolish before his lord MulLord, seek the Aradian out and tell him that King Ashkelon is going to attack at daybreak. He is going to come against the Polemmas army in the shadow of the tower," Sandor's voice was dispassionate. He said it in the same way one would report a fact of history, which had taken place a millennium earlier.

"How Sir, do you know that this will happen?" Rieve inquired.

"I saw it in my water jar when Professor Bozzez first entered the room," Sandor answered.

"In the water jar?" Rieve said with a tone of disbelief. "Sir, even if the officers were to believe the vision, which I doubt, not even the fastest Aradian in all of Entos could make it to the tower in time. A journey like that would take at least twelve hours. There isn't enough time," Rieve explained.

"I might have something that can help with that problem," Sandor said as he began looking around his office. He picked up jar after jar and can after can in a methodical, but slow process. Rieve was trying to remain patient, but Sandor's relaxed pace was beginning to unsettle him. Surely, he thought, Bozzez and MulLord would be at his door at any moment.

"Headmaster," Rieve said in a soft and low voice as he tried to hide his anxiety, "we're running out of time."

"Here it is," Sandor said. He took a little white cube out of a jar and handed it to Rieve. "Tell the Aradian to put this in his mouth, then chant the following incantation; *Tssadan eppon ereten, eppon hodian.*" Rieve repeated the

"Hasan Horan"

incantation out loud, then quietly to himself. It took a moment, but he was able to translate the incantation in his head. He rendered the translation, "*Run upon the earth upon or until the morning.*"

"Ye might also want to give him a bit of a conventional boost to send him off," Sandor suggested, then added. "Just make sure he is clear of all buildings. I didn't do that once and it took the poor Aradian months to heal up. It was a good thing he hit the healing arts building. The healers were able to tend to him in short order. I felt very badly about that incident, but a good lesson it was. Now take care and be off with thee," Sandor said as he touched his finger to the Entosian birthmarks on Rieve's head, lips, and breast. Rieve bowed his head in reverence to the blessing, then turned and made his way down the hallway.

"Oh, my son, I'm sorry, come back . . . I forgot something." Rieve stopped in his tracks and sighed a deep but subtle sigh. Sandor disappeared back into his office. Rieve turned around again. "Beat MulLord and Bozzez. At this pace I won't even beat the dawn's breaking light to my room," he whispered to himself.

Rieve walked to the threshold of the door and looked into the office, but saw nothing. He could hear Sandor scavenging about the deep recesses of the study, but could not see him. Books fell to the floor and jars and cans clinked together. "This might take some time," Rieve thought to himself. "I don't have an abundance of time at the moment. Perhaps," Rieve thought, "I should just leave and pretend as if I did not hear the request." He dismissed the thought and resigned himself to Sandor and Bozzez's schedules.

Rieve walked into the office and saw Sandor standing on a chair reaching for a dusty old jar on the top shelf. Rieve moved to help. He placed his hand on the back of Sandor to steady him. "I thank thee my, son, for thy thoughtfulness," Sandor said as he felt Rieve's hand on his back. Sandor took the jar from the shelf and climbed down from the chair.

Sandor walked over to the small round table piled high with old books and poured out the contents of the jar on a small bare spot on the table. A couple of rubies and several topaz stones tumbled out of the jar and onto the table. The stones were larger than most of the stones mounted on

The Oracles And The Jewels

jewelry, but still finely cut and small enough to be carried about without too much trouble.

"Here . . . this one belongs to thee," Sandor said as he handed Rieve the larger of the two rubies. "Now how many belong to thy little fellowship?" he asked, but before Rieve could answer, Sandor answered. "Oh there are six, so five more stones." Sandor counted out five topaz stones of various sizes. "The red is for thee and the gold stones distribute to the other members of thy fellowship. Tell no one about these stones. These stones will bring thee to me and thy friends to thee, should we find ourselves in need of one another. They will also warn the righteous who hold the stones of danger. The kind of danger that comes with the presence of Ashkelon."

"How do they work?" Rieve asked.

"I don't think we have the time for that discussion. The stones will teach thee when the time comes. Now go or we're going to be found out!" Sandor said. "Ye tarry here too long."

Rieve put the stones in his pocket and left the office in an obvious hurry. He was pleased to be on his way, but he couldn't help but think that it was already too late. He ran down the hallway and stairs. Once he entered the courtyard, he resumed his careful stroll across the yard. Within five minutes he was in his room. Much to his surprise he had enough time to wipe the sweat from his body and put on his sleeping robe. "Safe at home," Rieve whispered as he stretched out on his bed. "Now the only thing to do is to bring my breathing into a normal rhythm." A few moments later there was a knock at the door.

"Apprentice Rieve!" the shout came. The voice belonged to Professor MulLord. "Apprentice Rieve!" The second call was louder than the first. Rieve paused for a moment.

"See I told you," Professor Bozzez said with glee. "He's not here." Rieve rose from the bed, kicked the wastebasket on his way to the door, then shouted as if half asleep, "I'm coming! What's wrong?" he said with a manufactured tone of concern. Rieve opened the door. "Oh Professor MulLord and Professor Bozzez, I apologize. I was in bed. I hope I didn't sound rude."

"Hasan Horan"

"Understandable," MulLord snapped.

"Is there something wrong? Did something happen?" Rieve said as he poked his head into the hallway and looked around.

"Were you really in bed?" Professor Bozzez asked with a tone of interrogation.

"Sir," Rieve wiped the sleep from his eyes.

"I am sorry, Apprentice Rieve. It seems there was a mistake. Professor Bozzez was at the faculty building this evening and he swears that he didn't see you at Sandor's office."

"Excuse me, sir? Did you say, he didn't see me?" Rieve repeated as he hid his inner laughter.

"That's right. Professor Bozzez said he saw you in the courtyard this evening."

"That could be sir, I often take walks in the evening light and visit the courtyard quite often," Rieve explained. "But you said he didn't see me."

"That's right. Professor Bozzez swears that you were with Professor Sandor this evening and that he didn't see you there."

"Perhaps I'm still sleepy, but forgive me Professor Bozzez, that sounds a little odd."

"Indeed. Good night, Apprentice Priest Rieve Waynwright," MulLord said.

"Good night, sirs," Rieve said as he shut the door. "Headmaster," Rieve whispered, "you're truly a wonder."

Professor MulLord and Professor Bozzez started on their way down the hallway. "I apologize Professor MulLord for disturbing you at this late hour for this wild goose chase," Professor Bozzez said with a slight hint of fear in his voice. "But I am sure I..."

"Shut up, you stupid Adroitian," Professor MulLord said under his breath. "At least have the wits about you to wait until we are outside." The two walked down the hallway and out into the street in silence.

Once outside and a little way from the dorm, Bozzez opened his mouth to speak. MulLord interrupted.

"Professor Bozzez, I have no doubt that Apprentice Rieve was where you said he was when you said he was there. We have been watching him and I have kept my eye

The Oracles And The Jewels

on our former Headmaster myself," Professor MulLord said. " I just wish everyone would pay attention to the word former. Some of the City Fathers continue to argue that we did not have proper grounds for Sandor's removal. But if we can catch Sandor in open defiance of the City Fathers, we can settle the debate over who is really the Headmaster of the Academy. What I need," Professor MulLord continued, "is evidence. The City Fathers and the faculty are not going to turn their backs completely on my predecessor unless I can show that he has violated their edict. I had hoped you had hard evidence to that effect. But you have managed to let a great opportunity pass."

"My apologies, Headmaster. I will act more wisely in the future. I will also keep my eye on that apprentice."

"Join the crowd," MulLord replied. "The fact is, I have several people watching that apprentice. We have even enlisted the support of some of his fellow apprentices and a candidate or two. Sooner or later that young Demotic is going to make a mistake and when he does, I will be there to remove him from the Academy. Entos would be much better off if priests and conjurors like him and Sandor were removed from their offices. As for you, don't tell anyone about this little episode and keep your eye on that courtyard."

"Yes, sir," Bozzez said. "Good night."

"It could have been if not for your error," MulLord grunted. Bozzez turned to the left and MulLord to the right and both headed home.

Rieve waited just long enough for Professors MulLord and Bozzez to leave the building and get far enough away so that they would not see any lights come on in the dorm rooms. Rieve opened the door and looked into the hallway. It was all clear. He headed down the hall to the second to the last dorm room on the right. He knocked softly, but persistently, on the door.

"Who's there?" Candidate Nassar asked as he woke from his sleep.

Rieve had known Nassar for a few years. They had met in the latter years of grammar school two years before they had taken their exam. Nassar, an Aradian of the Edder tribe, was not well liked by most who knew him. He was a bit

"Hasan Horan"

overbearing, loud, too eager to please, and socially very clumsy. But for reasons unknown to Rieve, the two had become friends. Nassar often quoted Rieve in debates with other students and looked to Rieve in the way a much younger brother might look at his older, wiser, and braver brother. All of this Rieve found embarrassing as well as annoying yet friends they remained.

"It's Rieve. There's an emergency. Entos needs an Aradian," Rieve whispered. The door opened. Candidate Nassar knew what that meant. All Aradians knew what that meant. It meant someone needed a runner and messenger.

"What emergency?" Candidate Nassar asked.

"Ashkelon is going to attack the Polemmas Tower at dawn," Rieve reported.

"You're an apprentice priest and conjuror, not a military Procuron," Nassar said with some skepticism.

"I tell you as sure as the sun is going to rise, the attack will come," Rieve insisted.

"How do you know that?" Nassar asked.

"I can't tell you. It would be too dangerous," Rieve responded.

"Well then, good night," Nassar said with a yawn as he started to push the door close. Rieve countered the move with his right hand stopped the door from closing.

"Look, I saw it in the water in my sink," Rieve said feeling a little uncomfortable with lying to his friend.

"What?"

"I was practicing some incantations that, well I am not supposed to practice. It's from a book I found in the library about incantations concerning the future," Rieve told him.

"I didn't know that there was such a book. But if there is, it's not the kind of thing we are supposed to mess with," Nassar said rebuking Rieve.

"I know, but I did and there you have it. Now listen, I don't have a lot of time. If you won't run to the Polemmas Tower to warn them, then I will have to steal a horse so I can get there in time," Rieve responded.

"Can you ride a horse?" Nassar said raising an eyebrow.

"Not well. I rode one once or twice."

The Oracles And The Jewels

"I thought so. It's all a moot point anyway. Not even Arran the greatest and fastest long distance Aradian runner, could run sixty leagues in six hours. I believe his record was eight hours and seventeen minutes. I'm good, but not that good," Nassar explained.

"I've got that covered too," Rieve replied.

"Conjuring again," Nassar rolled his eyes.

"Yes," Rieve said, "but it is perfectly safe. Honest." Rieve said with an appeal in his voice.

"My mother told me that I should learn to say no." Nassar sighed and shook his head. "Okay, I'll go. This better not be one of those initiation rites I've heard about." There was no trace of humor in his response. Rieve reached for Nassar's running shoes, picked them up, and handed them to Nassar.

"Do you want me to put them on for you? You know me and my reputation. This is real and it is serious," Rieve said as Nassar took his shoes from Rieve's hand.

"I said I will go. What do I tell them when I get there?" Nassar asked. "If I have trouble believing you, why should they believe me?" As he spoke he put on his day clothing and his running shoes.

"When you get there go to the camp at the foot of the tower and ask for Cadet Brenz Clinton. Tell him that I sent you. Tell him that it has started. Tell him of Ashkelon's attack. He'll think of something to do. Don't worry about classes. I will attend your classes and take notes for you. I'll tell them you're sick. Now put this in your mouth and swallow."

"Put what where?" Nassar said objecting, but before he got the whole sentence out Rieve threw the white square tablet into his mouth and said, *"Tssadan eppon ereten, eppon hodian.* Now go!" Rieve pushed his friend into the hallway.

"Sugar. It's a sugar cube," Nassar said shaking his head. The revelation surprised Rieve. Nassar bent over and finished tying his shoes in the hallway.

"Ordinary things in ordinary Entosians," Rieve replied. "That's you and me. It is also those warriors at the Polemmas Tower. Need I say more?" Rieve smiled. "Have a good run."

"Okay, but I'm telling you, I don't think I can make it there in time." Nassar bolted down the hall with a speed that surprised him. He overshot the stairwell and managed to slow down enough to avoid hitting the wall at the end of the hallway.

"Sorry," Rieve said in a loud whisper, "I forgot about that part."

"What else have you forgotten?" Nassar said shaking his head.

"Nothing. Now get going," Rieve whispered. "Run well and to the glory of Entos."

"Yea," Nassar replied, then disappeared down the stairwell.

Rieve returned to his room. He looked out the window and saw his friend starting down the path in the direction of the Polemmas Tower. Rieve opened his window, took a little glitter in his hand, mumbled the right incantation, then threw the ball of glitter which hit his friend in the back. Nassar exploded in a burst of speed and disappeared into the night in a moment.

"I'm good," Rieve said in a rare moment of cockiness. Rieve looked at his clock. It was 12:15 in the dark. Nassar should reach the Polemmas Tower just at dawn. Would that be enough time? Candidate Nassar was a young and strong Aradian. He had both speed and endurance in his favor. Added to that the conjuring of the Headmaster and he should make it. Rieve could only wait to see what the morning light would bring. He lay down in his bed and sang a prayer before dozing off into a light sleep.

> *Boothos em Entos on, Borranon em ad kalloson.*
> *Katen Umat fahman etum ad tzaddam cullan Umat Eabben.*
> *Umim nabana Umat Naban atum Entos on senn hasan.*
> *Nabene Umat Naban etum kataloom ad katalam.*
> *Nabene Umat Naban etum ren ad Hoddan dem nogget anapalin ad skotana.*
> *Nabene Umat Naban atum ad gibbon demmim sussim.*
> *Umim nabana Umat Naban atum skootan mea hasan.*

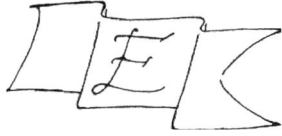

Chapter Nine
The War Begins

While Nassar ran, Rieve slept. When he awoke he was unsure as to the duration of his sleep. But as minutes turned to hours, it was clear that he hadn't slept long. As the night wore on, it seemed as if dawn would never come and the night would prevail. Woud Nassar make it in time? Would the guard let him into the camp? Would Brenz believe him? Would he know what to do? What if there were no attack? could Sandor be wrong? These were the thought chased away his sleep.

This was not so with Nassar. As he ran, he thought dawn was coming too quickly. As he ran he measured his progress by the land marks in the landscape. With the passing of each landmark, he ran a little harder and tried to gage his progress against the rising of the sun.

He had run all night and now the fires and night lights of the camp were in sight. "It won't be long now," he thought. The camp was just where Rieve said it would be.

As the woods turned into a gentle sloping field, his pace quickened and it only took a couple of minutes to reach the guard at the station just outside the camp.

"Halt! Halt there you, the Aradian!" a guard called out. He was a cadet, but he was still a guard who had been trained to take his duty seriously. He was also an Adroitian and had armed his bow even before he finished his command. Nassar slowed his pace and came to a stop a few feet away from the guard.

"Guard, I have an important message for Cadet Brenz Clinton. Do you know him?" Nassar asked.

"Everyone does, but I can't let you through until my commander gives you clearance," the guard explained.

"Look the message is very urgent. I left the Theological Academy at 12:15 in the dark to get here before the sun rose. I really need to talk with Cadet Brenz Clinton before the sun rises. It's urgent." Nassar pleaded.

The Oracles And The Jewels

"Sorry sir, I can't allow that until my commanding officer gives me orders allowing you to pass," the guard declared. "Besides, not even an Aradian can run that fast for that long."

"It's a long story. I don't really believe it myself. But I have an urgent message for Cadet Brenz Clinton and this is an emergency," Nassar said as he looked to the east. The dark morning sky looked like it would break into day within the next fifteen minutes.

"Sorry, sir. I can't let you pass," the guard insisted.

"This message must reach Cadet Brenz Clinton before dawn. If it doesn't something terrible is going to happen," Nassar said with a tone of sobriety. The guard looked eastward too.

"The sun is going to rise at any moment. I suggest you let me pass," Nassar said.

"I have orders," the guard replied. Nassar noticed a slight look of confusion and doubt in the eyes of the young guard.

"Then shoot me if you must!" he said. Nassar darted down the path toward the tents.

The guard stood stunned. No Entosian had ever blown by the guard post like that. Nor had an Entosian warrior ever been presented with the dilemma of having to shoot another Entosian. In the absence of anything else to do the guard shouted out, "Cadet Brenz Clinton is in the seventh tent on the right!"

"Thanks," Nassar replied, then sped down the trail. About forty-five seconds later Nassar burst into the seventh tent on the right. Brenz and his fellow cadets were just starting to wake. Nassar's abrupt entrance startled Brenz and, before Nassar was able to speak a word, Brenz had his sword at Nassar's throat.

A little winded but standing perfectly stiff Nassar asked, "Are you Cadet Brenz Clinton?" Brenz didn't answer. "Apprentice Priest Rieve Waynwright sent me with a message."

"Go ahead friend," Brenz said as he placed his sword back into its scabbard.

Nassar continued, "He said it's starting and he told me to tell you that Ashkelon is going to attack the Polemmas Tower at dawn, which is breaking as we speak." Brenz looked outside the tent door and to the east. It was true, the first beams of light were beginning to stretch out over the horizon. Dawn was upon them.

The War Begins

"Please get some water and help yourself to any food we have around the tent. Then I suggest you head back as quickly as possible. This is not going to be the place to be in about five minutes," Brenz said then turned to his four tent mates.

"Cadets, this is no drill. Apprentice Priest Rieve Waynwright is a conjuror, stronger than any other of his age. He also has friends in high places. If he said it is going to happen, it is going to happen. Our problem is, we're just cadets and by the time we go up the chain of command Ashkelon will be upon us."

"What you do suggest?" Cadet Keemon asked.

"Are you all ready for this?" Brenz replied.

"Yes, sir," Cadet Ansel said.

"I'm in," Cadet Durus followed.

"Ready to engage the enemy, sir," Cadet Karrena said.

"Okay then. We are going to take our first prisoner and our first piece of land." Brenz drew back the cloth door to his tent and pointed to the watcher on the wall. "There's our prisoner. He has the horn. We take him. He blows the horn. The warriors come running just in time to see Ashkelon's forces attack the wall." As he spoke Brenz and the members of his squad dressed in full battle gear.

"Fall in," Brenz said. They lined up behind him. Brenz took a deep breath. Keemon, Ansel, Durus, and Kerrena did the same, each in the order in which they stood.

"Let's go. Double time!" Brenz dashed forward. The others followed. They ran as fast as they could, being Kilposians and Demoticans, across the campground. Some of the other cadets were just waking, but a few saw the five running in full gear.

The word spread throughout the camp like wildfire. Something was happening and Brenz was leading it. That's all the cadets needed to know. They all began dressing and started to take up a defensive formation. They didn't know why, but their training had taught them to respond to unusual situations in such ways. The five cadets hit the stone steps at full run. Up and up they ran as their fellow cadets began to pour onto the formation grounds in full battle gear. The watcher on the wall stood motionless as the sight unfolded and as the cadets drew closer and closer to his position. Once they had reached the battlements, the watcher called out, "Halt, cadets!" They kept coming.

"Cadets. You don't belong here. Get down before I report you all!" the watcher protested.

The Oracles And The Jewels

"We can't do that, sir," Brenz informed the watcher as the five came to a stop just a few feet from him. "Sir, we need you to blow the horn."

"You need me to what?" the watcher objected with a shout.

"Blow the battle horn now sir or we will take you prisoner!" Brenz demanded. The watcher drew his sword. Brenz and his four counterparts did the same.

"Blow the horn . . . three times in rapid succession, sir," Brenz added.

"You don't know what you're asking. That will call ten thousand warriors to arms. You don't know what kind of trouble you're in for," the watcher said with a smile.

"Yes sir, we do. Ashkelon is coming and you can either be a hero, or you can get the blame," Brenz said. "But one way or another, that horn is going to be sounded."

"Look for yourself!" the watcher said and he turned toward the desert and pointed. "I don't see a thing and just in case you haven't noticed, I am a Fortian. If there was an army out there I would see it."

"He's there," Brenz said. "I don't know how he is concealing that fact, but he and his beasts are out there and closer than you think." The top of the sun was now above the horizon and in the eyes of the watcher. "He is coming now I tell you! Blow the horn, or I will."

"Okay cadet. Kiss your military career good-bye." The watcher looked past Brenz to his four friends. "That goes for all of you." The horn rang out three times and in rapid succession, precisely as needed to call all ten thousand warriors to arms and to set off a chain reaction. Over the next few minutes every watcher who had a horn stationed around the wall repeated the same cry. Warriors began to pour out of every doorway in the Polemmas Tower. The corridor along the top of the wall filled with archers, spearsmen, and swordsmen. The cavalry was busy readying their horses in the field below.

The colonel of the Polemmas army was making his way to the wall. He was accompanied by his personal staff. A Procuron major, a Fortian captain, and two lieutenants, one a Kilposian and the other a Demotic, were ascending the stairs, matching each stride made by the colonel. It took less than four minutes for every warrior of the Polemmas army to join the one hundred cadets who were already standing at the ready.

The War Begins

Cadets and warriors took their places and stood looking to the east as they stood at the ready. Their armor and weapons glistened in the rising sun. It was a cool morning and the breath of the warriors rose like a light fog over the green grass of the field. Silence took its place and only the whinny and gallop of the horses could be heard.

Brenz, Durus, Ansel, Keemon, and Karrena stood at the ready looking eastward. The Fortian watcher was pointed in the other direction. He was watching the colonel and his staff making their way up the stairs and along the battlements. The colonel and his staff joined the five cadets and stood motionless and silent looking to the east. Brenz's heart began to sink and a lump formed in his throat, although he did his best to hide the fact from his fellow cadets.

As the colonel, his staff, and the cadets stood motionless on the battlement, they looked to the east. There on the horizon was . . . nothing. The sun had risen, but they could see nothing. Brenz squinted and tried to make out any form. But in the glare of the sun, he could see nothing. Nor could a sound be heard. The watcher looked at Brenz with a smile and mouthed out the words, "You're in trouble now."

"Watcher, what do you see?" the colonel asked.

"Nothing, sir," the watcher replied. "Absolutely nothing."

"Nothing! What's the meaning of this?" the colonel barked.

"Ask the cadet, sir. It was his idea." The watcher pointed in Brenz's direction.

"Since when do you take orders from a cadet?" the colonel asked sharply.

"It was at the point of five swords, sir, that I blew the horn," the watcher answered. Brenz stood still as he peered into the desert wilderness. His sword was still drawn. Every muscle in his body stood at the ready. Everything about him showed unwavering confidence in his cause. But even Brenz was beginning to wonder what Rieve Waynwright had done to him.

"Cadet, explain yourself!" the colonel barked even louder.

"Ashkelon, sir. . . Ashkelon. He's coming, sir," Brenz said as he tried to bury his own increasing doubt.

"Oh really! How do you know this?" the colonel shouted.

"Faith, sir," Brenz answered.

"Faith! Did you say faith?" the colonel shouted.

The Oracles And The Jewels

"Yes, sir. Faith in the words of a conjuror," Brenz replied. "I know it's not much sir, but I have never known this conjuror to be wrong."

"I have known many to err. That is why there is a chain of command, an order that must be maintained!" the colonel shouted. At that moment, a thud was heard and the watcher was slammed backward as a large stone struck him in the chest and jettisoned him from the wall. The first stone was followed by a second, which hit the wall just below them, then a third that struck the two lieutenants who were standing to the left of the colonel.

The colonel turned to view the spectacle. Brenz looked eastward again. This time thousands of creatures from Bohow were materializing out of the blinding sun. Creatures from Bohow covered the land like a wide and dark river and winged creatures filled the now darkening sky. And all were running toward the wall and the gate below.

"Captain, dispatch one thousand of the spearsmen and swordsmen to the outer perimeter," the colonel shouted.

"Yes, sir," the captain snapped. He repeated the order to the signaler, who raised the appropriate flags. Five hundred spearsmen and five hundred swordsmen took up their positions outside at the base of the wall at the point where the main body would strike. The warriors fanned out and took up their formations. Once in place a conjuror took his position in the middle of the group and six healers took up their positions behind the conjuror.

Brenz and his friends stood on the top of the battlement next to the colonel watching the battle unfold.

"Is it wizardry or were they just hidden in the sun?" the colonel asked out loud. He looked to his Procuron major who stood silent without an answer. "The answer makes a difference," the colonel added. "Never before has Ashkelon possessed such power. And if it was wizardry, this is no raid."

The dust from the feet of the soldiers and hooves of the beasts began to rise from the desert floor and was taking on the form of a small storm cloud.

"Major, I need your best analysis. Is this a raid or is this Ashkelon?" the colonel asked.

"Sir, do you want me to figure the presence of these cadets in my analysis? It makes a difference," the major asked.

"I want you to tell me what you see down there," the colonel said with a hint of frustration as he pointed to the

The War Begins

approaching onslaught. "And up there," he pointed to the sky. "I want a basic reading of the situation, not an academic exercise!"

"It is too small to be an outright Ashkelon attack. I see no wizards despite the possibility of wizardry to conceal their presence across the desert floor. This attack is not organized in any recognizable formation. It looks more like a large raid. Ashkelon is not here, unless his presence is being hidden by some form of wizardry." The major paused and looked at the colonel's arm, which had just been hit by a small arrow.

"Continue," the colonel said.

"But the timing, stealth, size, direction, and composition indicates a level of planning not associated with a raid," the Procuron concluded.

"Do they have a sufficient force to breach the wall or to infiltrate Entos?"

"I do not believe so," the major said, "but that depends on how far in the winged creatures deposit their passengers."

"Captain, designate a dozen cavalry riders to chase down any soldier or beast that might be dropped behind our lines," the colonel said. "But first, ready the signaler!"

The Fortian captain repeated the command more loudly. "Ready Signaler!"

The signaler raised the flags ordering the archers to arm their bows. The archers armed their bows and drew the wire back. They stood motionless with their eyes fixed on the flags.

The Fortian captain and the cadets stared at the colonel, who himself was staring at the approaching enemy. Only a few seconds lapsed, but it seemed an eternity to Brenz. Winged creatures, gaint arrows, and large stones, which were loosed from catapults flew through the air over and along the sides of their heads.

"Loose!" the colonel shouted. The Fortian captain repeated the order. The signaler dropped the flags. The archers filled the sky with their arrows. Some of the winged creatures let out a shriek and fell to the ground. Some of the arrows found their mark in soldiers and beasts. Those who did not fall were bearing down on the swordsmen and spearsmen, who had just formed two semicircles, one inside the other, on the desert floor.

"They have the range. Fire at will," the colonel said. The Fortian captain repeated the command and the signaler

The Oracles And The Jewels

repeated the command with his flags. The archers complied and it began to rain arrows on top of the oncoming hoards. The charging mob smashed into the defensive line of the Entosian warriors. The line held and scores of beasts and soldiers fell as they were struck with Entosian metal.

"Tend to those cavalry riders," the colonel said.

"Yes, sir," the captain replied. He turned and left.

Some of the winged creatures deposited soldiers on and behind the wall. Boars, packs of giant wolves, beasts with horns, trolls, skulls, and mammothons were dropped in the encampment of the cadets and in the open field before them.

Prepared or not the cadets were now in their first real battle. Each cadet took up his position. The battle formations took on the shape of circles and the circles began to link together in a chain. Two and four-footed creatures landed, but found no safe refuge. As they hit the ground, the cadets cut them down. Several of the winged creatures were also struck fatal blows. The pace quickened, but between the Aradian archers and the cadets on the ground, the winged creatures could not keep up with their losses.

"Cadet, I don't know how you knew, we will have to talk about that later, but right now all of Entos is in your debt," the colonel said as blood seeped from the wound in his arm. "Now ready yourselves, cadets. Remember your training. Keep your heads. You'll be all right. You have had the best training possible. Now use that training. Here they come!" the colonel shouted. A moment later he was gone.

It had happened so fast the cadets didn't see which winged creature took him. Winged creatures and soldiers were now assaulting the battlement in force. Brenz looked up to the sky to see if he could see which winged creature had taken the colonel, but the sky was filled with so many creatures carrying soldiers, he could not distinguish the colonel's form from any other.

Brenz's eyes moved quickly from the sky to the ground below. Brenz had seen drawings of the battlefield formations, but this was the first time he had actually seen a real battle. The sight was sobering. He was impressed with the order and formation of the Entosian warriors and with the chaos that was being thrown against their lines. Entosian order seemed a sharp contrast to the chaos of Bohow and in that Brenz took heart.

"Does the chaos ever prevail over the order?" Brenz asked the Procuron as warriors began to repel the attacks at

The War Begins

the base and at the top of the wall. Brenz looked down at the base of the exterior wall where one thousand warriors were cutting down soldiers and creatures as quickly as they reached the line.

This was also the first time the cadets had ever seen their enemy in the flesh. Brenz was repulsed by their grotesque features, but impressed by the brilliance of their design. Each of the creatures had its own unique features.

The raid was led by wild beasts, mostly wild boars as large as a Pithosian. Just behind them, packs of wolves and several four – legged creatures with horns of various shapes and sizes were charging the line. The raiders of Bohow and soldiers of Ashkelon followed the beasts and had their swords drawn. Creatures of Bohow were as diverse in size as Entosians. There were creatures of every size and, like the Entosians, each group had unique natural abilities which had to be understood and for which adjustments had to be made if one was going to survive a such a battle.

Some of the creatures had smooth skin, but tough skin. Some were very hairy and others had scales that served as a natural armor. Unlike the wild beasts of Bohow that led the attack, creatures of Bohow walked upright, used weapons and tools, and killed Entosians out of sheer hate rather than hunger.

As Brenz stood watching the senseless massacre of so many creatures, he struggled to understand the hate that would drive creatures to wage such a war. Entosians did not understand this hate. The Land of Entos was very small compared to Bohow and the whole of Ashkelon's earth.

Ashkelon and his soldiers knew no fear except one. They feared the return of the King of Entos and they fought for no other reason than to destroy Entos. If there was no Entos, there would be no reason for the King's return.

Brenz looked to his fellow cadets. "The colonel was right, cadets. This is the real thing. This is hate enfleshed. Let's not fight for anything except for the love of Entos and hate of hate. Remember your training. Fight with reason and calm. Panic and rage are paths to defeat. Fight well and to the glory of Entos."

Brenz looked to the desert floor and saw the creatures falling as the Entosian swordsmen and spearsmen practiced their craft with precision. The outer line of defense had fallen back behind the second line of swordsmen.

Very few Entosian warriors fell in the initial clash of the two lines. The Entosian warriors struck down any creature

The Oracles And The Jewels

that came within their respective striking field. As the lines pressed together a few more Entosian warriors fell as a result of the overwhelming numbers that pressed in on them.

The wounded Entosians were pulled from the battle by their comrades. Once free from the main line a healer would move in and evaluate the injured warrior. Some were healed immediately and returned to the fray. The more severely injured were carried off through the gate.

The conjuror stood still in the midst of this great mass and bloodshed. As the circles began to draw in toward his position, he began to hurl balls of light and glitter into the backs of Entosian warriors.

The Procuron major and Brenz watched the battle unfold. Brenz looked over at him. "How are we doing?" Brenz asked.

"Well, very well," the Procuron replied. "My initial calculations place the death rate at one hundred twenty five to one. It is not a well-conceived attack. They are wasting creatures to no effective end. That's the difference, you know." The Procuron turned to the signaler. The signaler turned toward the warriors standing at the ready on the inside of the wall. He held up a signal flag ordering the artillery to open fire. With a wave of his arms the signaler gave the artillerymen the range readings. He waited about thirty seconds and then dropped the flag in one violent move. Immediately great balls of flames flew over the wall and the Entosian warriors' front line and smashed into the oncoming waves of Bohow's creatures.

"What's the difference?" Brenz asked as they watched the balls of fire sail over their heads.

"Chaos verse order. It's the definition of chaos. No order. No order, no purpose. No order shows no reason. That's what separates us from them. They do what they are told to do. They can be trained to fight and march. But when they are not following Ashkelon's orders, they follow instinct. Ashkelon doesn't waste his creatures like this. You were right about the attack, but as I see it unfolding, I think you are wrong about it being Ashkelon. It doesn't have his marks," the Procuron explained.

"Ready the cavalry," the major shouted to the signaler. The cavalry moved into position for a counteroffensive. The signaler held up the appropriate flags.

"Go," the Procuron said without emotion. The signaler dropped the flags. The captain of the cavalry blew the charge command on his horn. Immediately two hundred and

The War Begins

fifty cavalry riders charged out of the gate to the right of the main body and two hundred and fifty riders did the same to the left.

"Being in the right place at the right time and utilizing the right skills for the right occasion is how a battle is won," the Procuron explained. "It's the unexpected that frustrates me."

"Sir," Brenz said. "Look!" Brenz pointed to the sky just before them. A second wave of winged creatures had taken up formations to the right of the Polemmas Tower and were heading straight for the wall upon which the major and cadets stood.

"That looks like order to me," Brenz said. The winged creatures formed a tight formation along a straight line. This formation was more organized than the first wave. Most of the creatures were carrying soldiers and beasts. Some held large rocks in their talons. The rock-bearing creatures led the way. They dropped stones at the top of each stairway entrance, sealing the top of the wall off from reinforcements. The thousands of warriors and one hundred cadets stood useless for the moment. Some Pithosians ran to the stairs and began clearing away some of the stones, but winged creatures dropped more and started depositing mammothons in their path.

The winged creatures swooped down and deposited an array of creatures and soldiers on the top of the wall. Scores of Entosian warriors were trapped in the corridor on the top of the wall and soon bodies of beasts, soldiers, and Entosian warriors were falling from the wall.

Brenz and the other cadets readied themselves. "A pattern is emerging," the Procuron said. "One would expect this sort of thing from Ashkelon, but there are no battering rams, no use of fire, no columns, and no wizards. And there aren't enough of them. Interesting," the Procuron said as if speaking a mathematical equation.

At first the Entosians repelled the attacks from the creatures. They drove them back to the top of the stairs where the stones had fallen. The winged creatures began dropping stones in the corridor, effectively dividing the warriors into smaller more manageable groups. Several of the stones and boulders landed on top of some of the Entosian warriors. A couple of the warriors were picked up and dropped to their deaths by the winged creatures.

The Entosian archers redirected their fire to provide cover for the trapped warriors and cadets, but they needed to be careful. The archers had to anticipate the whole flight

The Oracles And The Jewels

path of their arrows, lest they start hitting Entosians. This often meant they had to move entire units to a different position to get a better angle.

Brenz stepped forward and immediately struck down three creatures. Three more took their place. The process continued for each of the cadets. The Procuron had stepped back behind the cadets to give all five room to practice their craft. Suddenly an arrow struck Cadet Keemon in the chest. The arrow was too large and hit him with such force that his breastplate could not stop it.

"Commander!" Durus shouted.

"Keemon!" Karrena cried out. The four cadets stood still in a moment of disbelief. As Keemon slid toward the floor, Brenz shouted out his name "Keemon Reus!" In that moment of distraction a swordsman of Bohow cut Brenz's cheek. Immediately Brenz felt the sting of the blade and the warm blood running down his face. Keemon's body slid down the wall of the battlement, then slumped over and came to rest on the walkway.

Brenz called out to the three remaining cadets, "D formation!" Without hesitation or thought, the cadets fell into formation. Their outline formed the shape of a diamond. Brenz took the lead position and constituted the point of attack. He advanced with great speed. The three cadets matched his speed and effectiveness. Brenz didn't seem to notice that the first creature in his way was a mammothon, named so because it was the largest and strongest of Ashkelon's soldiers. Mammothons stood nine feet tall from toe to the top of its head. Its shoulders were four feet wide and the average mammothon weighed four hundred pounds.

It was the tip of the mammothon's sword that had cut Brenz's cheek. A mammothon had smooth but very tough skin. Their muscles were so firm they served as their own armor. If caught by surprise, a mammothon could be cut. But if given time a mammothon could make himself ready to receive a blow and prevent the blade from penetrating too deeply. Brenz had moved with such quickness that the mammothon did not have time to ready himself at the point of attack. Brenz thrust his sword into the side of the mammothon. He withdrew his sword and delivered a second blow to the back of the creature's neck.

When the mammothon fell the other three cadets felt the impact under their feet. By the time the creature had fallen, Brenz had already advanced to the next two

The War Begins

creatures. They were sipedons. Sipedons were easily handled by a trained warrior. They were strong, but too slow to make good fighters. Their strength was in numbers and in the hard scales that covered their skin. They traveled and fought in packs and usually in open areas. They stood an average of six feet tall, were slim, but fought well when given the opportunity to fight along side of their own kind. They were able to communicate with each another with the slightest expressions and movements. When they were mixed with other soldiers, their ability to act as one was greatly diminished.

In the narrow walkways of the wall's battlements, they were out of place and at a great disadvantage. Brenz jumped between the two sipedons and struck the one on his right in its belly and the one on the left in its back. He did this so quickly, he was able to deliver two blows before his feet hit the stone walkway. The sipedons fell in the same order they were struck. Brenz allowed the next two sipedons to move by him so he could make an attack on a second mammothon, which was approaching quickly.

He had dispatched the first mammothon with speed and surprise. But there would be no surprise with this one. Their swords met. The mammothon swung his blade with such force he knocked Brenz back three steps. Brenz made a second charge, which ended the same as the first.

The mammothon smiled a big smile, roared, and took one step toward Brenz and closed the gap between them. He held his sword in his right hand and took his dagger in his left. Brenz drew his dagger as well, then quickly moved to the left of the mammothon. The mammothon took a stab at Brenz with his dagger, but Brenz was too quick. Brenz countered with a thrust from both his sword and dagger. The mammothon was ready for the sword but the dagger penetrated the flesh.

Three more creatures charged Brenz and he was now caught between the mammothon, which stood before him and a troll and two skulls that were closing in behind him. Brenz turned to his left, swapped his weapons so that his dagger was in his left hand and his sword was in the right. He lifted both evenly and point each weapon in the direction of his intended prey. With his dagger toward the troll and skulls and his sword toward the mammothon, he took a deep breath and readied himself for the attack.

Just then Durus loosed three arrows. The first arrow struck the mammothon in the back and stuck deep. The

The Oracles And The Jewels

second arrow penetrated the skin, but did not remain in the mammothon. The third arrow hit the mammothon, snapped in two, and bounced into the air. The mammothon roared, turned toward Durus, joined the two sipedons, and charged the other three cadets. Cadet Ansel struck the first sipedon. Before Durus was able to loose another round of arrows in the mammothon's direction a wild boar charged through the crowd and toward the cadets. Durus loosed several arrows into a wild boar and it fell. Cadet Karrena hesitated a moment until the second sipedon had entered her circle. Then Ansel and Karrena dispatched the two sipedons almost as quickly as Brenz had dispatched the first mammothon.

Durus, Ansel, and Karrena surrounded the mammothon. The mammothon roared a loud roar and raised its steel into the air. The three cadets swung and spun in classic battle style. The mammothon countered the first strikes, but the three cadets were simply too much for the creature, which fell from the wall in a few moments.

As Durus, Ansel, and Karrena eliminated their opponents, Brenz felled the troll and the two skulls. Durus, Karrena, and Ansel quickly rejoined Brenz and the four pressed forward until every creature in their section of the wall had fallen.

Once the four had finished, they returned to the body of their friend. They paused to rest a moment and to look upon their fallen brother warrior. The rest did not last long. The cavalry and the warriors at the base of the wall were cutting their way through the first wave of beasts and warriors. A second wave seemed to materialize out of the desert and was now flanking the cavalry from behind.

Winged creatures had also joined the battle and were attacking the horsemen. With the second wave, the Entosian line was in danger of breaking. If that happened the cavalry and warriors on the outside of the wall would be overrun and lost. The conjuror was so busy supporting the warriors, it appeared as if there were two steady streams of light coming from his hands as he rotated from one side of the semicircle to the other. The healers were equally busy healing warriors and sending them back into the fray. The more seriously wounded were being carried from the battlefield and through the gate.

The attack on the wall had distracted the Procuron major, whose attention was now completely devoted to the warriors below. "Fall back! Order them to fall back within the

The War Begins

wall!" the major shouted in a tone of urgency not often used by a Procuron officer. The signaler blew his horn and the horsemen, swordsmen, and spearsmen began to fall back through the large gate fighting as they withdrew.

"Let them in," the major said to the signaler. "Let them in and surround them on three sides. Now!"

The signaler turned and signaled. The warriors began moving into place. Seven thousand warriors formed two columns and marched in opposite directions. When they had created an open field of some one hundred yards, the columns turned and faced one another. The cadets were signaled to fall back two hundred yards and face the gates. The cavalry and the first legion retreated into the field and fell back to take positions with the cadets.

The creatures of Bohow followed as expected. They poured through the gates and into the open field with a mad passion void of any reason. The creatures pursued the retreating warriors with such blind hatred they failed to take note of the trap into which they had run. The creatures tore through the cadets' camp as they chased the retreating Entosians and took such delight in destroying things they failed to notice that they were now completely surrounded.

"A raid has rarely consisted of more than two thousand creatures," the major told Brenz. "Look, more than ten thousand are now pouring into the Demotic Valley to certain death. Something is happening here. Something historic. Something strange. This is neither a raid nor a full attack. This is something else. A test perhaps."

Once most of the creatures were inside the wall, the major issued the order. "Sound the counterattack!" The signaler did as instructed. The horn blew. The retreating warriors and riders stopped, turned toward their enemies, and began a counterattack. The cadets followed. The two columns of warriors marched forward. Within twenty-five minutes the battle was over. More than nine thousand creatures of Bohow had fallen in the valley. A few thousand more had died on the desert floor and the balance of Ashkelon's soldiers and beasts retreated back across the desert.

Entos had lost two hundred and two warriors, twenty-seven cavalry, and six cadets. Of the two hundred two warriors, one hundred fifty seven had fallen in the battle that took place outside the wall, seventy-five fell in the fight on the wall, and the rest fell in the final stage of the battle.

The Oracles And The Jewels

The colonel was the only known captive and no Entosian had been transformed.

As news of the attack made its way through the ranks of the military the attack shook the military establishment. The walls of Entos hadn't been breached in such a manner in centuries and an attack like this one was unknown in history.

Once the battle had ended, several Pithosian warriors gathered together to move the large stones that obstructed the stairs. One-by-one the stones were rolled away. With the colonel dead, or at the very least missing, the Procuron was the ranking officer on the wall.

"It is over, Cadet Brenz," the Procuron said.

"I don't think so," Brenz answered. "I think it is just beginning."

"This battle is over," the Procuron replied. "You and your fellow cadets fought well this day. Your friend died well. There is no reason for sadness here," the Procuron said. He put his hand on Brenz's shoulder. "Now go and get that cut taken care of before it leaves a scar."

"We have something to do first, sir," Brenz answered. The four cadets lifted their friend's body and slowly carried him down the stairs to the hospital tent.

The Academy of the Building Arts

It took about three hours for news of the attack against the Polemmas Tower to reach the heart of Entos. The news stunned the citizens. The details of the attack were not well known. What was known was that at dawn creatures of Bohow attacked the Polemmas Tower and wall. Reports that they had actually made it inside the wall were confirmed by city officials. The citizens were shocked and a bit frightened when they learned this information. For such a thing to happen the creatures must have attacked in force and in some kind of organized fashion. These were marks of Ashkelon, not of a raid. As to casualties, one rumor put the deaths at two dozen and another as many as two thousand.

The military planners spent the day evaluating the attack and assessing the damage. Not even the Procurons could agree over the nature of the attack. It bore the marks of a raid, but it also demonstrated an organization thought impossible for the simple creatures of Bohow. Yet it lacked the strength and military precision one expected from King Ashkelon. It was too strong and well organized for a raid, but too weak and disorganized for Ashkelon. No one knew what

The War Begins

Ashkelon looked like. He had not been seen in three generations. But all were agreed, no king-like figure was visible at the battle.

When news reached the City Fathers that the wall had been damaged and the gates destroyed, they dispatched engineers and builders from The Academy of the Building Arts to the Polemmas Tower. The City Fathers met in an emergency session to get a full report on the attack and to craft a statement for public posting.

As a result of the confusion over just what type of attack had taken place, President Botha urged the City Fathers to move the experimental moveable wall to the Polemmas Tower. The engineers, builders, and students assigned to the project expressed concern over the decision. They only had one prototype which had never been tested, not to mention they weren't even sure just how to move the moveable wall more than fifty leagues to the Polemmas Tower, a task that would take at best four days. Under President Botha's encouragement, the City Fathers insisted on, so the professors and students began working on the problem.

As one of the students involved in the design and construction of the wall, Breille assumed she would accompany the team to the Polemmas Tower. "The wall is not ready," she thought, but she was ready for an adventure. The trip would also give her an opportunity to see Brenz, if he was still alive. Of that she was reasonably confident. So she headed back to her house to gather her things.

Breille's father was waiting for her when she left the design building and stepped into the street.

"Hello, Father," Breille said. "Come to see me off?"

"No, Daughter. I came to tell you that you will not be heading off. You will be staying here."

"But Father, they need me. The wall isn't ready. It has some design problems. I know I am just a student, but I also know that I can help fix those problems and maybe save a few lives. The expansion system is my design." Breille said resolutely.

"I asked the City Fathers and your professors if you could sit this one out. They agreed. You've been assigned to help make the plans to move the wall, but you will remain here at the academy to provide technical support."

"Father, how could you?" Her big round eyes drew narrow with disapproval.

The Oracles And The Jewels

"Sorry, Daughter, but that's my decision. You're the only kin I have left and I would rather not take the risk," her father explained.

"But Father! It is perfectly safe and it would have been so much fun," Breille said in an uncharacteristic Procuron manner.

"That's enough, young lady. That's your mother's Demotic nature speaking, not your Procuron reason. I have to go. I have more briefings to attend. I'll see you at home tonight. Tend to your classes." He turned and walked back toward the city hall.

"You will see me tomorrow night and the night after that and the night after that," Breille said with a sigh of disappointment. She spent the afternoon pouting about her father's decision. But pouting turned to contemplation as the day moved along.

The little fellowship had previously agreed that should anything unusual happen they would all meet at the bridge at dusk. It was obvious to the other members of the fellowship that Tag and Brenz would not be allowed to leave their regiment, but Rieve, River, Blisse, and Breille rearranged their day so that they could gather at the appointed place and time. They, like all other students in Entos that day, spent the day watching the clocks in their classrooms. The faculties attempted to carry on as normal, but all of Entos sensed that things were not normal, although few would actually speak it.

River and Blisse met outside The Academy of Healing Arts and started to make their way down the slope toward the Demotic hamlet and the bridge, but before they left the Great Plateau they saw a city official posting the first official news report. They ran to the bulletin board next to the bench at the park by the crest of the plateau. The notice read,

Fellow Entosians

This morning at dawn creatures of Bohow conducted a raid against the Polemmas Tower. The creatures were successfully repelled and all is well in Entos. This was a raid and not an attack from Ashkelon as some have suggested. It is our judgment that it was a raid conducted for the purpose of harassment

The War Begins

and food. Entos is safe and the Polemmas army performed their duty bravely and with great skill. Unfortunately, some of Entos' bravest warriors have fallen in service to you. We honor those to whom honor is now due.

It is also with great pride that we have the privilege to bestow the Medal of Bravery upon Cadet Brenz Clinton, the Kilposian from the Clan of Lalage. Thanks to his quick thinking, bravery, and skills he demonstrated in the physical arts of combat, Cadet Brenz Clinton, the Kilposian of the Clan of Lalage, saved many Entosian lives. Cadet Brenz Clinton is the first cadet to be awarded such a honor. Join us in paying tribute to this Cadet in a parade in his honor upon his return.

Blisse and River read the news report with mixed emotions. They were saddened by the news of the attack and the fallen warriors, but they were excited and proud of what Brenz had done. It was in that spirit that the two of them headed toward the bridge. Blisse reached down and picked up a stick. "To arms! To arms!" She shouted and laughed. "I'm Cadet Brenz Clinton, slayer of the creatures of Bohow!" River looked around for a branch larger than the one Blisse had found, but all she could find was an even smaller twig. "I am Thayer Taggert and I am insanely jealous that Brenz has managed to become a war hero before me!" The two laughed and engaged in some sword play with their respective twigs as they made their way to the bridge.

Blisse and River arrived first. Just before dusk, Breille came down the path. In her right hand she had a rolled-up paper. Rieve was just behind her on the path. As the gap between Breille and Rieve narrowed, Rieve quickened the pace. The two reached the bridge at the same time.

"Did you two read it?" Blisse said with excitement.

"Read it!" Breille replied with a surprising tone of anger. "I have it in my hand!"

The Oracles And The Jewels

"You took it?" River asked.

"Yes," Breille replied.

"Don't you know that it is illegal to take down a posting for two days after it is posted?" River asked.

"Of course I do," Breille said. "It is a good law. It makes a lot of sense. It gives everyone time to read the news for himself."

"So you couldn't wait two days for a souvenir?" Blisse asked.

"It's not a souvenir. It's evidence," came Breille's reply.

"Evidence implies a crime," River said. "If it is evidence what is the crime?"

"The crime is a cover-up. This is part of a cover-up," Breille said.

"This is good news, well, it's kind of good news. Brenz is alive and a hero," Blisse said.

"Breille's probably right, not that Brenz didn't earn the medal," Rieve injected.

"I think we better start from the beginning," Blisse said.

"The entire military is on alert," Breille said. "If he leaves his unit now, that is desertion."

"So let's start putting some pieces of this puzzle together, shall we?" River suggested.

"This morning at dawn a raid was launched," River said.

"Well it begins before that and it was no simple raid," Rieve said. He then went on to tell them all that had happened in the Headmaster's office adding, "The Headmaster was clear. Ashkelon was behind this attack."

"Unless I miss my guess, and I usually don't, the attack was far more serious than the City Fathers have let on in this report," Breille said as she held up the paper.

"And what better way to hide a problem than to declare a hero and host a parade," River said.

"Exactly," Breille replied. "Brenz is a distraction. Something has the City Fathers worried. We have been attacked before. This is nothing new. It certainly isn't anything to create panic. But they regard this as so serious that they have ordered the prototype moveable wall into action in the Demotic Valley."

"You're going to the Demotic Valley," Blisse said with excitement.

"I was, but my father put an end to that plan," Breille said. "That is the other thing that doesn't make sense. If the danger is over and this is just an opportunity to test a wall

The War Begins

that is not ready to be tested, then why would my father keep me from going on a field trip?"

"The answer to that is obvious. Things are not as safe and under control as the City Fathers would like us to think," River mused.

"But would they be foolish enough to burden our warriors with a untested piece of military equipment in a time of great danger?" Breille asked.

"The answer to that question is obvious," Blisse replied with dripping sarcasm. "It would be the first bright idea they've had."

"What the City Fathers know and don't know is a matter of speculation," Rieve said. "I suspect they don't even know what's going on. It seems that the attack has them confused and they have chosen to err on the side of caution. They think their great wall will provide some safety and they welcome the opportunity to test it," Rieve suggested. "Perhaps they think the first attack is a probe meant to test our readiness for a full-scale attack from Ashkelon. Everyone has their eyes turned to the walls. The Headmaster also credits Ashkelon with this attack, but he also said there would be much more."

"Rieve Waynwright, have you been holding out on us?" River inquired.

"A little," Rieve confessed in a soft voice.

"A little," Blisse said again with sarcasm. "What does a little mean exactly . . . Rieve Waynwright?"

"In my first meeting with the Headmaster he said several things. At first I tried to dismiss them. But as history has unfolded, we seem to be getting closer and closer to the danger he spoke about," Rieve explained.

"Danger!" Blisse exclaimed, "just another little detail you forgot to tell us about."

"I didn't forget. I just didn't think the time was right to tell all that I knew. Besides, some of it I don't want Tag to know about. In my first meeting with the Headmaster he told me that this little fellowship would be in danger. That a great battle was coming and that this war would pit brother against brother, sister against sister, and father against son. I almost forgot about the last one until I saw my father with Professor MulLord. It seems my own father is on the wrong side of this battle," Rieve said.

"Which battle are we talking about? The battle with Ashkelon and his attack on the wall, or the battle between

The Oracles And The Jewels

the faculty and the City Fathers over the Academy and the new teaching?" Breille asked.

"I don't know. The Headmaster is not always clear about such things," Rieve explained. "What I do know is that the armies must fight with all their might against the attacks of Ashkelon or Entos will fall. But the Headmaster also said that I must not be distracted by that battle. Instead I was to be in the right places at the right times."

"I don't suppose the Headmaster told you where the right places are and when you're supposed to be at them, did he?" Blisse asked.

"No he didn't," Rieve answered.

"That would be too easy. That's not grandfather's way," Blisse said.

"Your grandfather also said that we would all end up in the thick of it all – in the very midst of the danger," Rieve explained. "That time for this danger must be very close now."

"What makes you say that?" River asked.

"Look." Rieve pulled the ruby and the five topaz stones from his pocket. "The Headmaster gave these to me," Rieve said.

"Oh, they're so pretty," Blisse remarked, "and big."

"I am supposed to keep the red one," Rieve explained, "and I am to give one to each member of our fellowship."

"The red one is a ruby and the gold are topaz," River said. Rieve handed each of the girls their stone.

"The other two belong to Tag and Brenz. I suggest you ladies figure out some way to fasten the stone to a necklace or something," Rieve said.

"Okay. I can see that and the best part is, I think it will go with most of my wardrobe," Blisse said with a smile.

"Same here," Breille added.

"I don't think they are meant to be a fashion statement, ladies. Although, they are pretty," River added.

"Now what are they supposed to do, Rieve?" Blisse asked.

"I asked the Headmaster the same thing," Rieve said.

"Oh great. What did grandfather say, as if that is going to be helpful," Blisse asked.

"He said that my red stone . . . ." Rieve responded.

"Ruby," River injected again.

"He said that my ruby will bring me to him when I am needed and when he is in trouble and your gold . . . topaz stones will bring all of you to me when I am in trouble," Rieve

The War Begins

said. "The Headmaster also said they will warn us of danger, the kind of danger that comes when Ashkelon is near."

"How does that happen?" This time the question came from Breille.

"I don't know, but I suspect one of these days, soon, we'll find out," Rieve said.

"It is getting late, so we best make some plans," River added. The four made plans to go to the victory parade together. It was left to Rieve to figure out how he would get the stones to Tag and Brenz, who were still encamped at their respective towers and a three day's walk from the Great Plateau.

The Polemmas Tower

The Polemmas army spent the day cleaning up after the battle. They had made temporary barriers to plug the holes in the gates, entrances, and wall. They were still strong and were confident that they could repel another attack of seventy five thousand creatures. But if Ashkelon attacked in force, they could not hold the wall for much more than three hours.

After the last major attack from Ashkelon, the engineers and builders of Entos designed and built a rail system into the lower half of the walls. Using a system of weights and counter-weights three large rail cars, which could hold one hundred fifty warriors each, would be catapulted along the rails at great speeds. In this way reinforcements could be sent where needed. The creation of the rail system reduced more than a full day's march of forty leagues to just a little under one hour. Even with the rail system it would take nearly three hours for enough reinforcements to reach the Polemmas Tower to make any real difference. That would be cutting it a bit too close.

The Polemmas army worked through the night. The Procuron commander worked out a rest and work schedule. Warriors were given three hours on and three hours off for rest. He did not know what the morning would bring. "But in the morning," the Procuron thought, "we will learn whether this was an Ashkelon attack or not. If this was an attack from Ashkelon, the king would certainly launch a second attack. He would not miss an military opportunity like this one." He hoped for the best, but prepared for the worst.

The sun rose and every warrior looked out on the desert floor and readied himself for another attack. But none came.

The Oracles And The Jewels

The same happened at the Hodia, Tarchus, Nuxia, Kanna, and Neggen Towers. Each hour on the hour the towers blew the "all clear," each in its order. By midmorning the entire city of Entos was breathing a little easier. Rieve, River, Blisse, and Breille went about their ordinary responsibilities. Tag and Brenz did the same.

But at 2:00 in the afternoon, the horns began to blow, three times. The Tarchus Tower was reporting an attack. It was a strange report. Of all the towers and walls, the Tarchus Tower would have been the least value to Ashkelon. The fall of this wall would give Ashkelon little strategic advantage. The mountain range in the northwestern valley and the lakes and canyons that cut across the plateau leading to the tower would hinder his progress. The fact that the Tarchus Plateau ran between the Fortian tribes and hamlets on the south and the Pithos tribes and hamlets on the north added to the challenges Ashkelon would face. By the time Ashkelon's army made it over the mountains and canyons and around the lakes, the armies of Entos would be waiting for him. Nor would the Fortians and Pithosians simply stand by and allow his armies to advance without inflicting major losses, since even Fortian and Pithos women and children were natural born fighters.

An attack on the Tarchus wall could only be a raid, but still Entos had not seen back-to-back raids of significant size in a very long time. Entos had never experienced raids on two exact opposite towers in so close a time span. The raids seemed coordinated and they set the city on edge.

By 3:00 in the afternoon the "all clear" signal was given by the Tarchus Tower. The attack had been a significant one consisting of several thousand beasts and soldiers, but had been repelled without any major damage to Entos. At 5:00 just before the sun started to set another attack was reported. This time against the Kanna Tower. By 6:00 the battle was over and the all clear was sounded. Three attacks in less than two days. A consensus among the military thinkers was beginning to emerge. The attacks were being orchestrated by King Ashkelon himself. There could be no other explanation. "But to what end?" was the question that ran through the ranks.

The Three Rings

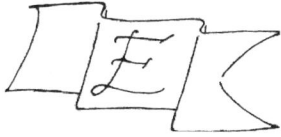

Chapter Ten
The Three Rings

City Council

"Order, Order!" President Botha called out as he banged the gavel on the wood block on the marble conference table. The City Fathers took their seats at the council table. It, like the table in the tribunal hall, was large and made of fine wood. This table was shaped in a large "U" and only had one podium in which the one addressing the council was to stand. Even before the meeting was called to order Professor MulLord was seated in the Headmaster's chair. General Witticor took his seat next to him.

"You've waited a long time to sit in that seat haven't you, Professor MulLord?" the general said with a disapproving voice.

"I earned this place, General," MulLord replied with equal firmness.

"You have done a lot to sit in that seat, but you have never earned it," the Wittcor barked quietly. "It is by subterfuge, not merit that you occupy that seat."

"How dare you speak to me that way!" MulLord snapped in a whisper.

"How dare you mock the King of Entos!" Witticor replied.

"This is not a time for panic and disorder," President Botha shouted over all the noise in the hall. "Thank you all for coming out this evening. I know it is late. We have much to do and I hope to conclude this meeting by midnight. That gives us about two hours to conduct our work. I have asked General Witticor to brief us on the events of the past forty-eight hours and to give us a military readiness report. General, the floor is yours."

"Thank you, Mr. President. At dawn yesterday morning, an attack was launched against the Polemmas Tower and its adjoining wall. The attack was unusual for many reasons. It was too large to be considered a raid, some forty thousand creatures strong. But too small by Ashkelon's standards. Colonel Muvel was killed in the attack. After his death, Major

The Oracles And The Jewels

Abolija took over command. He is a good warrior, a Procuron and not prone to overreaction. I know him personally. You have his field report in front of you. He handled the job well. I have appointed General Hokkan, the Demotic, to take over command. He is on his way to assume command of Polemmas as we speak.

"You also have the report from the commanding officers at the Tarchus and Kanna Towers. The attacks on those towers looked more like conventional raids, although slightly larger groups of ten to twenty thousand. If not for their timing and location, we would regard them as nothing more than uncharacteristically large raids.

"The Tarchus Tower was attacked by the larger force, but some of Ashkelon's elite soldiers participated. Two thousand of Ashkelon's monsters fell in battle. The Kanna Tower was attacked by a force of eight thousand. Same pattern. Three thousand seven hundred fell.

"It is our opinion that Ashkelon is testing the strength of the towers and walls. He is studying us in anticipation of a full-scale attack and invasion of Entos. But it appears he will attack us on several fronts, or at least he wants us to think so." The hall was silent.

"General, when is this attack likely to come?" City Father Derson asked.

"We don't know. It could be tomorrow. I suspect on the outside it would be within the month," the general answered. "We haven't sent out any scouts yet, but we have teams ready to go. We hope they will be able to provide some intelligence."

"Where will the attack come?" Professor MulLord asked.

"We have no reason to believe Ashkelon will change his primary point of attack. He will throw his main force against the wall between the Hodia and Polemmas Towers. He may engage several of the surrounding towers in an effort to keep us from reinforcing the wall at his main point of attack," the general stated.

"How can you be so sure, when you know so little else?" Professor MulLord said with the sound of disrespect.

"King Ashkelon is powerful, but he does have his limits. Moving small groups of a few thousand soldiers around to the Tarchus, Nuxia, and Kanna Towers is one thing, but moving an army of tens-of-thousands or of hundreds-of-thousands is another. Ashkelon is not a servant to his army. He is the master. He either can't or won't cause

The Three Rings

water to flow from desert rocks. Even creatures of Bohow and soldiers of Ektos need water and lots of it. Ashkelon is not going to spend his day feeding his army. He has more important things to do, at least to his way of thinking.

"His main water supply is the Oros and Yaash Rivers and they run through the forest opposite the Hodia Tower. He needs to be as close to water as he can be. His supply lines would not be able to reach to the west. It is the eastern walls of Entos that bear the greatest threat. Ashkelon will not go far from those rivers," the general explained.

"Are the armies ready for the attack?" President Botha asked.

"Yes sir, but there is more that needs to be done," the general said. "We are shifting some warriors and resources from the western towers to the east. We are also marshaling the interior forces to take up secondary positions to reinforce our warriors in the east. I would like the council's permission to relocate some of those western forces to the city.

"It will be very difficult for Ashkelon to break through the walls. Even if he does he can only pour so many creatures through the openings at a time. If he makes it through the wall between Hodia and Polemmas he will have to fight his way sixty leagues uphill and in an ever-narrowing pass. The closer he gets to the city, the easier it will be for us to defend the city and the harder it will be for him to enter it. The landscape forms a funnel. He will be funneled right into our metal. The city is not threatened by a conventional attack. He cannot march his army that far.

"Based on what we've seen from the attack on the Polemmas Tower, we believe that he will try to insert a significant number of soldiers and beasts by the air using winged creatures that have been spotted flying above. We believe that was the purpose of the attack on the Polemmas Tower. He was experimenting. What he didn't count on was someone sounding the alarm in advance of his air drop and landing his soldiers in the middle of the cadets' encampment. His creatures didn't have a chance. They were cut down before they could gain a foothold. He won't make that mistake again. We believe he will try to insert forces well behind the wall, perhaps as deep as twenty to forty leagues into the Demotic Valley. We are evacuating all women and children from the valley. Able-bodied males will remain as a militia force.

"What we suggest is that we divide our armies into three concentric circles. The main force will remain at the towers

The Oracles And The Jewels

and the walls in the east. Each army on the western wall will send half of their warriors to form a second semicircle about forty leagues from the eastern walls. Should Ashkelon successfully insert ground forces by using the winged creatures, our second line will eliminate them."

Secretary Scoderan spoke up, "General, you said three concentric circles?"

"Yes, Mr. Secretary I did," answered the general. "I would like to take a third group of warriors and form a very tight perimeter around the urban center, the city of Entos herself."

"General, do you lack confidence in your armies?" Professor MulLord asked.

"I do not," the general replied.

"Why three rings when two can do the job?" MulLord said. "Aren't you overestimating the power of Ashkelon?" The general felt at that moment as if he were being interrogated. His military judgment had never been questioned in such a manner before. Of course, he had never faced a full attack from Ashkelon before. But to have a plan opposed by Entosians who had no knowledge of or experience with war was unusual. In Entos laymen always gave more weight to the opinion of those who earned their living from the craft. A military man would never consider telling a builder how to go about building. A builder would not think to dissent from the learned opinions of a priest in regard to the Oracles. A priest left administrative affairs to the graduates from The Academy of Governance. If any thought to raise questions, it was for the purpose of understanding the recommendations and expanding the possibilities.

What was taking place in the council did not fit that description. The general was angered by the treatment and made even more angry by those who sat silent and allowed the challenge to go unchallenged.

"Call it caution. After all, Professor MulLord, if just a few of Ashkelon's elite soldiers make it to the city, the City Fathers, the Academy, and The Great Chamber itself would be in danger," the general responded in a voice that masked his true feelings.

"You forget, general. We have our own guards. All of whom were trained at your academy. They are the best of the best. The council selected them directly. I have the utmost confidence in them. We also have some new weapons created by our modernization program. Between

The Three Rings

our own guards and the prototype weapons, we will handle any attack on the city," Professor MulLord argued.

"'We will be able to handle any attack?'" the general repeated with a tone that mocked MulLord. "I would welcome the opportunity, Professor MulLord, to see you handle a weapon, new or ancient."

"General, we can do without the sarcasm," President Botha said. "Professor MulLord you would do well to speak to the general in a more respectful tone as well. We are all trying to find the best way to defend Entos. We are all on the same side here. Please continue, general."

"Thank you, Mr. President. I apologize for my tone. The military planners believe it would be best to create three concentric circles to provide adequate coverage over the greatest amount of territory. It also permits us to move our units and armies as needed. If no attack comes to the city, then it is a matter of moving those units down the Demotic slope to reinforce the second circle."

"General, if there is a significant force inserted twenty or thirty leagues behind the wall, wouldn't it be best to meet that force with overwhelming force and eliminate them straight away, rather than moving warriors back and forth? Then if no insertion takes place, the second line could advance and eliminate the enemy before he gets too far up the valley?" President Botha asked.

"Yes sir, but we do not know the range of the winged creatures. What if they could reach the city? Can they do so carrying Ashkelon's soldiers?" the general said.

"Never in the history of Entos has Ashkelon been able to penetrate this deep into Entos. He has never fully breached the walls," Vice President Mohhan said.

"With all due respect, General, I believe it would be best to put every available warrior into two concentric circles. Two strong lines rather than three weaker ones seems best to me," President Larrence of The Academy of Governance said. "Two stronger beams are better than three weaker ones in bearing a load. Isn't that true President Kuchen?"

"Depending on where the load is placed, yes," President Kuchen replied, "that is an accepted building principle, depending on where the load is placed."

"We are not building a building gentlemen with mathematical precision. We are fighting a war. That is an art and that art requires certain educated guesses, the gathering of information, and taking calculated risks," the general countered. "A war plan also needs flexibility. The

The Oracles And The Jewels

plan I am recommending plans for the worst, while giving us the ability to move resources and warriors to any battlefield where they are needed."

"I agree with Professor MulLord and with Presidents Larrence and Kuchen. I will take full responsibility for the protection of the academies and The Great Chamber," President Botha said.

"I agree. Two stronger lines would be best," Scoderan followed suit.

"With all due respect toward this esteemed council, I strongly urge that our entire plan be accepted. The cuts in the military forces have not yet taken effect. The modernization program of which you speak is incomplete and untested. We have enough warriors to do as we recommend," the general argued. After he spoke there was a long silence. The general walked slowly around the inside to the "U" shaped conference table. "This is not the time for experimentation. This is not the time to tell Entosians that the strength of Entos lies within their own hearts, good intentions, or modern machinery. This is a time of war. The power of the Oracles and a conjuror find their fulfillment in the flesh and blood of an Entosian warrior," the general shouted, "not in the mechanical operations of dangerous toys!"

President Botha was outraged at what he believed to be a direct assault on the good intentions and authority of the council. "General, you tend to the walls and countryside of Entos. Make sure Ashkelon doesn't make it past your lines. We will take it upon ourselves to secure the urban area. Things are tense enough. There is no need to worry the population by a show of force so close to The Great Chamber. Any objections from the council?" No one spoke a word.

"Then it is decided," Botha said.

"I request a full vote for the record," City Father Derson said.

"Is that really necessary?" Vice President Mohhan asked. "It's getting late."

"We insist," Simmjer, the Pithosian, said.

"Very well," President Botha said. The vote was taken. Nine votes in favor of President Botha's plan to form two lines of defense and three votes in support of the general's plan.

"General, you have a lot to do. Know that our thoughts and prayers are with you and your men," President Botha said. The general left the room and met his staff outside the hall in the courtyard.

"Major," the general said. "Begin the relocation of the western forces as we discussed earlier."

"I assume General, they approved the battle plan," the major asked.

"Part of it," the general answered. "They rejected assigning warriors to protect the city. They don't want warriors walking around in full uniforms worrying everyone. So major, here is what we're going to do. Recall the cadets from Krattos, Hodia, Polemmas, and Neggen. Bring them back into the city. The cadets at Borrhas, Tarchus, Nuxia, and Kanna are to fall back from the towers and walls forty leagues. I want them halfway between the city and wall and ready to move in either direction if needed. Cadets don't belong in a war zone. They aren't, properly speaking, warriors and they certainly haven't been assigned to combat-ready units. Officially we are bringing some back for urban training exercises and others for rapid deployment training. That's what we are doing," the general said as he grinned a little grin.

"While we are at it, we are also going to give Hodia, Krattos, Polemmas, and Neggen cadets some training in urban camouflage. The cadets are to be in uniform, but they are to wear their tribal robes over their uniforms. They will have to hide their armor and battle gear, but that can't be helped. Should they need their armor and weapons, make sure they can get to them in a hurry."

"Yes, sir," the major replied.

"The Pithosians and the Aradians are tall and large enough they can conceal their swords under their robes, but the rest of the cadets are going to have to be armed with only their daggers. That is as close to a sword as we can get. At least Entos will have three hundred fifty fighting men ready to defend her if things go badly. With the City Fathers' honor guard that should give us four hundred fighting men."

"Yes, sir," the major said. "Permission to speak freely sir?"

"Permission granted," Witticor snapped.

"Can they be trusted, sir? This is a pretty secret operation. If the council catches wind of what you are doing here, your career as commander is over. The cadets are still young, some of them only fifteen or so."

"That's what I am counting on. They owe no one. They are not invested in the system. They are idealists. They want

The Oracles And The Jewels

to fight. They want to prove to Entos that they are worthy to be called the best. They will do exactly what they are ordered to do. Get them into the city undetected. Once they are in the city, Colonel Fornoff and I will take it from there," Witticor ordered.

"It will take a couple of days to get them all back here," the major replied.

"We don't have a couple of days. I want them all in the Upper Theater of the Performing Arts Building at 7:00 in the dark, just after the sun goes down. I don't want to see even one uniform," the general barked, "tribal robes only."

"Yes, sir. We'll use the emergency evacuation system to retrieve the cadets. They should be here by 6:00, just as the sun is setting," the major replied. General Witticor and the major marched down the street and toward The Academy of the Ancient Warring Arts.

A House Divided

Chapter Eleven
A House Divided

A week earlier, the cadets had arrived at their respective towers. With the attacks on the three towers, Cadet Thayer Taggert and his squad were hopeful that they would see action soon. They were training harder than ever and were excited at the prospect of using their newly honed skills. Only a day had gone by since the first attack, but it seemed that everything was changing and rumors of more attacks were reaching the campus almost every hour. "Hodia," they thought, "could expect an attack at any moment." A copy of the bulletin announcing the attack on Polemmas and Brenz's citation had reached the camp in the late afternoon. The possibility of an attack and the news of Brenz's gallantry made it difficult for Thayer to sleep, for he wanted desperately to prove that he too was every bit as much a warrior as Brenz.

General Witticor obeyed the letter of the law by not positioning any warriors in the city, but in ordering the recall of the cadets he was violating the spirit of the City Fathers' will. The orders recalling the cadets went out at 11:30 that evening. By using trained birds the army could send messages between any tower and headquarters in just over two hours. At 1:45 in the dark the birds reached their goal. Cadets from the Hodia, Polemmas, Neggen, and Krattos Towers were ordered to break camp and double-time it to station #5, a military post ten leagues inside each tower and on their respective plateaus.

"Cadets, wake up. You're moving out in ten minutes," a voice snarled in the darkness of Tag's tent. "Be quiet about it. The regulars aren't to know." Before Tag could open his eyes, the warrior behind the voice had left the tent.

"Oh no," Tag whispered. "They can't do this to us!"

"Do what?" Cadet Marcus asked in a sleepy voice. "What are they doing?"

"They're moving us out and away from the battle. They're expecting an attack and they don't want cadets

The Oracles And The Jewels

caught up in the middle of it. There goes my chance. Brenz gets all the breaks," Tag complained. "He gets to become a hero and I have to get up in the middle of the night and march sixty leagues back to the safety of the city."

"Do you think that's it?" Cadet Kelila asked. "It just seems funny that they are moving us out so late at night and with the instructions to do it as quietly as possible."

"They just don't want us to wake them. They are probably going to be up and in the heat of battle by dawn," Tag said. The five cadets dressed, broke down their tents in the allotted time, and did so without uttering another word. Fifteen minutes later the fifty cadets were ready to move. They began their ten league run to station #5.

The same process on a larger scale was repeated at the Polemmas, Krattos, and Neggen cadet encampments. The Hodia Cadet unit was only half the size of any other. The Hodia army was the elite force. They were faster, stronger, and more mobile than the others. They not only protected the most crucial wall, but most warriors in the special forces came from the Hodia army. Each year only fifty cadets were accepted into the Hodia army. The balance of the Hodia army's recruits came from experienced warriors from the other armies. With the recommendation of their commanding officer, the very best were offered transfers to the Hodia army on an annual basis. About half of those who were recommended for the elite force accepted the promotion and moved on.

The Polemmas, Krattos, and Neggen cadet units had one hundred recruits each. But they were still very good fighting men. Moving them would take just a little longer than the Hodia army cadets.

During training and drills the cadets would sing to keep their steps in rhythm. This time under the lights of the three moons and the stars, they were ordered to remain silent. They did. Tag thought to himself about the pace. It was a hard pace. There was no way they could be expected to keep this pace up for more than ten or twenty leagues. The pace was well suited to a unit of Aradians, but they only had seven Aradians in their unit. They had ten Fortians, who were well suited for battles, but it was common for the Fortians to take up the rear on their longer runs. The Hodia cadet unit had ten Adroitians, who were the archers and disk throwers. They were quick, but they didn't fare any better than the Kilposians and the Demotics in a long distance run.

A House Divided

Long distance races between Demotics and Adroitians looked something like the proverbial tortoise and the hare.

The unit had six Pithosians who could be easily identified in the darkness of the night by their silhouette and the heavy thump of their feet as they ran along the path. The unit was fortunate. They had one Kicahian, who was very quiet and kept to himself. Kicahians tended to be of two kinds. They were either joiners who tried too hard to be accepted into a group or they were loners. This Kicahian was a loner. Tag's unit was rounded out by six Kilposians, eight Demotics, and two Procurons.

The unit was broken down into ten squads of five. Tag was squad leader and unit commander. As such he felt that even in their long distance runs he had to be in the front. On this run Tag was right behind the drill sergeant. The unit reached station #5 at 3:45 in the dark.

"Cadet Commander Tag," the drill sergeant said. "I will be returning to the Hodia Tower to help them. You're in charge from here on in. Get your unit to the city and in the Performing Arts Building and the Upper Theater by 7:00 in the dark. At station #1, ten leagues out from the city, you will all be given your tribal robes. Strip your unit of all armor. The Pithosians and Aradians may keep their swords, but they must keep them under their robes and out of sight. The rest of you will be issued daggers. Your mission is top secret and you are to enter the city unnoticed and blend in. Find a place to stow your armor and heavy weapons, but make sure they are in a place where you can get to them.

"Each squad needs to find its own hiding place. Make sure you are all at the Upper Theater on time. You will be joined by cadets from the Polemmas, Krattos, and Neggen Towers. The password to enter the Upper Theater is 'Youthful Enterprise.' Make sure all your cadets know the password.

"If you run into people you know in the city, just tell them that you've been given a leave until the Ashkelon matter settles down, but try not to be discovered in the first place. The evacuation units are just down the path. Any questions?" the sergeant asked.

"Yes sir, a lot of them, but I doubt very much you can answer any of them. I am clear on the immediate task at hand. This isn't a drill, is it sir?" Tag asked.

"If it is, cadet, it is the first time I've seen a drill like this. Take care, and if you must fight, fight well for the greater

The Oracles And The Jewels

glory of Entos." The two saluted and the sergeant began his run back toward the Hodia Tower.

The other forty-nine cadets watched the sergeant disappear down the trail in stunned amazement. Cadets were never without their drill sergeant before. They were sure that there was a rule someplace about that.

"Cadets, fall in!" Tag ordered with a voice that invoked images of the drill sergeant. They did as they were ordered. "Double-time!" The cadets began running down the path behind Tag. A minute later they entered a clearing and found five transports waiting for them. The transports were streamlined wagons, built to hold an average of ten Entosians at a time, depending on their size. Each wagon was pulled by a set of four steeds.

"Squads one and two board!" Tag shouted as he pointed to the first wagon on the right. "Squads three and four the next and so on, men. We don't have all night. Move it!" The cadets poured into the five wagons.

"Move out," the cadet commander called out to the drivers. No sooner was the order given than he noticed that the drivers were military men who, even at the lowest ranks, still outranked him.

"My apologies, sirs. I didn't realize . . ." At that the drivers shouted and the horses bolted forward. Tag was the only one unprepared for the moment and fell backward into the wagon where his squad was sitting. They laughed and Tag took it all in good spirit.

"Tag, what's going on?" Cadet Kelila inquired.

"It's Commander, Cadet," Tag said.

"Sorry, Commander," she replied.

"He can't tell us. He's in charge now. From here on, we're on a need-to-know basis. We don't need to know a thing until this wagon comes to a stop," Cadet Ailith, another member of Tag's unit said.

The five wagons raced along the path and toward the city with remarkable speed. The road was well-kept and smooth. The wheels of the wagon barely made a sound as they rolled along the path. The hooves of the horses pounded the path in a quick and regular rhythm. The pace would have made an Aradian proud. As the wagons sped along, snopes ran along the side, matching the speed and the silence of the wagons. They were a welcomed sight. The cadets watched the playful creatures. Occasionally, a cadet would pull some bread from his pack and throw it to the snopes who would snatch it up without missing a stride.

A House Divided

When the wagons reached station #4, they came to a stop just behind five identical wagons. "De-board and board," Tag ordered, not sure whether "de-board" was an actual military term. Cadets always walked. They never rode. His men knew what he meant, although they chuckled at the order. They flowed out of the first set of wagons and into the second set in just a few seconds. Tag took his spot with his squad in the lead wagon. Looking to the driver he said, "All aboard, Sir." The crack of the reigns set the train of wagons speeding down the path. The process repeated itself all night long and through the morning hours. The same process was being repeated for the Polemmas, Krattos, and Neggen cadet units. By daybreak the Hodia unit was a station and a half ahead of the rest. They would arrive in Entos before the others.

When the cadets of the Hodia Army reached station #1, there were no wagons waiting. "Commander," the driver said. "This is as far as we can take you. You are to walk in from here. Your orders are to walk, not run. Try to draw as little attention to yourselves as possible. I have been told that you know what you're doing from here on in."

"Everyone out of the wagons. We have a wardrobe change, men. Then we walk into Entos from here," Tag shouted. By now the cadets knew that they were being used for some secret and strange purpose. The order to change their wardrobe only added to the suspense.

"Fall in," Tag shouted. The cadets lined up in review formation. Tag explained what they were to do. "Your tribal robes are in the station. Put them on over your uniform and your armor. When we get to the crest of the Great Plateau, you are to take off your armor and swords and find a hiding place for your squad's gear. Everyone except Pithosians and Aradians will be issued daggers inside the station. The daggers will take the place of your swords. Pithosians and Aradians you can keep your swords. Your size and robes make it easy for you to conceal your weapons." As he spoke he walked the line and reviewed the cadets, playing the part of the commanding officer to perfection. "We will proceed into the city in our squads at ten minute intervals. My squad will go first. I will be waiting for you at the crest. You are to enter Entos unnoticed. Try not to be seen by people you know. If you are seen, tell them that your squad has been given a leave from the academy until this Ashkelon threat is passed. Your mission is top secret." Tag paused.

The Oracles And The Jewels

"We will likely arrive in Entos at 4:30. That will give you two and a half hours. You are to be at the Upper Theater at 7:00 sharp in the dark. Don't draw attention to yourselves or get into any trouble. Keep your uniforms on under your robes. In the event that trouble breaks out, you'll be ready.

"If you can get to your armor and sword do so, but only in the event of trouble. Cadets, you are still cadets, yet you are cadets in the finest army on Ashkelon's dark earth and you are ready for the challenge. You are better, smarter, faster, and more deadly than any creature of Bohow. You are officers and if Ashkelon comes, you will be warriors soon enough, even if you do not yet have the title or wear the warrior's uniform. I expect all of you, from the largest Pithosian," Tag looked up into the nostrils of the Pithosian standing before him, "to the smallest Adroitian," as he looked down on the head of the Adroitian standing to his right, "to conduct yourselves in the tradition of the Hodia Army. The password to enter the Upper Theater is 'Youthful Enterprise.' Take care and if you must fight, fight well for the greater glory of Entos. Fall out and suit up!"

Tag's squad was the first in the station house. They robed up quickly making sure to hide all their armor and weapons. They picked up their daggers and headed down the path without a word being spoken by any of the five. The ritual was repeated every ten minutes. Five groups of ten were now making their way down the path toward the city of Entos.

"Okay, Commander," Cadet Marrcus began, "we're alone now. Tell us what's going on."

"I wouldn't if I knew, but the fact of the matter is you all now know as much as I do," Tag said. "Anything I might say now is just a guess."

"So give us your best guess," Cadet Bonar, a Pithosian muttered.

"I don't know that I should, being the commander and all," Tag said.

"Since when did that ever stop you?" Cadet Kelila quipped as she gave him a push on the shoulder. "Come on, it's just us and we have all been guessing. You might as well too."

"Well then, let's all think this through," Tag said. "With the attacks on the Tarchus, Kanna, and Polemmas Towers the City Fathers and the military think-tank have come to the conclusion that King Ashkelon is behind all this and is testing the strength of the walls for a major attack."

A House Divided

"Nothing like beginning with the obvious. You're talking around the issue," Cadet Ailith said.

"I am just starting at the beginning. Didn't you know that's the sign of the good commander?" Tag laughed. "We have been ordered into the city to serve as a back up, a plan 'B' so to speak. The first possibility is that the City Fathers have ordered us back into the city in such a way that we do not alarm the population. They don't want to alarm the people as to the serious nature of Ashkelon's threat. That's the first possibility."

"What about the second possibility?" Cadet Marrcus asked.

"If the City Fathers haven't ordered us back, then someone pretty high up in the military establishment issued the order, maybe even without the City Fathers' knowledge," Tag answered.

"If it is without the City Fathers' knowledge, what would that mean?" Cadet Kelila asked in a rather sober tone.

"Let's suppose that we have been ordered back by one of the generals or General Witticor himself. We have been ordered back in such a way so that the City Fathers do not know about our presence," Tag stated.

"That would mean that there is a split between the military and the City Fathers," Cadet Ailith said with a bit of surprise. "Someone in the military knows something that the council does not or that the council does not trust the military's judgment."

"Or" Tag said with a pause, "we are looking at some kind of coup."

"If it is a coup, are we the good guys or bad guys?" Cadet Bonar asked as he lifted his right eyebrow.

"I think that we will find the answer to that question when we get into the theater," Tag replied.

The group continued to walk but mostly in silence. Tag was eager to get to the city and to The Academy of the Liberal and Performing Arts. The chances of seeing River were slim, but he thought it would be good to see her. Then he remembered that he was suppose to stay clear of people that he knew.

Yet they did have their little fellowship and the pledge that each member of the fellowship would meet whenever it was possible. Surely he could trust the other members to keep quiet. Meeting with them would also give him a chance to catch up on the events of the city, The Academy of the Theological Sciences, and to beat Entos' most recent hero

The Oracles And The Jewels

in a sword match. That last thought settled the matter. Tag would head to the crest of the Plateau for the Polemmas Tower to meet Brenz.

The Academy of Theological Sciences and Ancient Conjuring Arts

Candidate Nassar had returned to his dorm safe and sound late in the afternoon. He had just left the camp when the attack began. He stood on a hill about two leagues from the main battle watching the drama unfold. As he sat and watched the battle rage, many thoughts ran through his head. He was horrified at the carnage of war. Yet he had to admit that he took a delight in the destruction of such evil creatures.

"If Ashkelon were to succeed," he thought, "he would certainly take the Oracles and the Jewels from The Great Chamber and the Land of Entos would soon thereafter die. He and all Entosians, separated from the Oracles and the Jewels, would be transformed back into the creatures their great ancestors once were, creatures of Bohow." "How did Rieve know?" he asked out loud. "He could only know such a thing, by virtue of some great blessing," he answered.

There was no longer any doubt in Nassar's mind. Rieve was indeed a great leader, albeit he was at the beginning of his career. But Rieve had foreseen the attack, at least that is what Nassar had thought. Rieve and Nassar were already friends, but the events of the past several hours had convinced Nassar that Rieve was an Apprentice Priest who stood on the right side of the theological debate and who had already become an instrument of the Giver to deliver Entos from danger.

Nassar returned to his room about mid afternoon to find a series of notes left under his door from Rieve. Nassar laughed. Considering all that had just happened, missing classes looked pretty trivial, but Rieve had kept his promise.

As the morning had moved along and the news of the attack spread through the city, Entosians attempted to go about their business in an ordinary fashion. It was customary during such attacks for more Entosians to visit The Great Chamber and engage in some of the rituals as a way to petition the King of Entos to protect the warriors and intercede in the events of history. Battles kept everyone busy. The warriors and military first, the priests and conjurors in The Great Chamber second, and the City

A House Divided

Fathers third. Citizens went about their business, but took time to offer prayers and to check the bulletin boards for any news of the battle.

On the day after the attack on the Polemmas Tower, Rieve returned to his routine. He attended ritual practice with Professor Langward in the morning. He attended a lecture on the Maker, Giver, and King of Entos and the victory over Ashkelon in the age before Entos. He pretended to go to conjuring lab with Professor Etam, where he took a long nap and missed his last class of the day on the doctrine of stations in Entos. But his nap was interrupted.

"Excuse me, Professor Etam," a voice said from the hallway. Rieve stirred at the sound of an unfamiliar voice.

"I was expecting you, sir," Professor Etam replied. "I will leave you two alone, but don't be long. If anyone approaches I will let you know."

"Apprentice Rieve wake up. There's someone here to see you," the professor said. Rieve lifted his head and allowed his eyes to focus. As soon as he realized who was standing before him he jumped to his feet.

"Sorry, Sir," Rieve said. It was General Witticor. Rieve was stunned. "What could he want with me?" Rieve thought to himself.

"At ease, young man. You're not in the army, at least not yet," the general said in a tone that meant business. "Young man, I have a problem and I am told by a mutual friend of ours that you might be able to help me."

"Me? How?" Rieve asked.

"I have a secret force of military personnel making their way into this city as we speak. This secret force is without a conjuror. That is a bad thing. Every force needs a conjuror if they have any hope of victory. Unless I miss my guess, and that doesn't happen very often, they are going to need a first-rate conjuror," the general explained.

"Sir, don't you have a bunch of military conjurors at your disposal?" Rieve asked.

"Sure I do, but I can't use a military conjuror. I don't need one of those. I need a conjuror for a military unit, not a military conjuror. I need an unofficial conjuror who is resourceful and has friends ready and willing to help. Our mutual friend tells me that you are the kind of conjuror I need," the general said.

"What kind is that, Sir?" Rieve asked.

"The kind that loves Entos. The kind of conjuror who knows the difference between the new and old doctrines,"

The Oracles And The Jewels

he said with a smile. "The kind who plans ahead and happens to have some friends who meet frequently to share the information they've collected, while going about their ordinary lives. Our mutual friend tells me if there is anyone of an unofficial nature that I can trust, it is you. Is that right, Apprentice Priest Rieve?"

"Unfortunately for me that appears to the case, Sir," Rieve answered.

"Young man," the general said as he opened his hand exposing the second and small ruby from the Headmaster's jar, "I don't need to know the names of the members of your little fellowship, but it would be helpful to me to know what academies they attend. Can you tell me that?"

"We have pledged ourselves not to reveal the names of the little fellowship, that's all, Sir. I can provide the information you seek. One is at The Liberal Arts Academy, another at The Healing Arts Academy . . ,"

"Good, good," the general muttered. "I am going to need a few healers, the unofficial kind. I also need to get into the Upper Theater at 7:00 in the dark for a private party. Would you happen to know of someone who might be able to help me get in there?" the general asked.

Rieve responded instinctively and instantly. "River Kiernan, Sir," Rieve shook his head disappointed that he had just revealed the identity of one of the members of the little fellowship. "That wasn't fair, General."

"Don't worry, your secret is safer with me than it is with you," the general said with a slight grin.

"The fellowship also has a member at The Academy of the Building Arts and we have two cadets in your Academy."

"Very good," he said. "I have use for all of you." Just then Professor Etam stepped back into the room.

"General, a couple of candidates are headed down the hallway," Professor Etam warned.

"Two of your little fellowship will probably be at their respective crests toward their assigned towers. They should arrive about 5:00 this evening," the general opened his hand exposing the ruby a second time and whispered, "I will call you when I need you." He turned toward Professor Etam and the door and took Professor Etam's hand and shook it as the two students entered the lab.

"The military thanks you, Professor Etam, for your help at this time. If you could work on that bit of conjuring for us I think it might help put some of our fine warriors at ease."

A House Divided

"Yes, sir. I will get on that project right away," Professor Etam said as he played along. The general left the lab and walked quickly down the hall. "Good afternoon Candidates, I will be with you in few moments." Turning to Rieve, Professor Etam said, "Apprentice Rieve, sorry to keep you past your allotted time, but we need to perfect those skills. You're close, but you need to sharpen the recitation of those incantations."

"Thanks, Professor. I'll do better next time," Rieve said. Then he left the lab and walked down the hall in the opposite direction of the general. On his way out his mind raced, "Once again," he thought, "another meeting cloaked in secrecy and ambiguity."

As Rieve walked along he talked to himself. "Now what have I been brought into? What does the general want me to do? How am I going to explain this to the little fellowship? How am I going to meet Tag and Brenz at the Polemmas and Hodia crests at 5:00?" As Rieve ran through a list of questions and "to dos" he walked through the city streets and past his dorm.

Nassar was just getting up from a nap when he looked out the window and saw Rieve walking through the street below. Nassar splashed some water on his face and ran down the stairs and into the street.

"Rieve! Rieve Waynwright!" Nassar called out as he moved through the crowd. "Rieve!" Rieve paused and looked around. He saw Nassar coming down the street toward him.

"I thought you would have been in bed fast asleep by now," Rieve said.

"In bed! I can't sleep! I can't believe it! That was really exciting," Nassar exclaimed.

"What can't you believe?" Rieve asked.

"I can't believe that I had a part in such an important event. We could have been single-handedly responsible for saving Entos," Nassar replied.

"No, Nassar, we aren't single-handedly responsible for saving Entos. No one holds such a distinction and no one ever will," Rieve said with a tone of frustration. Rieve resumed his walk and Nassar followed along.

"Still, it was an amazing thing. How did you do it? It was just as you said. I was there, but I can hardly believe it! So how did you do it? I mean how did you really do it?" Nassar asked.

"Look, let's keep this matter to ourselves," Rieve said.

The Oracles And The Jewels

"I won't tell anyone. I promise. I swear myself to the seal," Nassar said.

"I can't tell you. If I tell you, I will betray a trust and you know I can't do that," Rieve said.

"Are you the one? Are you the next great leader?" Nassar asked.

"What a stupid thing to ask," Rieve replied.

"But with powers like yours, I believe you could be the next great leader of Entos," Nassar asserted.

"No. Absolutely not!" Rieve said firmly.

"Then how did you know?" Rieve looked at Nassar with frustration. "I know, you can't tell me," Nassar said with a tone of disappointment. But then his voice lifted again. "Listen Rieve, we've been friends for awhile. If you need anything, anything at all just let me know. I really want to be a part of this."

"No you don't. Nassar, you don't know what you're asking for. If I could give my part away to someone else more qualified, I would do it. But we are to do the parts assigned to us and that is all I am doing," Rieve said.

"But what about my part? What about me?" Nassar said as he stood with his finger pointed to his own chest.

"It's not about you. You've done your part for now and you've done it well. As for the future and your part in it, the King directs these things," Rieve said.

"Sorry, you're right. I apologize, Rieve. It was just so exciting being a part of something so grand," Nassar replied.

"Grand is overrated Nassar," Rieve answered. "Believe me when I tell you, if the need arises, I will call upon you. You have been a friend and will remain so. Now I hate to cut the discussion short, but I have an appointment to keep, a couple of them as a matter of fact."

"Can I come with you?" Nassar asked, then catching himself. "All right. I'll see you later. Thanks for the class notes." Nassar turned and walked back toward the dorm.

The Invisible Army

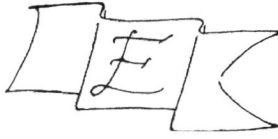

Chapter Twelve
The Invisible Army

The Academy of the Liberal and Performing Arts

It was 3:00 in the light when General Witticor entered the main theater. River was on stage rehearsing a new vocal arrangement for the Eighth Day Festival. The general stood patiently in the darkness of the unlit seats in the back of the theater. He didn't have to wait long, although he was running out of time and in a hurry. River's voice instructor offered a short critique of her performance, then dismissed her for the afternoon. River walked off the stage and up the aisle. She didn't see the general standing there until she was three rows away from him.
 "I don't know music as well as I ought to, young lady, but you sound pretty good to me," the general commented.
 "Thank you, sir," River replied.
 "Are you River Kiernan?" the general asked in a tone slightly above a whisper.
 "Yes, sir," she answered, "I am."
 "Apprentice Priest Rieve told me that I could find you here. I am looking for some young people Entos can trust. I have been assured that you are such a person." The general pulled the ruby from his pocket and showed it to her. "Can we talk outside for a moment?"
 "Yes, sir. I think we can," River replied. The two of them stepped outside, walked down the eight large steps connecting the Performing Arts Building to the street and started walking.
 The Performing Arts Building looked like a theater ought to look. Its walls were made of granite and only had few windows. It's granite walls rose elegantly, but firmly from the edge of the street and stood twelve stories tall. In those moments in the light of the three moons and at the break of dawned, when few walked the streets, the footsteps of even the smallest Entosian echoed with thunderous clarity. At

The Oracles And The Jewels

twelve stories tall, the Performing Arts Building was the second tallest building in the city.

There were four main entrances to the building. The west entrance led to a series of hallways and staircases, which in turn led to classrooms. The other entrances led to other lobbies and each lobby belonged to its own theater.

The Main Theater could seat twenty thousand at one time and took up more than half a city block by itself and it occupied the entire first floor of the Performing Arts Building, stood three and a half stories high, and was the grandest and most impressive public building in Entos second only to The Great Chamber. Above and toward the east wall was the Middle Theater. It was much smaller than the Main Theater, two stories tall, and seated five thousand. The Middle Theater was used for small public performances and ceremonies. Frequently, various tribes would use the Middle Theater to put on their own shows, hold meetings, and conduct tribal rituals honoring great Entosians who had been raised to do great things.

The Upper Theater was the smallest of the three. It was a charming little theater. It stood a story and a half tall and had only a thousand seats. The Upper Theater was not as grand and ornate as its two bigger sisters upon whose shoulders she sat, but it was still a worthy and valuable part of Entos' cultural life. This theater was used for academy functions like graduations and small school productions. The general selected the Upper Theater because, unlike the Middle and Main Theaters, the Upper Theater lobby was separated from the theater by a narrow stairwell and the theater itself had no windows.

It was surrounded by lecture halls, orchestra rooms, recital halls, rooms custom-made for Entos' many choirs, and prop and storage rooms for sets and scenery. The Upper Theater was large enough to hold the general's small secret army and it was soundproof. It was the perfect place for such a meeting.

It was perfect in every way except, there would be people coming and going all night long. It would be nearly impossible to get three hundred cadets into the theater without people taking notice. But General Witticor was not the kind of general who wasted his time on small details. Details were for colonels, majors, and lesser officers. The general surrounded himself with the best and most creative minds. Such problems belonged to those under his command.

The Invisible Army

The street below was crowded and the general walked at an even, but brisk pace. River had to step lively to keep up.

"How can I be of service, General?" River asked.

"At the moment, I need a small favor. Later, I think I will need something more substantial," the general said.

"First things first, General," River replied.

"I need the Upper Theater tonight from 7:00 till morning," the general said as his voice took on the sound of a general.

"Sir, that's easily done," River said. "Bring them over and I will let you in. There is a performance in the main theater tonight, but a friend of mine was planning on rehearsing in the Upper Theater at 7:00 and she owes me a favor. Just bring them to the south entrance and I will let you in."

"It requires a little more than that," the general said. "I need to get three hundred fifty cadets in and out of the Upper Theater without anyone seeing, hearing, or knowing that they were ever there."

The general noticed President Botha making his way down the street toward them. He gently took River by her elbow and turned down the street along the side of the Performing Arts Building. The streets were crowded and with his Fortian stature the general was sure that President Botha had not seen them. As the general took her arm and redirected her steps, River looked around to see who it was that the general was trying to avoid. She thought she saw President Botha out of the corner of her eye, but was unsure. She thought it best not to ask.

"General, with all due respect I think you need a conjuror, not a singer. I have a key to the theater. Getting in is no problem. Getting your cadets in and out without anyone knowing that they are there is a problem," River explained. "There is a performance in the Main Theater tonight and it is nearly sold out. There are going to be a lot of Entosians standing in front of the Performing Arts Building between 6:30 and 7:00. The streets will be filled with patrons and patrons mean vendors. Unless your army is invisible by 6:30, they will be seen."

"I hear you're a bright young lady. You'll figure something out. I am sure of it," the general said with a smile. Just then the general and River passed by the alley that ran behind the building academy. River looked down the alley and the answer presented itself to her. There in the work

The Oracles And The Jewels

yard of the building academy stood three sections of the moveable wall, twenty-five feet tall and one hundred feet long each. Together, the three panels were long enough to go halfway around a city block.

"Follow me, General," River said with a tone of optimism in her voice. The two of them made their way down the alley on the west end of the building then into the work yard. The walls were surrounded by two dozen academy students who were busily working on joining the three walls together by fastening two large hinges at each joint.

River stopped. The general did likewise. "General, I have the solution to your problem." The two of them stood there, looking at the three large walls. "What I don't have is seventy-five young men. Would you happen to know where I could find them?" River asked with a smile that betrayed how proud she was of herself. "I will need them here at 5:45."

"At 5:00 in the light at the crest toward the Polemmas Tower," the general said, "you will find what you need. But young lady, how are you going to steal them with all those students working on them and with the faculty watching over all that activity?"

"I'm not going to steal them, General. The Oracles don't permit such a thing. We are just going to field-test the wall," River said.

"One more thing, young lady. I understand you have a friend who is about to be in the healing business. I would like to extend an invitation to you and your healer friend to join my party this evening. When you see our conjuring friend, invite him as well. I didn't get a chance to do that." The general turned and headed back to his headquarters. As he parted he said, "Fight well, young lady. Entos needs you."

"Fight well General," River replied. She was in such a hurry that she didn't bother to complete the greeting. Instead she ran to the main entrance of The academy of the Building Arts. It was a very busy place. The academy was frantically working on the panels and trying to develop a system that would allow the panels to be linked together and be moved as quickly and easily as possible.

"Excuse me," River said as she tried to get the attention of one of the students standing inside the door. The student didn't hear her. She was a Procuron deep in thought. She was looking over some prints of the moveable wall. "Excuse me!" River said a little louder.

"Sorry," the Procuron said.

"I am looking for Breille Clarrice. Do you know her?"

The Invisible Army

"Sure, I'm assigned to her. She is working on the problem of moving the moveable wall," the Procuron said as she pointed in the direction of Breille.

"Thank you," River said, then ran across the lobby to a small room where Breille was doing some calculations.

"Breille," River called out, "Breille!"

Breille looked up and saw River running toward her. "Hello, River. What brings you here?" Breille asked as River came to a stop.

"We need to talk."

"Follow me," Breille said. The two walked out into the work yard and stood next to one of the panels of the moveable wall. It was late in the day, but as part of the war effort most of the students were planning to stay a little later. The professors of the academy were in the various drafting rooms that surrounded the main lobby. They were looking over plans and doing mathematical equations. Some of them were looking over the plan to attach wheels and a jacking system, which were to be installed on the following morning.

"General Witticor just enlisted the help of our little fellowship," River said. The information took Breille by surprise.

"What could the commander of the whole Entosian army want with us? How did he even know we exist?" Breille asked.

"As for the second question, he's been talking to Rieve. As for the first question, he needs your panels tonight, or at least these three panels tonight," River replied.

"They're not ready yet. Has the Polemmas Tower fallen?" Breille asked in a moment of panic.

"No. Relax. We need to help a small army disappear," River said.

"I think the general needs a conjuror, not a builder and singer," Breille replied.

"It's just plain scary how much I think like a Procuron," River quipped. "Look, we need to move these three panels around the south side of the Performing Arts Building so that we can get three hundred fifty cadets inside the Upper Theater without anyone seeing them. Can that be done?"

"Can it be done? Yes. We just need an army to carry the walls into place. How that can be done without the professors and students knowing is the challenging part." Breille said. "For my part, we have to make a few

The Oracles And The Jewels

adjustments before the panels can be moved even a few feet."

"I have to catch up with Blisse, then meet Brenz at the crest. I don't know how you're going to pull this off, but you're a bright girl. You'll figure it out," River said imitating the voice of the general.

"Thanks," Breille said, "You just bring me a hundred men to lift these panels."

"A hundred," River replied.

"Yes, a hundred. You're a bright girl. You'll figure it out," Breille said a voice imitating River's imitation.

It was now 3:45. That would be just enough time to retrieve Blisse and get to the crest. River ran through the streets and arrived at The Academy of Healing Arts at a little after 4:00. Classes had dismissed for the day, but River was sure she would find Blisse either at the library or in the courtyard talking to friends. If she was at the courtyard, Blisse would only stay there for a few minutes before heading home. If Blisse was at the library, then she would probably be there until 5:00. River made her way into the courtyard. Like all the academy courtyards in Entos it was a big place filled with trees, flowers, bushes, statues, and benches. River walked through the courtyard carefully looking for Blisse, but could not find her.

"You're Blisse's sister aren't you?" a voice said from behind her.

River turned and saw a Kilposian girl sitting on a bench with some notes on her lap. "Yes, I am. Have you seen her?" River asked.

"She was just here a couple of minutes ago, but I think she is on her way home," the Kilposian said.

"How do you know that?" River asked.

"She is a very predictable girl. She either goes through those arches over there," she said as she pointed to the arches at the end of the courtyard on the left, "or she goes through the arches at the other end of the courtyard on the right. That end on the left takes you to the library and the arches on the other end show her the way home. She went out that way." The Kilposian pointed behind her to the right.

"Thanks," River said. Then she ran through the courtyard and out the gates heading home. By the time she caught Blisse she was already over the crest and headed down the slope to their home. By this time River was pretty winded. She looked at her watch. It showed 4:30. It would be

The Invisible Army

a challenge to make it to the crest by five, but she had no choice.

The Hodia Cadets

Tag and his squad had the crest to the Great Plateau in sight. Their presence was concealed by a small cluster of trees. Between them and the Great Plateau there was nothing but open grass and a well-kept path.

"Well cadets, if we are going to shed our armor and swords, we better do it here," Tag said. The five of them took off their breastplates and shoulder and leg guards. They had already put their helmets in a bag. Cadet Bonar was so large that he had his own bag. He offered to let Tag put his armor in his bag and Tag accepted. That would make it easier for all of them to get to their armor quickly if needed.

As each cadet put his sword into the bag, he paused to give it one last look. They didn't like being without their swords. It put them at a great disadvantage. From the very moment they entered the academy, they were taught never to be without their swords. They felt naked without them. They often reached for it, touched it, and rested their hands on their swords. All of this had become second nature. If anything was going to give them away it was these kinds of habits.

The five of them made their way up the path to the Great Plateau. They walked a little way into the city and came upon a park. They surveyed the landscape and settled on hiding their gear under a little footbridge near the edge of the park. Marrcus and Ailith hid the gear while Bonar stood nearby obstructing anyone's view of the effort.

"Now what, Commander?" Cadet Kelila asked.

"First, and you're all going to like this, stop calling me 'commander' until I say otherwise. It's just Tag."

"Easy enough," Marrcus replied.

"Meet me at the Upper Theater at 6:30," Tag said.

"No sir, we think it would be best to stay together," Bonar said. Tag thought about it for a moment.

"I think you're right Bonar. Run ahead though to the crest and make sure the other nine squads make it on time and unnoticed. When you get there tell the cadets to hide their gear within a couple blocks of the park, or in the park. Then meet us over where the Polemmas and the Great Plateau meet," Tag ordered.

The Oracles And The Jewels

"Yes, sir," Bonar said as he started to salute, then catching himself he turned it into a scratch of his head. The four headed off to the Polemmas Tower crest. It was now 4:30.

"Blisse! Blisse Maia! Will you stop!" River shouted out in sheer frustration. About one hundred fifty yards separated the two girls, but Blisse was close enough to hear her sister's cry.

"What?" Blisse shouted back. All River could do was to wave her arm in a signaling motion beckoning Blisse to come to her. Blisse started to walk toward River. That caused River's arm to move more frantically. Blisse started to move a little faster. River's arm continued. Blisse started to run. That pleased River and she dropped her arm and took as many breaths as she could. In a few moments, Blisse was standing in front of her.

"Well, what?" Blisse said in her own frustrated style.

"Long story. You'll have to . . . wait to hear it with the others," River was still breathing very heavily, but was finally catching her breath. "We have to get to the crest by the Polemmas Plateau by 5:00."

"Nothing like giving us enough time. We're Demotics, not Adroits! Need I give you a lesson in anatomy?" Blisse said.

"Not now sister," River replied.

"Okay, let's go!" Blisse said as she accelerated up the slope. River followed and kept pace for most of the run. They raced over the Demotic Crest and dodged their way through the streets. Twenty minutes into the run, River was simply too tired to keep up the pace. A wide gap had opened between the two sisters before Blisse realized that River was no longer behind her. She turned and saw River walking so slowly through the street that most people were passing her.

"Go!" River yelled as she waved her arm and bent over to catch her breath. "Go to the crest!"

"And do what?" Blisse yelled back.

"Get there and wait! Tell them all to wait for me!" River shouted.

"Wait for who and tell who what?" Blisse responded.

"You'll see." At that River sat down. Blisse turned and ran. Blisse was out of sight in just a few moments. River got up and walked over to one of the sidewalk vendors. She pulled a couple of coins from her pocket and ordered a juice, "A lemon orange twist with a frosty foam on the top, please."

The Invisible Army

She sat down. "I don't think I'm cut out for this kind of thing." She took a couple of minutes to finish the drink. She thanked the vendor for his service, a common Entosian practice, and jogged off in the direction of the crest.

Blisse arrived at the crest five minutes before the hour. She arrived first and found no one there. "Oh great," she said, then in her sarcastic way continued. "Okay everyone! Stay put! Don't go anywhere! You can't go anywhere until my older sister, who seems to have lost her mind, gets here."

Blisse was standing with her back toward the city and her face toward the Polemmas Plateau. No sooner had she finished her little witticism when a voice from behind her said.

"River Kiernan's not the one talking to herself. Makes one wonder just who lost her mind." The voice was a familiar voice and it only took a second for Blisse to recognize it. Blisse turned and saw Tag, who had arrived with his cadets just a moment later, standing a few feet away with a big grin on his face. Blisse let out a little scream of joy and gave Tag a big hug and kiss on the cheek.

"Tag you look, you look great!" Blisse said. Tag had put on weight and muscle. His complexion had been darkened by the daily runs in the sun. He looked older and stronger than the last time she had seen him. She could feel the difference in his arms when she hugged him.

"But you also look like a civilian," she said. The other cadets looked at Tag to see if he was going to violate their orders; after all, they thought, he had just done that very thing in speaking to her.

"Well, they gave a couple of our squads leave until this Ashkelon thing blows over," Tag said as he was expected to say.

"I don't believe that for a minute Tag," she said. "Something is up. River just made me run here all the way from the Demotic Valley to tell you and everyone else who shows up to stay put until she gets here so she can tell you a long story that she wouldn't tell me."

"So much for a secret infiltration back into the city," Cadet Kelila said with a slight tone of jealousy. Blisse picked up on the sound, but Tag did not.

"It's okay, cadet. He is like a brother to me," Blisse said.

"It's not like that," Cadet Kelila replied quickly. "We are not suppose to be talking to anyone we know," Cadet Kelila replied.

"You aren't. You don't know me," Blisse answered.

The Oracles And The Jewels

"So what's going on?" Tag interrupted.

"I don't know. I only know that it is important for you all to wait here," Blisse said.

"That is going to be a problem soon. We are about to have a lot of people on this crest who aren't suppose to be seen together," Cadet Durus added.

"Comman . . . Tag, I am not okay with this," Bonar said.

"Bonar, something has changed. It is no accident that Blisse and River are here, or at least are suppose to be here. Something's up and we need to sit tight," Tag said.

"Look," Cadet Ailith said as he pointed down the plateau toward the Polemmas Tower, "a squad, minus one." It would be another couple of minutes before Tag and Blisse realized that it was Brenz's squad heading toward them.

"Blisse," Rieve shouted from behind the small group, "Look who I found all pooped out wandering the streets of Entos." Rieve was holding River's arm with his left hand and his conjuring staff in his right.

"Well, it looks like a reunion," Tag said.

"And I am still not comfortable with this. In fact, I am getting more and more uncomfortable every time a new friend of yours shows up," Bonar said as he stared into Tag's eyes.

"Cadet, relax. That's an order. I will sort this thing out in a few minutes. I take full responsibility in this matter," Tag said, regaining the voice he had when they were riding in the wagons.

Rieve and Tag shook hands. River gave Tag a more formal hug and kiss on the cheek than did her sister.

"It's Brenz," Blisse cried out. "It's Brenz and his squad."

"This is getting better all the time," Cadet Durus said.

Tag, Rieve, Blisse, and River walked to the peak of the crest and stood four-wide waiting for Brenz. Brenz broke from protocol and ran the last several yards to the place where the four stood. The four shook hands, hugged and kissed.

"I think you waited too long to tend to that cut Brenz. It's going to leave a scar," Blisse said as she peaked under the bandage that covered the cut.

"That's the idea," Tag replied. By the time they were done exchanging their greetings, the balance of Polemmas Squad One had caught up.

"This is sneaking into the city Commander Brenz?" Cadet Ansel said disapprovingly.

"I think I like this Polemmas cadet," Bonar spoke out.

The Invisible Army

"At ease, cadet," Brenz said. "If these four are here, something has changed."

"Are you two related?" Cadet Ailith asked.

"No, we're just good friends," Tag and Brenz replied in unison.

"This crest, cadets, is now our new staging area. What are the intervals between your squads?" Tag asked. Brenz was the commander of the entire Polemmas Cadet Unit, ninety-four in all. Like all the other cadet units, they had begun their training with a full complement of one hundred, but had lost six cadets in the first day's battle. The Hodia Army was superior in rank. As the ranking officer in the Hodia Cadet Unit, Tag outranked all the other officers in the cadet army. Although everyone understood that, they didn't like the fact that a cadet was changing that which had been handed down from full military personnel.

"Every five minutes two squads will enter the city," Brenz replied.

"Tell your squad to hold here and let's sort this thing out," Tag said.

Brenz did as ordered and the five members of the little fellowship walked into the narrow park that separated the city streets from the open field of the Polemmas Plateau. They moved far enough way so the cadets could not hear the conversation. Rieve quickly summarized his visit with General Witticor. River did the same. She explained the plan that she and Breille had created for getting the cadets into the Upper Theater unnoticed.

"Brenz, is there any way you can accelerate the pace? We have less than twenty minutes to get as many men in from the plateau as possible," Tag said.

Brenz looked around. He didn't see too many civilians in the area. Most had made their way down the slopes to their respective hamlets. "I can order Cadet Durus to blow the regrouping signal. That will bring anyone who hears it running. We run the risk of someone taking notice of it. They still have to hide their battle gear."

"They can hide their gear under the stage at the theater. The important thing is that we get to the building academy by 5:45," River said. The five of them agreed that the risk had to be taken. If questioned about it, they would simply modify their leave story. They returned to the crest where the waiting cadets were sitting down to rest. As Brenz and Tag approached, they stood up to receive their orders. While the little fellowship had been talking, Cadet Marrcus had

The Oracles And The Jewels

rejoined his Hodia squad and two squads from the Polemmas unit had arrived at the crest looking a little confused over what was taking place.

"Blow 'Regroup,' Cadet!" Brenz ordered.

Cadet Durus looked at the eighteen cadets already standing at the crest.

"A cadet commander should not have to repeat an order," Tag said with sternness in his eye.

Cadet Durus let loose with a blow that could be heard across the plateau. Some in the group looked toward the city to see if the sound of the horn had created any noticeable alarm. A few heads turned toward the crest, but their civilian clothing and their casual appearance seemed to set those who heard the horn at ease.

Within a few seconds, cadets started streaming in from the tall grass toward the crest. They still had their swords and armor under their tribal robes, but each had placed his hand on the butt of his sword ready to draw it from its scabbard.

"Blow the 'Regroup' every three minutes," Brenz ordered. By 5:25 they had about fifty cadets from the Polemmas Tower and the five cadets from Hodia gathered together at the crest.

"Listen up, cadets. There has been a slight change in your itinerary. You have twenty minutes to make it to the building academy across from the theater. You will see three large panels in the work yard on the north side of the building. Get there. There is a Procuron girl overseeing the panel project. She will be in the work yard, at least we think so. Take your instructions from her. Stay out of sight and do as you're instructed. You will be given additional orders once you are there. Break up and take different streets. Adroits and Aradians, take the long way around and leave the short routes to the others. Hodia cadets, if you see any of our own, bring them with you. We need all the help we can get."

"Commander . . ." Bonar said as he started to interrupt. But Tag continued his address.

"Cadets, General Witticor is expecting all of you to follow orders accordingly and to be at the theater at 7:00," Tag barked. "Do your best to keep your swords and armor hidden. You can stow them under the stage in the Upper Theater when you get there. Now get to the building academy and don't give yourselves away!"

Nearly fifty cadets ran across the narrow park between the crest and the first paved street of Entos. In just a few

The Invisible Army

moments they scattered into the various streets and avenues. Entos was a large enough city. Its downtown area was twelve blocks from north to south and eighteen blocks from east to west. A few hundred young Entosians could go unnoticed as long as they stayed in small groups and didn't draw attention to themselves.

Entos was large enough for any Entosian to go unnoticed, but it was also small enough that every Entosian from the time of his youth knew his way around the city. The Performing Arts Building was familiar to all Entosians. Entosians of every kind loved the performing arts. They loved music, plays, and storytelling. They had been in the theaters of the Performing Arts for citywide celebrations and tribal ceremonies. The average Entosian made it to the theater four times a year so every cadet knew exactly where he or she was supposed to be.

Rieve, Blisse, River, Tag, and Brenz began their walk back into the city. They took the short distance between the crest and the building academy. They walked at a brisk pace. River was glad it was a walk.

"So you're a hero now," Tag said.

"No. I am not a hero. Rieve is. I felt a little dishonest taking credit for sounding the alarm," Brenz admitted. "I felt like an actor pretending to be something I am not."

"So you're not a real hero," Tag said with a certain amount of joy in his face.

"Sure he is," Blisse said. "Look at his face."

"I wish I were what they said I am, but I felt guilty when they announced the citation and promoted me to commander," Brenz said.

"How did you explain the fact that you knew the attack was coming?" Rieve asked with a big smile. The five of them tried to walk together but the deeper they got into the city, the more difficult it was to stay together. They had to dodge traffic and had to constantly look around to make sure they stayed together. Each time the group was forced to separate, they fell silent and picked up right where the conversation left off once they reunited five abreast.

"I told them that I saw a winged creature with a scout mounted on it and that the rest was instinct," Brenz explained.

"That was the best you could do?" Rieve asked.

"I suppose I could have told them that a friend of mine, an apprentice priest conjuror sent one of his Academy

The Oracles And The Jewels

friends sixty leagues in six hours to tell me that an Ashkelon attack was imminent," Brenz answered.
"Would you two mind letting the rest of us in on the true story?" Tag said.
"All I did was follow Rieve's lead. He sent an Aradian to my camp to tell me Ashkelon was coming. By the way, did your friend make it back safely?" Brenz asked.
"Yes, he did. I think he is still sleeping." By now Brenz and Rieve were having a little fun with the members of their fellowship. They spoke slowly and added extraneous material.
"All I did was improvise and do what I was trained to do. Fight. For what it's worth Tag, the only reason I could fight as well as I did, was because they kept giving me you as an opponent," Brenz paused. "Still we lost six of our cadets and one of them belonged to my unit," Brenz looked down at the ground as he spoke, then lifted his head and continued, "Now I want to know how you knew."
"I wish I could say that my powers have developed to the point where I can see the future. But it was the Headmaster who saw the attack. He told me what to do. I simply did what he told me to do," Rieve answered.
"So here's an idea," River began, "Why not let all of Entos know that it was the Headmaster who saved the day? How could the City Fathers and the Academy faculty keep him out of his office then?"
"The main battle has not yet come. The Headmaster should probably remain hidden until that battle comes," Rieve answered.
"So if the main battle is yet to come, why are we walking away from the place where Ashkelon's main force will likely attack?" Tag asked.
"According to the Headmaster, Ashkelon will bring his army against the towers and walls, but that the most important battle will be elsewhere," Rieve said.
"Well, tell me where and I will be there." Tag said.
"That is still the unknown variable. For now we take one step at a time," Rieve said.
"River Kiernan, what exactly is up ahead?" Tag asked.
"The building academy has been working on a prototype moveable wall," she started to explain when Tag interrupted.
"We've all heard about that wall. It's a dumb idea. It will collapse and most likely on top of Entosians. The military doesn't like the wall. It was an idea thought up by City

The Invisible Army

Fathers who don't have the confidence they ought to have in the foot soldier."

"Well Tag, that wall is going to make three hundred fifty cadets disappear," River replied. "Right now Breille is hard at work trying to figure out exactly how we are going to relocate that wall without the entire faculty of the building academy noticing."

"What I don't understand is what am I doing here." Blisse said. She was starting to feel like a fifth wheel. It was clear enough to see how River was involved. The general needed the theater. Breille was being called upon to help hide the cadets. "It is obvious why River, Breille, Tag, and Brenz are supposed to be in the theater. But why did the general invite Rieve and me?"

"Every unit needs a conjuror and a healer or two if it is going to be a truly effective fighting unit," Tag said.

"That would mean that the general thinks there is a real possibility that we are going to see action," Brenz said as he dodged an old Fortian who had suddenly come to a stop in front of the five. Brenz bumped into the old man who let out a bit of a growl. "My apologies," Brenz said as he quickened his pace to rejoin the group which had continued unimpeded.

The little fellowship was now just six blocks away from The Academy of the Building Arts. They slowed down and started looking around for other cadets. Out of the corner of his eye, Tag saw one of his cadet squads at a vendor's juice stand. "Wait here," he told the others while he trotted across the street. His squad saw him coming, but pretended not to notice until he spoke with them.

"Fall in cadets. Stay about twenty feet behind me," he ordered. Tag turned and ran back to the fellowship. "We have more help. Keep walking," The squad members swallowed their newly purchased drinks, made their way across the street, and did as instructed.

The Academy of the Building Arts

Breille had spent the last ninety minutes directing the students under her supervision to take out the large hinge pins that tied the panels together. After the large hinges were removed, she sent the students home for the evening. She also had the braces and legs put on the three panels which would enable them to stand upright in the middle of the street. What she hadn't figured out was how she was

The Oracles And The Jewels

going to move these panels without the faculty noticing the seventy-five cadets carrying the panels away.

Breille looked at the clock. It was 5:35. In a few minutes River would arrive with her small army. Breille looked around the lobby. From the lobby windows all three panels were clearly visible through the six large windows that faced the work yard. The sun was starting to set, but there was still enough light to see the whole work yard. Breille started pacing back and forth as she considered the problem. She had to make the panels disappear without the faculty seeing them disappear. Back and forth she went, thinking and talking and talking and thinking.

"How? How?" she said out loud as she turned toward the building. Each time she turned toward to the west and the setting sun to trace her previous steps, the glare of the setting sun struck the metallic silver facade of the academy's exterior wall. The answer to her problem had been hitting her in the face all the time. "That's how!" she exclaimed.

She looked around and noticed small groups of young men and women collecting in the doorways, alleys, and on the street corners. She began systematically pointing to each group and then pointed to their respective destinations. She saw the little fellowship coming down the street and signaled to them. Five by five the cadets took up their positions behind the first panel and opposite the big glass windows.

"Hello, Breille," Tag said. "The faculty is still here. I hope you have this all figured out."

"Who needs conjurors to make things disappear?" Breille said. "Behold the power of the ordinary." She had directed twenty-five cadets to stand at the east end of the first panel. She walked over to the cadets with a posture of supreme confidence. "Lift, cadets!" she ordered as if she were their commanding officer. The panel was heavier than they thought it was going to be. The east end of the panel only rose just a few inches. "We are going to have to do better than that, cadets!" she shouted. As the twenty-five struggled to move the wall, more cadets joined the effort. After a third try they managed to raise the east end of the panel a few feet and began to turn the end of the panel toward the south and around the north east corner of the building.

"Now very slowly and very smoothly, take a step forward cadets." They tried, but nothing happened. "Another half step," Breille said as she stepped back to get a better

The Invisible Army

view of their progress or lack thereof. The second half step caused the silver flat surface at the end of the panel to catch the light of the setting sun and reflect it as if a mirror into the top two stories of the building academy.

"Stop!" Breille snapped. They did as instructed. "Now for the hard part," she said, "Grab the legs and the braces and tilt the wall forward. They did and the reflexed light moved its way down the side of the building until it came to a stop at the first floor. The light spilled through the windows and into the offices on the first floor and into the main lobby. "Hold it right there. Don't move!" Breille disappeared around the wall and walked into the main entrance of the front lobby. It was working. The light was temporarily blinding the faculty members whose desks and tables faced the work yard. Some of the Entosians inside had resorted to holding their hands over their eyes in an effort to block the light. Breille walked across the lobby in front of the windows.

"Breille is that you?" President Kuchen called out.

"Yes, sir," she replied with a tone of innocence.

"Those walls must have been moved a bit today. Could you draw the blinds on those windows?"

"Yes, Sir," Breille said.

"Thank you. It's late, young lady, why don't you head home?" President Kuchen suggested. Breille didn't expect that. An alibi, she thought.

"Thanks, President Kuchen. I am a little tired," she added as she released the blinds. They fell one by one and just in time. The glare was starting to fade. Either the cadets had moved or the sun was moving. She headed outside before the president could change his mind.

By now there were sixty cadets behind the panel. Breille moved quickly. It was 6:35 and a crowd was starting to gather in front of the Performing Arts Building.

"There's not enough," Breille said turning first to Tag, then to Rieve.

"Just do it!" Rieve said as he looked at the setting sun. "Blisse and River stand back here, behind me."

Brenz and Tag repeated Breille's orders. The first panel rose slowly from the ground, but too slowly. It was obvious they would not be able to carry even the first panel into place without frequent rests or another sixty cadets. The panels were heavier than they had first appeared to the cadets.

"*Kuzmonda, kuzmonda, kundere!*" Rieve lifted his conjuring staff and walked along the side of the cadets. Repeating the incantation and touching the sides and backs

The Oracles And The Jewels

of the cadets. With each touch of the staff the cadet straightened and the panel rose higher off the ground. With the last touch on the back of a Pithosian who stood at the end of the line, the panel surged forward, down the length of the academy building, around the back and was now heading toward the street. Blisse and River ran in front of the panel and into the street to clear a path. The large panel, twenty-five feet tall and one hundred feet long, startled the Entosians in the street as it was carried it along the Performing Arts Building and toward the busy Entosian streets.

"What's that?" a small Kilposian boy asked his father as a panel seemingly floated across their path. Blisse heard the little boy's question and responded.

"It's the moveable wall, well more specifically, it is a panel for a moveable wall for the army. It's being field-tested. Thank you for your cooperation." River heard the explanation and repeated it to another group of curious onlookers, who passed the information on to those standing behind them in the street.

The process was repeated at the next intersection. Breille, concealed behind the panel, directed the cadets as they turned the corner. Even with Rieve's little bit of conjuring, it took almost ten minutes for the cadets to move the panel a block and a half. But when they reached the south entrance to the Upper Theater, Breille had the leading edge of the panel placed against the exterior wall of the Performing Arts building and directed the back edge to be placed toward the middle of the street. She ordered the cadets to lower the wall to the ground and then the legs and supporting braces were locked into place. It worked. The wall stood firmly and securely.

The crowd standing in front of the Main Theater entrance watched with great interest. The panel seemed to move by itself. River was a familiar face around the theater so she had disappeared behind the wall, leaving Blisse to spread the disinformation. Again, Blisse explained to a few of the curious onlookers waiting to enter the theater that this was all part of the war effort – a field test, and thanked the people for their cooperation, adding this time that the military would appreciate it if the crowd would pretend as if the whole thing hadn't happened. "It's a secrecy thing," she told them. "Pass the word," and they did.

The cadets turned, and ran back to the work yard and took their positions at the second panel. Breille returned with

The Invisible Army

them and picked up two of the large hinges so she could tie the two panels together. That would give added strength and safety.

"Hey, conjuror," Tag called out as he took hold of one of the panel's ribs. "Do you think you could do that mumbling thing again. This time before we strain ourselves lifting this blasted wall."

"*Kuzmonda, kuzmonda, kundere!*" Rieve mumbled as he repeated the process of touching each cadet on their sides and backs. River, Blisse, and Breille repeated their efforts as well. They set the second wall in place and Breille slid the two large hinge pins in their sockets securing the two panels together and creating a wall now twenty-five feet high and two hundred long. It was a giant metal curtain which obstructed the view of the theatergoers and of those using the south street. The final panel would mirror the first and obstruct the view of anyone approaching from the west.

By 6:50 all three panels were securely in place. Breille left an opening between the back end of the third panel and the exterior wall large enough for a Pithosian to enter. While Breille was putting the finishing touches on the wall, River unlocked the south door to the Upper Theater and went inside. She turned on the lights in the lobby, the stairwell, and in the theater. She also opened the storage compartments under the stage.

In a few minutes the cadets were making their way into the building. Those who had not already stowed their battle gear were doing so under the stage. By 6:52, sixty to seventy cadets were seated in the theater, many with their eyes closed, resting from their labor. The whole project had begun on an uncertain footing, but once the first panel was put in place, everything came together like clock work.

Tag and Brenz stayed outside. Tag took up his position by the entryway between the panel and the exterior wall of the Performing Arts Building. Brenz went to the opposite corner of the intersection.

As squads appeared Brenz and Tag directed each squad to enter the theater through the path created by the panels. One group of cadets after another made their way down the path and spoke the password, "Youthful Enterprise." By 6:55 there was a steady stream of squads slipping their way between the panels and the wall of the building. At 6:59 a Fortian dressed in a traditional Fortian robe and carrying large rolled-up papers under his right arm approached the entryway.

The Oracles And The Jewels

"Excuse me, sir," Tag said. "You will have to go around. The Upper Theater is closed for the evening and the engineers are still securing and testing this wall." The man smiled but hesitated to speak. "It's a field test sir, conducted by the building academy. You can't come in here. It's for your own safety."

"Cadet, who do you think put all this together? What's your name?" General Witticor asked. When he spoke Tag recognized the voice.

"Cadet Thayer Taggert, sir!" he answered as he saluted the general. "I'm sorry. I have never seen you in civilian robes before, sir."

"Neither have my wife and children. Don't salute me, cadet. This is an undercover operation. You're the commander of the Hodia cadets aren't you, son?"

"Yes, sir."

"I have read some good reports about you. I am looking forward to seeing you handle a sword. I hear you're one of the fastest Demotics we have ever had." The general stepped around the corner to look down the street along the bright silver wall. "Very clever. I don't want to know how you all did this, or how you're going to undo this, but it's very clever. I commend you all."

"The credit belongs to Breille Clarrice, the Procuron, and River Kiernan, the Demotic," Tag replied.

"Very well. Carry on. I will see you inside on the stage. I want all the commanders on the stage before we start," the general said as he disappeared behind the wall.

"Yes, sir," Tag replied. More cadets arrived, each uttering the password.

Colonel Fornoff approached from the west side of the building. He had bought a ticket for the performance in the Main Theater. A uniformed colonel standing in line holding a ticket and waiting to get in to see a performance would not attract undue attention. The colonel arrived at the front of the building at 6:50. The theater had opened the doors at 6:30 and the patrons were making their way through the ticket takers. The colonel had been staring at the wall while he waited in line. He stepped out of line, excusing himself as he made his way upstream. He politely explained that his companion was late and he would need to wait for her.

Eventually he made his way down the street along the large silver wall until he found the entrance where Tag was posted. It was now 6:55 and time for Brenz and Tag to enter the theater. Brenz walked across the street to the entryway.

The Invisible Army

The stream of cadets had become a trickle. The trickle came to a stop. Brenz and Tag took one last look around. That's when they saw the colonel.

"Fine job cadets," the colonel said.

"Thank you, sir," they both replied. "Team effort," Tag added.

"Let's get inside," the colonel said.

"Yes, sir," they answered. They followed the colonel down the path and along the wall.

The colonel looked over the support system and the mechanics of the wall. "They won't work in battle, but it will take a collapse to convince the paper pushers. We will have to kill a few Entosians before they come to that conclusion. I will take well-trained and disciplined warriors with sticks over mechanical gimmicks any day."

The three were met at the door by River. After they entered, she looked down the pathway. It was empty. She locked the door and turned off the lobby lights. She did the same when the colonel, Brenz, and Tag reached the top of the stairs.

Tag and Brenz walked onto the stage and sat down on two empty chairs, next to the commanders from the Neggen and Krattos Units. The commander of the Neggen cadets was named Kyra. She was one of the only female commanders ever selected. She was an Adroitian. The commander of the Krattos Cadets was a Pithosian named Tabor. The chairs faced stage left. Opposite the commanders Rieve, Blisse, and Breille sat looking out of place. There was an open seat next to them. A few seconds after Tag and Brenz took their seats, River took the final chair. Also on the stage was a large board upon which notes and papers could be posted and a table.

The general and the colonel made their entrance onto the stage. The general had taken off his robe, under which he had concealed his full parade uniform. Immediately, the entire assembly stood at attention and saluted. The colonel and the general returned the salute. The general placed the papers he had brought on a table that he had River place on the stage upon their arrival.

"As you were, cadets. Please be seated," the general began. "I am General Witticor and as you know this is Colonel Fornoff. We have brought you back to the city and to this theater because the survival of Entos may rest on your young shoulders. You are here because the City Fathers have chosen to allocate all our military resources to two lines

The Oracles And The Jewels

of defense." The general paused and debated within his own mind as to how much to say about the actions of the City Fathers. He decided to continue without further comment.

"There is little doubt that King Ashkelon will attack the eastern walls, in all likelihood on the Eighth Day or shortly thereafter. We believe that we can hold Ashkelon's main force at the walls and towers. We also believe that King Ashkelon will open up a second front of attack by inserting large numbers of his best fighters inside the walls of Entos by the use of thousands of enormous winged creatures. We have taken steps to repel this threat as well. These two attacks alone will constitute the largest and most serious threat from Ashkelon that Entos has seen in more than five hundred years.

"You have been brought to the city to protect three potential targets. The Oracles and the Jewels in The Great Chamber, the priests and conjurors associated with The Academy of Theological Sciences and Ancient Conjuring Arts, and the citizens and city of Entos. Those are your three objectives and they are to be assigned priority in that specific order.

"Without the Oracles and the Jewels, the Land of Entos will cease to be and all Entosians, including you, will be transmuted into the creatures our ancient ancestors once were. Without a sufficient number of priests and conjurors, Entosians will cease to function as Entosians, each will do what is right in his own eyes, and Entos will die a slow but certain death. The wisdom of the ages has been handed down by each generation of priests and conjurors. Through them the Oracles and the Jewels preserve our collective ability to rightly understand, use, and speak the Oracles. If they are destroyed, we will be lost. The wisdom and strength of Entos lies in the teachers and conjurors. Because it is through them that the Oracles speak and the Jewels minister. Wisdom and strength do not reside within the good intentions and creativity of our own hearts and imaginations. Wisdom and strength certainly do not reside in the other academies.

"We can always write new plays and music. We can create new institutions of governance. We can rebuild that which Ashkelon's armies tear down. We cannot replace the Oracles. The Giver entrusted us with them until the return of the King. Nor can we manufacture the collective wisdom that has been handed down in The Academy of Theological Sciences and Ancient Conjuring Arts for more than five

The Invisible Army

thousand years. Without the priests and the conjurors our warriors will not be able to hold back the evil armies of Ashkelon.

"These two targets must be protected at all costs. If these are protected and secured, you are to do all that you can do to protect the lives of your fellow Entosians. This means if you are confronted with the choice of saving your parents, your brother or sister, or your beloved soul mate, or protecting the faculty of the Academy and the Oracles and Jewels, the latter is to be protected and the former commended into the hands of the King. Entosians can be replaced through the regular mating ritual of other Entosians. Cadets and warriors are also replaced in the same manner.

"Are we clear on these three objectives cadets?" the general shouted. The cadets, all three hundred fifty replied in one voice, "sir, yes sir!"

"Do not be fooled by the ordinariness of your surroundings. Things are not as they seem here in Entos. Ashkelon has a few surprises for us. But we have some of our own. You are one of those surprises.

"In a few days, perhaps more, you will hear of the great battle being fought at the walls. You will hear of the battles and skirmishes on the plateaus and in the valleys. When you hear of them, you will long to be with your fellow warriors. You will doubt whether your mission here in Entos is a worthy one because, while your comrades fight from morning to night, you will be walking these streets in ordinary tribal robes.

"You are here because this is exactly where Entos needs you to be. You will be my eyes and ears in Entos. You will spend your days walking the streets and going to the museums and parks. Each day your squad will return to The Academy for the Ancient Warring Arts where Colonel Fornoff will continue your military training. He will make sure that your skills remain sharp. He will work with you. Hand - picked conjurors will work with you, too, to improve your skills. He will brief you each day on where and what you are to do. You will brief him on any unusual activities you notice throughout your day.

"Remember, cadets, you are not a police force. You are not to be preoccupied helping Pithosian old ladies across the street. You are not to rescue critters from the trees. You are not to get involved in any activity that will draw undue attention to your presence in this city. The City Fathers do

The Oracles And The Jewels

not know you are here. No one outside this room knows you are here. It is to stay that way.

"At night some of you will sleep at the Academy. Others will sleep in the woods and fields near the city. Others will sleep in buildings that we know will be empty and safe. The colonel has worked all these details out and your respective commander will receive your daily assignments from him at the end of each day.

"Cadets, you are a military force, that I pray will not be called upon to fight. But if the battle horn blows, you are not to hesitate. The daggers are the best we can do for now. They are intended to provide you with a basic level of protection. The colonel will spend some more time training you in its use. However, cadets, if the horn blows, shed your tribal robes, put on your armor, grab your weapons, and come running. If you are confused, fight those who fight your fellow cadets, no matter who they are or who they appear to be.

"I will now turn you over to the colonel for your first briefing and your assignments for the next twenty-four hours." The general stepped aside and to the back of the stage.

"You know your own commanders," the colonel began, "learn the faces of the other four. Behind me and to my left I will now introduce you to four other individuals who you would do well to remember. They are specialists in their own right and they will prove very helpful before this war is over.

"First, Conjuror Rieve Waynwright, hand-picked by the Headmaster himself. He is going to put together a team of conjurors who will provide any assistance you need, both in battle and out." Rieve stood and faced the cadets. As he looked out over the theater, he hid his surprise at the announcement.

"Next is Blisse Maia, she attends The Academy of Healing Arts. She, likewise, will put together a small team of healers who will stand at the ready in the event that the battle comes." Blisse rose and took her place next to Rieve. She did not do as well at hiding her surprise.

"Breille Clarrice is the young Procuron whom many of you have already met. She is a builder and engineer. If you need anything in the way of repairs, special armaments, a ladder, bridge, or a three hundred foot wall at a moment's notice, you can find her at The Academy of the Building Arts." Breille stood next to Blisse.

The Invisible Army

"Finally, River Kiernan. Her speciality is the Liberal Arts and Performing Arts. For now she will be known to you as an intelligence and procurement officer. If you have a need or a problem she is going to take care of it for you." River stood next to the other three. River had been wondering how she fit into the grand plan. After hearing the introduction of Rieve and Blisse, she thought her role would be made more clear. The introduction did not clear up the matter and she felt a little uncomfortable standing among such a specialized and elite group. She was more of a general practitioner of knowledge and resourcefulness, but she didn't consider those qualities particularly useful for covert operations.

"These four civilians will become increasingly important to our operations as time goes on. I expect you all to show them the utmost respect and to protect them." River was now standing closest to the colonel. The colonel walked over to the table and took the documents the general had brought in. He handed two of the rolled-up pieces of paper to River and asked if she and Breille could post them on the board. They did as asked, while Rieve and Blisse returned to their seats. The two girls unrolled the papers. One of the papers was a map of Entos and the other a map of The Great Chamber and the Theological Academy.

"Cadets, we have created a plan to provide security for the key installations of the city day and night, eight days a week. As you can see from these maps, we intend to provide security for The Great Chamber, specifically to make sure the Oracles and the Jewels remain where the Giver left them. The Hodia cadets are assigned this task, with help from the Polemmas cadets, who will be right next door providing protection for The Academy of Theological Sciences and Ancient Conjuring Arts.

"Polemmas you will make sure that the priests, conjurors, and professors are protected in the event that Ashkelon achieves penetration. The City Fathers have their own guard, so city hall is not your concern, unless otherwise directed in the heat of battle.

"Krattos will patrol the northern half of the city and the hamlets to the north. Neggen you will take the southern half and the hamlets near the city. We have regular warriors about twenty leagues out from the city. In the event of an attack this close to The Great Chamber, Krattos and Neggen will provide our first line of defense. Polemmas and Hodia are our last and final line of defense. Between our regular forces and you, we have set up four lines. The first is at the

The Oracles And The Jewels

wall between Hodia and Polemmas towers. The second is in the Demotic Valley. The third is on the edge of the city. The fourth is around The Great Chamber and at the Academy. I wish we could say that we were confident that this would be enough, but the general and I have reason to believe it might not be. General, would you like to say more about that at this time?" the colonel asked.

"I am only prepared to tell you that we have intelligence reports that indicate Ashkelon has some significant surprises in store for us and we need you all to be on the alert and at your very best. You may have to fight the best of the best. You will also need to trust the instincts of your commanders."

"Thank you, general," the colonel said. "Cadets, I am giving your commanders your duty schedule. There are your patrol rotations, your assignments, and your training schedule." The colonel explained the basic outline of their day. A few squads from each unit would train together for two hours each day. In this way no area would be left unguarded. Squads from the Hodia and Polemmas units would train together. Squads from the Neggen and Krattos units would spar together. Every two hours throughout the day one-quarter of each unit would be relieved of patrol duty to report for training. After explaining to the cadets the basic outline of their duties the colonel asked, "Are there any questions?"

"Yes, sir," Cadet Kyra said as she rose to attention on the stage behind the colonel. "Permission to speak, Colonel Fornoff."

"Granted, cadet."

"Sir, how long will this duty last?" she asked.

"For the foreseeable future or until you're dead . . . whichever comes first. Any other questions?" No one dared ask another. The colonel turned to Breille and asked, "Miss Breille Clarrice, I assume these walls of yours must be returned this evening."

"Yes, sir."

"Cadets there are three panels. Those who are not scheduled for the first shift of patrol will help Miss Breille Clarrice return these walls. That should give you nearly three hundred cadets to help out. Once you're done helping with that task, take the time to stow your gear in locations near your assigned sectors and bed down for the night. Bed down in a place where you won't be causing any trouble. But

The Invisible Army

bed down near your sector. That is it for the evening, cadets. If you must fight, fight well to the glory of Entos. Dismissed!"

The cadets stood at attention and saluted. The colonel and general marched from the stage. River followed the two of them, unlocked the doors to the stairwell, turned on the lights, and did the same in the lobby. The general and colonel thanked her for her service and assured her they would be calling upon her again and soon.

A few moments later, Breille came down the stairs. Following behind her were nearly three hundred cadets in single file.

"Don't lock the door; some of us will be back in a few minutes," Breille said as she picked up the hammer she had left in the lobby. River stepped outside and held the door open as the cadets paraded by. As the cadets took their place next to the wall, Breille climbed the interior of the wall where the first two panels were connected by two large hinges. As soon as the first pins were removed the first of the three panels was freed. "Lift and forward!" Breille ordered. The first panel began moving. She ran to the second set of hinges and did the same. "Lift and forward!" she ordered again, this time looking to the cadets at the two remaining panels. Within a couple of minutes all three panels were making their way back to the work yard. It was dark out now, but the streets of Entos were always well lit. The three moons and the street lights on each corner made it easy for the cadets to find their way. Those same lights also made it easy for anyone walking the streets to see the panels floating down the streets and around the corner. By this time there were only a few people in the street. The performance in the Main Theater had not yet concluded.

Suddenly Blisse came running down the stairs and out into the street. By the time she made her way into the street the first two panels had made the turn and the third was about to do the same. Blisse overtook the last two panels easily and came to a stop in the street that ran along the south side of the building academy's building.

"Excuse us," she said to a few onlookers. "This is a field test of the walls. We appreciate your cooperation." The explanation had worked before, she thought it would again. She was wrong.

"Excuse me young lady. Who are you and what are you doing with those panels?" the Procuron said in a demanding voice.

The Oracles And The Jewels

The tone startled Blisse. "Excuse me, sir. Who are you that we should tell you? This test is strictly on a need-to-know basis."

"I am President Kuchen. The president of this academy and the man responsible for that wall. I need to know." The revelation shocked Blisse, but she continued nonetheless.

"Well sir, I thought someone would have sent you the memo. Are you sure you needed to be informed? You know how the military is, sir."

"I should have been informed! Now tell me who is in charge here!" President Kuchen started to step around Blisse.

"Careful, sir. One of those panels has fallen twice today. They are very unstable when moved in this way."

"Of course they're unstable young lady. We haven't attached the systems to move them yet."

"Well, that explains everything. You know these walls are getting a very bad write up. I wouldn't interfere at this point, sir."

"Young lady, get out of my way!" the president demanded.

"Okay sir, but Colonel Hafferling is going to be very upset."

"Colonel Hafferling. I never heard of a Colonel Hafferling," the president said. Blisse hadn't either. She made up the name in order to buy Breille and the cadets more time. By now River had made her way into the street. She was in earshot behind President Kuchen. She heard everything and knew what Blisse was attempting to do. River turned and ran in the other direction toward the east end of the work yard.

"Tell me where can I find him," the President asked.

"I don't know," Blisse answered.

"What does he look like? What tribe is he from?" President Kuchen asked.

"I don't know that either, sir."

"Is he one of those Fortians? I bet he's one of those Fortians. They are always charging forward and pushing others around," Kuchen said as he looked around to see if he could spot a Fortian general.

"Yes, sir. You know how strong-headed they are about their weapon systems," Blisse said.

"You're right about that, young lady. By the way, who are you?"

The Invisible Army

"Sir, all I know is that I got the same memo everyone else got. I saw your name on the memo too, sir. I was simply assigned to traffic control and safety. That's all I know," Blisse said. The trick worked.

"Memo. I don't remember any such memo," the President answered. "And I read all my memos."

"Well sir, you must be very busy with all that your academy has in development. The memo probably got lost in the volumes of paperwork in your office. Honestly sir, since this field test is top secret, I don't think we should be debating this matter in the street."

By now the panels had been placed back in the courtyard exactly as they were. Breille was replacing the hinges when River ran into the courtyard. "Get out of here! President Kuchen is coming!" Some of the cadets started to head back in the direction from whence they came. "No! Not that way! That way! And that way!" She pointed to the right and behind her as three cadets disappeared down every alley and street heading away from the president. Breille jumped down from the wall and she and River headed back toward the theater.

"You're right about that, young lady, now follow me. I am going to get to the bottom of this right now." Blisse saw River and Breille run across the street behind the back of the president.

"Yes, sir. After you," Blisse said. President Kuchen marched around the corner and along the back of the west wall of the Academy. He mumbled and grumbled all the way. Blisse followed, but she slowed each step until there was a sufficiently large gap between the two. Then she quickly and quietly ran down back toward the lobby of the Upper Theater.

The president turned the corner expecting to find several hundred military personnel standing behind the wall. "Where is Colonel Hafferling?" he shouted to absolutely no one. Stunned he stopped dead in his tracks. But his shout was so loud he disturbed two faculty members who had been working in their office. They did not understand the words, but they recognized the voice. They walked quickly into the work yard, fearing some kind of accident. Instead, they found the president walking back and forth from one side of the wall to the other looking to see if anyone was attempting to conceal themselves.

"President Kuchen," one of the professors said, "are you all right?"

The Oracles And The Jewels

"Did you see them?" he shouted.

"Who?" Professor Ashter asked.

"The warriors and that colonel!"

"We didn't see anything," Professor Enoss replied.

"They moved the wall! A field test, she said!"

"Moved the wall? That would take an army," Professor Ashter said.

"Young lady," the president shouted as he turned around expecting to find Blisse. He paused in a moment of surprise. She was gone. President Kuchen turned three hundred sixty degrees, stopping of course where he had started. "Where did she go?" he shouted.

"Who?" Professor Enoss asked.

"The girl in charge of traffic control! Don't tell me you didn't see her either."

"Sorry, we didn't," Professor Ashter answered.

"They were running around in the streets with our panels and no one but me saw them," he said placing his hands on his hips.

"President Kuchen. We have been working here all night and to the best of our knowledge those panels didn't move an inch. They would have had to go right past our office windows." Professor Ashter explained. "We didn't see them."

"We've all been working pretty hard trying to make these impossible deadlines, sir," Professor Enoss commented.

"Maybe you just need to go home and get a good night's sleep," Professor Ashter added.

"I agree with Professor Ashter, sir. It would be best if you just took the rest of the night off. Tomorrow is the field test. You need to be ready. You've been working pretty hard. After we get the lift system and wheels installed and the field test behind us, you'll feel better," Professor Enoss said.

"So you don't believe me! Gentlemen, I will get to the bottom of this," President Kuchen turned and left the work yard in search of Blisse, but she was nowhere to be found.

Professors Ashter and Enoss returned to their office, each with a large smile on his face. They sat down. Professor Enoss pulled from his desk a bottle of spirited juice.

"That General Witticor knows good juice when he sees it, doesn't he?" Professor Enoss said as he wiped the dust from the bottle.

The Invisible Army

"I was about to tell the general that we'd go along with the plan just for the fun of it. President Kuchen has been a real pain lately. But when the general sent this bottle over this afternoon, I just couldn't return it." The two settled into their chairs, opened the bottle, and poured its contents into their glasses. "I wonder what he needed those panels for anyway."

"I don't know and a few more drinks of this and I won't care either," Professor Enoss laughed as he took his first sip of the drink.

The Upper Theater

River and Breille had made it back to the lobby of the Upper Theater. A few of the cadets had also returned to the Upper Theater. By the time Blisse was able to return, the audience from the performance in the Main Theater was letting out and the streets around the Performing Arts Building were starting to fill up. It was easy for Blisse to lose herself in the crowd. River and Breille had the lobby lights off and stood at the door waiting eagerly and anxiously for Blisse's return.

"Do you think she is all right?" Breille asked.

"Sure she is. Blisse can talk her way out of anything," River said trying to hide her own anxiety.

"Even if she does get away, President Kuchen will be able to recognize her pretty easily," Breille said.

"That can be dealt with easily enough. Just a change to the hair. A little bit of makeup and he wouldn't be able to recognize her even if she was the only one in a lineup. He, after all, is a male Procuron."

"I see your point," Breille replied.

"And I see Blisse. She's right over there," River said. They both waited for Blisse as she made her way through the crowd. They looked around to make sure that no one was following her. Blisse reached the door just as River unlocked it. Blisse slipped in unnoticed from the street and River locked the door behind them.

"I can't wait to hear how you talked yourself out of this one!" River said.

"It wasn't easy," Blisse answered.

"Did the president get your name?" Breille asked.

"The only name he got was Colonel Hafferling's name."

"Blisse, who is Colonel Hafferling?" Breille asked.

The Oracles And The Jewels

"Exactly, who is Colonel Hafferling and what did he want with those walls?" Blisse said with a giggle.

"Don't forget, you were dealing with a Procuron. Procurons, by nature don't like questions without answers," Breille said.

"In that case, I sure hope there is no such person as Colonel Hafferling," River replied. "Let's get upstairs and see if there is anything else for which we are needed."

The three walked upstairs and onto the stage. The four commanders were working out some of the details of the next twenty four hours. Each commander was meeting with their respective squad leaders.

Commander Kyra was meeting with four squads, twenty cadets from Neggen. They were responsible for patrolling the southern approach to the city by night. Commander Tabor, of Krattos, was also meeting with his four squads, twenty cadets in all, to discuss the night patrol of the northern approach. While Neggen and Krattos had a much larger area to patrol, it was an easier task in some respects. A hundred cadets robed in tribal attire would not make a noticeable difference in the traffic patterns flowing in and out of the city during the course of an average day. But the cadets from Hodia and Polemmas would need to be careful not to put too many unusual faces in one place at the same time.

Brenz assigned three squads, fifteen cadets from Polemmas, for the night to patrol the campus and streets around The Academy of Theological Sciences and Ancient Conjuring Arts. Tag assigned only one squad, five cadets to watch over The Great Chamber. As each commander finished the briefing, the squads involved left the Upper Theater under the cover of night. River escorted each group down the stairwell and opened the front door. As each group departed into the night, River bade them farewell in the customary fashion. "If you must fight, fight well and to the glory of Entos."

After all the briefings were finished and all the squads departed, River returned to the Upper Theater. By now there were only the four commanders and their respective squads left, nineteen cadets in all, along with Rieve, Blisse, Breille, and River.

"Breille," Tag said. "I have drawn up a couple of ideas for a pair of new defensive weapons." Tag handed Breille two drawings and instructions. Breille looked at them for a moment and said, "Very clever."

The Invisible Army

"Do you think they will work?" Tag asked.

"If they are balanced right, they should," she assured him.

"If you can have them made out of the proper metal, they might come in handy in urban warfare."

"I don't think it will be a problem. It's simple. Wonder why no one has thought of them before," Breille replied. "I should be getting home," she continued. "You all know where to find me. Call on me if you need anything. Fight well and fight to the glory of Entos."

"Blisse and I need to be going too," River said.

"I can speak for myself, thank you," Blisse replied mocking her older sister a little bit. "I need to be going too."

"River, is this theater in use at dawn?" Thayer asked.

"No, it's not. I don't see why the rest of you can't sleep here tonight. Just be out by 7:00 in the light. Here's the key, lock up, and get it back to me in the morning," River said as she handed Brenz the key. "Thayer Taggert and Rieve Waynwright, would you follow us down the stairs? I want to show you how to lock the doors."

"Sure," Rieve said. Breille, Blisse, River, Tag, and Rieve made their way down to the lobby. They were all starting to feel the length of the day. They walked down the stairs slowly and in silence. River broke the silence only after they reached the lobby door.

"Thayer Taggert, would it be helpful if you had a little place of your own to serve as a command post?" she asked.

"It would," he said.

"I know of a room. It's a pretty large room in one of the old theater buildings. The building is only a block away from The Great Chamber and close to the Academy. It is used as a store now. At least the front part of the first floor is use as a store. The back part has an external staircase that goes up to the second story. The room is used as a storage area now for old sets and props. It was a small theater that held about a thousand seats. Most of the seats have been removed and used in other places. There are no windows so if you have lights on at night no one will know."

"Sounds perfect," Brenz said.

"It sounds perfect to me too," Rieve added. "After all, if I am going to get three or four more conjurors involved in this operation, they are going to need a place to practice the incantations and techniques for war. Naturally, Tag and Brenz, they will need some cadets on which to practice."

The Oracles And The Jewels

"Don't forget your healers," Blisse chimed in. "We are going to need a place to do some studying and practicing ourselves."

"I don't have a key to that room, but I think I can get one tomorrow," River said.

"Go ahead. Meet me here tomorrow at dusk and we will take a look," Tag ordered in military fashion. The three girls and Rieve left for the night. Tag and Brenz returned to the Upper Theater.

"Okay cadets," Tag shouted from the stage. The empty theater magnified his voice and startled some of the sleeping cadets. "We are going to bed down here tonight. We will rise at 5:30 in the light, just as the sun is rising and be out by 6:00."

The cadets settled in and the lights were turned off. The inside of the theater was as black as Ashkelon's own soul. Cadets and warriors were used to the light of the three moons and the stars. The blackness that blanketed the theater was alien to most Entosians. The cadets were not accustoms to such blackness so it took many of them a little longer to fall asleep.

"So," a voice said in the darkness, "this is what Ektos must be like." Another voice replied, "I suspect it's an even darker blackness." A moment later a light behind one of the stage curtains was found and turned on, casting a little light into the theater, especially at the stairwell door where it was needed most.

Chapter Thirteen
Expelled

Dawn came too early for most of the cadets. That was not true for Tag. He was eager to get on with the task at hand. While the rest slept, his mind raced throughout the night pausing long enough for him to get just a couple of hours of sleep. Tag was not only an exceptionally gifted warrior, he was also a brilliant strategist. He spent the night thinking of all the ways he would refine their patrols. When 5:15 came, he sprang to his feet, turned on the lights, and called the cadets to their new day. "Wake up cadets! Entos awaits your protection!"

"He's early," Durus said. "He's fifteen minutes early."

"He is a little slow this morning," Cadet Bonar replied. "He waited until 5:15. I believe that is about as late as I have ever seen him."

"Is he always this . . . this ready?" Cadet Durus asked as he stood up.

"I thought Commander Bronz was a little tight," Cadet Ansel said, "but your squad leader is even worse."

"Makes you glad that you didn't do so well on the placement examination, doesn't it?" Cadet Marrcus said as he looked at the cadets from the Polemmas unit.

"Now that you mention it, yes it does," Cadet Durus said, "I like my leaders reasonably assertive, not zealously committed."

"Are you cadets waiting for the show or just someone to find out you're here? Let's get moving!" Tag barked as he marched along the aisle. "The sun will soon rise and we need to be on the streets before she does!"

"I'll bet that our squad is out by 6:30," Marrcus said. "Any takers?"

"No," several voices replied.

By night The Great Chamber was guarded by two squads for each four hour shift. One squad patrolled the streets around the Chamber and other one patrolled the inside of the Great Chamber and the tunnels leading to and

The Oracles And The Jewels

from the Academy. By day two of Hodia's squads patrolled the outside of the Great Chamber and a third discretely worked its way through the inside of the Great Chamber and patrolled the tunnels that run below the main floor. Every four hours a new complement of cadets took over and with the rising of the sun, the whole rotation would begin anew.

By 5:45 all the squads, with the exception of Tag's, had left the Upper Theater and were on their way to their assignments. The Neggen squads headed south. The Krattos squads went to the north. Some of the Hodia cadets headed to the northeast toward The Great Chamber and the Polemmas squads made their way to the Academy. Shortly after sunrise the streets were a busy, active, and crowded place. But at 5:45 in the dark of the new day, barely a soul could be found in her byways therefore each squad took a different route so as not to arouse suspicions. Tag's squad left the theater after all the other squads. He led them out just before 6:00 to make his rounds to check on how some of the other squads had made it through the night.

It was no more than a ten minute walk from the Performing Arts Theater to The Great Chamber and the Academy. The first Hodia squad had begun their patrol at 10:00 and was relieved by the second patrol at 2:00 in the dark. Tag's squad had the 6:00 to 10:00 patrol and then was to report to The Academy of Ancient Warring Arts for two hours of intense combat training and drills.

Brenz's squad was on the same schedule. Polemmas had more territory to cover, but not by much. Unlike The Great Chamber, the Academy was constantly busy. It was filled with candidates, priests, professors, visitors, researchers to the library, and city dignitaries. They not only had to patrol the campus, but also had to patrol several adjacent buildings that were used by the Academy.

The cadets began the morning with great anticipation that something was going to happen, but the first part of the day passed without incident, at least as far as the city was concerned. The sun had risen and no reports of any attacks had reached the city. The cadets from the western wall had marched most of the night and still had fifteen more leagues left to go before they could make camp. Entos was quiet and going about her business as usual, but it was only an appearance. The armies of Entos were moving into position. The cadets were on their secret mission.

But the officers and armies of Entos were not the only ones getting into position. While the generals planned for the

Expelled

battle at hand, the City Fathers were gearing up for the battle yet to come. The immediate crisis had only served to strengthen their conviction that modernization and the new approach needed to be accelerated. They were moving resources to The Academy of the Building Arts at such a rate that it was hard for the administrators to keep all the paperwork and projects organized.

Professor MulLord was also wasting no time in his efforts to bring the Academy around to his way of thinking. The new approach would mark his administration. He immediately retained three new faculty members, one professor, and two conjuring priests to take over lecturing and some of the training of conjurors. All those who did not embrace the new approach were expected to remain silent about it. Any criticism of Professor MulLord's views and policies would trigger an investigation. The new policy applied to faculty, apprentice priests, and candidates and was called The Policy of Positive Suggestions.

The Academy of Theological Sciences and Ancient Conjuring Arts

Rieve attended the first class of the day as expected and as usual. Apprentice Priest Brenna was in Rieve's 8:00 class. Akimm's and Pandar's first class started at 9:00. The four of them usually met for their morning break in the commons, where they typically purchased a pastry and juice. Rieve needed at least two more conjurors to help with the cadet army. Brenna, Akimm, and Pandar were about the only three apprentice priests on campus that he trusted. The new approach had been successful in producing at least one thing at the Academy – a distrust among those studying for the priesthood. Behind the Oracles and the Jewels and the rituals of the Great Festival, trust was suppose to be the stock and trade of the Academy and of the priests. Conjurors had a sacred trust not only to use the power of Entos wisely and to her benefit, but also to use knowledge of both public and private things to the edification and safety of all.

At 10:00 Rieve, Brenna, Akimm, Pandar, and Yorrath met together in the commons in the usual manner. They sat down at their regular table, the sinners' table. As they sat, Rieve noticed that the candidates at the two tables to the immediate right and left of their table gathered up their books and their food and moved further away.

"Interesting," Rieve commented out loud.

The Oracles And The Jewels

"What's interesting?" Akimm asked.

"Our Academy colleagues are getting further and further away," Brenna said.

"Rather symbolic, don't you think," Rieve added.

"What do you mean?" Yorrath asked.

No one answered. Rieve noticed Candidate Nassar entering the room and looking for a familiar face with which to sit.

"Nassar," Rieve called. "Looking for a place to sit?" Nassar nodded his head and walked over to the table. Rieve introduced Nassar to the other four.

"Now that you have ruined my career by calling me over to sit with you, I might as well make myself at home," Nassar said with a smile.

"What's that all about?" Pandar asked.

"You guys don't know?" Nassar asked with a tone of surprise.

"I guess not," Rieve replied.

"Don't you know about the new policy of only positive criticism?" Nassar said.

"Who doesn't?" Akimm answered.

"Well along with that policy some of the professors of the underclassmen are telling the candidates to stay away from certain apprentice priests. That means priests like you," Nassar explained.

"Like us? What did we ever do?" Pandar said.

Nassar continued, "The first problem we are told is that you are blindly loyal to a distorted way of reading the Oracles. Second, you have challenged certain professors in the classroom in regard to the new approach. Third, it is said that you are loyal to the old Headmaster. Rumor has it you guys and others like you aren't going to graduate. Professor MulLord has guaranteed the powers that the Academy will only produce priests and conjurors who will go along with the emphasis."

"If all that is true, Nassar, you might want to get up and head to another table. There's no reason why you should risk your career before you get out of the Academy," Rieve suggested, knowing that Nassar would reject the idea.

"Too late. I am one of you guys. If that wasn't the case before the other night, it certainly is the case now," Nassar said as he looked at Rieve.

"The other night. What happened the other night?" Brenna asked. Rieve looked around to make sure that no other candidates or priests were in hearing range.

Expelled

Rieve noticed that Yorrath was getting a little uncomfortable. "Yorrath," Rieve said in a sober tone, "I don't think you are ready for this."

"I don't know what this is, but if you aren't comfortable with me hearing this, I will leave," Yorrath replied.

"I think that best," Rieve answered. Yorrath stood up and reached for Rieve's hand. They shook hands.

"Fight well and to the glory of Entos," Yorrath said as he departed.

Rieve waited a moment, then continued. "For the past several months, I have been under the tutoring of the Headmaster," Rieve said. The four of them sat in stunned silence.

"You could get removed for that!" Pandar said in a whisper. "Are you in your right mind?"

"I better start at the beginning. But before do, I must ask each of you for your pledge. I do this for Headmaster Sandor and Entos and not myself. For if you join us, you must never speak of these things to anyone. And if you walk away, the same must also be true. If you are not ready for what is about to be spoken, then take your leave now." The four looked at Rieve then at each other.

"Our pledge is given," Brenna said. Rieve looked at each one and each nodded his head in order.

"For better or for worse then, you're all in," Rieve said, then he started at the beginning. He told the four friends about the little fellowship, the first conversations that he had had with the Headmaster, the nightly trips to the Headmaster's office for conjuring training, the prophecy of the Headmaster about the attack on the Polemmas Towers and Nassar's service, and of the events of the past twenty-four hours. His five friends sat in uncharacteristic silence and in various levels of disbelief.

"Here's the big question. Are you interested in joining this secret army?"

"I'm in," Brenna said without hesitation.

"So am I," Akimm followed.

"Me too, although I don't have any conjuring skills yet. I will do what I can," Nassar said.

"Why not? Me too," Pandar said. "So now what?"

"Go about your ordinary business today. Tomorrow we will all begin our training as conjurors of the warring arts. I will let you know where to be and when to be there," Rieve told his friends. There was pride and joy in his voice.

"Do we need a password or something?" Akimm asked.

The Oracles And The Jewels

"That might not be a bad idea," Rieve replied. "The password is the Upper Room. I will make sure those guarding the door let you pass."

As Brenna sat content, the others began cleaning up the table.

"Oh, one last thing before we go, my friend the prophet," Brenna said looking to Rieve. "Pray tell me, prophet of old, who is pulling off all these practical jokes?"

"These things are hidden from me," he replied with a smile. "But odds are, it's a Fortian."

"That's an interesting smile," Nassar commented. "What does it mean? Dost thou knowest and simply refuse to reveal it? Or dost thou delight in childish pranks, as do the ordinary and impious country folks?"

"I just want to know who's that gutsy," Pandar said. "I mean printing and circulating a flyer filled with spoofs on all the new rules and regulations."

"I like the one where we are all supposed to line up behind Professor MulLord each morning to show all of Entos that we stand behind our new leader and the new teaching. What a hoot!" Brenna said with a loud laugh.

"I want to know who put Nassar's picture all over campus, suggesting him for president of the city council," Akimm added.

"The best one though was the Sandor's Office sign over MulLord's newly painted office door," Brenna said, then continued, "I get confused easily, but I got that one."

"My personal favorite," Pandar said, "is putting Sandor's Chair signs on all the faculty chairs on campus."

"I must confess, it's fun watching MulLord, Suedos, and Bozzez tear down every sign they come across and confiscate every flyer in sight. 'This must stop! Stop immediately it must!'" Rieve rejoined.

"Okay," Brenna shouted turning toward all the other students in the hall, "whoever is making fun of our new administration better knock it off before they get in trouble and have to go to the headmaster's office."

"You mean, Acting Headmaster," Pandar said in a slight whisper, which could only be heard by those gathered at the sinners' table.

"Yea, the Acting Headmaster's office," Brenna shouted.

"Well, time to go. We will revisit this great mystery at a later date. Learn and fight well to the glory of Entos," Rieve quipped.

Expelled

The hour had passed quickly and the 11:00 lecture would soon begin. Professor MulLord had reassigned Professor Ellery to take over Professor Wynnea's class on the Conjuring and the Warring Arts. This was unusual since Professor Wynnea had spent part of his career working with the armies and training conjurors to service the warriors. Anything Professor Ellery had to say about the subject was purely theoretical. Nor was Professor Ellery known for his courage. But Professor Wynnea, like Conjuror Stratia, was from the old school, experienced, and brave. He was a vocal critic of the new ways and believed they would lead to Entos' ruin.

"I hate to say it again, but Rieve is right. It is time to go gentlemen. We don't want to miss Professor Ellery's first lecture on a subject he doesn't understand," Brenna said.

"It would be best, gentlemen, if we all just go through the motions on campus. The real work is elsewhere. What we don't learn here we will learn there," Rieve said as he pointed in the direction of the War Academy. "Let's all meet at Diamond Park at 4:00 and we will go over to The Academy of the Ancient Warring Arts to meet Conjuror Stratia. I don't need to remind you, not a word about this to anyone."

Nassar went his way and the others headed off to class where they did as the new administration expected them to do. They sat silently and listened to Professor Ellery's lecture. In the afternoon Rieve was suppose to report to Professor Etam for his afternoon nap, but the events of the previous evening kept him away from the Headmaster so Rieve wanted to stop by the Headmaster's office. A visit in the day was risky, but that didn't seem to make a difference to him at this point. He asked Akimm to stop by Professor Etam's lab to tell the professor that Rieve would miss the afternoon session.

As expected, the faculty building was busy. Professors and students were coming and going. As Rieve entered the courtyard he saw Professor MulLord leaving the faculty building through the two large wooden doors of the main entrance. He hesitated until Professor MulLord had left, then made his way across the courtyard, through the two large doors, up the stairwell, down the hall, and knocked on Sandor's door.

"Come in," Sandor said. Rieve didn't waste any time. He entered as invited. "Hello my young apprentice. What brings thee to me in the light of day?"

The Oracles And The Jewels

"I wanted to apologize for missing our appointment last night," Rieve said.

"No need. Thou was otherwise engaged. This I knew. Now tell me, has thou enlisted the aid of thy friends?" Sandor asked.

"Yes, sir," Rieve answered.

"Whom didst thou select?"

"Brenna, Akimm, Pandar, and a candidate by the name of Nassar. Nassar was the Aradian who took your message to the Polemmas Tower. If we need more there is another by the name of Yorrath."

"Very good," Sandor said. "Thou hast chosen well."

"I do fear for their futures," Rieve said.

"Their futures are not in thy hands. They make their choices and must assume the responsibility. In so doing, they play their part," Sandor placed his hand on Rieve's shoulder and looked him in the eyes. "Always remember, they will do what is in their nature and thy must do what is in thine own nature."

"I will try to remember these things," Rieve replied, then he changed the subject. "Headmaster, have you heard the news about Professor MulLord's new policies?"

"No. Professor MulLord has made some new laws has he? That's always been one of his problems. He likes laws, especially his own. Entos has so few laws. She needs so few, but MulLord thinks he can make the city a better place through the creation of the right kind of laws. Strange that a school that accuses us of too many laws makes more than we could imagine. They seem to believe in a kind of theological reciprocity. What is the target of this law?"

"It is against Academy policy to critique or criticize the new approach or to dissent from the plans of the City Fathers. He calls it The Policy of Positive Criticism," Rieve answered.

"The new way is not content to take old words and redefine them. The new way does do that, but it must also go about creating new ways of speaking. Such words have nothing to do with the Oracles. MulLord and his students can dress it up with whatever words they like. It is what it is. It is also what it is not, the words of the Oracles."

"A gag order," Rieve answered quickly. "Cooperate and graduate. Critique, question, or challenge the new or the officials and you risk expulsion."

Expelled

"It is more than that. It is law dressed up as grace. The untrained ear will not hear the difference. Entos has been such a gracious place . . . for the most part."

"Headmaster, may I ask you a forthright question?" Rieve said in a soft voice.

"Indeed," Sandor replied in a voice that matched Rieve's.

"Why do you sit here day-after-day doing nothing about what they are doing to the Academy? Why don't you go and take back this Academy? There are hundreds of priests loyal to the ancient ways and to you. You have done so much for so many and I know they would come to your aid. But they cannot fight for you if you will not take the field."

"Dost thou believe it is that easy?" Sandor replied.

"Isn't it?" Rieve asked. "I know that many students will stand with you, if you only ask."

"Thou has much to learn. It has been a long time since faculty members have been asked to pay a price and they fear loss of position and popularity. The support of students is easily earned, but it will be like a flower that wilts in the heat of the day. Do not think less of them. Support for that which is good and right in good times is an easy task. But to stand and do what ought to be done in the face of great evil and at great cost to one's own person is quite another. For hundreds of years it has been easy to do the right thing here in Entos. But the time for testing has come."

"So they don't believe what it is they teach?" Rieve asked in a voice of disappointment.

"Dost thou think believing is easy? It is hard. Very hard and each has his own weakness. The professors have sharp minds and know the difference between the new and the old, but their spirits have never known hardship. They are untested and will remain so for a little while longer. If students are willing to stand and speak, it is only because they do not understand the risk they take in so doing." Sandor sat down and peered through the window. Rieve thought he saw a tear roll down Sandor's left cheek in the reflection of the window, but he was unsure of what he saw.

"Headmaster, I too am untested," Rieve said softly, "yet you have selected me to risk my standing in this place."

"I did not pick thee," Sandor replied in an equally soft voice. "If it had been up to me, I would have spared thee all the trouble that is now falling upon thee. No, my son, I did not choose thee. Entos chose. Entos chose both of us," Sandor set a large old jar of water on the little round table. He picked

The Oracles And The Jewels

up a glass stirring rod and began to stir the water with a circular motion. Rieve watched the water in the jar with great interest.

"The new teaching did not produce the evil that now lives within the walls of Entos. The evil produced the new teaching. Not every Entosian is an Entosian. They only appear to be. The testing that is coming upon us will separate those who are from those who are not."

"How will we tell the difference between the imposters and those who are true?" Rieve asked.

"Everyone will show himself to be what he is in the course of time." By now Sandor had created a strong whirlpool in the jar and had withdrawn the stirring stick, yet the whirlpool was not losing its momentum. In fact, it had gained momentum and was becoming more violent.

"What I can show thee is what will be if things continue as they are in this moment. This vision is for thee, thine eyes only shall see what is here." Sandor picked up the jar. "Peer thee into the water. The waters show all things. It makes clear that which is unclear, and clean that which is unclean." Sandor lifted the jar.

The water turned cloudy and began to move about. Images began to take shape. Rieve looked into the jar. At first he saw nothing. Then suddenly the image of King Ashkelon and his army of hundreds of thousands appeared. They were attacking the walls. He saw Entosian warriors and creatures of Bohow falling in battle. He saw the streets of Entos running with blood, buildings ablaze, and fallen cadets, some of whom he thought he recognized. He saw winged creatures carrying Professor Etam away. He saw the body of Entosian warriors lying in the jungle and swamps of Bohow and Entosian citizens fleeing to the mountains of Oros. He saw Thayer lying dead on the steps of The Great Chamber and Sandor lying dead in the resting place of the Oracles. The last two images were more than Rieve could bear.

"No!" Rieve shouted. He looked to Sandor. "No, no, this can't be! This must not be!" Rieve looked back to the large glass jar. He had only looked away for a moment, but that was long enough to break the spell. The images were gone and the whirlpool was slowing.

"What have I just seen?" Rieve asked with fear in his voice.

"Only what thou was meant to see."

Expelled

"Did you not see it?" Rieve asked with panic in his face. "Did you see?"

"No. These things were for thee, only thee," Sandor sighed. "I wish that I could bear these visions in your stead, but they are not mine, but thine."

"Have you seen such visions?" Rieve asked.

"I have seen what belongs to me," Sandor replied.

"Can these things be changed?"

"Maybe, maybe not. But all things run their course, just as they must," Sandor replied.

"How then will I know if I have acted in a way that prevents these things? How will I know which actions lead to these things and which actions will lead to better things?" Rieve asked.

"It is not for thee to know," Sandor said. "It is only for thee to do thy part."

"Why then do you show me these things if I can't do anything about them?" Rieve asked. "Surely, the Creator, King, and Sustainer is greater than fate."

"Our place and doings are all part of the greater mystery." Sandor put the jar back on the table and sat down. "It is a mystery that we may never be permitted to comprehend. What we do know is that each one of us fits into his own place and is fulfilling the duties of our stations. Thou has seen these things, so that thy may know what is at stake. This burden has been placed upon thee and thy friends. Do thou thy part. In so doing, Entos will continue toward her destiny and we toward ours. We will not change her destiny, but we can affect ours. This we know for the Oracles have declared it to be so."

"But Entos can never fall. This the Oracles teach," Rieve replied.

"Indeed, it is as thou has said. But this is also true. Entos can be placed under the foot of Ashkelon. She can also be delivered from him. If she is to go forward, we must go with her." Sandor took a small cup and dipped it into the water in the jar. Without saying a word he put the cup to his lips and drank, then he placed the cup to Rieve's lips.

"The rest is for thee to drink," Sandor said. "I cannot take this burden from thee. It belongs to thee. But I can share thy burdens for as long as I am with thee." Rieve took hold of the cup and drank it ever so slowly. Although Rieve did not see it or feel it as he drank, the youthful face of a boy began to fade away and his face began to show a maturity uncommon for

The Oracles And The Jewels

his years. The change was subtle, but the change was not imperceptible to Sandor.

"The battles for Entos have always been fought by the young. Entos is a peculiar creation in that way. In times such as ours, she spends her young and steals away youth, so that the old may go on and another generation may come forth. In thy sacrifices, all the rest will live. Thee and thine will have more to do with the future of Entos than this old conjuror or that old fool who now reckons himself the headmaster of the Academy."

"Perhaps, sir, it would be best if I were to stand at your side when the attack comes," Rieve suggested.

"Ye have thy duties. To these thou must attend. I have mine. Now here, take this. Take it in thy hand." Sandor handed Rieve a very old staff, not unlike the one that Sandor had leaning against his own desk.

"This belonged to the conjuror who trained me. This belonged to my lord and master. When he died, he entrusted it to me so that he could give it to thee."

"To me?" Rieve said in surprised humility.

"Yes, to thee. It has been waiting for thee for a very long time. It has stood in the corner of my many studies for more than fifty years."

"Are you sure that I am the one for whom it has waited?" Rieve asked. Sandor went to hand it to him, but Rieve hesitated.

"Ye are not merely my student. Thou art my fulfillment." Rieve stood still in a long moment of silence. "Take up thy staff, my son," Sandor repeated in a gentle but firm voice. "The choice is not ours. This staff belongs to thee. This thou shall see when thou hast taken it up into thine hand."

Rieve swallowed hard and whispered. "Yes, my lord." Rieve said the words without thinking about them in advance. "My lord," he thought after the words had spilled from his lips. Such an address was an ancient custom, rarely used in modern times. It felt awkward, but the words came out on their own. Rieve thought the words sounded arrogant, yet given the circumstance in which they were spoken, they seemed appropriate. Rieve understood that he and Sandor were joined together in a sacred office and holy commission. Rieve was being given a great and awesome opportunity to serve Entos as one in a long line of conjurors whose line formed a chain going back to the Days of Old.

In taking up the staff and in speaking that phrase, "my lord," Rieve felt that he was contributing to the decline and

Expelled

The Oracles And The Jewels

perhaps even to the death of Sandor. These thoughts were as hard to bear as the visions he had just seen.

"I know the thoughts thou thinketh. It is better to yield and to serve joyfully, than to fight against that which has been ordained from the beginning. Do not worry too much. It was many years after I received my staff that my lord departed this realm," Sandor smiled.

Rieve set his apprentice staff against the wall. He looked at the staff, then at Sandor. His eyes moved back and forth between the two. Rieve slowly moved his right hand toward the ancient staff. Finally, he took hold of its grip and when he touched it he knew that it belonged to him. The doubt that had welled up in him vanished. He did not understand why he had been chosen or how Sandor knew that the staff belonged to him, but there was no doubt in Rieve's mind the staff was his and he felt its ancient history and the touch of its power. He felt the centuries through which the staff had traveled and knew it had done great things. It was ancient and the fingers of all those who had possessed the staff before had worn grooves into its shaft. Yet, his own hand was a perfect fit.

"See, it does belong to thee," Sandor said with a slight smile. "It would be more accurate to say that thou now belongs to the staff, as I belong to mine." Sandor looked at his staff as it leaned against his desk. He held out his hand toward it. The staff slid across the floor and came to rest in the palm of his hand.

"When death finds its prey in me , thou must giveth this staff," Sandor held up his staff, "to the one to whom it belongs and to the one thou wilt train many years from now."

"How will I know him who is to receive the staff?" Rieve asked.

"The staff will show thee to whom it belongs. His name will be Sandor."

"Your name?"

"My former master's name was Sakkan, which means good steward. Sakkan is an ancient name. What does your name mean?"

"Good steward," Rieve replied.

"Yes, your name is the Demotic form of the ancient name Sakkan. It is always important to do homework. It is good to know the ancient languages. It would be a terrible thing if thou were to give this staff to the wrong conjuror," Sandor smiled a gentle smile. "Always do thy homework." Sandor turned and looked out the window toward the east.

Expelled

"They don't see him yet, but I do." Rieve walked to the window and looked eastward as he stood along the side of Sandor.

"I don't see anything," Rieve said, "just the Entosian sky." Sandor gave Rieve a light slap on the back of his head, as if trying to knock something loose. Rieve looked again. This time he squinted.

"I still don't see anything," Rieve said.

"I know," Sandor said with a giggle. "Thy sight wilt improve once thou leaves the Academy. Then thou wilt seeth things with a keener vision . . . only then and after some suffering," Sandor turned away from the window and walked toward the door. "Now be on thy way," he said with a lighter and more cheerful tone. "I have a friend of ours to see. Fight well and fight to the glory of Entos."

"Fight well, my lord, and to the greater glory of Entos," Rieve replied.

The Hodia Tower

It began as a subtle shadow on the eastern horizon, barely noticeable. The sentries for the morning watch did not report the phenomena because its subtlety caused too much doubt. But by 10:00 in the light, the phenomena was becoming noticeable to the warriors stationed on the battlements. The watcher sent for the commander of the Hodia Tower, General Raggnar.

The door on the south side of the tower opened and the general, a Pithosian, walked quickly along the battlement. His staff, which consisted of a Procuron major, a Fortian captain, a Kicahian lieutenant, and Conjuror Taphar followed closely behind.

"What do you see, Corporal?" the general said to the watcher, a Fortian.

"There, General," the corporal said as he pointed to the southeast of the tower and handed the general the looking glass. "I don't know what it is, but it doesn't look like a storm front. It rises from the ground to the sky. Not from the sky to the ground. But...," the corporal paused.

"But what?" the general asked as he peered through the looking glass toward the sprinkle of blackness on the eastern horizon. His voice made his question sound more like a command rather than a question.

"Sir, it sounds like rolling thunder to me. But it is constant. It is more like a groan."

The Oracles And The Jewels

"Taphar, is that him?" the general asked, although he had already come to his own conclusion.

Conjuror Taphar answered the question without hesitation and without any doubt, "Yes, that is King Ashkelon."

"Major, how long before he is within striking distance?" the general asked.

"At this distance Sir, it would be hard to guess. It depends on the size of his army and the size and number of artillery pieces," the major answered.

"For the sake of estimating his arrival, let's say he has an army of two hundred fifty thousand and artillery to support a full assault against the wall. How long before he is in place?"

"Three and a half days, maybe four," the major answered. "I place him along the Oros River on the eastern side of the Skattos Forest."

"When do you think the cloud will be visible from the city?"

"Tomorrow by noon people will probably start noticing it," the major said, "but they won't be sure until sunrise the next day."

"Corporal, if you or any other watchers see anything at all, report it immediately. Especially keep your eyes to the sky for the winged creatures," the general instructed.

"Yes, sir!" the corporal responded.

"Captain."

"Yes, General," the Fortian said.

"Do you see what we see?"

"Yes, General. He is coming, but the darkness is not dust from their feet. It is something else," the captain said.

"What?" the general asked.

"My answer would only be a guess," the captain said.

"What do you think the rest of us are doing?" the general snapped. "Take your best guess, captain."

"Winged creatures," the captain said.

"That is a pretty good guess. Captain from this moment on, I want one hundred archers on this wall at all times. They are to shoot down any creature that comes within range. Shoot first, then report to me."

"Yes, sir," the captain answered as he saluted and ran back toward the tower.

"Taphar," the general said.

"What do you see?" the general handed him the looking glass. Conjuror Taphar looked through the glass.

Expelled

"Evil, general, pure evil," Taphar said, then added. "I see a real fight and much death."

"Lieutenant," the general called.

The lieutenant stepped forward and saluted. "Yes, sir."

"Take your special force and head out across the desert and take cover in the forest. Gather intelligence on the size and composition of Ashkelon's army. Send the information to me by bird and get back here in a timely fashion. Don't get too close to Ashkelon. We are going to need you back here for the fight." Just then a private, an Adroitian, ran out of the tower and along the battlement.

"Sir, a message," he said as he handed the message to the major. The major read the message and handed it to the general and he read it.

"Lieutenant, the Polemmas Tower spotted Ashkelon's movement an hour ago. They have already sent a probe out to the forest. Krattos will probably do the same. If you have to engage make sure you're not shooting at your fellow Entosians."

"Yes, sir," the lieutenant answered. "It will be good to have company, sir."

"Fight well and fight for the glory of Entos," the general said as the lieutenant saluted. The general returned the salute and the lieutenant marched back to the tower. The general took another look at the approaching horde, then left the battlement and entered the tower.

A few minutes later a carrier bird was loosed from the tower and flew toward the city. A moment later a second bird headed to Krattos Tower and a third to Polemmas. The process would be repeated. Within a couple of hours all eight towers would be notified of Ashkelon's coming.

Within fifteen minutes, the lieutenant and his scouts were riding hard across the desert floor toward the forests of Bohow. A small cloud of dust followed them as they rode toward the faint green landscape of the forest twenty-five leagues away.

The Land of Entos was surrounded by a small desert which averaged forty leagues wide. The mighty River of Oros began in the Oros Mountains, which were northwest of the Land of Entos. The Oros Mountains were twice as high and even more dangerous than those found in the Pithosian Valley or on the Plateau of Tarchus. So dangerous were they that only a few creatures had made their home in the cliffs and caves of the great mountains. So high were they that snow remained on them year around. The melt joined

The Oracles And The Jewels

with the springs which flowed from the sides of their great cliffs and fed the mighty Oros River, which ran across the northern side of Entos, then turned southeast toward Mount Ektos.

Beyond the desert of Bohow was the black forest called Skattos Forest, which was a seven days' journey from the west to the east. East of the Skattos Forest was Pachhad, Ashkelon's jungle, in which some of Bohow's mightiest creatures dwelt. The Oros River divided the Skattos Forest and the jungle in half, but did not provide safe travel due to the numerous rapids and waterfalls.

To the southeast of the Pachhad Jungle lay the Rochabba Swamps where, it was said, no son of Entos had ever crossed without sinking into the depths of despair. The River Oros ran beyond the swamps to the middle of the Land of Barren Rock where rivers of magma flowed back and forth to no end and took no rest.

In the midst of the Land of Barren Rock, the Oros River divided into the Yaash River, which turned to the northeast and ran through the Land of Yaash, and the Moowth River, which turned to the southwest and cut through the rough Land of Moowth. Yaash was a land filled with plateaus, canyons, and mighty rivers. Many creatures of Bohow and a few Entosians had fallen to their deaths in the Land of Yaash. The Land of Moowth was a desolate and barren place of rocks and sand.

In the five thousand years since the creation of Entos, only a very few had dared leave the comfort of Entos. Over the centuries, many warriors and priests had made the journey across the desert and into the forest and jungles, but less than half had ever returned. Such was the brutality of Bohow and every scout who was sent that day knew it could be his last.

The Academy of Healing Arts

The division between the old and the new was much more identifiable in The Academy of Theological Sciences and Ancient Conjuring Arts than it was in The Academy of Healing Arts. Students who held the ancient ways would sit together at the same tables for lunch and in the lecture rooms. Everyone not of the old school sat everywhere else.

Such a visible division was not obvious in the other academies. Blisse had many friends in the healing academy. She was to select from among them a few

Expelled

devoted friends who shared her concerns for Entos and who would be willing to take risks. Finding such people would not be easy. Those who went into the profession of the healing arts were generally not adventurous types. They would regard such intrigue as political posturing unhealthy for the life of Entos. What she could count on was the common desire to heal wounded Entosians.

Blisse was looking for students who were in large part blind loyalists who, because of their love and devotion to relieving suffering, would simply come when called and go when sent. Surely, she thought, if she could fool an academy president she'll to be able to pull this off. Blisse arrived at school on time, although sleepy-eyed. She spent the morning surveying her classes to see which of her classmates or professors possessed the right qualities. They have to be loyal, able to keep a confidence, and a little naive. She settled on two of her classmates. Her first choice was an Adroitian girl by the name of Sabinnee. Sabinnee possessed two out of three of the criteria quite well. She was loyal and naive. Whether she could keep a confidence was uncertain. Blisse decided it was worth the risk.

Blisse's second choice was an Aradian student by the name of Chaiva. If there was anyone in The Academy of Healing Arts who would welcome the opportunity to become involved in such an adventure it would be Chaiva.

"Good morning," Blisse said as she approached Sabinnee's desk.

"Hello, Blisse. How are you doing this morning?" Sabinnee asked.

"Fine. But there is something that I would like to talk to you about," Blisse replied.

"What about?"

"It's a secret, but an important one. It might even be a little hazardous."

"Hazardous? A secret? That is what I like about you Blisse. You always make things more enjoyable than if they had taken place without you."

"The word enjoyable may be the last word you might want to apply to this situation. You know Ashkelon is coming. Well there is some concern in official circles that he might even penetrate as far as the city itself."

"What does that have to do with us?" Sabinnee said.

"That is the secret part. Can I trust you? Would you be willing to give your pledge?"

"The pledge? This must be serious."

The Oracles And The Jewels

"Yes, it is," Blisse said.

"Well then, you have my pledge."

"I have been asked by a general to help put some contingency plans into place in the event that some of our Entosians are hurt in an attack."

"That's strange. Why would they ask you?"

"Because the officials are not supposed to know these plans are being made. It has something to do with the fight between the new and the old. As healers it makes no difference to us whether they are of the new or old school. An injured Entosian is an injured Entosian."

"So Blisse, what do you need me to do?" Sabinnee asked.

"I need you to be ready. That's all. I need you to go where I send you and come when I call. I need you to always have your healing pouch fully equipped and to have your incantation booklet in your pocket."

"Easy enough, I guess," Sabinnee said. "Who else is involved?"

"Just the two of us at the moment. I will be talking with Chaiva to see if she would be willing to help out."

"I think she will do just fine," Sabinnee said. "Tell your general friend to feel free to call on me anytime."

"Thanks Sabinnee. Now all you need to do is to run when and to where you hear the horn," Blisse said, "I need to find Chaiva and I have to go to class. I'll talk to you later." As Blisse walked away from Sabinnee's desk, she thought to herself, "That was too easy. The appeal to the healing oath to heal any Entosian in need is a pretty powerful tool. Oh well, one down and one to go." Blisse knew she would find Chaiva in the courtyard, sitting on her favorite bench under her favorite tree.

"Good morning, Chaiva," Blisse said as she approached Chaiva who had watched Blisse traverse the path that cut through the middle of the courtyard.

"Good morning, Blisse. I've been waiting for you," Chaiva said

"Really? Why?" Blisse asked.

"I understand you're involved in some clandestine operation," Chaiva said in a whisper. The disclosure surprised Blisse and left her speechless for a moment. Finally she spoke.

"How did you know? I didn't tell anyone except Sabinnee," Blisse said.

Expelled

"I will tell you my secret if you tell me yours," Chaiva said.

"You first," Blisse said as she stood before Chaiva with her hands on her hips.

"Sit down," Chaiva said. Blisse took her place next to Chaiva on the bench. "My uncle is General Witticor. He stopped by our cottage last night and told me that if you did not find me by noon today, I was supposed to find you."

"Did he say anything else?" Blisse asked.

"Not really. I tried to get him to do some talking, but if it is official there's no way he is going to utter a sound. What can you tell me?"

"I have been asked to help put some contingency plans into place in the event that some of our Entosians are hurt in an attack on the city," Blisse started to explain.

"There hasn't been an attack on the city since the creation of the walls and towers," Chaiva commented. "Uncle must have some top secret intelligence information if he is worried about that. But why enlist the help of students instead of professors?"

"I suppose General Witticor thinks we're a little more trustworthy. But questions like those are above my station. I only know that I need healers who will come and go as I direct and as needed. So you're volunteering," Blisse said.

"Sure am. I told Uncle that last night," Chaiva answered. "My pouch will always be full and my medical booklet will be with me at every moment of the day. You just tell me when and where to be and that is where I will go."

"Run when and to where you hear the horn. That is the only thing I know at the moment," Blisse said.

The Academy of the Ancient Warring Arts

At 8:00 squads from the Krattos, Neggen, Polemmas, and Hodia units had reported for training as scheduled. It was now 10:00 in the light and the first group was leaving and the second group of cadets was trickling in. The Academy of the Warring Arts building was one of the largest structures in the city. It was a round building symbolic of the battle circle and entrances dotted its exterior. The warring academy was located on the near northeast side of the city toward Hodia and Krattos. The eighty to ninety cadets who were wandering into and out of the building every two hours went largely unnoticed.

The Oracles And The Jewels

The morning patrol for all the units went well and without incident. From all appearances, their mission was off to a good start. Tag's squad entered the building from the south at 10:15. Brenz's squads came from the north at 10:20. By 10:30 seventeen squads, eighty-four cadets in all, were assembled in the Hall of Combat waiting the arrival of Colonel Fornoff. They didn't wait long.

"Attention!" Tag shouted as the colonel entered the hall.

"Good morning, cadets!" the colonel said. "Each day you will report here as scheduled. Inside these walls you will be expected to shed your tribal robes and wear your uniforms. Your training will begin with a briefing, followed by thirty minutes of physical fitness training, then special weapons, combat training, working with a conjuror, and the last thirty minutes of your time here each day will be reserved for showers, change of uniforms, and squad meetings."

"Cadets, let's get started. Shed those tribal robes now!" The cadets did so and threw them against the walls, then lined up in formation and stood at attention. With their robes off, most of their daggers were clearly visible. Some had tucked the dagger in the waist of the pants. Others had put the daggers in the boots. Still others had affixed them to the their backs and others concealed them under their robe, but on top of their uniforms.

"Cadets, a dagger is not a sword. It is what you have always been taught that it is. It is a defensive weapon to be used to block the blade of your opponent. If you try to use your dagger as a sword, you will likely die. The dagger will be effective because your opponent will not expect it. But you will only surprise him once. The dagger is most effective when it is not seen. That means you will have to be so close to your opponent that you will smell his breath and his sweat. The dagger is effective when thrown well, but once you throw it, it no longer belongs to you. It belongs to your target. If you throw it, you will be without a weapon. Throw it only if you must to save the life of another."

The colonel walked over to a set of armor and a sword hanging on the wall. He took the display from the wall and walked over to Tag.

"Cadet Thayer Taggert. Put these on and attack me." Tag did as he was instructed. It only took him a few seconds to put the armor on and take the sword in his hand.

"Too slow, cadet!" the colonel shouted. "Before this morning is out you will all learn to suit up faster than that."

Expelled

Tag stood in front of the colonel, sword in hand, and leaning forward as if paused to attack. The colonel was old and large, even by Pithosian standards. Tag was an average size Demotic.

"I see hesitation in your eyes, cadet! Why?" the colonel shouted.

"You're unarmed, Colonel," Tag replied in a firm voice.

"I said attack!" Before the colonel had finished the whole sentence, Tag launched forward thrusting his sword toward the colonel's stomach. The colonel produced a dagger, caught the tip of Tag's sword with the dagger at the point where the blade and dagger's handle were joined. He pushed the tip of the sword to his left. Tag was a bit faster than the colonel had anticipated and the sword sliced the colonel's uniform and left a shallow cut in the colonel's side, but the colonel did not react to the cut. As the sword continued passed him, the colonel spun to his left and brought the dagger to bear against the side of Tag's neck. The two stood motionless.

"Good," the colonel said as the cut made itself known to him. "This cadet is fast, but if this were real this cadet would also be dead. That is how you use the dagger. Use it for closeup work and use it fast. Your opponent should not know you have it until it is too late. Any questions?"

"Sir," Cadet Tabor said.

"Yes, cadet?" the colonel replied even though he was now walking to the first aid cabinet on the wall.

"Can we carry more than one dagger?" Tabor asked.

"Help yourself. Just don't clunk when you walk. Cadet Thayer Taggert. Come here. You did this. You can help me wrap a bandage around it."

"Yes, sir. Sorry, Colonel," Tag said.

"Don't apologize for following orders and doing your best," the colonel said. "It is getting harder these days to find Entosians who strive for excellence. We want everyone to feel good these days . . . feel good about slop," the colonel grumbled.

"In that case, Colonel, I do owe you an apology," Tag replied.

"For what?" the colonel barked.

"That wasn't my best, sir," Tag said, not knowing whether to smile or fake humility. Tag took one end of the bandage and held it as the colonel turned three times in a three hundred sixty degree circle, wrapping himself in the bandage.

The Oracles And The Jewels

The cadets spent the balance of their time practicing and sparring with their daggers. When their time was up, they headed to the showers and suited up in clean uniforms. At 12:15 the cadets reassembled in the combat hall to put on their tribal robes. Cadet Tabor and a few others had raided the weapons room for additional daggers. They were busy attaching them to various parts of their uniforms, bodies, and robes when the colonel and General Witticor entered the hall.

"Attention!" Tag shouted. Every cadet snapped immediately into position and the room fell silent.

"As you were," the colonel said. "General Witticor would like to speak to you."

The general stepped forward. Colonel Fornoff opened up a small case that held a ribbon with a combat metal attached to it.

"Cadets," The general said. "I have some good news and some bad news. As to the good news, Cadet Brenz Clinton, step forward." Brenz did.

"Who do you name as your second?" the general asked.

"Cadet Thayer Taggert, sir," Brenz said in a clear and resounding voice.

"Entosians know," the general said, "that there is no such thing as a self-made warrior. We all owe what we have become to the King and to those the King has placed in our lives. Cadet Brenz Clinton has selected Cadet Thayer Taggert to be his second. Why do you so name this one as your second?" the general asked.

"I sharpened my skills against his sword, sir. Cadet Thayer Taggert has always pushed me to be and to do my very best. Although I cannot beat him without the aid of a conjuror, he has challenged me and inspired me by his skill and spirit," Brenz explained.

"Cadet Thayer Taggert, step forward." Tag did so.

"Cadets! It is my privilege to present to Cadet Brenz Clinton of the Polemmas army his first medal, the Medal of Gallantry, for actions taken two days ago. Without his quick thinking and courage in battle, many more Entosian warriors would have been lost." General Witticor handed Tag the medal. It was customary for the second to pin the one being honored. Tag did as expected. As he did he looked at Brenz, gave a slight smile, and stuck him with the pin just deep enough to produce a silent chuckle from both cadets. Tag stepped back and saluted Brenz. Brenz returned the salute.

Expelled

At that the hall erupted into the traditional reply. "This one has fought well and to the glory of Entos!"

"Congratulations Cadets Brenz Clinton and Thayer Taggert," General Witticor said. The two cadets saluted and returned to the line.

"Now for the bad news. Forty-five minutes ago we received a message from Polemmas. Ashkelon is marching on Entos. That report was confirmed by Hodia just a few minutes ago. It is believed that he has made his way into the Skattos Forest and will launch a full-scale attack in three days. This information is not to be spoken of outside this academy. The City Fathers will post an official notice only when the fact can't be hidden from the people any longer. They don't want panic and neither do we. Carry on!" With that order, the general concluded his presentation and briefing.

"You know your mission. Ashkelon is coming. Stay vigilant. Fight well and to the glory of Entos. Cadets dismissed!" the colonel shouted. The squads regrouped and each squad headed out the same doors through which they had entered.

"Cadets Thayer Taggert and Brenz Clinton, General Witticor would like a word with you," Colonel Fornoff said.

Tag and Brenz remained at attention. General Witticor approached the two. "At ease men," he said. "I understand you two are part of a little fellowship. Is that right?"

"Sir," Tag said "we can't comment on that question."

"You just did. You also know by now that we are on the same side. Cadet Thayer Taggert, I assumed you were a part of this little fellowship because your brother the conjuror/priest and I have become good friends. For the record, he didn't tell me who you were."

"Permission to speak, sir," Thayer asked.

"Permission, granted," General Witticor answered.

"How did you know?"

"I knew that two of my cadets, one from Hodia and one from Polemmas, were members of this little fellowship. When Cadet Brenz Clinton picked you as his second, that provided the final piece of the puzzle. So you can help me, help you, to help Entos."

"Sir, yes Sir," Brenz and Thayer replied in unison.

"Good. May I communicate with your little fellowship through the two of you?"

"Yes, Sir," they replied again in unison.

The Oracles And The Jewels

"Good, otherwise I will have to waste a lot of time tracking down your friends every time I need something . . . something like a healer or a builder," Witticor smiled. "By the same token, if the little fellowship needs something, I am not without friends. Am I clear on that?"

"Yes, sir!" Tag and Brenz said again in unison.

"Now, do your cadets have everything they need so far?" the general asked.

"Yes, sir!" they said.

"Anything I should know at this point?" the general asked.

"Sir, tonight we are going to look at a place to set up a base of operation. If it proves workable, we will let you know," Thayer said.

"Do that. Carry on, cadets." Tag and Brenz saluted. The general returned the salute and then the colonel and general left the room. Tag and Brenz reunited with their squads, robed up, loaded up on supplies, and headed for the Borrhas Plateau.

Unlike the Hodia and Polemmas Plateaus, the Borrhas Plateau had trees, bushes, and rolling hills that came right up to the city's edge. Several squads had planned to conceal themselves in Borrhas' cover. They would be able to enter the city at a moment's notice without having to cross a large open field. They reached the woods of Borrhas at 1:00 in the light. On their way, they spotted patrols from Krattos making their rounds. They exchanged nods and went their way.

Once they reached the woods, all there was to do was wait. Squads from their respective units were covering their patrols. They were under orders to remain out of sight and to do all they could to minimize being discovered or recognized. The cadets who had just left the Warring Academy had picked up food from the commissary and were now disappearing into alleys, parks, valleys, and the woods near the city to eat, sleep, train, and rest.

Tag and the members of his squad queried Brenz's squad and the other members of Polemmas about the events two days prior. They questioned the Polemmas cadets about the battle for two reasons. They wanted to learn as much as they could about the methods, strengths, and weaknesses of their opponents from Bohow and Ektos. They also wanted to revel in the glory of battle, but as Brenz and his fellow cadets described the horror of battle and the death of six of their own Tag, Marrcus, Kelila, Ailith, and

Expelled

Bonar began to realize for the first time that the glory and honor of battle is a sour and harsh kind of glory.

The Academy of Theological Sciences and Ancient Conjuring Arts

Rieve left Sandor sitting in the courtyard reading a book. It was just before 3:00 in the light when two candidates approached him.

"Apprentice Priest Rieve Waynwright," one of the candidates said in a nervous tone.

"Yes," Rieve replied.

"Headmaster MulLord would like to see you in the Tribunal Hall. We have been sent to bring you to him," the second candidate said with arrogance in his voice.

"Okay," Rieve said.

"I have also been ordered to take your staff from you," the second Candidate said. Rieve's staff was leaning against the bench. The second candidate reached to take the staff in hand, but the staff began to slide along the arm of the bench and away from the candidate's hand. The movement of the staff startled him and he withdrew his hand. He made a second attempt to take the staff in hand but the staff moved again. Rieve watched the process with as much surprise and curiosity as the two cadets.

"Are you sure you want to take that staff from me?" Rieve said with a smile. "What if the staff doesn't want to go with you?"

"I demand you stop this trickery and give me the staff!" the second candidate said.

"Haven't you heard, a good priest does the bidding of his staff, not the other way around," Rieve said. "Here, I will carry it for you." Rieve held forth his hand and the staff flew quickly into it. "Let's go," Rieve said, then stepped in front of the two candidates and led them across the courtyard to the Tribunal Hall. Rieve was nervous and worried, but he had promised himself that he would not show it, not to the candidates, and certainly not to MulLord. He would do his best to conduct himself in a manner that would make Sandor proud. As he walked across the courtyard he repeated a truth under this breath recorded in the Oracles. "A student is not to be treated better than his master." The saying comforted him and gave him courage for he knew that Sandor had been wronged and now he would be too.

The Oracles And The Jewels

The candidates opened the two wooden doors to the hall and Rieve entered therein. They closed the doors behind him and remained outside. The hall was empty except for MulLord, who was sitting in the presiding judge's chair. Rieve walked to the Podium of the Respondent and took his place in the box.

"Young man, you're in a lot of trouble. I think I can help you out if you cooperate with us." Professor MulLord began in a voice that sounded like that of a caring father.

"If there is anything I can do to help solve whatever problem there may be, I will gladly do so," Rieve said.

"I have received reports that you have been in contact with Headmaster Emeritus Sandor. In fact, I myself just saw you moments ago standing next to the Headmaster Emeritus looking out his window. Do you deny this?"

"No, sir. I do not deny this," Rieve said.

"What is your relationship to Sandor?" Professor MulLord asked still in the voice of a concerned father.

"He is my father," Rieve replied.

"Is he your teacher?" MulLord asked.

"He has taught me much and that is what a father does for his children," Rieve replied quickly.

"That was not the question," MulLord said.

"I am unsure as to how to answer that question," Rieve responded.

"As I said, we have information from at least one of your fellow students that you have been under the regular instruction of Headmaster Sandor. We have information that you are going to use this knowledge and the training you are receiving from Sandor to incite your fellow students against the new leadership. It is also said that you have engaged in the black arts and have seen things that do not belong to you."

"That sir, is a lie!" Rieve answered firmly. "No one in Entosian can see what does not belong to him, since the seeing is given by the King. That accusation, sir, is false on the face of it."

"Don't lecture me on the will and power of the King," MulLord snapped.

"What is the name of this student? I am entitled to see him and to question him myself if he is the source of these accusations."

"No you are not. We have new procedures in place now. Procedures that have been designed to protect you," MulLord replied, "and those who help us protect the

Expelled

Academy. Apprentice Priest Rieve Waynwright, are you aware that it is against the rules for Sandor to be teaching you anything?"

"I know that Headmaster Sandor has been banned from teaching in the classroom," Rieve said. He paused for only a moment, "Banned unjustly in my judgment."

"It is not your judgment that matters. This ban means that he is not to teach anyone under any condition and students are not to seek his instruction," MulLord's voice was now taking on a different tone. It was hardening in the same way that matched his face.

"With all due respect, that is not how the ban from the City Fathers reads."

"That is what the ban means!" MulLord shouted. "In a few minutes faculty members will be walking through that door," he pointed to a door to his right. "They are going to vote on whether you should be removed from this academy or merely placed on probation. They have heard the testimony of one of your own friends and that testimony is devastating. It constitutes cause for removal. However, the panel will take into consideration my recommendation. Do you understand what I am telling you?"

"Yes, I believe I do," Rieve said.

MulLord arose from his chair and walked around the "C" shaped table. He walked over to the Podium of the Accuser and leaned against it. The hall was filled only with the sound of their own heartbeats and breathing. The silence seemed to last forever. MulLord meant it to.

"If you tell me all that you and Sandor have talked about, I will recommend probation and I will save your career. If you will not cooperate, I will have to report that too. Your fate is in my hands. Headmaster Sandor cannot keep you in this Academy. Only I can do that. So tell me, what has Sandor taught you? What have you two been talking about? Has he taught you the black arts?"

Rieve was silent. MulLord repeated himself again and again. Each time louder than before ending in a shout, "What has Sandor taught you!" Rieve remained silent.

A moment later MulLord noticed the ancient staff. He reached for it. The staff rushed against Rieve's body. Its movement surprised MulLord and caught Rieve off guard.

"How dare you deny me. Give me that now!" MulLord stepped forward and reached for the staff.

The Oracles And The Jewels

"No!" Rieve shouted with a shout that surprised even him. The sound echoed throughout the hall. "Where did that come from?" Rieve thought to himself.

"What an outrage! An outrage for you to speak to me in such a tone! It is not yours. It is mine. It belongs to the Academy!" MulLord tried to take it a second time. He grabbed the staff with his right hand about six inches below Rieve's hand. A second later MulLord yelled in pain. The air filled with the smell of burnt flesh. Immediately MulLord let go of the staff. The inside of his hand, palm, fingers, and thumb were burnt. He held his right wrist with his left hand. The yell was so loud four faculty members came running into the hall.

"Headmaster MulLord, are you all right!" Professor Ellery called out.

"What is going on here!" Professor Bozzez yelled. Ellery and Bozzez were followed by Suedos and Paddan.

MulLord took a deep breath and stepped back from Rieve. "I'm all right, gentlemen. Please take your seats." They did as instructed. MulLord stepped into the Podium of the Accuser. "I wish I could report that this young Entosian has cooperated with my investigation. But this is not so. Apprentice Priest Rieve Waynwright has been decidedly uncooperative. Dare I say, even rebellious. He stands accused of seeking and obtaining instruction from an unapproved conjuror, an offense punishable by expulsion from The Academy of Theological Sciences and Ancient Conjuring Arts and a stripping of his priestly privileges. By the testimony of one of his own friends and classmates, we have established that he has on at least one occasion, perhaps more, engaged in the use of black arts. In addition, he has refused to yield the staff he now holds in plain view and to return it to the Academy. He has added to his problems by shouting in disobedience to the Headmaster and by inflicting an injury on the Headmaster's person." MulLord held up his hand and showed the panel his burns. "He has used his power, as you can see, to inflict harm upon a fellow Entosian. This is itself a confirmation that he is engaged in the use of the black arts.

"We have spared nothing to give this apprentice priest the opportunity to repent of his ways and to provide this committee with the information it needs to resolve this matter.

"Gentlemen of the Disciplinary Committee, I have investigated the matter thoroughly and have found him guilty

Expelled

of these offenses. It is my recommendation that he be punished to the fullest. The matter is now in your hands. What say you?"

"I object!" Rieve said. "There are only four faculty members present. I am entitled to a full hearing by a full panel of judges."

"Law, law, law. Rules and regulations. That seems, gentlemen, to be the only thing these young priests of ours understand these days. That has been the problem with this Academy for some time now and that's why Entos is so troubled. Here we are trying to help this young Entosian see his way clear to comply with the spirit of the law, the spirit of cooperation, and what does he do? He quotes rules and regulations. I bid you vote," MulLord said. "All in favor of expulsion signify by saying 'Aye.'"

At that moment, the door behind and to the left of the table opened. Three faculty members entered. Professors Langward, Worett, and Scarre rushed in. Rieve's heart was lifted in that moment. He looked to see if his own father was among the intruders, but he was not and the joy that had filled his heart quickly dissipated.

"Professor MulLord, what is the meaning of this?" Professor Scarre asked.

"What has this student done?" Langward added.

"Professors, this is none of your concern! This is the Disciplinary Committee," MulLord replied.

"I beg to differ, Professor MulLord," Worett said. "I am a sitting member of the Committee, as is Professor Scarre."

"You are mistaken. You were members of the Disciplinary Committee when Sandor was Headmaster of this Academy. But I am now the head of this Academy and this is my Disciplinary Committee. Furthermore, these proceedings are confidential. They are confidential because we want to protect the privacy of this young priest. They are confidential so as to save the accused public embarrassment. I demand that the three of you leave this hall immediately!" MulLord shouted.

"So that you can unjustly remove this priest from this institution?" Professor Worett said.

"I warn you Professor Worett. Speaking untruths about your Headmaster is grounds for your own removal," MulLord said as he struck his fist against the tabletop.

"Speaking untruths against this apprentice priest is no less an offense to Entos," Langward said.

The Oracles And The Jewels

"That is quite enough. You are all ordered to leave!" MulLord shouted again.

"We will not!" Langward replied.

"Guards! Guards!" MulLord called out. The honor guards, who were standing outside the main doors, entered.

"Remove these men from these chambers!" MulLord ordered. Scarre and Worett looked nervously at one another and began to make a slow retreat toward the door.

Professor Langward lifted his conjuror's staff in their direction and thrust it gently forward. The guards fell backward. Scarre and Worett stopped in their tracks.

"Remain, gentlemen," Langward said.

"Langward is right. This priest has the right to witnesses. We shall remain here," Scarre said.

"Guards!" MulLord shouted. He looked at the guards who were still sitting on the floor. "Get up!" he shouted. They did not move. They looked to Langward and then back to MulLord.

"Their spirit is willing, but their flesh is too weak," Langward said as he smiled at MulLord.

"Suit yourselves! It will change nothing," MulLord said with a huff. "Now, gentlemen of the committee, it is time to vote. All in favor of the divine dismissal of Apprentice Priest Rieve Waynwright of Timaho Clan as a student of The Academy of Theological Sciences and Ancient Conjuring Arts signify by saying 'Yea'." All four professors responded with the affirmative.

"Apprentice Priest Rieve Waynwright, you are no longer a student here at the Academy," MulLord said with great satisfaction.

"I call upon the committee to cast a second vote in favor of divesting this apprentice priest of his staff and all the powers and privileges thereof. Signify by the customary sign, 'Yea'," MulLord directed. Immediately four 'yea' votes were spoken.

"Surrender the staff, Rieve Waynwright, collect up your things, and leave campus immediately. Speak to no one on your way out."

Rieve stood in stunned silence. It all happened so quickly. He still held the staff in his hand, but stood confused and did not know what to do or what could be done. He had hope Professors Langward, Scarre, and Worett would be able to delay the inevitable, but they looked as confused as did Rieve.

Expelled

"Surrender the staff!" MulLord commanded sharply as he held out his hand. "Now!" Rieve lifted the staff to give it to MulLord. Suddenly the main doors flew open. Sandor stepped into the hall. Everyone in the room looked into the light that had broken through the doorway. They could not see his form in the bright light, but they all knew instantly who it was that had entered.

"This is none of your concern, Sandor!" MulLord shouted. "This is no longer your jurisdiction! Leave now!"

"This priest is my charge," Sandor replied in an equally firm voice. "He no longer belongs to the likes of thee."

"By what authority is this boy your charge?" MulLord shouted in return.

"By sacred right, by holy tradition, by divine institution!" Sandor said in a firm and clear voice. "Tell me please, that thou still remember such things. Or hast thou forsaken these as well?" MulLord said nothing in reply.

"Thy ignorance dost not negate the truth of the matter. Rieve Waynwright is now a conjuror and priest. This conjuror and priest is my charge, for I have called him and sealed him in his office. He has been ordained by one who was ordained long before thee and whose power has been confirmed by the King."

"Then this is your fault. You have brought this upon this boy by your actions!" MulLord yelled.

Sandor's face took on a stern and angry form. Ellery, Bozzez, Suedos, and Paddan rose to their feet and stepped back from the table. To stand against Langward, Worctt, and Scarre was one thing, but to stand against Sandor, the most powerful conjuror in Entos of the past five hundred years was another. Faced with his presence their courage fled and they looked for an escape.

"Stand, you cowards!" MulLord yelled. "You are the Disciplinary Committee. You belong here! They do not! If you leave you're finished in this Academy." The threat accomplished the purpose for which it was sent. Ellery, Bozzez, Suedos, and Paddan stopped their retreat and took their seats again.

"Leave the boy alone," Sandor commanded.

"He has already been expelled!" MulLord shouted. "You are too late. The vote has been cast. It cannot be undone. The only business left is that staff. He has been ordered to turn it over. But by black magic he refuses."

"Remove him from this Academy, this ye can do. Remove him from the priesthood, this ye cannot do. Defame

The Oracles And The Jewels

him, this ye can do. But dishonor him, this cannot be done by anyone but himself alone. Expel him, this ye can do too. But take his office and his power, this ye cannot do! These things can only be done through me! I trained him. I placed him under orders. I gave him his staff, a staff that has been passed from generation to generation, from the one to whom it belonged and to the one to whom it rightly belongs now."

Sandor's tone change. He now spoke slowly and in a low tone, "So I say it again, and I say it for the last time, leave this priest alone." He breathed a heavy breath and looked at the two guards standing near him. The two guards retreated into the recesses of the hall.

MulLord stepped forward and took hold of the front of Rieve's robe. Sandor lifted his staff and struck its base on the granite floor. A rumble rolled across the room and a crack the width of his staff opened up and ran across the floor and between the two podiums, then turned to the right and continued in front of the podium and between the four judges and Rieve. As the crack traveled across the floor, a spray of water went forth from it and water filled the crack. When the crack had finished separating Rieve from his five judges, Sandor commanded, "Come thou, my young priest. For thou hast been expelled from the Academy." Then Sandor said with a voice filled with happiness. "Be of good cheer. Thou is in good company. So am I." Sandor looked at Rieve and smiled, then continued. "If I know MulLord, he will see to it that we will not be lonely."

The two exited the Tribunal Hall and walked into the courtyard. As they entered the courtyard, every eye fell upon them and silence overtook the yard. The breeze stopped and the birds ceased their singing. Rieve looked eastward and saw Brenna and Nassar sitting on a bench. They sat motionless and stunned. Rieve looked to the eastern sky above their heads.

"I see him. Now I see him. You're right, my lord. Ashkelon is coming," Rieve said.

"Indeed, Thou has been removed from the Academy. Thou wilt see things more clearly now," Sandor said. "Fear not, young priest. What thou has they cannot take from thee. Thou has been set in place. Thou hast become what thou now is."

Rieve glanced back to Brenna and Nassar. Brenna gave a slight smile and a nod of his head. Rieve returned the glance and nod.

Expelled

"My lord, what about the Great Ritual? Now that I have been removed I won't be permitted to preside in The Great Chamber," Rieve said

"Thou wilt just have to wait a bit longer than the others. Waiting is a good thing, my son. Waiting is sometimes a very good thing."

Cadet Headquarters

The afternoon passed slowly for the cadets. At 4:00 Tag and Brenz led their squads back into the city. They passed The Academy of the Theological Sciences and The Great Chamber. As they walked by each squad, the squad gave their commanders the all clear sign. All was going well and so far it appeared that the authorities had not discovered their presence. The plan was working. They were, for all practical purposes, an invisible army on a crucial mission. The nine cadets made their way through the city and to The Academy of the Building Arts.

"Wait here," Tag told the two squads. "I want to see how Breille is coming with my new toys." He walked across the street and into the main entrance of the academy. The others dispersed into the various shops and into the open market near the Performing Arts Building on the other side of the street.

"Good afternoon," Tag said to the Procuron sitting at the reception desk inside the main entrance.

"What can I do for you?" the receptionist asked.

"I am looking for Breille Clarrice. I am a friend of hers and was just in the area and wanted to stop by to say hello. Is that all right?" Tag asked politely.

"Of course it is. Classes ended an hour ago. She is probably working on a project of some kind. You will find her in the student project manager's office along the back wall to the left."

"Thank you," Tag said. He made his way through the large lobby and the crowd of workers to the back wall. Breille was right where the receptionist had said. The door was open, but Tag knocked anyway. Breille turned around and saw him there.

"Hello Tag," she said.

"Hello Breille," Tag replied. "Did you get into any trouble over last night?" he asked as he stepped into the little workroom and closed the door.

The Oracles And The Jewels

"No. But President Kuchen is pretty angry. If he knew who to throttle, he would. He has been asking everyone if they've ever heard of a 'General Hafferling'."

"I wouldn't want to be General Hafferling when Kuchen finds him," Tag said with a soft laugh. "I came by to let you know that there are only a couple of days left. Those toys might be needed in three days."

"I drew up some plans and they are in the machinery. The prototype lab should be producing about two dozen of them in the next day or so. I will have them put in a cart and left in back of the building when they are done."

"Can all that be done without anyone noticing?" Tag asked.

"That's no problem these days. The modernization program is turning out all kinds of prototype 'toys' to replace our warrior boys. No one is going to notice," Breille explained. "If trouble starts, where do you think would be the best place for me?"

"Assuming River Kiernan is able to get us into that old little theater, we will set up our headquarters there. If you hear a horn blast and see youths running through the streets, we will probably need you at headquarters. We are meeting River at the old theater in about an hour. Do you want to come along?" Tag asked.

"Yes. Two or three days. That's all," Breille said softly.

"That's all. But we're ready."

"Give me a few minutes to put some things away and I will walk over with you," Breille said.

"I'll be outside. Brenz's squad and mine are waiting for me. We will wait for you."

"See you in a couple of minutes," Breille said.

Tag walked outside to the open market. The two squads made their way to his position.

"Did you talk to her?" Brenz asked.

"Yes. She's coming with us. We need to wait a couple of minutes." Breille emerged from the building and joined the group. They headed due west and then turned north approaching the west side of The Great Chamber and the old theater from the south.

The Conjurors

Akimm, Brenna, Pandar, and Nassar arrived in the park a few minutes early. Rieve's news had been leaked to the entire student body for the purpose of intimidating the rest of

Expelled

the apprentice priests and candidates. All were now expected to comply with MulLord's new expectations.

Rieve had picked up his books from his cabinet at the Academy and had moved them to the Headmaster's house just off campus. As he walked from the Headmaster's house to the park on the northeast side of The Great Chamber to meet the other four, he walked with his head high, still wearing his priestly robe and carrying his staff. He looked confident and unashamed of what had happened. Yet, even though he had done nothing to merit his expulsion, he could not help but feel embarrassed. As he walked passed the Academy and The Great Chamber he felt as though every pair of eyes fell on him. He couldn't help think that every whisper and laugh that found his was directed toward him. He looked like a priest on a mission, but inwardly he was conflicted. Angry and sad over what happened, yet proud to be associated and convicted with the Headmaster. He felt lonely, but he had never known such a friend and teacher as Sandor. He counted it a privilege and a burden to suffer the same fate as his master.

As Rieve walked, he played the entire trial over in his head, wondering if there was something he could have or should have said. As he approached the park, he saw his four friends standing under a tree waiting for him. He looked around. "Too many people here," he thought. He shook his head no and pointed in the direction of the Warring Academy. The others understood what he meant. He did not want Academy students or faculty seeing them with him. He was alone now, at least that is what Rieve wanted MulLord to think. That was also the way Rieve felt.

All five walked briskly down the street to the warring academy. The four were about a half block in front of Rieve. By the time they were six blocks away from the Academy and The Great Chamber it was safe for Rieve to join the other four, but he elected not to do so. When the four arrived at the Warring Academy building they stopped across the street and waited for Rieve to catch up.

"Is it true?" Pandar asked.
"I am afraid so," Rieve answered.
"Isn't there an appeal process?" Akimm asked.
"Sure there is. He can make an appeal to MulLord and the City Fathers," Brenna said. "A lot of good that will do."
"Sorry, Rieve. You don't deserve this," Nassar said.

The Oracles And The Jewels

"Rumors say you were thrown out because you were using an unauthorized conjuror and practicing the black arts," Pandar reported.

"Believe what they will. Those who know me know better than that," Rieve said.

"Yes, but what are we to say in return?" Pandar asked.

"The truth," Brenna maintained, "just speak the truth. Some say that you were betrayed by a friend and a classmate."

"It that true?" Pandar asked. Rieve did not answer. "Do you know who it was?"

"Yes, I believe so," Rieve said. Tears welled up in his eyes. He looked away hoping that his friends did not notice.

"Who was it?" Pandar said insistently.

"How Rieve, can we defend you? How can we help you?" Nassar interrupted.

"Don't say anything. Don't defend me. Don't try to win the argument. Time will vindicate me if I need vindication. Just keep your eyes on the real battle and the real battle is not over me. This is just the side show. Let's go meet Conjuror Stratia." Rieve led the four across the street and into The Academy of the Ancient Warring Arts. The five of them approached the receptionist's desk.

"Good afternoon. Where can we find Conjuror Stratia?"

"He is in the basement in the office in the center of the building," the Kilposian cadet replied.

"The very center, I suppose," Rieve commented.

"As a matter of fact, yes. Just go down the stairs over there and work your way to the middle of the building."

"Thank you and good day," Rieve said. The other four also thanked her. When they had finished thanking her, she said, "Fight well gentlemen and to the glory of Entos." The blessing struck them as strange. When spoken by a warrior or cadet, it was always spoken to another warrior or cadet. They were neither.

The five of them headed down the stairs and made their way to the middle of the building. The office was not hard to find. His office sat in the middle of a large empty room, obviously an old training room. The office itself was constructed of wood and glass and was in the shape of The Great Chamber. It had eight sides and eight windows. The conjuror was able to see all the way around the room by simply sitting on his chair and spinning in the desired direction. Conjuror Stratia saw them coming and turned on the lights in the old hall.

Expelled

"Well fellow sojourners," he said with a smile. "The general told me to expect a visit from some apprentice priests. Which one of you is Rieve Waynwright?"

"I am, sir," Rieve said softly.

"I am honored to meet such a young warrior who has already shown himself in his young life to be a friend to Sandor and to the old ways," Stratia said as he approached them.

"The honor is mine," Rieve replied.

"Who are these?" Stratia asked.

"This is Brenna, Akimm, Pandar, and this is Candidate Nassar." As Rieve introduced each of them Stratia placed his hand on the shoulder of each and gave him a little shake. Stratia looked to Nassar, "Any powers at all?"

"Not yet, sir," Nassar said. A feeling of uselessness fell over him.

"That's okay. I am sure you will prove useful soon enough to someone. Everyone is useless to someone, at sometime," Stratia said as he removed his hand from Nassar's shoulder.

"Thank you, sir, I think," Nassar said.

Stratia walked into his office and over to a pipe with a funnel-shaped end that came down from the ceiling. He shouted into the pipe, " Send down eight cadets for conjuring practice!

"Gentlemen," he began, "we don't have a lot of time. This is likely going to be your only lesson before things get moving around here. So it is very important for you to listen to me and to do exactly what I tell you to do. Should there be a battle in the city, I will come out of retirement and give aid where I can. But you will likely be on your own and the lives of cadets will depend on your ability to master three simple movements and incantations.

"Those movements are as follows. The boost. It is a ball of energy that enables your target to maximize his full physical potential and to push him beyond those limits so that he will be stronger and faster than those around him. He will accelerate, but from his own perspective everyone else will slow down. The duration of this boost depends on several variables. The strength of the target; the type of activity in which the target is engaged; and the quality of your magic." Stratia looked at Rieve. "Not all conjurors are equal in their power and not all work equally hard in training that power. If Headmaster Sandor has chosen you, he sees great potential in you." Stratia turned to the others.

The Oracles And The Jewels

"The second movement is the push. You will be able to move objects and creatures away from you as if you pushed them. The third movement is the pull. It is of course, the opposite of the push. The push and pull movements can be combined into energy that produces a throw. But once an object has been impacted by your energy, you have no control over its flight path. It is exactly like throwing a ball. You cannot steer it.

"The same principles that apply in other realms of conjuring apply here as well. There must be two things present for wizardry to work. The spoken words and the elements. You cannot think it. You cannot wish it. You cannot bring something about by remembering it. These cannot and will not work unless you attach the words to a physical element, even if that element is not so obvious – like sound, or air, or water. The kind of conjuring that takes place here in Entos is the kind that attaches itself to means, to creatures, and to substances.

"In this regard we are at a disadvantage. Ashkelon enjoys no such limitations. He can send destructive energy from his own will, the source of which is his own hate for you. With a wave of his hand he can throw you anywhere he wills."

As Stratia finished his introduction, eight cadets entered the training room. They were suited up in training gear so that every inch of their bodies was protected. They were armed with practice swords, whose blades were blunted. Rieve, Akimm, Pandar, and Brenna were each assigned two sets of combatants. Four sets of the cadets took the floor and the other four took positions against the wall to wait their turn. Conjuror Stratia placed a stand in the middle of the floor. A shallow dish, which contained dust of gold and silver, had been attached to the stand.

"This is how this works. Rieve you are facing off against Brenna. Akimm and Pandar are opponents. The combatants who stand between you are mere instruments. You are the warriors here and they are your weapons. Do not break your weapons. If they fall you may well, too. When I shout engage, speak this word over your dish of dust and make sure your breath disturbs the elements in the dish. Speak *exnatellon* and begin immediately. Ready. Engage!"

The four did as instructed. Brenna's combatant hit the floor first and within five seconds. Akimm and Pandar proved equally inept in their first attempts to help boost and move

Expelled

their cadets. Their match continued, while Brenna and Rieve regrouped.

"You've done this before," Brenna said.

"You're right," Rieve said with a smile. "Probably one of the reasons kicked me out of the Academy?"

"That's just a small part of it," Brenna said

"Are you cadets all right?" Rieve asked. The cadets nodded their heads signaling they were fine and ready to start again.

Rieve and Brenna took their positions behind their combatants. The conjuror shouted 'engage' again. This time Brenna was fast enough to grab a fist full of glitter and provide the needed boost for his combatant. Rieve's combatant prevailed again, but this time there was at least a fight. For the next thirty minutes the four conjurors and their combatants practiced again and again, each time achieving a new level of proficiency. Toward the end of the training, all four were beginning to master the three basic movements, but time was running short. Rieve needed to meet the little fellowship at the old theater, which was an easy twenty minute walk.

"Conjuror Stratia," Rieve began, "I must apologize. I must excuse myself. I would appreciate it if you would continue to work with my three friends. Nassar and I have an appointment that we must keep at 6:00. Thank you very much for your time and service. Since I am no longer a student at the Academy I suspect I will be spending a lot more time in this basement. I hope to see you tomorrow." Conjuror Stratia nodded his head as if to say good day. Rieve reached for his staff and the staff returned to its place. Nassar and Rieve walked across the floor, up the stairs, through the lobby, and into the street.

"Nassar," Rieve said. "You don't have to be involved in this. Without the ability to conjure, you're at a distinct disadvantage."

"I want to help. I consider it a privilege to serve with you and I want you to know that you can trust me. Even if all others fail you, I will not," Nassar said as he put his hand on Rieve's shoulder.

"Do not swear such a thing," Rieve replied. "These are dangerous times and we will fail each other."

"You can trust me," Nassar said.

"If that is the case, I can think of one thing you can do to help out," Rieve replied.

"What's that?" Nassar asked.

The Oracles And The Jewels

"I still have my clothes and personal items in my dorm room. I need to get them over to the Headmaster's house," Rieve said with a smile.

"Top secret stuff. As I've said. No task is too big or too small. I'll take care of that," Nassar said.

"I have one place to stop first. If you can get started, I will be there shortly," Rieve assured him. The two parted company. Rieve turned left and headed south. Nassar continued straight toward the Academy dorms.

He walked quickly through the crowded streets occasionally looking back over his left shoulder and eastward at the darkening sky. With the passing of every hour Rieve could see the coming of Ashkelon more clearly. It would probably be another day before most Entosians would be able to see the darkening sky, but it was becoming clearer to him. The armies on the eastern walls could see the darkness approaching from their perch high upon the battlements, but the Entosians in the city could not see the approaching danger. The beauty and lights of the city shielded their eyes from the darkness that would soon envelop the land.

The Scouts

The scouts pushed themselves and their horses hard all day so they could cross the desert before dusk. They reached the edge of the forest, dismounted, and made their way on foot into the deep darkness. The scouts from Polemmas reached the forest at 5:00, Hodia at 6:00, and Krattos at about 6:30. The forest was strangely quiet. Only a few of the warriors had ever been to the forest, but all knew that the kind of quiet they now heard was unusual. It was still with the calmness of death. The only sound they heard was the sound of their own footsteps shuffling through the undergrowth.

The scouts from Polemmas had expected to encounter some of the beasts and creatures that had attacked the wall two days earlier, but all they came across were the carcasses of beasts, creatures, and fighters that had retreated across the desert only to succumb to their wounds during the retreat. It was as if the entire forest had been vacated by every creature that had the power of mobility.

The sun had set and the light of the three moons was concealed above the canopy of the forest. It was almost too dark to advance, but advance they did. All three squads

Expelled

wove their way through the forest until well into the night. At 12:00 in the dark, each of the squads bedded down and posted one guard to keep watch while the others slept.

The Hodia scouts were the last squad to bring their movement to a stop for the night. The force consisted of the lieutenant, the Kicahian named Arokim, two sergeants, one Fortian named Benjaminn and the other Justin, a Demotic, and three corporals – Tor, a Pithosian; Mead, an Aradian; and Gavvin, the Adroit.

To be a member of a special force like the scouts, a warrior had to achieve the highest proficiency rating in overall battle skills. They had to demonstrate an exceptional ability to work together and to anticipate the thoughts, desires, and actions of the other members of the unit. These warriors were the best of the best, but this would be their first journey to the Skattos Forest.

"Mead, you take the first watch. Justin, you have the second. We will all be up at dawn," Arokim ordered, "whatever dawn looks like in such a place as this."

"Yes, sir," Mead replied.

"Lieutenant," Justin said, " Where are we headed in the morning?"

"To the southeast," the lieutenant answered. "It is my intent to get as close as possible, as soon as possible, to the leading edge of Ashkelon's army. If things work out well, we should bump into the scouts from Polemmas. After that, all is improvisation."

"It certainly doesn't look like we will have to do any fighting between here and there," Gavvin said. "The forest is empty."

"Don't be fooled by the silence," Mead said. "I hear something, but it is distant. I can't make it out yet. But there is something out there."

"Well, if it is at a distance, we should get at least one night's sleep," the lieutenant said. "Don't worry about what's out there. There are enough dangers in these trees to keep us all alert. Now shut your mouths and close your eyes. We have an active day ahead of us."

The Cadet Base

As Rieve approached the old theater from the northeast, Brenz, Tag, Breille, and their squads approached from the south. River and Blisse were already at the theater cleaning up from the years of neglect.

The Oracles And The Jewels

"This place should serve as a perfect headquarters," River told Blisse as they cleaned up.

"I bet only about twenty Entosians actually know this place still exists. It certainly doesn't look like anyone has cleaned the place in twenty years," Blisse said. "I didn't know that part of my service for the cause would be spent as a maid cleaning up after dead actors."

"You keep cleaning. I'm going outside to look for the rest," River said. "It is starting to get dark. They're going to need a little help finding the place." River stepped out onto the metal grate at the top of the metal stairs which ran along the back of the building in a narrow alley where few traveled.

Cadet Ansel, a Fortian, was the first to spot River standing on the metal grate.

"There she is," he said. "On the top of those steps." The group was still three blocks away.

"Keep those Fortian eyes on River," Brenz said. "I don't think she can see us yet." The group began to walk a little faster. The alley was narrow and the platform upon which River stood was three stories aboveground. Unless people were looking down the alley and almost straight up, they would not have noticed her. As it was, River didn't notice the little band of ten until they entered the alley. She signaled that all was clear and they could ascend the stairs.

Rieve came down the alley from the opposite direction, the northeast. He saw the line of ten making their way up the staircase and each one disappeared behind the heavy metal door. River saw Rieve as well and waited for him to join the group. Once inside, River secured the door.

"What do you think? Will it do?" River asked.

"This is perfect," Tag said. "It is large enough to practice, soundproof, no windows, and is just one block away from The Great Chamber and the Academy. We can use the stage for our armory. That balcony will do just fine for sleeping quarters for Hodia and Polemmas."

"And what about you, Rieve?" Breille asked. "Will it suit your purposes as well?"

"It will, provided we can clear a large enough spot in the middle of floor so that the combatants and conjurors can train together," Rieve answered.

"I have an idea," Breille said. "Tomorrow, when Tag's toys are ready, I will send a work crew over to deliver the toys, remove the rest of the seats, and clear the middle of the theater."

Expelled

"Can you do that without them being missed?" Brenz asked.

"Thanks to the City Fathers, we have so many students at the building academy that we don't know what to do with all of them. We have more workers than we do ideas at the moment," Breille explained. "Besides, they start moving the panels out of the city tomorrow and that puts a lot of us out of work. I'll write it up as a field trip."

"Well, if you're taking orders, I have a few ideas of my own," Blisse said as she looked over the possibilities. "Can you create a field hospital here?"

"That depends on what you need," Breille said.

"I need a couple of tables, medical cabinets, a lift of some sort so that we can get the wounded up here and in the door quickly, and some better lights. I will send a couple of my recruits over tomorrow afternoon with all the medical supplies we need in the event of a battle."

"Okay, then I will send over an entire civil engineering department," Breille said.

"Brenz," Tag said, "Send out your squad to let all the Hodia and Polemmas squads know that this is now our base of operation. Everyone is to report here, sleep here, and help put this place in order. We don't have much time. Two days at best."

"Yes, sir," Brenz repeated the command to his own squad, who immediately left the old theater to spread the word.

"Two days," Breille repeated. "Is that an official estimate?"

"I put it close to three days," Rieve said.

"What intelligence do you have?" Tag asked.

"I can see him coming. He is in the eastern part of the forest, but his army is so large, part of it is still making its way through the jungle."

"You can see him?" Tag said with some disbelief.

"Yes."

"When did you acquire that gift?" Brenz asked.

"Right after they expelled me from the Academy, just as the Headmaster said it would be."

"They expelled you! On what grounds?" Tag asked.

"My loyalty to the old school and to the Headmaster, I guess. These days they don't really need a reason. They just need an accusation."

"Where are you going to live?" Blisse asked.

The Oracles And The Jewels

"Are you going to move back with Mother and Father?" Tag asked.

"No. Father might be part of the problem," Rieve answered. Rieve thought the revelation would shock Tag, but Tag didn't respond at all. "Headmaster Sandor has taken me into his own home," Rieve continued, "for the time being, which reminds me. I need to clear out my dorm room. I am out of my element here, so I will leave all of you to your work. I will bring some conjurors over tomorrow after classes so they can get some practice."

"I need to go too," Blisse said. "I will walk out with you Rieve." Rieve and Blisse walked down the stairs and headed off in two different directions.

Breille remained in the old theater measuring the walls and looking over the rest of the room. River went about reorganizing the mess so that there would be no confusion between props and real armor and weapons. Throughout the night cadets from the Hodia and Polemmas units reported to the old theater and helped clean. Tag and Brenz worked through the night to help prepare the room for its new life, short as it might be. Breille and River left at 10:00. At 12:00, they all turned in for the night.

Rieve walked back to his old dorm. It wasn't a long walk, only three blocks. It just seemed like a long way. He arrived at the door through which he had always entered. It was the door on the south end of the hall. Two candidates were standing outside talking. That was unusual for this time of night. As Rieve approached the door, the two candidates stepped into his way.

"Professor MulLord has barred you from the hall," the first candidate said.

"I have only come to retrieve my things," Rieve said. "Certainly theft of personal property, even of one expelled, is still wrong."

"Your personal belongings have been impounded until Professor MulLord and the authorities go through it all."

"To what end?"

"I suppose they are looking for evidence of the black arts," the second candidate spoke. "Now be on your way." Rieve hesitated, again unsure about what he ought to do.

"Now move along and don't worry about your friend Nassar. He was told your dorm room was off limits."

"Is there a problem here?" a third candidate asked. MulLord had posted two candidates at each entrance just to be sure. The two at the south entrance were now joined by

Expelled

the two from the north entrance. They took up positions surrounding Rieve.

"No, there is no problem," Rieve said. "I have just come to collect my things. The presence of these gentlemen suggested to me that Professor MulLord hasn't had time to plant evidence of the dark arts in my room yet. So I guess I must wait."

"Now a comment like that is uncalled for and will be reported to the proper authorities," the third candidate said.

Rieve turned and looked the third candidate in the eyes and said, "I am a faithful priest of Entos, a conjuror, to whom you owe respect and loyalty. You owe respect to all who hold such a staff, and especially to a priest who tells the truth."

"Fellow candidates, show this priestly imposter off the grounds," the fourth candidate said. Two of the candidates took hold of Rieve's arms and began to push him down the sidewalk.

"Gentlemen, is this really necessary?" Rieve asked. One of the candidates struck Rieve on the cheek.

As the scene unfolded, two cadets from the Polemmas army watched. They had recognized Rieve from General Witticor's introduction at the old theater and were shocked to see a priest handled with such irreverence. The sight of a priest being struck was too much. The two cadets converged upon the site.

"Excuse me, candidates," the first cadet shouted. "What is the problem here?"

"None of your concern, citizen," one of the candidates replied. "We are just tending to Academy business."

"There must be a problem," the second cadet rebutted. "For I have never seen any Entosian treat a priest and conjuror in such a poor fashion."

"And I have never seen a layperson touch a priest, except as an expression of respect, love, or in the giving of aid," the first cadet said.

"This is not your concern," the fourth candidate said as all seven came to a stop on the pathway. "Be on your way, the both of you!"

"It is a concern to all Entosians when a priest is treated in such a fashion. For have you not heard the old axiom. An attack upon the King's servant is an attack upon the King?" the first cadet said.

"For what you do to one of His, you do to Him as well," the second cadet said. "And that should be a matter of concern for all of Entos."

The Oracles And The Jewels

"Strangers, I will only ask you once more. Move off this path. Tend to your own business or we will remove you ourselves."

"I shall only ask you once more. Take your hands from this priest," the first cadet replied. "Or it will become necessary for you to remove us from your path."

One of the candidates gave the cadet a shove. The cadet was a Fortian who was dressed in a tribal robe that hid his large arms and imposing chest. The candidate pushed, but the cadet did not move even an inch. The candidate made a second attempt to push the cadet out of his way, but that effort set off a series of movements that left all four candidates on the ground gasping for air and moaning in pain.

"What are your names?" Rieve asked.

"I am Pio of the Minnos Tribe and a cadet in the Polemmas army," the first replied.

"I am Cort of the tribe of Barinn," the second cadet answered.

"Thank you gentlemen for your assistance." Rieve looked back at the four candidates still lying on the ground. "Are they going to be all right?" Rieve asked.

"They'll be all right," Pio said.

"Sir, is there anything we can to do help you?" Cort asked.

"I could use a little help getting my personal items out of my room. It would be pretty hard for MulLord to plant evidence to frame me in an empty room."

"I will go get some help," Cort, the Adroitian said. In a moment he was gone. Rieve and the Fortian walked back to the dorm entrance. The four candidates began to get up.

"Gentlemen," Pio shouted from the step. "I suggest you just sit down for a few minutes. A few of my friends will be along to help this priest. It would be best if you all just sat this one out." The four Candidates nodded their heads in agreement, staggered over to a nearby bench, and sat down.

Cort did not have to run far. The incident attracted the attention of his squad, who in turned signaled a second squad to stand by. Several cadets were now gathering at the door of the dorm.

"Sir, lead the way," Pio said as he swung his arm and gave Rieve a little bow.

"Thank you," Rieve answered as he stepped inside. The ten cadets followed.

Expelled

Several students poked their heads into the hallway to see what was happening.

"Sorry, sir," Cort said. "It appears we've drawn a little attention to ourselves."

"There is no reason to be sneaking around. The more witnesses the better. Everyone will know that I collected my things and in so doing I prevented Professor MulLord from planting evidence against me."

"Good evening, my friend," Nassar said as he poked his head into the hallway. "Can I be of service?"

"No need. I have plenty of help," Rieve said as he opened the door to his old room. "It appears I have already found new friends and they are more helpful than many of my previous classmates. Go back to your studies; you need it."

"Good night Rieve. Don't hesitate to call upon me. You still have a few friends in this place. Not many, but a few," Nassar said as he closed his door.

It only took a minute. Rieve didn't have many material possessions. Priests in Entos didn't need much. The citizens tended to their needs and gave them what was needed. The cadets marched down the hall, descended the staircase at the south end of the building, and followed Rieve to the Headmaster's home, where upon reaching the door Rieve knocked.

"Come in, my son," Sandor said. Rieve opened the door and the cadets filed in. "Well, it seems you have found some worthy friends," Sandor said. "It is good that there are still some among us who respect a faithful priest. Put his things in the back room, gentlemen. I thank thee for thy service."

"Our privilege," cadet Pio replied, "especially after seeing the way they treated this priest. I have never seen such disrespect in an Entosian before."

"I trust that thou and thy friends rendered a good service to those misguided Entosians and taught them respect," Sandor said with a smile.

"Yes, sir. I think we did. But I am afraid it is the kind of respect born out of fear rather than love."

"When the one fails the other must succeed," Sandor said as he nodded his head signaling his sadness.

"Keep up the good work. We only have one more day before things start moving along," Sandor said.

"We will be ready Headmaster," Cort snapped. "And we will not fail you." As cadets filed out of the house, Sandor touched each one on his birthmarks. As he touched each

The Oracles And The Jewels

one pictures flashed in his mind and he whispered a unique blessing befitting each one's fate.

Sandor gave a sigh, stepped onto his porch and said. "How sad."

"Sad, my lord? How so?" Rieve asked as he followed Sandor onto the porch.

"So young, but they have so little time."

"Are they going to die? How do you know? Did you see something?"

"Yes," Sandor said. "Sometimes, it happens that way when death is close."

"They are all going to die?" Rieve asked with a tone of disbelief in his voice.

"Not all, but most," Sandor answered.

"Surely, we must do something," Rieve sad with a slight tone of urgency in his voice.

"Always wanting to do something, when there is nothing to do," Sandor said. "What dost thou suggest? Tell them to neglect their duty? Should we tell them to run away when the enemy comes? Should we tell them to beg for their lives and turn them into something less than true Entosian warriors? To be an Entosian warrior one must be willing to die. Shall we tempt them to give up that which they have wanted all of their lives? Or perhaps, we should simply step aside and let Ashkelon take whatever he wants. What are we to do? We are to do what is required of priests and conjurors. We are to do what all the priests and conjurors before us have done. Those fine young boys who just left, they . . . they are to do what all fine warriors have done before them in times of war. They are to fight and even die so that Entos will go on. We will talk more in the light of day. We both need our rest this night."

Sandor turned to enter the house. "Oh," he said as he turned around again. "Thou servants of MulLord and the City Fathers, who stand watch over this house by the light of our moons, the young priest and I are retiring for the evening. Remain faithful to thy duty. I will let ye know when we both awake. Ye are free to rest this evening. Ye will have another day of life in Entos before fate finds ye." Sandor turned to Rieve. "After thee, Conjuror Rieve Waynwright." Sandor said then entered the house, and closed the door.

"I guess I will sleep with one eye open," Rieve said looking out the front window trying to get a peek at those to whom the Headmaster spoke.

Expelled

"Two Kicahians. Boys, really. Just doing what MulLord and the City Fathers tell them to do. They won't bother us," Sandor said.

"How do you know that?" Rieve asked.

"On the first night that they were here, I walked about the outside of my house speaking gibberish. I told them that I had placed a spell on the house that would follow them to the third and fourth generations of their children."

"You didn't," Rieve said.

"Of course not. As I said. They are just boys doing their duty. The real guards watch me by day. Sleep well."

"Good night, my lord," Rieve said.

"Thou art now a priest. Thou may call me Sandor. We are equals. In public we retain the formal, but in private thou may use the familiar."

"You are the first among equals, my lord, my father in the faith, and that is how I will continue to address you . . . 'my lord'," Rieve said as he bowed his head slightly.

"Good night," Sandor said as he shook his head slightly. "To be young again. How wonderful."

"Good night, my old Lord," Rieve answered. He smiled and shook his head in the same way as did Sandor.

The Academy of the Building Arts

Breille was up early and at work in her project room. The three panels that Breille had borrowed were joined by three more. All had been equipped with a lift system and wheels and were now being rolled into the streets in the direction of the Demotic valley. President Kuchen was overseeing the first leg of the journey. Several professors and students were also assisting in the project. Fortunately for Breille, there were still plenty of students willing and ready to get to work on new projects. Breille had created the necessary plans, filled out the required paperwork, and was about to submit the requisition forms to secure the needed supplies for the old theater. The list was impressive, as was the request for workers. What she didn't have was a signature of a sponsoring faculty member. Missing signatures was not uncommon and would only pose a problem if someone questioned the project.

As students of the academy started to show up, Breille began to recruit workers. That was not difficult either. Each morning students would check the project board to see if there was a particular project of interest. They would read

The Oracles And The Jewels

the project description, the listed of needed skills, and other basic information. The project sheets also listed the professor in charge and student project manager who would be directly in charge of the students involved. Breille listed herself as the student project manager, but the sheet did not have a faculty member's signature.

Breille listed the project as a renovation for military purposes. That was all that was needed to create interest among the students. Military projects were quickly becoming the way to get noticed at the building academy and, thanks to the modernization program of the City Fathers, almost half of the new projects were related in some way to the military. Field trips were also an opportunity to get out of lectures and avoid a day of pure mathematical equations. Within thirty minutes she had the four dozen students she needed to finish the project in one day.

Rieve gave them a short briefing and all were instructed to be back in the main lobby at 9:00. By 8:30 the supplies and equipment for the project were being placed in carts that now lined the alley behind the building. Several faculty members took notice of the activity and the supplies, but they assumed the materials had something to do with the wall and had the necessary authorization.

But as the materials began to pile up, one of the professors started to have her suspicions. Professor Tamikka prided herself on keeping up with the various projects of the academy. She had arrived on campus just before 8:30 and couldn't help but notice several students starting to gather around the reception area. She went from office to office asking her colleagues if they knew anything about the materials piling up in the alley way.

"Excuse me," Professor Tamikka said to one of the students.

"Good morning, Professor Tamikka," the student replied.

"Is there a field trip this morning?"

"It's a field project. It must have been a last minute project. It was posted this morning," the student explained.

"Who is in charge?" the Professor asked.

"I don't know who the professor is, but the student manager is Breille Clarrice," she said.

Breille was sitting in her project room looking out her window at the conversation between the professor and student. "Now what am I going to do? Do I sit in here and wait for Tamikka to interrogate me, or do I go out there and

Expelled

bluff my way through?" she thought to herself. "I'll bluff," she said out loud. Breille took a deep breath, got up, picked up the pile of papers pertaining to the project, and walked confidently into the lobby.

"May I have your attention please," She said at the top of her voice as she approached four dozen students gathered in the lobby. "Good morning. I want to thank you all for volunteering to help with this project. We have a very busy day planned and have a great deal of work that needs to be done before sunset. This project came up at the last minute and it is very important we finish the job today. This morning we will be renovating a large room for use as a military operation center, a field hospital, and a training hall."

"Excuse me, Breille Clarrice!" Professor Tamikka interrupted.

"I will be with you in a minute, Professor," Breille replied. "We have a very tight schedule this morning and I must get these students briefed and on their way. If you could just give me a movement." Breille turned back toward the students.

"The key to this project is speed. As I said the entire project must be completed today. The military is overseeing this project and will be timing us," Breille explained. The students were getting more excited all the time. "This is not only a project, it is a challenge," Breille added.

"Excuse me, young lady. I must insist that you take a moment to talk to me or these students aren't going anywhere!" the Professor insisted.

"I will be back in a moment," Breille informed the group. "In the meantime, please pass these plans out and directions. I apologize for the delay." Professor Tamikka took Breille by the arm and pulled her away from the rest of the students as Breille finished her last word.

"Young lady. I have talked to almost every professor in this building and no one knows anything about this project... There is no signature on this page!" Tamikka held up the project form she had taken from the board. "Where is your authorization for this project?"

"Here is all my paperwork, Professor Tamikka. If you would like to look through it all you're welcome to. I just need to get these students moving while you do that. As I said, this is a timed exercise," Breille answered.

"No one is going anywhere until I see the proper authorization," the professor said as she frantically sorted through the volume of paperwork Breille handed her. Breille

The Oracles And The Jewels

was on the verge of panic, or as close to it as any Procuron could get. The form the professor was looking for was in the pile of papers she had given to the professor, but it had no faculty signature. Without the signature, Breille would be considered little more than a common thief, stealing supplies, and students' time. Breille was coming to the realization that in just a few more moments, in just a few more turn of the pages, Professor Timikka would find a blank form and Breille's career at The Academy of the Building Arts would come to an end as abruptly as did Rieve's the day before.

"Here it is," Professor Tamikka said proudly. "Just as I thought! Young lady! There's no signature here! Explain yourself!"

Breille looked to her right and saw four dozen sets of eyes looking at her in great expectation and panic.

"Professor, could you step into the office so that I can explain this," Breille said.

"I demand an answer here and now," she replied.

"But this project is . . . It is a military project . . ." Breille said struggling to keep her composure.

"Military projects need authorization too, young lady and you know that. Without a sponsoring faculty member, this is an unauthorized project and you are a thief and a liar!" Timikka said with great satisfaction.

"But . . . but . . . this one," Breille started to say.

"This one is top secret and none of your business Professor Tamikka," a strong male voice said. The speaker approached from behind Breille. Tamikka's countenance fell. "This is my project and your interference is slowing the whole thing down," Professor Enoss said. Enoss came to a stop between Breille and Tamikka. "I apologize, Breille Clarrice, for putting you in such a difficult position. I should have been here on time. Please accept my apologizes for any embarrassment I might have caused you," Enoss said.

Breille stood stunned for a moment then responded, "No Professor, I should be apologizing to you. I am already behind schedule. If I had been on time, this whole encounter would have been avoided."

"This young lady was under orders by me to keep this project as quiet as possible," Enoss said. He looked straight into Tamikka's eyes and clinched the muscles in his jaw, as if in great frustration. "Thanks to you, Professor, the project is off to a rough start and not much of a secret either. Here we are at the edge of war, and you are running around the

Expelled

place making public that which is suppose to be confidential."

"Professor Enoss, you know very well that none of this should have been done without your signature on this authorization form first. This form is blank and that is a violation of procedure," Professor Tamikka asserted as if she were the ranking faculty member. In truth Enoss had been at the academy for many more years than her and chaired one of the departments charged with military development. Tamikka was one of the newer faculty members and had received her placement from the City Fathers to help expedite the transition from the older technologies to the newer ones.

"Professor, may I remind you that I am one of your supervisors. I suggest you act like a Procuron and speak in a tone more befitting a subordinate. This project came to me late last night. I needed to be home and was not able to complete any of the paperwork. This young lady was kind enough to work through the night to assist me. Knowing her as I do, I am sure everything is under control. Now Professor Tamikka, I believe you owe Breille Clarrice an apology. Once you're done apologizing, you ought to thank her for the extra effort. Given who her father is, I would think that might be a good career move too." Enoss took the pile of papers from Tamikka and signed the authorization form.

"I will not apologize," Tamikka said.

"Then excuse us. We have work to do," Professor Enoss replied. Professor Tamikka turned and walked away in a huff and to the smiles of several students.

"Young lady, I don't have a clue about what you're doing, but I assume General Witticor does. He does, or doesn't he?"

"Sort of, sir," Breille whispered back.

"Sort of is close enough. Now get out of here before anyone else takes notice. I don't outrank everyone around here."

"Thank you, thank you very, very much, Professor Enoss," Breille said. "You won't be sorry." Breille joined the rest of the students gathered in the lobby. "May I have your attention. I apologize for the delay and thank you for being patient. There are twelve wagons full of supplies behind the building that need to be transported to our work location. I trust that the maps, plans, and detailed instructions have been passed out. We will head over to the work site

The Oracles And The Jewels

immediately. I am sorry for the delay and we will need to work extra hard to make up the time."

Breille and four dozen workers walked out to the back alley, picked up the carts, and marched down the street at a hurried pace. They headed west, then turned north toward the old theater. It took about twenty minutes for the students to reach the site. It was 9:30 when they opened the door and entered the theater.

The students broke down into the respective work crews and headed inside. Breille set up some signs in the alley. The signs read, "Building Academy At Work, Renovations In Progress. Do Not Enter." She placed one sign at each end of the alley. The signs were commonly seen in the city and attracted little attention. They would assure that the day's work would go on uninterrupted and so it did.

Sandor's Home

Rieve awoke at 7:00 in the light. Sandor had been up for two hours and had already made breakfast. It had been a long time since Rieve had slept that late. He felt guilty about it. He walked into the breakfast area and saw Sandor setting a plate full of food on the table.

"Good morning, young priest," Sandor said. "It appears thou had a very good night's sleep."

"I apologize for sleeping so late," Rieve said. "This is not a very good way to start off in my master's house."

"Thou wilt earn thy keep soon enough," Sandor said. "We have much to talk about this day before the morrow comes. It is time to learn what is about to take place and where thy duty lies. The next two days are going to separate the true from the false. A great evil has taken hold and tomorrow is the beginning of a long and painful journey."

"I am beginning to see what you mean," Rieve said. "Professor MulLord for example, is one of them. Isn't he?"

"One of them?" Sandor asked.

"A creature of Bohow," Rieve answered.

"Thou sounds so sure in thy judgment?" Sandor replied in the tone of a question.

"Do you not share my judgment?" Rieve asked. His voice took on the sound of uncertainty.

"I can only see his outer form. His outer form tells me that he is an Entosian. His form is that of an Entosian. His conduct is that of a bad Entosian. The rest is hidden, even

Expelled

from me. But what is also true is that the work of Ashkelon is not hidden, for he uses the deeds of good and bad Entosians alike to achieve his own ends. Many Entosians, either knowingly or unknowingly, are proficient at helping him," Sandor explained as Rieve began to eat his breakfast.

"Which is the greater danger?" Rieve asked. "The army that now marches west against the eastern walls of Entos or the Entosians in this city who seem unaware of the danger they have created?" Rieve took another bite as he waited for the answer.

"They are both dangerous and they could end in the same result. The first way is quicker and more obvious. The second way will take time and will claim more casualties."

"Why has Ashkelon chosen now, this moment of history, to launch such an attack?" Rieve asked.

"He must believe that his agents in Entos have divided us in such a way to make an attack successful. If the reports from General Witticor are correct, Ashkelon has trained a new generation of soldiers in the art of war. He has created a union between the creatures of Bohow, the wild beasts, the fowls of the air, and his own solider, which he created and bred for one purpose. To destroy Entos and to cast the Oracles and the Jewels into the fires of Ektos."

"Can he destroy the parchment upon which the Oracles are written? Can he crush the Jewels?" Rieve asked.

"No one knows. What we do know is that if the Oracles and the Jewels are taken out of the Land of Entos, neither the city nor the land can survive for very long. But the Oracles give power to the Jewels and if the Oracles are kept here," Sandor touched the birthmark on Rieve's head, then he touched the birthmark on Rieve's lips and said, "and are spoken here, then faith is kindled here in thy heart," Sandor placed his hand over Rieve's heart and continued, "and in the hearts of all who still have Entosian ears Entos is saved. Light and life itself is created and sustained by the Oracles and the Jewels. Entos exists to serve and to protect the Oracles and the Jewels, the Entosians who dwell in her land, and the Land of Entos herself. The general believes that the primary target of tomorrow's attack is the Oracles and the Jewels. We also believe that fellow Entosians may, knowingly or unknowingly, aid Ashkelon in that endeavor."

"Professor MulLord?" Rieve asked.

"He may be one of Ashkelon's helpers, but I don't believe he is Ashkelon's primary agent in this treachery."

The Oracles And The Jewels

"Why not Professor MulLord?" Rieve asked. "He is the one who has brought the fight to us."

"Ashkelon surrounds himself with brilliant and cunning creatures. Ashkelon loathes incompetence almost as much as he does righteousness. He wants the best and the brightest of his kind to lead." Sandor paused for a moment, dropped his head a bit, then said in a softer voice, "Entosians used to want the best and brightest too. No longer though." Sandor resumed his previous posture and continued. "The dim-witted and base are merely tools for Ashkelon. He uses their bodies and wastes them as he sees fit. Ashkelon needs Entosians like MulLord. He needs them to divide. He enjoys dividing brother against brother and sister against sister. He takes delight in the look of betrayal and enjoys more the look of pain in the one who has been betrayed. But he doesn't like the fact that he must rely on Entosians."

"I don't like it very much either," Rieve added.

"Now tomorrow when the attack begins, it would be best if thou would tend to The Great Chamber. If the general and I are right, the Hodia cadets are going to need the support of the best conjurors."

"Where will you be?" Rieve asked.

"On campus, watching all things from my perch in the faculty building," Sandor answered.

"But wouldn't it be best if you were in The Great Chamber?"

"Battles such as this one are won by priests and cadets who are young and who have not lived long enough to have their weaknesses exploited by the statesmen and elder priests. Now promise me, my young priest, that thou wilt not worry about me. Tend to The Great Chamber."

"I cannot promise," Rieve answered. "I do not know what tomorrow will bring and I will not make a pledge based on an option of 'either/or.' It is my desire to do both."

"Indeed, but both thy cannot do," Sandor said. "Thou wilt have to chose."

"What have you seen?" Rieve asked.

"I don't need to see it. This is how things work." Sandor replied. "Now finish eating and we shall walk around this beautiful city and look at her that we may remember her as she is now, in her present state, before the scars and ugliness are inflicted upon her."

Chapter Fourteen
Skattos Forest

"Wake up. We move out in five," shouted Lieutenant Arokim, a lieutenant in the Hodia army. Sergeant Justin had prepared some warm soup for breakfast, but it didn't last long. Within three minutes breakfast was gone. Each took his turn relieving himself a little distance from camp while the others cleaned up the area.

"Sergeant Benjaminn, take point. Those Fortians eyes of yours must serve us well today."

"Yes, sir," Benjaminn said.

"Corporal Mead, do you hear anything different this morning than you did last night?" Lieutenant Arokim asked.

"They're just a little closer, but not by much. They didn't make much progress last night."

"Corporal Gavvin, take your horse and the rear. Stay back a little ways. We don't want the horse to be heard before we hear them," Lieutenant Arokim explained.

In the light of day the squad could now see the forest as it actually existed. It was an unpleasant place in every way. Moss and mold blanketed the ground like grass. Every step left an imprint. If the toes or heels of their boots dragged upon the surface with even the lightest touch, a scar was left upon the ground. This would make tracking the enemy easy, but it also meant that the enemy could track them just as easily.

The trees weren't of the kind found in Entos. The trees of Skattos Forest were grotesque. The roots began above the ground and stretched out in all directions, often breaking through the surface of the ground, making the terrain all the more difficult to pass. The bark was hard and as sharp as razors. Moss covered much of the trunk and the leaves did not have a rich green color to them. They were a pale and dirty green, starved of light. The air too was stale and had the odor of death.

As the squad began its journey through the Skattos Forest, it became clear that this was not going to be a fast journey. Their path was often blocked with downed trees,

The Oracles And The Jewels

twice as large as any in Entos, giant roots, and large vines that often reached for them whenever they drew too close.

"I don't know how he does it," Corporal Gavvin said as he pulled himself over the top of a large root that crossed the path.

"Who does what?" Corporal Mead asked.

"How does Ashkelon move an entire army through this forest?" Gavvin asked.

"It is said that he simply orders the paths to be made smooth and the vines move," Benjaminn answered.

"That will be a sight to see," Gavvin said as he dropped to the other side of the root behind Benjaminn.

"Now that you have your question answered, don't you think you ought to shut-up before one of Ashkelon's trolls hears you? Some say their hearing is more acute that an Aradian's," Lieutenant Arokim said as he dropped to the same side of the root as Benjaminn and Gavvin. The squad fell silent and barely spoke a word for the rest of the day. Arokim believed that they would run into Ashkelon's army was still far off and that they would likely find his Ashkelon's army later in the day. But he had heard stories of creatures that lived in the top of the trees who could speak and who were used by Ashkelon to pass messages to and from their king. If the stories were true it made no difference whether they spoke or not. Ashkelon would already know they were in his forest.

The Great Chamber

Tag and Brenz's morning went as expected. They maintained their patrol without incident and arrived on time for their briefing and combat training. Breille was hard at work changing the theater into a base for operations and a field hospital. Blisse started her day in the normal way and attended her morning classes. She made arrangements for her two assistants to meet her at three so she could take them over to the old theater to begin setting everything up for the battle that was soon to come.

Rieve and Sandor left Sandor's home in the bright light of the morning sun. They walked slowly and looked at the beautiful buildings, which were a mixture of the ancient and contemporary. As they passed each building, Sandor told Rieve of its history and the meaning of its architecture and the colors of Entos. He saw in all things, natural or Entosian made, the intent and intelligence of the designers.

Skattos Forest

Sandor led Rieve through the streets, into the parks, and into the museums and art galleries. Rieve was impressed with the knowledge of his teacher. There was no question about Sandor's knowledge of the Oracles and of the sacred history of Entos. Rieve knew that Sandor was the wisest theologian in all of Entos, but he was awestruck by what Sandor knew concerning art and architecture. Sandor saw all things through the eyes of the Oracles and he saw that all in Entos was beautiful. As they walked, Rieve noticed two of the council's honor guardsmen following them.

"Are they here for our protection or are they here to protect Entos from us?" Rieve asked as he watched the two guards watching him.

"That all depends who picked them. If General Witticor was able to arrange their assignments for the day without MulLord, Botha, Scoderan, or Mohhan finding out, they are here to protect us. If, on the other hand, MulLord, Botha, Scoderan, or Mohhan discovered Witticor's influence, any one of them, or any number of other people would put their own men in place to do the opposite. We won't know until the moment of truth comes. Then we shall find out," Sandor explained with a smile and with a tone of complete acceptance.

"Sir, how can you live so happily and with so much ease not knowing whether those near you are friend or foe, whether they will run you through with a sword when you turn your back or strike down the one who moves to strike you?"

"It will all unfold as it should. Why be anxious about it? That will do nothing except make the day more unpleasant and for those with whom I converse in that day. See there," Sandor pointed to the eastern sky, which was beginning to show signs of Ashkelon's approach, although few within the city had taken notice of the tint of grey that was creeping into the eastern sky, "we could have spent the last two days worrying and fretting over the darkening sky, and indeed many will, but that hasn't changed the fact that all things have been set in place for the sky over Entos to be blackened by the evil of Ashkelon."

"But sir, have we not taken the steps to change what would have happened had we not known of the attack? Have we not fretted, so to speak?" Rieve asked.

"I have not. I hope as a young priest thou has not. Thou ought not. What we have done, what thou hast done, what I have done, indeed what General Witticor and all his agents

The Oracles And The Jewels

have done is simply their duty in light of the coming evil. That is all we can do. And those two there," the Headmaster pointed in the direction of the two guards, "they are doing their duty, either for ill or for good. But we will not know which it is until the time comes," Sandor said as he came to a stop at the bottom of the steps of The Great Chamber. The two looked up at the beauty and stature of the place.

"Come, let us see the prize that is esteemed by Ashkelon," Sandor said as he began to ascend the stairs to The Great Chamber. "It is a sad day my son, when Ashkelon understands the power and significance of the Oracles and the Jewels more than those who have been touched by them."

Rieve followed Sandor up the stairs. A few moments later, the two guards did the same. Rieve and Sandor spent the balance of the morning in The Great Chamber. Sandor told the stories of the Great Windows and of the contributions of the great conjurors who had helped the armies of old win the battles that forged out the Land of Entos.

"Close your eyes, my son," Sandor said. Rieve did. "Now place thy hands over thy eyes." Rieve did that too.

"Where we now stand there was once only darkness. A darkness darker than what thou does see now," Sandor began. "There was a sun over King Ashkelon's earth before the Ancient of Days, but its light did not reach Ashkelon's earth. His earth and the place where thou now stands was full only of evil and of darkness."

Rieve took his hands from his eyes and opened them. The two stood before the first window in The Great Chamber. The window depicted the moment when the light and the King came into Ashkelon's dark earth.

"Fire and smoke," Sandor continued, "rose from the two greatest mountains in Ashkelon's earth. Those mountains were called Mount Ektos, which means 'out of' and Mount Tophos, which means 'despair.' The smoke that poured out of them blanketed all of Ashkelon's earth. This place, where you now stand, was the place where Mount Tophos once stood. It stood higher and was more powerful than Ektos. Here in the time before the Ancient of Days, there was once nothing but darkness and despair. Then suddenly, and without warning, the light broke through Ashkelon's black sky." Sandor pointed straight up to and through the glass roof. "In a moment and with a crack louder than lighting, came the Light and Hope." Sandor pointed to the cradle in which the scrolls of the Oracles and the Jewels lay.

"In those dark days before the Ancient of Days, Ashkelon wandered his earth free of all that was good and right. He ruled over all the darkness and was master to every creature that walked, crawled, flew, talked, or grew on his earth. Slaves all and all slaves. In bondage to evil and content in the same." Sandor was filled with drama, hope, and expectation.

"The King came into the darkness. His very being pierced the darkness and he called forth to Ashkelon's earth. The King who had been King over so many kings in so many other worlds, the King who was King before there ever was a King Ashkelon had come to this place in His time. He came in peace, but knew that Ashkelon knew nothing of peace and would have no part of it.

"They came – the Creator, the Giver, and the King, from the north. They came from over the Oros mountains and stood at the foot of Mount Tophos. He spoke His words to the mountain, 'Be closed up!' and the mountain closed its mouth and fell silent, and the gods of the mountain fled into the forest and to Ashkelon and Ektos. For they were in fear of the King because they were gods, but they were not the Creator, Giver, and King. He spoke and the elements listened to his voices.

"Not even Ashkelon has the power to command the elements, not in this way. Ashkelon's words have the power to kill and destroy. His presence causes living things to recoil for fear of him. But he is the taker and user of life. He is everything that the King of Entos is not. The King of Entos is everything Ashkelon is not."

"Yet, Ashkelon is still a king," Rieve interjected.

"Indeed, a king he is," Sandor said. "King Ashkelon is the antonym of the King of Entos. Ashkelon lives because others die. Ashkelon has no dominion over life. Death, darkness, violence, and storms go before and follow him wherever he goes. Ashkelon's power stops at the winds, rain, earth, and sky. Ashkelon has created nothing, not even his own earth.

"As the Ancient of Days broke over the earth, the King of Entos spoke to the sky and commanded it, 'Be open.' The sky above Mount Tophos cleared and the light of the sun fell upon Ashkelon's earth for the first time. The gods of Tophos made haste to Ashkelon and told him of the mighty King and the great light. Ashkelon made haste to Mount Tophos and

The Oracles And The Jewels

looked upon the light that encompassed his mighty mountain. In that moment, Ashkelon knew that his enemy was more than his equal. He knew that his earth had been invaded by a mighty King whose very word could close the mouth of his mighty volcano and open the skies above his earth.

"Enraged Ashkelon returned to Ektos, gathered his army, and marched upon Tophos to drive the Invader from his earth. He summoned his eight most formidable creatures from the eight corners of his earth to slay the King of Entos.

"While Ashkelon gathered his army and marched westward, the Creator, Giver, and King reached His hand into the heart of Mount Tophos and took from it three diamonds and spoke a third time, 'Be made low.' Mount Tophos was no more. In the place where Tophos once stood, a great light shone down from the sky and the ground formed a mighty plateau which stretched out and pointed to the eight corners of the earth. There the King lived and waited for the attack from Ashkelon and his terrible creatures.

"When Ashkelon came to the place where Tophos once stood, he looked upon the light and issued forth a great cry, 'Be gone from my land for it was given to me!' " Sandor paused for a moment and led Rieve to the second window.

"Be gone from my land for it was given to me!" Sandor continued. "But the King replied, 'You have held this land in darkness long enough. The hour has come.'

"'It shall never come!' The words exploded from Ashkelon's mouth with fire and with such force that even the creatures that stood before him were consumed by its flames." Sandor had told the story thousands of times, but the repetition never dulled his telling of it. His voice was filled with drama and his eyes became like those of a little boy.

"Ashkelon ordered his eight terrible creatures to drive the King from the plateau and from his earth. The King stood firm atop His plateau and where there was one, there were now three Kings. One-by-one the three slew the eight. 'Depart from me, you one and you three!' Ashkelon spoke as he threw his spears into the side of the Kings." Sandor pointed to the words inscribed on the bottom of the second window. 'Depart from me, you one and you three!'

Sandor and Rieve moved to the third window. Sandor continued, "But our King did not depart. 'Kill this one and these three!' Ashkelon ordered all the creatures of his dark earth. As the creatures of Bohow and the soldiers of Ektos

Skattos Forest

charged forward toward the King, the King knelt down and touched the slain creatures from the eight corners of Ashkelon's earth, once upon the forehead, once upon the lips, and once upon the breast and spoke the ancient words that we speak unto this day." Sandor paused took a breath and chanted the words, *"'Horrom sarrach ek chooshem. Bassar mimim bassar. Essem mimim, essem."*

Rieve softly spoke the translations as Sandor sang, *"My Light arises out of darkness. My flesh is brought forth from my flesh. My bone is brought forth from my bone."*

Sandor and Rieve moved to the fourth window and Sandor continued to tell the story. "One-by-one the eight new creatures arose, the first of those raised were the first Entosians, and the first warriors. As each took his former weapon into his hand, the weapons were transformed from the crude metal objects into beautiful swords, shields, and armor that shown with the Light of Entos.

"The eight marched forward to meet the creatures of Bohow and the soldiers of Ektos. They stood together arrayed in a glorious light and eight abreast. In that day the eight warriors of Entos were given their names according to the gifts that the Giver had given to them. Their names were: Adroit, Arada, Demot, Fortan, Kicah, Kilpos, Pithos, and Procuro.

"When the battle was over, Ashkelon's army had been laid to waste. But Ashkelon turned to the eight who had betrayed him and vowed an eternal vow to drive the King, the Light, Entos, and all her beautiful residents from his earth.

"The King walked among Ashkelon's dead and spoke his words and touched eight more creatures of his own choosing. He brought them to his warriors and gave them one to the other and they began to multiply. The King lived among the creatures He had created. He taught them the way of His light. He taught them to fight. He taught them how to read, write, and to use his Oracles and Jewels to change their offspring from enemies of Bohow into brother and sister Entosians. The King lived among His people on the Great Plateau.

"Then one glorious morning at dawn, the King returned to the place from whence He came. He departed over the Oros Mountains and returned to the Land of the Kings. From that first day to this one, light pierces the darkness each morning and a new day begins.

The Oracles And The Jewels

"Each day that the sun rises, Ashkelon's hate for its glory rises too. Ashkelon has spent more than five thousand years trying to extinguish the Light of Entos. But the words of the King remain, so the sun remains too." Sandor looked straight up at the glass ceiling above him.

"The Oracles and Jewels are so much more than words and stones. They give this place its divine light and life. They keep us from being what we once were. Without them, the darkness will return." Sandor put his hand on Rieve's shoulder. "The Oracles and Jewels must be protected at all costs or all will be lost. Even if that means you must forsake me and everything else you hold dear in this world."

"Can Ashkelon take them from us?" Rieve asked.

"Yes. There are many ways to take them. Some obvious and others not so."

"Are the rumors true?" Rieve asked.

"Which rumors?" Sandor replied.

"The rumors that some want to change the rituals, the language, the music, and the words of The Great Chamber."

"Yes," Sandor said.

"The Oracles too?"

"Indeed. Although they deny it," Sandor answered.

"What will happen if they do such a thing?"

"It shall be our undoing. I have seen it." Sandor answered. He paused as he surveyed the windows again. Rieve did the same. "Let us sing," Sandor said, "The Hymn of the Land of Entos." Sing they did. All who were offering their prayers in The Great Chamber in that hour joined Rieve and Sandor in their hymn of praise and intercession. This is the song they sang.

The Hymn of the Land Entos

She is the bright and beaming Light; Amidst the darkness of this world.

She is our mother who gave us life, she gave us birth; She keeps us in this true life and saves us from this evil earth.

She is the cradle of His words; She is the stable of the Jewels.

She is the bride arrayed in white; She is the glorious maid of might.

The King gave us His Truth and Light; And the King who taught us how to fight.

She is the fortress in which we delight; She is the land of beauteous Light.

She is the product of the sun: She is the land who made us one.

She is the Land of Entos fair; She is the city of splendid glare.
She is the Land of Entos fair; She is the city of splendid glare.

Rieve and Sandor spent the balance of the morning singing some of the hymns of The Great Chamber that told of the Ancient of Days and of the Days of Old. When it came time for lunch Rieve and Sandor returned to the house and ate together. After they had finished Rieve walked to the Warring Academy to work with Conjuror Stratia. He was joined later in the afternoon by Brenna, Akimm, and Pandar. Sandor walked to his study in the faculty building where he spent the afternoon.

The Academy of the Ancient Warring Arts

The day went slowly for Brenz and Tag. They had completed their training and were collecting food in the commissary when Colonel Fornoff and General Witticor approached the two cadets. Immediately Brenz and Tag snapped to attention.

"At ease, cadets," the general said. "I understand you have a base presently under construction someplace near The Great Chamber."

"Yes, sir," Tag replied.

"You have some very creative and motivated friends," the colonel added.

"Yes, sir," Brenz answered.

"They have guts too," the general said. "The building academy is going to have to submit a request for additional funding if your friends keep re-appropriating supplies and I am going to owe Professor Enoss some of my finest wine."

"You seem to be on top of just about everything, General," Brenz said.

"I know everything except where the blasted thing is," the general laughed. "Wherever it is, it is well hidden."

"Would you and the Colonel like to see it sir?" Tag asked.

"That might be helpful," the general said.

"Can you meet us at the south entrance to The Great Chamber at 5:00 sir?" Tag asked.

"I believe that can be arranged," the general responded. "Is that all right with you Colonel?"

"Yes. By the way," the colonel added, "You two don't know anything about two missing disk targets and a sharpening stone would you?" the colonel asked.

The Oracles And The Jewels

"No, sir," Tag and Brenz answered in unison.

"Just thought I would ask. Carry on cadets," the colonel said. The two cadets saluted and the colonel and general turned and marched from the room.

"Did you take the targets?" Brenz asked Tag.

"No, did you take the sharpening stone?" Tag asked Brenz.

"No, but I think our cadets are getting into the spirit of this thing. Let's get our squads and see how things are shaping up at the base," Tag suggested.

"Yes, sir," Brenz snapped.

The Scouts

Ashkelon's army had marched through the night and was approaching the halfway point in the forest. The scouts from Hodia had spent the morning on a heading east by southeast. The scouts from Polemmas were on an east by northeast heading. Not only was the gap between Ashkelon and the Hodia narrowing, the gap between Polemmas and Hodia was also narrowing. The Polemmas scouts made the first contact with the leading edge of Ashkelon's army.

"Lieutenant," Sergeant Celsus, a Fortian, whispered, "Yafet has made contact!" Lieutenant Hadrian, an Aradian crawled along a small ridge that separated the scouts from a column of mammothons marching toward them. The column was still at a distance. Hadrian crawled up next to Celsus. The two of them peered down the narrow path. Ashkelon's army was moving along the path and as they walked the roots that normally obstructed the path and prevented a smooth march through the forest moved out of the way of the advancing army, like snakes slithering into their holes.

"Where is Yafet?" Lieutenant Hadrian asked in a voice that could barely be heard.

"He's standing up against that tree . . . straight ahead." Celsus pointed to the Kicahian who was pressing himself hard against the trunk of the tree.

"I can't see him," the lieutenant said.

"What's the point of having a Kicahian in your squad if you can see him? They fight like trolls, but if you need them to infiltrate enemy lines, a Kicahian is a good soldier to have around. They can't be seen or smelled."

"I'll trust those Fortian eyes of yours. Signal him to hold his ground. Let them come to us," Hadrian ordered. Celsus used the designated hand signal to order Yafet to hold his

Skattos Forest

position. Hadrian signaled Sergeant Faggon, an Adroit, to take up a position on the right flank. Then he signaled Corporal Durrant to take a position to the left. Ora, the Pithosian, was assigned to support any team member who might need help. The six froze in position and waited for their enemy to approach. They did not have to wait long. As the column of mammothons drew closer, the ground began to vibrate.

"Lieutenant," Celsus whispered, "a problem." He pointed to the tree trunk against which Yafet was leaning. A vine had been disturbed by the vibration of the mammothons and was working its way down the trunk to investigate. Even though a Kicahian could mirror his environment and appear invisible, physically they occupied space in the same way any Pithosian would. In a few more seconds the vine would detect Yafet and take hold of him. He would not only be discovered by the vines, but his presence would be known to the mammothons.

"Nail that vine to the tree," the lieutenant ordered in whisper. Celsus loaded his cross bow. The lieutenant signaled Faggon to drawn his bow. Hadrian did the same. The three took careful aim at the vine snaking its way toward Yafet, who was now feeling the presence of the vine. He tilted his head upward and watched the vine creeping its way toward his head.

Hadrian loosed his arrow and hit the tip of the vine, pinning it to the tree about one foot above Yafet's head. A moment later, Celsus and Faggon loosed their arrows and pinned the main body of the vine to the tree. The three reloaded and loosed three more arrows into the vine completely immobilizing the plant. Yafet looked to the mammothons to see if they had noticed the arrows. They had not. The marching, groaning, and talking of the mammothons was so loud that no one heard the sound of the arrows striking the tree. Yafet breathed a sigh of relief.

"Keep your eye on Yafet," Hadrian said to Celsus. "We don't want to lose him to anything as silly as a plant." The lieutenant signaled the rest of the team to keep an eye out for any vines that might drop in on them.

It took twenty minutes for the mammothon column to pass. They moved at a surprisingly quick pace. After they had passed, the scouts could hear the distant sound of an even larger army. Hadrian looked down the path to see if the vines were returning. They did not. "Ashkelon's main army must be close," he thought to himself.

The Oracles And The Jewels

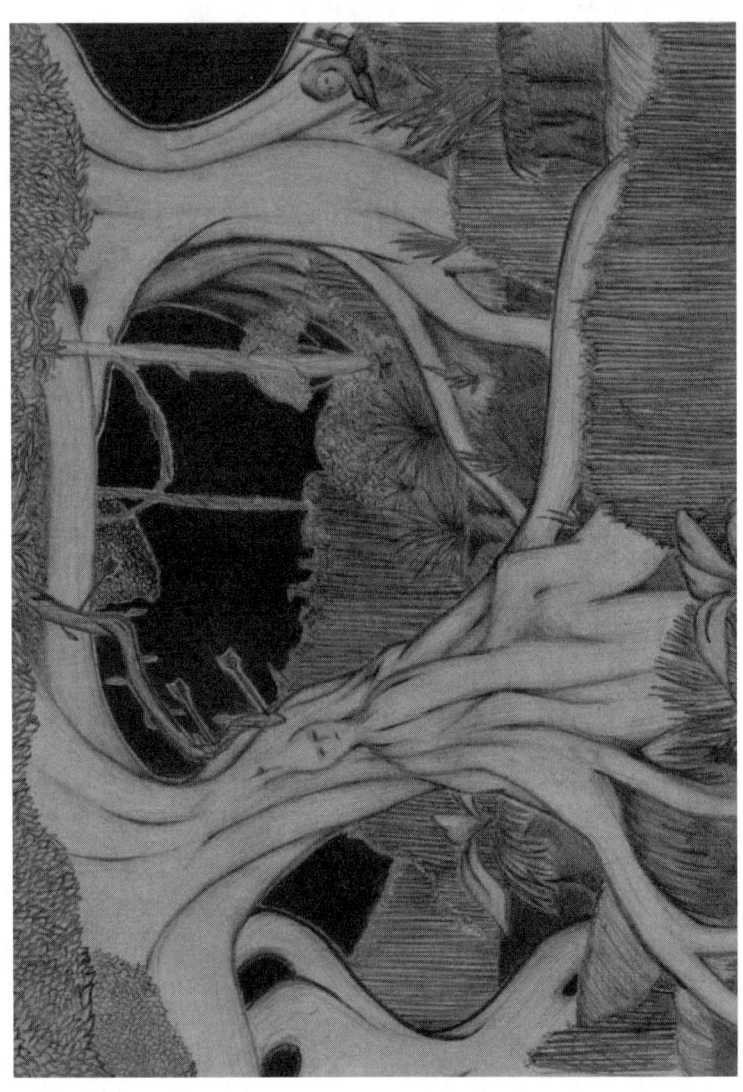

Skattos Forest

"Lieutenant," Celsus said as he peered down the path in the direction from whence the mammothons had come, "I can see them. Thousands and thousands of them. Skulls, beasts with troll riders, sipedons, mammothons, and even priests of Ashkelon. Sir, if we don't move now they are going to find us. In a couple of minutes this forest is going to be filled with the ugliest collection of creatures you ever did see."

The lieutenant looked skyward to the forest canopy, which was now starting to sway back and forth and a thunder of wings rolled across and above the top of the canopy.

"What's that?" Celsus asked.

"The winged creatures, I think," Hadrian whispered. "They must be large creatures indeed."

"There must be a lot of them," Celsus replied.

The sound was getting so loud that the two found themselves having to speak louder with each word. Suddenly a little rock bounced off the back of the lieutenant. It startled him. He turned in its direction and drew his sword. The rock had been thrown by corporal Ora. Hadrian looked at her. She was pointing behind her. A column of trolls riding beasts had suddenly appeared behind them.

Lieutenant Hadrian stood up and with a wave of his arm ordered his team to move to the northwest. Hadrian ran down the path to Yafet.

"Sergeant it's your call," Hadrian said. "Stay here and see what you can see, then try to catch up with us in a few hours, or you can move out with us now."

"Are you leaving the forest?" Sergeant Yafet asked.

"We're going to send off a bird and try to find Hodia. We will keep just ahead of Ashkelon's army, but we will try to stay behind that lead unit of mammothons. If they stay on this heading they will be poised to attack the wall between Polemmas and Hodia shortly after dawn tomorrow."

"There is so much we don't know. It would be better for Entos if we were able to send back detailed intelligence. We can only do that if we get really close," Yafet explained.

"It's your call. What is it?" Hadrian asked. Hadrian looked sternly into Yafet's eyes. "I need you to say it."

"I am going to stay here, sir. Take my horse. I will hang in here, so to speak, as long as I can. After all, what good is a Kicahian, if you can't get him behind enemy lines," Yafet said with a small grin.

"Do you want me to leave one of the Fortians with you?" Hadrian asked.

The Oracles And The Jewels

"No sir. A fortian is the last thing I want around when I am trying to hide. He will only get me found," Yafet said with a smile that widened across his face. "Those Fortians are clumsy creatures."

"They are indeed. Remember, we are headed that way." Hadrian pointed to the northwest. "We will see you later my friend. Fight well, sergeant, and to the glory of Entos," the lieutenant said. The lieutenant hurried to catch up with the rest of the unit, then took one last look at the tree which concealed Yafet before the team began weaving their way through the forest to the northwest. Ten minutes later the main force of Ashkelon's army began to pass Yafet. Just a few moments earlier the forest was virtually empty, but now there seemed little room for the plants and trees that blanketed the forest floor.

Over the next two hours, thousands and thousands of Ashkelon's soldiers and beasts of Bohow passed by Yafet without seeing or smelling him. One mammothon even leaned against the tree to rest for a moment, but still they did not detect Yafet. In the third hour the artillery pieces began to roll by. Three enormous battering rams, two dozen catapults, wagons piled high with grappling hooks, a dozen giant crossbows, contraptions that Yafet had never seen in any military textbook, and ladders that were long enough to scale even the tallest sections of Entos' walls passed by.

"Halt!" a voice shouted from behind the one of the artillery columns. The voice could be heard even above the rumble of the wagons, the thunder of the winged creatures above the trees, the snorts of the beasts, the grunting of the trolls, and the sound of morses pulling the wagons. A morse was so named because it was so much more than a horse. They were horse-like creatures, but much larger, covered with fur, and possessing teeth which were meant to eat flesh and bone. A morse was large enough for a full-sized mammothon to ride and could easily be ridden by four trolls at one time. At the shout of the general's voice the entire column came to a stop.

"Silence," the voice spoke again. A mammothon, a general in rank and mounted on a morse, moved up the column and stopped a spear's throw away from the tree where Yafet was hiding. The general looked at the vine that had been nailed to the tree above Yafet's head. He stared at it for a moment.

"Entosian arrows," he said under his breath. "Master, they are here – a Kicahian."

Skattos Forest

"Kill him! Kill them all!" the voice echoed in his ears.

He drew his sword and threw it straight into the tree three feet below the tip of the vine. When the sword struck the tree the general let out a roar of excitement thinking that he had struck his quarry. He expected to hear the scream and see a dying Kicahian turn back into his natural, albino form. But all that could be heard was the roar of the mammothon and the thud of the sword as it struck the tree.

"Where did he go? Find him! The Kicahian! Find him and bring him to me!" the mammothon general shouted in an angry rage. "Entosians are here! Find them, kill them, and cook them for dinner!"

Several trolls and skulls left the path and began searching the forest, but to no avail. Yafet was nowhere to be found. It didn't take long for some of the trolls to find Polemmas' tracks. "General. Tracks," one of the trolls reported. "There are five of them and five horses. They are in front of us."

"Take your ugly little troll and a skull unit and catch them. Don't let them send back a bird! Fail and you die!" The general growled as he shouted the orders. "Send a roguerunner to Captain Sagamond's mammothon column. Tell him they are being followed and they are to turn and destroy the enemy!"

A roguerunner was a small wolf-like creature as ferocious as any badger and as quick as any bird. A roguerunner sprinted to the side of the troll. The troll wrote a short message, rolled it up, slipped it into a cylinder, and placed it into the roguerunner's teeth. He gave the beast a kick and off it ran.

The troll shouted for his unit and commanded a captain from among the skulls to bring fifty of his own fighters with him. In a few minutes one hundred fifty fighters were following the tracks of Polemmas.

Meanwhile Lieutenant Hadrian and the rest of his team were pushing hard to stay ahead of Ashkelon's main army, but not so fast that they would overtake the first column of mammothons who continued their hurried march to the northwest. About three hundred yards past the point where Polemmas had left Yafet, they came across the tracks left by the mammothons. Lieutenant Hadrian ordered his team to hide their tracks in the tracks left by the mammothons, but this did not fool the trolls and skulls.

The trolls and skulls fell in behind Polemmas and began their pursuit. The troll units were about three hours behind

The Oracles And The Jewels

Polemmas, but they had the advantage of speed. They could run as fast as their feet would take them. Polemmas had to gauge their pace by the mammothons in front of them.

At the same time the mammothons were walking into a position wherein they would be surrounded on two sides by warriors from Entos. Polemmas was just to their southeast some five hundred yards behind them and Hodia was to the northwest just over three thousand yards in front of them.

"They're close," corporal Mead said. "I can hear them."

"From which direction?" Lieutenant Arokim asked.

"Just where you said they would be," Mead replied.

"How far?" Lieutenant Arokim asked.

"Twenty five hundred, maybe three thousand yards away. They are moving fast, too fast for an entire army," Mead answered.

"It is probably a patrol of some kind," Arokim said.

"It is pretty large for a patrol."

"That's Ashkelon's way. He thinks power is in numbers," Arokim said.

"Sounds like Ashkelon and the City Fathers have something in common," Tor quipped.

"You don't say much Tor, but when you do, you do," Justin said with a smile.

"Gentlemen, this is not the time nor the place to discuss the bigger is better policy of the City Fathers," the lieutenant barked. "Hodia. We'll stop here. There is no sense in going any further. They are coming to us. Dig in and take cover. Clear any of the hungry vines from your area so we don't have any problems once that unit gets here. Corporal Gavvin, you have the smallest hole to dig. I want you to take the horses back about two hundred yards to the right. Tie them up there and clear the area of any vines. I don't want our horses turned into anyone's or anything's lunch."

"Yes, sir," Gavvin said then he went about collecting up the horses and headed back from the direction they had just come. Gavvin made it back in plenty of time to find himself a hiding place.

"They're getting pretty close now, sir," Mead reported.

"They are close enough for me to see them," Sergeant Benjaminn said. "Just great! They're mammothons. Several hundred of them by the looks of it."

"Take cover, warriors. Remember, we are to do whatever we can to avoid contact. We are here for information." Arokim said.

Skattos Forest

As each member took his position he felt the ground begin to tremble and saw the path begin to widen. The roots started disappearing under the ground. Unfortunately for Gavvin, the root behind which he had taken cover disappeared like a serpent under a wave and he was left completely exposed in an ever-widening path. He immediately rolled behind a second root only to have it disappear as well. The rest of the team looked upon the little Adroit with amusement at first, but as the mammothons drew closer, Gavvin's teammates began pointing frantically to other possible hiding places.

Gavvin's third try proved to be stable, but by now he was on the opposite side of the path completely separated from the rest of his team and the approaching column of mammothons who were now too close for him to risk another move. The mammothons drew closer. As Benjaminn looked down the path he saw the first mammothon riding a morse. The column drew closer. Five hundred yards became four hundred, four hundred shrunk to three and three to two.

"Halt!" the captain shouted. "Fall out. You have ten minutes to rest, eat, and relieve yourselves. Then we march to the desert. We are close. Light your torches and stay alert!" The captain dismounted and took from his saddlebags a large ball of flesh and bones. He sat down in the middle of the path and looked straight ahead as he ate. Occasionally, he tore a piece of bone off and gave it to his morse.

Lieutenant Hadrian stopped in his tracks and thrust his hand downward, giving the signal for Polemmas to stop.

Celsus ran to Hadrian's side and looked down the path. "They've stopped, sir. I can't really see them. There is a hill in the way and it's getting dark, but the movement of their lights is from side to side. They are not moving forward," Celsus said.

"The main column must be about an hour behind us," Hadrian said, then added, "We can wait for a few minutes." An hour was not much time and Hadrian was not comfortable with the decision, but they needed the rest. He signaled Polemmas to sit. They did. It had been four hours since they had left their friend Yafet, the sun was setting and the blackness of the night would soon take over the forest. Creatures of Bohow were used to this kind of blackness. Their eyes were well suited for it. This was not so for Entosians. In the full light of day, Entosians had the advantage, but in just thirty minutes the Entosian warriors

The Oracles And The Jewels

would have to depend on the light of their enemy's torches to illumine their way through the forest. This would mean that they would have to draw closer to them.

As the Polemmas scouts sat waiting for their order to advance, each one turned his thoughts toward Yafet and offered whispers of well wishes for their brave brother. He had seen the composition of Ashkelon's army. They had two remaining birds, but had nothing more to report. If Yafet did not return, the mission would be almost worthless and their journey in vain.

"Fall in!" Captain Sagamond shouted. The mammothons were slow to move. "I said fall in!" His voice rumbled through the forest and most of his soldiers quickened their steps. But one mammothon did not heed the command of his captain, at least not with the immediacy desired by Sagamond. Sagamond shouted, "You dare delay when I issue an order?" at that Sagamond drew his sword and severed the mammothon's head from his shoulders. The column immediately took shape.

Tor chuckled just loud enough for Hadrian to hear him. "Lieutenant," he mumbled under his breath, "that's one less we need to worry about."

The mammothon column began to march forward again. One hundred yards soon became fifty, but before fifty yards became twenty-five, the roguerunner ran along the side of the column, passed the captain, stopped at the hoof of the captain's morse, and growled.

"Lieutenant," the captain called, "that beast has a message for me. Retrieve it now!"

The lieutenant ran to the creature, took the cylinder from the roguerunner's teeth, opened it up, and handed the message to the captain. The captain read it, growled, and grinned. "They are here!" he shouted with great excitement. Entosians are here in the forest. They are behind us. We will eat tonight! About face," the captain shouted as he turned his morse and gave it a hard kick. The captain charged down along the column with his sword drawn.

"Lieutenant," Tor whispered. "How can they know we are here?"

"They don't! They are headed the wrong way. They don't know about us. They must have discovered Polemmas. Follow their commander and stay out of sight!" The Hodia scouts began to move as quickly as they could behind the column. They had their bows at the ready as they moved from tree to tree.

Skattos Forest

The captain rode along his column yelling, "Find them, kill them, and bring them to me. Hurry you lazy rabble!" The column ran down the path toward the Polemmas scouts. Hadrian and Durrant were the first to see them approaching.

"They know we are here!" Hadrian shouted. "Circle up now!"

"How do they know?" Durrant shouted.

"They must have discovered Yafet," Celsus answered.

"It's not important how they found out," Hadrian answered. "What is important is that one of us survives to tell the story."

The remaining warriors from Polemmas formed their circle and crouched down amidst the roots in a vain effort to conceal themselves. But the roguerunner had smelled them out and was the first creature to throw itself into the battle. Faggon matched the roguerunner's speed and cut it in half as it launched itself through the air toward the circle. There was no hiding now. Within a few moments the scouts from Polemmas were surrounded on all sides. One enraged mammothon after another fell as Captain Sagamond stood back and watched the battle unfold.

The Hodia scouts had a clear view of what was taking place. They looked to Arokim and awaited his order. Arokim debated within his own mind as to what he ought to do. His mission was to collect information and make sure that information made it back to Entos. Yet his fellow warriors were in danger of being overrun and killed. They had come from behind that the column. They had more information than Hodia, but their presence was no longer a secret. The debate took only but a moment.

"Attack," he whispered to himself. Arokim raised his arm and with his index finger pointed forward to the mammothon officers.

Tor had managed to approach Sagamond from behind. When Arokim gave the order to attack, he stood up, raised his sword, delivered a fatal blow across the captain's back, then thrust his sword into the belly of the morse. The two creatures fell to the ground without any of the other mammothons taking notice. Arokim pointed to Justin, then to the second in command. The mammothon lieutenant was standing with his back to Hodia watching the battle with the Polemmas warriors unfold. Justin struck him down in the same manner. Benjaminn did the same to a mammothon sergeant standing nearby. The other Hodia warriors followed suit. They systematically and quickly approached

The Oracles And The Jewels

one mammothon at a time and killed one officer after another. Then they began cutting their way to the middle. When the rest of the mammothons realized that they were being attacked from behind, many turned and took the battle to the Hodia warriors.

The warriors from Polemmas had been divided and each was fighting for his own life. The Entosian warriors fought quickly and made maximum use of the cover provided by the forest. They moved about jumping and running and with each movement they countered the attacks of the mammothons and landed their own blows.

But there were too many mammothons for the small band of Entosians to handle. The first to fall was Corporal Durrant, the Fortian. He had been backed into a tree. As he swung his sword and fought off the attacking mammothons, a vine took Durrant by the neck. In that moment a mammothon's sword found its mark and Durrant's lifeless body was pulled up into the canopy.

Hadrian was the second to fall. He was crushed when a mammothon lifted a broken tree trunk and threw it over the heads of his comrades on top of the lieutenant. Corporal Mead of Hodia was the third to fall. She fought well, but had gotten her foot tangled in some vines that ran along the ground. Unable to turn in a complete circle she left her back exposed and a mammothon took advantage of her limitation.

"To the northwest!" Arokim cried out. "Fight your way to the northwest! To the horses! Diamond formation on Tor!" Tor moved to the point of the formation and struck down any mammothon that attempted to cut off the escape route. Ora moved to the rear of the formation and all the others took up a position within the formation. Arokim left the formation and concealed himself against a tree.

As soon as the Entosian warriors had all taken up their positions, they began to move to the northwest and did so effectively and quickly. A few dozen mammothons ran past Arokim, but did not see him. One mammothon even stepped on Arokim's leg, but still did not see him.

Arokim waited for the mammothons to pass, then pursued them from behind. He took one unsuspecting mammothon after another. As the mammothons pursued the Entosian warriors, Arokim pursued them. Suddenly, there appeared beside Arokim an Entosian brother - a Kicahian. It was Yafet, who was now matching Arokim's kill for kill.

Skattos Forest

"Sergeant, I don't know where you came from, but I'm sure glad to see you. It would've been better for you if you had just sneaked out of this blasted forest."

"That's not the Entosian way. Besides, I need to get one of those birds hanging off Ora's hip. I got a very good look at Ashkelon's army and those birds are much faster than I am, Lieutenant," Yafet explained as the two marched forward working their way through the pursuing mammothons.

Mammothons were large and the most difficult of Ashkelon's soldiers to kill, but they were like buffalo. If their leader fell, they were easily confused and quickly became a disorganized mob. Any strategy they had in mind was quickly forgotten and unless someone shouted out the instructions they would simply move forward into the Entosian blades. With Sagamond and their officers dead, they were like any other creature in Bohow driven by rage and the desire for Entosian flesh.

They would pursue the little band to the last. The command by Arokim to move toward the horses was working. Now that Yafet had joined Arokim behind the pursuing mob, mammothons were falling quickly at both ends of the formation.

"Lieutenant," Yafet said, "I hate to have to tell you this, but we have one hundred fifty trolls and skulls closing in behind us."

"How much time do we have?" Arokim asked as he killed another mammothon.

"Thirty minutes. Maybe forty-five," Yafet answered.

"I suggest you hurry up," Arokim shouted as he pushed forward with even greater speed.

It took the scouts nearly thirty-five minutes to fight their way to the horses. By the time they reached them there were less than thirty mammothons left and darkness was descending.

"Light up the place up!" Arokim ordered. The Entosians wrapped some cloth around some of their arrows, struck their flick rocks together to start a fire, set them ablaze, and loosed them into the trunks of the trees.

Corporal Gavvin mounted Tor's steed and began riding between the remaining mammothons. As he rode he alternated between his bow and his sword and selected one unsuspecting mammothon after another to fall.

The others took their bows and began felling the advancing mammothons with volleys of arrows. With the fall of the last mammothon the forest fell silent.

The Oracles And The Jewels

The Entosians joined the silence. Three of their own had fallen. In time, they would grow accustomed to losing brothers in arms, but at the moment such a thing rarely happened. Their temporary victory was bittersweet.

"How many birds do we have left?" Arokim asked, breaking the silence.

Ora took down the small cage strapped to her hip. "One dead and one a little frazzled. But she'll still fly," she said.

"Why should she be any different than the rest of us?" Arokim added.

"What about Hodia?" Ora asked.

"We have three birds, but in our zeal to find and rescue you, we left them with the horses," Arokim replied.

"What were the names of your fallen comrades?" Yafet asked as he looked to Gavvin, who was still seated on Tor's horse.

"Mead, Corporal Mead," Gavvin replied. And the names of yours?" Gavvin asked in return.

"Lieutenant Hadrian and Corporal Durrant," Celsus answered quickly and with a tone of pride.

"Know this, no one here this day has died in vain. Hodia meet Sergeant Yafet. He got a very good look at Ashkelon's army and has the information we were sent to collect. Corporal Gavvin, ride back and collect Hodia's horses." Arokim looked at Celsus.

"Sergeant, what's your name?"

"Celsus, sir," he replied.

"Take my horse over there and help Gavvin collect your horses," Arokim ordered. The two wasted no time. In a moment they were gone.

"Sergeant Yafet, write down what you know." Arokim handed Yafet a writing tool and the parchment paper.

"When Gavvin and Celsus get back we will have four birds left. We are going to send three with identical messages. The one from Polemmas will carry the original in Yafet's handwriting. The other two birds from Hodia will carry the copies. We will keep one bird just in case we need it later. Justin and Tor copy exactly what Yafet writes. Justin, yours is copy number one and Tor, yours is copy number two."

Yafet completed his task quickly, then read it out loud for the other two. They copied the message exactly as it was dictated. As the three recorded the messages, the other scouts retrieved their arrows from the bodies of their victims and from the trees of the forest.

Skattos Forest

The message read:
M.C. E. A. full force.
Est. 150,000 – 200,000 L.C.
Unknown # W.C., L.F.
3 B – rams, 24 CP, 12 bows, ladders, water wagons
Ashkelon with them
Attack est. 9:00
Hodia+Pol. – 3 under attack

Once they had finished writing the messages, they handed the three parchment papers to Arokim and began to collect arrows and additional weapons. Fifteen minutes later, Celsus and Gavvin returned with the horses from Hodia and the cage with the four messenger birds.

Arokim attached the messages to the bird, while Benjaminn held each bird. Suddenly an arrow pierced Benjaminn's armor and he fell to the ground wounded and grunting in pain.

"Trolls and skulls," Yafet shouted. Arokim took the bird from Benjaminn's hand and stuffed the message in the leather pouch, then attached it to the bird's talon. While the others moved to defend Arokim and Benjaminn, Arokim handed Benjaminn, who was in pain but was still able to assist, the first bird.

"Wait!' Arokim shouted. "Don't release yet!"

Corporal Gavvin gave his horse a kick and charged toward the oncoming trolls.

"That's my horse," Tor shouted. "Bring him back!"

"I promise!" Gavvin shouted in return.

"I mean now!" By the time the words were out of Tor's mouth Gavvin was too far away to hear. Arokim attached the second message to the second bird and handed it to Benjaminn. He took the third bird from its cage and attached the third message.

"On my word, release all three at once," Arokim said to Benjaminn as a volley of arrows descended upon the group.

"Arrows!" Arokim shouted to the other warriors. "On my command!" Celsus, Ora, Justin, Yafet, and Tor readied their bows. "When we release the birds, shoot any skull that takes aim at them. Benjaminn's eyes began to close as his breath started to go out of him.

"Benjaminn!" Arokim shouted. "Don't leave us yet. We need you!" Benjaminn opened his eyes and gave a slight smile.

The Oracles And The Jewels

"Yes, sir," he said in a voice too low for Arokim to hear or notice.

"Archers. Ready?" Arokim shouted.

"Yes, sir," they all replied.

"Benjaminn release!"

Benjaminn tossed the birds into the air with his last bit of strength. Arokim tossed his bird gently into the air, then immediately took his bow and armed it with an arrow.

A skull shouted out, "Shoot the birds!" and a dozen archers took aim.

"Loose!" Arokim shouted. The six Entosians loosed their arrows and struck six of the skull archers in the chest. The others loosed their arrows and one of the Hodia birds fell to the ground. As the skull archers took aim for a second time, each was struck in the back with arrows from Gavvin's bow. In the time it took them to rearm their bows, Gavvin had fired and rearmed six times. Tor let out a shout, "Fine job, little fella. Now bring back my horse!"

But Gavvin's little victory was not without a price. A troll's spear struck Gavvin in the side and knocked him from the horse.

"No!" Tor yelled, then loosed his arrow into the chest of the troll.

Tor's horse stopped next to his fallen rider. Gavvin was wounded badly but was able to take hold of the horse's tail. "Go," he said. "Go to your master" The horse moved forward toward Tor.

"Felda come!" Tor yelled. The horse looked toward her master. "Felda, come!" The horse began to move toward her master. As she wove her way through the forest, a small arrow struck the horse in the side. She flinched, but kept moving. The Entosians and skulls exchanged volleys of arrows as the trolls advanced toward the Entosian position. Felda slowly moved through the battle pulling Gavvin behind her until she returned to her place with the rest of the horses.

"Two birds have been sent. Our mission is accomplished. There is no failure possible now," Arokim shouted. The others looked at him and nodded in consent. "Then let us take the battle to them! These are just trolls and skulls. Why didn't we hear them coming?" Arokim asked.

"We don't have any Aradians left, sir," Celsus replied, "and I couldn't see them. It's too dark."

"Well let's light up the place," Arokim said. "They loosed a second volley of flaming arrows and achieved the desired effect.

Skattos Forest

"Now that we can see them, let them hear the sound and feel the cut of Entosian metal!" Arokim said. He took his sword in his right hand and his dagger in the left. The others did the same. As they did, they glanced back at Benjaminn's now lifeless body and tipped their swords in respect.

"Full attack. Move at will. Ready?" Arokim said.

"Sir! Wait! Look!" Celsus pointed to the northeast of their position. "I didn't hear them, but I see them."

"I can't believe it!" Ora said. "This day will be ours yet!" She laughed. "Krattos, the Krattos scouts!"

"What is their composition?" Arokim asked. Celsus looked around and took inventory.

"Three Aradians, one Adroit, and a Kilposian or Demotic," Celsus said.

"No Pithosian," Ora replied.

"How do you think they got here so fast?" Yafet said.

"At least we can fight," Tor replied.

"Are you going to be picky?" Justin asked.

"I like humor as much as the next Entosian, but let's finish this fight before we start mocking one another," Arokim said. "Sergeant Celsus, is Krattos set?"

"They are waiting for our mark."

"Watch for arrows. Block them as they come in, engage the enemy, and keep their attention. Krattos will take them by surprise. On my command! Attack!" Arokim shouted. The six leaped over the root behind which they had taken cover and ran toward the trolls and skulls. Arrows flew toward them, but the Entosian warriors were so well trained and fast they were able to deflect as many as came. The skulls drew their swords and ran forward. The two sides met in an open area. The skull fighters fell in behind the trolls. The Krattos scouts loosed a volley of arrows into their enemies, then drew their swords and daggers in hand and charged.

In ten minutes all one hundred fifty soldiers from Ektos lay dead. Tor's horse survived the wound, but Gavvin did not. He and Benjaminn would be the last Entosians to fall in battle that day. Of the twelve Entosian warriors from Hodia and Polemmas that had entered the forest the day before only seven remained. The remaining seven were joined by five warriors from Krattos.

"Welcome Krattos. Allow me to introduce what is left of our units. From Polemmas that is Sergeant Yafet, Corporal Ora, Sergeant Faggon, and Sergeant Celsus. I am Lieutenant Arokim of Hodia and this is Sergeant Justin and Corporal Tor."

The Oracles And The Jewels

"Good to meet you, brothers. Sorry we took so long. The horses slowed us down. We released them and made it here under our own power. I am Lieutenant Roggan and this is Sergeants Cedric and Tita. The Demotic there is Edris and the little Adroit is Magnus, apparently his parents had a sense of humor when the little guy was named."

"Big or small, we're glad to see you all," Arokim said. "I wish we had more time to visit, but we don't have much time do we, Yafet? How far behind us is Ashkelon's main force?"

"Four hours. They can see in this blackness and we can't. I suspect we will all reach the desert at about the same time – dawn," Yafet said.

As he looked around the forest floor covered with dead bodies, Roggan said, "Well I doubt that Ashkelon is going to just sit by and let us run around his forest leaving dead bodies lying about."

"Those bodies won't be here by the time his main force arrives. The vines and roots will clean up this mess. This forest is a very brutal, but efficient place," Arokim said. He pointed to a few vines that were already dragging the bodies up the tree trunks toward the canopy. Roots were also starting to pull some of the dead into the ground.

"What of our fallen comrades?" Ora asked.

"I wish we could give them a proper burial in Entos, but we cannot. It would do no good to bury them under stones. The roots will take them anyway and we will give Ashkelon a marker. If we try to take them back with us, they will slow us down and Ashkelon's creatures will find them by their smell. Their eyes are his eyes. We will have to commend their souls into the hands of our King and their bodies to this wicked forest," Arokim said with a note of sadness in his voice.

"Now grab a torch and let's get moving. That way, straight west until we hit desert. I am pretty sure two of the birds made it. It's our job to get back." The remaining scouts collected their horses and torches, retrieved as many arrows as time permitted, and began their long and dark march through the pitch black forest.

Chapter Fifteen
Make Ready

The Cadet Base

Inside the city of Entos things were as normal as could be and the day progressed as expected. It was now 3:00 and Tag and Brenz stood at the south entrance of The Great Chamber waiting for General Witticor and Colonel Fornoff to arrive. Blisse, Sabinnee, and Chaiva had brought their supplies to the field hospital and were working with Breille and River.

Rieve ascended the metal stairs, entered the room through its heavy metal door, and was surprised at the transformation that had taken place in just a few hours. The hall no longer looked like an old theater. It didn't look like a theater at all. It looked like a fully equipped military base and field hospital. The weapons were neatly ordered on newly built racks and tables. Some of the students from the building academy were polishing and sharpening the armor and weapons. Tag's new toys were laid out on a table. Food and water were stockpiled, and four conjuring stands and dust were ready. They had also created a map board upon which was a large map of the entire city. A second smaller map board had maps of the valleys and plateaus surrounding the city. Brenna, Akimm, and Pandar were already practicing their battle conjuring with some brave cadets who were now wearing a few bruises.

"Well done, ladies," Rieve said.

"Hello, Rieve Waynwright," River said with a smile.

"Thank you, Rieve," Breille said. "But, as you can see we had a lot of help."

Rieve turned in a three hundred sixty degree circle. His jaw lowered in stunned amazement. "I thought conjurors were suppose to be miracle workers. The Headmaster couldn't have done this . . . How do you do this stuff without getting caught?" Rieve asked.

The Oracles And The Jewels

"That's a long story and I am just too busy to repeat it again. Let's just say that General Witticor has friends in key places and I am very, very grateful for that," Breille replied.

"River, can I talk with you privately for a moment?" Rieve asked.

"Sure, Rieve Waynwright." The two walked over to a corner away from all the activity of the room.

"I have a favor to ask you about tomorrow."

"What kind of favor?" River inquired.

"I would like you to stay with Headmaster Sandor. No matter what happens. I need you to stay with him. I would do it myself, but if a battle breaks out in the city I will be too busy to look after him," Rieve explained.

"Is there something wrong with Grandfather?" River asked.

"I get the sense that the Headmaster thinks he is going to die tomorrow," Rieve answered.

River was visibly stunned by the comment. "I'm sure there's nothing to worry about. There is no one equal to Grandfather's power in all of Entos," River said as she tried to reassure herself as much as Rieve. "What makes you think Grandfather's life is in danger?"

"It's just the way he has been talking for the past couple of days. There is a foreboding about him. He is speaking as if his time is very short," Rieve answered.

"He is always talking about how his time, everyone's time here in Entos is short," River replied.

"The past couple of days have been different, almost prophetic and I am worried that something might happen to the Headmaster if we don't take extra measures to protect him. I thought you might be able to keep him company and send for help if anything does happen."

"Okay. Okay. While you are all making your way to glory, I will sit with Grandfather," River said.

"Come to the house at dawn and we will eat breakfast together. Your grandfather makes a great breakfast."

"Rieve, did you see that?" Pandar shouted from the middle of the room. Rieve stepped to the side of River to get a better view. "I am getting the hang of this. I think I have found my calling!" Suddenly Pandar's warrior was knocked to the ground.

"Concentrate!" Rieve shouted back. "It is true . . . pride goes before the fall."

"His pride, my fall," the cadet mumbled. Pandar leaned over his warrior and apologized. "My mistake, cadet. Sorry.

Make Ready

We were doing so well together for a moment." The cadet nodded his head as Pandar helped him to his feet.

"Time for a rest, fellas," Brenna said. "I need to talk to Conjuror Rieve for a minute."

"Conjuror Rieve Waynwright," Brenna called out. He trotted over to where River had once stood. "I have some interesting information for you. MulLord told his classes today that Professor Scarre is filling in for him tomorrow. Akimm told me that Professor Ellery is also taking the day off tomorrow. He has made arrangements for Professor Etam to take his classes on the history of the Conjurors and the Warring Arts."

"That is interesting," Rieve said. "Did either man offer an explanation for their absence?"

"Ellery said something about a faculty search meeting," Akimm said as he joined the other two. Pandar followed Akimm to complete the circle.

"Let me guess, all the faculty members who support the new approach are on the search committee and will be behind closed doors tomorrow," Rieve said.

"I'll bet most, if not all the faculty members advocating the new way are taking the day off tomorrow," Akimm said.

"Don't be betting" Pandar replied. "MulLord's last edict on improvement said we can't bet, even in jest, lest we offend or cause our brethren to stumble."

"So many rules these days, it is hard to keep track of what we can and cannot do," Brenna added. "I'm so confused."

"Scheming and contriving doesn't seem to be against the rules," Rieve added. "Thanks for the information. When I see the general, I will pass the information on. I will also make sure Tag knows."

"If tomorrow is the big day, what are we supposed to do?" Akimm asked.

"There is no time like the present. I might as well take charge now," Rieve said with a tone of regret in his voice. "Brenna, you stay with Polemmas at the Academy. You're their conjuror starting now. Pandar will take the Neggen cadets; Akimm, you have Krattos, and I will be with Hodia. Should you hear the battle horn, get to your assignments as soon as you can. . . and Pandar, don't forget to take your sand and dust. If you remember your means like you remember homework, those poor cadets won't have chance."

The Oracles And The Jewels

"Okay, cadets, are you ready for some more practice?" Brenna shouted. "Rieve, did you notice my cadet has the fewest bruises on him?" Brenna said with a smile. The cadets signaled their willingness to start again and so they did.

The general and the colonel were a little late, but Tag and Brenz didn't mind. The day seemed like a waste to them. They assumed that special forces and scouts were at work, but didn't have any first-hand information or part in those operations.

"Are you ready for battle again?" Tag asked Brenz as they sat on the steps to The Great Chamber.

"I was more ready the first time. It was more than I expected. It was less than I expected too," Brenz said as he reflected upon the battle three days earlier. His face was still dressed with a small bandage that Blisse had made up for him. It was time for the dressing to be changed, but Brenz did not worry much about such things. Blisse was always checking on it and redressing it for him. He assumed, and rightly so, that he would see Blisse soon and she would tend to it all over again. She would make a fuss over the wound and he would make a fuss over the attention she would give to the wound.

"Did you know Cadet Keemon well?" Tag asked.

"I knew him as a fine cadet and a loyal member of my squad. I didn't know much about him from his days before he became a cadet. You know how it is. Cadets and warriors don't think or talk much about what they were. They only know what they are now," Brenz said, "and they are proud and humble to be warriors in the service of Entos."

"That is as it should be," Tag replied. "Even now, that boy I once knew who use to run and jump off the top of the 'Faces of the King' is slipping away. When I see Rieve I see him differently now. He seems less and less like my brother and more and more like a conjuror/priest whom I must get to know more about."

"The boy I once knew did not slip away. He seemed to vanish all at once on that wall three days ago," Brenz said.

The two looked to the east at the gathering darkness. By now it was obvious to everyone that something very bad was on the horizon. The City Fathers had posted an official statement on the bulletin boards around the city in an effort to calm the Entosians. It was short and simple. Short and smiple statements usually meant that the threat was real and close at hand.

Make Ready

Fellow Entosians

An attack from Ashkelon seems imminent. We expect the attack in the next forty – eight hours. We encourage you all to visit The Great Chamber to offer prayers to the King, Giver, and Maker of Entos. But rest assured the armies stand ready and will repel any force that can be brought against us.

The City Fathers

The post was having the desired effect, at least in regard to The Great Chamber. The foot traffic that passed by Tag and Brenz alone was remarkably heavy. The post was driving them to the Chamber to offer their prayers, but it did not have the calming effect. Entosians knew that the leaders of Entos were no longer united, but were divided. Now they would learn if the division would matter when facing a foreign enemy and an attack from outside.

"Everything seems to change, everything except what takes place in there," Tag said as he pointed over the back of his shoulder toward The Great Chamber. "To think, Entosians come and go. We are born, we change, we grow old, eventually we die, and that process goes on century after century, millennium after millennium, and what takes place inside there just keeps going. We fight and die so that the Great Rituals continue. I used to think that warriors were the most important of all the citizens of Entos. Sitting here, I am now realizing that the real battle is the one the priests and conjurors are fighting to keep all the new innovations from taking hold inside The Great Chamber."

"Good," a voice said with great boldness and pleasure. It was General Witticor. Colonel Fornoff was with him. The two cadets snapped to and came to their feet. "I'm glad to see that you are not only learning the skills of sword play and intrigue, but that along the way you two are developing good old-fashioned theological wisdom. We are here because of her," he said as he nodded his head toward The Great Chamber and because of him." He looked to the east. "Now let's leave things at that for now and let the real theologians do the theologizing. Show us the new headquarters of the cadet army."

The Oracles And The Jewels

"Yes, sir," Tag said. "This way." Tag and Brenz led the way. They walked two abreast with the general and colonel following. They headed west down the street toward the old forgotten theater.

"So how are things with the cadets?" the colonel asked.

"Fine, sir," Brenz answered.

"I suspect they are already getting a little bored," the general said.

"Some are, sir," Tag replied.

"Boredom is easy enough to spot. We know warriors are getting bored when they start arguing about whether it is important to argue about theologizing," Colonel Fornoff said as he looked to his right at General Witticor.

"The cadets don't know what an exciting time they live in, Colonel Fornoff," Witticor began. "They only see tension and conflict. They, like so many Entosians, tend to regard these theological debates as sophistry. Unfortunately, most think all this theologizing and study of the Ancients is at its best nostalgia and at its worse harmful to the unity of Entos. Do you remember Colonel, the days when warriors used to study the Oracles at the feet of their conjurors and how we could talk theology and history for hours while standing guard?"

"Yes, General, I remember. I suppose that's why old warriors like us can see that these cadets and warriors have an opportunity to make history this day," the colonel answered. Tag and Brenz pretended as if the conversation was none of their business. But as the general and the colonel spoke these things, their hearts were filled with a quiet pride.

"Colonel, should these cadets deliver a defeat to Ashkelon, that will give the old demon a moment of pause," the general said.

"We wouldn't be the officers we are today without boredom and repetition," the general concluded.

"Sirs, if you try to inspire the cadets and warriors to battle with a speech like that, well you might not like the results," Tag said with a hint of humor in his voice.

"Son, never underestimate the ordinary, mundane, and common. They breed patience and contentment. Everything is as it should be. Our job now is to wait for the evil ones to manifest themselves," the general pontificated. "There are many among us, but we will not know who they are until their deeds are made manifest."

Make Ready

"Sir, we turn left here," Brenz said. The four of them walked around the sign. The general read it out loud as he walked by, "building academy at Work, Renovations In Progress. Do Not Enter." The general shook his head approvingly and smiled. "Boys, those girls are really something, especially that Procuron girl. If I were your age, I think I would consider marrying her."

"No thank you, sir," Tag said. "You're welcome to her."

"Sorry, but we are already married," the colonel said.

"The military is a great vocation, but she makes a poor bride. Remember that. A hard-working, creative, and understanding female is a good mate for a warrior," the general said. "Think on that. Entos always needs more Entosians." The four turned and headed up the metal staircase. They had to work their way up the steps. Several of the students from the building academy were carrying materials out, others were carrying materials in, and others were heading home.

"Secret base," the general said. "Everyone knows where this place is except me," the general said.

"Sorry, General, it was on a need-to-know basis," Tag replied. The four of them entered the room. The general and colonel walked slowly in and were completely amazed at what they beheld. The theater was a hub of activity and fully equipped. Conjurors and cadets were practicing, two Adroit cadets were practicing disk throwing at one of the targets, which had been procured from the Academy of Warring Arts, some were sharpening their weapons, others were polishing their boots, belts, and decorations, and still others were throwing daggers. Witticor and Fornoff climbed the stairs, walked passed the makeshift armory, and walked to the map board.

"What are these?" the colonel said as he picked up two heavy rectangular-shaped metal pieces with a modified chain that held the two metal pieces together.

"Oh, those are my idea, Colonel. I don't know if they work. Procuron Breille Clarrice made them for me." Tag explained.

"What are they supposed to do?" the colonel asked.

"I haven't tried them yet, but I suppose we could give them their first field test right now," Tag said.

"Here, Colonel," Tag handed the colonel a Pithosian sword. "If we are going to test this, we might as well test it on the biggest sword in the place." By now the four conjurors and cadets had stopped to watch the test. Tag picked up a

The Oracles And The Jewels

belt and his own sword and put them on. Then he picked up two sets of his metal creation, one at a time and hung them on his belt. They were heavy, heavier than he had expected.

"Colonel, please," Tag said. Tag led him to the middle of the floor.

"You aren't going to cut me again son, are you?" The colonel said with a smile.

"No sir, but you aren't going to cut me either, at least not if these things work," Tag replied. "Colonel, attack when you are ready." He did immediately. As before, Tag met the colonel's sword with his. When the colonel swung a second time Tag met the colonel's sword a second time, but this time he pulled the set of weights from his belt and threw them in such a way that the blade of the colonel's sword was caught by the chain that held the weights together. The metal weights were magnetic. They wrapped around the colonel's sword and slowed his third swing. Tag repeated his movements with the second set of weights. With the weights attached to the colonel's sword it was now more than three times its weight and slowed down the colonel enough that he would have been easily dispatched.

"I see the point," the colonel said as he dropped the sword.

"You're a Pithosian," Tag said, "I suspect on an unsuspecting skull or troll, one set would do the trick."

"If we are stuck with these daggers, I wouldn't mind having a set of these," Brenz said.

The general picked up a set. Breille walked over and explained the changes she had made in the original design and showed him the unique features of the rope-like chain. The general was duly impressed.

"How many of these did you make?" the general asked.

"A couple of dozen, but more are being made today," Breille answered.

"Good. Keep going," he said to Breille. He turned around and shouted out to all the cadets in the hall, "If one of you doesn't end up marrying this girl, you aren't fit for your uniforms." Several of the cadets paused for a moment and took a good look at her. The hospital beds and tables caught the general's eye. He walked across the floor and approached Blisse and River.

"Ladies, you are responsible for this?"

"Yes, General," Blisse answered. He took another look around the room.

Make Ready

"Well done. Is there anything you need?" the general said.

"No, sir," Blisse responded. "We have everything we need right here."

"When you're all done with your formal training, you all have a future in the military corp," the general announced. The old theater organ caught the general's eye. Organs in Entos were pipe organs. They sounded like pipe organs, but when played well and right they not only gave off the sound of an organ, they also gave off a sound like a fine piano. The case of this particular organ was made from the timbers of Tarchus, sturdy and hard. The general loved music and had an affection for the older style organs.

"You decided to keep the organ," the general said.

"That's my sister," Blisse said. "Some of the students from the building academy wanted to get rid of it, but River would not permit it. Besides Breille pointed out that we didn't have the time to disconnect and move the thing. So there it is."

"Does it work?" the General asked.

"River played around with it a bit. It is a little out of tune," Blisse said.

"Colonel, it looks like everything is under control here. We are in the way here," the general said. He paused for a moment and looked at the clock which now read 3:53.

The colonel shouted, "Commanders and Conjuror Rieve!" Rieve immediately excused himself from his training. Brenz and Tag put down the blade weights and presented themselves at attention before the general.

"Everything is shaping up here just fine. I will be leaving the city in a few minutes for the Demotic valley. I plan to be at the wall in the morning when Ashkelon attacks. I have several things I must oversee. Upon my departure Colonel Fornoff will be the ranking officer in the city. Fornoff and Fornoff alone is the only officer in the city that you are to trust. Headmaster Sandor and Conjuror Stratia are the only conjurors from whom you are to take orders. It that clear?" the general said in a stern voice.

"Yes, sir," Brenz and Tag replied.

"Yes, General," Rieve said.

"When the sky grows dark, Conjuror Stratia will leave the Academy and join up with the rest of Hodia and Conjuror Rieve at The Great Chamber. Should anything happen to the colonel here, Cadet Thayer Taggert you will be the ranking officer in this secret army."

The Oracles And The Jewels

Thayer Taggert looked surprised at the announcement. "I don't like the idea either," the general said noting Tag's response, "but that is how it must be. You two are as ready to assume warrior status as any two cadets I have ever seen," He paused, took a step toward Rieve and continued, " and you are a full conjuror." When I leave this city at 4:30, the only thing that will stand between Ashkelon and the Oracles is you and your men. Remember three objectives. Remember your training. Trust your instincts and always conduct yourself in the Entosian tradition – faith, honor, and courage. Fight well and fight to the glory of Entos. Colonel, let's go," the general said. Brenz and Tag saluted. The general and the colonel returned the salute. The general led the way across the room and the colonel followed.

"You're in charge now Tag," Brenz said as he saluted the highest ranking officer in the cadet army.

"Great, that's just great," Tag said with a tone of doubt in his voice and he returned the salute, "if the city falls I will go down in Entosian history as the cadet who failed her."

"It is good to be just an average cadet from the Polemmas army," Brenz said with a smile.

"Remember, if I fall you're in charge," Tag answered. Brenz's smiled disappeared as Tag's smile manifested itself.

"Attention please," River shouted from the stage. "We appreciate all the work you have done today. I think you even exceeded Breille Clarrice's schedule and her expectations. We want to remind you that this project is top secret and judging from the reaction of General Witticor this afternoon, this project has been a success. Before we finish for the night, Breille Clarrice, do you have anything to say?"

"Yes," Breille answered. She made her way to the area that was formerly the stage. "I want to express my appreciation for all your work. For all practical purposes, the job is finished and two hours ahead of schedule. I would appreciate it if any of you returning to The Academy of the Building Arts would return all our tools, leftover materials, and carts. I will work on your performance reports tonight if time permits and will turn them in to Professor Enoss within the next couple of days." Breille knew that if things unfolded as the general thought they would, by tomorrow afternoon no one would care about the reports. If nothing happened, she would still have plenty of time to complete them.

"Again, thank you all for helping today. We will all meet at the academy tomorrow for a debriefing on the project."

Make Ready

The students from the building academy spent the next thirty minutes finishing their projects and collecting their materials and tools. By 4:30 the only people left in the hall were forty cadets, the four conjurors, and the little fellowship. At 5:00 Brenna, Akimm, and Pandar concluded their practice sessions and dismissed the cadets.

"Rieve," Brenna began, "we have our assignments. I assume we begin the morning as if it were a normal day."

"It sounds like a plan to me, unless, of course, you want to take a day off," Rieve answered. "Although tomorrow will be the first time in a long time that you will have real theologians and conjurors teaching class. I might even be tempted to sneak onto campus. All the administration can do is ask me to leave."

"It's 5:00. It is dinner time, ladies," Brenz announced. "Breille, River, and Blisse, I think the cadets owe you dinner."

"Listen up cadets. It's time to pitch in and reward these young ladies for making your lives easier. We're accepting donations so that your commanders and your conjuror can take these ladies to dinner. Here's a cap. Your donations are welcome," Tag shouted. Forty-five cadets lined up and each dropped a few coins into the cap. Priests were known for their thriftiness. Not so for warriors. They were among the most generous group in Entos and the same could be said of cadets. They collected so much money they were able to pay for a first-rate meal for the ladies and buy additional food and drinks to distribute to the cadets who came to the theater to rest.

"Thank you very much, cadets. Your generosity will be well rewarded this evening when we bring back some of Entos' epicurean delights. If you're really good, I might even be able to persuade one of Entos' rising stars, Miss River Kiernan, to perform for you this evening right here in this old theater. So pass the word and see how many of your fellow cadets are interested in a free show."

"Thayer Taggert," River said, "It would've been nice if you asked first."

"Would you have refused?" Tag asked.

"Of course not," River said.

"So the result is the same," Tag said with a smile. "Part of being a good leader requires the leader to look to his warriors' morale. So it is settled, Blisse will play the piano and River Kiernan will sing."

The Oracles And The Jewels

"I am sorry I will not be able to go to dinner with you," Breille said. "I still have a few details that I need to tend to before I go home for the night and I probably should get started on the reports."

"Breille, you do not have anything else left to do tonight," Brenz said.

"I think you've done enough for the day," Rieve joined in. "You can take forty-five minutes off for dinner and the evening off for a show."

"Are you insisting?" Breille asked.

"Yes, we are," Blisse said. "All work and no play will make you a very successful Procuron, but a very poor member of the fellowship."

"Play is required of the fellowship?" Breille asked. Her tone was such that the others did not know whether she was kidding or serious.

"Very much so," Blisse replied. "Ask the Headmaster's charge."

"Rieve Waynwright. Is this true?" Breille asked, then smiled a small smile.

"Most certainly, Breille Clarrice. Play is the cure of all manner of spiritual ill. When during the day you have given your all, play, play, play, till dawn does fall."

"Dawn doesn't fall. Night falls. Dawn rises," Breille rebutted.

"Look, I just made it up. Don't expect too much," Rieve replied.

"You have been out-voted. You are coming to dinner with the rest of us, or haven't you heard I am second in command in this cadet army?" Tag said as he looked at the clock.

"When did that happen?" Breille asked.

"It went into effect about 30 minutes ago," Brenz said. "Haven't you noticed him watching the clock?"

"When did Entos become a democracy?" Breille said.

"Okay, it's a dictatorship and I am the ranking conjuror of the cadet army and I order you, a conscript, to dinner with the rest of your comrades," Rieve said. "So now the ranking officer and the ranking conjuror have both ordered it." Brenz and Tag took Breille by each elbow and lifted her off the floor and carried her out the door, which was no small feat since a female Procuron was every bit as tall as male Demotics and Kilposians.

"I yield," Breille said.

Make Ready

"If it makes you happy, there is one small thing you can do when we get back," River said as she held the door open. "You can check out the amplification system to see if it still works. Now that we stripped the place and put all these beds and pads, and military stuff in here, I'm not sure that the acoustics are suitable for a performance. I will probably need some amplification."

Rieve, Tag, Brenz, River, Blisse, and Breille went down to the street to eat dinner at a street café near The Great Chamber. The café was virtually empty. In light of an impending attack by Ashkelon it appeared that most Entosians had gone home early and were going to stay there. The six took turns ordering and tried not to look at the eastern sky. But as darkness fell, none of the six could keep their eyes off the sky. As the sun was setting in the west, the darkness of the eastern sky began to take on a more ominous look.

"Why is the sky dark?" Blisse asked. "I know. It's because Ashkelon is coming, but I want to know what is it that makes the sky so dark."

"Some say it is dark with Ashkelon's winged creatures," Brenz answered.

"But don't the Oracles say the blackness follows him wherever he goes?" Blisse asked.

"Blackness is the natural order in Ashkelon's earth. The darker it is the more at home Ashkelon and his creatures are. Light, virtue, righteousness, and love are alien qualities in Ashkelon's earth. Blackness and Ashkelon go together. Where the one goes the other follows. If there are winged creatures in that black sky, that only adds to its blackness," Rieve explained. "Entos and Entosians are merely pilgrims in this dark world. Mount Ektos cannot generate enough blackness to overcome the sun's light. It does, however, generate enough to keep Ektos in darkness and to surround Ashkelon with darkness."

"Do you believe that tomorrow the streets of Entos will be the scene of a great battle?" River asked.

"The general wouldn't go to all this trouble if he weren't convinced that an attack in the city wasn't a real possibility," Tag said.

"He's a general. One of the best in our history. His job is to consider all military possibilities and to prepare for them," Breille said.

"That is true. But the general is not the only one speaking and acting in such away. This morning I took a

The Oracles And The Jewels

walk with Headmaster Sandor and we spent the morning just walking and looking at the buildings of Entos and The Great Chamber. It was almost as if the Headmaster was saying good-bye to the city he has known for his entire life. The Headmaster certainly sees something coming," Rieve explained.

"So tomorrow everything changes," Blisse said.

"Yes," Rieve said quietly, "everything except the Oracles and the Jewels."

"Well, there is no sense in sitting here worrying about it. Being anxious over what might happen tomorrow won't change what will happen tomorrow. So let's just eat, drink, sing, and have a good time tonight," Tag said. "Tomorrow will take care of itself."

"You sound like someone else I talked to this morning, Cadet Thayer Taggert," Rieve said.

"Who would that be?" Tag asked.

"The Headmaster," Rieve said.

"Now you sound like a general I talked to today," Tag said. The fellowship finished its meal and went in search of a market that had not closed it doors. They found one three blocks to the west of the old theater and went inside.

"Fruit, I think the cadets would like fruit," Blisse said. "They need healthy food for tomorrow."

"That's tomorrow. This is tonight. I'm a cadet and I know what I want tonight. I want sweets, chocolate, bread with cheese, juice, and frozen cream," Brenz said.

"The conjurors will give you a boost. You don't need it from your food. You need good healthy food," Blisse countered.

"Blisse Maia and Brenz Clinton, I suggest a compromise. Besides, I want those cadets in a good mood when I sing this evening."

"River Kiernan, I'm not unreasonable. As long as we put some fruit on the menu," Blisse said.

"As long as we have sweets, chocolate, bread with cheese, juice, and frozen cream on the menu, I can be reasonable too," Brenz said. The group finished their shopping and walked back to the old theater. Dinner and shopping had taken almost two hours. When they returned to the old theater they found one hundred fifty cadets from all four units.

"I don't think we have enough food," Brenz said to Blisse as they walked over to two empty tables and began to put

Make Ready

out the food. Within a couple of minutes a crowd of hungry cadets descended on the two tables.

"I told you we needed more fruit," she replied.

The cadets from Hodia and Polemmas had drawn the more comfortable duty of the four units. They were free to walk among the shops, markets, and restaurants and eat as their bellies desired. But the cadets from Neggen and Krattos did not have that advantage. They stayed on the outside edges of the city and slept in the slopes and on the plateaus so that they could hear any battle cry from their fellow cadets. They ate what they could carry from their occasional trips into the city.

Upon returning, Breille immediately checked the amplification system and lowered the curtain they had left on the stage to conceal the weapons. River looked over the music she had in her case. She selected *The Hymn of the Land of Entos*, a piece from The Great Chamber, and *The Battle Hymn of Entos*.

Tag looked over to Breille, who nodded her head to let Tag know that all was ready. Then he looked over to River who was handing Blisse the music. River indicated that they were ready. Tag climbed up on the old stage.

"Cadets, ladies and gentlemen, all!" Tag said. "I want to thank you all for coming this evening. First I want all the cadets who pitched in for the ladies' dinner to know that they ate well. We brought back some food, but it looks like it didn't last. So all we have to offer you tonight is an evening of fine music, entertainment, and camaraderie. Tomorrow may well be our moment of truth. I know that you will all bring honor to the uniforms that you wear under those tribal robes.

"Now I would like to introduce to you one of the finest talents in Entos today, River Kiernan, who will sing for you and her sister Blisse Maia who will accompany her on the organ. Please welcome them."

The cadets whistled and lightly stomped their feet, which was the customary way of expressing gratitude and appreciation of public performances River took her place on the stage. Breille dimmed the lights and directed one of the three spotlights, which had been converted to medical lights hanging over the hospital tables, on River. Blisse began playing *The Hymn of the Land of Entos*. Immediately the cadets fell silent and stood at attention. In unison they snapped their right hands over their right brows, and held their salute until River had finished the anthem.

The Oracles And The Jewels

The importance of the moment began to weigh on River's emotions, but she fought back the tears that wanted so desperately to free themselves from her eyes. She opened her mouth and began to sing. The strength of her voice surprised the other members of the fellowship. Blisse was the only member of the fellowship who had ever heard her sister perform.

When River had finished the hymn and the last note of the organ faded away, the cadets stood in perfect silence, then in unison they snapped their right hands down to their sides and sat down. Many of the cadets struggled to keep the tears from rolling down their face. Those who lost that battle wiped tears from their cheeks as they lightly tapped their feet on the floor.

As Blisse began playing the second piece, the door opened and Headmaster Sandor appeared. Blisse immediately stopped as all eyes looked to the door. Most Entosians had only seen Sandor from afar while he presided over the great rituals. As soon as the cadets realized who it was that had entered the room, each one took to his knee and bowed his head. Tag approached the Headmaster and knelt down on one knee and bowed his as well. Tag did as the Headmaster requested and all in the room followed his lead.

"Headmaster Sandor, on behalf of this humble and ill-equipped cadet army, I welcome you. It is a great honor to have you with us," Cadet Thayer Taggert said.

Sandor placed his hand upon Thayer's head and said, "Thank you my son. It is I who am humbled by all of thee. Please stand, ye all, stand please and hold thy heads high this night. I don't want to interrupt the performance. I just wanted to come to hear my granddaughters sing and play. And of course, I wanted to see all of thee, the ones who are going to save Entos tomorrow. Now please granddaughters continue. . . . Blisse Maia play. River Kiernan sing." The Headmaster walked over to the snack table and stood facing the stage. Thayer stood next to him. As River continued to introduce her second selection, the Headmaster snuck an occasional crumb from the table.

"The next piece I would like to perform for you is a new composition. In fact it is so new that it is still a work in progress. It is a piece that I hope one day will be included in the Great Ritual of The Great Chamber. I haven't finished all the stanzas yet, but I would like to perform for you what I have finished. I hope you like it," River said. "The title isn't

Make Ready

very original. This song is about the old things that have made Entos the wonderful creature that she is supposed to be. It is simply called, *The Oracles and The Jewels, The Things of Old.*"

The Oracles and The Jewels

1. We were but ghastly creatures, lost in darkness, without redeeming features. Alive but dead, a life oppressed, a life of hate, a life of dread.

To the Chamber we were brought, in the Chamber were we bought. From our mother's womb were we born of flesh and blood to be entombed.

In our father's arms we're held, to the rail he beheld. Then to us the priests did speak, the Oracles as to the meek.

Touched us with the Jewels did he – the brow, the lips, the heart, the three. The things from old are always new; the things from old are always new.

The things of new come from the old; the things of new come from the old.

2. Then we behold the Oracles and Jewels to see the beast destroyed by Thee. And from the womb of Entos we, The Great Chamber, the Oracles, and Three.

He made us free to see the sky so rich with blue, to see the words of His so true. In the ancient rituals were we born, Entosians all to be free from him.

The things of old create the new. The things of old create the new. To us the priests did speak of old, the Oracles as to the meek.

Touched us with the Jewels did He – the brow, the lips, the heart, the three. The things from old are always new; the things from old are always new.

The things of new come from the old; the things of new come from the old.

3. From the dead did we arise as with the sun of the eastern skies. From the Ancient of Days we have beheld, the love, the light and its rays as well.

From the Days of Old the words have stayed, for from those words all was made.

From the Ancient of Days Land has come, from the Days of Old the sun has won.

To us the priests did speak of old, the Oracles as to the meek. Touched us with the Jewels did He – the brow, the lips, the heart, the three.

The Oracles And The Jewels

The things from old are always new; the things from old are always new.

The things of new come from the old; the things of new come from the old.

Blisse started to play for the fourth stanza, but River interrupted, "Sorry, Blisse. Sorry, cadets. That is as much as I have written. I have been a little busy lately, but I hope you liked it."

The cadets stood in stunned silence. It had been such a long time since anyone had composed such a beautiful new hymn praising the things of old. Suddenly the silence was broken and the cadets whistled and stomped their feet with such enthusiasm.

"Thank you," River said. The applause continued and was so loud she could not be heard. She tried again to calm the crowd. "Thank you, thank you." She paused for a moment and the noise began to settle. "Thank you, but if you get any louder it will be impossible to keep this secret army secret. Although," she said as she looked at her grandfather, "it appears that this place isn't a very well-kept secret. Now if you liked the first two hymns, I am sure you are going to like the last hymn for the evening. It is, after all, your Battle Hymn. As is the custom from the Days of Old, when your army is named in the hymn please stand, so that we civilians may salute you who keep the peace."

The Battle Hymn of Entos

Though ten thousand foes now arise: and we His children they despise. Our faith, our hope, our confidence; the Oracles shall never forsake.

For us He came to stay and make; from Him the foe will never take. Until the day of victory hast come; the Battle Hymn is always sung.

Our souls ascend upon the high; while the King of Entos draws ever nigh. We are but pilgrims here on earth; the King draws ever near the earth.

Should we fall in battle here; we fall for all that is right and dear.

Fight on Hodia, Krattos, Kanna, Fight well Polemmas, Nuxia, and Borrhas Fight to the glory Neggen and Tarchus

Fight well ye citizens of Light. Fight well thy warriors with all thy might. To the glory of Entos thy shall fight, for all that is good and right.

Make Ready

Warriors of Entos now arise, the Sun has lit the morning skies.
Warriors of Entos now arise, the Sun has lit the morning skies.

As the hymn was sung, cadets from Hodia, Krattos, Polemmas, and Neggen stood. The few civilians in the hall, the Headmaster included, saluted the cadets and, as they did, everyone in the hall, the Headmaster included, fought back the tears. Once River had finished, the applause overwhelmed her and she was easily convinced to sing a half-dozen more songs before Tag stepped in to bring the night's events to an end. Tag stepped on the stage. Brenz called the group to order.

"Attention!"

"At ease, cadets. I hate to be the one to bring this evening's festival to an end, but the next day or two may prove to be all we can handle. I want to thank River Kiernan and Blisse Maia for their contribution this evening . . . and, of course . . . Breille Clarrice who made sure all things went well. I especially want to thank Headmaster Sandor for coming. His presence here means a lot to all of us. If you become confused over which side of this battle you ought to fight on, just remember Headmaster Sandor's appearance here tonight. His presence and blessing should serve to remind us all that we are fighting on the right side.

"Cadets, outwardly nothing should change. You will continue your rotation as normal, unless you are called to arms. Neggen and Krattos, should that call come, half of every squad is to head immediately to the combat area. The other half of your squad is to get to your weapons' stockpile and join your squad in battle as soon as you can. Be quick about it. Remember, your fellow cadet is armed with only a dagger or two and will not be able to hold the enemy at bay for very long.

"Due to this room's proximity to The Great Chamber and the Academy, you will be able to pick up your armor and weapons here. Breille Clarrice has created a lift system. The first to arrive here will transfer the weapon racks to the lift and lower them to the alley below. You will not need to climb the stairs and suit up here. You can do it in the alley below. Once all the gear is lowered to the street, the lift system will be used to lift the wounded and move them into the field hospital. Blisse Maia is in charge of the field hospital. Once the battle starts, in this room she is in charge. If you find

The Oracles And The Jewels

yourself in here for any reason, you will do as ordered. If she asks you for help, you give it to her.

"As for the balance of the evening, please double-check your gear. I see we have some interesting new tools in the armory. Feel free to check them out. Practice with them a bit before you hide them in your robes. You're welcome to take any weapon with you as long as you can conceal them. We want you ready, but not obvious. There are enemies here we do not know. Once you check your gear get some rest. Those of you who are sleeping here tonight will be awakened at 5:30 and will be out just before dawn. Regardless of where you're stationed, do your best to get some rest. Tomorrow might be a long day. Any questions?... .. Dismissed."

The cadets filed out the door one by one. As they did, the Headmaster stood at the door with Rieve at his side. As each cadet passed, Sandor touched the cadet's forehead, lips, and breast with the diamond mounted on the top of his staff. As he touched the cadets, he spoke a blessing. "May the King of Entos use you well to the glory of His bride Entos." Rieve could have well joined in giving this blessing, but he knew that every cadet to a man wanted to receive these words from the Headmaster himself so he simply dismissed the cadets saying, "Fight well and to the glory of Entos."

Once all the cadets had either left the old theater or bedded down for the night, Rieve and Sandor walked back to Sandor's home. Rieve initiated the only verbal exchange between the two conjurors in the four-block walk. "The night sky is very dark tonight." "Indeed," replied Sandor. The two entered the house and went to their bedrooms where they fell fast asleep.

River, Blisse, and Breille bedded down for the evening in the ladies' quarters in the loft, while all the male cadets bedded down on the floor. Tag and Brenz were the last two to put their heads to rest. Surprisingly, they both fell fast asleep and slept soundly all night at peace with the day and the morrow.

While the cadets were being entertained for the evening, General Witticor made his way to the front lines. He rode all night, changing horses every five leagues at prepared riders' stations. Along the way he passed President Kuchen and the small army of engineers and military bureaucrats who had struggled all day long to move their six panels only twenty-three leagues.

Make Ready

"President Kuchen," the general said as he sat upon his horse, which was puffing and breathing heavily from their run. "May I speak with you for a moment?"

"Certainly, General," he replied. The two moved away from the rest of the group so they could speak freely.

"You haven't made very good progress," the general said in as respectful a voice as he could muster.

"We have had a few problems along the way General, but we are working those problems out. Tomorrow we will do better," the president said.

"With all due respect, Mr. President, if you try to reach the east wall you will be killed. You aren't going to make it. At this pace you just might end up unprotected between two fronts of combat. There is a good chance the Ashkelon is going to drop soldiers in the open fields of the Demotic Valley. You and your people could end up right in the middle of Ashkelon's drop zone."

"With all due respect to you, General, we intend to test this wall at the main point of attack. Should Ashkelon breach the great wall, this wall is your only hope to contain him. You can use these to make a fortress within a fortress," the president said.

"Mr. President. If we must hide ourselves behind a wall within our own walls, we would have already lost the day," the general replied.

"You, sir, have tried to discourage this project from the first day and I will not yield to this last-ditch effort to stop us from testing this wall as it was meant to be tested."

"Mr. President! This is no schoolboy's test. This is a war. I don't care about your blasted wall. I am concerned about the fact that you and your party, especially those young students of yours, are going to be killed as a result of your foolish pride. What I suggest is that you travel through the night until you reach the inner ring of our defensive line. Stay with them. Maybe they will have a use for your panels or wall, whatever you wish to call it!"

"General! We will not only travel through the night, but will do so without so much as a momentary rest. We will reach the great wall tomorrow afternoon. If you are so worried about our well-being you have the authority to reassign a hundred warriors from the inner line of defense to escort us to our final destination," the president shouted. The tone of the conversation had increased to the point that many of students could hear the argument clearly.

The Oracles And The Jewels

"I won't do that, Mr. President. Our defenses are already dangerously thin. I still have troop movements taking place and do not have the ability to move my warriors at will to make up for your stubborn pride. The best thing for all concerned is that you reach the inner defensive line by 1:00 in the dark and bed down there for the night. They will protect you and maybe find a use for your toy fortress."

"General, you do not have the authority to override my mandate. That mandate is from the city council!"

"You're right, President Kuchen, I don't have the authority to stop you from taking these panels to the wall and getting yourself killed, but I do have the authority on a field of battle, which is what I now declare the entire Demotic Valley to be! Under the rules of engagement, I have complete control over every citizen of Entos in this valley with the exception of any other City Father; that would be you!"

The general gave his horse a slight kick and galloped to the middle of the moving party. It was evening and the night sky had grown darker with the approach of Ashkelon, but there was still enough light from the sky reflecting off the panels so that all could be seen by the general and all could see the general.

"Hear me now!" he shouted "I am General Witticor. The highest ranking officer and commander of the warriors of Entos and one of the City Fathers. My first set of orders are for the military bureaucrats among you. You are charged with the protection and safety of these civilians. That was your original calling into this army. I am now ordering you to honor that solemn duty. Your orders are to join up with the interior defensive forces about ten leagues ahead and take up defensive positions. Ready yourselves for an attack and provide protection for these civilians. There are no paper pushers in the Entosian army this day. Today you are all warriors. Some of whom will live and some who will die. Therefore, you will obey my orders. Now you are to place any civilian of any rank who interferes with these orders under arrest for treason.

"As for the civilians among you, you have a choice, you may advance these panels to the interior defensive line and offer them and your labor in defense of Entos or you may turn around right now and walk as quickly as you can back to the city. If you do the latter, do not stop to rest this night. Go all the way back to the city and hope that you arrive before Ashkelon does.

Make Ready

"The only person among you who is authorized to advance these panels to the great wall is President Kuchen. If he wishes to carry these panels one-by-one on his own back he may do so. But you may not go with him! Those are my orders. I expect them to be followed. If you don't, you will be dead by 12:00 in the light." The general gave his horse a slight kick and galloped back to President Kuchen.

"Mr. President, you have cost dearly this night. I do not have time to deal with arrogant fools who want to play army," the general growled as he gritted his teeth. "I will inform the commander of the interior line, Major Gaynor, that he should be expecting you. I will, out of the mercy of the Maker and for the sake of our King, ask the major to protect your worthless butt. Although I will not fault him in the least if he should let you fend for yourself."

"General, in all my life I have never been spoken to in such a fashion! I will take this matter up with the City Fathers and I will work for your removal from the City Fathers!" The president shouted.

"I certainly hope so, Mr. President, because that would mean you are still alive. At the moment, I doubt very much a man as stupid as you is going to live through the next twenty-four hours." With that comment the general kicked his horse hard and resumed his night ride to his next horse station.

General Witticor reached the east wall near the halfway point between the Hodia and Polemmas towers. Warriors, horses, and artillery had been flowing into the area all day and night. An old command station which had been used in previous battles had been cleaned up and prepared as the general's field headquarters. His staff was already in the building when he arrived and so were the messages from the birds sent to both Hodia and Polemmas towers. As the general entered the room all the students snapped to attention and saluted him.

"At ease," the general said. "Have we heard from the scouts?"

"Yes sir, General," a Procuron colonel named Tarrant said as he handed the two messages to Witticor, who proceeded to read them and translated them out loud.

"Made contact. Enemy army is a full force.
Estimate 150,000 to 200,00 large creatures
Unknown number of winged creatures, but large force
3 battering rams, 24 catapults, 12 large crossbows, ladders, and water wagons

The Oracles And The Jewels

Ashkelon with them.
Attack estimated at 9:00
Hodia has hooked up with Polemmas. Minus three warriors. Under attack

"Colonel, what's your reading of 'minus 3 under attack?'" the general asked.

"I believe, General, that Hodia and Polemmas together have already lost three warriors and they were writing the message while under attack. Identical messages were received at the Hodia and Polemmas towers at approximately the same time. The messages are exact duplicates."

"Colonel Tarrant, is this all the intelligence we have? Have the others reported anything?"

"No, General . . they haven't," the colonel replied with a tone of disappointment.

"Good, very good," the general quietly mumbled. "If the scouts are still alive, one can only hope that they bump into the others. They have done a fine job. Entos is in their debt."

"Yes, General, we are," the colonel said. "On the positive side of things, General, you have done well thus far. You have anticipated Ashkelon's attack. You have been pretty accurate all along. One wonders whether we just wasted six scouts securing information that you probably knew," the colonel said.

"I was guessing. You need more than a guess. This information not only confirms what I suspected. It now commits us to taking up particular positions," Witticor replied as he leaned over a table covered with a detailed map of the terrain.

"His main attack will be right here," the colonel pointed to the middle of the wall between Hodia and Polemmas towers. "He is bringing with him an army fit for an invasion and an occupation. He will attack by land and air and will likely drop several thousand of his soldiers into the interior of Entos.

"He has more in mind than a simple two front attack. I know it!" Witticor said as he walked around the table peering at the map. Two hundred thousand isn't near enough to breach the walls and march sixty leagues to the heart of the city, even if he were to drop a third of them behind our first defensive line. He either has three times the number reported here, two hundred thousand, or he has something far more dangerous in the works."

Make Ready

"Dispatch a bird to the Kanna and Neggen expeditionary forces," Witticor ordered. "Give them the word – *Annan Velotis* – *Proceed with all haste.*"

"We should be able to repel an attack here at the wall and any attack that might come to the interior of the Demotic Valley. It will be difficult," the colonel said.

"Indeed, it will," the general replied.

"The only question is the city," the colonel said.

"I believe the city is in good hands as well," the general replied. "But do we have enough of those hands and are those hands experienced enough?" Witticor sighed. "Those cadets certainly have the heart for this battle. Is the artillery in place?"

"It is being moved there now," the colonel replied.

"What about the rail system, is it holding up?" the general asked.

"We had a couple of problems overnight. One of the catapults between here and Polemmas broke down. No one was hurt, but the system was down for about two hours. It's back up and running and we're continuing troop movements," the colonel explained.

"What about the evacuation lifts?" the general asked.

"Without builders and engineers from the building academy, I am not as confident in them as I would like to be," the colonel said.

"Get used to it, Colonel," Witticor replied. "The days of a unified front and intra-branch cooperation are history. Each academy, discipline, and industry will need to become self sufficient from this day forward. The days of the military engineer are returning."

"We had to create a design of our own making for the lifts. We couldn't get the steel we needed. The lifts are made entirely of wood, with the exception of nails and plates refashioned from old armor."

"Have they been tested?" Witticor asked.

"They will probably be ready in an hour," General Raggnar answered. "The problem is, General, we could not build the lifts as large as we wanted. The timber wouldn't hold."

"We're an army of one hundred thousand strong on the brink of the biggest war in five hundred years and we can't get the steel we need," the general said in disgust. "I should have assigned the job to that little Procuron girl, Breille Clarrice, and the cadets. So what do we have?"

The Oracles And The Jewels

"We have eight lifts and each one can hold an average of one hundred twenty five warriors."

"We had planned on sending two thousand warriors to meet Ashkelon's front line on the desert," the general said as he shook his head in frustration.

"But we can only evacuate one thousand of them over the wall. If we send more they will have to retreat through the gates," the colonel explained.

"That pretty much defeats the purpose," the general said.

"Yes, General, but the only other alternative is to reduce our front line by one thousand," the colonel replied.

"Are you sure we can't use the evacuation lifts more than once?" the general asked.

"We might be able to make a second trip with the two lifts in the middle, if we reposition some of our resources and counterweights immediately after the first lift," the colonel answered. "We could deploy as many as twelve hundred fifty. We could use the two lifts in the middle to evacuate the wounded and the first two hundred, assuming the line holds, then we could send the middle two down for a second and final trip. But we would leave the balance of our forces on the ground for five to ten minutes longer than we expected."

"I don't want to have to use the gates at all. Those gates are to be sealed until the time we allow them to be breached. If we can get through them, they can get through them. If they are going to breach this wall, they are going to have to knock part of it down. The only warriors we will put on the desert floor are the warriors we can withdraw over the top of the wall. If we can evacuate twelve hundred, then we will only deploy twelve hundred to the desert floor. What is the projected casualty rate?"

"The Procurons think we are going to lose eight percent," General Raggnar answered. "With only twelve hundred on the ground we will be stretched pretty thin and that will increase our casualty rate."

"Here is what we are going to do. We will deploy twelve hundred warriors to the desert floor. On my signal two hundred warriors are to be immediately evacuated. The two middle lifts will be reinserted and the remaining one thousand will be evacuated in as systematic a manner as the situation permits starting with the outside lifts and moving to the middle.

The six outside lifts are to be raised first and loaded with flammables, set ablaze, and dropped on top of those poor

Make Ready

devils as each lift is made ready. Make sure our warriors understand they must hold a tight circle around the middle lifts so that we don't drop the lifts on top of our own warriors. Once the beasts and soldiers regroup and surge forward against our warriors, the super-structures for the outside six lifts are to be cut loose from the wall. That will likely cause a momentary fall back. That should buy our men on the ground a few precious moments to regroup and start filling the last two middle lifts. We also don't want to make it any easier for Ashkelon to scale our wall with our own equipment. General Raggnar, are you clear on the plan?"

"Yes, General, but those lifts are going to be overloaded with men, some wounded. We are going to have to make a couple of modifications."

"Make them," Witticor said,

"I will get on the project straightaway," Raggnar said as he saluted and marched from the building.

The Scouts

The scouts' progress through the night was slow. They wove their way through the forest by the light of their torches, pulling the five remaining horses behind them. Occasionally one of the scouts would be caught in a vine, but cutting themselves free was a normal routine and the event no longer stirred excitement.

As the night passed, the scouts knew that the gap between Ashkelon's front line troops and themselves was closing too quickly. The forest parted for them and the darkness was no problem for their eyes. As each hour passed each member was coming to the conclusion that they were losing the race. They would not be able to return to Entos before the attack.

"All right, I will bring the subject up if no one else is going to do it," Sergeant Justin said. "Lieutenant Arokim, what's the plan?"

"We keep moving, that's the plan," the lieutenant said.

"That is the short-term plan. What is the long-term plan?" Justin asked.

"I am flattered that you think I am such a good squad leader that we have need for a long-term plan," Arokim said.

"The term 'long' is a relative term, sir," Justin answered.

"Okay, sergeant, let me hear your assessment of our situation and your plan," lieutenant said.

The Oracles And The Jewels

"At our present pace we will reach the desert about an hour before sunrise. At sunrise we will be standing in the open, flat, barren, and defenseless desert floor. Ashkelon and his army, including the winged creatures, will be about ten feet behind us. At that moment we will turn our five remaining horses and will launch a full attack against a superior force estimated to be one hundred fifty thousand to two hundred thousand battle-hardened soldiers. We will destroy the entire army and go out in a blaze of glory!" Justin cried out.

"That doesn't seem to be a very practical plan, but if it is okay with all of you, I'm all for it," Sergeant Celsus said.

"I thought you Hodia types were optimists," Lieutenant Roggan quipped.

"That was the optimistic picture," Justin said.

"I think Sergeant Justin understands the situation just fine," Lieutenant Arokim said. "He has the right idea, just not the right strategy. So here is what I propose. We're going to proceed to the place where the desert and forest meet. We're going to move south just far enough to allow Ashkelon's army to march by. We will remain concealed in the tree line and attempt to disrupt his rear units and supply lines. If we perform well, we will likely make two or three attacks on his artillery units before we are discovered. If we can rob him of the use of some of his artillery, we will have done well and saved many Entosian lives. The more resources we can draw away from Ashkelon's main attack, the better it will be for Entos and our fellow warriors on the wall."

"It sounds like a plan," Lieutenant Roggan concurred.

"Now that we, and Ashkelon's forest, are all clear about the plan, let's get moving," Arokim said.

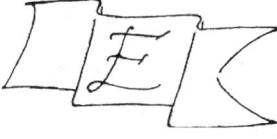

Chapter Sixteen
King Ashkelon Attacks

The sun rose at 5:35. It was the darkest morning Entos had seen in five hundred years. Despite Ashkelon's nearness, the sun managed to pierce through his dark canopy and all could see that morning had come. By 5:00, the general was standing at the point of attack, halfway between the Hodia and Polemmas towers, on a battlement from which he could see the entire battlefield.

General Raggnar, a Pithosian, the new commanding officer of the Hodia army stood at Witticor's left. General Hokkan, the Demotic commander of the Polemmas Tower army, stood at his right. All three generals stood inside the battlement looking through their field glasses at Ashkelon's large army. Once they had cleared the forest and made it to the desert, the army was able to move more rapidly. The cool of the night helped the pace as well.

Ashkelon's army was made up of fifteen legions formed into fifteen distinguishable rectangles. Each legion had between eight and ten thousand soldiers. Mammothon regiments led the way for each of the legions, one thousand mammothons per line. Behind them there were four or five rows of sipedons. The sipedons were followed by two or three rows of trolls. The last two rows of each unit consisted of skulls.

In addition to the fifteen legions that made up the main body of Ashkelon's ground army, there were two larger units of fighters, numbering some twenty thousand soldiers and beasts each. One was to the north of the main body and the other to the south. These soldiers wore special harnesses over their armor which had handles that rose from the shoulder of each fighter. Most of these fighters were trolls and skulls. There were a few mammothons, maybe five

The Oracles And The Jewels

hundred in each legion. Hovering above the ground forces were thousands of winged creatures, both large and small.

"General Witticor," General Hokkan said. "That is the most terrible collection of beasts and creatures I have ever seen."

"I didn't know that so many damnable creatures existed in Asheklon's black earth," General Raggnar said. "It is a good thing that none of those warriors on the ground behind us can see this ungodly sight. We taught them not to be afraid, but we have never shown them a sight like this."

"In about three hours they won't need field glasses to see this sight. They will be looking into the eyes of those damnable creatures themselves," Witticor said. "All that can be done has been done. Now we simply wait and watch the evil come."

"Is Ashkelon down there?" General Hokkan asked as he moved his field glass across the breadth of Ashkelon's army.

"He's down there someplace," Witticor said. "I am sure of it." Witticor surveyed the army too. A few moments of silence passed.

"There he is," Tarrant said.

"Yes, I see him," Witticor replied. "He is right in the middle of the whole damned army." It was hard to see the details of Ashkelon's features, but his presence was unmistakable. In the third column of the second row rode a figure, twice the size of any mammothon or Pithosian. He wore full body armor and a helmet which extended over the upper half of his face. He was mounted upon a morse that was larger and blacker than all others. From his left hip hung a two-edged axe and a whip of chains. A huge black steel sword hung from his right hip. These are not the weapons of one who engages in the art of war. These are the weapons of sheer brute force and the power to cut down many warriors with one full swing.

"Can that devil even be felled?" Hokkan asked.

"The Oracles tell us that he will one day fall, but not at the hand of any Entosian warrior's blade," Witticor answered. "He will fall at the hand of an Entosian priest, the likes of which Entos has not yet seen. The best that we can do in the meantime is to destroy each army he sends against us."

King Ashkelon Attacks

"If he can't be killed by an Entosian blade, then why doesn't he just march into the heart of Entos, destroy the city, take the Oracles and Jewels himself, and be done with us all?" Tarrant asked.

"He has his limits, just like all other creatures. He is not a god. He just thinks he is," Witticor replied. "He can be felled, otherwise he would have no use for lesser creatures. But he must always live in fear that the priest who can fell him may live within these walls."

"There is no shortage of lesser creature that's for sure," Tarrant commented.

"No, there's not. He has plenty of agents through which to work his evil. There are plenty of them out there beyond the walls and too many behind these walls. It is our task at this moment to tend to those out there, so here is what is going to unfold, gentlemen," Witticor continued. "Ashkelon will send those first five legions against the wall below us. He will send a second wave shortly thereafter. He will hold the remaining five legions until the wall is breached."

"And the two large units to the north and south?" Hokkan asked. "Those are the troops he is going to insert by air."

"Yes, but he won't do that until our archers are busy providing cover fire. He will wait until the battle is well underway, then he will insert them. If our archers are busy engaging land forces, he will get more of the airborne fighters behind our line and we will need to show restraint. Instruct our archers to shoot down winged creatures when the opportunity presents itself. Their main targets, however, must be the main body. We will have to trust our second line to engage Ashkelon's airborne legions. The question is, how far . . . . how far can they fly with such a heavy load? That is the variable that places Entos at risk," Witticor said with a tone of concern.

Sandor's Home

A knock came at the door at 5:25. Sandor opened it. River and Blisse stood outside.

"Good morning young ladies, welcome. What a pleasant surprise," Sandor said greeting the girls. He took

The Oracles And The Jewels

River's hand in his right hand and Blisse's hand in his left. "Come in, Granddaughters. To what do I owe this rare visit?"

"Rieve Waynwright invited me over for breakfast. I hope you don't mind. I asked sister to join us," River Kiernan said.

"No, I don't mind," Sandor replied.

"We hope you have enough for all four of us. We don't want to deprive you of anything," Blisse said.

"Rieve Waynwright said you always prepare a feast in the morning," River said.

"Yes, I always prepare more than I need. It's an old habit. You never know when you are going to have guests. In days gone by it was common for students to visit in the evening, stay the night, and eat breakfast with me in the light. It was also common for visiting scholars and the conjurors from the various armies to stay overnight and eat breakfast with me. But those days are long gone."

The three of them walked into the breakfast room. A few minutes later Rieve joined them. He was dressed in his priestly robe and carried his staff. River and Blisse were surprised by his looked. It was more than the wearing of the robe and the carrying of the staff. Rieve had the look of sobriety and maturity. He looked out the window toward the eastern sky and held his breath for a moment.

"That is the darkest morning I have ever seen. Today is the day," Rieve said.

"It was a quiet and uneasy walk over here this morning," Blisse said.

"Master," Rieve began, "I might as well confess. I asked River over for breakfast this morning because I also asked her to stay with you all day today."

"Thank you for your concern, my son, but I am sure she has better things to do than to look after an old man."

"The old man is my grandfather," River said. "It is my duty and calling as your granddaughter to tend to you, Grandfather. I would hope that a priest would not encourage a member of his own family to neglect her duties. Besides, Grandfather, my work is pretty much done. This day belongs to Rieve Waynwright, Thayer Taggert, Brenz Clinton, Breille Clarrice, and Blisse Maia. Today belongs to the warriors, conjurors, and healers. I would just be in the way."

King Ashkelon Attacks

"I doubt that, young lady. Thou hast proven to be very resourceful and quite helpful," Sandor said. "It would be best if thy sought the places of safety. If I know me, trouble will seek me out this day."

"All the more reason, Grandfather, for River to spend the day with you," Blisse said. "Besides, if she gets in the way or something, just make her disappear or turn her into some little creature or something. You have my permission."

"Thank you, Blisse Maia, for your helpful suggestions," River said.

"So it is settled," Rieve said. "River Kiernan will stay with you, Master. Blisse will tend to the field hospital. I will tend to The Great Chamber and Hodia. And you, Master, will sit high atop your perch in the faculty building watching over the Academy and the streets below."

"Now that it's all settled, can we actually eat?" Blisse said. The four sat down to an uneventful, yet pleasant breakfast together. When they had finished, Sandor and River walked the short walk from his house to the faculty building, but as with every morning they were not alone. Two warriors from the honor guard followed at a short distance.

Rieve walked Blisse to the old theater, then made his way to The Great Chamber. Along the way he saw Tag and Brenz eating breakfast at a breakfast café.

"Good morning Cadets," Rieve said. "You're out early."

"That shouldn't come as a surprise," Tag replied as he pointed upward toward the dark morning sky.

"Are you carrying the fellowship stones?" Rieve asked. Brenz and Tag pulled their topaz stones from the pouches that hung from their belts and showed them to Rieve.

"Just checking," Rieve said.

"If you're checking up on us, we want to see yours," Brenz said. Rieve pulled the ruby from his pouch and showed it to the two cadets.

"Now there is just one question left," Tag said.

"How do they work?" Brenz and Tag said in unison.

"I don't know, but I will bet you that by the end of the day we will know," Rieve said.

"Did you eat breakfast yet?" Brenz asked Rieve.

"Yes and I am full. The Headmaster loves to cook and eat. If I live with him long enough I am going to start looking

The Oracles And The Jewels

like a very short Pithosian. Besides, you two look like you're just about finished."

"We are," Brenz said as he picked up the crumbs from his plate and put them into his mouth."

"You don't have to report for duty for another hour and ten minutes. So what's the plan?" Rieve asked.

"We were going to check in this morning with Conjuror Stratia. We thought he would be here, but he hasn't shown up yet. Colonel Fornoff was right. He is a great conjuror, just a little slow getting places. So we're going to check in with the colonel, retrieve the old conjuror, and walk him over."

"Do you think it is safe for me come along, or should I stay at The Great Chamber?" Rieve asked.

"We haven't heard any battle horns from Polemmas or Hodia yet, so I don't think the attack has started. We probably have an hour or two before things get busy. I also saw Professors Etam, Worett, and Scarre go in The Great Chamber a little while ago. If something does happen before we get back, there are enough trustworthy conjurors around here to handle things," Tag said in a surprisingly relaxed way.

Brenz left enough coins to cover the bill and Tag added a generous tip for the waiter.

"Since when did little brother become such a big spender?" Rieve commented.

"The waiter had the courage to leave home and open up shop this morning," Tag answered. "Courage and devotion to duty should always be rewarded. Now, I could let a conjuror leave the tip, but everyone knows that conjurors are the worst tippers in all of Entos. Besides, by tomorrow I might not need money," Tag said with a bit of morbid humor.

"Whatever the reason, I am glad to see you being so generous," Rieve replied.

The three walked briskly to The Academy of the Ancient Warring Arts. They arrived at 7:30, just as the receptionist was taking her place at the lobby desk.

"Good morning, gentlemen," she said.

"Good morning, Cadet Charis," Tag replied. "I didn't expect to see anyone here this morning."

"Until the horn blows, it is business as usual. But don't worry, when that horn blows the few of us left in the academy

King Ashkelon Attacks

have our orders to join ranks so we can save your hides," she said with a bashful smile.

"Is Conjuror Stratia in yet?" Brenz asked.

Cadet Charis looked over at a sign-in board. "Yes he is, signed in about a half hour ago."

"What about Colonel Fornoff?" Tag asked.

"He came in about the same time."

"Anyone else in the place?" Brenz asked as he looked around at all the dimly lit hallways and dark offices. "Or is this place always this dark?"

"Usually by now it is filled with instructors, but the City Fathers scheduled some kind of presentation on the armies and their place in the future of Entos," she reported.

"Strange, this is the first time we've heard anything about it," Tag said. "I would have thought that Colonel Fornoff or General Witticor would have said something about it."

"It was scheduled a couple of weeks ago, then the attacks began and it was canceled at General Witticor's request. Well, as you know the general left the city yesterday afternoon and shortly thereafter a memo was sent over from the Academy of Governance stating that an abbreviated version of the presentation would be held this morning over breakfast. So the few instructors left in the place are over there eating breakfast and being briefed on the new and improved Entos," Charis explained.

"I take it that Colonel Fornoff and Conjuror Stratia weren't interested in attending," Rieve said.

"The Colonel and Conjuror Stratia pretty much do what they believe is helpful. No more and no less. They don't waste their time in bureaucratic meetings."

"Sounds to me like Cadet Charis isn't particularly thrilled with the prospect of a new and improved Entos," Brenz replied.

"My interest remains in those things that have always been and those things that have made Entos great. The Oracles, the Jewels, the ancient traditions, and eventually a good husband with whom I can raise some traditional little Entosian warriors. Is it safe to assume you and I have the same interests?" Charis said as she smiled not so bashfully in Tag's direction.

The Oracles And The Jewels

"I share some of your interests," Tag replied. "My friend here Cadet Brenz Clinton shares all of those interests. Perhaps the two of you ought to compare notes on your interests sometime."

"Speaking of time," Brenz said, "We are running out of it."

"We will see you on our way out," Rieve said as the three of them headed to the stairs. They hurried up three flights, but before they reached the second floor Brenz and Tag were engaged in a race for bragging rights. Brenz had the natural advantage. Kilposians were fleet of foot, but Tag gave him a race. Brenz hit the third floor door with a bang and shouted, "I win!"

They waited but a moment then opened the door and started down the hallway toward the colonel's office. They were about halfway down the hall when Rieve finally made it to the third floor. As Brenz and Tag approached the colonel's office they noticed broken glass and bits of wood scattered about the hallway.

"Something's wrong," Tag said. Brenz and Tag sprinted forward and through the broken doorway leading to the colonel's office. As they ran, their right hands reached beneath their robes and gripped their daggers.

"Colonel!" Tag shouted. The colonel had been cut several times and was bleeding. "Colonel!" Tag shouted a second time.

The colonel opened his eyes. "I must be getting old. I didn't hear them. They were dressed as cadets, Hodia cadets. I think there were six of them, but it happened too fast."

"Colonel, you're cut pretty badly. We need to get you to a healer in a hurry," Brenz said.

"It looks worse than it is," the colonel replied as he struggled to sit up. Tag held him down.

"Wait here, Colonel," Tag said. "Don't move. Sir, it's worse than you think."

"I'll give the orders here, Cadet," the colonel said.

"Not until I am sure you're all right, Sir," Tag countered.

Rieve had heard the shouting and ran down the hall to the office. "What happened?" Rieve asked.

"The Colonel was attacked," Tag said.

King Ashkelon Attacks

"How long ago?" Rieve asked.

"I was knocked on the head. I don't know, but I am still alive. They must have heard you coming."

"Conjuror Stratia," Rieve said quietly.

"Stratia!" the colonel repeated with alarm. "Stratia. Go! Go!"

"You go," Rieve said looking to Brenz and Tag. "I'll take care of the colonel."

Brenz and Tag bolted from the office, down the hall, and into the stairwell. This time their daggers were drawn. As they raced down the stairs, Brenz landed on every other step. Tag took larger jumps opting to hit every third or fourth step to keep pace. When they reached the main floor, Brenz was slightly ahead. He opened the door to the main lobby and shouted, "Cadet Charis! The colonel's been attacked. He needs a healer!" He didn't wait for a reply. Cadet Charis immediately left her post and ran out the back entrance of the building. Cadets from Krattos often used the yard as a resting place. This morning was no different. Three squads were suiting up to report for an 8:00 patrol.

"Cadets!" Charis shouted. "The colonel's been attacked. He's wounded and needs a healer! Come with me!" Immediately, fifteen cadets fell in behind her and ran to the colonel's office.

Tag and Brenz reached the basement stairwell at the same time. They exploded through the door to Stratia's practice hall, but the room was silent and dark. They stopped. The light was on in Stratia's eight-sided office in the middle of the hall, but they did not see anything of Stratia. Tag made his way to the wall and leveler for the lights. He turned the leveler to the 'on' position, but none of the luminaries on the walls brightened.

"Conjuror Stratia," Brenz said. There was no answer. "Sir," Brenz said a second time. "Are you down here?" Then a moment later.

"Yes, here I am," Stratia replied as he entered the hall from the opposite stairwell. "What's all the fuss about?" he asked as he walked slowly toward Brenz and Tag.

"Sir, the Colonel's been attacked," Tag said. "Some warriors dressed like cadets tried to kill him."

"This is terrible," Stratia said.

The Oracles And The Jewels

"We came down to check on you," Brenz said. By now the light from Stratia's office illuminated his face.

"On me? What would anyone want with me?" At that moment Stratia let out a groan and looked down at the sword upon which he was now impaled. Brenz and Tag stood motionless for a moment as they saw the horror unfold. The moment did not last but an instant. Five more swords flashed toward them reflecting the light from Stratia's office.

Tag and Brenz began to jump, turn, and twist, using their daggers to block the incoming blades. The sword that had been holding up Stratia withdrew itself from his belly and Stratia's lifeless body fell to the floor with a thump. The five swords were joined by the sixth. Three struck violently at each of the cadets and with each blow they drove the two further and further apart. Their tribal robes were being cut to pieces, but both Tag and Brenz had managed to avoid being hit with a direct blow. It was only a matter of time, each thought. Daggers were no match for six swords.

The hall was dimly lit, but the light that was there was reflecting off several sets of practice armor and swords hanging on the wall. Surrounded on three sides, Tag threw his dagger toward the shadowy figure before him. The figure let out a cry and the sword dropped to the warrior's side. Tag delivered a blow to the figure's head and in so doing cleared a path to the swords hanging on the wall. In a instant, he had turned the tables. He grabbed a sword in each hand and ran toward Brenz.

"Polemmas!" he shouted as he tossed the sword to Brenz. Before the sword reached his hand, Brenz threw his dagger at the shadowy figure over whose head the sword was soaring. Tag kept running toward Brenz and took a swing at the warrior on Brenz's right. The figure blocked the strike, but fell backward. Brenz and Tag took up positions back-to-back. Two of their attackers were now wounded and had withdrawn from the fight, but the six combatants still left in the battle were fighting to a stalemate.

By now the battle had lasted nearly five minutes. It took less than four minutes for Cadet Charis and fifteen cadets from Krattos to reach the colonel's office.

"I need a Krattos squad," Rieve said.

"Reporting!" snapped one of the squad leaders.

King Ashkelon Attacks

"Follow me!" Rieve snapped back.

While Cadet Charis and the others applied first aid to the colonel, wrapped his wounds, and placed the colonel on a stretcher, Rieve quickly made his way down the four flights of stairs to the basement with five Krattos cadets right behind.

As Rieve reached the bottom of the stairwell, he could hear the crashing of the metal blades. The five cadets drew their daggers and readied themselves. Rieve opened the door and looked into the dimly lit room. He could make out six shadowy figures engaged in mortal combat.

"Hold fast," Rieve ordered. "Wait till you can see." Rieve ran unnoticed into Stratia's office. He grabbed a luminary and struck it against the desk. He repeated the process two more times. When all three luminaries were lit, he tossed them in the direction of the combatants. The attackers were dressed in Hodia uniforms, but their faces were concealed by old practice face guards. The light caught the attackers by surprise and for fear of being discovered, the attackers charged the five cadets who blocked their exit, exchanging blows with the cadets as they fled. The cadets turned to pursue the attackers and Brenz moved to join them.

"Stop, Cadets!" Tag ordered. Immediately they stopped.

"But, sir!" shouted Brenz. He took another step.

"Stop, Cadet!" Tag ordered again. Brenz looked at Tag with frustration in his eyes and they locked eyes in an angry stare.

"As much as I want to go after them too," Tag shouted, "we can't go running around the city. We are not a police force. We have a mission and we are to remain invisible to the rest of Entos. We must keep our primary mission in mind. These assassins will make themselves known again and we will deal with them when the time is right." Tag turned aside and saw Stratia's body lying lifeless on the hardwood floor.

The three luminaries provided ample light and all the cadets walked toward Stratia's body. Rieve knew the effort was in vain, but he knelt and placed his fingers along side Stratia's neck to see if there was a pulse. There was not. The wound was too great and his life had been poured out on the wooden floor. Rieve returned to the office where he found a

The Oracles And The Jewels

small blanket, then slowly walked back to Stratia's corpse where he placed the blanket over Stratia. "You have done well, good and faithful steward. You fought well and to the glory of Entos. May the King receive you according to his work."

"How is the Colonel?" Tag asked.

"He will be fine," Rieve answered. "Cadet Charis rounded up several Krattos cadets. They will be carrying him off to the field hospital any moment." The three walked quickly to the stairwell. The Krattos cadets followed.

"Krattos," Tag said. "Keep what has happened here to yourselves. The mission is first."

"Yes, sir," they replied.

As they climbed the stairs, they heard the colonel yelling at the cadets, who were obviously having a difficult time maneuvering the colonel, a big Pithosian, down the narrow stairwell on the stretcher.

"Yes indeed," Rieve said. "He will be all right."

Tag, Brenz, Rieve, and the five cadets ascended the stairwell and entered the lobby where they stood waiting for the colonel's stretcher to meet them. A couple of minutes later it did. The colonel saw the three standing by the reception desk.

"Stratia? How is Stratia?" the colonel asked.

"We failed you, Colonel. He is dead," Tag said.

"No son, you did not," the colonel replied. "Things are as they are ought to be." The colonel looked at the cuts that had been sliced into Tag's robes. "By the looks of those robes, you didn't run from the fight."

"No, sir. Nor did we win it," Tag answered.

"You have so much to learn, young warrior," Fornoff sighed.

"Colonel," Cadet Charis said. "Sir, that will be enough talking for now. You are injured more badly that you think. You will need your strength." Colonel Fornoff closed his eyes and fell asleep. His breathing became shallow. Charis called out, "Cadets! Double-time!" The cadets immediately responded and began a well-synchronized run out the door and into the streets. They headed straight west until they reached the Headmaster's house on the corner, then turned left. They sent an Aradian ahead to inform Blisse of the

King Ashkelon Attacks

colonel's imminent arrival. By the time they reached the field hospital, the evacuation lift was waiting for the colonel. The cadets placed him onto the lift and the counterweights were released.

"I'm going to need six of you up here to help us get him in the room," Blisse said. The six largest cadets ran up the metal staircase where the colonel and Blisse were waiting. They removed the colonel from the lift, carried him over, and placed him upon one of the hospital tables. Rieve, Tag, and Brenz followed the stretcher into the old theater. As Blisse went to work on the colonel, Brenz and Tag replaced their torn and tattered tribal robes with new ones. Rieve stood beside Blisse ready to assist her if needed. The colonel opened his eyes and looked at Blisse.

"Hello, young lady," the colonel said. "It's nice to know a pretty little thing like you will be taking care of me."

"Your reputation for flirting is well known Colonel. All talk though, from what I hear," Blisse said with a smile.

"Oh, if I were young again missy."

"If you were young again sir, you probably wouldn't be in this shape," Blisse said and smiled.

"How true," he replied softly.

"Sorry, Colonel. I wish we had someone with a little more experience working the floor. Someone with any experience at all would be an improvement."

"You'll do fine young lady," the colonel said. "There's nothing like a young attractive healer to bring an old colonel back to life."

"What happened, Colonel?" Blisse asked as she prepared her wraps and ointment.

"Just a little espionage and a botched assassination attempt," the colonel said. "I sure hope I didn't train those assassins. I would be ashamed to be their C.O."

"Now we've talked too much Colonel. Time to sleep." The colonel closed his eyes and fell asleep.

"Espionage and assassinations," Blisse said with a tone of disbelief as she turned toward Rieve. "Why would Entosians kill fellow Entosians? What in Ashkelon's earth is happening to Entos?"

"Headmaster Sandor said that not all Entosians are really Entosians," Rieve explained.

The Oracles And The Jewels

"So, who are the real Entosians and who are the pretenders?" Blisse asked.

Blisse started with the deepest cuts first and worked on them one at a time. As she applied the medicine, she spoke in the sacred language and used the words of the Oracles to heal and pressed on the open wound.

"Aman aham rafa pasa emen," Blisse chanted in a soft voice.

Rieve translated the song under his breath. *"A faithful friend heals the wounds of the other."*

It only took a few seconds for each wound to stop bleeding and close up. She repeated the process seven more times, eight in all, then covered each wound with a bandage.

"He will be okay," Blisse said as she turned to Rieve. "He lost a lot of blood and will probably sleep the rest of the day."

"Cadet Thayer Taggert, did you hear that report?" Rieve shouted across the room. "The colonel will be all right, but he is out of commission for the day."

"That means you're the ranking officer," Brenz said.

"I know," Tag replied rather quietly.

"Stratia dead and the colonel out of commission. This morning's events raise a lot of questions, don't they?" Brenz said.

"Yes they do. Do our enemies know about us? Do they know about our secret army? Was this an attack on our command structure so as to cut us off from our leaders? Or was this an attack to get a powerful conjuror out of the way?" Tag asked.

"If this was about cutting us off from our command structure, then someone who is not supposed to know we are here knows we are here," Brenz replied. "If it was not an attack on us, then was Stratia the first in a long line of conjurors and priests who are going to be killed so as to further weaken Entos?"

"Makes one wonder what else they know and what else they are willing to do," Tag said.

King Ashkelon Attacks

The Battle For the Eastern Wall

Generals Witticor, Raggnar, and Hokkan stood watch all morning from the Eastern wall and battlement. They watched as Ashkelon's army inched its way across the desert floor. It was 8:30 when Ashkelon's march came to a stop. All seventeen legions came to a stop, but the legions to the north and to the south paused only for a few minutes, then advanced further.

"What do you make of that, General Witticor?" General Raggnar asked. "The airborne legions advance, while all those in the desert stop and wait."

"That tells me that Ashkelon knows exactly how far his winged creatures can penetrate our perimeter. The closer they are to the wall when they are picked up, the further they can fly into Entos and drop their cargo. That is an encouraging sign. They have their limits."

"Unless I miss my guess, General," Hokkan began, "When those legions on the north and the south stop marching, Ashkelon's attack will commence."

"That sounds like a pretty good guess to me," Witticor said. "It's time, generals. Blow the horn and send the birds."

Each of the generals turned to their colonels and passed the order. The colonels passed the order to their majors, who called out to their respective watchmen. "Sound the alarm!"

Instantly, the horns sounded. Each tower's horn had a distinctive sound. When blown in combination, everyone understood that the attack was coming between the towers and against the wall. In a few minutes the entire Land of Entos would know that the attack would be against the wall in the Demotic Valley. All would also know for whom to pray.

The horns triggered a reaction that rolled across the whole Land of Entos from east to west. By the thousands, the warriors of Entos took up their battle stations and positions. The horsemen ran to their waiting steeds. The artillerymen ran to their heavy equipment and began the process of drawing back the bow strings on their giant crossbows and the arms of their catapults. Each piece of equipment was loaded. The horsemen rode into their formations and the infantry took up their positions. Once

The Oracles And The Jewels

each division had taken up its position on the field, its conjuror marched into the midst of them. The twelve hundred spearsmen and swordsmen who were assigned the duty of meeting Ashkelon's first wave of attack on the outside of the wall ascended the stairs and took their positions on the battlements. One thousand of them stepped into the lifts and were lowered to the ground outside the wall. The remaining two hundred repelled down the wall. Once they were on the ground their ropes were pulled up behind them. Twelve hundred warriors stood five deep, awaiting the order to advance and take up their positions in a semicircle. As they stood on the desert floor, they looked across the desert at the mighty army of Ashkelon.

"They are so many," one warrior said as the fear began to well up.

"They are like locusts," another said with his voice shaking.

"Yes they are!" a captain shouted. "They are a great plague upon the land. With their numbers, they could easily overwhelm all of Entos. But you. . . you warriors of Entos, you conjurors of The Great Chamber, you are the hand of the mighty King who has kept this land safe for five thousand years. What are locusts compared to our King?" The captain looked into the eyes of his warriors. His words had helped, but he still saw doubt in their eyes. "Sing, you sons and daughters of the King. Sing courage, sing faith, sing confidence that the locust will fear thy King!" Sing they did.

The Battle Hymn of Entos

Though ten thousands foes now arise: and we His children they despise. Our faith, our hope, our confidence; the Oracles shall never forsake.

For us He came to stay and make; from Him the foe will never take. Until the day of victory hast come; the Battle Hymn is always sung.

Our souls ascend upon the high; while the King of Entos draws ever nigh. We are but pilgrims here on earth; the King draws ever near the earth.

Should we fall in battle here; we fall for all that is right and dear.

King Ashkelon Attacks

Fight on Hodia, Krattos, Kanna, Fight well Polemmas, Nuxia, and Borrhas Fight to the glory Neggen and Tarchus
  Fight well ye citizens of Light. Fight well thy warriors with all thy might.
  To the glory of Entos thy shall fight, for all that is good and right.
  Warriors of Entos now arise, the Sun has lit the morning skies.
  Warriors of Entos now arise, the Sun has lit the morning skies.

The Scouts

The scouts from Krattos, Polemmas, and Hodia had spent the night dodging Ashkelon's army. They had remained undetected and had managed to move far enough south so that his army passed by without noticing the warriors, who now found themselves behind two hundred thousand beasts and soldiers.

"Well, gentlemen," Arokim began, "the time has come. It was a pleasure serving with you in the King's righteous army. Aradians on foot and the rest mount up. Our target is that division right there." Arokim pointed to the closest division in Ashkelon's main army. "The Aradians will set the pace, but let's try to create as little dust as possible. If they spot us at a distance, they will think that we are just some tardy soldiers who lost their way in the forest. When they figure out who we are, I will give the order for a full attack. Our objective is to set aflame their heavy ammunition wagons first; the light ammunition wagons second; and if any of us survive that, take out as many of those poor devils as we can. Let's go."

The three Aradians from Krattos set the pace and the riders followed. They ran for a few minutes in silence, then Sergeant Justin began singing *The Hymn of the Land Entos*. The others joined in. Once they had finished that, Lieutenant Roggan began sing *The Battle Hymn of Entos*.

Suddenly, in front of the Aradians several Entosian warriors rose up out of the desert floor. The twelve remaining scouts instinctively drew their swords or armed their bows. The warriors waved their arms. One of them put his index finger over his mouth in an attempt to silence any statement before it was made. The warriors wore the colors of Kanna.

The Oracles And The Jewels

"Halt!" Arokim ordered. Immediately the twelve scouts came to a stop and stood in silent disbelief.

"Come here!" the warrior said. He was dressed in a colonel's uniform. "Look." He pointed to an opening in the desert floor. There was a small trench that had been camouflaged from the top. The trench was just barely large enough for two squads.

"Lay those horses down and get in here before they see you or you will wreck the whole thing!" Arokim and the rest did as they were instructed, though they found it hard to believe what their ears were hearing and what their eyes saw.

The scouts laid down on the desert floor with their horses and threw dirt over themselves and the horses in an effort to hide their presence. The others, Arokim included, crawled into the trench.

"What are you doing here?" Arokim asked.

"We are the advance team for our offensive force."

"Offensive force?" Arokim repeated.

"Yes, offensive force. You don't think we are going to let you go out in a blaze of glory all by yourselves. Or do you think you're so good you don't need any help?" he said with a smile. "Ten against two hundred thousand. No one is that good. I am Colonel Sollon, with Kanna."

"I am Arokim. It is good to see you. We gladly accept any help you have to offer. But where's the rest of your army?" Arokim asked.

"In the forest right behind us. It is a combined force of Kanna and Neggen, ten thousand strong. I was just about to give the signal to advance when you guys showed up and almost wrecked the whole thing. Now stay put for a moment." The colonel crawled out of the trench and held up a green and red flag, then he crawled back into the trench.

"How are you going to get ten thousand Entosian warriors across an open stretch of this desert without being noticed?" Arokim asked.

"We are going to walk right up behind them," the Colonel answered. "Do you have a better idea?"

"You're going to walk right up behind them?" Arokim repeated.

King Ashkelon Attacks

"You guys must have had a rough couple of days out there in that forest. You keep repeating everything. Take a look," Solon said.

Solon lifted the edge of the camouflage canvas and pointed. Emerging from the forest were Entosian warriors covered in animal skins, dressed in armor from the soldiers who had fallen in the battle four days earlier. Many of the warriors had covered themselves with dirt and mud. Others were wearing skull caps. Up close it would be easy to see that these were disguises, but by the time they would be seen for what they really were, it would be too late. For the next two hours they would look like another advancing division of Ashkelon's army.

"Who thought of this?" Arokim asked

"General Witticor. He built his career on being committed to the old school, but creative enough to take the battle to the enemy. We just might win this day," the colonel said. "Of course, the key was to know where to be and when to be there. Your message helped in that regard. Witticor took a big risk. There are only a few warriors left on the western walls. Witticor divided his forces. If Ashkelon attacked from the west, Entos would be lost. But the sacrifice of your scouts has been well repaid."

The scouts and squads from Neggen and Kanna waited in their trench until the Entosian division was marching over them. Then they fell into the formation and marched toward the nearest Ashkelon division.

The Eastern Wall

"General Witticor," General Hokkan said as he looked through his field glasses, "The northern and southern legions have stopped." Witticor looked through his field glasses to see the movement.

"Look to the southeast," General Raggnar said. "I think that is Kanna and Neggen."

"They're right on schedule," Witticor commented.

"It doesn't look like they have been spotted yet," General Raggnar said.

"No, it doesn't look like they've been spotted yet," General Witticor answered. "Even if they are, their presence

The Oracles And The Jewels

will have the needed effect. Ashkelon will have to fight us on two fronts," Witticor said with a slight smile. "That fight is about to begin in earnest right now. Here they come."

The three generals lowered their field glasses and stood upright on the battlement.

"Signal the front line to advance and take up defensive positions. Ready the archers," Witticor ordered. The signalman turned his attention to the warriors standing outside the wall. He gave the signal to the twelve hundred warriors standing almost directly below them. The spearsmen and swordsmen fanned out into a semicircle, six hundred in the outer line and four hundred behind them. The Hodia warriors constituted the northern half of the circle and the Polemmas the southern half. Once they had readied themselves for the wave that was bearing down on them, ten conjurors took up their positions. They stood shoulder-to-shoulder and mirrored the larger formation of warriors.

Looking down from atop the wall, the twelve hundred Entosian warriors standing on the desert floor looked powerless and insignificant in light of the tens of thousands of creatures charging toward them. But this was how it had always been. Against such overwhelming odds and all the power of Ashkelon, the very survival of Entos was a mystery.

The two lines of Entosian warriors stood their ground. Each warrior stood motionless and looked straight ahead. Their faces were marked by resolve and gallantry. They held their finely sharpened and polished swords, each sword a work of art, over their right shoulders. They gripped the handle with both hands and readied themselves to strike any creature that threw itself into the sword's domain.

The spearsmen too stood fast. Each spearsmen had three spears, two of which had been thrust into the ground. The third spear was held in the warrior's hand and was ready to find its mark. Two of the spears were smaller than the third. These were throwing spears. When the beasts and creatures were within range the spearsmen would throw the first two spears at selected targets. The third spear was heavier and was meant to be used in battle to supplement and reinforce the swordsmen at whose side they stood ready. As Ashkelon's first wave bore down upon the

King Ashkelon Attacks

warriors, the warriors continued to sing the Battle Hymn. The conjurors began to speak words of encouragement and courage to their warriors. They reached into their pouches and began to utter the sacred words.

In the centuries that had come before, many conjurors had been killed in battle, but legend held that every one of them died with words from the Oracles still fresh on their lips. There was little doubt that on this day conjurors would fall. On this dark day, warriors would learn for themselves whether the legend was true.

At General Witticor's command the signalman turned and signaled the archers to arm their bows. The two thousand archers on the ground and the one thousand on the wall, most of them Adroits, did as directed.

"Signal the artillery to set the artillery balls aflame," Witticor ordered. The second signalman held up the proper flag and immediately twelve artillery balls were lit. It seemed to take forever as the beasts, riders, and soldiers bore down on the small band of warriors standing outside the wall. The ground shook and thunder rolled. The sound seemed to come from both the ground below and the sky above. The beasts and creatures from Bohow screamed and yelled like the wild, irrational, bloodthirsty beasts Ashkelon had made them to be.

Witticor issued his third order. "Commence artillery firing. Fire at will." The second signalman dropped the flag and instantly twelve large flaming balls soared over the generals' heads against a backdrop of the blackened sky, over the one thousand Entosian warriors on the ground, then smashed into the oncoming line of beasts and creatures.

"Loose arrows. Fire at will," Witticor ordered as if ordering an appetizer at a restaurant. The first signalman began to drop the appropriate flag, but before it hit the ground two thousand arrows from behind the wall blanketed the sky, and another one thousand were loosed from atop the wall toward the oncoming beasts. The initial burst was immediately followed by a continual stream of Entosian arrows. Beasts, riders, and soldiers began to fall. The sight of it was encouraging to the warriors standing outside the wall on the desert floor.

The Oracles And The Jewels

Ashkelon's artillery returned fire just as his beasts, riders, and soldiers crashed into the Entosian front line. The conjurors went to work just as quickly as the first wave of Ashkelon's creatures engaged the Entosians. Their function was to thin out as many of the advancing soldiers as possible, then retreat to repel the inevitable breeching of the wall.

The generals stood atop the battlement watching the battle unfold.

"General Witticor," Tarrant said as he pointed to the northern division. The winged creatures were swooping down and lifting Ashkelon's creatures off the ground. Once a soldier was airborne, the creature flew in a circular pattern.

"Ashkelon is not going to make the same mistake twice. This time he is going to deposit them behind the walls in force," Hokkan commented. When half of the soldiers from the northern and southern division were gathered up, the winged creatures flew over the wall just to the north and south of the main battle. The archers nearest the creatures loosed several volleys of arrows. Many arrows hit their mark striking down either the winged creature or the cargo it was carrying, but there were so many, their efforts made little difference. The winged creatures continued inland.

By now the first line of Entosian warriors had fallen back and the second line of spearsmen and swordsmen were cutting down their enemy as if they were a machine. As Entosian warriors fell, the circle tightened and grew smaller. The process repeated itself two more times until the remaining warriors were standing with their backs to the evacuation lifts.

"General Witticor," Tarrant said. "Ashkelon is sending another three legions against the wall." The three neatly divided rectangles surged forward and merged into one large mob. With the continual pounding against the wall from Ashkelon's artillery, the roar of the battle was so loud the generals now had to shout to be heard.

"They'll be overrun!" Hokkan shouted.

"Evacuate. Pull them back. Evacuate," Witticor said with a calmness that seemed out of place. He looked to his right at Hokkan and repeated the order. "Evacuate. Pull them

King Ashkelon Attacks

back." He turned his head to the left and spoke the same order to Raggnar, "Evacuate before we lose them all."

The two generals moved in opposite directions to take direct control of the evacuation, but before Hokkan could issue the order to his engineers to evacuate, a large arrow struck him in the shoulder and knocked him off his feet. He was stunned for a moment. Colonel Tarrant was standing nearby and ran to his aid.

"General," Tarrant said, bending down to help Hokkan.

"Don't worry about me! Evacuate immediately!" Hokkan grunted as he pushed the colonel's hand away. Colonel Tarrant stood and repeated the order as he ran along the battlement. "Evacuate! Evacuate!" Once the order was being carried out, Tarrant yelled, "Healer! Healer! General Hokkan is wounded."

By now the commanding officers on the ground were looking for the evacuation signal. The platforms reached the Hodia warriors first and they began to retreat onto the four platforms on their side. The arrow strike on Hokkan had caused a slight delay in getting the platforms lowered for the Polemmas warriors. The delay was significant enough to affect the withdrawal. The Hodia warriors retreated onto the platforms and were being lifted from the desert floor, leaving the left flank of the Polemmas warriors with an unprotected.

As Hodia's lift left the ground, several of Ashkelon's soldiers penetrated the left flank of Polemmas, cutting several Polemmas warriors off from their retreat. Scores of beasts and soldiers poured into the breach and filled the space between two dozen Polemmas swordsmen. Some were overwhelmed and cut or trampled. A few others were barely holding their ground.

The four platforms were now sitting on the ground, but most of the Polemmas warriors were unable to reach them. Witticor stood high above the unfolding disaster, directing fire down from the Entosian archers in such a way as to suppress an additional surge. But even though Entosian arrows rained down on the creatures of Bohow and Ashkelon's soldiers, the Polemmas warriors did not have much time before they were completely overwhelmed.

"Choose your targets carefully," Witticor shouted, "but hit them! Your brothers are depending on you!" So many of

The Oracles And The Jewels

Ashkelon's soldiers had poured into the breach that several of Ashkelon's blades found their mark in the Polemmas conjuror whose body was torn to pieces by a beast before it could fall to the ground. With the conjuror dead, the warriors were left to their ordinary skills.

Six Hodia warriors jumped from the platform to the ground below and began fighting their way through the mass of creatures. Hodia's conjuror followed the six and took up his position. The six were joined by a dozen more Hodia warriors who had been unable to get onto the platforms. The Hodia warriors and their conjuror cleared the line and restored the perimeter on the left flank. Working in unison, the archers and spearsmen on the wall, the Hodia warriors and conjuror who had returned to help their brothers, and the warriors of Polemmas were able to clear an escape route and to reestablish their defensive line. With order restored, the semicircle began to constrict in an orderly fashion as the Polemmas warriors took their positions on the last remaining platform.

As the battle unfolded below, the Hodia warriors were disembarking from their four platforms at the top of the battlement. As soon as a platform was emptied, oil was poured over the structure, it was set ablaze, then the platform and its superstructure were cut from their moorings. The flaming structures crashed down upon beasts and soldiers of Bohow below in rapid succession. Dozens of beasts and soldiers were killed and the rest fell back in a momentary retreat.

As the Hodia platforms fell downward, the four Polemmas platforms were on their way up. Three of the platforms were full. The fourth platform was half empty. The casualties were greater than Witticor had expected. Only one thousand fifty six of the original twelve hundred warriors had managed to survive the initial onslaught. But they had decimated Ashkelon's first wave and caused him to send an additional three legions into battle before he was able to breach the wall.

Ashkelon's first volley of artillery had missed the wall. Most had fallen short, landing on and killing most of his own soldiers. But the second volley was faring better than his first. They had made the proper adjustments and now the

King Ashkelon Attacks

large stones were finding their mark. The large doors and walls around the doors began to give way. As Ashkelon's artillery struck the walls, doors, and battlements, Witticor directed his artillery to fire upon the main body of the attack.

With the Entosian warriors evacuated from the desert floor, Ashkelon's soldiers began assaulting the wall with ladders, battering rams, and other devices designed to breach the wall.

The burning wreckage from the eight lifts and Entos' artillery forced Ashkelon to attack along a wider section of the wall than they had intended. Witticor too had to make adjustments in the placement of his own warriors. A battle that had initially been confined along an eight hundred foot section of the wall was now being fought along a section of the wall more than twice that distance. With the exception of the loss of too many warriors on the desert floor, the battle was unfolding as Witticor had predicted.

"Are they going to make it, General?" Tarrant asked.

"I think so," Witticor replied.

"General Witticor," Hokkan said. "Permission to return to duty."

"Are you all right, General?" Witticor asked.

"Yes, sir. The healer did his job well," Hokkan answered.

"Your uniform is a bloody mess, General," Witticor replied with a smile.

"Yes, sir, my apologies. I will tend to that as soon as we send that damnable Ashkelon back to where he belongs," Hokkan answered.

"Permission granted, General," Witticor snapped.

"Gentlemen, we must hold this wall for another ninety minutes. We must give Kanna and Neggen time to launch their attack on Ashkelon's rear guard and reserves."

"We have managed to spread them out over a pretty long stretch of the wall, General," General Raggnar said.

"They have done the same to us. We can't defend that much ground for very long," Witticor said. "Send the cavalry to attack both flanks. Let's see if we can't bunch them up in the middle."

"Yes, sir," Hokkan replied.

The Oracles And The Jewels

"Generals, we don't want to lose too many of those boys. We are going to need to get inside the wall before the wall falls. Give the order to withdraw if things start to go wrong. Don't forget the plan. We want them to enter the valley according to our time schedule and through a narrow pass," Witticor reminded them. "Make sure your cavalry commanders understand that the battle will be won or lost in the Demotic Valley not on the desert floor. Once the cavalries push them around a bit, thin them out, and bunch them up both units are to withdraw to the top of the slope in the Demotic Valley."

"Yes, sir," the generals replied.

Thirty minutes had passed since the first beast fell in Ashkelon's main attack. The battle had settled into a pattern. The artillery exchanged volleys at regular intervals. Ashkelon sent a continual stream of replacements against the wall, but time and time again his beasts and soldiers fell. Those who tried to scale the wall with ladders were being successfully repelled. Those who made it to the top of the battlements were cut down just as quickly. The winged creatures were beginning to return from their first sortie and were picking up the additional soldiers from the northern and southern legions.

It was a ten minute ride to the nearest set of doors to the north and south of the battle. It took another fifteen minutes before the cavalries were ready to launch their attack on Ashkelon's two flanks.

"General Witticor," Hokkan said. "The cavalry has started its attack on the southern flank. The north Hodia cavalry is in position and will engage in just a few minutes."

"Good," Witticor replied.

"The first reports are positive. We're holding them, General," Hokkan said.

"Only because Ashkelon is letting us hold them," Witticor responded. "He is holding back. He's waiting for something," Witticor mumbled.

"What, General?" Tarrant asked.

"For an opening in the wall or for the beasts and soldiers he airlifted into the interior. Perhaps he is waiting for something to happen in the city. Probably all three," Witticor

King Ashkelon Attacks

replied as he thrust his sword into a skull that had managed to make it to the top of the ladder.

The Demotic Valley, The Phanos Forest

Unlike the attack that came four days earlier, the winged creatures were being more selective in where they deposited their passengers. This time the creatures sought out areas free from enemy patrols and camps and deposited, although not very gently, their passengers in open areas where they were able to regroup. The southern legion was regrouping in a field about one league from the Entosian line in the Phanos Forest. This line made up the second ring of defense.

The Phanos Forest was nearly fifteen leagues wide, but only six leagues deep at its thickest point. The forest was named after the millions of moths, which were named Phanos (an ancient word that means "to illumine") that dwelt in the canopy of the forest. The creatures were nocturnal and glowed with a soft yellow light. Their presence at night cast a soft and wonderful light upon the ground. The sun provided the light by day and the moths illumined the forest at night. Like other places in Entos, the forest had never known true darkness.

As the soldiers and beasts from the southern legion were being dropped into the Azura Field, the soldiers and beasts from the northern legion were carried over the heads and well out of the range of the Entosian warriors below. Several of the Entosian warriors had loosed their arrows, but only a few found their mark, even then inflicting only minor wounds.

President Kuchen was standing with the warriors in the Phanos Forest. He, like the warriors whose protection he now needed, peered through the canopy above and watched the creatures soar overhead and toward the city.

"Where are they going, major?" Kuchen asked.

"I imagine they are on their way to the city," Major Gaynor, a Kilposian, answered.

"The city. The city has never been attacked before. Not since the construction of the walls," President Kuchen said.

The Oracles And The Jewels

"There is a first time for everything, Mr. President," the major said.

"But the city is unprotected!" Kuchen exclaimed.

"I doubt that," the major replied.

"Yes it is. The City Fathers denied General Witticor's request for warriors to guard the city."

"Yes, we know," the major said calmly as he looked up through gaps in the forest canopy and watched more of the winged creatures passing overhead. "General Witticor always finds a way."

"I order you to fall back to the city now!" President Kuchen shouted.

"You have no jurisdiction here. I take my orders from General Witticor alone."

"I order you now!" Kuchen shouted.

"Order and shout all you want, sir," the major said, "Besides there is no way we can reach the city in time, unless someone has created a flock of really big Entosian birds. Don't worry, Mr. President, the honor guard is still in the city," the major said with a grin.

"But look at how many there are," he said pointing to the sky. "The guard will be overwhelmed. We must fall back," Kuchen said softening his tone.

"Mr. President, I have my orders. I am to hold the line here and prevent whatever comes my way from crossing our line and advancing on the city. I have one thin line stretching from the Polemmas Plateau to the south and the Hodia Plateau to the north. That means I have about twenty-five leagues to cover. That makes for a very thin line indeed. Ashkelon's troops are going to pick one primary point of attack and try to break through."

"But the city? What will happen to the city?" Kuchen said with a voice of regret.

"General Witticor would not have left the city unless it was protected. Despite what the bureaucrats ordered, the general would have found a way to do his job, while at the same time obeying the council. That is the kind of leader he is. Besides, don't you want to see how your walls work?" With that comment the major struck a nerve and the softening tone of President Kuchen disappeared and he resumed his shouting.

King Ashkelon Attacks

"I must object to the manner in which you are using these panels! It's an insult to everyone associated with this project. I appeal to you to reconsider!"

"Even if I wanted to reconsider, and I don't, I don't have the time to do so," Major Gaynor said. "I suspect the enemy will be upon us in the next thirty to sixty minutes. Maybe in the future, if you have a future as a city father, you will allow the military to do its job while you tend to the proper duties of The Academy of the Building Arts."

At that moment a Fortian captain approached Gaynor. "Major!" Captain Konnar said.

"Yes, captain," the major replied.

"Our Kicahian scout has just arrived. She reports that thousands of soldiers and beasts are being dropped into Azura Field one league to the southeast. When she left the area she estimated the force to be in excess of five thousand and there was no sign that the troop deployment was letting up. They are still pouring in. The force consists of skulls, trolls, and several beasts, many fitted with saddles. There were few mammothons and no morses. She reports that they haven't started marching yet. They're just waiting and cutting down the wild flowers."

"They are waiting for the rest of their legion," the major replied.

"Sir, if we were to break camp and march on them now we might be able to hit them before they reach full strength," the captain recommended.

"We could do that. But since we don't know what full strength is or when they will be dropped in, we could also arrive at exactly the wrong time. No, captain. We will wait right here where we can make use of the forest and the president's panels," the major answered. The two officers smiled at each other. President Kuchen did not.

"Thank you, captain. Send the scout back and let us know as soon as they march. Send four squads of Adroits on horseback to provide some harassing fire and provide further incentive for them to come our way. We want them to take the paths we cut for them without them realizing we cut paths for them," the major said with a smile. "Is that enough for everyone to understand?"

The Oracles And The Jewels

"Yes, sir," Captain Konnar answered, then saluted and left. "As clear as clear can be."

"Yes we do," the major said. "Now, Mr. President, if you will excuse me, I must tend to my lines. I suggest you find yourself a sword for personal protection and withdraw to the rear."

Over the next hour the entire southern division of Ashkelon's army had landed and had regrouped in Azura Field. The Kicahian scout had reported back to Gaynor once the landings were complete. She estimated the size of the force to be ten thousand creatures in all.

The legion formed up in two squares. Once in formation, they began their march on a heading to the northwest where the forest was thinnest and more passable. When they came to within a quarter of a league of the tree line, the twenty Adroits, who were armed with bows, rode out into the clearing twenty abreast and in plain view. The commanding officer of Ashkelon's legion saw the twenty riders emerge from the tree line.

"Riders!" he shouted, "Attack!" as he pointed to the enemy. "Attack and bring one back alive!" A hundred trolls and the beasts upon which they sat charged forward.

"Full march!" the mammothon commander ordered. The order was repeated through the massive columns and the whole legion began running toward the tree line.

"Ready yourselves," the Adroit sergeant ordered. The twenty archers loaded their bows, two arrows each.

"Loose!" the sergeant ordered and immediately forty arrows soared across the darkened sky, over the heads of the charging trolls, and landed in the main body of the legion, killing or wounding twenty beasts and soldiers.

"Hold your positions Entosians!" the sergeant shouted as the trolls bore down upon them. "Take the nearest one! Loose!" This time the warriors were deadly accurate. Every warrior hit his mark, wounding or killing twenty of the charging trolls.

"Hold your positions. One more time. Loose!" Several more trolls or the beasts upon which they were riding crashed to the ground.

"Fall back! Follow me!" the sergeant yelled so he could be heard over the thundering sound of the charging beasts.

King Ashkelon Attacks

Then he kicked and turned his horse toward the tree line. By the time all twenty had turned their horses and had accelerated to a full run, the remaining trolls were less than one hundred feet behind them.

The Entosian line was only a quarter of a league within the tree line. The thundering hooves of the Entosian horses and the beasts of Bohow could be heard before the warriors could be seen. Twenty-five Entosian warriors lined each side of the path and took cover behind trees and bushes to wait for their orders.

"Stay hidden!" Gaynor shouted. "Wait for them to come to us! Hold your fire! Hold . . . Hold . . . Hold."

"They're all yours, major!" the Adroit sergeant shouted as his horse flew past Gaynor, who was standing in the middle of one of the three large paths they had cleared the day before. Once the twenty Entosian riders had cleared Gaynor, the troll leading the attack fixed his eyes upon the major who turned his body toward the charging trolls, drew his sword, raised it above his right shoulder, and planted his feet. The troll grinned and growled with delight.

At that moment the major dropped the point of his sword to the ground. The movement loosed a hailstorm of arrows, spears, and throwing disks. The beasts and trolls fell to the ground and Entosian warriors descended upon those who had survived the first volley. The troll leading the attack looked back in surprise and, as he turned around to look for the major, his beast met with the major's sword. The beast crashed headfirst into the ground and the troll was catapulted from its back and slammed into a tree. The twenty riders had brought their horses to a quick stop and turned around readying themselves for a counter charge. But the action was unnecessary.

"Sergeant!" the major called. "Give the order for the flanks to begin their swing." The Adroit sergeant turned to his right and rode along the back of the line. "Forward at forty-five," he shouted. As he rode to the right, one of the other riders did the same to the left. Several hundred Entosian warriors began a quiet march forward at an angle to the three paths, which were now filling with Ashkelon's creatures.

The Oracles And The Jewels

By the time the last of the troll riders fell, the first group of five thousand Ektos soldiers were entering the tree line and could hear the ensuing battle. At first they assumed that their comrades were successfully completing their mission, but as they drew closer they saw fifty Entosian warriors standing over the dead bodies of their kind.

"Full attack!" the mammothon commander yelled, enraged at the sight. "Full attack!" With that order five thousand screams went up and a wall of Ektosian soldiers and beasts of Bohow surged across the forest floor toward the fifty warriors.

"Fall back!" the major ordered and the fifty warriors retreated to their original line, then assumed their starting positions again. The riders took up positions behind the fifty warriors. Gaynor stood in front of them all.

Like the desert floor outside the eastern wall, the forest floor shook with the pounding footsteps of the beasts and the soldiers, and like the warriors who stood on the desert floor facing an enemy of overwhelming numbers and of brute force, these Entosian warriors stood firm. If fear was rising up inside of these warriors at the ungodly scene bearing down on them, and it probably was, they did not show it. Each warrior stood stalwart with his eyes fixed straight ahead looking to see which of the attackers would enter his sphere and thus be the first to feel the sting of his sword.

"Stand fast!" Gaynor shouted. "Blow the horn!" A Procuron lieutenant pulled the battle horn from his side and blew a long blast. Suddenly there emerged from behind the trees, bushes, and from holes dug in the ground a line of Entosian warriors stretching to the north and south as far as the eye could see. The fifty were now joined by one hundred on the right and one hundred to the left. They now stood two hundred fifty across. With the order "forward at forty-five" two hundred more warriors were marching into formation, thus creating a three-sided box into which Ashkelon's legion was unwittingly pouring itself.

The two lines clashed. Soldiers, beasts, and warriors began to fall in battle. The forest was filling quickly. The three paths were so densely populated that the beasts and Ektosian soldiers were finding it difficult to maneuver and

King Ashkelon Attacks

many of the soldiers and beasts became sitting targets. The eighteen archers on horseback loosed volley after volley of arrows into their enemies with such staggering speed the eye could barely see the movement of their hands as they reloaded. Trolls, skulls, beasts, and mammothons fell with regularity.

"Release panels one and two!" Gaynor shouted as he fought off one attacking soldier. "Release panels one and two!" he repeated.

Six Kicahians, who had concealed themselves along each side of the three paths, picked up their axes and in unison cut a rope, which had been secured to the base of each tree on the outside of each path. In a moment three large panels, which were secured on one end by two large ropes, swung from the forest canopy straight down the middle of each path. The heavy walls hit the Ektosian soldiers and beasts with such force, scores of them were killed, crushed, or sent flying across the forest floor.

The release of the first three panels triggered the release of the second three panels, which swung down from the opposite direction, having an even more devastating effect upon the enemy. These panels came crashing into soldiers and beasts attempting to flee the first set of panels. Gaynor was surprised by the effect of the panels. "Who would have thought," he said to himself.

But once the panels came to a rest, they functioned as three large curtains that obstructed his view and divided his forces into six sections.

Gaynor gave the order to advance. The three sides of the box began moving forward, pushing Ashkelon's soldiers into a smaller area. But the push did not come without price and great difficulty. The battle was by no means won. The mammothon commander was rallying his forces and organizing them into defensive positions. The battle lines became fixed. The advancing movement of the Entosian warriors stalled.

The Entosians were still greatly outnumbered and soldiers and beasts were still pouring in from the field. The riders were running low on arrows so the eighteen archers on horseback drew their swords and charged forward into the thick of the battle. Reenforcements were on their way,

The Oracles And The Jewels

but they had to be drawn from the line that stretched across the width of the forest.

No one had noticed, but within moments after giving the command to advance, Gaynor lay dead on the ground with three skull arrows planted in his chest. The panels not only obstructed the view of the Ektosian soldiers, but it also made it difficult for Gaynor to see three skull archers who had taken aim at him.

As was the case with the battle at the eastern wall, the battle in Phanos Forest settled into its own pattern and began to consume evil creatures and good men alike.

The Academy of Theological Sciences and Ancient Conjuring Arts

Tag and Brenz had reported to their patrols, Brenz to his daily patrol at the Academy and Tag to the streets surrounding The Great Chamber. Rieve had made his way to the inside of The Great Chamber where he was content to wait for the events of the day to find him. It didn't take long for the events to find any of the members of the little fellowship.

"Hello, fellow expellee," a voice whispered from behind Rieve.

"Brenna, Akimm, Pandar? What are you doing here? You're suppose to be in class," Rieve whispered back.

"The best-made plans and all that," Akimm said.

"We were all pink–slipped this morning," Pandar added.

"What is pink–slipped?" Rieve asked.

"It's one of MulLord's new streamline procedures. In order to save the candidate or apprentice priest the embarrassment of a tribunal, they hold hearings behind closed doors and then notify you they held the meeting and have removed you from the Academy," Brenna explained.

"We showed up this morning and each of us was given one of these," Akimm said as he pulled a pink slip of paper from his pocket and handed it to Rieve. Rieve read it.

Apprentice Priest Akimm,

We regret to inform you that a hearing was held by the disciplinary committee and as a result of:

King Ashkelon Attacks

1. Your impenitence
2. Persistently offensive conduct
3. Your refusal to be obedient to Headmaster MulLord who only desires all that is good for your well-being and the well-being of Entos
4. Engaging in unauthorized conjuring activity and
5. For associating with a conjuror who has been previously removed for insubordination and suspicion of practicing the black arts

You have been removed from The Academy of Theological Sciences and Ancient Conjuring Arts effective immediately. You are to remove all personal items from campus and leave the same by 10:00 in the light this very morning.

If you wish to appeal, you may set up an appointment with me and must supply all requested information upon demand.

Signed
Headmaster MulLord

"You see. They were trying to save us from the embarrassment you faced when you had to walk out of the tribunal," Akimm commented.

"Professor MulLord, always thinking of the other guy," Brenna said. "He is such a good Entosian."

"Sorry, brothers. I didn't mean to bring this on you," Rieve said.

"We knew what we were getting into," Brenna said.

"Well, that settles it. They know," Rieve commented.

"Who knows what?" Pandar said with an anxious tone in his voice.

"This morning Conjuror Stratia was murdered and Colonel Fornoff attacked in a failed attempt to assassinate him. Tag and Brenz were able to save the colonel, but not Stratia."

"Colonel Fornoff, Conjuror Stratia, and the expulsion of the three of you all in the same day, the very day Ashkelon attacks adds up to treachery in downtown Entos," Rieve explained.

"What about the Academy?" Brenna asked. "I've been expelled. If I hang around campus today, the honor guard will haul me off."

The Oracles And The Jewels

"Akimm and Pandar, report to Krattos and Neggen on the outside of the city and take up your positions with them. Brenna, you stay here and look after the Oracles, the Jewels, and Hodia. I will tend to the Academy."

"They're not going to let you on campus either," Akimm said.

"I will figure that problem out once I get there. Now let's all get going," Rieve said. Rieve marched outside with Akimm and Pandar. Each headed off in the direction of his assignment. Rieve headed for the Academy, but didn't find Tag along the way so he circled around The Great Chamber counterclockwise a second time. This time Rieve spotted Tag on the northeast side of the Chamber sitting at a small street café across from Diamond Park.

"Tag," Rieve said.

"What's wrong?" Tag asked.

"Brenna, Akimm, and Pandar were kicked out of the Academy and off campus grounds this morning," Rieve told him.

"They know about us then," Tag replied.

"It looks that way."

"Well, they know about us but they don't know exactly which ones we are. We will stay concealed until there is an attack on the city, but I will pass the word that we are no longer a surprise. I suspect by now every cadet knows that Stratia is dead and the colonel is out of the picture."

"It might not be a bad idea to start the rumor that the colonel is dead. No one is going to try to assassinate a dead man," Rieve suggested.

"Good idea," Tag replied. He lifted his hand and signaled for cadets Marrcus and Kelila to come to his side.

"Yes, sir," Kelila asked.

"Pass the word. They know about the cadet army. Colonel Fornoff has died and everyone needs to be careful, stay sharp, and stay hidden." Tag said. Just then they heard the faint sound of a battle horn. The streets fell silent. "Pass the word. That's the Demotic Valley battle horn. The Demotic Valley is under attack. Pass that information along as well. Marrcus and Kelila, be ready and watch your backs."

The two headed off in opposite directions and could be seen talking to some of the cadets. The information went

King Ashkelon Attacks

through the ranks quickly. It spread through the streets around The Great Chamber and the information worked itself outward through the Krattos and Neggen cadets. It seemed to move faster than the messengers could walk.

"Where are you headed?" Tag asked Rieve.

"Brenna is going to keep his eye on The Great Chamber and Hodia. I am going over to the Academy to watch over Polemmas. I might even call on the Headmaster."

"Well, that will be interesting and should start something rolling this morning," Tag said with a chuckle.

"See you later, little brother," Rieve said.

"Take care, big brother," Tag replied. The two shook hands and parted. Rieve headed to the Academy and Tag started for his headquarters in the old theater. Along the way he stopped to talk with squad leaders and encouraged them. It was a little past 10:00 in the light. He walked as casually as he could. He assumed he was being watched.

Sandor's Study

"Well, Granddaughter," Sandor began, "thou hast grown up into a lovely young lady. Thou reminds me so much of thy grandmother."

"I wish I had known her," River said. "She died quite young."

"Yes, she died when she was thirty-seven," Sandor replied.

"Giving birth to Mother, wasn't it?" River asked.

"Yes."

"Mother doesn't talk about it," River said.

"She shouldn't. It wasn't thy mother's fault. Dying young even in childbirth is rare, but it happens when it fits the will of the King."

"Why didn't you remarry, Grandfather?"

"It is best to remain as thou are in such circumstances. After thy grandmother's death, I dedicated myself to my studies and to conjuring. It was at that time that my powers and my insights began to increase beyond the ordinary. And now, my Granddaughter, events are about to take hold of us."

"What do you mean?" River asked.

The Oracles And The Jewels

"They are coming."

A moment later five men dressed in priests' robes and tribal clothing burst into the office.

"Young lady," a Pithosian said. "Come with us. We have business with the Headmaster."

"I will not. I intend to stay with my Grandfather! Who are you and what do you want?"

"That is none of your concern, young lady," the Pithosian said.

"If you think you're taking him away, you have another think coming," River said as she put her hand on the chest of the Pithosian. The Pithosian brushed her aside with the back of his hand and though it was not his intent, his hand struck her on the cheek. And though he did not intend to, he did not apologize for it.

"I am warning thee. Do not touch her again," Sandor said. River stood up and stepped between Sandor and the Pithosian.

The Pithosian stepped forward to push River aside for a second time. Sandor placed the top of his conjuror's staff between River's shoulder blades and gave her a push. River thrust her hand forward into the chest of the Pithosian with such force he was thrown across the study and landed against a bookshelf filled with books and glass jars, all of which came crashing down on the Pithosian and floor. The four remaining men pulled their swords from underneath their robes.

"Enough!" Sandor said.

"Headmaster, we know the limits of your power. This girl is unarmed and untrained in the arts of combat. Do you really want us to cut this young girl down? We urge you to come with us peacefully."

"And my Granddaughter?" Sandor asked.

"We have no interest in her. We will simply escort her out of the city. But we need you to come with us now."

"River, do as they direct. Thou wilt be okay," Sandor said as he put his hand on her sore cheek.

"I am not worried about me, Grandfather."

"No, but I am thy Grandfather and the rightful Headmaster of Entos. Thou wilt do as I say," Sandor said in a firm tone.

King Ashkelon Attacks

"Yes, Grandfather," River said as she knelt and kissed his hand.

Two of the men took River by the arm and escorted her down the hallway and out the back door. The other two waited for a moment, then took Sandor by the arms and forced him in the opposite direction.

As Sandor and River were taken from the building, Rieve crossed the street and stepped onto the campus. He didn't hesitate. The campus was usually busy. The faculty and theological students also seemed to be in a heightened state of activity. Apparently the word of the attack in the Demotic Valley was out and the normal class schedule was being altered. Rieve made it by the first building of classrooms and entered the courtyard from the east. He headed for the faculty building and as he walked he looked up to the Headmaster's window, expecting to see River or the Headmaster in the window. They weren't there. He stopped for a moment and looked around. He thought he felt his pouch growing warmer, but before he could give it a second thought, two honor guardsmen spotted him and rushed to block his path.

"Halt, priest," one of the guards snapped. "We have orders not to permit you or your friends on campus. This is by order of Headmaster MulLord. Leave immediately or we will have to escort you from the property."

"Gentlemen, there's no need for hostility. I've come to see Professor MulLord," Rieve responded. "I have a matter of great importance to discuss with the professor." The request caught the two guards by surprise.

"He's in class right now," the other guard replied.

"That's okay, I will wait," Rieve said. "I'll just sit right here and wait." Rieve sat down on the nearest bench.

"I demand you leave," the first guard said.

"I can do as you wish, but believe me when I tell you that Professor MulLord will be very upset when he finds out that you sent me away. I have some information that he desperately wants." The two guards looked at each other, hoping the other would resolve the problem.

After a moment of uncomfortable silence the second guard said, "I will locate Headmaster MulLord and tell him you want to see him." The guardsman turned to his

The Oracles And The Jewels

comrade. "Keep Rieve Waynwright here. Don't let him out of your sight."

As Rieve sat quietly on the bench awaiting the return of the guard, River was being escorted by two guards out the back door of the faculty building and ushered down the street toward the Neggen Valley. Sandor was being taken in the other direction toward the Aradian Valley. The guards who were escorting River were wearing tribal robes and the two taking Sandor had disguised themselves as priests. All four concealed their weapons, but had made it clear to both Sandor and River that failure to cooperate would result in the use of their weapons.

As Rieve sat awaiting the return of the guard, the pouch which carried his stone had become so warm that Rieve couldn't help but feel its heat through his robes. He took the pouch and opened it ever so slightly. The stone was red. "Sandor is in danger," he thought to himself. "River too." Then suddenly the sound of battle horns echoed through the city streets. The horn was loud and clear and came from the southeast, from the edge of the Demotic Valley.

"With all due respect," Rieve said to the guardsman, "Don't you think you ought to answer that call? It's a battle horn and it is coming from over there." Rieve pointed in the direction of the Demotic Valley and Hodia Plateau. "The city is under attack." The guard stood perfectly still. "It's your duty to answer that call." Still the guardsman did nothing.

Rieve looked up and saw winged creatures soaring high above the city. Some of the creatures were carrying soldiers. Others carried nets filled with stones and still others carried nothing at all.

"Doesn't that mean anything to you?" Rieve said in as firm a voice as he could muster. He pointed to the sky. The guard looked up. He stepped back and placed his hand on his sword. Rieve noticed blood seeping through the guard's uniform on the right side.

"You're bleeding, warrior, and the battle hasn't even started yet." Their eyes met. "You were up early this morning weren't you, traitor?"

"I don't know what you're talking about!" he snapped back. "I don't know what you're talking about!"

"Thou protests a bit too much," Rieve said.

King Ashkelon Attacks

The guard drew his sword and thrust it toward Rieve. Rieve blocked the first strike with his staff. A second blow was delivered and again Rieve blocked it with his staff, but the force of the blow knocked him to the ground. The guard lifted his sword a third time and was about to bring it down upon Rieve when a dagger pierced the guard's arm. The guard yelled in pain and the sword dropped to the ground. Immediately two Polemmas cadets descended upon the guard who was yelling in pain as he held his arm. One of the cadets grabbed the dagger and pulled it from the guard's arm which produced a greater shout of pain.

"Conjuror, are you all right?" one of the cadets asked Rieve.

"Yes. Thank you very much."

"What is this all about?" the other cadet asked.

"By the looks of his uniform, he is one of the assassins who helped kill Conjuror Stratia this morning," Rieve replied. "Gentlemen, we all have a lot to do." Rieve pointed to the sky. "I'm going to check on the Headmaster and River."

"What should we do with him?" one of the cadets asked.

"I don't think we have any plans for prisoners," the other said.

"He can't be reasoned with. I don't think he is one of us," Rieve replied. "If he lives, he will hurt another."

"Can we do that?" the first cadet asked. There was a tone of horror in his voice.

"You must," Rieve answered. The two cadets hesitated and looked at each other.

"I am not going to kill an unarmed warrior!" the second said.

"We must. The conjuror has ordered it," the other replied. As the two debated the issue, Rieve reached into his pouch, pulled from it a smaller pouch, and opened it. He took a small pinch of black powder and held it with his left fingers.

"Here then," Rieve said as he picked up the guard's sword and gave it back to the guard. "He is no longer unarmed." The instant that the sword was placed in the guard's hand, the guard broke free of the cadets, turned, and moved to strike down Rieve. Rieve threw the powder onto one of the cadet's hands, and shouted, *"Katala Katalam!"* Immediately the cadet's hand thrust forward,

The Oracles And The Jewels

burying his dagger into the heart of the guard. It all happened so fast, the cadets barely comprehended it. The guard fell to the ground and, when his life had gone out of him, he changed into his true form, a skull. The cadets stood in stunned silence.

"That was pretty risky," one of the cadets said.

"No, it wasn't. You were here," Rieve replied. "Besides, I didn't have the time to convince you. The Headmaster and his granddaughter are in danger. Know this, only death shows the creature for what he really is." Rieve turned and ran into the faculty building and up the six flights of stairs, down the hall, and into the Headmaster's study where he found the Pithosian on the floor atop broken glass and scattered books.

River and her two escorts were proceeding unnoticed down a street filled with cadets and citizens running every direction imaginable. Tag was among those running. He was a block away from the old theater when he saw River. In his excitement he did not notice that she was being followed by two men.

"Are you headed for the old theater, River Kiernan?" he called out, but River ignored the call. "Keep walking," one of the escorts ordered.

"River Kiernan," Tag shouted in a volume that could not be denied. "Are you going to the old theater!"

"Answer him!" the escort said.

"Yes, Tag," she shouted back. "Yes, Tag, I will see you there in a little while!" Tag continued on his way crossing the intersection through which River and her escorts had just passed. The escorts breathed a sigh of relief.

"Good, young lady. Well done," one of the guards said. "You just saved your own life, not to mention the life of your friend."

"Now, it's time for the two of you to think about saving your own lives," Tag said as he poked his dagger first into the back of one of the escorts and then into the back of the other. "Hands up, gentlemen." They put their hands up slightly above their shoulders. Cadets Ailith and Bonar had been shadowing Thayer. When the two guards raised their hands Ailith and Bonar descended upon the position.

"Thank you, Thayer Taggert," River said.

King Ashkelon Attacks

"You're welcome and please never call me Tag again, unless you're in trouble. Now, tell me what do we have here besides kidnappers?"

"There are two more. They took the Headmaster!" River answered.

"Where?" Tag asked.

"I don't know," River said.

Suddenly the sound of a whistle could be heard. River and Tag looked in the direction of the sound and saw an officer in the honor guard blowing a whistle and pointing in their direction.

"More honor guards!" Tag said as two more guards began running in their direction.

"You're under arrest," one of the escorts said. "You better drop the knife. If you do, I will tell them to go easy on you."

"Sorry, I can't do that," Tag said, "I have orders." Ailith and Bonar turned toward the approaching guards who had drawn their swords and readied themselves for the fight.

"We have orders too. They are from President Botha," the first escort said. "We are to arrest any cadet who disobeys our orders and, above all, we are to protect The Great Chamber from any intruder."

Thayer looked around again. The two guards crossing the street had now been joined by three more.

"River! Go! Weapons!" Tag shouted. The two escorts stood perfectly still. They smiled at River, knowing that time was now on their side.

"By the time you get back, your friends will be dead," the first escort said.

"Go," Tag said.

"Understood!" River shouted and turned toward the old theater. She had taken only six steps when an arm jetted out from a doorway and grabbed her by her hair. "Halt!" a voice shouted. River let out a yell, "Ouch! Let go!"

Tag immediately threw his dagger into the arm and River's yell paled in comparison to the howl loosed by the man in the doorway. He let go of River's hair and she turned with a slight look of disbelief at Thayer. The wounded guardsman started for Tag, but a Hodia cadet, who was

The Oracles And The Jewels

nearby stepped into his path, drew his dagger, and put it against his opponent's side. "Relax, guardsman," he said.

"Go!" Tag shouted to River, "Bonar, sound the alarm!" The two guardsmen turned toward Tag, dropped their robes to reveal their honor guard uniforms, and drew their swords. The uniforms revealed their rank. The first was a sergeant and the second a lieutenant. As Bonar pulled his battle horn from beneath his robe and let loose with a blast, Tag dropped his robe revealing his Hodia cadet uniform. Ailith and Bonar did the same.

"You should have surrendered," the first guard said. By now Tag, Ailith, and Bonar were surrounded by no less than seven honor guardsmen, whose swords were poised to thrust.

"We are under direct orders from General Witticor," Tag explained. "We are here to protect Entos from enemies both foreign and domestic. We intend to do that and we are prepared to forfeit our lives, but yours will do too."

"So it shall be," the ranking officer said.

"This is your last chance," Tag added. "You can join with us or fight us. If you fight us many good Entosians will die today at the hands of other Entosians. We don't have much time. Ashkelon's creatures are here. They are in the Demotic Valley and they are in the sky." Tag pointed to the sky. "It won't be long before they start landing those beasts on top of our heads. So sergeant, I suggest you make up your mind."

The intersection filled with Hodia cadets, honor guardsmen, and Polemmas cadets. Some of the cadets were on their way to retrieve their weapons from the old theater. The honor guardsmen were outnumbered three to one, but they had the swords. By now the streets were nearly empty of civilians who were seeking shelter in public buildings, The Great Chamber, and shops.

"Now where are they taking the Headmaster?" Tag asked.

"If I knew, I wouldn't tell you," the first guardsman said. "We have our orders and they have their orders. You're only a cadet, but you know how it works."

"Then don't waste my time," Tag barked. "Hodia! Polemmas! To your weapons and your posts!"

King Ashkelon Attacks

"Attack!" the lieutenant shouted. The fight began immediately. Bonar and Ailith used their daggers to block the first thrusts of their opponents' swords. Tag was unarmed, but moved quickly to avoid being struck. He successfully dodged the first thrust, but the lieutenant's blade cut him on his left arm with the second.

Several daggers flew through the air and hit a variety of targets. Two daggers found their mark in the lieutenant. Three of the remaining guardsmen were also wounded. The other three rushed to the aid of their wounded comrades and pulled them from the intersection.

Tag held his arm as he shouted, "Leave them. To your weapons!" Twenty-five cadets bolted down the street and into the alley where Blisse, River, and Breille, who arrived at the old theater shortly after the first battle horn had sounded, were lowering the platform to the street. The platform was filled with swords, armor, and helmets of every size and grouped according to their colors; white for Hodia and red for Polemmas.

It only took a minute for the platform to empty and the three girls were hard at work pulling the platform up where they could restock it. River and Blisse raised the platform while Breille rolled out a second rack of gear. The system worked smoothly, although not fast enough for some of the cadets who were standing below waiting for gear. "Hurry up, up there!" one of them shouted.

"It's coming, cadet," Blisse shouted back. He started for the staircase. "Stay there cadet. The stairs are for medical personnel, commanding officers, and the injured. If you get in my way, you'll be among the injured! Save it for Ashkelon!" Blisse shouted as she pulled on the pulley rope in rhythm with River. As the platform reached the top, Blisse saw Tag walking down the alley toward the stairs with Bonar and Ailith who were carrying the lieutenant between them. "Ladies, you're going to have to handle the gear. I have work to do." It was then she noticed that Tag's uniform was bloodied as well.

"Breille," Blisse shouted, "Take my place at the rope. Tag's injured!" Blisse started down the stairs.

"It looks worse than it is," Tag shouted. Take care of the lieutenant first." To prove his point Tag accelerated his pace

The Oracles And The Jewels

and ran up the staircase. Bonar and Ailith followed as they carried the injured lieutenant.

"So do you need me or are you going to close that up yourself?" Blisse said in her typical tone.

"I would rather have it done your way, but without all the talk and without your own distinctive bedside manner," he replied with a smile as he reached the threshold of the door. Blisse gave him a little push in the back to move him along.

"How is the colonel?" Tag asked.

"He's fine."

"We passed the word that he died of his wounds. That should help keep him safe for the day."

"Good idea, although I don't like people thinking I lost my first patient," Blisse replied. "Now sit down." Tag sat on the table next to the colonel, who was sound asleep and lying flat on his back with his large nose pointing straight to the ceiling.

King Ashkelon Attacks

"That's one big nose," Tag said as he looked at the colonel. "It looks big when he is standing upright. In that position, it looks like it could rival Mount Oros."

"Be quiet," she said as she wiped off the blood revealing the cut. "You're right, it's not too deep." She dipped her fingers into the same jar of cream she had used earlier on the colonel, then applied some of it to Tag's cut. As she rubbed the cream into the wound she spoke the sacred language for the second time that morning. *"Aman aham rafa pasa emen."* The bleeding stopped and the wound closed.

Bonar and Ailith entered the hall and placed the wounded and unconscious lieutenant on the third table.

"Are you the only healer here this morning?" Tag asked.

"I'm sure that Sabinnee and Chaiva will be here soon. The battle horns have started blowing all over the city. They'll be here."

"Good. I think we are going to need all the help we can get today. The guardsmen kidnaped River and attacked us. Now we have two adversaries about which we must worry. We have the creatures from Bohow and Ashkelon's soldiers and we have to fight our own. If you end up treating more honor guardsmen, close their wounds but put them to sleep for the day. We will heal our own, but we aren't going to send them back to fight us."

"All right," she said as she wrapped a bandage around the arm. "You're ready."

"Thanks. See you later."

"Be careful," Blisse said as she touched Tag on the shoulder.

Tag hopped off the table, suited, and loaded up. Blisse began working on the lieutenant. He had lost a lot of blood. She repeated the process she had used for the colonel and Thayer, but his wounds were deeper. *"Aman aham rafa pasa emen"* she repeated again and again, but joined that sacred utterance with another. *"Borran amets umat gibbon cullan umat palanan dekkim adam demmim laccam or Um."*

"What does all that mean?" Tag asked as he suited up for battle.

"It translates, *Almighty, heal Thy warrior with Thy wonders that he might fight for Thee.*"

The Oracles And The Jewels

"Just make sure he ends up fighting on the right side," Tag.

"I'm just duty bound to heal all who are brought to me," Blisse said. "You're in charge of who's on which side." At that she returned to her chant as she bound his wounds and gave the warrior a potion to drink.

"Commander! Commander!" an Adroit corporal from Neggen shouted as he burst into the room. "Where is Commander Thayer Taggert?"

"Over here," Tag replied. The Adroit corporal bolted to the stage.

"Sir, a large force of Ashkelon's beasts and soldiers are marching up the Demotic Valley toward the city. They are using the Three Faces of the King as their staging area." The corporal's voice had the sound of panic and uncertainty in it.

"They are that close?" Tag asked.

"Yes, sir," the corporal snapped.

Tag heard the fear in the cadet's voice. "What's your name, corporal?" Tag asked.

"Veris, Cadet Veris of the Adroit tribe and the clan of Nyssa."

"Relax, Cadet Veris. You have had all the training you need to get the job done and you have all the help you need," Tag said.

"Yes, sir," the cadet replied, still unsettled.

"How many are there?"

"It is hard to tell, sir. When I left, there were maybe two to three thousand, but they were still coming out of the woods and others were being air-dropped into the field. Commander Kyra believes they are amassing a significant force and she is not sure we can hold them on our own."

"Can you make it to Krattos?" Tag asked.

"Yes, sir!"

"Tell Commander Tabor to send seventy-five Krattos warriors to reinforce Neggen at the entrance of the Demotic Valley. On your way, tell Commander Brenz Clinton at the Academy to send twenty-five of his Polemmas warriors to the valley as well. Hodia and Polemmas will handle whatever lands or makes it into the city. Tell Commander Kyra that Neggen must hold the line at the edge of the plateau. Don't worry about those who make it past the line

King Ashkelon Attacks

and into the city. We will handle whatever comes our way. But your line must hold. Are you clear on the orders, corporal?"

"Yes, sir!" the corporal responded. His voice now had a tone of confidence. He snapped a sharp salute and a small grin lifted the sides of his mouth.

"Go," Tag ordered as he returned the salute. The Adroit dashed out of the room, down the staircase, and up the alley toward the Academy.

"Breille. I need every warrior I can spare. Can you get some classmates from the building academy over here to help out?"

"Already done, Commander Thayer Taggert. They should be here soon."

"Good. Hold the fort, ladies." Tag hurried down the stairs where Marrcus, Kelila, Ailith, and Bonar were now gathered awaiting their leader.

"To The Great Chamber. Move out!" Tag shouted. The five ran in the "V" formation with Tag at the point. They moved through the nearly empty street and up toward The Great Chamber at a full run. By the time Tag's squad reached the chamber, most of the Hodia cadets had drawn their swords and taken up their positions outside the eight entrances to The Great Chamber. Each entrance had one squad and two squads patrolled the perimeter of the Chamber. Tag's squad had been assigned the perimeter between The Great Chamber and the Academy.

The cadets stood still and silent in their defensive positions. They looked skyward as the winged creatures circled above, waiting to deposit their deadly passengers.

"There are a lot of them," Marrcus said.

"What are they waiting for?" Cadet Kelila asked.

"Timing. Timing isn't everything, but it counts for something," Ailith responded.

"When they do start landing, don't go chasing after them. Our mission is to protect The Great Chamber first, the Academy second, and the citizens third. Keep that in mind," Tag commented.

The Oracles And The Jewels

The Academy of Theological Sciences and Ancient Conjuring Arts

Rieve had left Sandor's study and had run into the courtyard as he frantically looked for any sign of his Headmaster. Polemmas cadets were clearly visible. Some were in their cadet uniforms and others in armor. Students of the Academy had gathered in the courtyard to see what was going on.

Brenz was standing the middle of the courtyard.

"Commander Brenz Clinton! Where is Commander Brenz Clinton?"

"Over here, corporal," Brenz shouted and raised his hand. Cadet Veris pushed his way through the gathering crowd.

"Sir, Commander Thayer Taggert has ordered twenty-five of our warriors to the Demotic Valley. Neggen is facing a significant force."

Brenz called out five names. "Chor, Saulon, Kellach, Genea, and Fortinus!" In a few moments all five were standing before Brenz.

"Neggen needs support. Take your squads to Demotic Valley and show those Neggen cadets how to fight. You better stop at headquarters on the way and pick up some extra weapons."

"Yes, sir!" all five shouted and headed off in the direction of their squads. Cadet Veris saluted and headed off to the northern edge of the city for the Krattos Commander.

Rieve made his way through the crowd. "Commander! Commander! Have you seen Headmaster Sandor?"

"No," Brenz answered.

"They are missing," Rieve reported, "and look." Rieve pulled the stone from his pouch. It radiated with anger.

Brenz immediately called out three more names. "Ahba, Kefsen, and Salis." Three more cadets presented themselves before Brenz. "Take your squads and search the campus. If you find any faculty members send them to the archives in the basement and post guards. We must keep them safe. If you hear the battle horn, come running quickly."

King Ashkelon Attacks

"Yes, sir," the three replied and headed off in different directions.

Brenz and Rieve looked to the sky and to the top of the buildings.

"Brenz, it is imperative that we find Sandor," Rieve said.

"I know. But where could they have taken him?" Brenz asked.

"Have you seen any of the professors in the past thirty minutes or so?" Rieve asked.

"I saw Ellery and Millaran heading for the basement."

"What about the rest of you?" Rieve shouted as he turned in a three hundred sixty degree circle.

"Suedos. I saw Suedos," a Polemmas cadet said.

"Bozzez is downstairs," Nassar said as he stepped into the courtyard and looked skyward.

"What about Etam, Langward, Worett, Atteowe, or Scarre? Has anyone seen them? Nassar have you seen them?" Rieve asked.

"No, now that you mention it, I haven't." Nassar answered.

"Commander, we have to find them," Rieve said.

"Commander! Look!" a Fortian by the name of Javvan shouted. He pointed to the top of the library building, which was located to the northeast of the courtyard.

"I'm not a Fortian, Javvan!" Brenz shouted. "All I see are winged creatures. What am I looking at?"

"The winged creatures are taking Entosians off the top of the library building! They have put some kind of harness around them and the winged creatures are swooping down to pick them up."

"Javvan, stay here and prepare to fight. You're in command. My squad, follow me!" Brenz shouted. Immediately Brenz, Ansel, Durus, and Karrena ran from the courtyard and toward the library building. Rieve followed as best he could, but they were too fast for him. The squad reached the building well ahead of Rieve and ascended the stairwell with equal speed.

The library building was the shortest building on campus. It stood only three stories tall and located a half a block away from the buildings that surrounded the courtyard. Its unique features made it clearly visible from the

The Oracles And The Jewels

air and it was far enough from the taller buildings that marked the skyline near The Great Chamber.

Brenz, Ansel, Durus, and Karrena reached the top of the stairwell and paused. "Ready warriors. On my count, diamond formation. . . three, two, one, go!" Karrena kicked the door open with all her strength. Brenz led the way and the four took up their formation and moved quickly toward the other end of the roof.

They could see clearly now. There were five honor guardsmen holding three remaining professors at the tip of a sword. Professors Etam, Scarre, and Sandor stood at the end of the roof with their hands and feet bound and a harness secured around their shoulders.

"Release them or die," Brenz shouted as the four advanced. Just then a shadow of a winged creature passed over and before them. "Durus! Take it!" Brenz shouted as he pointed skyward without moving his head and without breaking eye contact with his prey. No sooner had the words left his mouth and Durus had his bow loaded and drawn. Immediately, three arrows found their mark in the underbelly of the winged beast. It let out a cry that echoed through the streets, then fell to the ground below.

"Durus! Stand fast! Strike any winged creature that descends!" Brenz ordered. A moment later Brenz, Karrena, and Ansel were engaged in a fight for their lives and the lives of the remaining professors. As the eight warriors fought with swords, daggers, and throwing disks, Durus loaded and loosed arrows one right after the other as several winged creatures attempted to snatch the remaining professors from the roof.

Brenz engaged two of the guardsmen. Karrena and Ansel paired off against the two others, while the fifth stood guard over the professors. At about two minutes into the battle, Brenz was able to deliver a lethal blow to one of his opponents. Karrena had been badly cut, but was still holding her own. Ansel had not been struck, but it was becoming evident that he was no match for his opponent.

"Kill them! Kill them!" one of the guardsmen shouted as he looked to the fifth guardsman. "Sandor first!"

The fifth guardsman raised his sword to deliver the deadly blow when he was immediately struck in the side,

King Ashkelon Attacks

then the back with two arrows from Durus' bow. The guard fell from the roof. At that moment, the winged creatures were given an opening and did not waste the opportunity. Before the guardsman's body had hit the street below, Professors Etam and Scarre had been snatched from the roof. A third was about to snatch up Sandor when Durus loosed another volley of arrows into the air. A second beast fell.

Rieve had reached the roof just as Etam and Scarre had been taken. "No!" He called out. He looked to Sandor who stood helpless. The sight stunned Rieve. Sandor was the most powerful conjuror in all of Entos, yet he seemed so helpless. Rieve did not understand. He hesitated and stood motionless.

"Conjuror!" Sandor yelled. The voice shook Rieve from his confusion. "Conjuror!" Sandor shouted and nodded his head in the direction of Ansel, who was now bleeding from his right arm. Rieve reached into his conjuror's pouch and took a pinch of glitter. *"Gibbon laccam sussim,"* Rieve said as he thrust his hand and the glitter forward to Ansel. *"Gibbon laccam sussim,"* as he did the same toward Karrena. Before he could repeat the process for the third time, Brenz felled his foe. Karrena and Ansel had done the same upon receiving the elements.

A moment later the four warriors and two conjurors stood still and looked in silence at their fallen enemies and three fallen winged creatures that now littered the roof top. Suddenly one of the winged creatures let loose a very loud screech and the other winged creatures began depositing beasts and soldiers into the city. Four soldiers were dropped onto the roof in seconds after the screech.

"Take them!" Brenz ordered, then he and Rieve ran to Sandor to cut him loose from his binds. As they did Durus loosed the balance of his arrows into any winged creature that came near the roof. Karrena and Ansel quickly dispatched the four soldiers that had been deposited on the roof. They all stood motionless for moment. Brenz turned to Sandor. His head dropped a bit to mirror the posture of his eyes.

"My apologies, Headmaster Sandor," Brenz said. "I have failed you and Entos,"

"How so my son?" Sandor asked.

The Oracles And The Jewels

"Your faculty. They have taken them from us. It was my charge to protect you and them."

"This is not thy fault. Who could have foreseen this? I did not even see it," Sandor replied. "No son, this is not thy fault. Thou hast performed well. All of thee hath performed well."

"Thank you, sir, but the facts are plain enough. I have failed," Brenz said as he bowed his head deeper in shame. Sandor placed his hand on the young warrior's head. "Thou cannot stop what has been set in motion. Thou has done what needed to be done, when it needed to be done. Thou will only shame yourself and thy comrades if you yield to defeat in thy soul. There is still so much to do. The war has just begun and I pray all perform as well as thee." Sandor looked to Rieve and said, "Now do any of thee know what has become of my granddaughter? They took her too."

"She's okay, sir. She is at our base," Karrena answered as she approached the three. "Sorry, Conjuror Rieve Waynwright. I didn't have a chance to tell you that Tag has saved her. She was helping distribute weapons. Commander, Ansel is badly wounded," Karrena continued. "Permission to take him to the healer."

"Permission granted," Brenz replied. "Karrena, make sure he gets back safely. Bring Durus a supply of arrows and meet us at the Academy."

"May I suggest that ye meetest us at the sanctuary at The Great Chamber," Sandor said. "They hath taken our best teachers. They will no doubt try to seize the teachings too."

"Karrena, meet us at The Great Chamber," Brenz repeated.

"Yes, sir," Karrena said as the group walked quickly across the roof.

The Battle at the Wall

The sky was black with clouds. The air was thick with the smoke and the smell of burning oil.

"Colonel Tarrant, do you have a status report on Neggen and Kanna?" Witticor asked.

King Ashkelon Attacks

"Neggen and Kanna are within one thousand feet of their objective, sir. They have come to a stop. I assume they are waiting for our signal," Tarrant reported.

"Well, it is time to find out if this plan is going to work, or if we are all going to die this day. Give the signals," Witticor shouted.

Tarrant repeated the order. "Launch signal Oracle! Send the word!"

Hokkan turned to the signaler on his side. "Give the signal Jewel. Send the word." Raggnar did the same.

Three balls of fire were loosed from three catapults in the direction of the Hodia Tower. The signaler to the right of Witticor turned and began waving a series of flags to the thousands of warriors standing at the ready inside the wall. Immediately the warriors began to march away from the wall and up the slope.

"Sound the withdraw for the cavalry," Witticor said. General Raggnar and Hokkan repeated the order. A moment later horns were sounding the retreat.

The Desert Floor

"That's the signal!" Colonel Sollon shouted as he pointed to the three large fire balls flying toward the Hodia Tower.

"Warriors! Ready on my command! Fight well and to the glory of Entos. Archers to the front." Two hundred Aradian archers ran to the front. "Arm bows! Draw! Aim!" Sollon shouted. In an instant two hundred arrows were pointed skyward and toward the nearest division of soldiers and beasts.

"Loose!" Sollon shouted. "Fire at will!" Before the first volley of arrows had hit their marks, two more volleys were launched. Arrows rained down on the rear division of Ashkelon's army. The division was thrown into chaos as the soldiers and beasts tried to determine from whom and what direction the arrows had come. As the shouts and screams of pain ascended from behind Ashkelon, the mighty king rose from his throne.

Ashkelon had been seated on a viewing platform which rose fifteen feet above the desert floor. Ashkelon sat high

The Oracles And The Jewels

upon his throne, yet even sitting he towered over his generals who stood one on each side of his chair. To the right of Ashkelon stood his greatest general and the underlord of the Skattos Forest, General Ya'ar. To his left the underlord of the Pachhad Jungles, Deabbon. Next to General Ya'ar stood the underlord of the swamps, Shaqqa, the most loathsome in appearance of all Ashkelon's underlords.

From his platform and throne high above the crowd, he watched the battle unfold and issued forth his orders. Up until this moment he had done so with a cold and calm irascibility. But as the screams rose from behind him, Ashkelon stood up and turned in angry disbelief. He said nothing. He marched to the back corner of the platform to survey the battle that was just beginning.

Ashkelon was ten feet tall. King Ashkelon towered above all others on the battlefield. His skin was dark, but his eyes were red with the fire of Ektos. His body was covered from head to toe with heavy black armor, which had edges and points as sharp as razors. The black and purple robe that hung from his neck dragged along the floor behind as he walked quickly across the platform. The sword that hung from his side was six feet long and so heavy no Entosian could swing it and no sword fashioned in Entos could withstand a blow from it. As he marched across the platform, he drew the sword. It was so large and heavy it made an unmistakable sound as it left the scabbard.

The crown on his head was large, made of steel and iron with black rubies which were mounted in the base of the crown. The crown was as large and grotesque as Ashkelon himself. Several spires rose from the base and towered above Ashkelon's head. It looked more like a weapon than a crown. Ashkelon stared in the direction of the Entosian division. His eyes glowed red and the breath from his nostrils was so hot that it could be seen.

"You, you, and you," Ashkelon shouted as he pointed to three officers standing at the base of the platform. "Send your divisions there!" He pointed to the Entosian division. "I don't want even one Entosian warrior to survive. Wipe them from the face of my earth!" His voice shook everyone and everything around him. "Now go!" The officers vanished in

King Ashkelon Attacks

an instant. Within a few minutes, three divisions, plus the one under attack were organizing to launch a counterattack on the Entosian division.

"General Witticor," Hakkon shouted. "Look. It's working. Three! No! Four divisions are moving to the southeast to attack."

"Good. From the Ancient of Days, divide and conquer. Are the warriors ready in the valley?" Witticor asked.

"Yes," Tarrant answered. "Everything is ready."

"Let them in," Witticor ordered. Hakkon and Tarrant shouted the order. "Open the gates!" Again the order was repeated and the large beams and stones that had been placed against the gates to reinforce them were removed. Within a few minutes Ashkelon's battering rams were breaking their way through the gates and soldiers and beasts were pouring into the valley.

"General, I suggest we withdraw to higher and safer ground," Tarrant said.

"Yes. It is time," Witticor replied.

"Evacuate the wall!" Tarrant and Hakkon repeated the order. "Regroup at the edge of the woods."

"Warriors, I have good news. General Witticor's plan is working. We are dividing Ashkelon's forces and four divisions are moving to attack us!" Colonel Sollon shouted. "Battle formations!" The large square formation broke apart into a standard Entosian battle formation of five large circles.

"Colonel," Arokim said, "Where do you want us?" The remaining scouts stood at Arokim's side, weary and soiled from their long journey, but ready to fulfill their duty.

"Lieutenant," the colonel said with a smile. "Your team can cut your way through the middle ten thousand. We will handle the rest."

"Very well, Colonel," Arokim said and returned the smile.

"Lieutenant."

"Yes, Colonel," Arokim replied.

"We will begin in a defensive posture to thin the enemy out. But when the order to attack is given, I want your team to have the honor of leading us home. Get us there as fast as you can, while sending as many of these cursed creatures to their damnable reward," Colonel Sollon said.

The Oracles And The Jewels

"Yes, sir!" Arokim snapped. Arokim turned to his remaining scouts and shouted, "Scouts to the left and the front." Celsus, Ora, Justin, Yafet, Tor, Faggon, Roggan, Cedric, Tita, Edris, and Magnus followed Arokim and moved into the gap between the two circles at the front of the formation.

Once the remaining twelve scouts had formed their circle, they looked at the wall of soldiers and beasts which was now just a little more than one hundred yards away. Arokim spoke one final word.

"Stand firm, scouts. You are the best. It has pleased our glorious King to send ten thousand fellow Entosian warriors to guard our backs. Now fight well and to the glory of Entos. May our God unite us again safely within the walls of Entos or in His realm which has no end."

The twelve scouts raised their swords. The ten thousand warriors behind them did the same. They stood motionless, like statues frozen in time, awaiting the wall of beasts and warriors to break upon them. And break upon them they did.

Soldiers and beasts began to fall in predictable and statistical fashion. By the hundreds they fell as the Entosian metal proved itself. Entosians fell as well.

The little circle formed by the scouts did not last long. Yafet was the first scout to fall when he was overwhelmed by five mammothons. Celsus made an attempt to help Yafet, but was wounded in the leg with a troll's arrow. As he fell to the ground, Celsus watched the mammothons strike Yafet down before they tore his body to pieces.

The mammothons moved to finish Celsus, but Tor placed himself between the advancing mammothons and his comrade. As Tor engaged them from the front, Edris quickly circled behind them and struck the unsuspecting mammothons. Without saying a word and without hesitation, Tor took hold of Celsus' leg with his left hand and the shaft of the arrow with his right. In one smooth and powerful movement, Tor snapped the arrow off just above the flesh, then helped Celsus to his feet. Edris provided the needed protection for the two.

"Thank you, my friend," Celsus said.

King Ashkelon Attacks

"It's only a temporary fix. We will all be joining Yafet soon enough," Tor replied.

"I am in no hurry," Celsus replied.

The Battle in the Demotic Valley

"Cadets!" Commander Kyra shouted. "Form a straight line. We will use the ridge to our advantage. Do not form circles. Form your line and hold. Reinforcements from Krattos and Polemmas, you will fill in the holes in the line should they appear and take out any soldier or beast that breaks through the line. Are we all clear?"

"Yes, sir," the cadets shouted.

"Form up!" Kyra yelled. Nearly two hundred cadets took up their positions on the edge of the plateau.

Ashkelon's beasts began to advance up the slope. By now they had set ablaze the nearly two dozen homes in the valley, including Rieve's and Tag's home near the edge of the woods.

Every warrior had been given a bow and at least three dozen arrows. "Hold your fire!" Kyra shouted.

A few beasts broke ranks from the advancing columns and were running toward the line.

"Adroitians. Shoot anything that breaks ranks. The rest of you hold your fire until I give the command!" As Kyra shouted orders she marched behind the line with her sword drawn. She was a tiny and beautiful Adroitian, but that did not matter. What mattered was the way in which she spoke and conducted herself. She, like all others who had been awarded the rank of cadet commander, had demonstrated extraordinary talent for the job. As she walked and repeated her commands, the Adroitian archers picked off each beast that broke ranks and charged up the hill.

The column continued to advance and when it was close enough to feel the ground rumble under their feet, Kyra gave the order. "Loose arrows!" Hundreds of arrows filled the air. "Fire at will!" The order was repeated up and down the line. Beasts and soldiers began to cry out and fall. Yet the column did not break. Usually under such conditions, discipline broke down and a premature charge would take shape. But this time, the column held its shape and

The Oracles And The Jewels

continued their march. At three hundred yards their march accelerated to a trot. At two hundred yards the trot graduated to a run. The cadets continued their volley of arrows and had managed to drop several hundred of the enemy, still several thousand strong.

"Cease fire!" Kyra shouted. "Draw your weapons! Your choice! Fight well and to the glory of Entos!" Most of the line held, but at great cost. The left flank of the line was almost completely wiped out, and before the reinforcements could fight their way to the flank and restore the line, a few hundred soldiers and beasts had made it into the city, which was now on the verge of chaos.

The Battle In The Phanos Forest

The battle in the Phanos Forest was not going well for the few Entosian warriors that had been dispatched there. The Entosian warriors had succeeded in their primary mission, which was to cut off and hinder any reinforcements from reaching the city or inflicting any further damage on the dozens of villages scattered through the Demotic Valley, but the forces deployed along the edge of the forest were not sufficiently strong to eliminate the threat completely. Major Gaynor lay dead and the battle had largely disintegrated into disorganized pockets of battles. The cavalry was attempting to chase down any soldier or beast that had managed to make it out of the forest into the field toward the city.

The battle had stirred millions of Phanos flies that resided in the canopy of the forest and it was so bright hardly a shadow could be seen. The sound of millions of wings humming provided a strangely soothing sound to those who listened to it.

"Captain!" the conjuror cried out. "Major Gaynor is dead! You're the ranking officer. I suggest you start acting the part!" A young captain looked at the conjuror in a moment of disbelief.

"Yes, you, my son, are the ranking officer here. I'm afraid if you don't bring some kind of order to this mess, we run the risk of being overrun and failing in our mission," the conjuror said.

King Ashkelon Attacks

The young captain looked around to survey the sight. The battle had been reduced to a brawl on every side. The young captain could see no clear way of bringing order out of chaos to form a clear line of defense.

"Conjuror," the captain said, "I need a surprise, some kind of miracle to bring order out of this chaos. Sir, miracles are your job."

The conjuror looked skyward with a look of frustration and hopelessness. As he stared at the Phanos moths, the look of frustration disappeared and a small smile took shape.

"Conjuror!" the captain called. "Look out!" The captain sprinted toward the conjuror with his sword in his left hand and a throwing disk in his right. He loosed the disk and it hit its target, a troll, but it was too late. The troll had planted a spear into the side of the conjuror who was now falling to the ground. The captain finished the troll with a blow from his sword. He took the head and shoulders of the conjuror in his arms and shouted. "Healer! Healer!"

"Save your breath," the conjuror said. "He's dead and I will see him soon enough."

"I've failed you," the captain said.

"You have not. I will not fail you," the conjuror said. "Use this miracle well captain." The conjuror lifted his finger toward the sky and whispered, *Ophann phanos. Ophann phanos demmim gannon.* Should it be granted, use this miracle well, Captain, and save your warriors." The captain laid the body of the conjuror on the ground and looked toward the canopy, then to the battle below. He marched forward and shouted his warriors. "The healer is dead! The conjuror has joined him. Fight well, Entosian warriors, and we shall see one another on the other side." He entered the thick of the battle and cut down one soldier after another.

The hum of the Phanos wings began to increase. The light began to grow brighter, but none of the warriors noticed the increase in volume or light. But Ashkelon's soldiers and beasts were not accustomed to the light and, as the light increased, their vision was impaired.

Suddenly, millions of moths swooped down on the clusters of Ashkelon soldiers. The soldiers began falling back in blindness and confusion. The warriors began to

The Oracles And The Jewels

advance toward the retreating soldiers. The captain stood stunned for a moment as he watched the scene unfold.

"Even the littlest creatures of Entos fight for her with their light," he whispered to himself. He looked over at the body of the conjuror. "Thank you. Thank you. I will use it well," he said.

"Fall back! Regroup! Form the line," he shouted. "Do it now!"

"But they are on the run, sir," a lieutenant pleaded.

"Fall back! Regroup! Form the line," the captain repeated as if he hadn't heard the appeal. "Cavalry fill the ranks!" The warriors did as ordered and the line reformed. The warriors were stunned by their losses. Their numbers had been cut in half.

"Chaos is our enemy. Order is our comrade," the captain shouted above the noise as he mounted his horse. "We will not yield to chaos and we will not fail this day. How can we fail? Even the moths of Phanos Forest have joined this battle! Too many Entosians have fallen this day! Too many have shed their blood. No more will fall under my command! You, the faithful few stand in a long line of faithful warriors who have spilled their blood on this sacred ground. They did not fail us and we will not in this hour of need fail them. Generations will speak of this day and of your part in it. They will tell their children of your faith and courage. They will tell their grandchildren about the day that the King turned you, the defeated, the weary, the wounded into the victors! Will they speak of you when they speak of this day?"

"Yes, sir," the warriors replied in one voice.

"Advance in stride then and hold the line," the captain shouted. He turned his horse and guided her to the front and center of the line. "Advance!" The line moved forward.

The soldiers and beasts of Bohow were in a state of confusion and were falling back and fleeing from the moths. As they retreated they swung wildly at the moths.

"Advance, double time," the captain ordered. The gap between the retreating soldiers and the warriors was closing. As the warriors closed the gap between the two lines they began cutting their enemies down. Step-by-step Ashkelon's soldiers fell back toward the field from whence they came. But as the soldiers thought they were going to be

King Ashkelon Attacks

freed from the forest, the moths blocked their retreat and drove them into the blades of the oncoming Entosian warriors until they were none left.

The Battle For The Great Chamber

"Commander Brenz Clinton," Thayer began as they entered the street.

"Yes, sir," Brenz replied.

"Shake it off. No matter how you feel about it, you did not fail and the loss of the conjurors was not your fault. It was a completely unforeseeable event."

"Yes, sir, if you say so," Brenz replied with a tone of disbelief.

"Who among us would have thought that our own honor guard would have betrayed our conjurors into the hands of Ashkelon? No one. In fact such a thing could only happen with the highest possible authority. I didn't foresee it. Conjuror Rieve did not foresee it. Not even Headmaster Sandor could predict that such a thing would happen. It would be very unreasonable to place this matter on your shoulders." Tag explained.

"Yes, sir," Brenz replied again in a tone as unconvinced as the first.

"Commander!" Tag yelled. Durus, Rieve, and Sandor were caught by surprise at the outburst. Brenz looked at the surprise in their eyes, then dropped his head.

"Commander Brenz Clinton! I need you. All of you. Every ounce of you in this fight. Do you see those soldiers and beasts?" Tag pointed to a group of soldiers and beasts some three blocks away and marching toward The Great Chamber. "They are the least of our problems commander! Our biggest problem is the guardsmen. They have the same training and skills as do we and we do not know if all fifty are involved in this conspiracy or if they are on our side. We do not know who to trust and who to kill. But they know that we are an unauthorized military force and their orders and our orders do not match. Make no mistake about this. They are the best of the best. They will be able to cut right through our lines and enter The Great Chamber if that is what they are ordered to do. You are the second best swordsman in the

The Oracles And The Jewels

cadet army and the best commander on the ground. Are you ready for this fight or shall I appoint another?"

Brenz stiffened and raised his head. "I am ready, sir. I will not fail or disappoint."

"Good! Now take point and make sure that no one, be he a beast, soldier, guardsman, or Ashkelon himself comes anywhere near the Headmaster or Conjuror Rieve. Our mission is to get them into The Great Chamber, then to secure it against anyone else entering therein. Are you clear cadet?" Tag shouted.

Brenz returned the shout. "Yes, sir!"

"Move out!" Tag ordered.

"Durus! Take the right side of the street. I will take the left! Go!" Durus and Brenz ran a half-a-block ahead of the other three.

"Rieve and Headmaster," Tag said. "Stay a half block behind those two. They will clear the street and make it safe for you. Follow their directions. I will take up the rear. When we get to The Great Chamber, we will regroup before we cross the street."

"Indeed, fight well and to the glory of Entos, young Cadet," Sandor said.

As the five drew closer to The Great Chamber, Brenz and Durus encountered more and more of Ashkelon's soldiers. Occasionally, a beast or soldier had the misfortune of turning the corner and finding itself behind Sandor and Rieve and being cut down just as quickly by Tag.

The attack in the city was not organized. But it was a lesson in chaos and destruction. As the beasts and soldiers went through the streets, they broke the windows of the buildings and set many of the buildings on fire. On occasion they would run across an Entosian civilian, kill, and eat him. The soldiers and beasts were converging on two specific targets. A smaller force was attacking The Academy of Theological Sciences and Ancient Conjuring Arts, but the main concentration was converging on The Great Chamber. It took ten minutes for the group to reach the street circling The Great Chamber. When they did, they were surprised by what they saw.

Soldiers and beasts were circling The Great Chamber in two rings running in opposite directions. Many of the trolls

King Ashkelon Attacks

had mounted beasts and were riding wildly around The Great Chamber. The sky over the chamber was darker than the rest of the already blackened sky. Ashkelon's soldiers and beasts were screaming and roaring, but they had not yet launched an attack on The Great Chamber itself. Before the circle had closed, the Hodia cadets had had time to take up their positions at each of the eight entrances. A few guardsmen had also managed to make it into the circle. Several guardsmen had taken up positions on the inside of the ring between the cadets and the beasts. The thunder of the beast's hooves and soldier's boots on the stone street made it necessary for all to shout if they were to be heard. As time went on more and more soldiers joined their comrades.

Brenz and Durus reached the edge of the street first. They motioned for Rieve and Sandor to join them. Once the four were together, Tag joined them. The five stood confounded for a moment at the sight they beheld.

"There are so many of them," Durus said. There is no way so few cadets can keep them from the chamber."

"Where's Brenna?" Brenz asked.

"He is probably on the south side of the chamber," Rieve replied.

"At his very best he can only provide assistance to cadets at two entrances. But that's his problem at the moment. We have our own."

"Commander," Brenz shouted. "How do you propose we get from here to there without being trampled?"

"We could go back to the Academy and use the tunnels," Tag shouted.

"Take too long," Sandor replied in an equally loud voice.

"Headmaster, if you have any ideas, I'm open to your recommendation on this matter," Tag replied.

"It would seem the answer is obvious," Sandor answered. "So obvious perhaps Conjuror Rieve Waynwright might have the answer. No offense intended."

"None taken. Although I am unsure of the answer," Rieve said.

"Think, my son," Sandor replied.

"There can only be two possibilities, my Lord. We either go through them or we go over them," Rieve answered.

The Oracles And The Jewels

"Those are the only two options I can imagine," Sandor said. "Now Commander, pick one."

"I would prefer over, Headmaster, but I do not know how such a thing is possible," Tag replied.

"Nor do I, but that has little to do with it," Sandor said. "Pick one of thy number."

"I will go first. Just in case it doesn't go well," Brenz said.

"I suggest the little guy, Durus," Rieve said. "Practice."

"What do you want me to do?" Durus asked.

"Run and jump," Sandor said.

"Commander?" Durus said with a question in his voice.

"Run and jump. That's an order, warrior," Tag shouted then smiled. "Cadet Brenz, you will go next. Then Conjuror Rieve. Then . . . then, Headmaster, how will you get across?"

"Cadet, my jumping days are long gone. But as with all such things, something will change and make it possible."

"My Lord, if you do not make it across, then I will not either. I will remain at your side," Rieve said.

"Thou wilt be needed on the other side. It is for thee to be there. It is for me to stay here," Sandor said.

"But how do you know that?" Tag asked.

"Because thou chose to go over," Sandor answered.

"But . . ." Tag started to say.

"Don't bother, little brother. You can't win this debate. Soon we will be involved in a lesson on free will and did you really pick over rather than through, or was it ordained from before the foundations of Entos were made. We really don't have time for such a debate. I think it would be best to simply stay with the first choice – over," Rieve explained. "Something will happen and all will be as it ought to be."

Sandor smiled. "You're learning quickly, my son."

"Durus. Back up. Get a good running start and jump," Brenz said.

"Yes, sir." Durus swallowed hard and took a deep breath. He walked about thirty feet. Then with a sudden burst he ran forward and just as he was about to crash into the outer ring of beasts he jumped. At the same moment Sandor shouted, *"Fanan Gibbon,"* and a sparkle of glitter struck Durus in the back and propelled him over the two rings and spilled him out on the sidewalk on the other side.

King Ashkelon Attacks

The Hodia cadet guarding the north entrance watched in disbelief, as did the guardsmen in view of the event.

"Fanan Gibbon," Sandor said looking at Rieve.

"Fanan Gibbon," Rieve repeated.

"Ready?" Sandor asked.

"Ready," Brenz replied. "You might as well go too Commander Thayer Taggert," Sandor said.

"Two at once?" Tag asked.

"There are two conjurors here and perhaps showing off a bit might discourage some of these guardsmen from opposing us."

"Okay," Tag replied. Brenz and Tag walked back about thirty feet. They looked at each other.

"Ready?" Tag asked.

"Ready," came Brenz's reply.

"Go!" Tag shouted and the two of them burst forward.

"Fanan Gibbon," Sandor and Rieve shouted in unison as they threw balls of glitter into the cadets' backs. Brenz and Tag flew over the beasts and soldiers and rolled onto the sidewalk on the other side. Their landing was more graceful than was Durus'. They rolled onto their feet and drew their swords as they came to a stop. It was an impressive display, smooth and graceful. Brenz and Tag were surprised by their entrance, but they hid it under a facade of professional determination.

Durus had been surrounded by four members of the honor guard who were holding him at the point of their swords. The sight of Tag's and Brenz's entrance into the circle stunned them. They stepped back for a moment, then resumed their stance.

"Warriors," Tag said. "Stand down. We are all Entosians here, aren't we? They are our enemies." Tag pointed his sword to the circling beasts and soldiers.

"We have our orders, Cadet," one of the guardsmen answered. "Our orders come from President Botha. We are to protect The Great Chamber from all enemies, foreign and domestic. That means from rogue cadets, especially rogue cadets."

"Gentlemen," Brenz said. "We have killed four of your fellow guardsmen today. Men who betrayed the teachers of Entos into the hands of Ashkelon."

The Oracles And The Jewels

"Liar!" shouted one of the guardsmen.

"It is no lie," Tag snapped back.

"Unless you step aside we will have to double that number," Brenz said as he stared into the eyes of the guardsmen. The muscles in his jaw tightened. He raised his sword and readied himself for the attack.

As the guards stood peering into the faces of Thayer, Brenz, and Durus, Rieve floated over the rings and into position right behind the three cadets. As he touched the ground he tapped his staff three times on the stone sidewalk.

"Is that you, big brother?" Tag asked without looking behind him.

"Yes, little brother. I am here."

"Are you ready?" Tag asked.

"I am ready, if these four warriors are ready to die," Rieve said. He opened his hand revealing the glitter in the palm of his hand.

"Now gentlemen, either use those swords, or take up your positions and be prepared to repel the coming attack. Those creatures are not going to run in circles forever."

"At ease," the captain said. "We will take this matter up later, once we have dealt with these creatures."

"Wise choice," Tag said. The four guardsmen backed slowly away and took up their former position halfway between the Hodia cadets at the entrance and the beasts in the street. Tag, Brenz, Durus, and Rieve ran up the stairs to join the cadets at the north entrance. Once they were high enough they could see Sandor leaning against a building across the street.

Tag and Rieve stood on the steps staring at Sandor on the other side. "I don't like it, brother," Tag said.

"I don't either, but it will work out just as he said. We have to keep our eyes open for that little window of opportunity to bring him to us."

"Time to go to work," Tag said.

"Indeed," Rieve replied. "Fight well and to the glory of Entos."

"Indeed," Tag snapped. "Durus. Pass the word. Tell the men to stay at their posts. They are to fight where they stand. At the entrances of The Great Chamber. No one is to go in or

King Ashkelon Attacks

come out of The Great Chamber. Not beast or soldier of Ashkelon and no guardsman is to enter or leave the chamber. Conjuror Rieve and I will enter The Great Chamber momentarily to make sure all is secure. The cadets are to use arrows and throwing disks to thin out the enemy. Aim for the soldiers first and the beasts second. Fight guardsmen only if attacked. Fire at will at the soldiers."

"Yes, sir," Durus barked and sprinted to the next entrance to pass the orders on.

Rieve had joined the Hodia cadets at the top of the stairs near the two large doors of The Great Chamber. Thayer and Brenz took their stand between their Hodia cadets and the guardsmen.

"I'm more concerned about them," Brenz said as he lifted his sword in the direction of the guardsmen, "than I am about Ashkelon's hordes."

Tag turned toward the five cadets behind him. "Fire at will, warriors. Soldiers first and beasts second." A moment later arrows and throwing disks began finding their marks. Soldiers and beasts began to fall with regularity, yet they did not attack or break their pattern. The Hodia cadets loosed volley after volley into the circling soldiers and beasts.

"What are they waiting for?" Tag asked out loud.

"It makes no sense at all!" Brenz shouted back over the thundering sound of hooves on the stone street.

"Conjuror Rieve," Tag shouted above the thundering hooves, "let's secure the Oracles and the Jewels." The two turned and began toward the doors of The Great Chamber.

"Move aside, you little pest!" a voice unlike any ever heard in the Land of Entos said. It was a voice with its own echo and a voice that shook the bones of those who heard it. Rieve and Tag stood stunned and speechless as he looked at the robed figure standing in the doorway. He was flanked by two guardsmen, each holding one of the large doors.

"I said move aside! You have caused me enough trouble this day." The voice rumbled above the noise of the hooves, above the shouts and screams of the soldiers and beasts, and even above the heartbeats that were now pounding in the ears of the warriors. Brenz turned toward the voice and stood still in shock and surprise.

"Botha," Brenz said in disbelief. "It is Botha," he repeated in a hushed voice.

The Oracles And The Jewels

The same thought came to Thayer. "It looks like Botha, at least mostly like him," Tag said to himself before shouting, Botha! It's Botha!"

"He's too big. His eyes," Brenz replied.

"It's Botha, or what use to be Botha," Tag answered. "He is the betrayer."

Rieve looked frantically for Sandor, but could not find him in the chaos of the moment. He turned back toward Botha.

"You're the betrayer," Rieve said.

"I will not speak it again!" Botha replied.

"You will not pass," Rieve said with a resolve befitting a priest of The Great Chamber. He looked strong and confident, but inwardly he was hoping Sandor would deliver them all from their fate.

"Yes, I will pass," Botha roared, then with a wave of his hand he launched Rieve into the air several feet. Rieve hit the pavement a moment later and rolled down the steps below. Tag started to take a step toward Rieve, but Rieve lifted his hand and nodded his head, signaling that he was okay. The Hodia cadets withdrew from their perch on the top step and retreated to a safer distance.

"Stop, you beasts of Bohow! Cease, ye soldiers of Ashkelon!" Botha ordered. At his word the circling hordes brought themselves to a halt and silence fell over the city. All eyes fell upon Ashkelon's wizard.

"I am Botha, a prince in Ektos, an underlord of Bohow. You beasts and soldiers know me. I am the one for whom you have been waiting. I am the one who has been concealed. I am the one in whom Lord Ashkelon has placed his hope! Hear me now."

Immediately, the beasts and soldiers fell to their knees and bowed their heads. Botha breathed a deep and hot breath, then continued. "I have the treasures for which we came." Tag glanced at the four guardsmen. Two of them had fallen to their knees. The other two looked on in horror and disbelief.

"See the spoils of your sacrifice!" Botha roared. "Look upon the gifts we shall bring to our Lord Ashkelon." Botha stepped aside and four more guardsmen brought out a large chest, set it on the ground, and opened the lid. "See the

King Ashkelon Attacks

Oracles and the Jewels!" Botha cried. "The life of Entos belongs to us and no one shall take it!"

Tag, Brenz, and Durus charged forward. They were joined by the two guardsmen who had not bowed their knees to Botha. No command had been given and no cry of defiance came forth, for none was needed. As the five Entosians charged forward, Botha's four guardsmen moved just as quickly. Swords clashed and a guardsman fell. Brenz, Tag, and Durus held their own, but could not make progress toward the chest. The two Entosian guardsmen had drawn their swords against the two guardsmen who had bowed their knees to Botha. In a matter of seconds, one good guardsman and an evil one lay dead on the steps of The Great Chamber.

Rieve rose to his feet and spoke an incantation, *"Velotis amet aman gibbon,"* and threw his spell into the cadets. They exploded with speed and power and cut down the guardsmen, then walked up the steps and stood before Botha, who stood alone with the chest. Botha smiled at the boys standing before him.

"Away!" he shouted and waved his hand. The cadets and guardsmen were thrown backward towards the beasts and soldiers. "Kill them! Kill all of them! Destroy this temple. They have no need of it any longer!" Botha called out as he raised his arms in victory. The screams and shouts went up from the multitude surrounding The Great Chamber and Ashkelon's army rushed forward. Soldiers, beasts, and most guardsmen rushed the door. The cadets on every side of The Great Chamber began to cut down all the unholy creatures whose hooves and feet defiled the Chamber. The battle for The Great Chamber was under way.

Rieve repeated the incantation again, *"Velotis amet aman gibbon,"* but this time the mere speaking of the words produced the desired effect. Brenz, Tag, the remaining guardsmen, and the last three cadets at the north entrance burst to their feet and began striking down the beasts and soldiers that had rushed forward.

Two mammothon soldiers made it to the top of the stairs where Botha stood. They took hold of the chest and followed Botha down the steps. As Botha moved through the surging crowd the creatures parted and formed a protective ring

The Oracles And The Jewels

around their master. Botha took the chest from the soldiers and held it high above his head. A winged creature circling above gave out a loud screech and began descending toward the chest.

"Commander!" Rieve shouted. He pointed to Botha, then to the winged creature.

"Hodia! Brenz!" Tag shouted. "Diamond formation." Rieve took his position in the middle of the formation. They fought their way through the mob. Most of the soldiers and beasts attacked the warriors, but many others bolted up the stairs and into The Great Chamber. Stones and arrows began smashing the windows from within and from without.

"We aren't going to reach them," Brenz shouted to Tag. The two looked at the winged creature. In a few moments the chest would be gone.

"Throw them!" Brenz shouted.

"What?" Tag shouted back.

"Throw them!" Brenz replied. His eyes directed Thayer to his belt and to the weapon Thayer had designed. Thayer took one set from his belt and tossed them to Brenz. He took hold of the second set.

"Protect us," Brenz ordered. The guardsmen and cadets moved into position as quickly as the order had been given.

"Now!" Tag shouted. The two threw the oddly shaped weapon and each struck one of Botha's wrists. The chest fell to the ground just as the winged creature tried to snatch it.

Botha turned and looked at the warriors with rage in his eyes. He growled and took a sword from one of the mammothons and marched toward the remaining cadets.

"You've done it now. You've made him really mad," Rieve said. He smiled. "Well done," he added.

"A strange time to find your sense of humor, brother," Tag replied.

As Botha drew near, the beasts and soldiers withdrew. With a wave of his hand Botha knocked all the cadets to the ground. Rieve alone stood before Botha. It was only a moment, but it seemed like such a very long time to Rieve. He had no powers of his own to fell the mighty underlord. He had only his natural ability. Botha took a swing of his sword. Rieve jumped to one side, but the sword cut him at his ribs.

King Ashkelon Attacks

Tag and Brenz sprang to their feet and charged. Again with the wave of his hand Botha knocked them to the ground. He struck Rieve a second time hitting him on the opposite side of the first strike.

"I will cut you to pieces," Botha roared as he took a step towards Rieve. Tag and Brenz charged a second time only to be thrown back again.

"Wait your turn!" Botha said. "This conjuror is first!" He raised the sword a third time and swung it with all his might. But the sword seemed to take forever to reach its destination. So slow did it seem to Rieve, that even wounded he was able to move out of its reach. As all looked on, Rieve's movements were so fast, they could barely comprehend what was taking place.

"Prince Botha! Underlord of Bohow! You shall not take possession of the King's gifts. They do not belong to you or your kind. Nor does this conjuror belong to you this day. He has been appointed for another." All eyes turned toward the voice as Sandor spoke.

"Sandor," Rieve said still not comprehending what had just happened to him.

"Away with you old fool!" Botha roared and waved his arm. Sandor was thrown backward, but no sooner had Sandor hit the ground when Rieve shouted, *"Fanan!"* The word lifted Sandor to his feet.

Instantly Sandor shouted, "Strike!" Tag and Brenz sprang forward. Botha swung his sword blocking Brenz's blade, but Tag's strike severed the hand which held the sword. The hand and sword fell to the ground.

Botha yelled in pain, "Kill them all!" Botha moved forward and raised his remaining hand.

"No!" Sandor shouted. "Away with you! You slave of Ashkelon." Sandor struck his staff on the ground and the stone pavement rolled like a wave and broke under Botha's feet. He was thrown to the ground.

The masses surged forward toward the small band of warrior cadets. The two mammothons pulled Botha away from the battle. Tag and Brenz made a final charge to the chest and took it under their possession. Rieve stumbled up the stairs away from the battle. Sandor followed him.

The Oracles And The Jewels

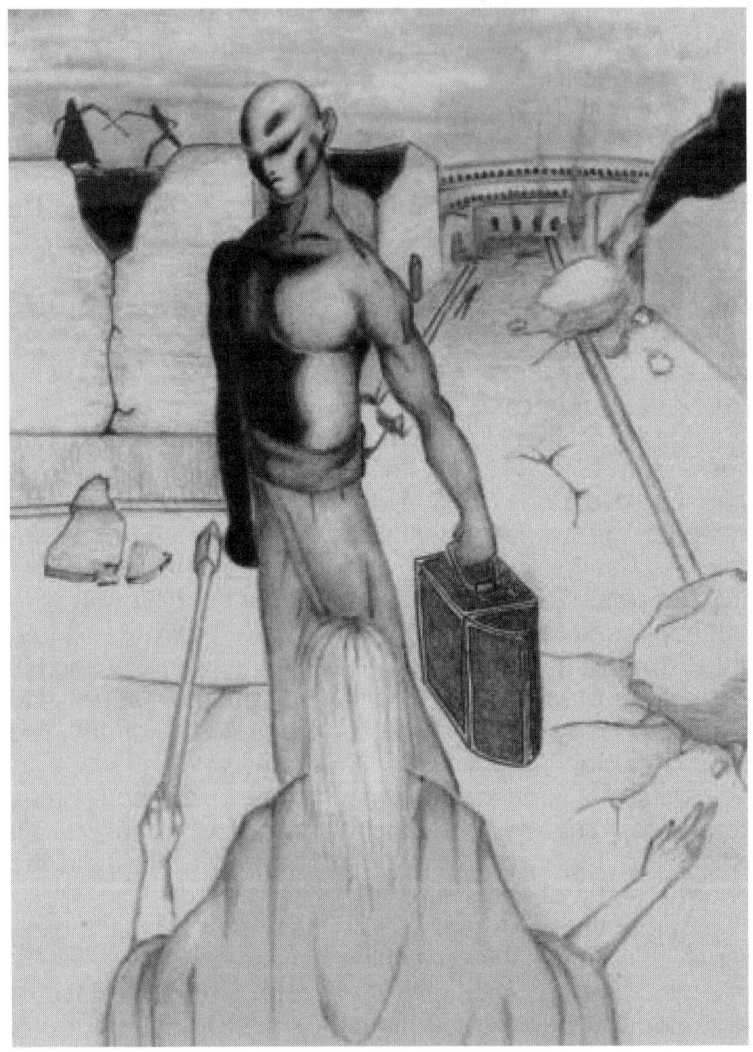

"Help them," Rieve said as Sandor checked Rieve's wounds. "Help the cadets."

"Help is here, my son," Sandor replied. He pointed his staff to the north, east, and west. As he did, Polemmas and Krattos cadets came pouring into the street surrounding The Great Chamber. The sight of fallen cadets at the entrances of The Great Chamber, the traitorous guardsmen, and the

King Ashkelon Attacks

vandalism being inflicted upon The Great Chamber were the only inspiration the cadets needed. Dozens of cadet warriors battled their way toward the entrances of The Great Chamber. Akimm was close behind, watching after all in his charge. Healers and helpers from the field hospital were also among the reinforcements.

"Granddaughters," Sandor called out. "Here, over here!"

Blisse, River, Breille, and several other healers and students were making their way through the streets distributing arrows, disks, and swords where needed. Colonel Fornoff and several mildly wounded cadets from the hospital provided protection for them as they cleared a path for their civilian warriors. As Breille and River made their way through the streets they found it necessary to use some of the weapons they were carrying to help a warrior. On occasion they would have to fend off a charging beast.

Colonel Fornoff began shouting orders to the cadets. He was bringing order out of chaos and victory out of defeat. His voice and large stature strengthened the warrior cadets who were now fighting with a renewed spirit. Durus and some archers formed up on his command. They perched themselves on the high ground at the chamber's entrance. The colonel directed their fire as they began to break the enemy's back.

By the time Blisse reached Rieve, he was unconscious. A pool of blood began running down the stairs and the color had gone out of his face.

Blisse paused for a moment. "Granddaughter, fear not. This is not his time. Work well and to the glory of Entos," Sandor said.

While Blisse began working on Rieve, Breille continued to make war on any creature that came near them. River continued to distribute supplies to the archers, while Brenz and Tag carried the chest toward Sandor.

"Here, Headmaster. They are safe," Brenz said.

"Well done, cadets," Sandor answered.

"Rieve? How is he?" Tag asked as he bent over his brother and placed his hand on his head. "He's so cold."

"He has lost so much blood," Blisse said as she cleaned the wounds. "It's bad, very bad. The cut is very deep." Her

The Oracles And The Jewels

face wore the look of calm panic. "He's dead," she thought to herself. "Should I say it or leave it for all to see." She debated the question in her mind as she tried to hold back her own grief. She would have said it, but her mouth was busy speaking the incantations, *"Aman aham rafa pasa emen."* She repeated it again and again. Every third time she added, *"Borran amets umat gibbon cullan umat palanan dekkim adam demmim laccam or Um,"* as she had done for the wounded guardsman earlier that day. The guardsman survived his wounds thanks to Blisse, but there was nothing to be done for Rieve.

Blisse didn't have to say it. Tag saw it in her face. "He's dead . . . He's dead, isn't he?" Tag asked in a soft grief-stricken voice. River and Breille joined the small group just in time to hear the question.

"No," River said. "It can't be!" Blisse closed her eyes and a tear ran down her cheek. "No," River repeated in a softer voice.

"No," Sandor answered firmly. "He's only asleep. It is not his time." When Sandor spoke the little fellowship heard anger and defiance in his voice. Sandor's face was almost as pale as Rieve's. Tears were welling up in his eyes and the hand holding his staff trembled.

"No, I tell you. It is not his time. It was to be my time. I waited outside for Botha. He should have been outside, not in the chamber. He is not dead. Bring him. Bring him now into the chamber. Bring the chest into the chamber. Hurry, hurry."

Brenz ordered two of his cadets to bring the chest. Tag, Brenz, Breille, and River lifted Rieve to their shoulders and followed. Sandor hurried up the steps.

"Colonel, I need the chamber cleared of all the damnable beasts and servants of Ashkelon now."

"Yes, sir," the colonel replied. "Warriors follow me," he shouted. He stepped inside the chamber. More than two dozen cadet warriors followed. Sandor fell in line behind the cadets, the chest behind Sandor, and the little fellowship carrying Rieve followed the chest in which the life of Entos dwelt. As they carried Rieve, Blisse continued to speak the words and apply her oil to his wounds, but did so only because she had hope from Sandor's words.

King Ashkelon Attacks

"Depart from His holy place," Sandor shouted at the nearly two hundred soldiers and beasts that were still in the chamber. The cadets scattered in every direction to drive the creatures from the hallowed ground.

"Be gone, you damnable creatures. This day belongs to Entos!" the colonel shouted as he quickened his pace and raised his sword. The soldiers and beasts fled before the swords and determined cadets pursued their enemies. A few moments later the Chamber fell silent and lay in a state of disrepair and ruin.

"Guard the doors," the colonel shouted. "Don't let anyone in."

Sandor led the group to the rail. The cradle was empty, but was still draped with the white blood-stained robe. The Great Chamber was darkened by the absence of the Oracles and was lit only by the gray sky above.

"Open the chest," Sandor ordered. The two cadets did as instructed. Sandor took the Oracles and placed them in the cradle and said, *"Oracium ren koboon."* Light began to break in the Chamber and the darkness left through the doors and to the sky above. Sandor then took the Jewels and restored them to their resting place with these words, *"Eabben ren koboon."*

"Place the conjuror here!" The little fellowship laid Rieve down next to the altar, then they left the inner circle and stood outside the rail. Blisse retreated to the outside of the rail with the little group.

"Granddaughter, it is as I spake. This conjuror is not dead. Continue thy work," Sandor spoke. This time his voice had a gentle tone to it, but the tear that ran down his cheek sent a different message.

Sandor began to read, then sing the words of the Oracles. He spoke in the ancient language and lifted his voice. His words could not be understood by the little fellowship. They were unfamiliar even to the colonel, but the tone of Sandor's song was not. It was the song of an angry and sad mourner. It was a voice rarely heard in the Land of Entos, but it was an unmistakable sound.

As Sandor sang his song and spoke the words of the Oracles a scream of pain came forth from one of the balconies. "No! No!" the soldier screamed. "Leave me as I

The Oracles And The Jewels

am! Leave me as I am!" The soldier's cry echoed along with Sandor's chant.

Colonel Fornoff looked around in an attempt to locate the source of the sound. "He's in the second balcony in Tarchus!" the colonel shouted and pointed. Tag and Brenz turned in that direction and ran as quickly as they could. Sandor continued uninterrupted and seemingly unaware of the events round him. As Sandor continued, his voice grew stronger, the volume louder, the tone more confident, and the voice less mournful. As Sandor continued, the voice of the soldier grew weaker, the volume softer, and the tone more contrite. A few moments later the voice fell silent.

Sandor's chant continued without rest and each line more loudly than the previous. Suddenly, he collapsed. River rushed forward toward her grandfather. Rieve gasped for air and opened his eyes for a moment.

"Blisse," Breille said calling her attention to a waking Rieve, but Blisse's attention was fixed on Sandor.

"Sandor . . . I am," Rieve said in a voice hardly audible, then closed his eyes again. Breille knelt down next to Rieve.

"I'm here, Rieve," Breille said. She felt his head. It was cold. She felt for a pulse. It was weak, but improving.

"Grandfather!" River said as she rushed forward. Blisse reached Sandor first.

"Blisse, what's wrong?" River asked.

"I don't know. I don't know," Blisse said as she looked for a wound. She listened to his heart. She put her ear to his nose and mouth to listen for breath.

"Is he alive?" River asked. The colonel joined the two of them at Sandor's side.

"Yes," Blisse answered. "But barely. We need to get him to a healer, a real healer. There's no wound. There is no bruise. We can't treat this at the field hospital. We need to get him to the academy hospital. He needs the best"

The colonel ran, as best as he was able, out of the chamber and into the street. The soldiers and beasts were retreating through the city toward the Demotic Valley. The Neggen, Polemmas, and Krattos cadets had suffered significant losses, but they had held the line and inflicted heavy casualties on the enemy who was now retreating toward the woods in the Demotic Valley.

King Ashkelon Attacks

The colonel returned to the chamber with several cadets. "Take the Headmaster and the conjuror to The Academy of Healing Arts immediately. Keep your swords drawn and strike down any creature or Entosian who stands in your way," the colonel shouted. "These two must live," he added. "Young lady," the colonel said as he looked to Blisse. "I have other warriors in need of a healer. I will send your sister to accompany the Headmaster and Conjuror Rieve Waynwright. They will get the best care possible."

"Yes, sir," Blisse replied.

"Oh, and miss, thank you for saving my life," the colonel smiled a big smile as he placed his hand on her cheek.

"You're welcome," Blisse said. She glanced back at Rieve and Sandor as they were carried out of The Great Chamber.

"River Kiernan!"

"Yes, Colonel," River replied.

"Go with your friend and grandfather to The Academy of Healing Arts. Seek out a healer by the name of Kallos. Commend the Headmaster and your friend to his care. Tell him that there are many Entosians, civilians, and warriors in the streets who need their help."

"Yes, sir," River said. "Thank you." A slight smile came over her face.

"Breille Clarrice," the colonel said. "We could sure use a few dozen engineers and builders to put out these fires and secure these buildings before they start falling down on top of us. Can you make those arrangements?"

"Yes, sir," Breille replied.

"Colonel," Tag shouted from the second balcony.

"Yes, Commander," the colonel replied.

"Sir, there's a Pithosian warrior up here. He's unconscious and dressed in an enemy uniform and carries the weapons of Ashkelon."

"Praise be to the King," the colonel said with big smile. "It still happens."

"What still happens, sir?" Brenz asked.

"The Headmaster spoke the words of the Oracles and the words transformed that damnable creature into our brother," the colonel answered.

"But, sir. What of all the screaming?" Brenz asked.

The Oracles And The Jewels

"No one comes from the darkness into the light willingly. It hurts too much. You have to be dragged into it against your will. Those were the screams of birth. Now bring that fellow citizen down here. Go find a priest and get him sealed with the birthmarks of the Jewels before he wakes up and we lose that warrior to Ashkelon."

"Yes, sir!" Tag replied. "But, sir, are there any good priests left in the city? The only two I know are on the way to the hospital."

"They don't have to be good ones. They just have to do the job right. That's where you two come in. You stand with swords drawn and if that priest cheats this new creature out of his new life, kill the priest and get another. Keep doing that until you find one who does the job right."

"Yes, sir!" Tag said.

"Welcome to the new ways cadets!" the colonel shouted and laughed. "There's one more thing; you two need to give that new citizen a name."

"A name, sir?" Tag replied.

"An Entosian name. You have the authority to name him. Use that authority well. Congratulations. You're the proud parents of an new Entosian. Now excuse me. I have a cleanup operation to run."

"A name? Any ideas, Commander Thayer Taggert?" Brenz said as he grabbed one arm of the unconscious Pithosian.

"Not a clue. Any ideas, Commander Brenz Clinton?" Tag replied as he grabbed the other arm and began dragging the Pithosian up the aisle of the balcony.

"Oh, Pithosians are the heaviest creatures the Maker ever created," Brenz grunted.

"That's it," Tag said.

"What?" Brenz asked.

"His new name. In the old language, I think it would be . . . Kabbed Burus or would it be Burus Kabbed. Roughly translated, 'the really heavy one.' "

"Don't you think we ought to find out before we name him?" Brenz asked with a grunt as he pulled the Pithosian forward.

"We don't have time. There's a cleanup operation underway. So Burus Kabbed it is," Tag said.

King Ashkelon Attacks

Brenz and Tag did as they were ordered and Entos' newest citizen was so named. There was no need to kill any priests. They were happy to do the job right, albeit at the point of two blood-stained swords. Once the new Entosian had been marked by the Jewels, they turned their new brother over to some healers who were collecting the dead and wounded from the streets outside The Great Chamber.

While Tag and Brenz oversaw the marking of the new Entosian, Blisse began tending to the wounded who were lying on the steps outside The Great Chamber. Few were still alive. Most of the Hodia cadets lay dead alongside of the honor guardsmen who had slain them. She moved from body to body, checking each cadet and guardsman for any sign of life. When she found such a sign, she applied her oils, spoke her incantations, placed the appropriate tag on his collar, and moved on to the next. She repeated the process over and over again as she followed the path of the battle from The Great Chamber to the edge of the city at the Demotic Valley. Chaiva and Sabinnee did the same. The three worked independently, but the path of the bodies led down the same streets and toward the same destination.

As Blisse knelt over the body of a Polemmas cadet, she heard Brenz. "Blisse," he said softly as he and Tag approached from behind. "Are you all right?"

Blisse looked up at Brenz and Tag with a tear in her eye. "So many of them are dead. And the wounds are not from the crude blades of soldiers. Their wounds were made by Entosian blades. Our own guardsmen killed most of them. How can they do such a thing to their brothers?"

"I don't know," Brenz answered.

"That question will have to wait for now," Tag replied. "Commander, there is still more fighting that needs to be done."

"Yes," Brenz sighed.

"Blisse, take care and stay alert," Tag said softening his tone. "There might still be some of Ashkelon's beasts and soldiers wandering the streets."

"I will," Blisse said as she placed her hand over the eyes of the dead cadet she had been kneeling over. She closed his eyes, then put the appropriate tag on his collar.

The Oracles And The Jewels

Brenz and Tag ran down the street toward the Demotic Valley. As they made their way to the battle, they struck down any stray soldier or beast that had the misfortune of crossing their path. By now there was a steady flow of warriors working their way through the streets to the valley. Once they arrived they took a position in the line and began to push the beasts and soldiers off the plateau and toward the Demotic Valley from whence they came.

The Battle of the Wall

Ashkelon's soldiers and beasts poured through the gates and into the field. Witticor's plan was working. Ashkelon had to divide his forces to fight on two fronts. Forty thousand of his soldiers and beasts had turned toward the desert and attacked the ten thousand warriors on the desert floor. His forty thousand were no match for the ten thousand Entosian warriors. Ashkelon knew that. He had sent these legions to their death to buy time for his main attack on the wall and to protect himself from a direct assault against his own person.

While the forty thousand marched eastward, tens-of-thousands more were charging into the valley. Allowing Ashkelon's army to breach the wall and enter the Land of Entos was a gamble Witticor had willingly accepted and his gamble was paying off. By opening the gates and allowing Ashkelon's soldiers free access to the Demotic Valley, Witticor was effectively controlling the number of soldiers his army had to face. The relatively small opening of the gates slowed Ashkelon's advance and provided the Entosian archers and artillery a smaller target area and prevented the possibility of being overrun.

All was going as Witticor had planned. Ashkelon's attention had been redirected to his rear guard. No one was controlling the forces now pouring through the breach in the wall and his army was being destroyed in a predictable fashion. Ashkelon's soldiers and beasts were rushing into the valley and to their deaths through the three gates.

Through the eyes of a winged creature flying above The Great Chamber, Ashkelon had seen Botha being driven from the steps and the chest being reclaimed by Sandor. In

King Ashkelon Attacks

that moment, Ashkelon roared a great roar, the likes of which had not been heard in Bohow in five thousand years. His roar shook the ground upon which both Entosian and Ektosian now stood. The roar almost drove the courage and faith from the hearts of the scouts and warriors who fought on the desert floor. "Cursed, cursed, is the ground of Entos," he cried. Ashkelon's voice rolled through the ground upon which he stood and to the hill upon which Witticor was now standing.

"Something has happened," Witticor mumbled as he stood in the valley watching his warriors make quick work of the invaders. "Something very good," he thought. "Victory must be at hand."

The Desert Floor

In that moment, King Ashkelon unleashed the full weight of his rage against friend and foe alike. He turned his attention away from the scouts and toward the battle at the wall.

"Attack! All of you! Forward! Destroy them all!" Ashkelon shouted. Enraged, he pushed and threw his officers toward the battle.

"Loose the artillery against the walls and the gates," he ordered. None of his officers dared point out that, in so doing, Ashkelon would kill many of his own soldiers. They knew that the battle had been lost and in time Ashkelon would make for himself replacements.

So enraged was Ashkelon at the loss of the chest, he took up his own sword, jumped from his platform, and marched toward the Entosian warriors on the desert floor. Ashkelon charged forward toward the warriors, striking down and throwing aside any who had the misfortune of being in his path. Ashkelon fixed his eyes upon Colonel Sollon. Arokim and his scouts fixed their eyes upon Ashkelon.

As Ashkelon marched toward the colonel, his eyes grew brighter and his passion was all the more aroused. Beasts and soldiers hurried to get out of his way. Those that did not hurry quick enough, hurried no more.

The Oracles And The Jewels

"Arokim!" Ora shouted. Arokim turned toward the voice. Ora pointed at Ashkelon. "What are your orders, sir?" she cried out.

Arokim hesitated for a moment. The scouts could intercept Ashkelon, but all knew they could not defeat him. At best, their sacrifice would serve as an alarm for the colonel and perhaps buy the colonel a few minutes. Colonel Sollon had not yet seen Ashkelon bearing down upon him and unless something was done in the next few seconds, the colonel would most certainly be dead or worse.

"Sir!" Ora cried out.

Arokim hesitated no longer. "Intercept and destroy!" he shouted as he pointed his sword to the mighty king.

The scouts moved quickly through the battlefield dispatching all soldiers and beasts between them and their prey. Celsus loosed one arrow after another at the monstrous Ashkelon, but most bounced off his heavy armor.

Magnus was the first to reach Ashkelon, but Ashkelon matched the Adroit's speed with a swing of his hand. The blow launched the Adroit several feet into the air. None of Magnus' comrades saw where he landed, but there was little doubt that he had landed in the midst of hundreds of beasts and soldiers and certain death. Arokim the Kicahian, Justin

King Ashkelon Attacks

the Demotic, and Roggan the Aradian were next. They took up their positions three abreast between the king and their colonel. A dozen sipedons moved to defend their king, but were struck down in rapid succession by the three scouts.

Ashkelon paused for a moment to watch and wait for the remaining scouts to take their positions. Tor, Ora, Tita, Cedric, and Edris joined the other three. Arokim stood in the middle. Justin to his right and Roggan stood to his left. Tor moved to Arokim's far left and Cedric to Tor's right. Edris stood to the far right of Arokim and Tita stood to Edris' left. Ora fell in behind Arokim. Celsus stood off at a distance and loosed an arrow into any soldier or beast that approached the scouts from behind.

More of Ashkelon's soldiers and beasts poured into the gap that had opened up between their king and the Entosian warriors. One after another threw itself into the small wall of Entosian metal.

"Stand firm," Arokim ordered. "Hold your ground, you Entosian few!"

Ashkelon looked up and fixed his eyes upon Colonel Sollon. Sollon locked eye with Ashkelon and in that moment the order to attack Ashkelon almost broke through Sollon's lips, but sound judgment prevailed.

"Attack, sir?" one of Sollon's officers asked.

"No, Captain," he said softly. "No. Order the army to advance to the left and to the right flanks. Go around Ashkelon and head for home."

"But, sir, the scouts!" the captain cried.

"Give the order, Captain!" the colonel shouted in anger and frustration. "Go around that bastard king!"

The captain reluctantly but firmly repeated the order to the trumpeters. A moment later the trumpets sounded and the flagmen directed their respective units in the way they should go. The Entosian warriors began to cut their way around Ashkelon and toward the walls of Entos.

"Captain!" the colonel shouted above the clash of steel and flesh. "Send a conjuror to the scouts!"

"Yes, sir," the captain shouted in reply and in so doing a small smile broke upon his face. The order was fulfilled and the captain began cutting a path toward the scouts. The

The Oracles And The Jewels

conjuror and the captain took up positions behind the scouts.

As Sollon's army began to move to the right and left of Ashkelon, the king looked down upon the small band of scouts, then looked upward to consider the colonel again. But the colonel was not to be found. He had disappeared into the mass of warriors.

The small wall of scouts had held against Ashkelon's soldiers and beasts. It was a small and momentary victory, but a victory nonetheless. They had accomplished the purpose for which they had thrown themselves into the breech. Colonel Sollon had escaped and the Entosian desert army had avoided certain annihilation. Ashkelon himself was stunned by the event. His revenge had been stayed, but his wrath would not.

Ashkelon stepped forward and raised his sword. The sword was the length of a Entosian Demotic and its weight was greater than the same. The warrior scouts raised their swords in defiance. They looked Ashkelon square in the eyes. The warrior scouts and the conjuror who now stood behind them saw what no Entosian had seen before. Each of them swallowed hard. The conjuror spoke. "Fight well ye warriors and to the glory of Entos. The King awaits our arrival."

Ashkelon took another step toward the scouts. As he did, he growled. The ground under their feet shook. When Ashkelon took his third step toward the scouts, each of them took a step backward.

Arokim debated the situation in his mind. By Ashkelon's third step, the debate had ended.

"Retreat!" Arokim shouted. "Retreat!"

Before any of the scouts could act upon the order, Ashkelon's heavy sword took Edris and Tita. The power of Ashkelon's sword was well known in Entos. His strength and size had been well documented in the history and military books of the warring academy. But the speed with which Ashkelon wielded the sword stunned the scouts. He was as quick and as graceful as any Adroit, but more powerful than any Pithosian. Edris and Tita were struck with such celerity that they did not feel the sting of the blade.

King Ashkelon Attacks

As Ashkelon withdrew his sword to swing it again, a flash of light struck each of the remaining scouts in the back. The conjuror's energy had found its marks. The scouts exploded forward with a burst of speed and with such power that each landed a blow. Arokim struck Ashkelon's arm. Ora struck one leg and Cedric struck the other. Justin and Tor landed blows against Ashkelon's body. Roggan struck Ashkelon's right arm. Each blow had landed with such force sparks flew from the clash of metal. Had these blows landed on any other creature, the creature's fate would not be in doubt. But against Ashkelon's armor, they left not even a mark.

The scouts landed on the back side of Ashkelon and immediately turned to strike a second time. Ashkelon was ready. He struck Ora down with his left hand and brought his sword to bear against Arokim. As Ashkelon's sword met Arokim's, the conjuror had found his mark. Arokim was spared, but the force of Ashkelon's blow knocked him to the ground. He hit hard and with such force the breath was driven from his lungs. Arokim lay on the ground in a moment of confusion.

Cedric, Justin, Roggan, and Tor had followed Arokim in the second attack. The thrusts from the other four were quickly and successfully countered. The scouts fell to the ground not far from where Arokim was laying.

"Enough of you!" Ashkelon roared. He threw his dagger into the chest of the conjuror with such force that the conjuror's body disappeared into a crowd of beasts and soldiers. Arokim saw the conjuror fall. Celsus had too. He had managed to limp toward his fallen comrades. With one last step, Celsus placed himself between Ashkelon and his fellow scouts. Celsus loosed three remaining arrows toward Ashkelon's heart, but Ashkelon matched their speed with his sword, deflecting the first and the second. The third bounced and broke on Ashkelon's breastplate.

"Retreat!" Arokim said so softly no one could hear. Arokim struggled to his feet. Ashkelon stepped toward Celsus and lifted his sword. Celsus lowered his bow and stood still. Ashkelon drew closer. Suddenly, with the speed of an Adroit, Celsus armed his bow, dropped to one knee, and loosed an arrow into the left eye of the mighty king.

The Oracles And The Jewels

Ashkelon bent over, cried out with a shout that could be heard across the battlefield. He pulled the arrow from his eye and covered the wound with his left hand. Then he straightened up and swung his sword with his right hand. Celsus drew his sword to block Ashkelon's blade, but Ashkelon's blade severed his sword and then cut Celsus himself in half.

As Ashkelon moved to strike Celsus down, Arokim shouted "Retreat!" but the shout was in vain. Celsus' body was falling to the ground before he had finished the command. Arokim closed his eyes and cursed himself for not shouting the command sooner and more clearly. "Retreat!" Arokim shouted a third time. This time there was no hesitation or lack of clarity. "Retreat. Warriors, to the walls of Entos!"

"On my point," Justin shouted. Cedric, Tor, Roggan, and Arokim ran away and around Ashkelon. There was no point in pursing the scouts now. The day had been lost and Ashkelon had resigned himself to returning to Ektos. As the scouts disappeared into the battlefield, Ashkelon roared, "Come! Now! To Ektos!" General Sloan repeated the command, but no trumpeter sounded out since there was no sound for retreat in Ektos.

Ashkelon called for his morse, mounted the beast, and rode away from the battle. Generals Ya'ar, Deabbon, and Shaqqa mounted their creatures and followed, leaving their beasts and soldiers to face the end of the day without their commanders.

Arokim, Justin, Cedric, Tor, and Roggan tightened their formation and cut their way through the pockets of beasts and soldiers whose ranks were now caught up in the chaos of retreat. As the scouts moved closer and closer to the wall, they were joined by an increasing number of warriors from the desert army. With the addition of each warrior, they grew stronger and their advance accelerated. But the wall was still a long way off and thousands of soldiers and beasts stood between them and the safety of the wall.

The Demotic Valley

King Ashkelon Attacks

General Witticor watched as his artillery, cavalry, and warriors drove Ashkelon's soldiers from the valley and back onto the desert floor.

"General," Hakkon said pointing to retreating soldiers. "They are retreating toward the forest."

"Ashkelon has had enough. We have won the day," Witticor replied.

"Thanks be to the Creator and King of Entos," Tarrant said with a tone of relief.

The Oracles And The Jewels

"Indeed, we have won," Witticor said then added, "but at what price?"

"The necessary price," Hakkon answered. "No one, General, is going to second guess you on this one. If the city held, this will go down as the greatest military victory in more than five hundred years."

"I agree, General Witticor. This has been a great victory and our losses can't compare with what has been gained today," Tarrant added.

"The day is not over," Witticor said. "Order every tower, all eight, to send two hundred warriors to sweep their way through the valleys to The Great Chamber. They are to kill any creature or soldier of Bohow they come across. A healer and conjuror is to go along and provide assistance to any wounded they find."

"Yes, sir," Hakkon snapped.

"Colonel Tarrant," Witticor said, "I will be leaving at once for the city. Assemble a squad to accompany me."

"Yes, sir," Tarrant replied.

"General Raggnar," Witticor said. "We still have warriors on that desert floor. They will be fighting their way home. Send one hundred riders into the desert with some wagons to provide support. Let's get as many of those boys back as we can."

"Yes, sir," Raggnar said as he snapped a sharp salute.

"General Hakkon."

"Yes, General Witticor," Hakkon replied.

"I leave you to clean up this mess and secure the wall."

"Yes, sir," Hakkon replied.

"General Hakkon, tell the warriors that they fought well and brought glory to Entos today," Witticor said. The generals and their staff exchanged salutes and each headed his own way.

The Aftermath

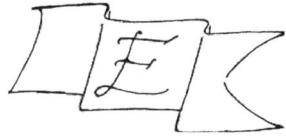

Chapter Seventeen
The Aftermath

Healing Arts Building

While the battles raged on the edge of the city, several of the cadets carried Sandor and Rieve to The Academy of Healing Arts. River followed closely behind. The hallway was filled with the injured and with the families of the injured. Never had The Academy of Healing Arts been so busy or so full. The cadets were ushered down the hall and into a treatment room. A few minutes later they presented themselves to River, nodded in respect and appreciation, and made their way out of the academy.

"Excuse me," River said with a timid voice.

"Yes, young lady," the receptionist replied.

"Headmaster Sandor and the Priest Rieve," River began.

"What about them?" she snapped.

"I would like Healer Kallos to treat them, please," River said sheepishly. The receptionist looked at her with mild scorn. " . . . if you don't mind," River added.

"Young lady, we are very busy and I can assure you that all of our healers are well qualified," the receptionist said.

"I have instructions from Colonel Fornoff," River said now in a fully adult voice. A look of firmness took over her face. "Healer Kallos will be assigned to treat the Headmaster and Conjuror Rieve Waynwright. That is by order of Colonel Fornoff. Am I clear on that point?"

"Colonel Fornoff, so it shall be," the clerk replied and so it was.

"Colonel Fornoff has also asked me to inform the staff that there are many wounded and dead in the streets who need to be cared for," River said.

"We will do what we can, young lady," the clerk said.

River settled into the waiting room to wait and worry about the fate of the two priests. She was not alone. The waiting room was filled with sisters, mothers, fathers,

The Oracles And The Jewels

husbands, and wives of those who had been injured or killed in the battle. Many of the injured were civilians who had been attacked by beasts or who had been injured in the many fires that were burning in the city. Soon more of the injured would be brought in from the surrounding villages. News of the field hospital had already reached the Healing Academy and, while all knew that some would call for an inquiry on the establishment of a clandestine and unsupervised hospital, it was, at the moment, a great blessing. Cadets and citizens with minor wounds were being directed to the field hospital, while the critically wounded were being treated at The Academy of Healing Arts.

River settled into a big, soft, blue chair before noticing some blood on her left hand and forearm. It was Rieve's blood. She walked over to the fountain in the middle of the room and gently washed the blood from her own flesh. Upon finishing, she started to return to the chair, but an older, stately, worried-looking lady, a Kilposian had taken her rest there.

"Oh excuse me," she said. "Was this your chair?"

"No. I was just keeping it for you," River replied with a gentle smile. But the woman started to rise.

"No, please stay," River said as she took the lady's elbow and helped her back into the chair.

"You're River Kiernan, aren't you?" the Kilposian asked.

"Yes, I am," River replied.

"I've seen you perform at the Grand Theater," she said. "You have a wonderful voice. I haven't heard talent like yours in more than fifty years."

"Thank you," River replied.

"Your voice has a way to sooth the most troubled soul."

"Thank you again," River replied.

"There seems to be a lot of troubled souls in this room," the old lady added.

"Indeed," River replied.

"Would you?" the lady asked with a smile.

"Would I?" River replied with a note of confusion.

"Sing? Sing for us and calm our troubled souls, for we are greatly worried for those whom we love and for our beloved Land of Entos."

River looked around the room, which was falling silent, as if to await her reply.

"Forgive me, madam, but I don't feel much like singing at the moment. My grandfather, Headmaster Sandor, and a

The Aftermath

dear friend have been gravely injured and I am not sure if I can sing at this moment."

"Dear child," the old lady said with a slight sigh, "these are the moments for which the Creator made the song and the singers. Conjurors are the vehicles by which Entosians are made and preserved. The Healers are the instruments by which our bodies are protected. And you my child, you too perform a great service. The songs that come forth from thy mouth comfort the mind and give peace to the troubled. . . . Is there any doubt that we are now in a time of trouble?" She paused and looked around the room. River also looked upon the crowded but still room.

The old lady continued. "Dear child, some of us shall be told this very day that our beloveds have left us to be with our King. Only a song, bearing the words of the Oracles, can comfort us when such news comes. So sing child, sing softly, and I will close this mouth, these weary eyes, and open these old ears to hear the comfort of thy song. For I have seen and heard so much folly on this day."

"Very well," River said. Then she knelt beside the old woman, took her hand, and took a deep breath and sang.

To thee, My child, who mourns below, whose loss is due to battle and woe. To thee, My child, I do come to rescue thee from the wicked one.

Ye mourn the lost and fallen ones; But mourn not for thy dear sons.. Mourn for those whose life is death; Mourn for those who know no rest.

Mourn for those who know not love; Mourn for those whose deeds are death. For tho' tribulation fall us fast; Our Lord our God shall come at last."

Though sin and evil still oppress; The King of glory and heavenly best. Shall come to thee in thy distress; To speak His words the heavenly blessed.

For in thy struggles ye shall see, the greatest of all victories.

So we count our losses but gains to see; and loss of fame and miseries. The blood of martyrs preserves the land; freedom is this blessed band.

Tho' tribulation fall us fast; Our Lord our God, shall come at last. In the last battle the King shall come; To shed the blood of the evil one.

Hear these words thy mournful child; thy blood has not in vain been spent. For His good land and cause defend, thy body and thy blood has lent.

The Oracles And The Jewels

Tho' tribulation fall us fast, Our Lord our God, shall come at last. To thee My child who mourns below; Thy trouble and thy woe shall pass.

His glory is secured at last. His glory is secured at last.

River looked around the room. All sat silent. As her eyes met the worried and the injured, they each in turn whispered their "thank you." With each offering of thanks River bowed her head in respect.

"Well said, well sung," the old woman said. "Now, I am well readied."

"Readied?" River replied. The old woman squeezed River's hand. "For what?"

"For whatever news they bring me of my beloved son," the woman answered. River sat down on the floor next to the old woman. The old woman put her hand upon River's head. "Rest, my child. Listen to the words of your own song. I can feel the weight of the whole world upon your shoulders. It is a terrible weight. It is a weight that is not yours to bear. You and your friends are to help him bear this weight. But, Daughter, it is not yours to bear."

"I know," River said.

"Rest now, daughter. The news will come to both of us. May each of us will that which has already been ordained."

The Plateau at the Demotic Valley

Tag and Brenz stood shoulder to shoulder and methodically worked their way into the lines of beasts and soldiers. Thayer Taggert had taken command of the line of cadets which was growing stronger and more numerous with the passing of each minute. Cadets from all over the city were converging on the plateau. They joined the line and, on Tag's command, the whole line would move forward step-by-step. With each step forward more of Ashkelon's soldiers fell to the ground. It was only when Tag reached the edge of the plateau overlooking the Demotic Valley that he realized this was his home. Then he remembered his own house and his mother.

He froze in time. The promise he had made to his mother not so long ago echoed in his ears. "Mother, as soon as I am in the Warring Academy, you need not fear any creature from Bohow or soldier of Ashkelon. You have my word."

The Aftermath

Brenz shouted, but Tag heard him not. As his words rang in his ears, he stood motionless looking over the devastation that had been his home and the valley in which he once played. A soldier charged forward to strike Tag, but Brenz interceded and struck the creature dead. Tag didn't notice.

"Commander!" Brenz shouted. "Commander!" he shouted a second time before he realized what had taken Tag's thoughts captive. Brenz grabbed Tag by the back of his shirt and pulled him from the line. The hole was filled by two more cadets. The violent motion startled Tag and his shock turned to rage. Brenz could see it in his eyes.

"Forward," Tag said. "Full attack." The words were barely noticeable.

"No!" Brenz shouted. "Stay the course. Stick to the plan!"

"No yourself!" Tag shouted back. "Attack! Attack! Charge!" he yelled with all his might then he charged forward toward a breech in the soldiers' line. Brenz took hold of his arm, but Thayer turned and knocked him to the ground.

"Cadets, forward!" Tag shouted. He ran past the cadet line, pulled a dagger from a cadet's belt on the way and, with a sword in his right hand and the dagger in his left, he charged into the line of the soldiers. Brenz picked himself up from the ground and followed Tag.

"Commander! She's already dead!" he yelled, but it made no difference. Tag had disappeared into the mob of soldiers and beasts.

Brenz turned toward the cadet line and with his back toward his enemy he shouted, "You heard the command!" "Advance! Full Attack! Follow me!" Brenz turned and charged forward. The cadet line surged forward like a cutting machine and the enemy line broke in a matter of moments.

"Kill them all!" Tag shouted. "Advance!" There was a rage in his voice that Entosians were not accustomed to hearing. They responded nonetheless. A second wave rolled over the enemy. Cries of retreat could be heard from Ashkelon's soldiers. Never before had such a cry been heard from Ashkelon's soldiers and it news of such a command ever reached Ashkelon himself, it meant certain death to the whole unit.

Confusion and panic had taken hold of the Ektosian soldiers. The beasts were the first to turn and run. The soldiers began to do the same. Tag too ran forward toward his house. Brenz followed. As they ran up the path to his

The Oracles And The Jewels

house, the two struck down any soldier or beast that had the misfortune of retreating across their path.

The cadets followed Tag's example and broke free from their formations. Each pursued his own target and each was successful in overtaking it.

Tag had run up the trail and toward his house a thousand times before, but he had never made such quick work of it and never with a look of rage in his eyes. A few minutes later he stood before the smoldering ashes of his house.

"Mother!" he called out, but there was no answer. Brenz had followed his friend up the path, but could not keep pace. He heard Tag call for his mother. He knew there would be no reply.

"Tag!" Brenz called out. Tag heard, but did not answer.

"Mother!" Tag shouted again. "Mother! Mother!" He began to search wildly amidst the ruins, but could not find her. His desperate search yielded no results and she answered not.

"Tag!" Brenz said as he approached his friend from behind. "Tag," Brenz said in a softer voice as he touched Tag's shoulder. Tag jerked away.

"Leave me!" Tag said.

"I will not," Brenz replied.

"I don't need your help!" Tag snapped. "It was my responsibility to protect her."

"No!" Brenz said softly, "it was your responsibility to protect Entos and that is what you have done this day."

"I said leave me!" Tag yelled. "That is an order!"

"It is an order I will not obey, since you yourself have mixed duty with personal interest," Brenz answered. "I am not leaving until you do."

Tag reached for his sword, which he had placed in its scabbard moments earlier. The movement surprised Brenz, who had been standing at the ready with his sword in hand. Brenz thought for a moment, then put his sword back into its scabbard. Tag turned away and began his search again.

As Tag looked through the ruins of the house, Brenz wandered into the backyard. There he found a blood trail and some pieces of clothing, but he said nothing. He knew what he would find. Soldiers, beasts, and morse feed on the flesh of their victims. Brenz knew that he would not find Arete the wife of Tedmund amidst the smoldering ashes of the house.

The Aftermath

The beasts of Bohow and the soldiers of Ektos had held that ground for most of the day. Ashkelon's army was always wild with hunger and would not waste raw flesh. Brenz followed the trail to the place where the yard, creek, and forest met. At his feet he found a pool of blood. He looked up slowly until the ungodly sight invaded his view of the otherwise beautiful landscape. But he could not bear to look long at the sight. He grew instantly weak and did not know how, or if, he should summon his friend to behold the sight. But he knew that he could not hide it.

Brenz stepped back a few steps and spoke softly, "Commander." Thayer heard the whisper and immediately stood still. Thayer knew what that whisper meant and braced himself for what had been discovered. Brenz turned his head toward his friend and with a tear in his eye called out a second time more clearly. "Tag, I've found her." Tag ran toward the place where Brenz stood. Brenz stepped in his way and reached out to grab him, but the effort was only half-hearted. "Commander, don't trouble yourself." Thayer Taggert ran past him, then suddenly slowed and came to a stop.

As Thayer came closer the details of his mother's fate were more clearly seen. He fell to his knees in the bloody soil. The moment of silence was broken by Thayer's scream, "No! No!" Unlike Brenz, Thayer could not take his eyes off the remains of his mother, nor could he bring himself to touch them or cut them down. "I've failed you, Mother. Forgive me. I've failed you," Thayer repeated again and again as he wept.

The time passed slowly for both cadets, but more so for Brenz. He had never seen nor heard such mourning. Brenz sat down in the yard, wept for his friend, and sang a lyric from an Entosian hymn, "Weep not this day, for the blood of innocence shall be our stay, the blood of innocence shall be our stay." Brenz repeated the lyrics several times, but Tag heard not the hymn. But the sound of mourning and Brenz's song gave way to the business of war.

"Sir," a voice said.

Brenz turned and saw a cadet, a signalman, standing in front of the ruins.

"Yes," Brenz replied.

The signalman looked toward Thayer, who was still lamenting the death of his mother, although in a more subdued manner.

The Oracles And The Jewels

"Cadet, I am second in command here," Brenz snapped. "What is it?"

"Sir, the men are scattered all over the valley. Some of the cadets have followed the creatures into the woods," the cadet explained.

"Yes," Brenz said in reply.

"Sir, is that a good thing? I mean to leave the city unprotected and to have our cadets scattered all over the place."

"No, it is not a good thing," Brenz replied. "Well done, cadet. Sound the 'Recall.' Call the cadets back to the city. We will regroup there. Send word to Colonel Fornoff that we stand at the ready and await his orders."

"Very well, sir," the cadet said. He lifted his horn to his lips and loosed two long notes that would bring order out of the chaos. The sound had the desired effect upon all who heard it, all but Thayer Taggert who seemed oblivious to all around him.

The signalman sounded his call as he walked his way down the path and toward the city. The cadets answered the call as they had been taught.

"Commander . . . Commander Thayer Taggert," Brenz said in a firm voice. "The time for weeping is over. It is time to return to your duties, sir."

"Yes, it is," Thayer responded. His voice was cold and without emotion. The sound of it caught Brenz off guard, but he welcomed it as an improvement.

Thayer stood up and turned toward the city. His uniform was splattered with the blood of his enemies, but his knees and hands were covered with the unmistakable blood of his Entosian mother.

"Sound the recall," Thayer commanded.

"Already done," Brenz snapped.

"Send word to Colonel Fornoff!"

"Already done," Brenz snapped again.

"Well done, cadet. You see I am not needed as badly as you think," Thayer said as he stepped onto the path.

"It is not a question of being needed, sir," Brenz replied, "It is a question of office and duty."

"Yes, it is, and when the day comes that I must fall, it is good to know that those under my command will be well cared for. Now enough talk, let us get to the city."

Thayer tried to hide the deep trouble that had been stirred in his soul, but Brenz could still hear a quality in his voice that had not been there before. Something had

The Aftermath

changed in Thayer and a grief and anger had arisen that was unusual for an Entosian.

The Academy of Healing Arts

"River Kiernan," a voice softly said in the tone of a question. River opened her eyes. "River Kiernan," the voice said a second time in a louder and firmer tone.

"Yes, I am River Kiernan," she replied. River stood up quickly. "I'm sorry I must have fallen asleep."

"Are you Headmaster Sandor's granddaughter?" Healer Kallos asked.

"Yes, I am," she answered. River looked around for the old woman, but she was gone. The waiting room that had been so full was now mostly empty. "I must have slept for some time," she said.

"I am Healer Kallos. Colonel Fornoff is a good friend and I am very glad you were so insistent that I treat the Headmaster. He was in very critical condition when he arrived. It appears that Headmaster Sandor will remain among us for a bit longer. He is stable, but very weak," Kallos explained.

"What is the exact nature of his illness?" River asked.

"Illness? The Headmaster was not taken ill. He lost a terrible amount of blood," Kallos answered.

"Blood?" River repeated in disbelief. "But how?"

"Yes, blood. His wound must have been very deep." Kallos said. "I understand that was your younger sister Blisse who treated him on the battlefield."

"Yes, it was Blisse, but . . . " River began

"She healed him so well," Kallos continued, "and so quickly that not a mark has been left upon his body."

"But the Headmaster was not struck down by a soldier's sword. Grandfather received no wound," River interrupted. "With all due respect, you must be confused. The young conjuror Rieve Waynwright is the one who received the wound."

"Yes, he did and it was deep. But Miss River Kiernan, I examined both of them and there is no doubt in my mind both spilled blood this day and a lot of it. They will both require several days of rest, food, and incantations."

"May I visit them?" River asked.

"Yes, but please make it short. They are both very tired," Kallos answered.

The Oracles And The Jewels

"Thank you, Healer Kallos. I am in your debt," River said as she bowed her head.

"No, young lady, all of Entos will be in your debt, yours and your friends," he replied and bowed his head. "Follow me," Kallos said, "and I will show you the Headmaster's room. The Conjuror Rieve Waynwright is just across the hall from the Headmaster."

The two walked briskly down the long hallway. It was a long walk. Kallos had had Sandor and Rieve placed in the two rooms at the end of the hallway away from the noise and traffic of the nurses station and the waiting room. But the rooms were not only quieter, they were more secure.

"I assigned them the last two rooms at the end of hallway," Kallos began, "and I have sent word to Colonel Fornoff to post a sentry outside their doors to guarantee their protection."

The statement surprised River, but she said nothing in reply. As they approached the rooms, the implications of the healer's order began to take hold.

"They will be safe here, won't they?" River asked.

"Yes, young lady, they will. Colonel Fornoff will post his most trustworthy warriors and I have given my staff very specific instructions as to the care of these two. Here we are. Conjuror Rieve Waynwright is on the right and your grandfather is on the left. I leave you to them."

"Thank you again," River said. She slowly entered the room. It was dark but not so dark that one could not see. Sandor was asleep and his complexion was very pale. River had never seen her grandfather look so fragile. She took his hand and rubbed it gently.

"Grandfather," she said softly. There was no response.

"Grandfather," she said in a firmer voice, "it is me, River Kiernan, your granddaughter."

"I knoweth the names of my granddaughters," Sandor said in a voice soft and frail. A small smile came over his face. A larger smile took hold of hers.

"How has Entos fared this day?" Sandor asked as he opened his eyes and turned his head toward his granddaughter.

"The news is good, Grandfather. Entos has been spared. But only by the grace of the King, the wits of General Witticor, and the bravery of our warriors, cadets, and conjurors."

The Aftermath

"And my charge," he asked as the smile disappeared from his face. "How is the Conjuror Rieve Waynwright? Were my petitions answered?"

"He is alive, Grandfather. Healer Kallos says that you both lost much blood and are very weak, but in time both of you will recover."

"It is good that the King has answered me thus," Sandor whispered. "The boy will recover quickly. As for me, I am no longer necessary."

"I take issue with you on that, Grandfather, but I will not waste my time or your energy debating the point," River said gently rebuking her grandfather.

"Perhaps now, Grandfather, they will listen to you . . . to the old teachings. Perhaps now, having been delivered by the ancient ways in our most desperate hour, they will trust again."

"No, Daughter, even in this hour they trust not," Sandor took a slow deep breath. "For they cannot," then he fell asleep.

So was the beginning of the last days of old Entos.

The End

Appendix
Vocabulary for Sacred Language

Articles & Prep.

Ad = the
Adon = of the
Atum = therefore/consequently
Cullan = with
Dekkim = that or so that
Demmin = will/to do
Eppon = Over, upon, on top
Etum = and
Em = of
Hasan = being made
Horan = not seen
Mea = not
On = /be/being/existing
Or = For
Orad = For the
Senn = was

Verbs

Fanan = fly
Kataloom = destroy
Nogget = push
Ren = send
Rafa = heal
Tssada = run

Pronouns

Um = you
Umim = you (plural)
Umat = your
Adam = he

Nouns

Aham = friend
Aman = True/Faithful
Amet = strength
Amets = strengthen
Anapalin = back
Annan = Proceed
Borranon = Giver
Boothos = Helper
Borran = Maker
Eabben = Jewels
Emen = Other
Ereten = Land
Fahman = creation
Gabbom = Greater
Gibbon = Warrior
Hodia = day
Hoddan = Light
Kalloson = Good
Katalam = destroyer
Katen = Protector
Koboon = glory
Laccam = fight
Mellom = King
Nabana = spake
Naban = Word
Nabene = speak
Oracium = Oracles
Palanan = Wonders, mysteries
Pasa = Wounds
Paaran = honor
Pission = faithfulness
Sammar = Praise
Skotan = dark
Skotana = darkness
Skootan = Evil Foe
Strattem = Soldier
Tzaddam = children
Sussim = Well/Fine
Yaddann = knowledge
Velotis = speed

Rieve's Song

Boothos Em Entos On

Boothos em Entos on, Borranon em ad kalloson.
Katen Umat fahman etum ad tzaddam cullan Umat Eabben.
Umim nabana Umat Naban atum Entos on senn hasan.
Nabene Umat Naban etum kataloom ad katalam.
Nabene Umat Naban etum ren ad Hoddan dem nogget anapalin ad skotana.
Nabene Umat Naban atum ad gibbon demmim sussim.
Umim nabana Umat Naban atum skootan mea hasan.

Helper of Entos

Helper of Entos, Giver of the good things.
Protect Your creation, and the children with Your Jewels.
You spake Your Word therefore Entos was made.
Speak Your Word and destroy the destroyers.
Speak Your Word and send the Light to push back the darkness.
Speak Your Word and the warrior will be well.
You spake Your Word and the evil foe is no more.